ZACHARY GOLDMAN PRIVATE INVESTIGATOR

Cases 5-7

P.D. WORKMAN

ISBN: 9781989415986 (Kindle)

ISBN: 9781989415993 (ePub)

ISBN: 9781774681398 (KDP Print)

ISBN: 9781774681404 (IS Paperback)

ISBN: 9781774681411 (IS Hardcover)

pdworkman

THEY THOUGHT HE WAS SAFE

Zachary Goldman Mysteries #5

For those who are lost or invisible.

CHAPTER ONE

The little family gathered around the dining room table was about as far from a traditional nuclear family as one could get. Lorne Peterson had been Zachary's foster father for a few weeks when he was young, following the house fire that had been the last straw in the break-up of his biological family. But Zachary and Mr. Peterson had kept in touch, connected in part by a love of photography and his former foster father's darkroom facilities.

Mr. Peterson—Zachary tried, but could rarely bring himself to call him Lorne—had gone through his own family dissolution a few years later, when his wife had become aware of his alternative relationships. They had lost their certification to foster, and separation and divorce followed soon after.

Zachary remembered the initial shock when he had stopped in to visit Mr. Peterson and get some film developed and he realized that Pat, the other man in the apartment, was not a neighbor who had stopped in for coffee, but Mr. Peterson's partner. He had known that Mr. Peterson was seeing someone named Pat, but had mistakenly assumed that Pat was a woman. More than twenty years later, Lorne and Pat were still together, and society had changed enough that they were able to live together openly in the mainstream rather than keeping their relationship quiet.

Pat was between Zachary and Mr. Peterson in age, still muscular and vital, though he was definitely looking more distinguished than he had in his twenties, gray creeping in at his temples and fine lines mapping his face. Mr. Peterson's deeper wrinkles all pointed up, ready to burst into a sunrise when he smiled. He was losing his hair, and the fringe that was left was almost pure white. But even as his body got older, he remained energetic and young at heart.

They had been a constant in Zachary's life for two decades and, despite the fact that Mr. Peterson had only been his foster parent for a few weeks and Pat never had been, they were the closest thing to family that Zachary had. He hadn't kept in touch with any of his other foster siblings or parents, and much of his adolescence had been spent in youth centers and group homes. With his severe ADHD and PTSD, he hadn't been an easy kid to parent.

Tyrrell's face at the table was a new one. In spite of the fact that he was Zachary's biological brother, they had not seen each other from the time that Tyrrell was six until he and Zachary had been reunited on Christmas Eve.

As Christmas Eve was the anniversary of the fire that had destroyed their family more than thirty years previously, it was always a dark time for Zachary. Some years he had almost not made it through the holiday. Being reunited with his brother had been the fulfillment of what he had thought was an impossible dream. He had been sure that he would never see any of his biological siblings again. Even being a private investigator, he had never looked for them, never daring to interfere with what might be happy lives to remind them of the horrible thing he had done in causing that fire.

Tyrrell's facial features were similar enough to Zachary's to recognize a family resemblance, though Zachary's face was still gaunt, not yet filled out following his pre-Christmas depression. Tyrrell's hair was dark like Zachary's, but longer and shaggier. He was clean-shaven. It was his eyes that Zachary found startling. In spite of the hard life that Tyrrell had been through, they were still the shining blue eyes of the six-year-old brother he remembered.

They gathered around the table to exchange stories of Zachary's and Tyrrell's separate lives, comparing notes and getting to know each other again. Zachary needed an environment where he felt safe to share in spite of any flashbacks or surges of emotion brought up by the retellings. A restaurant or bar would just not have worked. Some of their experiences were similar, and others were not. Tyrrell had been younger at the time of the family's dissolution, and therefore less damaged than Zachary, and he had been able to stay with the two younger kids for most of his childhood, so he'd had that constant in his life. Zachary had been alone, bounced from one family to another so quickly that he'd been known to return to the wrong family after school, forgetting where he was supposed to be.

But in spite of the smiles around the table, Zachary knew there was something wrong.

――――――

At first, Zachary hadn't been able to put his finger on it. He thought that maybe Mr. Peterson and Pat were just awkward having a new 'son' at the dining room table. They were used to Zachary and his quirks, but Tyrrell was a recent addition and they didn't know enough about his past to know what might trigger him, or about his interests to know what questions to ask to encourage his participation in the conversation.

But it was more than that.

There were a number of looks exchanged between Lorne and Pat that didn't seem to follow the rhythm of Tyrrell's participation in the conversation. Mr. Peterson put his hand over Pat's as they ate, something Zachary had rarely seen him do at the table. Their natural cheer was diminished, as if there were something pulling them away from the conversation to think sad thoughts. Like someone who had recently lost a loved one but was trying to act unaffected.

He watched the two of them more closely, but didn't call them out in front of Tyrrell. Obviously, whatever was going on was something they didn't want to share with Tyrrell. Maybe not with Zachary either.

Tyrrell didn't know Pat and Lorne like Zachary did, and didn't seem to notice anything amiss. He tried to catch Zachary's eye.

"Do you remember that?"

Zachary hadn't realized how distracted he had become from Tyrrell's story. He licked his lips. "Uh… sorry… I missed that."

Tyrrell looked at him for a minute, nonplussed. He shook his head. "About time to top up your Ritalin?"

"Uh… not taking any ADHD meds right now," Zachary admitted. "Sorry."

"I didn't mean..." Tyrrell flushed pink. "I wasn't serious. It was just supposed to be a joke. Because you were distracted."

Zachary flashed a look toward Mr. Peterson and Pat, noting that their hands were again touching, and Mr. Peterson was giving Pat a questioning look as he thought Zachary was occupied by a separate conversation. Zachary swallowed.

"I try to only take them if I really need to focus on something. I don't like to have to take them all the time, and they can interfere with other meds. So I just take them when I really need to."

"I didn't mean you to take it seriously..."

"What were you talking about? That I missed?"

Tyrrell looked like he didn't want to cover the same ground again. Mr. Peterson put down his fork and jumped in.

"It was about your sister Jocelyn. I gather she was sort of a second mother to you guys?"

Zachary nodded, glad to segue to something in the past rather than focusing on the issues he still battled. "Yeah, she was really bossy. I resented it, because... well, who do you think got most of that bossiness? It wasn't the little guys; she was pretty patient with them. But me... she figured I was old enough that I should have figured out how to behave myself. We were supposed to pay attention to her and fly straight, but... I was always going off-script."

Tyrrell chuckled. "Is that what you call it?"

Zachary felt his own face get warm. "I tried, but... I wasn't any better at following her rules than I was anyone else's." He included Mr. Peterson and Pat in his broad shrug. They had either experienced or heard the stories of some of his more disastrous choices.

"Joss was a little bossy," Tyrrell admitted. "But she really helped me to figure out what I was supposed to do. I really wished that we'd been able to stay together when we went into foster care. She would have been able to help me to figure out the rules when I was in a new home. I often heard her little voice in my head, telling me how to behave properly, when I was trying to sort it out."

Zachary often had too many little voices in his head, and they all told him different things. But it wasn't usually until *after* he'd impulsively done something that he actually heard them. The voices of Joss, his parents, his social worker, or some other authority in his life, telling him that once again, he'd done something exceptionally stupid and that there were going to be consequences.

Zachary shrugged and looked down at his plate. He ate a couple of bites, forcing himself to eat despite the bubble of anxiety in his stomach from trying to figure out what Mr. Peterson and Pat were so worried about. As he'd told Tyrrell, he was off of his ADHD meds, so he actually had an appetite, and Pat was a good cook, but the unspoken tension in the room was getting to him.

"Have you had any contact with her?" Mr. Peterson asked with interest.

"A little," Tyrrell said. "Mostly just email or social media, you know. We haven't gotten together face-to-face. I think... she's got her own life and isn't that interested in reconnecting. It can be hard... stirring up old memories. She's got her own life now."

"You guys should have a reunion, get everyone together. It sounds like you know where everyone is now."

Tyrrell nodded slowly. He glanced sideways at Zachary. "I have ways to contact everyone now. But I'm not sure if everyone wants to get together. They're all living their own lives."

"But you grew up with the younger ones. You guys must have a pretty good relationship."

"We were together until I was fourteen or something, so yeah, we have a lot of shared memories, but then we didn't have anything to do with each other because we were in different homes until we were adults. It's a real hodgepodge of relationships."

"I can't imagine what it must be like not to know where your siblings are," Pat contributed. "I just have one sister, and we've always been in contact, even if she didn't particularly approve of my 'lifestyle choices.' It would be hard, not even knowing where they were."

There was a suspicious crack in Pat's voice that set alarm bells ringing for Zachary. Pat didn't usually get emotional about his family. He laughed about their attitudes, mentioned them now and then, but even when his father had died, he hadn't cried about it. Not in front of Zachary, anyway. With the number of times that Zachary had broken down around Pat, Pat certainly shouldn't have felt awkward about shedding a few tears in front of Zachary.

Zachary studied Pat closely, and then Mr. Peterson. Lorne apparently caught the significance of the look. He made an infinitesimal shake of his head, which might have even been unconscious, and Zachary knew it wasn't the time to ask what was going on.

"I guess it's a different experience," Tyrrell agreed, "but I've never known anything else, so for me, that's just the way families are. You spend a few years together, and then you don't have any contact for a decade or more. Now with the internet, you have these opportunities to touch base again and find out what people have been occupying themselves with. We're all adults now, so it isn't like we're looking to live together as a family again."

"I'm glad you reached out to Zachary," Mr. Peterson said. "It's been really good for him to have contact with someone from his family again."

Zachary nodded reflexively.

"I think everyone needs to know that they have somewhere they belong," Mr. Peterson went on. "Not just somewhere like this," he spread his hands to indicate his home, where Zachary was a welcome part of the family any time, "but biologically, too. I've heard that a lot of people who are foster or adopted kids really miss that biological connection, even if they never met their biological family before. There's just a hole where they feel like they don't belong or aren't a part of the family who raised them."

Zachary let his eyes linger on Mr. Peterson for a few moments. It was only natural that, as a foster parent, he would be aware of the needs of foster kids to find some kind of genetic connection. But he didn't want Mr. Peterson to feel like he hadn't been a good enough parent or friend to Zachary.

Tyrrell gave a shrug. "I guess so. I always knew I had biological siblings out there. Even parents, if I wanted to look for them. But I was more interested in building a family of my own. Getting married, having kids. I guess that was my way of having a genetic connection with someone. My own kids."

Zachary felt a pang. He hadn't told Tyrrell his own history with his ex, Bridget, and the issues that she'd had with having children. Zachary had always thought that he would have a family, a house full of kids to remind Zachary of the family that he'd lost. To make up for the pain that he'd caused.

Even though Bridget had said from the start that she didn't want kids, he'd thought that she would change her mind. That biological clock would start ticking, she would see what a great father Zachary would make, and she would decide it was time.

He'd been sadly mistaken and things had not ended well.

Mr. Peterson flashed a look at Zachary, knowing the history. Maybe that too was part of what he had read. How kids with no biological heritage longed for children of their own. Maybe it was an established pathological desire.

CHAPTER TWO

They got through the evening. Zachary found the time went much more slowly than usual as he watched Mr. Peterson and Pat, waiting for a flash of insight into what was going on with them. He was intuitive, skilled at reading body language and facial expression, and he knew Lorne and Pat well, but he couldn't quite put his finger on what was going on.

After saying his goodbyes, he walked out to his car, and waited until Tyrrell got into his and drove away. Then he returned to the house.

Pat opened the door, looking at Zachary with surprise. "Forget something?" he asked, looking behind himself to see if Zachary had left a book or bag.

Zachary shook his head. He hesitated. "I just wanted to see if there was something I could do…"

Pat looked at him for a minute, then stepped back. "Come in."

Mr. Peterson came around the corner. "Oh, Zachary. What's up? I thought you were on your way."

Pat looked at him, communicating something by his manner. Mr. Peterson nodded slowly. "I guess I should know better than to try to get anything past you." He led the way to the living room and they sat down. Mr. Peterson normally liked his easy chair, and Pat was usually back and forth, preparing coffee or checking something in the kitchen, playing the part of the diligent host. But they both sat down together on the couch, holding hands again.

Mr. Peterson looked at Pat. "You want to start?"

Pat blinked, looked down, then nodded. "Sure." He cleared his throat. He looked at Zachary, gaze steady. "A friend of mine is missing."

"Oh." Zachary thought about that. "I'm sorry. How long has he been missing? Have you talked to the police?"

"I talked to the police... they weren't really that interested. They said that they would look into it, but as far as I can see, they haven't done much. They said they would get back to us if they found anything, but..."

"You haven't heard anything back from them," Zachary finished. "They can keep their investigations pretty close to the chest, sometimes. If you're not the next of kin, they don't have any requirement to report back to you. They haven't said anything?"

"They don't think there's any foul play. They think that he just... left town."

Zachary nodded. "Could he have?"

"He didn't," Pat said with certainty. "I know Jose, and he didn't leave town. He would have said something to me if he'd been planning on leaving. Even if it was something unplanned, he would still have called."

"Where do you know him from?"

Pat looked at Mr. Peterson, and then back at Zachary. "We know him from the community. He's gay. Someone we get together with now and then to do something with."

They didn't often talk about their social life, so Zachary didn't know how large their group of gay friends was, or how long they had known this Jose. Zachary had never heard either of them mention him before.

"How long has he been missing?"

Pat swallowed and rubbed his forehead. Mr. Peterson patted his back and filled in the details. "As far as we can tell, it's been a week since anyone has seen him."

"A week." Zachary didn't like that. He could understand the police not being too concerned if it had only been a day or two, but a week should have been raising some red flags. "Have you talked to his work? His family?"

"He doesn't have any family here. He has a wife and kids back in El Salvador, he sends money home to them. Here, he doesn't have anyone... steady. Just friends, casual encounters."

"He's gay but he has a wife and kids in El Salvador?"

Pat shrugged and nodded. "Sometimes it happens that way."

Mr. Peterson had previously been married to a woman and had foster kids, so Zachary supposed he shouldn't have been surprised. People chose to do the socially acceptable thing, and then later decided that they couldn't maintain appearances.

"And work? Does he have a job?"

Pat nodded and took over again. "He did day labor, cash pay, but it was with the same company every day, not going from one job to another. I talked with the foreman and he said that Jose just stopped showing up."

"Was he surprised about that?"

"No… but that doesn't mean that he was right. If you had a worker coming in every day and then they just stopped coming without a word, wouldn't you be concerned?"

"I would," Zachary admitted. "But I don't deal with day laborers. I guess they probably have a pretty heavy turnover. Is he… legal?"

"No. Undocumented."

"So if there was trouble, he might have just disappeared."

"He could… but like I said, he would have at least given us a heads-up that something had happened."

"If he could. But sometimes there isn't any warning, they just get arrested and put into a facility awaiting deportation. You don't know that he would be able to call you. Or that he would. He might have been limited in the number of calls that he could make, or he might have figured there was no point. You couldn't do anything for him, so why bother?"

"I still think he would have told us if he could."

"Did the police check in with ICE? See whether he had been picked up in a sweep?"

"They haven't gotten back to us. I think if they had found his name on a list like that, they would have at least said that he was okay, even if they didn't give us any details."

Zachary nodded. In theory. But sometimes the police dropped the ball and didn't call back, especially if it were just a random friend and not the next of kin. Sometimes they got distracted by other cases or bogged down, and just clearing the case was all they could do, without making a bunch of reports to the friends or family.

"You don't think he went back to El Salvador? What if his wife said she needed him to come back? She or one of the kids was sick. Something that sounded like an emergency."

"He would have let someone know." Pat shook his head. "He didn't live by himself. Most of these illegals don't make enough money to get a place of their own. Especially when they're sending as much home as they can. So he had roommates. He didn't tell them where he was going. He just didn't come home one day."

Zachary found himself pulling out his notepad to start making notes. His brain was grinding through the possibilities. If Jose hadn't gone home, then ICE was still the most likely possibility. Someone had tipped them off and he had been nabbed on his way home from work, at a bar, or even at the grocery store.

But there were other possibilities. He was mugged or had an accident, and was in the hospital somewhere. Maybe under his own name and maybe as a John Doe. Similarly, he could be in the morgue. Going home to El Salvador was less likely. He would probably at least have told his roommates what was happening if he were going back home. There would be no reason not to tell them. He would have had to make arrangements; he wouldn't have just been able to hop on a plane and fly back in a couple of hours. Zachary scratched down a few thoughts. He looked up to see Mr. Peterson and Pat watching him intently.

"Do you have the name of the officer who investigated it? A case number?"

"Yeah. Just a minute." Pat got up and retreated to the bedroom to get the details.

Mr. Peterson gave Zachary a smile. "Thanks for this, Zachary. We've been very worried."

"You should have told me. I could have gotten started on it earlier."

"You have a lot on your plate. One undocumented worker disappears… it's not exactly at the top of the priority list."

"Not for the police. It would have been for me."

Mr. Peterson smiled. "Thank you."

They waited for Pat to return with the information about the policeman. "He and Pat were pretty close?"

"They clicked. Sometimes you just meet someone that everything falls into place with. You start a conversation with them, and it's like you've known them your whole life. You know?"

Mr. Peterson didn't sound jealous, but Zachary couldn't help wondering just how far the friendship went. He had never seen any cracks in the relationship between Mr. Peterson and Pat, but people hid that kind of thing. Zachary hadn't known that Mr. Peterson and his wife were getting divorced until he had shown up at the house one day to be told by Mrs. Peterson that her husband didn't live there anymore. He had seen, before that, that the two of them were not terribly compatible. They had very different personalities and viewpoints. If Mr. Peterson had had his way, Zachary probably would have lived with them longer than he had. Maybe not for years, but a few more weeks. They would have tried for longer to work things out. Mr. Peterson understood Zachary and his issues better. His wife had only been concerned about Zachary's behaviors and how they might affect the other foster children. As a mother, of course that was something that she had to consider.

Pat returned with a piece of paper. He handed it to Zachary. Detective Dougan, a phone number, and a case number.

"Thanks. Tell me the information you can about your friend. His full name, where he worked, where he lived, anyone else in your group I can talk to."

Pat sat back down. He pulled out his phone. "His name is Jose Flores. He worked for A.L. Landscaping." He read off a phone number and address for Zachary. "The roommate that I talked to..." He tapped around on his phone for a minute. "His name was Nando Gonzalez."

"Do you know him?"

"No. I hadn't ever met him before. I hadn't ever been in Jose's apartment. But I knew where it was. We had picked him up before and I knew what the apartment number was. So I just went and knocked on the door..."

Zachary processed this. He tried to envision what had happened, and how Nando might have felt about the broad-chested white man showing up without warning at his door. He would have been nervous. Anxious about being turned over to Immigration. Suspicious of whether Pat were actually a friend of Jose's, or someone playing a part. Nando probably wouldn't have told Pat everything he knew. Even if he knew from Jose that he and Pat were friends, he probably would still have hung back. Illegals had to be wary even of friends. There was no telling what Pat's true motivation might have been.

"Do you mind me looking into it? Going back and talking to him?"

"No, of course. Go ahead. I'd really like to know what happened to him. I'm worried. He wasn't that kind of guy, you know, the kind who would just disappear. I know some people do that. But Jose… he was dedicated to his job. He wanted to make things work in America. He wanted to help his wife and kids come here."

"This roommate that you talked to, he wasn't someone from your community, then?"

"No. We didn't know him."

"The two of them were not a couple?"

"No." Pat gave a smile and shook his head. "I doubt that he knew Jose was gay."

"Why not? Had he not… come out?"

It seemed like an antiquated term in a society where sexual orientation was no longer supposed to be taboo and gay marriage was legal. Was there still a reason for men and women to be in the closet and hide their orientation from their families and friends?

"It's different for men of color," Pat said slowly. "There is a belief that the word 'gay' only applies to white men. That it's not just sexual orientation, but race and class as well. The type of gay men that you see on prime-time TV. White, limp-wristed, lisping, middle-to-upper-class, sweater-wearing men. And people like Jose… aren't that. So they tend not to even identify as gay."

"Really?" It had never occurred to Zachary that the term meant anything other than a same-sex attraction. "I… I had no idea."

"How would you?" Mr. Peterson gave a smile. "Unless you spend a lot of time in those circles, you don't really hear what people think or what their prejudices are."

"So how would he identify himself?" Zachary asked curiously. "If he wouldn't say that he is gay, because only white guys are gay, then he would say that he is…?"

"MSM is a term they have borrowed from medical literature. During the initial years of the AIDS epidemic, medical practitioners found that a lot of non-whites said that they were not gay, even though they were having same-sex relations. So they had to change their language in order to properly identify the risk factors. Not 'are you gay,' but 'have you had sex with men?' MSM was the medical shorthand. Or WSW for the women."

Zachary wrote MSM down so he wouldn't forget it when he started to talk to people that Jose knew who might be part of the gay—MSM—community. Language was a powerful thing, and he didn't want to risk offending someone who might have information to share. Say the wrong thing, and he might never hear anything more from a witness.

Pat handed Zachary a photo. A group of men around a table. Pat and Lorne and others Zachary didn't recognize. Pat pointed to the Hispanic man beside him.

"That's Jose."

He was well-dressed, not what Zachary would have expected for an illegal worker. He had on evening wear, like the other men, a suit or dinner jacket and blue tie. He had a wide, pleasant smile, and looked comfortable, part of the group. Zachary raised an eyebrow at Pat, and when he nodded, kept the photo.

"Have you talked to his wife?"

"I don't know how to reach her. We never talked about it. I don't know her name or where in El Salvador she lives."

"Did *she* know that he was... MSM?"

"I doubt it. A lot of men like him keep it pretty quiet. Other than the people that they hook up with, they don't tell anyone. They live two lives, and keep them very separate."

"How did you meet?"

Pat and Mr. Peterson looked at each other. Not in a way that suggested they had something to hide, but just that they had to think about it and might need a memory jogger.

It was Mr. Peterson who answered first. "I think... the first time we met up was at a club downtown. There was a very popular lounge singer who was doing a night there... it was very busy, a lot of people wanted to see him. We went well ahead of time to get a table. The place was so packed, they were asking patrons to share tables. Jose ended up at our table, and we struck up a conversation."

"That's right," Pat's face cleared. "I'd forgotten all about that. We've done so many other things together. It was just one of those cases where everything fits together, and it was such a comfortable conversation... by the end of the night, it was like we had always been friends."

"And you've spent a lot of time together since then? How long has that been?"

"About... four months... five?"

"And the three of you together, or just Jose and you?"

Pat raised his eyebrows. "I'm devoted to Lorne, Zachary. This was not a hook-up."

"So the three of you?"

"Yes, the three of us. Usually other people as well. A group of guys getting together at a bar or club, or even a museum or gallery. Christmas shopping together. Just… things that friends do together."

Zachary nodded, getting a more clear picture of the relationship. "Can I talk to one or two of your friends? Or would that be intrusive?"

There were several seconds of hesitation, the silence drawing out.

"I'll have to talk to them first," Pat said eventually. "I'll get you names and numbers once I've had a chance to."

"Okay. Did the police talk to anyone else?"

"I don't know who they talked to. They didn't ask for the names of any other friends. Just for his boss at A.L. I think that's where the investigation stopped."

CHAPTER THREE

Lorne and Pat's house was a couple of hours north of Zachary's, and he was later getting back to his apartment than he had expected, but he was calm and hyperfocused on the investigation during his drive back. He could barely even remember his time on the road.

He was glad he had gone back in to find out what was wrong. If he hadn't, his own anxiety would have been through the roof by the time he got home, and he probably would not have slept that night. Going back had been the right choice. Zachary hadn't wanted to kick Tyrrell out to talk to Lorne and Pat privately, but he had needed to find out what was bothering them. It had been too obvious that something was wrong.

It was too late to start making phone calls on the case, especially not to the police officer. Zachary wouldn't even be able to get patched through. They would just tell him to call back in the morning.

But he could start by running Jose's name through the databases he had access to. He didn't expect to find much. Jose would not show up as a property owner or having a driver's license. He wouldn't have any arrest records. No credit history. But something still might pop up somewhere, on a news page, social network, or some other site. He should have asked Pat about an email address as well, which might have given Zachary access to Jose's email or social accounts if some of his data had been breached in the past.

There were a couple of social media accounts that might have been Jose's, but the avatars were cartoons rather than his face, so Zachary couldn't match them to the photo that Pat had given him, and their activity was private rather than public, so if he was to get into them, he'd have to have a password, or the police would have to deal with the providers to get access to them.

Eventually, his eyes were getting too gritty to look at the computer screen any longer, and he knew he needed to get to bed. He still felt wired, so he just took one sleeping pill and nothing else with a couple swallows of flat Coke from the fridge, and headed to bed. He would really get into gear in the morning.

———

He slept restlessly, but that was normal. If he got a few hours of sleep, he was doing well, especially with a new investigation buzzing in his brain. So when light started to make its way through his window signaling the impending dawn, he got up. He shuffled into the kitchen to put on some coffee, took his morning meds, and woke up his computer again. At least the computer didn't require a certain number of hours of rest. It was too early to call Detective Dougan, so Zachary checked his email. He hadn't checked it the night before.

There was a short email from Tyrrell saying that he had enjoyed having supper with Zachary and his extended family, and one from Mr. Peterson thanking Zachary for looking into Jose's case for them. Just casual, polite emails, but Zachary savored them, appreciating the touchstones. After all of the horrible email he'd gotten from Devon Masters before Christmas, it was a huge relief to be able to open his email inbox without feeling like he was facing the firing squad. Those casual little polite emails were the best remedy in the world. So he fired one back to each of the men and sipped his coffee. He took a glance at the morning news. Nothing much happening that would impact him.

He went back to his email and sent one to Kenzie as well. Nothing big or important, just touching base with her too. She had been a rock during his pre-Christmas depression, and now that things were back to normal, he wanted to pay her back in some way. There wasn't any big, life-changing thing he could do for her or give her, so for the time being, he would have to do the little things, and hope that they added up to something meaningful to her.

When she had first started seeing him, she'd had no idea what kind of a mess she was getting herself into. She'd been looking for a casual date, a fun time, and instead had ended up with him. She deserved a prize for not dumping him after the first confrontation with Bridget. Maybe part of that had just been the entertainment value Bridget provided, since Kenzie had never really considered her a rival, but had been amused that Bridget claimed to hate Zachary when, as far as Kenzie was concerned, Bridget was still attracted to him.

Zachary could have told Kenzie that wasn't the case—and had, in fact told her so several times—but Kenzie stubbornly refused to believe it. She said it was up to Zachary to boot Bridget out of his life, which wasn't something that he could do. It wasn't exactly polite to admit to his date that he still had feelings for his ex, but Zachary couldn't help that. He and Bridget had been apart as long as they had been together, but he still couldn't let go of the life that he had thought they would have together.

His current therapist had traced his inability to let go of the relationship back to Zachary's love for his mother and the fact she had abandoned him as a child, which was a pretty obvious parallel for anyone to draw, but being able to see the similarities between the two relationships and being able to get over his pining for Bridget were two different things. Until he could, Zachary was determined to 'fake it until he could make it,' to show Kenzie the attention she deserved and pretend that Bridget was out of his life and didn't mean anything to him.

Kenzie wouldn't be checking her email for a couple more hours, so he started to work his way through the stack of paperwork on his desk. If anyone had told him how much paperwork there would be as a private detective, he might not have set his sights on becoming one. He had never done well in school, his ADHD causing too many problems in any classroom setting. At least at home, he didn't have to deal with the distractions of thirty other people coughing and sniffling and shifting around in their seats. He worked through some routine skip traces, added paragraphs to reporting letters, and drew up invoices for cases that he had closed and needed to collect on. As much as he hated accounting, he wasn't going to get paid without them.

The hour hand finally crept around to eight—or since he didn't actually have an analog clock, the display on his phone and computer screen read eight—and he figured it was worth seeing if he could get Officer Thurlow Dougan. He dialed the number that Pat had given him and listened to the ringing, fully expecting that he would end up in Dougan's voicemail and have to explain what he wanted to the machine. He was scripting it in his head when the line was picked up, not by voicemail, but by a real person.

"Dougan."

"Oh, Detective Dougan. You don't know me," Zachary fumbled a little. He hated dealing with people by phone, where he couldn't read their facial expressions and body language. "I've been talking to Pat Parker about Jose Flores, the man that he reported missing…?"

"Right," Dougan said, his voice taking on an edge. Too early in the morning and he apparently didn't have his morning coffee on board yet. "And who are you?"

"Pat is my step-father," Zachary said, fudging the relationship a bit, but he knew Pat wouldn't mind. In fact, he would have been delighted. "And I'm a private investigator."

"I see."

"I know you're busy and you have plenty of other cases that demand your time and attention. I wondered if I could get a report from you on anything you were able to find, and then I'll do a little follow-up investigation, see if I can put Pat's worries to rest."

"I don't suppose Mr. Parker explained to you that Jose Flores is an illegal immigrant."

"Yes, he did. And I know that makes him a lot harder to trace through the usual channels."

"It makes him damn near impossible to trace. These guys don't leave a trail. Like I told your father when he made the report, this guy probably just got worried about an Immigration investigation and decided to move on to another location. Or he decided to go back home. It happens all the time. With undocumenteds, there's really nothing we can do."

"Yeah," Zachary agreed, trying to sound as sympathetic as possible, "and you've got plenty else on your desk to worry about."

"Darn right I do." Dougan sounded a little mollified. A few more minutes, and Zachary would have him volunteering everything he knew. The man didn't want to have to investigate it any further and he didn't want to waste his time in reporting to Pat that he hadn't been able to find anything. He just wanted it off his desk.

"I'm wondering what you were able to cover. Did you talk to his boss?"

"Sure. First place I went. As usual, the guy wouldn't admit that Jose even worked there. Of course he doesn't hire illegals. Everything he does is above board. But a little pressure and he did admit that he knew Jose, but hadn't seen him since your friend had. He just stopped showing up one day. Nothing unusual for these guys. They come and they go, and they don't say what they're doing. They just disappear. They're ghosts."

"Yeah. Pat said that he was sure that if Jose went back to El Salvador or to a different job, he would have said something about it, and he never did…"

"Pat doesn't deal with these guys on a daily basis. That's just not the way it works. It's pounded into these guys. *Don't tell anyone where you are or where you're going. It's too dangerous. ICE will get you. Don't leave a trail.* So even though Pat may think that it's a suspicious disappearance, that is not my opinion."

"Got it. And how about the roommate?"

"Roommates," Dougan corrected. "You never get just two of these guys in one place. You get whole families living in one room. With single guys, you get half a dozen or more in one apartment. They sleep in bunk beds, on couches, on the floor. Anywhere there's room."

"Uh-huh. Did you find anyone over there who was willing to talk to you?"

"Just got the same line everywhere. *Jose doesn't live here anymore. Maybe Jose went home. Maybe Jose found a better job.* Nobody knows anything. But they're not worried about it, either."

Zachary nodded to himself. It was going to take more digging to get anything more out of the roommates or friends. More time and effort than a police officer had to pursue such things.

"Did you find anything at all that indicated that he had planned to leave? Or anything that didn't jive with what the roommates were saying?"

"No. It was all pretty much what I expected. Nothing suspicious."

"Any enemies? Jealous—uh—lovers? Any risky behaviors?"

"No. No hint of any foul play. I gather from your, uh, step-father, that they were under the impression he was gay, but I didn't find any hint of that."

It didn't surprise Zachary that Jose had kept that part of his life a secret. It sounded like it was less acceptable in his circles than it was for Lorne and Pat. And they hadn't been comfortable with being openly gay for a lot of years.

"I'll take a closer look at that," he told Dougan. "Is there anything else that you would look at more carefully if you had the time to spend on the case?"

Dougan didn't answer immediately. Zachary wondered if he had pushed too fast. He didn't think he'd have Dougan's attention for long, so he didn't want to waste any time. He hadn't implied that the police weren't putting enough effort into the case, just that they didn't have unlimited time.

"I'd take a harder look at the roommates," Dougan said finally. "They're all undocumented, of course, so there's no way to check criminal records or follow their histories without getting federal agencies involved… but when you are trying to encourage them to talk, getting the feds involved is counterproductive."

"Yeah. That makes sense. Was there any roommate in particular that gave you a bad vibe? The one that Pat mentioned was Nando González."

"He seemed okay. But some of the others… I honestly couldn't even tell who was living there and who was just visiting. It seems like a free-for-all. If it was me, I wouldn't want to be living there with people coming and going in my room all the time. I wouldn't feel like I had any security."

"Yeah." Zachary thought about some of the foster homes he had been in, where there had been no sense of personal space or ownership, and if there was anything he didn't want anyone else to get their hands on, he had to keep it on his person. Like his camera. Places like that, the neck strap didn't leave his neck, not even while he was sleeping. "I wouldn't like that either." He let silence draw out for a few seconds. "Was there anything else that bothered you about the case? Anything that felt discordant?"

"We don't usually get missing persons reports for illegals. So that was a bit different. Not bad or wrong, just unusual. When we've got a case involving illegals, it's usually a body in the morgue, smuggling, human trafficking… we're not looking for immigrants that have gone missing."

Zachary jotted a few quick notes. "Great. Thanks for your time, Detective Dougan. I'll let you know if I run into anything you would want to act on. Feel free to call me if anything comes to mind later that didn't seem right or that you couldn't pursue at the time. Did I give you my number?"

He hadn't, but it was a way for Dougan to feel like he was still in control of the flow of communications. As if Zachary were acting for him, taking just one thing off of his desk that he didn't have to worry about anymore.

Dougan grunted that he hadn't, so Zachary gave it to him, and repeated his name, first and last. "And can I call you if I have any other questions? I promise I won't become a pest. But just in case something comes up that I need to get your read on."

"Yes, fine. I suppose. But if you do start harassing me, I'm going to block your number."

"Fair enough," Zachary agreed. Probably he wouldn't need Dougan for anything else, but he wanted to leave the lines of communication open and to leave a good impression with Dougan in case Zachary ever had to deal with his department again. He knew how much cops hated investigators who interfered with their cases. He had both friends and enemies in his own local precinct. He couldn't always avoid stepping on toes, but he did the best he could to keep relations friendly.

"Thanks for all of your help, Detective Dougan. I appreciate you taking the time."

CHAPTER FOUR

Mr. Peterson and Pat had never talked very much about their social life or the gay community in Vermont. Zachary had always assumed that they lived a fairly reclusive life, mostly doing things with each other. He didn't get invited to large dinner parties, and things like Christmas were always quiet, private affairs. Not that Zachary had ever been there for Christmas, other than the most recent one. He'd always turned down the invitations before. It wasn't because he didn't appreciate them, but Christmas was just such a difficult time of year for him, he could never bring himself to make plans ahead of time, and once Christmas Day arrived, he just wanted to recover his equilibrium.

But Pat and Loren obviously had a social life. They didn't just stay at home reading, cooking, and gardening. They went places, saw shows, and went out shopping with friends.

Zachary didn't imagine there was a big gay community in Vermont, though there were an increasing number of couples moving into the state following marriage equalization. Zachary fired up his browser and after anonymizing his IP address, started to do some research.

It occurred to him that if there were any foul play involved, even though the cops didn't think there was, there might be some hint of it in the community. Other people might have been targeted but never reported. There might be more information available if a more well-known gay white man had been targeted than there would be with an unknown, dark-skinned illegal. Zachary started with some general searches to see where the various gay bars, lounges, and other gathering places were in the nearby towns. There was a good amount that he turned up with just regular web searches. He could have someone else do some deep web exploration for him later on to see what was hidden in webpages that weren't cataloged by Google.

After making note of some locations, events, and festivals that were going on or had taken place recently, he started to dig deeper. Looking for signs of gay men or women who had disappeared, been assaulted, or murdered. If someone had targeted Jose, he was probably not the first person. More than likely, if there were a kidnapper or murderer out there, he had worked his way up gradually from threats and assaults, through other attempts and violent acts, until he had success on a higher level.

There were bulletin boards, many of them requiring a new account to get access. Zachary created a new email address and used it to apply for memberships. Most of them were automated and he was allowed immediate access. Not really secure if the participants really wanted any kind of shield between themselves and the general public. A couple of the boards indicated that his membership was pending, and he wondered whether there would actually be someone checking the profile out to see if he were a real person, or whether all the moderator would do was look at his name and email address and click 'approve.'

He started digging into the forums, looking for any sign of trouble. And it didn't take long.

———

Within half an hour, he'd amassed enough information to occupy a special task force. He wasn't sure how he was going to sift through all of it to find anything useful. There were specifics given about people who had caused disturbances at events, people who ordered gay prostitutes just to beat them up, neo-Nazis who had threatened violence and, in some cases, had followed through. It wasn't going to be a matter of trying to find someone who had committed crimes against the gay community, but sifting through all of the potential suspects to find someone who might be connected with Jose. He wasn't sure how he was going to do that.

It was late enough that Zachary knew Kenzie would be at the morgue, sorting through the email that had collected over the weekend, having downed at least one cup of coffee. She might be too bogged down to talk on the phone, especially if they'd had a number of bodies come in over the weekend, but he could leave a message and she could get back to him when she felt like it.

He dialed her number on the phone without looking it up or relying on a saved speed dial number. It rang a few times, but then was picked up.

"Zachary. Hey."

"Hi. How crazy is it over there today?"

"The bodies are practically walking themselves in today. I thought we were past the busy season once Christmas was over and done, but apparently some people managed to stick it out through Christmas, but couldn't stand the cold, dark months after that."

Zachary sighed. He could sympathize with her new clients. Christmas and the long, cold nights of January and February were daunting. Even those who were mentally healthy complained about how cold it was and how they were depressed by the snow and the cold.

"But, you don't want to hear about that," Kenzie said cheerfully, realizing that it wasn't the best approach to take with someone who regularly had problems making it through the cold, dark months. "I'm at your service. What's up?"

"Maybe I just called to talk."

"You wouldn't just call me just to talk on a Monday morning. You know it's a busy time, and I'm sure you have weekend emails and other jobs to catch up on as well. If you were going to call me just to visit, you'd wait until the end of the day."

"I suppose."

"So, what is it? You got a new case? Zachary Goldman is out to get justice?"

"Yes to a new case… though I don't know whether it will go anywhere or if there was any injustice done. For now, just a missing person."

"Okay. And what do you need me for?"

"You've taken some psychology courses, right?"

"Sure. I'm not as up with it as my forensics, but I can help with some basic questions."

"Okay, well, this one is about how to tell the difference between

29

someone who's just blowing hot air and someone who really intends violence. Or has committed violence. How can I sort through possible threats to find the people who are really dangerous?"

"Yikes. You don't think that's a little deep for a Monday morning? I'm sure there are a lot of people who would like to know the same thing. But the fact is, you can't really tell. If you know enough about the person you might be able to construct a profile and have an idea of who is dangerous and who is not, but you couldn't tell for sure. Those TV shows you see where they build detailed profiles and predict who is committing a string of serial murders, that's fiction. There's no way to construct something so specific. People are going to do what they're going to do, and some of them are very good at masking what they feel. Or the fact that they don't feel."

Zachary thought back to the bullies and psychopaths that he had encountered in foster care or in school. Or even in the police force. Some of them were very good at looking innocent, even vulnerable. Some of the worst bullies hid behind their masks of age, femininity, or friendliness. They made you think that there was nothing to worry about, and then they brought down the hammer.

Someone like Mrs. Phipps at one of the group home he had been in would have the social worker eating out of her hand, thinking she was the sweetest little old lady anywhere, but as soon as the social worker was out of the house, would turn around and whale on Zachary with her cane for some infraction. Danger could lurk behind just about anyone's innocent-looking eyes.

"Can you think of some warning signs you might see? In, say, a serial killer or someone who had committed violence repeatedly, but managed to keep it under the radar?"

Kenzie made a clicking noise with her tongue. "I'm going to have to think about that one. Psychological profiling can give you some ideas. A serial killer is most likely to be a man, probably comes across as charming and self-effacing, maybe still lives with his mother or helps to take care of someone else. Sometimes it's someone who has a connection with crime, like a dispatcher or firefighter. Probably not a cop, but someone who would like to be, that sees things in black and white and sees themselves as the only one who can fix society's ills. As far as age goes, I can't help you there. Some of them start out very young. They've probably committed some kind of violence by their teenage years, if not actually killed someone, and either served time or got away with it."

"So, someone wouldn't just start at thirty or forty."

"Not as likely. They might not get caught until then, but chances are they started much earlier."

"And they tend to like a certain type, right? Like all of the victims are girls with long blond hair…"

"Maybe. But not necessarily. You'll usually see them sticking to one particular gender, maybe age range, but physical type is not as important as they make it out to be on television."

"Okay. I'm not sure how I'm going to get through all of this information, then. If you had to sort through a bunch of unrelated data to figure out who was a serial killer, how would you do it?"

Kenzie considered. He could hear her tapping away while she filled out forms. "Well… to tell the truth, I probably wouldn't use psychology at all. Because you're not going to be getting interviews and psychologist's report for each of the suspects, are you? Even if you were, I'm not sure it would help. What I would do is… I would try to match up their schedules with the victims'. Who doesn't have a good alibi? Whose long-haul trucking route or time off of work matches up with the distribution of the victims? You'll probably have a lot easier time narrowing it down that way than by a psychological profile. You're not going to be able to tell who is hiding behind a mask. You need to look for the physical evidence."

CHAPTER FIVE

It would take a couple of hours to drive to Jose's residence. Zachary eventually bit the bullet and just headed out. He hadn't gotten far with the list of suspects from the discussion boards, but he had everything saved to the cloud so he could look it up on his computer, tablet, or phone when he needed to. If he happened to run across any of the accused bullies in Jose's apartment or at his work, he would at least have somewhere to start.

As it was, he didn't know where any of those names were going to lead or if any of them were going to be helpful. Other than to establish that there was still a lot of bullying and violence against the gay community, in spite of how it was supposed to be better for them now. He felt bad that there was still so much prejudice against gays. He remembered how careful he had been when he'd first met Pat, afraid of hurting his feelings—or worse, Mr. Peterson's—with the wrong reaction or by saying something insensitive. They were two of the nicest, most stable people that he knew, and he could never understand how people could be so prejudiced. Maybe it was because Zachary had grown up in so many different homes, meeting people of many different races and persuasions. He'd learned that everybody was just an individual, and to judge them by the way that they behaved and treated others rather than by any preconceived notion.

The address that Pat had given him was not in a nice area, which wasn't a surprise. Where else could the illegals afford the rent? It wasn't going to be a fancy neighborhood. Zachary drove around the block a couple of times getting the lay of the land before choosing where to park, a little distance away from the apartment, where it wasn't quite so sketchy looking. Then he walked back to the apartment, eyes peeled for any gang activity or other hazards. Eventually, he stepped into the building.

It was dim inside and he stood there blinking for a few minutes before his eyes adjusted to the lighting enough to go on. He didn't want to be walking in blind. The apartment was on the third floor, and there was no evidence of an elevator, so he climbed the two flights of stairs and looked at the numbers on the doors. Most of the apartments didn't have any numbers at all, so he counted them off and hoped he picked the right one. If he didn't, he supposed the resident would point him in the right direction. What were they going to do, beat him up because he knocked on the wrong door?

He knocked a couple of times before the door was answered. It was a short man with black hair and dark skin, Zachary guessed he could be Mexican or El Salvadoran or any one of a number of different nationalities. Zachary smiled and didn't make any movements that might be taken as aggressive.

"Hey," he said. "Is this Jose's place?"

The man looked at him suspiciously, then shook his head. "Jose doesn't live here anymore."

"So this is the right place. I wonder if I could come in and talk to you and any of the others who are around for just a few minutes. I'm trying to find out where he went."

The man shook his head and started to close the door. Zachary quickly stuck his foot in the crack to keep it from closing all the way. "I'm just trying to find out what happened to him. Once I know he's okay, that's it. I just want to make sure nothing happened to him."

"Nothing happen. He just go"

"I don't think that's true."

The man looked at him, brows drawing down. "Why?"

"Because he didn't tell anyone where he was going. If he was going to go back to El Salvador or off to another job, he would have told his friends."

"No. He not tell anyone. He just go."

"I'll just be a minute. Let me come in and have a look around, then I'll go and I won't bother you again. Are you Nando?"

"No."

"Is Nando here?"

The man looked over his shoulder. "Nando is out."

"When is he getting back?"

"Don't know."

"You must know something. Is he at work? Or did he go out shopping or to eat?"

"He just out. You go. You call him later."

"I need to talk to him. I'll just wait here." Zachary stubbornly didn't pull his foot out of the doorway. What were they going to do? Call the police on him? They wouldn't want anything to do with the cops. They wouldn't want to draw attention to themselves.

The man stood there, dithering about what to do, his eyes going up and down the hallway as if worried that someone was going to happen by. Finally, shaking his head in frustration, he opened the door and allowed Zachary to step in.

"Thank you," Zachary said politely. He looked around the apartment.

Detective Dougan had warned him that it would be crowded. He hadn't been kidding. There was no living room furniture in the room Zachary walked into, just cots and mattresses with barely enough room to walk between them. Zachary tried not to give away his shock at the conditions. The place smelled like onions cooked on a hot plate, mixed with stale instant coffee and body odor. Even though it looked like they were careful not to leave garbage around the apartment, Zachary could see cockroaches creeping along the floorboards under the cots. Anyone who had a mattress right on the floor was taking the risk of having them crawl right across him. Zachary gave a little shudder. But he pasted a smile on his face and forged ahead.

"Thanks for letting me in," he said, as if it had been the man's choice and he hadn't just been forced into it. "So, where was Jose's bed?"

There were other men there, all more or less the same racial profile and body shape. All men who spent the day working hard, who slept and ate little. They watched him with suspicion that Zachary pretended not to notice.

The man looked at him, rolling his eyes and shaking his head. "Jose not here anymore."

"I know that. Which bed was his? Was he in here or one of the bedrooms?"

"Who are you?" demanded one of the other men, older than the first, his face rounder as if he hadn't missed quite as many meals.

"My name is Zachary Goldman," Zachary said, offering his hand. "Are you Nando?"

The man nodded. He didn't take Zachary's hand. "And who is Zachary Goldman?"

"I'm a friend of Pat Parker's. Pat and Jose were friends, and Pat's been worried about what happened to him, so I came by to see if I could find anything out."

"Pat," Nando repeated.

"Yes, did you ever meet Pat?"

"No, I know Jose talked about a Pat." Nando showed rotten teeth with a grimace that might have been an attempt at a smile. "Pat and Lauren, a couple of girls that he went out with sometimes." He gave Zachary a wink. "I always thought he was doing pretty well to have two girls who would go out with him at the same time."

Zachary didn't correct his misapprehension. Jose may have told him that he was going out with girls because he hadn't been comfortable coming out about his status. If that was the case, it wouldn't do Zachary any good to tell Nando that he'd been lied to. That would just make him resentful and he wouldn't want to talk to Zachary or disclose anything else that he'd been told that might be a lie.

"Pat is worried about Jose," Zachary repeated. "Jose didn't say where he was going, he just disappeared without telling anyone. Pat wants to make sure that he's not hurt."

Nando shrugged his shoulders. "Jose goes where he goes. I don't know where he went. Maybe he went home."

"He wouldn't do that, would he? He needed to earn money here to send home to them. He wanted to take care of his family and maybe find a way for them to join him here someday, right?"

Nando pursed his lips. He folded his arms in front of his chest. "You don't know Jose."

"No, I don't. Tell me about him. Were you surprised when he left? Were you surprised that he didn't tell you where he was going?"

"No. People come, people go. Especially around here. Nobody stays forever."

"So you just came home from work one day, and all of his stuff was gone…?"

Something changed in Nando's eyes. He looked around the room as if he might have said something wrong, even though he hadn't yet answered.

"He did take his stuff with him, didn't he?" Zachary prompted.

"Who are you? Are you the one who sent that policeman around? We told the policeman; he took all of his stuff with him. Cleared everything out. There wasn't anything of his left behind here."

"Oh." Zachary considered that. He supposed that a place like that was probably similar to a foster home. Whatever you didn't take with you when you left, everybody else took at the first opportunity. Zachary had been taken out of the Peterson's home while he was at school. His social worker had packed his bag for him, but she hadn't known to pack his camera. She hadn't packed his meds either, but Zachary hadn't been concerned about those. He had only been worried about his precious camera. Mr. Peterson had kept it safe for him until he was able to go back and get it. At any other foster home, that wouldn't have happened. Whoever wanted the camera would have just taken it. "So what did he leave behind? Any personal papers?"

Nando looked around the room, meeting the eyes of others of the roommates, all of them trying to communicate by facial expression and body language as to what he should say or do.

"I don't care if you're using his things," Zachary reassured them. "I'm not going to take away blankets or clothes or anything. I'm just wondering whether there was anything personal. Anything that you were surprised he'd left behind?"

Nando scratched stubble on his jaw. "He didn't leave anything."

"What? Money? A journal?"

"He wouldn't leave money!" One of the other men barked with laughter. "Nobody leaves money here. If you have money, you keep it with you. You wouldn't leave it somewhere anybody else could find it."

"You don't have lockers or drawers or anywhere secure where you can store your own things?"

"Some people have a box," Nando said. "But you don't leave anything valuable here. If Immigration come one day... if you can't come back because something happened. Anything important, you take it with you."

"So, what did Jose leave?"

"He leave nothing," Nando insisted again. But every time he insisted, Zachary was more convinced that he was lying. Jose had left something behind.

Zachary took a slow look around the room. Then he headed toward the back hallway where the bedrooms were. Alarm showed in Nando's face and several of the others'. Zachary kept going. As long as they weren't physically stopping him, he was going to have a look around and find out what he could.

There were two bedrooms, and they looked pretty much the same as the front room, with cots and mattresses taking up the majority of the space. There were a few boxes, as Nando had said. Little cardboard boxes and a few metal boxes like a business would use for petty cash. There were no dressers and no clothes hanging in the closets. Extra clothes were neatly folded on each of the beds. Maybe to be used as pillows during the night.

There were no mattresses that were obviously unoccupied. Zachary looked at each bed carefully, analyzing whether there was anything out of place.

"You can't be in here," Nando said more urgently from Zachary's elbow.

Zachary keyed in on his tone. "I won't be long. Which bed was Jose's when he was here?"

"You can't be in here."

"Is this where Jose was?"

"He is gone."

Zachary took a slow walk around the room, watching Nando's face for some change in expression. Like a game of hot and cold. Nando was trying not to tell him anything about where Jose's bed had been, but he got more agitated as Zachary got close to it. Zachary bent down over one of the cots.

"This one?"

"No, you can't touch other people's things. It's time for you to leave."

Zachary picked up the clothes and shook each piece of clothing out, one at a time. Nothing hiding there. No cash in the spare socks. Nothing left in the pockets of the owner's pants. Zachary folded them again and put them down. He pulled back the blanket over the cot. Again, there didn't seem to be anything hidden there. There was a thin mattress over the top surface of the cot, and Zachary peeled it back to have a look underneath. There wasn't anything hidden under the mattress, but he could see a metal box underneath the cot. He got down on his knees to retrieve it and tried not to handle it any more than he had to, touching his fingertips to the corners in case there were other fingerprints that should be collected, such as Jose's or those of someone else who lived in the little apartment. Maybe someone who had something to do with Jose's disappearance.

It didn't have a lock, but it had a latch. Zachary flipped it up and opened the hinged lid. There were a few pictures, a little notepad, a piece of fabric that might have been a handkerchief. Zachary picked up the photos by the edges and studied them. A couple of young children, a woman in a flowered dress, smiling tiredly at the camera.

"Is this Jose's family?" Zachary asked.

Nando stared at him sullenly.

"That's his family," said another voice. Zachary turned to see a younger man in the doorway. He was maybe eighteen, no older than that. He had an easy smile and a friendly manner. "How did you know Jose?"

CHAPTER SIX

"How *did* I know him?"

A look of realization crossed over the young man's face, but then was quickly gone. "My English is bad," he said humbly. "How *do* you know him?"

"I'm a private investigator," Zachary said, "looking into his disappearance."

The younger man looked at Nando and glanced around the room. "A private investigator?" the boy repeated with interest. "Like on TV?"

"Yes, like on TV," Zachary agreed. "And I'm going to find out what happened to him. What can you tell me about the day he disappeared?"

Nando shook his head at the boy, warning him.

"Why don't we go out somewhere?" Zachary suggested. "We can go talk somewhere more private. I'll take this," he indicated the box to Nando, "and keep it safe. Then you won't have to worry about it anymore."

The boy looked at Zachary and Nando uncertainly. He shrugged. "You want to buy me pizza?"

Zachary couldn't help laughing. "Of course, I'd be happy to buy you pizza."

He handled the box carefully, trying not to destroy any evidence. It had a handle on the top that he unfolded and hung on to with two fingers in an effort not to get more fingerprints on it. He and the boy walked back through the apartment and out the door. Nando didn't follow or make any threats. Zachary breathed a sigh of relief when he was out of the oppressive atmosphere of the apartment. While no threats had been made, they had not wanted him there. If they had decided to gang up on him, he wouldn't have been able to protect himself from all of them. As the apartment door shut behind them, he turned to the younger man.

"I'm Zachary."

"Philippe. Nice to meet you."

"Thank you for letting me know about Jose's box. I'm sure he would have wanted it to be taken care of."

Philippe looked sideways at him and didn't comment.

"How long has it been since you have seen Jose?"

"A week. Maybe a little more. Hard to remember, I don't keep track of him."

"No, of course not. You have a job and he has his and the two of you don't have a lot of time to hang out together."

Philippe nodded his agreement. "The days run together... I can't keep track."

"And Nando? He didn't want you to talk about it?"

Philippe laughed. "Nando doesn't want me to talk about anything. He is always saying to keep my mouth shut. *Don't talk to anyone about anything. Don't give them something to remember. Just keep your head down and don't make waves.*"

"I guess he has lots of experience. But still... you can't always live your life that way, hiding from everybody else."

"It's not normal for me," Philippe agreed. "I am a very friendly person; I like to talk to people. I like to have fun and have parties. Nando says *none of that. Don't let anyone see you.*"

"That would be very hard," Zachary said encouragingly. Though personally, he would much rather be holed up in his apartment alone most of the time, not out partying or visiting. But Philippe was naturally gregarious and it would be difficult for him to live that way. "So were you and Jose good friends?"

"We talked sometimes. He didn't spend much time at the apartment. But when he was around, we would talk. He liked to talk to people too."

"He was good friends with a couple of friends of mine."

Philippe cast a sideways glance at Zachary. He was following Zachary's lead back to where his car was parked, but didn't ask where they were going.

"What friends?" Philippe asked eventually.

"Pat Parker and Lorne Peterson."

Philippe nodded slowly. He didn't say anything to indicate whether he knew who they were or whether, like Nando, he thought they were girlfriends. Zachary decided to approach it from another direction.

"Jose had family back home?"

"Yes," Philippe nodded eagerly. "You saw his picture. A very nice family."

"It must have been hard for him to be away from them."

"Of course. He loved his wife and children very much. But he couldn't make the money they needed to survive in El Salvador. He came here to make a better life. They were supposed to follow him sometime."

"So when you didn't see Jose, did you think he'd gone back to El Salvador?"

"Back there? No, why would he go back? He needed to work here to support them."

"There wasn't an emergency back home? They didn't call him to say that he had to go back to see his family? Maybe one of his children was hurt or they were in some kind of danger?"

"No. Nothing like that." Philippe shook his head, eyebrows drawing down. "Who told you that?"

"The first thing everybody says is, 'Maybe he went home.'"

Philippe shook his head with certainty. "He would never go back."

"Not even to visit? Not even if something had happened to his children?"

"If he went back, they would all be killed. He could never go back."

Zachary raised his brows. "He would be killed? By who?"

"He had trouble with one of the cartels. His family was safe as long as he left, but if he went back…"

Zachary thought that through. They walked in silence for a while. Zachary indicated his car as they walked up to it. "This is mine. I want to put this box away. Where do you want to go for pizza? Do you have a favorite place, or just anywhere?"

"Wherever you want," Philippe said agreeably.

Zachary stowed the box away and they both got into the car. He looked on his phone for a pizza place in a slightly nicer area of town and started the engine. He didn't want to ask Philippe too much until he was a captive audience. Once he was eating, Philippe wouldn't want to interrupt his meal just because the questions were getting uncomfortable. He'd want to eat all he could while he had the chance. Zachary suspected he was probably not getting enough to eat on a daily basis.

Once they were settled and the pizza was being baked, Zachary continued the discussion. "What do you think happened to Jose?"

Philippe pursed his lips, thinking about it.

"Nando says that people leave all the time. They can go on to another job or they might be running away. If ICE showed up at his work, he wouldn't stay around. He wouldn't go back to the apartment; he would just leave."

"The police officer who was investigating his disappearance said that Immigration was not involved. They don't have Jose and, as far as we can tell, they weren't investigating his work or anywhere that he was involved with. So why would he just disappear like that?"

"Nando says…"

"I want to know what you have to say. You seem like a bright young man. You seem like you were friends with Jose and care about what happened to him. I don't think Nando does."

Philippe didn't say anything for a while. "Nando does care," he said eventually. "But he is always worried about how things are going to affect him. He doesn't want to have to run away. He wants to make money. He makes good money because he works hard and he is the one who rents the apartment, so everybody's money goes to him."

"And he makes more than it takes to pay the landlord?" Zachary asked. There were a lot of beds in that apartment. If fifteen or twenty men were paying a hundred dollars apiece for rent, Nando could be socking away a good amount of money just from the rent.

"He is the one who runs the risk," Philippe said with a shrug. "So he gets paid something for it."

"Do you think that Nando had something to do with Jose's disappearance?"

Philippe looked shocked by this suggestion. His eyes widened comically, and he shook his head vigorously. "No, no, Nando wouldn't do anything to hurt Jose. He is a good man. He takes care of us. If someone is sick or hurt, he is the one who helps. He will get medicine or a doctor, or he can help someone escape, if there is word on the streets that someone is looking for him. Nando is a good man. Just very careful."

Zachary nodded slowly. The waitress brought out their pizza, and both men helped themselves. Zachary didn't see how he was going to be able to eat more than one slice of the huge pizza. Philippe could have his fill and take the leftovers home to the other men at his apartment.

"But Nando doesn't know what happened to Jose?"

Philippe shook his head. "He kept Jose's things. Didn't get someone else in there to replace Jose right away, in case he came back. But… he is not coming back."

Zachary chewed a mouthful of pizza, unable to answer right away. He swallowed. "How do you know he's not coming back?"

"If he was coming back, he would have by now. There wasn't anything to keep him away from the apartment. Not for this long. Maybe a couple of times he stayed away with a friend overnight. But not a whole week. And he didn't go to work. So… I don't know what happened, but I don't think he is coming back."

"Do you have an idea of why not? What might have happened to him?"

"This land… sometimes it just eats men up."

Zachary considered all that Philippe was saying or not saying. "Do you know Pat and Lorne Peterson?"

Philippe took another piece of pizza. Zachary wasn't even halfway through his.

"I met them," Philippe said finally, cautious.

"Nando thought that they were Jose's girlfriends."

Philippe laughed. "Jose did not have any girlfriends."

"He didn't date anyone here? Because he had a wife back in El Salvador?"

Philippe looked at Zachary over his piece of pizza, studying him closely. "You know Pat and Lorne?" he asked.

"Lorne was my foster father."

Philippe took another bite of his pizza, thinking about that. "You know that Jose dated men," he said finally.

Zachary nodded. "Yes. I know that. A lot of people might find that shocking, but I don't. Did other people in the apartment know that about him?"

Philippe shook his head. "I do not think so. The only people who know are people he goes with. Socially."

And that included Philippe himself, Zachary realized. He raised his eyes to meet Philippe's. "I'm sorry. I didn't realize you were that close."

Philippe nodded. "He thought I was too young," he confided. "He said I wasn't old enough to know what I wanted. But I have always known."

Zachary wasn't sure what to say. He let Philippe's words roll around his mind for a few minutes. He took out his notepad and pencil. "I need to write a few things down before I forget. I'm not going to write down your name. You can look, if you want to."

Philippe shook his head. "It doesn't matter. You can write my name."

"Do you have an idea what happened to Jose? Do you think he just left on his own?"

"No... he would not have left unless he was in trouble. And if he was in trouble, the rest of us would be as well. Me and Nando and everyone else who worked or lived with him. Or socialized with him."

Zachary nodded.

There was silence as Zachary wrote his notes.

"There have been other men," Philippe said.

CHAPTER SEVEN

Zachary didn't want to misinterpret Philippe or put words in his mouth. He answered cautiously. "Other men?" he repeated. "You mean, you have seen other men?"

Philippe shook his head. "I have. But I meant... other men who have disappeared."

Zachary couldn't help readjusting his chair and leaning forward, wanting to connect with Philippe and not take any chance of misunderstanding him. "Tell me about these disappearances. Who has disappeared? Other undocumenteds, like Jose?"

"Some of them undocumented. Some with documents. But other men... who are not white... who are part of this community."

"Gay men?" Zachary pressed, then corrected himself. "MSM, I mean? Like you and Jose?"

Philippe nodded. He put down his pizza for a moment, which told Zachary that he was very serious about what else he had to share. He also leaned toward Zachary. "Jose was not the first one. There have been men disappearing... for some time."

"Did you tell the police this?"

Philippe's eyes flashed. "Why would I tell them anything? They haven't done anything. They think they solve the problem by arresting people.

Having raids of bars and lounges and other places we gather. They don't want to stop the disappearances. Just the complaints."

"Do you think they know who is behind it? Or do you think the police themselves are behind it?"

"No. I just think... they don't want to hear it. They don't care if a few men go missing. It isn't worth it to investigate."

"Have you talked to others about this?" Zachary assumed that he must have. If men had been disappearing for years, then Philippe certainly wasn't old enough to remember them. He couldn't have been part of the community for more than a year or two, if that. Someone else in the community must have talked to him about it, and shared the information about the police cracking down on gays instead of trying to help them out.

"Yes. Of course."

"I'd like to talk to somebody who remembers about other men who have disappeared. I want to know what's going on."

"Nobody knows, though," Philippe said. "If they knew who it was, they wouldn't have to be afraid. They could turn them over to the police. Or they could do something about it themselves."

Zachary nodded. "I understand that. But if I can get information about the victims, these other men who have disappeared, I might be able to figure something out. A pattern. Somebody who knew all of them or was involved closely with them."

"How would you find anything out? If the police can't find anything, how would you? They are not going to give you their files."

"Did the police find out that Jose had left his box of personal items behind?" Zachary challenged.

Philippe shook his head. "No."

"And did the police find out that you and Jose were... close friends?"

"No."

"I found those things out. Today is my first day on the case, and I know more now than the police. I can investigate. I can't promise that I'll figure out who it is, but I can't figure it out if people refuse to talk to me. I need you and the other men in the community to talk about what's going on. I already have a list of men who could be involved. People who have made threats or who have been violent. I may not have the databases that the police have, but I have a start. And I can find out more."

Philippe raised his brows. "You have suspects?"

"Yes. Potential suspects. I need more details before I can point the finger at anyone seriously, but I have a start."

Philippe picked up his pizza again. He ate it more slowly, chewing thoughtfully. "I will ask around," he agreed.

"I need more than that. I don't live here and I want to be able to get started on the investigation today. I don't want to have to go home without anything, and then to come back in a few days when you turn somebody up who is willing to talk when the trail is colder. If somebody took Jose a week ago, and either harmed him or locked him up somewhere, then that person is here now. Close by. He's looking over his shoulder and thinking that nobody can punish him for what he's done. He's laughing at you."

"Not laughing at me," Philippe insisted, sounding offended.

"Yes, he's laughing at you and everybody else in the community who knows that something is going on but doesn't know who the monster is behind it. He's laughing at you and everybody else who is afraid to go out at night. He gets a kick out of it, out of knowing that he's smarter than you or anyone else."

"He isn't that smart."

"He is if he has been getting away with kidnapping or murdering men in Vermont for years. Enough men for the people in the community sit up and take notice. There are bound to be men that no one has tied to this guy too. People who were expected to go somewhere else, so they were never missed at the time. However many men you know of who have disappeared, you can bet there are more. Maybe twice as many. Serial offenders operate for years before anyone catches them. We never know how many victims there really were."

Philippe took another piece of pizza. "Why do you believe me?"

Zachary was taken aback by the question. He considered it from Philippe's point of view. He was young, barely old enough to be called a man. He offered a wild story about men disappearing with no corroborating evidence. As a young man and an immigrant, he was used to being ignored and pushed aside.

"I believe you because I believe Pat," he said slowly. "I've known him for a lot of years and I know he's not the type to get hysterical or imagine things or make them up. If he's concerned, then I know there's reason to be. He didn't tell me that there were other men who have disappeared, but that might just be because he didn't want to taint the investigation or sound like he was telling wild, unverified stories."

Zachary took a sip of his soft drink.

"And I believe you… because you took the time to answer my questions and you care enough about Jose to find out what happened to him. I'm not going to brush you off because of your race or your age. I've had that happen to me too many times. I believe you and Pat that Jose has disappeared. And I did my own preliminary investigating this morning; I know there are a lot of people who are making trouble with the community and could be dangerous. Just because it's not out in the open, that doesn't mean it's not there. There are still plenty of people who feel threatened by the growing acceptance of the gay community. A lot of people who would not balk at violence to stop it."

Philippe was nodding along with him. He took several big bites of pizza, so it was a minute before he could talk. "I will see if I can get someone to talk to you… if you really think you can find something out. I don't know what you can do when they just disappear. How would you find anything out? There are no clues."

"The more similar cases we can find, the more clues we'll have. We'll find a pattern. Somebody had contact with all of them."

Philippe stopped mid-bite, sudden realization crossing his face. "If it is someone who knew Jose… then it is somebody I know."

"Well… more than likely. We don't know for sure where they met or how well this guy knew his victims, but chances are… it's somebody who has crossed your path as well."

Philippe gave a shudder. "That is creepy."

It wasn't funny, but Zachary had to laugh at Philippe's accent and expression. "Sorry. Yes. It is. I wouldn't want to think this guy was looking at me."

"Looking at me…" Philippe repeated, shaking his head. "I do not like this."

"You need to know. You need to be careful… I don't want *you* disappearing."

"But how can I know who is safe and who is not?"

"We'll try to narrow down where they were when they disappeared. That will give us some clue. Just… try not to go places by yourself. Especially not when you're leaving somewhere that is known to… cater to men like you."

"It's more safe to be with someone? To look like a couple? That attracts more attention. People don't have to guess whether you are there for... purposes."

Zachary thought about that. "I don't know. I still think it is safer to be with someone than to be alone. The men who have disappeared, they haven't disappeared as couples...?"

"No," Philippe agreed after a moment, "only one at a time."

"Then I'd expect you to be safer walking with someone else."

Philippe nodded thoughtfully, but didn't immediately buy in. "It's a bad world," he said finally. "If you walk as a couple, you attract skinheads and other gangs who want to stomp out the... men like me. But if you walk alone, you might just disappear."

Zachary didn't like to think of what it would be like to live in that world. He'd been in dangerous situations before, but to be in danger just because of who he was dating or where he chose to drink or take in entertainment seemed totally unfair. Philippe and Jose and Lorne and Pat should all be able to walk where they liked and with whom they liked without being targeted.

"Be careful. We know there are predators out there, whether these disappearances are related or not, so please just be careful."

The boy nodded.

"Do you think you could get your friend on the phone?" Zachary suggested. "I'd really like to talk to him before going home again. If you'd like some privacy, I could go outside for some fresh air while you chat..." He motioned to the sidewalk in front of the pizza shop.

Philippe shook his head. "He won't be able to talk right now. He is working. You don't have anything else to do while you are in town?"

Zachary considered his options. "I need to talk to Jose's boss. And if there are places that you know Jose hung out, I'd like to visit them, ask some questions."

"You don't want to go these places," Philippe said, shaking his head.

"I need to. I need to talk to people who knew him, see what people saw, what they know. If he was being targeted because of his preferences, then there may be people around those places who might have seen whoever is... making these men disappear."

Philippe's eyes were big. "Why don't you say killing them?" he asked. "That's what you think, isn't it?"

Zachary looked for some other explanation, but couldn't find one. "With one person... he could have just gone somewhere. Or had an accident. Gotten hit in the head or mugged or even run away with someone. But if there is a pattern here, and other men like him are disappearing... then I have to think that yes, it is the work of a serial killer."

"But there are no bodies."

"Just because they haven't been found... that doesn't mean there aren't any. They just haven't been left somewhere that someone could discover them. He may have a field he buries them in, or a basement or storage warehouse. Who knows? Sometimes these guys kill for years and years before they ever get caught. They don't leave the bodies where they can be found."

"So you think Jose is dead."

Zachary met Philippe's eyes, dark and shiny with emotion. "After he has been gone for a week or more... yes. Now and then you hear about a kidnapper who has kept his victims alive for years... but that's pretty rare. And usually the victims are women. I can't think of any where men have been kept alive for years. If this is the work of a serial killer—and we really don't have any evidence of that yet—then I doubt he would have been kept alive for more than a day or two."

Philippe nodded his agreement. "I think this too."

"I'm sorry. That's not what you wanted to hear."

"I wanted to hear the truth. If I want to hear stories, I can go home and talk to Nando."

"What does he think happened?"

"That Jose just went away. He doesn't know about us. He doesn't know Jose at all."

"If he had found out, how do you think he would have reacted?"

Philippe smiled a little. "You want to know if he would have killed Jose?"

"I want to know what you think."

"No. Not Nando. He is my mother's brother. If he found out about Jose and me, he would probably kick Jose out and call my mother. He is supposed to be looking after me. Making sure I don't get myself in trouble."

"You don't think he would have blown up and attacked Jose? It's possible, you know, if he thought that Jose was taking advantage of you and that he had let your mother down. He could have blown his top."

"No. Nando, he talks tough, but he is not physical. He does not get violent. He uses words and his brain, not his hands."

Zachary nodded, but jotted the thought down anyway. If it turned out that Jose's disappearance wasn't related to other men in the community disappearing, it was possible that it was a one-off. Manslaughter when Nando discovered that one of the men he trusted had interfered with the nephew he was supposed to be protecting.

"I have the information about where he worked," Zachary said, "but I need you to tell me about the other places he went, whether he went with you or on his own or with others. I can ask Pat too, but I think you probably were closer to Jose and will be able to give me more information."

Philippe nodded. He was obviously reluctant to pass the information on, but he seemed resigned to it.

"I won't mention you when I talk to them," Zachary promised.

Philippe listed a few of the places that he and Jose had gone and Zachary wrote them down. He closed his notepad, and when he slid it back into his pocket, he pulled out a business card.

"Please call me once you have contacted your friend about the disappearances. I'd like to talk to him tonight if I can. It may already be too late… but I don't want to be accused of taking my time when someone might have been in danger. I think the chances that he is still alive are pretty slim, but I have to act like he is and time is of the essence."

Philippe agreed. He took the business card from Zachary and studied it. Zachary stood up, leaving plenty of money on the table. More than was needed for the pizza and the tip. He felt bad for Jose's young friend.

Zachary stopped, his hand on the back of his chair after he pushed it in. "Uh… one more question. Were you aware whether Jose was seeing anyone else?"

"Yes," Philippe admitted. "We were not exclusive. We both saw other people."

"Anyone who might have been jealous about Jose seeing someone else?"

"I don't know. I didn't hang around with any of his other… friends."

"Did he ever complain about domestic violence? Anyone who had hit him or choked him? Anyone he didn't want to have anything to do with anymore?"

Philippe shook his head. Then Zachary could see that he was reconsidering. Philippe looked at him, frowning.

"Choked him…" he repeated.

Zachary waited for him to process the memory. Philippe thumped his fingers on the table. "One day… he had bruises on his neck and he was hurt… his ribs…"

"Did he say where he got the bruises?"

"No. I asked, but he said it was nothing, not to worry about it. I kept asking him… and he said it was just rough play." Philippe shrugged, not meeting Zachary's eyes. "So I let it go."

"How long ago was this?"

"A couple of weeks ago, maybe a month."

"Not too long ago. It's worth looking into. Do you know anyone else he was seeing? Or anything about them?"

"We didn't really share that… we didn't want to hurt each other…"

"If you think of anyone, let me know. Even if it's just someone you got a vibe from… you know, you had the feeling that maybe they had met before or gone out sometime."

Philippe nodded. "Okay. I don't think so… but I'll think about it."

"Thanks. Put me in contact with your friend as soon as you can. I'll check out his work next, but that probably won't take long. We need to keep this moving as fast as we can."

CHAPTER EIGHT

Zachary reached A.L. Landscaping and looked around. It was mostly just a front office with a receptionist on hand to deal with the public. There was storage space in back for materials and equipment, but it wasn't the type of place that had a storefront. The receptionist was white, apparently not an illegal immigrant. When Zachary came into the office, she raised her brows like she thought he had walked into the wrong place.

"Can I help you?"

"I'm looking for Art McDonald."

She looked surprised. "Do you have an appointment?"

"No, I'm afraid not. I'll wait if he's got someone else with him."

"Mr. McDonald doesn't see anyone without an appointment."

"Does he have any time this afternoon?"

She looked sour at this. She looked at her computer screen and considered her answer. "What is this concerning?"

"I'm looking into the disappearance of one of his workers."

Her eyes flicked over to him. "I beg your pardon?"

"One of his workers has gone missing. I'm a private investigator looking into it. We may have a situation on our hands."

Her hands left the keyboard and she stared at him. "A situation? What are you talking about?"

"I'm sure you want to keep everything quiet, but we may be dealing with… a serial killer."

Her eyes widened in alarm. "Are you pulling my leg?"

"Sorry, ma'am, I don't mean to scare you, but we really do need to address this immediately. I realize that he was an illegal immigrant, but I'm not here about immigration or your business practices. I'm here about a man's disappearance, maybe a whole series of deaths."

She looked unsure of what to do. Zachary tried to look impressive. She glanced toward another office, trying to decide whether to interrupt her boss, which was obviously something she wouldn't have normally done. After a few more minutes of hesitation, she stood up. "Please wait here," she instructed. She smoothed out her skirt, gave it a little tug down, and went into one of the other offices. Zachary listened, but couldn't hear her voice as she went to McDonald to explain the problem to him. In a few minutes, they were both back.

McDonald was a large man. Tall, florid red cheeks, too heavy around the middle. He looked strong, but also like he spent most of his day sitting around.

"What is this nonsense?" he demanded.

The receptionist looked around her front office as if there might be someone to overhear him, and that he should not be talking so loudly, but of course there was no one else there and he was the boss, so she couldn't exactly kick him out or tell him to tone it down.

Zachary offered a businesslike hand to shake and produced his business card for McDonald. "Zachary Goldman. Thank you for seeing me."

McDonald stammered something out that wasn't quite "I didn't agree to see you," but tried to be something more gracious. Then he returned to his previous line. "That is this nonsense about a serial killer? Is this some kind of joke?"

"No, I'm afraid not. I know that this is inconvenient for you, but if we're going to be able to prevent others from being killed, we need to find this guy. We need to identify him and get him off the streets so that he can't keep killing."

McDonald gave a distracted nod. He looked at his receptionist and then back toward his office. "I suppose you'd better come with me."

Zachary followed him back to his office. A tiny space, plain beige with few pictures or decorations. Lots of filing cabinets and loose papers. It looked more like an accountant's office than what Zachary would expect a landscaper's office to look. But he was a business owner, not the guy who was actually mowing lawns and designing flower borders.

"I really don't know what this is about, Mr. Goldman." He needed to look at the business card to prompt himself with Zachary's name. "But I can assure you that there is no connection between my business and any serial killer." He shook his head. "I wouldn't allow anything like that to go on!"

As if he thought that he would have any control over it.

"No, of course not. I'm certainly not accusing you of anything. This is just the latest development in a long chain of murders that has been going on for years. I'm not accusing you or anybody that you have hired. I'm sure this all went on completely outside of company time. But since the latest victim was one of your employees, I really do need to follow up with you and see if there is anything that we can find that might be helpful in our investigation."

McDonald sat down heavily behind his desk and motioned for Zachary to have a seat. Except that the chairs on the other side of his desk were all covered with papers. Zachary looked at them, trying to decide whether to shift one of the piles of paper somewhere else, then elected to stay standing. It gave him a psychological position of power over McDonald.

"I really do appreciate you taking the time to help me," Zachary said. Even though McDonald had agreed to nothing of the kind. "I'm sure you must know how hard it is to track down any information about illegals. You deal with them every day, so you must understand what it's like."

McDonald didn't take the bait. He just shook his head. "Who is it you're talking about here?"

"This is about Jose Flores."

McDonald's eyes flickered in recognition. "I already told the police; I don't know what happened to him. He just disappeared, didn't come in one day."

"But you didn't find anything suspicious about that behavior?"

"No. Why would I? These people come and go, they don't give any notice. They just leave you in the lurch. I have no idea where he was going or why."

"That puts you in a position, doesn't it? You rely on them to come in every day, you have everyone's schedules arranged, and then he just doesn't come in. Pretty inconsiderate."

"Yeah, well, that's just the way it is in this business. You have to be flexible. But there are always new people who are willing to work. You can find them as fast as you lose them."

"But then you have to train them."

McDonald nodded. "Yeah. That's true. It feels like a never-ending battle sometimes. But I'm trying to help these people out. It's not just something I do for myself."

Zachary balked at the idea that McDonald was just hiring illegals out of the goodness of his heart, that it was some kind of cause for him. Of course that was a big, fat lie. He just stared at McDonald for a minute, letting him feel foolish for having made such a statement, then went on.

"I realize that you already told the police everything you know; I just have a few follow-up questions for you. As you can understand, every little piece of information could be important. We don't have any way of knowing what may lead us to our killer."

"That Dougan was a pain in the neck. Treated me like I was breaking the law by hiring illegals. How am I supposed to run a business without workers? And how are they supposed to live if they don't get jobs? I'm keeping them off the streets. The government doesn't have to support them. People don't have to see them sleeping on the sidewalks and begging for money. It benefits everyone."

"I'm sure Jose was very grateful for his job. He had a wife and kids back in El Salvador that he was trying to support?"

"Yeah, something like that. One of those countries."

"He was happy working here, as far as you know?"

"I never had any complaints."

"And he was a pretty regular worker? He showed up here every day? Didn't just pop in casually now and then? Didn't miss Monday mornings because of a hangover?"

"No, he was here every day," McDonald said grudgingly. "He was reliable."

"That's what I'm hearing. How did he get along with the other workers? Were there ever any signs of trouble? People he argued with or wouldn't work with?"

"No, nothing like that."

"You never had any fights between him and someone else?"

McDonald considered for a moment, his eyes narrowing. Then he shook his head. Zachary wasn't sure whether he believed the answer. McDonald still seemed to be hiding something. "No, no fights."

"Nothing that concerned you?"

"I wasn't with them every day. I have foremen, designers, people who work with them every day. I'm just the guy that makes sure they have jobs to go to and that they get paid. I'm not the one working side-by-side with them."

"Who was? I should probably be talking to them too. And maybe to some of your other workers. They would know things about Jose that you would never have the opportunity to hear about, stuck here in your office."

"You're not talking to anyone else on my staff. I'm giving you my time and that's more than I think you deserve. I think this line about a serial killer is just that, a line. You don't know what happened to Jose. You don't know he's dead. You think I wouldn't have heard about it if the police found a body? Even if it didn't make it into the papers, the cops would still be back here waving their hands around and saying that I should have known."

"You couldn't have known that he was going to be targeted, and I doubt it had anything at all to do with his job. But we have to check everything out. It is possible that the killer first met Jose on the job. He could be another worker or he could even be a client. And at some point he made a connection with Jose, one thing led to another, and…"

"You're serious about it being a serial killer. Why haven't I heard about this before now? It seems to me if there was a serial killer, we would have heard about it. You can't keep something like that quiet."

"You can if everyone who is killed is undocumented and just looks like they have disappeared."

McDonald thought about that for a minute. "So you don't know it's a serial killer," he said finally.

"We've got a pretty good idea what it is that we're looking at," Zachary said seriously. "Just because we can't produce the bodies yet, that doesn't mean they're not there." He looked at McDonald significantly. "I'm sure you heard about that killer up in Canada who hid the bodies in landscaping planters."

The red color drained out of McDonald's cheeks. His eyes widened and he shook his head. "That couldn't happen here. We would know if anyone was tampering with planters. There's no way that could happen here."

"In that case, it was the owner of the landscaping business that was the killer. He had full access whenever he wanted."

"Are you accusing me? That's ridiculous!"

"I'm not accusing you. I'm just pointing out that… this is one of the first places we have to look at. Is there any possibility that the bodies might have ended up in garden plots? Concrete pads or borders? Planters? There are a lot of places that you could hide a body, if you were so inclined."

"But I'm not out there. Like you said, I'm here in the office all day long. I couldn't do anything like that."

"Maybe. You still have access to equipment and the work orders at night or on days off. But I'm not accusing you. There could be someone else on your staff… or it could be nothing to do with your business at all."

"There isn't anything. You know there isn't any connection with the business."

"I don't think there is," Zachary agreed slowly. "But I would like to have some questions answered."

CHAPTER NINE

"So ask your questions," McDonald barked. "This has nothing to do with my business."

"When did Jose come into work last?"

McDonald pulled out a handwritten ledger and looked at it, making sure that Zachary understood he was taking the question seriously and not just answering off the cuff.

"The twenty-third. That's a week ago last Friday."

"And he didn't tell you that he was going to be missing time or was taking vacation or going away somewhere."

"He didn't tell me anything. And as far as I know he didn't tell any of the supervisors either. But these people don't. They don't take vacations, and if they're leaving, they just go. They don't tell anyone."

"So you weren't surprised when he didn't show up for work the following Monday."

McDonald pursed his lips indecisively. "He had been a reliable worker until then, showing up for work every day. I was surprised to hear he hadn't shown up. But I wasn't concerned."

"Did you call him?"

"Call him? Why would I do that?"

"To see if he was sick or was coming back."

"No, I didn't call him."

"Did you have a number for him?"

McDonald glowered at him. But he got up and went to one of the filing cabinets and thumbed through the files there. He pulled one out and returned to his desk. He opened the slim file and looked over the information.

"Yes, we had a number for him. No way of knowing whether it was a legitimate number or not."

"You could call it and see if he answers."

McDonald said nothing.

"Did you give the police that number?"

"No."

"And you've never called him?"

"No."

"Could I get it from you?"

"I don't know about giving private employee information to anyone who asks. You are not the police."

"I can give you Detective Dougan's number and you could give it to him. Then either he could call it, or he could give it to me. Or you could call the number and see if he answers. It seems a little silly to sit on the number without *somebody* calling it."

McDonald could no doubt see that calling Dougan to tell him that he'd had Jose's phone number all along and had not provided it during their investigation would put him in a bad light. He'd already said that he didn't want to give it to a private party. That left only one option. He picked up the receiver on his desk phone and held it between his shoulder and his chin. He jabbed at in the numbers in his file, his irritation clear. He waited for a few seconds, then hung up again.

"Out of service," he said. "Probably it was a fake number from the start. They've usually got a burner phone, but they don't give the real number to anyone."

"Detective Dougan would be able to check it out and see if it's a real number and what the last few calls made on it were. You could say that it just came to your attention, or one of the other workers gave it to you because they were starting to get concerned about not having heard from Jose."

"I could," McDonald said morosely, not giving Zachary the impression that he would. But Zachary didn't want to push it yet, or he'd get kicked out before he got a chance to ask the rest of his questions.

"Did Jose have any friends in particular? Was he always on with someone else?"

McDonald shrugged. "No one that I'm aware of."

"What did he do? Did he have any particular specialty?"

McDonald looked at the file folder again, his eyes skimming over the information there. "He was a hard worker, did pretty much anything. Mowing, carrying, loading and unloading, handyman work. But he wasn't a skilled laborer. He didn't have any particular training or certifications."

"You don't know what education he might have had back in El Salvador? Did he ever say that he was an accountant or engineer or anything like that?"

"What would he be doing working at a landscaping company?"

"People do, you know. They get here and they can't use the education they had in their home country. Doctors and lawyers too."

"Well, he wasn't any damn lawyer, that's for sure."

Zachary gazed toward the open file on McDonald's desk. "I don't suppose I could get a copy of that, could I? Any information you could give me on Jose would be very helpful."

"You don't have a warrant. There's nothing in here you could use, anyway. There's hardly anything here."

"Do you have his next of kin? Contact information for his wife?"

McDonald looked at the file, then shook his head. "No. We have an emergency contact—I believe his roommate. But nothing back in El Salvador."

"Is the emergency contact Nando González?"

"Yes."

"Okay. I've already talked to him. Is there anything else? Anything that concerned you or that came up with the police?"

McDonald looked at his watch. "I think we're ready to wrap up here. I wish you all the best on your investigation, but I don't think there's anything else I can help you with."

Zachary waited for a few seconds, letting the silence draw out, seeing if there was anything else that McDonald had to contribute.

"How about that phone number? Do you want to give it to Dougan or me?"

"Why would I give it to you?"

"You might find it easier than talking to Dougan. Some people don't like talking to cops."

"What are you going to do with it if I give it to you? The number is no good. It isn't going to lead you anywhere."

"I may take it to Dougan myself and see if he can find anything out about the last people that Jose talked to, or if there was someone particular who had that number. It may not be a fake number. It may just have run out of minutes or battery by now. He's been gone for over a week. If it wasn't plugged in, the battery would be dead."

"If you tell Dougan it came from me, he's just going to be back here getting on my case and asking why I didn't give it to him in the first place."

Though that would be a good question for Dougan to ask, Zachary didn't want to antagonize McDonald. "I can say I got it from a friend of Jose's. Then it's off of your conscience, because you passed it on, but you won't have Dougan here asking questions. If you want to know the truth, I don't think Dougan is interested in putting any more time into the case. Not unless I can turn something up for him to look at."

McDonald pondered this for a few minutes, then shrugged. He turned the open file folder around so that it was right side up for Zachary. "There it is. You can copy it down."

Zachary skimmed the rest of the page as he slowly got his notepad out and flipped through it, looking for the next blank page to write the number down on. He wasn't a fast reader and he didn't have a photographic memory, so there wasn't a lot that he could get from the form in the time it took for him to write down the number. But he did his best, quickly skimming past Jose's name and address. No SSN, of course, and the birthdate was also blank. The phone number that didn't work. Nando's name and phone number. A short list of the safety and hazardous materials training Jose had received from the company. There was nothing filled in under medical conditions and allergies. A few codes at the bottom of the page that Zachary didn't understand. Probably his pay level and other terms of employment. Zachary painstakingly scrawled out the phone number, reviewing the page for any other clues. When he was done, McDonald took the file back again.

"I appreciate you taking the time with me," Zachary told him.

McDonald stretched, then took a drink of his coffee, as if he'd just been released from a tedious meeting. "Tell me the truth… you don't think that Jose was actually killed by a serial killer, do you? That's just something you said to get in the door?"

"I'm afraid it is something I'm looking at. I'm meeting with someone shortly who can hopefully give me a head start on that. You'll let me know if you think of anything else? Or if anyone else seems to be showing interest in Jose and what happened to him?" Zachary slid another business card across the desk for him. "Just give me a call if you think of anything. It doesn't have to be proven. Random facts are fine. You never know what might trigger a connection."

McDonald nodded, but didn't pick up the card.

———

Zachary called Philippe to see where he was on getting ahold of his friend who had inside knowledge of the men who had disappeared. Philippe said that he had talked to him, but that he needed some time to prepare before meeting with Zachary. Zachary hoped that didn't mean that he was spooked and on the run.

"You're sure he's going to get back to us?"

"He will, he will," Philippe assured him. "He wants someone to listen. For years, he keeps telling everyone about these men disappearing, and no one will listen. He wants to talk to you."

"Okay. Well, I need to keep moving forward with the investigation, so have you had a chance to think about places that Jose might have spent time?"

"I don't think it's safe for you to go to these places. You were just telling me not to go anywhere alone."

Zachary had a hard time coming up with an argument to that. "I'll just be asking questions as a private investigator. Nobody is going to think that I'm gay."

"Who are you kidding? People see you coming out of a gay scene, they're going to think that you're gay."

"I'll be careful," Zachary promised. "Now, give me a few places to check out."

Philippe sighed and complied, giving Zachary the names of a few establishments and where they could be found. Zachary could practically hear him shaking his head. "But you be careful, bro…"

"I will." Zachary put his phone away. For a moment, he entertained the idea of calling a friend to go with him to the bars. But he was away from home and couldn't think of any friends that he would have invited to go to a gay bar with him anyway. All of the cops he knew well were out of the jurisdiction and weren't going to drive a couple of hours out of their way to humor Zachary's whims.

Tyrrell wasn't that far away, but Zachary couldn't imagine taking his baby brother into such a place. Mr. Peterson and Pat were, of course, the logical choices, but they were getting on in years and neither would want to be seen as being on the prowl. Being seen crawling gay bars with a much younger man like Zachary might irreparably damage their reputations.

So he went alone, like he had planned to do from the start.

CHAPTER TEN

When he got to The Night Scene, it was just opening and there were only a couple of patrons there ahead of him. Zachary looked around, feeling a little awkward, knowing that he must stand out, both because he didn't belong there and because it was the first time he'd ever been there. The bouncer eyed him, but let him in without any questions. The long-haired bartender watched his approach with heavy-lidded eyes.

"Uh, hi," Zachary greeted. "Get a Coke?"

The bartender nodded and got out a glass. He filled it from the fountain, added a lime wedge to the rim, and placed it on a square napkin in front of Zachary. Zachary slid a bill across to him.

"Don't think I've seen you here before," the bartender commented.

"No. This is my first time."

"You meeting someone here?"

He had a feeling that the bartender was trying to figure out if he belonged there or had just wandered in from the street, thinking it was a regular bar.

"Actually, I'm looking for people who might know a missing man. Name of Jose Flores."

"Missing?"

"He seems to have dropped off the face of the earth more than a week ago. I'm trying to figure out what happened to him."

"That happens sometimes," the bartender said cautiously.

"Maybe so. If he's just gone on to something else, that's fine... but he has friends who are worried that something might have happened to him."

The man scratched the back of his neck. "That so?"

"Yeah." Zachary passed his card across the bar. "I'm Zachary."

"Paul." He didn't give his last name, but there was no reason he should. It wasn't like Zachary was the police or it was an official interrogation. He didn't need to provide any information he didn't want to.

"Nice to meet you, Paul. Did you know Jose Flores?"

"Might have. How do you know him?"

Zachary considered how best to answer it. He didn't know whether Mr. Peterson and Pat had ever been to the bar, or whether it was just somewhere for unattached young men to meet each other. Their names might mean nothing to Paul. But on the other hand, if he fudged on how he got the case, Paul might not see any reason to help him out. A private investigator looking into a disappearance for no obvious reason was very different from a private investigator looking into it for a friend who was concerned.

"A friend of mine asked me to look into it," he said slowly. "But I don't know if he has ever been here. I got the name of this bar from someone else."

"Who is your friend?"

"Patrick Parker. He is sort of a step-father to me."

Paul considered that, saying nothing. He polished a smudge on the bar counter that was invisible to Zachary. "He doesn't come around here," he said, "but I know him."

Zachary nodded, relaxing a little. "If you want to ask him about me, he'll confirm it."

"I believe you."

"So did you know Jose?"

"Not very well, but he did hang out here. Him and a couple of other immigrants."

"Was there ever any trouble that you saw? Anyone give him any hassle? Or did he ever get in a fight or cause trouble for you?"

"He wasn't that kind of guy. He was pretty quiet. Just wanted to meet people, have a drink and maybe a dance. Go somewhere else to take it any further."

Zachary breathed slowly. He took a sip of his Coke. "The guys he came with, they ever cause any trouble? Give you a bad vibe?"

"No. Nothing I can remember. They were regulars. Nothing suspicious."

"And was he always with them? Did he ever come by himself?"

"Might have. I didn't keep close track of him. As long as he was ordering drinks and not causing any trouble, why would I care who he was with or what he was doing? This is a place where you come to be yourself. We don't interfere with patrons unless they're being disruptive."

Zachary nodded. "When was the last time you saw him?"

"I couldn't say. A week. Two. Couldn't be sure."

"He's been missing from work for about ten days."

Paul nodded. "Somewhere in there."

"You ever talk to him? Discuss any interests? Home? Hopes and dreams?"

Paul chuckled. "Like I say, he wasn't here to talk to me. We never exchanged more than a few words."

"He was from El Salvador."

"Uh-huh."

"He never talked about it?"

"No, can't say he did."

"Never talked about going home?"

"Going home? No. Never. Nothing like that."

"You got the feeling that he intended to be here permanently."

"I don't know what his plans were, but I don't think going back to El Salvador ever entered into it."

"He had a wife and kids there."

Paul gave a grin. "All the more reason never to go back."

"I guess so. Do you get a lot of men in here who have families? Who hang around here but aren't... out?"

"Probably half the people who come in here, my friend. If they can't be themselves at home, they need somewhere they can be. This is that place for a lot of people. Leave the mask at the door and show who you really are and what you really want."

Zachary shifted uncomfortably. He looked around briefly. There were a few more customers trickling in, but things were not picking up yet. The music sounded too loud. Later, it would be drowned out by conversations. One patron, a big bear of a man with grizzled black and gray whiskers stared at Zachary, his face curious and challenging. He seemed to be a customer rather than a bouncer, but he looked like he would be perfectly happy running Zachary out of there if he felt like it was necessary. Zachary took a few more swallows of his Coke, trying not to let the man's stare unnerve him.

"Did he have any particular friends, other than the other immigrants that he sometimes came with?"

"No one particular. He hadn't settled down."

"So he didn't have a steady date."

"No."

"I was talking to Philippe earlier."

"I figured."

"How?" Zachary was taken aback that Paul would know who he had been talking to.

"Most people know to keep their mouths shut. That young pup Philippe… he hasn't learned yet."

"He's concerned about Jose. I'm someone who could help. It's not like he talked to someone untrustworthy."

Paul looked at him thoughtfully, then nodded. "Still… the boy needs more experience. I'm afraid he's going to say something to the wrong person. Something that will have consequences."

"Do you know who the wrong person would be? Is there someone around here you would not trust?"

"There's always people around here you can't trust," the bartender said slowly. "And once you say something, you can't take it back. Things could happen." He traced a white scar that ran down his neck.

"Is that what happened to you?"

"I was a young pup once too. The lessons can be harsh. Luckily, I survived. Not everyone does."

"Who cut you? Did you get in a fight? Were you attacked?"

"It was a long time ago. He's not around anymore."

"But there could be other people around here who would hurt someone like Philippe if he said the wrong thing."

Paul agreed. He left Zachary to attend to other customers, moving down the bar and then back again eventually. Zachary watched the patrons around him. He knew he couldn't tell who was safe and who was dangerous just by looking at them, but there wasn't anyone in the bar yet that he had a particularly bad feeling about. He would have felt comfortable talking to any of them. At least, under the right circumstances. Maybe not in a gay bar, but if they were sitting next to him on the bus or at a conference, he wouldn't have felt like they were dangerous.

"Philippe said that there have been other people who have disappeared. Other men like Jose," he said when Paul was back down at his end of the bar.

Paul busied himself with the till and the bar, serving drinks and making change as more people started to flow in through the doors. It was picking up faster than Zachary would have expected. Paul returned to where Zachary sat and leaned closer to him, bringing him a second Coke. "I wouldn't discuss that here."

Zachary looked around. The man who had been staring at him was sitting down, nursing a drink of his own, and no longer staring at Zachary, though he still glanced over while Zachary was examining him. Zachary looked around for anyone else who might be listening in or showing an interest in their conversation. No one looked particularly concerned with his being there.

"I don't suppose you'd want to discuss it another time and place," he suggested.

"No," Paul agreed. "So maybe you'd best just drop it. You don't need to be panicking people, making them think this is not a safe place."

"No, I didn't mean that. I didn't mean that anyone had disappeared from the bar. Just from town."

"People come and go all the time. Someone hangs out here for a few weeks or a few months, and then one day you think, 'I haven't seen that guy lately. I wonder whatever happened to him.' And probably, you never find out."

"Sure," Zachary agreed. "They find somewhere else they like to hang out, or they start a serious relationship and aren't here looking anymore. People aren't static."

"No. And it's best not to start talking about people disappearing, like something bad happened to them. There's a difference between disappearing and just not going back to the same bar."

Zachary drained his first Coke and pulled the second toward him. He needed to pace himself, or he was going to end up having to use the public restroom, and he really didn't think he wanted to risk that. He took a very small sip to show that he was still drinking and passed another bill to Paul to pay for the second drink.

"But Jose *did* disappear. He didn't just stop coming here. He hasn't been at work or at home. No one has seen him. The police have been brought it on it."

Paul cocked an eyebrow. He pushed the long hair on the right side of his face back over his ear, showing off several earrings. "The police haven't been around here."

"No, I didn't think so. I don't think they're actually very interested in finding out what happened to Jose. He's… a nonperson to them."

"We're all nonpersons to the police."

Zachary dragged his finger through the condensation on the side of the glass. "Is it that bad? The police don't get along with anyone who is gay?"

"I imagine some of them get along just fine with people who haven't come out yet. But the police departments and the gay community around here do not have a good track record."

"I'm sorry to hear that. The officer I talked to seemed pretty decent. He didn't put much time into it, but he didn't tell me to get lost. He didn't tell me that it didn't matter, even if he didn't believe that there was anything wrong. He still filed the report, did the initial legwork."

"Then they are doing more than they have done in the past. In past years… you try to get them involved in something, and you're more likely to get the wrong end of the baton, so to speak. It's best not to ask for help."

"There must be gay police officers. They don't treat you any better?"

"How do you think *they* would be treated if they did?"

Zachary nodded slowly. "I suppose if there's that much animosity, there would be resentments."

"As a cop, you don't want to be assigned all the dirty or dangerous calls. You don't want to be stuck at the bottom of the ladder and never able to advance. So you toe the line and you don't make allowances for people like us."

"I thought things would have gotten better since the Marriage Equality Act was passed. There has been an influx of gay couples…"

"Enacting a law doesn't change people's opinions. Not that quickly, anyway. There's a lot of resentment about that influx, if you're on the side of the Christians or the Nazis."

There were a number of curious glances in their direction at his words. Zachary felt his cheeks heating at the attention. "I'm sorry to hear that. I thought it would make things better."

"It has in some respects; not in others."

CHAPTER ELEVEN

The large man who had been watching Zachary picked up his drink and approached Zachary at the bar.

"Don't think I've seen you here before," he observed.

"Uh, no. I'm Zachary." On instinct, he didn't give his last name or the fact that he was a private investigator.

"You can call me Teddy."

It seemed a rather cuddly nickname for such a formidable man, but Zachary nodded and didn't ask why. He turned to look at Paul, but he had withdrawn to the other end of the bar and was serving customers there, not looking at Zachary.

"So are you new in town?" Teddy inquired. "Or just to The Night Scene?"

"I'm from out of town. I come down this way now and then to visit my father. A friend mentioned the bar to me today and I thought I would check it out."

Teddy's eyes raked him from head to toe, and Zachary had the uncomfortable feeling that the man saw him for what he was. Zachary knew that there wasn't any physical trait that could give him away as straight or gay, but he must look as uncomfortable as he felt hanging out in a gay bar and being approached by a stranger.

But Teddy didn't confront him and say he knew who he was and what he was after. He didn't even challenge Zachary on whether he was actually gay, or maybe had just ended up in the wrong bar.

Glancing around, Zachary noted that there were some women around. Or people he assumed were women. Everybody wasn't paired off. He could conceivably have walked into the bar without realizing that it was a gay bar. His so-called friend might have set him up there as a joke.

"So what do you think so far?" Teddy asked. "It will be a little while before everybody gets warmed up and the place will be hopping. Pretty quiet right now."

"I don't mind quiet. I wanted to get a feel for it before it was too busy."

"What were you talking about with Paul? You seemed to be having a pretty involved conversation."

Zachary shrugged. "Nothing, just small talk."

Teddy wasn't buying it. He motioned for another drink. Paul gave him a wave but continued to take care of drinks down at the other end of the bar.

"Are you a Vermonter?" Teddy asked.

"Yes. Just up north."

"And… unattached?"

Zachary considered the question. Teddy was moving a lot faster than Zachary would have expected. But if The Night Scene was a hookup joint, maybe that was expected. He found himself thinking about Kenzie rather than about the appropriate answer to give Teddy. They were closer than they had ever been, but Zachary had noticed a change since Christmas. Was it because she had been ready to take their relationship further when he had not been, too mired in his case and pre-Christmas depression? Or having had a taste for just how low he could go, had she finally decided that a relationship with him wasn't in the cards?

"Earth to Zachary…"

"Oh." Zachary brought his attention back to Teddy. "Uh, sorry, I was just thinking…"

"About who? That was a pretty deep dive."

"Yeah. Well… things didn't really work out between us the way I'd expected. Probably my fault."

"Maybe you just weren't compatible."

Zachary took a sip of his Coke. "Yeah. Maybe not. It's just that it looked promising for a while there… but maybe I'm not very good at long-term relationships." There was Bridget. He'd been with her for a couple of years.

But that had ended up so disastrously that he couldn't consider it a successful long-term relationship.

"So maybe what you're looking for isn't long-term," Teddy suggested. "Maybe right now, what you really want is something quick and intense." He leaned closer to Zachary. Zachary couldn't help readjusting to increase the space between them. No matter what role he was playing, his reaction to Teddy being in his personal space was visceral.

Teddy grinned and drained the rest of his glass. He put it down on the bar with a hard thunk, attracting Paul's attention. Paul made his way back over to them and gave Teddy a refill. He glanced at Zachary. "And you're okay, Zachary?"

Zachary sensed the double meaning. Paul wasn't just checking on refills, but whether he was okay with the big man talking to him. He nodded. "Yeah, I'm good. Thanks."

"Let me know if you need something." He drifted back away, getting busier as the bar got more crowded. A couple of other bartenders arrived, tying up their aprons and positioning themselves along the bar so that Paul didn't have to handle everything himself.

"I was wondering if my friend was going to be here tonight," Zachary said, "But I don't see him."

"The night is young. The place barely opened. Who is your friend?"

"Jose Flores."

Zachary was watching carefully for Teddy's reaction to the name, but Teddy didn't betray any surprise or concern. "Oh, yes. Well, he's not here every night. Did he tell you he would be here tonight?"

"No. I was just thinking it would be nice if it worked out that way. Have you seen him lately? I hope he hasn't gone off again."

"No, I can't say I've seen him recently... maybe a few weeks. He's 'gone off' before?"

"Yeah, he kind of disappears from the scene every now and then. Maybe he's shacked up with someone."

"I wouldn't hang your hopes on seeing him tonight, then. Leave yourself open to... other possibilities."

He hadn't moved perceptibly closer, but Zachary again felt like Teddy was too close. The man was just being friendly. If Zachary had been attracted to him, he was sure he would have felt completely different about his proximity and the signals he was sending out. As it was,

Zachary didn't think he could push the masquerade much further with Teddy. He should circulate and talk to a few other people. Get a feeling for who else might have known Jose or had concerns about what had happened to him.

Teddy saw Zachary's glance around the bar, and looked around himself. He jerked his head toward the door. "There's my date. I'll see you around. Happy hunting."

Zachary watched him make his way across the room to a younger man with a Hispanic cast to his features. They greeted each other warmly and found a table to sit down at. Zachary stared at them, a little shocked that Teddy had moved so quickly from flirting with him to cozying up with the man he was apparently there to see. The people Zachary normally spent time with were not the type to jump from one love interest to another in mere seconds, and it threw him off balance. He shook his head and had another sip of his Coke, looking around.

———

Zachary had asked a few other people about Jose. Everyone seemed to be friendly, but shrugged and shook their heads at his questions. It would seem that no one had seen Jose or knew where he might have gone. No one knew of any plans he'd had and, despite what Zachary had told Teddy, Jose had never dropped out of sight before. He didn't run into anyone who had been mentioned in the forums as possibly being dangerous.

It was getting late and the crowd was getting louder. Zachary had had enough of people standing too close or touching him while they talked. He just wanted his own space, peace and quiet.

He headed for the door, and was startled to have his way barred by a large man stepping into his path. He focused on the intruder and realized it was Teddy. He'd obviously had a few more drinks. His eyes were rimmed with red and his movements were sloppy.

"Come with me."

Zachary balked. "What?"

"Come. Come here."

Zachary looked around. Teddy grabbed his arm, pulling him back, away from the door. "Come on. Stay with me."

Zachary followed, resisting all the way, not wanting to walk right into some encounter with Teddy. Teddy pulled him over to the table that his date was sitting at and motioned to him and an empty chair.

"Here, sit down. Talk with Dimitri."

Zachary hesitated, looking at the other man. "Uh… Dimitri?"

The younger man nodded, showing off a row of very white teeth. "Hi."

"What is it… what is this about?" He still couldn't shake the instinct that Teddy wanted to pull him into something. A threesome, maybe.

"Teddy says you were talking about Jose. I know Jose."

"Oh." Zachary nodded. He sat down carefully, worried that doing so might mean he was committing to something more. "How do you know Jose? Have you seen him lately?"

"He's been very naughty," Dimitri shook his head, smiling at Zachary, showing off how charming he was. "He was supposed to meet me, and he didn't. I think he's avoiding me."

"When were you supposed to meet?" Zachary resisted the urge to pull out his notepad. He was there incognito; he would have to remember the important points to note down later. A casual friend of Jose's would not haul out a notepad and start taking notes.

"A week ago. But he never showed up. Left me here all alone."

Teddy nodded along. "I remember. Because I saw you later that night."

"At least Teddy doesn't stand me up. What happened to Jose?" Dimitri asked Zachary. "Do you know? Did he run off with some floozy?"

Zachary gulped. "I don't know. I haven't seen him. I thought he might be here tonight." Playing the part of a friend who had been out of touch, he couldn't very well say that he knew no one else had seen Jose within that time period.

"He hasn't been here. He must have some new beau who is keeping him busy." Dimitri's voice was falsetto, setting Zachary's teeth on edge.

"I guess he might have. I haven't been able to get him on the phone for a few days… Did you try him?"

"Every time I call, it just goes to voicemail. Like he's rejecting my calls."

"To voicemail?" Zachary sat up straighter. "What number do you have?"

It took some cajoling, but Dimitri eventually agreed to text it to him, which Zachary suspected was a ploy for Dimitri to get Zachary's number. Dimitri sent it through, and it was the same number as Zachary had gotten from McDonald. Zachary frowned. "And you get his voicemail? That's not what I was getting."

He tapped the number, selected 'call,' and listened to see what would happen. As McDonald had said, it went to a system message saying that the customer was not available.

"I get a message saying the phone is offline," he told Dimitri. "Do you remember what day you called him and got his voicemail?" Getting Jose's voicemail suggested that the phone had still been charged and online. That might give them a better fix on when Jose had disappeared. And if Dougan could get any information from the phone company records…

Dimitri shook his head. "I don't know."

"Can you think about it? What day was it when you tried to call him last?" Teddy was giving him a strange look, but Zachary didn't want to back down on the request. "It could be important."

"Why is it important? Obviously Jose doesn't care for me or for you. He's found some sugar daddy."

"Was it on the weekend? Or the week before? What were you trying to call him about? What day was he supposed to meet you?"

"Talk about needy!" Dimitri gave him a superior look. "Honey, if you're going to hang all over him like that, he's just going to kick you to the curb. If he hasn't already."

"Maybe his phone is broken," Zachary suggested. "Maybe he's not ignoring either one of us. Maybe he changed his number because someone was harassing him." Zachary opened his mouth to tell them about Harding, his last big case, and how he had tried to shake loose from his stalker by getting a new phone and number. But Zachary wasn't there as a private eye, so anything he happened to say about a case was going to come off sounding strange. "If his phone was broken, wouldn't he have called to give you his new number? And wouldn't he still show up here when you were scheduled to meet?"

"I would expect him to."

"You really don't know what day you called him and got his voicemail? When was your date scheduled for?"

Dimitri considered this. He gave Teddy a flirty look and made eyes at him, apparently wanting to impart to Zachary that Jose was not his competition. Jose was long gone, after all.

"Wednesday," he said finally. "Wing night. But he didn't show up. I called him, but every time it just went to voicemail. He could have just answered and said he couldn't come or changed his mind. He didn't have to treat me like that."

"No," Zachary agreed, trying to soothe his feelings. "You're right. I would expect better from Jose. He doesn't usually play games."

Dimitri nodded, fake-sniffling. "That was very naughty of him."

Zachary decided it was time to move on. He nodded to Dimitri and stood up. Teddy was still standing there, and looked for a moment like he wasn't going to let Zachary past, but then he gave a quick nod and stepped aside.

CHAPTER TWELVE

Zachary was exhausted as he left the bar. It wasn't because he had been up too long or been doing physical work, but just the emotional effort it took to deal with all of the people and the noise and to act like someone he was not. And it was more than just letting people believe that he was gay. He was really not a 'people person,' and large crowds were difficult. A few close friends at a quiet venue was something he could manage for a while, but strangers were difficult, and especially having to deal with them in one-on-one interactions. He had stretched his social muscles about as far as they could be stretched.

He stopped near the doors of the bar to jot down a few more notes before going out. He didn't want to forget anything important.

He slid the notepad back away and stepped out the doors. In spite of the time of night, the street was brightly lit with streetlights and the signs of other nearby bars and venues. There were a good number of cars and people on the street, reassuring him that it was safe. He wasn't walking down a dark alley where predators might be waiting for him.

He had parked his car a little way away, though. He hadn't wanted to leave his car in the parking lot of a gay bar and risk it getting vandalized. So he'd found a place he could park a couple of blocks away.

At first, that didn't seem to be a problem. There were plenty of people around in spite of the cold weather. On their way home or going out to party. As he turned down the last street, however, Zachary could hear boot heels behind him. Nothing to be concerned about, just some woman in heeled snow boots. Zachary glanced back a couple of times, and couldn't see her. There was a small group of twenty-something young men behind him, and he thought the boot-heels came from behind them.

But the men, who had been talking, quieted when he looked back toward them. It was suddenly a little too quiet and he could still hear the boot heels and not see who it was making the noise.

He kept going. He wasn't far from his car. The young men would go on to wherever their vehicle was parked or to their clubbing destination and Zachary would be fine.

He started to walk just a little bit faster. Once he was in his car he could regroup. The speed of the footsteps increased as well and the group of young men seemed to be getting closer. Zachary risked one more glance back at them, noticing this time that they wore long brown coats and the sound of the boots was not a woman walking behind them, but one of the men wearing jackboots. Zachary swallowed. It was cold out and they were wearing hats, so he couldn't see for sure whether they were skinheads, but his instincts told him they were.

Skinheads who had followed him from a gay bar.

Zachary's short walk to his car had taken him farther away from the crowds and the bright lights. There were a few people around, but not many, and they walked quickly, heads down, not looking at each other. Zachary looked quickly around. He needed somewhere with more people. He would be safer in a crowd. The skinheads would get bored and go away, looking for other quarry.

But his walk had taken him away from the bars and storefronts into an area that was single family homes and low-rise apartment buildings. Nothing where crowds of people gathered. All was quiet and still, except for the clomping of the jackboots behind him.

If he ran, they would give chase and would bring him down. He'd never been a good runner, and since the car accident, he hadn't regained the ability to go much faster than a trot. The more he thought about his gait, the more likely he was to trip and fall. If he stopped to engage with them, they might draw the confrontation out longer, but they weren't going to be dissuaded from their goal by any argument from him. They would just be amused by him trying to talk them out of a beating, and then they would hurt him.

He tried to increase his speed just a tiny bit, so that they wouldn't notice. Put just a few more feet in between them by the time he got to his car. They didn't know which car was his, so they wouldn't know when to start closing in on him. If he could keep going at a quicker pace until he got to his car, he might be able to jump in before they had a chance to catch up. If he were lucky.

But he knew that wasn't going to work.

They could probably tell by his quickened pace and his narrow focus that he was getting close to his car. There were a couple of laughs as they spoke among themselves, planning out the fun ahead. Zachary swallowed hard. He fingered his phone in his pocket. He wasn't going to be able to get it out and call emergency or someone to help him before the skinheads managed to get it away from him. He couldn't figure out any other plan. Throw his wallet on the ground and hope that it distracted them and that one of them would go after it, giving him another half-second to get into his car? Yell at them like he was crazy and see if they were freaked out by it or he could attract the attention of some passerby? His throat was so dry, he didn't know if he'd be able to raise a croak, or if it would be like those dreams where he screamed and screamed and no sound came out.

His car was just three spaces away. Zachary found his keys in his coat pocket and pressed the unlock button.

The taillights flashed and his car gave a friendly chirp.

If he survived, he was going to have to take it to Jergens to get that feature disabled.

The skinheads were on him in a second, before he could get past the first car. A couple of them slammed him into the side of a red Nissan crossover with a crunch that shook Zachary from head to toe. He expelled a puff of air and a groan that sounded like a dying warthog. Zachary tried to fight back, to protest, but they had his arms pressed back against the car so the was spread-eagled, unable to move. He could try to kick them, but they'd know what he was doing as soon as he shifted his weight.

"What's going on?" Zachary demanded. "Let me go!"

"Little fairy thought that he was home free," one of them mocked, getting right in Zachary's face, eyeball to eyeball so that Zachary could smell his foul breath and see the tattoos inked all over his face. Swastikas, teardrops, numbers that Zachary didn't know the meaning of. He struggled to free himself, but they weren't going to let him go that easily.

"Thought no one saw him coming out of the den of iniquity," the man in his face crooned. "Thought that he'd pulled one over and no one would know what filthiness he'd been up to. Well, we know, little fairy. We know what you've been up to. And we're not going to allow it. It's an offense against God."

"I didn't do anything," Zachary protested. "I was looking for someone. A missing person. I'm not gay, I wasn't doing anything."

"*I was looking for someone,*" the man echoed in a high voice. The others were egging him on, throwing in their own remarks and encouraging swift and severe violence. "You were looking for someone, all right. Someone to fill your unwholesome desires."

"I'm looking for a missing person. He used to go to that bar."

They laughed again. Zachary tried to pull out of their grips, but he knew it was useless. His body wouldn't hold still even though his brain knew he couldn't get away.

"You want to know why he's missing?" the chief skinhead asked. "Maybe he's one of the ones that we got."

"Let me go. I don't have any problem with you guys. Just leave me alone."

"We have a problem with you. And you need to be taught a lesson. You need to be taught not to sin. Man shall not lie with man. It's right there in the Bible. We can't allow this to go on. Just because the government says that two fairies can get married to each other, that doesn't make it right. We're here to defend God and the Constitution."

Zachary knew they were just mouthing the words. They didn't believe in anything. He tried to tell them that Lorne and Pat were better people than the skinhead neo-Nazis would ever be. Simultaneously, he fought to hold the words back and his impulsive brain tried to push them out, so that he just stammered, which was probably the best possible outcome.

"Just let me go," he begged. "I'm not from around here. I'm not going to be back here again. I am just looking into a missing persons case."

"You're not no cop."

"No, no, I'm not. I'm just trying to help out a friend."

"Yeah, a friend," one of the skinheads sneered, and he was the first one to hit Zachary.

CHAPTER THIRTEEN

His fist hit Zachary's cheekbone with a crunch and Zachary's head hit the van behind him. He saw bright stars and dark splotches and fought to stay conscious. Though why would he want to be conscious for the beating? The skinhead stood there shaking out his hand, obviously having hurt his poor knuckles on Zachary's face.

One of them pushed the first aside and kicked a knee up into Zachary's solar plexus. He would have hit the ground if he hadn't been supported by the gentlemen who had his arms pinned to the side of the van. As it was, he drew his feet up off the ground, all of the wind driven out of him, reflexively trying to curl up into a ball. There was laughter from the little group. There was nothing Zachary could do to protest or to fight back. He couldn't draw in a breath to reinflate his lungs. His legs were so weak that even when his feet touched the ground again, he couldn't hold his own weight or kick one of the men in the knee.

His head was spinning. There was a flurry of other blows. Zachary couldn't keep his eyes open or break the beatdown into a blow-by-blow analysis. They came from all directions at once and he couldn't even cry out.

There was a shout from somewhere. Zachary's head was spinning so badly he didn't even know which way was up.

"Let's go!" one of them said.

Another shouted something in German.

They dropped him to the pavement, kicked him a few times for good measure, then were off and running.

The Good Samaritan, whoever he was, didn't chase after them, but stopped to examine Zachary.

The first word out of his mouth was a curse, and Zachary knew he probably didn't look too good. He still couldn't get his breath back, and it seemed like a long time since he had breathed. His body should be reinflating his lungs and taking in oxygen, but he seemed to have forgotten how. Maybe the skinheads had reinjured Zachary's spine. Maybe there had been some small flaw in it that the doctors weren't aware of, and he would be paralyzed for life.

Which wouldn't be long if he didn't start breathing again soon.

"Can you hear me?" the man shouted, kneeling over him. "They're gone now. You're safe. I'm going to get help."

He clutched at the man's coat, not wanting to be left behind. If the man went to find help and left Zachary there on the ground, the skinheads might come back again and continue their lesson on morality.

"It's okay," the man told him again. He patted Zachary's clutching hand. "I'm not going anywhere. Just let me get my phone out."

Zachary loosened his grip and the man went through his various inside and outside pockets before he found his phone and called for help. He described his location and Zachary's condition the best he could, and then knelt there over him, murmuring soothing words and trying to keep Zachary quiet until help could arrive.

Zachary wasn't sure when it was he started breathing again.

"It's going to be okay," the man said. "Did you know those guys? Were they trying to mug you?"

Zachary shook his head, which made him woozy. "Skinheads," he breathed. "Thought I was… gay."

His savior swore again. He tried to make Zachary more comfortable, straightening out his splayed limbs and wadding something up under his head. "They shouldn't be very long. They'll take good care of you."

As Zachary lay there, he thought that it probably wasn't the worst beating he'd ever suffered. It was superficial. He'd have bruises for a few weeks, but no permanent damage. No broken bones. No internal bleeding. He'd be perfectly all right once he could get on his feet again. But it was going to be a while before he felt steady enough to get to his feet. He raised his hand and touched his face, feeling the sticky, warm cut over his cheek. It was bleeding. But it had been a punch and not a cut with a blade. Probably wouldn't need stitches. Maybe just a strip of suture tape.

"It's going to be okay," he whispered, unconsciously echoing the man's own words, trying to reassure him that there was no permanent damage. He was breathing.

When the ambulance approached, Zachary thought his head was going to split right open, the discordant sound of the siren bouncing around between his ears, making them pulse and his head throb and swell. Then the siren turned off, and the paramedics got out of their ambulance.

Ever so slowly. He didn't know why it was that on TV paramedics were always running and moving quickly, when in real life, they always seemed to go super slow, as if they were on a reduced speed from the rest of the world, carefully considering every step, getting their medical kits out, surveying the scene and discussing risks before they even got close. There was another set of sirens and a couple of police cars arrived. The cops moved faster than the paramedics, asking the rescuer what he had seen and if either one of them had any weapons.

"Weapons?" the man demanded. "Do you think I did this to him? Do you think he'd let someone do this to him if he was armed?"

"We have to ask," the cop said irritably. "You don't know how many times police get to a scene and find that people are armed when they aren't supposed to be and all kinds of bad stuff can go down. What about him? Are you armed, sir?" he asked Zachary loudly, bending down over him and opening up his coat so that he could check for himself.

"No," Zachary assured him, breathing heavily. The attack had happened too fast for him to get really scared and to think about what could happen to him in realistic terms. But the cops kept asking for more details, and each question ramped up Zachary's anxiety more. How many of the skinheads had there been? Which direction had they gone? Were they carrying weapons? Had they said anything? Were they known to him?

Once they had determined there were no weapons on the scene and that Zachary and his rescuer were not going to leap up and attack anyone, they allowed the paramedics to get in close to assess Zachary's injuries. They shone lights in his eyes, looked at his face and his head, and kept asking where it hurt the most. Zachary's head throbbed from the sirens and their demanding voices as much as from his injuries. He tried to shake his head, but that hurt too much.

"I'm okay," he told them. "I'll just go home."

"You're not going home. Where did they hit you? Just in the face? In the body?"

They felt all over his arms and legs and body, looking for blood and feeling for any breaks or flinching that would direct them to more serious injuries.

"Please…" Zachary just wanted them to stop touching him. "Please stop."

Eventually, they got a gurney out. Zachary didn't know where the police had taken the man who had rescued him, but once the paramedics had Zachary on the stretcher, the Good Samaritan appeared over Zachary's face once more.

"You're going to be okay," the man said, smiling reassuringly. "I'm sorry this happened to you."

Zachary gave his best attempt at a smile and thank you before the man disappeared from his range of vision again.

"He said it was because he was gay," he told the police as they continued to ask him for more details. "He must have come from that bar a couple of blocks away and they followed him. We don't usually have gang activity in this area. It's supposed to be a safe place to live."

Zachary tried to protest that he wasn't actually gay, but no one was listening to him. They couldn't care less what his sexual orientation was. The paramedics rolled the stretcher into the ambulance, and one of them got in back with him while the other got in front to drive.

"Hang in there, bud," the one in the back said to him, patting him on the shoulder. "You're going to be okay. We'll get you to the hospital and get you all checked out. You're safe now."

––––––––

He felt a lot better when they got him to the regional medical center and got some Demerol into him. The pain receded to a more bearable level and his heart rate started to slow. He tried to relax his muscles, aware that he had been gripping the bars of the gurney tightly as if he might fall off. The nurses twittered over him and washed the blood off his face and put an ice bag over his cheek. He was parked in a hallway where they were waiting for someone to take him to x-ray. One of the cops towered over him, trying to get a coherent story out of him.

"I was in the bar," Zachary repeated patiently. "But I'm not gay. They just thought I was. The skinheads. But I'm not." He wasn't sure why it was so important for him to establish this point. He didn't think there was anything wrong with being gay. He admired Mr. Peterson and Pat for their devoted relationship and all of the good things they did with their lives. But he didn't want to be misidentified. He wanted them to see the person he really was, and not a role he had just been playing.

"Then what were you doing at the bar?" the cop asked impatiently, rolling his eyes.

"I'm investigating a missing person. Jose Flores. He frequented that bar, so I was asking questions about whether anyone had seen him or where he might have gone, if he disappeared on his own."

"You were investigating this. You're not a cop."

"No, I'm a private investigator." Zachary tried to slide his fingers into his inside pocket, but they wouldn't seem to work the way they were supposed to.

"May I?" the cop asked, his hand hovering above Zachary's.

"Yeah. Just… my pocket there…"

The cop inserted a couple of fat fingers and pincered Zachary's notebook and small stack of business cards between them. He drew them all out and looked at them. Zachary couldn't see them very well as the cop spread them out over Zachary's chest. His business cards, a few other cards he had collected during the investigation. His notepad. The cop picked up the notepad and started to flip through the pages without asking. Zachary supposed that he had already given the man permission to look at what he wanted to, so he held his tongue. It wasn't like there was anything incriminating in the notepad, or even anything very interesting. Just the messy, somewhat cryptic notes that he had made as he found out little tidbits about Jose's life and thought of more questions and avenues to investigate. He supposed it probably didn't look much different from the cop's own duty notepad. As the cop gathered everything back together into a stack, Zachary's phone started to ring.

"Can I keep one of these?" the cop asked, holding up one of Zachary's business cards.

"Yeah." Zachary patted at his pants pocket, trying hard to corral his phone. The cop didn't offer to help this time. Zachary eventually managed to pull it out and answer it before it went to voicemail. He saw Philippe's number on the screen. "Hello."

There was a silence for a moment from Philippe. Maybe he had already hung up, thinking that Zachary wasn't going to answer.

"Philippe? Are you there?"

"Is this Zachary?" Philippe sounded confused.

"Yeah. What's up?"

"You sound weird. Where are you?"

There was a call over the PA system for a doctor, and Zachary didn't think there was any point in trying to keep his location a secret. "I'm at the medical center. Did you get ahold of your friend?"

"Yeah. He says he'll talk to you. I told him it's gotta be tonight. Is that still okay? Did something happen?"

"That's good. Thanks."

"Why are you at the hospital? Did you find Jose?"

"No… I, uh, ran into some trouble."

"Are you okay?" Philippe's voice cracked like he was still thirteen. "What kind of trouble? Is it the guy you think killed Jose?"

"No…" Zachary looked at the cop, who was listening with interest, and wondered how much of Philippe's side of the conversation he was able to hear. "At least… I don't think so. I think if it was these guys, they would have just left him there, like they did me. I don't think they would go to the effort of dragging him away somewhere."

"These guys? What happened? What guys?"

"Skinheads. Neo-Nazis. Followed me from the bar."

"I told you to be careful! Didn't I tell you not to walk alone?"

"I never saw them until it was too late. I was being careful."

"You never know who is going to be hanging around these places."

"Yeah. Thanks."

Philippe didn't say anything for a minute. "Are you okay?" he asked finally. "You're talking, so you must be okay. Did they do any permanent damage?"

"I don't think so. Waiting for x-rays."

"So you probably don't want to talk to my guy tonight. You're not going to be able to see him."

"I still want to. Can he come here? I'm probably just going to be laying around here for hours until they decide I'm okay to go home or I sign myself out."

"Really? You want to see him at the hospital?"

"At least we will be safe. There won't be anyone hanging around like at the bar."

"Huh. Unless one of those skinheads broke his knuckles on your face and decides to go in to get them treated."

Zachary remembered the skinhead shaking out his hand after hitting Zachary in the cheek and didn't think it was so funny. He took a quick look around, nervous, but he couldn't see the emergency room waiting area from where he was. He couldn't see very much of anything from where he was. Just the cop standing over him, waiting for him to finish the call so he could ask more questions.

When he hung up, the cop raised an eyebrow. "Not much slows you down, does it?"

Zachary thought about how much he sometimes had to fight against himself just to get from one day to the next. Working through physical injury was nothing compared with fighting his own brain and emotional state.

"I guess. I mean, it's not that bad with the Demerol. I don't think anything is broken. I'm a little loopy, that's all."

"Who is this guy that you want to come talk to you tonight? What's that all about?"

Zachary didn't see what that had to do with his assault case, or what business it was of the cop's, but he answered anyway. Maybe there was a way to persuade the police that there was something to Jose's disappearance.

"A witness that says that more men have disappeared than just the one I'm looking for. That there have been a long series of similar disappearances."

"What does that mean?"

Zachary figured the cop already knew exactly what it meant. "That we might have a serial killer on our hands."

"We?"

"If there's a serial killer operating in Vermont, then the police are going to have to be involved sooner or later."

"What makes you think there's a serial killer? That's quite a reach."

"I don't know yet, not until I talk to this guy and look into it further. He says there have been others. That's all the information I have so far. That and my missing person... doesn't feel right. I don't think he just took off without telling anyone."

"Has a report been filed on him?"

"Yes. The officer in charge is..." Zachary tried to bring the name up, but the Demerol was having a bigger effect on him than he had thought. "McDougall? No—Dougan. I already talked to him. He doesn't think there's anything to it."

The cop grunted. "So, these neo-Nazis that attacked you," he said, going back to the investigation at hand. "Do you think they had something to do with your missing guy? Were they trying to warn you off from the investigation?"

"No, I doubt it. They wouldn't know about the questions I was asking inside, they just thought I was gay. Unless they have someone planted inside, and I don't think these guys are that subtle. They're just out to do some damage. Pick off easy targets."

"You might want to reconsider going to night spots like that. Especially alone. Take a friend with you. A few friends. Don't walk to your car by yourself."

Zachary sighed. He didn't exactly have anyone he could take with him.

The cop shook his head. "Well then, you might want to get a permit and start carrying. At least you would have a way to defend yourself."

Zachary had promised himself that he would never own a gun. It would be far more hazardous to his safety than it would be a benefit.

"Thanks," he said. "I'll think about it."

"That doesn't mean I want you going around shooting up every skinhead you see... but you do have the right to protect yourself."

CHAPTER FOURTEEN

ometime between when the cop left and when Philippe's friend made it to the hospital, Zachary fell asleep. He wasn't normally quick to fall asleep in strange places; it was hard enough at home. But the Demerol and the aftermath of the adrenaline rush apparently combined to make him sleepy, and he fell asleep right in the hallway as people walked by talking and shouting instructions to each other. He woke up a few times, but then closed his eyes again and just drifted off, feeling warm and comfy and drowsy.

He was eventually taken in for his x-rays, and then moved to another curtained area while he was waiting for the results. He'd been there for some time, sliding in and out of sleep, when a man showed up at his bedside.

At first, Zachary took him for a janitor or an orderly. A tall man with black skin and sharp, angular features. He looked down at Zachary and said his name a few times before Zachary realized that this was someone he actually wanted to talk to. Zachary tried to sit up and the man helped to readjust the pillows and raise the head of the bed. Then he sat down in a chair he dragged into the curtained area from somewhere outside.

"You are Zachary Goldman," he said firmly.

"Yes," Zachary nodded. "Sorry. I didn't mean to fall asleep there. You're Philippe's friend?"

The man looked at him suspiciously. "His friend, yes. I am."

"Good. He said that you had told him about other men disappearing, and I wanted to hear about that. It's important."

"I have tried to tell people that it is important, but everybody just blows it off." The man made a sweeping gesture with his hands.

Zachary nodded. He was starting to see how that was the case. No one yet had shown any concern over what had happened to Jose, other than Pat and Philippe. "Yes. But I want to hear. I don't know if I'll be able to do anything to make anyone else pay attention, but if these disappearances are related, I want to know about it. There's no point in chasing down dead ends if there are a bunch of related disappearances that could lead us to the killer. Or whatever he is."

Philippe's friend nodded.

"What's your name?" Zachary asked him.

"Jama Mwangi, but you can call me John."

"Okay, John. What can you tell me about these missing men?"

John had a soft-sided briefcase with him. He opened it up and pulled out a writing tablet which had a long list of carefully hand printed names in a column from the top to the bottom. Zachary took it from him, looking over the list. There were so many names. He had expected two or three more, not a full page. He scanned through the names. They were not names that he recognized. Nothing that had been in the news. A lot of them were Hispanic names, maybe some African or Middle Eastern. Zachary worked his way through them, trying to break them down by ethnic groups, to start seeing patterns even before he had any more information than the names.

He rested the list on his lap. "Are they all illegals?"

"No, not all. Some have documents. Some were even citizens, born here. But none of them were white."

Zachary thought about that, letting his mind drift. If they were all immigrants, or looked like immigrants, then the perpetrator had picked them because of that. He wanted men who would disappear more easily. Men that the police would discount, just as they had Jose, as someone who was *other* than they were. Someone who could be written off as unimportant and insignificant. People like that just came and went. They could just disappear one day, but there was no reason to be concerned. They just did that kind of thing.

"Can you tell me anything else about them? Did you know all of them? Did any of them get reported to the police as missing or end up in the news?"

John looked at Zachary, his eyes piercing. Zachary tried to keep his eyes steady and not to blush under the close examination.

"You believe about this?" John demanded.

"Yes, I believe it. I want to know if they're related to each other and Jose. I need more details in order to investigate them." He let his eyes run down the list again. "This is a lot of people."

"It is not all this year," John explained. "Only a few every year. Between two and six. But it has been going on for years."

"How did you find out? How many of them did you know?"

"There had been talk in the community. Rumors, stories that men disappeared and no one ever knew what happened to them. I didn't know what to think. I thought it was just urban legend. *You need to be careful, or the man with the hook will get you.*" He gave a laugh and looked at Zachary to see if he understood.

Zachary nodded. "A cautionary tale. Trying to help people to stay safe."

"Then there was Amelio..." John pointed to one of the names on the page, two thirds of the way down the list. "He and I were seeing each other... not exclusively, but regularly, every week or two... and then he stopped showing up. No one had seen him. I asked everyone. But he was just gone. They said that he had just stopped coming around. Maybe ICE got him..."

Zachary nodded. Same old story. "But you were sure that he hadn't been caught, or gone off somewhere on his own?"

"I couldn't be sure one hundred percent, but..." John gave a little shrug. "I knew him. I didn't think he would just leave without telling me. Or somebody. And there wasn't any word that it was Immigration. Usually, there are at least rumors. Someone saw it go down. Someone knew that they came to the apartment or to his work. But no one had seen or heard anything."

"Did he have a family? Here or wherever he came from? Back home?"

"No, he was single. There have been others... some of the men on that list had wives, children. Usually not here. Usually, they were still sending them money, or trying to arrange to bring them here."

"How many did you know personally? Just Amelio?"

John shook his head. "No. A few others…" He went down the list, pointing to each of the names after Amelio's, indicating how he knew them or knew about their disappearances. Zachary looked at him, feeling the deepening frown lines across his own forehead.

"How do you know so many of these men?"

Sometimes serial killers liked people to know what they had done. They liked to rub it in the face of the officials. Could John be one of those men, proudly showing Zachary all of the men that he had killed in the past years to see his reaction?

"I didn't know all of them," John said quickly. "I did know a few of them. I am… attracted to that type. Dark, slim, kind men… I was drawn to them. But they kept… disappearing."

As if someone else were drawn to them too. Zachary nodded. He had talked to Kenzie about the traits that the missing men might share. The type that the killer might obsess on.

"Do you have more details than this?" he asked, thinking of John's brief-case, which looked like it had held a lot more than just a few sheets of paper. John didn't look like a lawyer or accountant. "If I'm going to investigate it, I need to know everything. Trying to track down everything you already have would take time, and it would take that much longer to find Jose and whoever took him."

John let out his breath. "It's too late for Jose. Isn't it? Don't you think?"

"It may be," Zachary admitted, "but if you've already gathered data, I don't want to waste time trying to find out the same information."

John searched his face once more, then nodded. He reached into his briefcase and pulled out a thick pile of papers, all sorted into files and rubber-banded together. There were sticky notes protruding out the sides and tops of the folders. Zachary reached for it eagerly. It wasn't very often he had so much to go on. If John knew what he was talking about and wasn't just a paranoid conspiracy freak, the files were a treasure trove.

John laid the stack of files in Zachary's lap. Zachary pulled the rubber bands off and opened the top folder. Background notes on one of the more recently missing men. Surveillance records. Notes about his acquaintances and finances. Zachary couldn't believe his luck.

"You have all of this information and the police still wouldn't listen to you?"

John shrugged. "I haven't… exactly… gone to the police."

"How could you not give them this information?"

"If I went to the police, they would deport me."

"If you were helping them to solve a crime, especially one of this proportion, they wouldn't turn you in. They could help you get a visa to let you stay here, for helping them."

"They don't do that."

"They can," Zachary insisted.

"But they don't."

Zachary couldn't argue with that. He knew very little about what it was like to live as an illegal immigrant. John would know far better than he did how the police or government would respond to an illegal offering information and asking for asylum. Zachary had no idea how they would be treated. From what John and Paul the bartender had said, they wouldn't be welcomed with open arms.

"Can I borrow these files? Make a copy?"

John shook his head. "I don't want them out of my sight. You can look at them, but I don't know what will happen to them if you take them away. This is the only copy."

"We could go somewhere to copy them. A library. Office store."

"Nobody will be open this late. And you don't look like you are going to be going anywhere soon."

Zachary looked down at himself, still bruised and muddy and tired after his long night. He could get himself released, but he should at least find out whether he had any broken bones. And he probably shouldn't drive while he was still foggy from Demerol. His heart was thumping quickly, excited by the prospect of looking through all of the information that John had compiled about the missing men. But there was no way he would retain everything he read, even if he could read through everything in one night. What he thought he would remember might disappear as soon as the Demerol wore off. Drugs could do funny things with memory.

"I don't know… we need to find a way to copy them. Do you think that one of the nurses would let us use a photocopier?"

John raised an eyebrow, looking at Zachary and shaking his head slightly as if Zachary were crazy. And he supposed it had been a stupid question. The hospital wasn't going to let them borrow a photocopier. If he could just capture what was on each of the pages… but even trying to write down the important points on each page would take hours, and there was no guarantee that he would get everything relevant. At some point, he'd find he needed to go back to the originals, and that would mean arranging to meet John somewhere and then paging through all of those papers again for what he had missed.

"A snapshot," he said suddenly.

"What?"

Zachary started patting his pockets. He looked around. At some point, they had changed him out of his street clothes into a hospital johnny. They must have done that before taking x-rays, though he couldn't remember it. During that period that he'd been in and out of sleep.

"Where are my clothes? Do you see them?"

John opened a skinny cupboard. "In here."

"In my coat, check the pockets. I have a digital camera."

"A camera?" John repeated doubtfully, patting the coat.

"It's small. Smaller than a cell phone."

John looked through the pockets more carefully, and eventually found Zachary's tiny digital camera, which he always thought of as his spy camera. It was like the novelties listed in the backs of comic books when he'd been young, only it was far more sophisticated than anything that had been invented back then. Higher resolution than a cell phone camera. Removable storage cards so that he could take as many pictures as he needed to without filling the camera memory up.

Zachary checked it over. It was a little banged up after his encounter with the skinheads, but the lens and the viewfinder were unmarked, so it should work. Hopefully. He held it over the page of names and clicked the shutter button. A moment later, the document appeared on the LCD screen, edges smoothed and square, nice high resolution.

"Perfect. I'll take the pictures; you turn the pages. It will take a few minutes, but it's easier than finding a copy shop in the middle of the night."

John hesitated, taking the list of names from him.

"It will be okay," Zachary told him, trying to soothe any worries that John had. "You've done a lot of work and you probably don't feel like letting it go... but you want to do something for these men, don't you? You want us to be able to put them to rest, and to know what happened to them. And to catch whoever is doing this. We can't just keep watching from the side-lines as more men disappear."

John nodded his agreement. "Yes, you are right... But you're sure you can use them? You can get the police to do something about it this time?"

"I will. I know cops and I'll find someone who will take another look at it. I'm not going to give up until they've taken another look at these cases. It's one thing when there's one missing man. But this many... we need to catch who is doing this."

CHAPTER FIFTEEN

The doctor returned to find Zachary covered with John's papers while he photographed them to make sure that he had every last piece of information on the missing men as he could get. The doctor shook his head slowly.

"What's all this? Shouldn't you be resting?"

"I have work to do," Zachary told him. "Can I go home now?"

"The x-rays are clear. You don't have any bones that need to be set. But I wouldn't recommend resuming your normal activities for a few days. You're going to be pretty stiff and sore. You need to give your body the chance to recover before you go off… doing whatever it is that you do."

"Great. Do I get a prescription painkiller?"

The doctor pursed his lips, looking as if he were trying to decide whether Zachary was a drug-seeking addict. He looked down at the clipboard in his hand containing Zachary's chart, and nodded. "Yes, it would probably be a good idea, at least for a few days. I'm only going to prescribe a small number of pills. You'll need to go to your GP if you need a longer prescription, and he can decide what you need. You're on… other meds…?" he trailed off, apparently seeing the list of prescriptions that Zachary had provided.

"I don't take them all every day. But I figured you'd need to know all of them because of interactions."

"Yes, you're right." He looked at Zachary again. "You have someone who is managing this protocol? You're not getting different meds from different doctors?"

"Yeah. Just one doctor. You can call him if you want."

He nodded, looking relieved. "As long as you've got someone who knows all of what you are taking and is making adjustments when needed. I'll leave that to him." He took out a prescription pad and scribbled down the details of the painkillers for Zachary. "You're going to need to be careful if you're taking that with any kind of tranquilizer or sleep aid. Talk to your doctor or pharmacist first. I'll get the staff started on checking you out."

"Okay, thanks."

He was glad that he wasn't going to need to stay overnight. He knew that the Demerol was still masking the amount of damage that had been done to his body, but he didn't want to have to put the investigation aside while he recovered. Those missing men needed him. And other men who might be in peril if Zachary didn't figure out who the predator was.

"No driving," the doctor advised as he scratched his initials onto the chart. "You'll need someone to pick you up."

Zachary had been afraid of that. He looked at John, who shook his head. Zachary didn't know if he even had a car. He might have gotten to the hospital on the bus, or a friend might have dropped him off as a favor. Zachary could call a cab, but then the next question was where to stay. He didn't particularly want to be by himself in a hotel room. Not after the encounter with the skinheads. He wanted to be with other people, not walking down a lonely street again, listening to footsteps behind him.

"I'll... uh... I'll sort something out."

"If the nurses see you are driving yourself, they will call the police."

"I don't even have my car here. It's back at the bar where I got beaten up."

"Get it tomorrow when it's light out and you have someone with you."

———

He ended up calling Mr. Peterson. He hated to do it. He knew he and Pat would be in bed, and a ringing phone in the middle of the night would worry them. But if he didn't want to spend the night alone, there was only one couple in town that he could call.

"Zachary?" Mr. Peterson's voice was concerned. "Are you okay?"

"Yes. Everything is okay. I'm fine. But... I need somewhere to stay tonight. And a ride."

"Certainly, of course. Are you still working? It's got to be..." there was a pause as Mr. Peterson checked the time. "Three o'clock in the morning."

"Yeah. I'm sorry to bother you so late. I wouldn't have if I could have called anyone else..."

"You know that we're happy to have you over any time. Where do you need to be picked up?"

Zachary cleared his throat, preparing for further concern from his former foster father. "Well... I'm at the Regional Medical Center."

"The hospital?" Lorne's voice peaked louder.

Zachary could hear Pat in the background, asking about what was going on. Mr. Peterson muffled the phone while he answered Pat. Then he spoke to Zachary again.

"Are you hurt? Did you have a panic attack? Tell me what happened."

"I got hurt. It's fine. There's nothing broken, they're releasing me. Just a few bruises. I'll tell you all about it."

"We'll be right there. The hospital is about fifteen minutes away."

"Don't rush. It always takes an hour to get checked out. I'll be out front once I've been released. You don't even have to come in."

But he knew that wouldn't stop Mr. Peterson from coming in. He'd want reassurance from the staff that Zachary wasn't checking himself out against medical advice and to know whether there were any special instructions to follow. If they knew about the other medications. Zachary was a grown man, but bring his foster father into the picture, and he might as well have been eleven years old again, when he'd had a bad reaction to his meds and Mr. Peterson had been the one to rush him to the emergency room in his pajamas and sneakers.

Zachary went through John's papers one last time to make sure that he'd seen everything and captured it all on his camera. He brought up the images on the camera to make sure they were saved. Then he thanked John for all of the work he had done and for bringing it to Zachary in the middle of the night. Once John was gone, he dressed slowly and gingerly, and headed to the desk to sign all of the release forms and waivers.

———

He managed to get to the front doors at the same time as Mr. Peterson was walking up. Zachary smiled and waved and Mr. Peterson stopped where he was and waited for Zachary to exit the hospital. Even under the too-dim exterior lights of the hospital, Mr. Peterson could obviously see the damage done to Zachary's face. His mouth fell open.

"Oh, Zachary! What have you done to yourself?"

He took Zachary by the arm to walk him to the car where Pat was waiting, as if Zachary were the sixty-year-old instead of in the prime of life. They walked slowly, Zachary reducing his speed to accommodate Mr. Peterson's pace, and Mr. Peterson slowing his even more to adjust for whatever injuries he couldn't see.

"I'll tell you about it when we're on our way," he said. "I'll just have to repeat it for Pat otherwise."

He hobbled to the car, where Mr. Peterson insisted that Zachary get into the front where there was more legroom and more comfortable seating, even though Zachary was a small man and would have been just fine in the back.

Pat turned his head to look at Zachary as he got in, and exchanged looks with Mr. Peterson. They helped Zachary get his seatbelt on. Pat shook his head.

"Did you have a tussle with a bear, or what? You look awful, Zachary, and those bruises haven't even set yet. You'd better sleep with ice on your eye tonight, or you're not even going to be able to open it in the morning."

"It looks worse than it is. They hit my cheek, actually, not the orbital…" Zachary trailed off.

"They?" Mr. Peterson asked. "Who exactly is *they*?" He climbed into the back seat and pulled his door closed.

"I kind of got mugged," Zachary hedged. "It's okay. I'm fine and they didn't steal anything. They got interrupted."

"You're not fine. Where were you? Why were you out somewhere so dangerous late at night?"

"Err…" Zachary had hoped not to have to give them any details, knowing it would just make them feel worse. "I was… investigating…"

"Investigating what?" Mr. Peterson shot back. And then Zachary heard the intake of breath behind him as Mr. Peterson suddenly realized why Zachary would be in town conducting an investigation late at night. He swore softly. "Not Jose's disappearance?"

"Yeah."

"You shouldn't have… did you have to go out so late? You could talk to his roommate and his boss during the day. You didn't need to go anywhere else. You didn't need to go somewhere dangerous."

"It wasn't really dangerous. I was fine while I was there. It was just when I left… it was dark, and I didn't see… I was parked a few blocks away and I didn't realize that I'd been followed."

"By who? Do you know who it was that did this to you? Was it a witness? Someone trying to shut you down?"

"Just… no, nothing to do with the investigation. Just some kids looking for trouble, that's all. It was nothing. Really."

"Kids? Like a street gang?"

"No… a group… of young men. Not an actual gang, I don't think. Just the kind who band together…"

Pat looked over at Zachary as he pulled out of the hospital parking lot. "Zachary," he said, in a low, even tone that meant that they knew Zachary was trying to obfuscate. It was time to fess up and tell the truth.

"It was… a group of skinheads."

"Skinheads," Mr. Peterson repeated. "Why would you have any trouble from skinheads? You're white. You're not Jewish or…" He trailed off, understanding.

"They followed you from The Night Scene," Pat said flatly.

"Yeah."

Pat thumped the steering wheel in frustration. As a man who normally had endless patience and sangfroid, it was an emotional outburst. "This would never have happened if you hadn't been trying to find out what happened to Jose!"

"It's not your fault," Zachary hurried to reassure him. "It was just one of those things. It could have happened to anybody at any time."

"But it didn't. It happened to you when you were investigating a case that I gave you. And I'm not even paying you! You need to drop it now. It's not worth something happening to you. It's bad enough that Jose has disappeared, but I would never forgive myself if something even worse than this happened to you because you were following up on a lead."

"It's late and I got you out of bed," Zachary said. "You're tired. It's really not that big a deal. You'll feel better about it in the morning."

"I won't feel better about it. We'll talk in the morning, but you'll drop it. Wherever Jose has gone, we're not going to get him back. He's made his own choice."

Zachary was silent. He wasn't going to tell them that it was a serial killer. Not yet. Not until he knew more details. He had a lot of research to go over before he could come to that conclusion. But if it was a serial killer, there was no way Zachary was going to just let it go.

CHAPTER SIXTEEN

He did his best not to let Lorne and Pat see the extent of his injuries, but by the time they got back to the house, the Demerol was wearing off. Zachary got ready for bed and took one of the painkillers they had filled at the pharmacy on the way home. It was obvious he wasn't going to get any sleep without them. As it was, he had a restless night, tossing and turning to find a comfortable position when everything hurt. He was up by the time the gray light of dawn started to fill the room, hurting too badly to go back to sleep. His mind was already whirling as he tried to sort out the details he knew of Jose's life and his disappearance. He wanted to get started on John's research as soon as possible, but first he would have to get everything off of the digital card and print it out.

Mr. Peterson looked in on him when he got up and found him poring over his notepad, reviewing everything he had written down and trying to pull all of the threads into something that made sense.

"Up already?"

"Yeah, couldn't stop thinking about it."

Mr. Peterson shook his head.

"I know it looks bad." Zachary put his hand over his cheek and black eye, as if hiding them from sight would erase them from Mr. Peterson's memory. "But it really isn't as bad as it looks. I'm fine."

"You always say that. You won't admit when you are really hurt."

"Well…" Zachary trailed off, not sure what to say about that. He'd dealt with debriding and skin grafts following the fire when he was ten. That was a kind of pain he couldn't even begin to describe. When he compared that to the damage inflicted by fists and feet, even by several men, there was just no comparison. Even broken bones were not that bad. "It hurts if I move the wrong way or if I touch it," he tapped light fingers over the lump that was normally his cheek, "but I've had worse. The doctors checked to make sure nothing is broken and there's no internal bleeding. It's just a matter of time for the cuts and bruises to heal."

"Have you taken a painkiller already this morning? What can I get you? Breakfast?"

"Yes. I'm not hungry. Coffee would be good."

"You need more than coffee in your stomach if you're taking painkillers. You need real food."

"Just… just a piece of toast."

"Okay. I'll put it in the toaster in a minute."

Mr. Peterson went on to the bathroom and then in a few minutes was in the kitchen, getting the coffee and toast started. Pat was the usual cook for dinner, and Mr. Peterson for breakfast. Lunch was usually every man for himself. Mr. Peterson obviously got the light end of the cooking chores. Zachary was surprised that Pat wasn't up yet, but he might not have had a good night's sleep after having to get up in the middle of the night to fetch Zachary from the hospital. He'd been pretty upset when he'd gone back to bed.

Zachary wandered out to the kitchen as the smell of coffee started to waft through the house. He sat down at the table, continuing to read through his notes and make additional ones as Mr. Peterson put a buttered slice of toast in front of him. He put out jam and honey, but Zachary nibbled the toast without.

"What are you working on?" Mr. Peterson asked.

"Just looking through my notes; the interviews yesterday. Figuring out where I need to go next."

"You're not going to drop the case, are you?"

Zachary looked up at him. "No. I couldn't." He glanced in the direction of Pat's closed bedroom door. "It may be more than just Jose."

"What do you mean, more? You mean there is some kind of conspiracy?"

"No… someone who is… making people disappear."

"People?"

"Gay men of color, especially illegals… it's been going on for a number of years."

Mr. Peterson sat down. He stared across the table at Zachary. "You don't mean it."

"You haven't ever heard any rumors? Any talk about men disappearing?"

"I know there are people who have talked about it… but I always figured it was just tall tales. People seeing patterns where there weren't any. As a general rule… we like to classify things, give them names, sort out patterns. We're a species that likes logic and predictability and tries to create it."

"And that may be all it is," Zachary agreed. "I have to work through the data and see what I can find. Do you know if Jose was seeing anybody regularly? I have one young man who says they were, but I'm wondering if there was anyone else. Or if it was just random hook-ups."

"I don't know if I would say regular… but there were a few men. Probably more that I didn't know about. He didn't seem like he was ready for any kind of commitment. Men who have been married often fear settling down with someone again. Taking the risk of calling a relationship permanent."

Zachary wondered if Mr. Peterson had experienced that. It had seemed to Zachary that he had transitioned immediately from Mrs. Peterson to Pat, but Zachary hadn't been aware of anything that was going on while the Petersons were still married. What kind of relationships Mr. Peterson had pursued before the marriage broke apart.

"The boy I talked to, Philippe, he said that Jose had bruises on his throat one day. Like he'd been choked."

Mr. Peterson's face turned even paler than usual. He took a fortifying sip of coffee. "Who would do that?"

"I don't know. I don't know whether it was a regular partner, or someone he had just encountered. I don't know whether Jose normally participated in that kind of thing, or whether someone talked him into it or did it without his permission. Or as a threat or part of a fight. I just don't know." Zachary shook his head. He had more questions than answers; it was too early in the investigation to know anything.

"If he was into asphyxiation… I wasn't aware of it. But that's not something people usually share casually. I never saw him with bruises." He turned his hands palms-up and shrugged. "We talked about *music*."

Zachary nodded. Pat had said that they were just a social group. Jose had done his dating outside of that group, and perhaps they had not known each other as well as Pat had thought.

"Is Pat okay?" Zachary nodded toward the bedroom.

"He'll be all right. He's worried about you, but he still wants to know what happened to Jose. He was up most of the night after we got back, fussing about it."

"I'm not going to drop it. Especially not if this is a serial killer."

"If you have evidence that it is, you get the police to take over. You don't need to be putting yourself in some psycho's crosshairs."

"Sure, of course. You know me. I'm not a cowboy going in, guns blazing. That's TV, not real life."

Mr. Peterson nodded, and took a sip of his coffee, looking more reassured. "This thing last night has got us both pretty worried about you. We thought it would be a few inquiries on the phone, nothing dangerous. You getting attacked like that… brought it too close to home. We don't want you getting hurt. I don't know if you've looked in the mirror this morning, but you look like you collided with a train. I don't want you doing anything risky."

"I won't. The first thing I need to know is whether I could use your computer for a bit. I have some digital photos to process and it would be easiest if I could just do it here."

"Of course. Process away."

"You've got a digital memory card reader?"

"Doesn't everyone?" Mr. Peterson smiled.

Zachary had been introduced to photography by Mr. Peterson when he had given Zachary a used camera for his birthday. They had processed a lot of film together in Mr. Peterson's darkroom, even when technology had shifted to digital. Now they both used digital cameras most of the time, though they both still had analog cameras for more creative work.

Zachary ate a couple more bites of his toast and left the rest on the plate.

———

Zachary retrieved his camera from his jacket pocket and pressed his thumbnail into the card slot to pop the card out. It didn't come out. He tried again, and it still didn't pop free like it was supposed to. Zachary took a closer look to see what was going on. The camera had been banged up and dented during his altercation with the skinheads, but everything had seemed to be in working order when he had taken the pictures of John's documents the night before. Looking at it more closely, however, Zachary saw that one of the dents pressed into the card slot, and was pinning the memory card in place. Zachary tried to pry it loose with his fingernail, but that didn't work. He went into the bathroom and found a pair of tweezers, and tried to use them to pull it out. It still wouldn't budge. Zachary tried to push it farther in, and then to pull it out, but nothing was budging it. Zachary went back out to the kitchen where Mr. Peterson was reading the newspaper. Lorne looked up at him.

"What's up?"

"Have you ever had this happen before? I can't get the memory card out."

Mr. Peterson took it from him and examined it closely.

"Hmm… it certainly is stuck in there, isn't it? I'm not sure what I would suggest. Maybe take it to a camera repair store and see if they can retrieve it. Can you still access what's on the card?"

Zachary tested it, worried that after pushing and pulling the memory card around it would no longer be connected to the innards of the camera, but he was still able to pull the images up on the LCD screen.

"Yeah, see? They're still there."

"Can you transfer them to camera memory and use a USB cable to connect with the computer?"

Zachary looked over the camera. The mini USB port was just below the card slot, and it too had been deformed by the violent attack the night before. "I don't think that's going to work either. Even if we can bend it back into shape…"

"You'd best not mess with it. Leave it to the repair shop to take a look at, they have a lot more experience with that kind of thing."

Zachary sighed. "I'd better see if I can get ahold of my witness again. Maybe meet him at a photocopy shop to get a hard copy of the documents.

I thought taking the pictures was a good idea last night, but it seems like it was just a waste of time. I wasn't thinking clearly. Didn't even notice the damage."

"I'm sure they can still be recovered, but you might want to follow up with him just in case."

"Okay. Do you have a shop nearby that you'd recommend for repairs? My little place back home is pretty basic."

"Yeah, I can take you over there this afternoon. Why don't you see if you can get a bit more sleep this morning? You look all in."

Zachary shook his head. "I've got too much to do. And if this is the work of a serial killer, every hour could make a difference."

"Serial killers don't kill every day. That's not the way it works. You have time."

Zachary considered this. Mr. Peterson was right, of course. The difference between a serial killer and a mass murderer was the cooling off period between kills. A mass murderer might kill more people all at once in one angry rampage, but a serial killer killed, had a cooling off period, and then eventually ramped up to kill again. If Jose had been taken just over a week before, and John had suggested that two to six men a year had disappeared, then he wasn't likely to kill again in the next month. Zachary wasn't racing against the clock to get the case solved in one or two days. It would take longer than that to sort out what was happening and get the police onside.

"Okay. But I still can't sleep during the day. I slept at the hospital last night, too. Not just here. So I've had enough to get me through the day."

Mr. Peterson shrugged and shook his head, giving up.

———

Zachary returned to the bedroom and picked up his phone. He didn't have John's direct number, which meant that he would have to go through Philippe again, and if John were at work during the day, then he was going to have to wait until the evening again before being given an opportunity to talk and discuss his needs. But Zachary might as well get started right away. Maybe he would be lucky and it would be John's day off. He'd been at the hospital quite late, so maybe he had known that he wouldn't be at work the next day and could stay up late.

Philippe answered the phone after quite a number of rings, and sounded out of breath. "Zachary?"

"Yes. Sorry, did I get you at work?"

"Yes. It's okay for a minute, but I can't let the boss see me talking on the phone. What's going on? Is everything okay?"

"I wanted to get John's number from you. Or if I can't get that, if you would get him to call or text me. He's got my card, but I didn't get his numbers."

"You met with him last night, right? Why do you need him again today? He'll need to keep his head down. Not let anyone figure out what is going on."

That was probably a bit paranoid. There was only one killer, not a big conspiracy. The chances that John would somehow tip off a serial killer as to where he had been the night before and the information he had shared with Zachary was highly unlikely.

"I need to get another copy of his documents. I ran into a problem with the pictures I took. Can you let him know? I really need to start going through all of that information. See if I can verify his findings."

"I'll call him, man," Philippe said, sounding frustrated, "but I don't know if he'll be able to do that. He works hard, and he was already out last night. If he does too much sneaking around, someone will catch on. They'll know that he's up to something."

CHAPTER SEVENTEEN

Zachary didn't want to put the case aside while he waited for a response back from John, so he considered the information he already had, and then called Detective Dougan. The policeman answered his phone with a testy 'Dougan.'

"Uh, yes, Detective Dougan. It's Zachary Goldman. I wanted to talk to you about Jose Flores for another minute, if you have the time."

"I told you that if you harass me, I'm just going to block you. What is this about now? We just talked yesterday."

"Yes, sir, and I don't intend to harass you at all. I have had a couple of developments and I just wanted to follow up with you and keep you informed."

"Have you been drinking?" Dougan asked suspiciously.

Zachary paused, frowning. "No. I haven't had anything to drink today."

"You sound like you're slurring. You haven't had anything at all?"

"Oh… no. I ran into some trouble last night, and I have a fat lip… that must be what you're hearing."

"You ran into some trouble?"

"It's unrelated," Zachary said, not wanting to have to explain again or to distract Dougan from the case at hand. "I don't want to take up any more of your time than I need to."

"Okay. Go ahead. What have you got?"

"During the course of your investigation, did you get Jose's cell phone number?"

"No, I was told he didn't have one. I figured it was bull crap. Everybody has to have a phone number these days to hold down a job. But he wasn't the registered owner of any phone number, and his landlord said he didn't have one."

"I got it from his boss and Dimitri, a friend. Same phone number from both, so it looks like it's legitimate. Dimitri says that it was working up until Wednesday. It was going to voicemail, but it was still in service. Sometime since then, it has started getting the 'not in the service area' message, so I'm assuming that's when it ran out of juice."

"I doubt it will help to shed any light on the case, but go ahead and give it to me and I'll take a look."

Zachary read the number off to him. "I thought maybe you could see who he's been talking to on the phone… maybe someone on his call logs will know what happened to him."

"Yeah. Possibly. But probably a wild goose chase. Give me this *friend's* number as well."

Zachary gave him Dimitri's number. "I'd offer to go through the logs myself, if I thought you'd give them to me."

"Unfortunately, not something I can do. We'll have to run them down ourselves. Is that it, then?"

"I wanted to ask you… and this is only very preliminary, not something I have any proof of… but has there been any investigation into rumors of gay immigrant men disappearing over the past few years? Like maybe there is someone targeting them…?"

"What?"

"I am hearing talk of quite a number of men who have disappeared in the last few years. They say that the police won't pay any attention, but I don't know if that means that the police have looked into it and discounted it as a possibility, or whether that means that they haven't looked into it."

"First I've heard of it," Dougan growled. "I can check to be sure, but I think I would have heard about it if there was an investigation underway. I don't like to get involved in finger pointing, but you should understand that every time there is a bust at one of these lounges, the gay community immediately starts whining about relations between the police and the gays and how we're always too quick to bust them and slow to listen to anything about how they are being victimized. So yeah, you do hear about violence against them whenever there is a bust. But that doesn't mean that there's anything to it."

"No, of course not. There are always going to be a lot of... different perspectives on community policing."

"Yeah. If you want to put it that way."

"I don't have anything on this yet, but... I am going to be looking over some documents on these disappearances. So this is just a heads-up that I might have something to discuss in a day or two, once I've had a chance to go through the data. I don't want to surprise you."

"You're going to find out that there's nothing to it, I can guarantee that."

"Good. I hope there isn't. I'd rather not think that someone could have been operating here for that long. I'd rather not think of the friends and family who have been left behind finding out now, years later, that it wasn't ever dealt with at the time."

"Is that a threat?"

"No." Zachary bit his lip. "I didn't mean that at all. I'd like to put this to bed just as much as you."

"I doubt that. Let me just warn you, if you get anything, you'd better be bringing it directly to me, and not discussing it with anyone else along the way. If something like this leaks out to the public, there will be widespread panic. I do not want to have to deal with the consequences of something like this getting out into the wild."

"I think you'll find that it already is in the gay community. But maybe not in the mainstream. I'm not going to give the information to anyone else. Just to you."

"See to it."

———

Despite his assertion to Mr. Peterson that he'd had enough sleep and wouldn't be able to sleep during the day, Zachary fell asleep while he was holding an ice pack across his eyes. He had apparently been conked out for a couple of hours when Lorne came into the room to see if he was ready to go to the camera repair shop.

"Do you want to sleep longer? We can put this off for another time."

"No." Zachary blinked his eyes, trying to clear his vision, knowing that if he rubbed them, the bruises would make him regret it. "I want to get those pictures processed as soon as I can. I haven't heard back from Philippe yet about what John said." He picked up his phone from the bed beside him and looked at it. There were several missed calls from Philippe. The ringer was turned off and with the phone on the bed, the vibration hadn't been enough to wake him up. "Oh, I guess he did. Hang on a sec, I need to see what he has to say."

Rather than checking the voicemail messages that Philippe had left, Zachary just called him. Philippe answered almost immediately this time. "Zachary? Where the hell have you been? I thought he got you too!"

"Thought who got me?" Zachary asked, a knot tightening in his stomach.

"I've been calling John and calling him. He doesn't answer. I checked with one of the guys who works at the same site as he does and John didn't show up today! He never misses work, but he didn't show up today. No one knows where he is. Every call just goes through to voicemail, and he's not returning any of them. It's just like with Jose, Zachary! What's going on?"

Zachary looked over at Mr. Peterson, who could probably hear Philippe's panicked voice, even though Zachary didn't have it on speakerphone.

"I don't know what's going on. Maybe he is sick today. Do you know where he lives? Or who he lives with?"

"They said he didn't go home last night. He went out to the hospital to see you, and then he never went home."

"He would have had to go home," Zachary said blankly.

"I know, but he didn't!"

"He had all of those papers. He would have gone home to put them away somewhere safe. He had put all that time and effort into all of that research. He wouldn't have let anyone else get their hands on it."

"He's missing!" Philippe insisted.

"I hear you… are you going to report it to the police?"

"He wouldn't want me to."

"Why not?"

"Because, we don't report each other to the police. If he was just somewhere else… I would get him in trouble. I don't want to get him in trouble."

"He could already be in trouble. Not with the police, but with someone who intends to do him harm. You need to report it."

"No, I can't. Nando told me to stay out of this. He'll kill me if he finds out that I talked to you and that I've been talking with John. I'm just supposed to be going to work, not getting myself in the middle of something like this!"

"Nando would want you to tell if you knew people were being victimized. He'd want to know about Jose and the others."

"No, he wouldn't! He would tell me to mind my own business unless I wanted to disappear too!"

Zachary didn't know what to say to that. He let the words just hang in the air. Did Nando know something about what had happened to Jose and the missing men? Or did Philippe?

"I'm going to have to get the police involved," he said finally. "They can do more if they start while the trail is fresh."

"You're just going to cause more trouble!"

"Then I'm going to cause more trouble," Zachary agreed. He hung up the phone. He looked at Mr. Peterson. "You heard?"

"Who is this John? He's the one who let you take pictures of his research?"

"Yes."

"Maybe he changed his mind. Maybe he decided that dealing with you was too dangerous and he needed to go underground."

"I hope so. I'd much rather think he was in hiding than that something had happened to him."

———

Dougan didn't answer the phone when Zachary called him again. Zachary wondered whether he had already blocked his number, or whether he would because Zachary had called twice in one day. But he tried to stay calm about it, left a message about John and his unexpected disappearance, and he got ready to go to the camera repair place.

Pat was up and gave Zachary a careful hug, trying to be mindful of all of his bumps and bruises. "You're a good man, Zach. Please be careful and don't do anything risky because of this case. I wouldn't want anything else to happen to you."

Neither of them had told Pat yet about the call from Philippe. Zachary was still hoping it was a mistake, and that they would soon hear that John was okay.

"I'm just fine," he assured Pat. "I know it looks bad, but... I've dealt with worse. We're just going over to the camera store. Nothing is going to happen there."

"I've been to the camera store with Lorne," Pat said, his eyebrows drawn down in a dramatic scowl, "and every time he goes, they empty out his wallet."

Zachary laughed. "Well, I can't promise they won't do that," he agreed. He might find one or two things he needed to add to his collection while he was there too. There was nothing that was quite so much fun as a camera store, especially if they had vintage cameras and parts as well as modern digital.

"I don't know if it's a good idea turning the two of you loose in a camera store," Pat said. "It's akin to taking a couple of alcoholics to a wine tasting."

In spite of Zachary's reassurances, Pat still patted his shoulder and clucked over him like a mother hen, always protective of his family.

"We won't be long," Zachary promised.

"Oh, I've heard that one before. You won't be back until you've cleaned the whole store out."

———

The owner and staff at the camera store gaped at Zachary's ugly bruises, and then tried to pretend they weren't staring every time they looked at him. Zachary tried to ignore the looks and just to talk to them as if everything were normal. Mr. Peterson greeted the owner as an old friend, then gestured to Zachary.

"Rocky, this is one of my of foster kids, Zachary. The only one who inherited my love of photography."

"Hi," Zachary shook hands with him. "Might have had something to do with the camera you gave me for my birthday."

Lorne waved his hand. "I knew you had the eye. That's why I gave it to you. You were a watcher, always observing everything."

"Well, it was the first birthday present I ever got, so even if I hadn't had an innate talent for it, I think I still would have pursued it as a hobby."

Mr. Peterson cocked his head. Zachary replayed what he had just said in his head. "What?"

"You mean it was the first birthday present I ever gave you?"

Zachary shook his head. "No, the first birthday present I ever got. First one I can remember, anyway. Maybe I got things as a baby, from welfare organizations, but our parents never had any money for gifts."

Mr. Peterson considered this seriously. "I never knew that."

"We didn't always have enough *food* to get by."

"Well… I guess I'm glad I got you that camera."

Rocky, the owner spread his hands in inquiry. "So, what can I do for you today?"

Lorne explained. "Zachary's got a camera that's had a little accident. We need to recover the pictures on the memory card."

"Let's have a look."

Zachary brought out the little camera and showed Rocky the card slot, with the digital memory card wedged firmly in place. Rocky examined it and also the damaged mini USB port, his mind following the same logic as Mr. Peterson's. He pulled out some tools.

"How important are the pictures and how important is the camera itself?"

"The pictures are more important. If the camera has to be replaced, I can deal with that. But the pictures are of some important documents, and I don't know if I'll ever be able to get my hands on the originals again."

Rocky nodded. "We'll see what we can do, then." He started unscrewing the tiny screws that held the camera together.

Zachary browsed through the store, not wanting to stand there staring at Rocky as he worked on the camera. He would do his work best without someone hovering over him. In a few minutes, Zachary was lost in the world of photography accessories just like a kid in a toy store.

His phone ringing pulled him out of his happy wandering. He pulled it out and looked at the display, which was a blocked number. He answered the call, his heart speeding.

"Zachary Goldman."

"It's Detective Dougan, returning your call."

"Thanks for calling back. Did you get my voicemail…?" He wasn't sure whether he needed to start at the beginning or if Dougan was already up to speed.

"Let's skip the preliminaries. I believe your John Jama Mwangi matches up with my John Doe."

"Your John Doe?" Zachary repeated, heart sinking.

"Deceased black male, six foot four, slight build, mid-forties to early fifties."

"Yes… that could be him. What happened?"

"Vehicle fire. He's in the morgue."

Zachary was shocked. He was horrified, but at the same time, relieved that John's disappearance did not follow the same pattern as the rest of the disappearances. It was just a coincidence. It was horrible, but a victim of the serial killer would have just disappeared.

"How did it happen? An accident?"

"I would say not. Looks like the car was torched with him in it. It will be some time before we hear from the medical examiner whether he was alive or dead when the fire started."

Zachary's legs went weak. "When did this happen? Where?"

"It happened in the hospital parking garage, early this morning."

He looked for somewhere to sit down, and hobbled over to a chair that had been set up by a camera on a tripod, struggling to catch his breath.

"But that's… he came to see me at the hospital last night. He must have… that would be right after he left…"

"Sounds like it," Dougan agreed.

"But… what could have happened? It wasn't an accident? It was torched?" Zachary echoed Dougan's words, trying to make sense of them and to form a picture of what had happened.

"I'd like to know how this connects up with your missing persons investigation."

"He is a witness… he believed that these other missing men were all related. He had done a bunch of research into all of the other disappearances, tried to tie them all together."

"And you believe him? That they were all related?"

"I don't know. I haven't had a chance to read through all of his research yet."

"You have his papers?"

"I took digital photos of them. He didn't want to part with the originals."

"And he had them in his briefcase?"

Zachary thought of the papers in the car. In his mind's eye, he saw the briefcase full of papers catch fire. The whoomp as the fire reached the bundle of papers and started to burn higher and brighter. The flames would rise and jump and spread to the upholstery, consuming the whole car.

And then he was there. Not in the car, but in his childhood home as the Christmas tree went up in flames, the fire jumping to the curtains, furniture, and carpet, consuming everything in its path. The air was sucked from the room and Zachary was burning up in it, trying to crawl under the couch and to protect his face with his arms, while the fire roared around him like a living monster.

CHAPTER EIGHTEEN

"Zachary, you're okay. Come on back. You're not there. You're in the camera store. Open your eyes. Look around."

Zachary became aware of Mr. Peterson's gentle touch and his calm, even voice. If Mr. Peterson was there, then the fire was long extinguished. He could breathe again. Zachary sucked in lungfuls of cool, sweet air. He pried his eyes open and took in the camera store around him, a couple of the employees gawking at him like he was some sideshow freak. Zachary held Mr. Peterson's arm, trying to ground himself back in the present.

"You're okay," Mr. Peterson repeated.

Zachary nodded, unable to speak yet. He focused on breathing slowly in and out, trying to slow the pounding of his heart. Mr. Peterson stood there waiting patiently.

"Sorry," Zachary apologized.

"You have nothing to be sorry for. You can't control the flashbacks."

"I should be able to. After this long, I should know better than to let myself think..." he trailed off, trying to force his mind away from thoughts that would take him back down that hole.

"See anything you're interested in buying today?" Mr. Peterson looked around at the shelves of camera accessories, trying to distract Zachary.

"Plenty," Zachary agreed, forcing a smile. "Just like Pat said, I could spend all of my money here."

"I'm thinking of a macro lens."

"Yeah. Those are cool."

"Were you… talking to someone?" Mr. Peterson nodded to the phone in Zachary's hand. He looked down at it and realized the call was still live. He put it back up to his ear.

"Uh—hello?"

"Mr. Goldman? What the hell is going on? Where are you?"

"I, uh… I get flashbacks sometimes. Sorry."

"Flashbacks to what? Were you a soldier?"

"No. A fire." Zachary tried to gloss over it, to focus on other aspects. "So everything was destroyed. All of John's original research."

"I would say so. Did he have a suspect? Who knew he was coming to see you?"

"I don't know who might have known about it. Just me, and him, and Philippe as far as I know. He didn't have a suspect… not that he mentioned. I'll have to see what's in his papers, but I would think that if he had a name, he would have told me, even if he couldn't prove it."

"And Philippe? Give me his info."

"He was a friend of Jose's. He's not the one."

"You can't rule out anyone Jose knew. It's a lot easier to get someone alone if they trust you."

"He's just a kid. Eighteen, maybe."

"I need to talk to him. Whether he is a suspect or not, I need to know who he talked to or who might have overheard him. If only three people knew where our vic was going to be, then one of you either torched the car or told the person who did."

Zachary sighed. He knew it was true, but he couldn't imagine Philippe having anything to do with Jose's death, not even because he had accidentally let slip to the wrong person where John was going to be. He reluctantly gave Philippe's information to Dougan.

"I want copies of all of the papers you took pictures of. They could be the key to this case. How soon can I get them?"

"As soon as I can. The camera got damaged and we're trying to recover them right now."

"The camera got damaged."

"Yes. The photos are on the memory card, they're still just fine. But we can't get the card out. I'm just at the repair place."

"You want to tell me what happened last night?"

"I told you, John came to see me at the hospital. I took pictures of his research. Then he left, and I guess that's when—"

"Back it up. I want to know the rest. Why you have a fat lip and were in the hospital last night and how your camera got damaged."

"Oh. That."

"Yes. That."

"I had… an encounter with the local skinheads."

"I see. Did you report it?"

"I talked to a cop… I don't remember his name. I might have been a little doped up on Demerol at the time."

"How badly were you hurt?"

"Cuts and bruises. Nothing broken."

"Except your camera."

"Yeah," Zachary agreed.

"As soon as you recover the photographs, I expect you to get them to me. Can you email them?"

"Sure, of course. The minute I get them."

When Zachary ended the call, he bowed his head, letting out a long breath. Mr. Peterson was still nearby, browsing the accessories and keeping an eye on Zachary. He glanced over and raised one eyebrow. "Okay?"

Zachary nodded.

"I've got it out," Rocky announced. Zachary looked over at the service counter and saw Rocky holding up the memory card with a pair of tweezers. Zachary got up, his legs still a little wobbly, and went over to him.

"And everything is accessible?"

"Let's have a look." Rocky inserted the card into a card reader and watched the computer monitor. "Looks like it's loading."

They watched the file list populate the screen. Zachary breathed out a sigh of relief. "Can you print them out so that we have a hard copy?"

"There's quite a bit here." Rocky changed the view to thumbnails. "Are they all documents? Cheaper to print them on copy paper rather than photographic paper."

"Yes. Copy paper is fine. I'm just anxious to have a hard copy right away. It's easier for me to read than a computer screen. And could I borrow your computer to email out a copy?"

Rocky hesitated. "I don't normally let customers use my computer. It's not a public terminal."

"It's important," Zachary insisted. He pulled the first page from the printer as it dropped into the tray. "Look," he showed Rocky the list of names. "These are all missing and probably murdered men. I need to get copies of all of this to the police for them to use in their investigation."

Rocky's eyes widened as he took in the length of the list. He looked at the printer as it whirred and continued to drop pages into the tray. "You can just take it home and email it from there."

"Just let me use your computer for thirty seconds," Zachary snapped.

Rocky looked taken aback. Mr. Peterson shot Zachary a surprised look from across the store.

Rocky stepped back from the computer, turning it a few degrees toward Zachary for him to use. Zachary opened the web browser and uploaded them to his cloud account then logged into his email and shared them with Dougan.

Rocky had moved away to talk with Mr. Peterson, and Zachary realized they were discussing Rocky's fee to retrieve the memory card and print the files.

"I'll pay for that," Zachary said quickly. "You don't need to do that."

"Zachary, we asked you to look into this case. If we were proper clients, you'd be billing us back for your expenses anyway, wouldn't you? There's no reason you should have to eat the costs just because we're family."

"But…"

"Zachary, let me cover it."

Zachary gave in. He was exhausted after the flashback and wanted to go somewhere he could be alone to recover. He had sent the files to Dougan. The police would be reviewing them and they would open an investigation into the missing men. Zachary would review the files too, in time, but in the meantime, the police could get started on the information John had compiled. They would probably tell Zachary to stay out of the case altogether, and his involvement would be at an end.

CHAPTER NINETEEN

He leafed through the papers as Mr. Peterson drove home, making sure that everything he could remember from the night before was there, captured from the camera. The digital memory card was safely in his wallet. He wanted to analyze everything and start figuring out the case, but his head throbbed and he was tired from the flashback. He just wanted to close his eyes and recover. Mr. Peterson had been talking, but Zachary hadn't been listening to him. He looked over when Lorne stopped talking, startled by the silence.

"Are you okay?" Lorne asked.

Zachary swallowed. He nodded. "Yeah. I'll be fine."

"I know you will be… I just want to make sure."

"Yeah. It always tires me out… but that's all. It will be okay."

He sat and listened to the radio and looked through the papers again, worrying that there would be one page missing, the key to solving the disappearances. John's copies were gone. If Zachary hadn't taken pictures the night before, then they would have been completely in the dark when the originals were destroyed. Even the list of who had disappeared. Men were forgotten after a while. They had no families and no one knew what had happened to them, and eventually everyone forgot they had even existed.

Back at Mr. Peterson's house, they reported to Pat on the recovery of the files. Zachary skipped supper and went to the guest room where he had spent the night before, shutting the door so he could let himself go without being observed. He knew his foster father was not far away if he needed his stabilizing influence, but his immediate need was for space to just be alone with his own thoughts and memories. The next day, he would start compiling the evidence and seeing what he could come up with.

————

Zachary awoke in the morning to his ringing phone. He had taken a sleeping pill the night before and had slept through the early dawn when he usually woke. But it wasn't late. Zachary rubbed his gritty eyes and looked at the screen. It was a blocked call. Dougan.

"Zachary Goldman."

"Goldman, I should throw your butt in jail. What do you think you're doing, spreading your theories to a reporter?"

Zachary blinked and tried to figure out what Dougan was talking about.

"What?"

"You act like you're being helpful and cooperative, and then you throw the police department under the bus! How are we supposed to conduct a proper investigation when you tell everybody what's going on? If we ever had a chance to get close to John Mwangi's killer without alerting him to our suspicions, that's out the window now. I can't believe that you would be so irresponsible!"

"Detective Dougan... I don't know what you're talking about."

"You don't. No one else had this information. It could only have come from you. You couldn't even give us a few days to look at the evidence and pull things together. You just jump in with both feet and put everything in jeopardy."

"I don't know what you're talking about. I haven't talked to any reporter. I haven't talked to anyone."

"That's clearly not true. It wasn't Mwangi who went to the press. He didn't have time after talking to you. And he's been sitting on this information for months already. Why would he suddenly release it after talking to you? He wouldn't. Because *you're* the one who did."

"I haven't talked to anyone."

"You're the only one who had the documents."

"Yes. As far as I know."

"Then how did they get all over the morning paper? That list of names has gotten everyone in a panic. The phone has not stopped ringing. They want to know how the police could have sat on the news of a serial killer for so long without letting the public know the risk. We haven't even determined that there is a serial killer! That's your theory, and it hasn't been proven in any way."

"It's not even my theory. I haven't gone through everything yet either. I haven't even verified that all of the men on the list are missing."

"Well, you've thrown it all into the public eye now, and that doesn't make it easier for us to investigate, it makes it harder."

"I didn't give it to anyone." Zachary tried to sort out what Dougan was telling him. "They had the list? I don't understand... As soon as we got the documents off of the memory card, I printed them off and I emailed a copy to you. That's it. No one else has seen them."

"Who else has access to your computer?"

"It wasn't my computer."

Zachary's heart sank as he realized that it must have been Rocky or someone else on his staff. Zachary had lost his cool and told them about the missing and murdered men. Rocky had either copied what was on the card onto his hard drive, or Zachary had left his email box open in the browser, giving him access to what he had sent to Dougan.

He swore under his breath. "I didn't want to wait until I could get to another computer to send it to you. So I borrowed the camera shop's computer to email them to you right away. He must have kept a copy."

Dougan swore as well. "Brilliant, Goldman. Just brilliant."

CHAPTER TWENTY

Zachary opened the web browser on his phone to look up the local news site to see how bad the exposure had been. Maybe it would just blow over and after the initial panic, everyone would just go back to whatever they had been worrying about before the story broke. If people hadn't cared about the missing men before, then why would they worry now? After the initial shock wore off, people would decide that they were in no danger themselves and would go back to their own lives.

But the story had broken big. He immediately saw that it was not only on the local news, but had been reported in the national papers' websites as well. They were all just regurgitating what the local paper had said and adding that the police had no comment, but it was everywhere. It wasn't going to just blow over.

Some of them had done a little digging and had sidebars on Zachary's attack by the skinheads and on the fire that had killed John. Once the first one had reported that Zachary had been attacked after leaving The Night Scene, the rest of the articles had reported that he was gay himself, and that was what had sparked his interest in the case. Pat's and Lorne's names were also mentioned, reported as being 'prominent men in the gay community.'

Zachary felt sick.

He opened the bedroom door and walked to the kitchen, where Mr.

Peterson and Pat sat with their coffee and a newspaper. Zachary could only hope that the story hadn't made it to the printed news before the deadline.

But Pat's ashen face told him that his hope was vain.

They both looked at him without a word. Without the usual cheery morning smiles.

"I'm sorry," Zachary said. "I didn't talk to anyone. I swear. It wasn't me."

"How did they get this, then?" Mr. Peterson asked.

Zachary licked his dry lips. He glanced over at the coffee machine. "It must have been Rocky or someone on his staff. They had the recovered files."

Mr. Peterson shook his head slowly. "Good grief. I never would have expected Rocky to do something like that. That's my fault, Zachary. I should never have taken you there."

"You had no way of knowing. We just went there to get the camera fixed. They shouldn't have used it for their own purposes."

"No."

Pat was still looking at Zachary with wide eyes. "Do you really think this is the work of a serial killer?"

"I don't know. I haven't spent enough time going through the documents. I don't even know yet if John was right and they are all missing. Some of these guys could be reading about their own deaths right now and be pretty surprised. I need to go through and verify everything."

"I would guess the police will be doing that now. They have more manpower than you do."

"They haven't even opened an investigation into this," Zachary said. "They just got the information yesterday, and like I said, it has to all be verified before we go jumping to any conclusions. I do think... that it is more than coincidence that ties all of these men together. It looks too much like a pattern. But it's way too early to tell."

"The paper says there is an investigation underway."

"I know... but they're wrong. There are two investigations right now. Jose's missing persons case and John's death. I don't know if any missing persons files were ever opened on any of the other men. But there is no serial murder investigation. There's no task force, at least not as of five minutes ago. And just in case you're wondering, I am not gay."

Pat cracked a smile at that. "I think I know that. I get your point. They haven't gotten all of the facts right. This is just so shocking." He shook his head in dismay. "I had no idea, when we talked to you about Jose, that it would lead to any of this."

"How could you? I'm just following the evidence, seeing where it leads. There wasn't any way to predict it." Zachary poured himself a cup of coffee. "I guess I'd better hit the books."

"Do you need any help?" Mr. Peterson asked. "Reading, collating information, anything?"

He knew that reading wasn't Zachary's strongest suit. But Zachary's skills had grown and developed as a private investigator, and he had gotten accustomed to reading and managing large amounts of paperwork when he had to.

"I'll take my ADHD meds so that I can focus on it, and I'll start a database or wiki on the computer to tame all the facts. It's a big job, but I can manage it."

"Well, if you need anything, just let me know. You can rest your eyes and I can read some of it to you. I'm not so much good on the computer, but you can bounce ideas off of us. Talk about theories, see what fits."

"Thanks. I'll let you know." He had worked out how to make his computer read digital documents aloud to him, so he didn't need Mr. Peterson for that. But he might take him up on brainstorming ideas together.

"And you need more for breakfast than just coffee."

"One piece of toast," Zachary conceded.

"You eat the whole thing."

"I'll try."

When Zachary walked through the living room to get back to the guest bedroom, he saw unusual activity out the front window and stopped for a closer look. There was an assortment of trucks that didn't belong there, with satellite dishes on top and people milling about with cameras and boom mikes. Zachary stared at them.

"I see you've noticed our visitors," Pat observed.

"How long have they been here?"

"Since before we got up. That security system of yours woke us up when they got too close to the house, so I chased them back over the property line. They've been pretty good since then, but we're leaving the system armed so we know if they start getting too close again."

"Why would they be here?"

"To interview you."

"Or the prominent citizens in the Vermont gay community," Mr. Peterson added, smiling.

Zachary rubbed his temples. "Oh, man… I'm so sorry about this."

"This isn't anything you did, Zachary. This is something that we all walked into. It's part of finding out what happened to Jose. If he was the victim of a predator who has been killing other gay men for the past few years… then this is what we need to do. We can't back down just because it's inconvenient."

"I should have been more careful, though. I should have made sure that Rocky hadn't copied anything to his hard drive. Made sure that I logged out and cleared the web browser. I shouldn't have emailed the files from there at all. I don't know what I was thinking. Just that the faster I got them to Dougan, the sooner we could start getting some answers."

"Zachary, we're all in this together. Pat and I fully support you on this. Pat asked you to look into it. I took you to the camera shop. None of us could have predicted this outcome, or we might have approached it differently. But you didn't do anything but follow the evidence. If you've found more than the police did, that just shows what a good investigator you are."

———

Zachary remained hyperfocused on John's papers for most of the morning, pulled out of it once or twice due to the whoops of the security system when the crowd outside got too close to the house. He had his phone turned to airplane mode so he wouldn't be interrupted by reporters or other curious inquiries. When he took a break, he turned his phone back on to collect his messages. He saw that one of them was from Kenzie and gave her a call back.

"Oh, so you are deigning to speak to the rest of us common folk?" Kenzie teased when she picked up.

"Sorry. Had to turn the phone off to get anything done this morning."

"I don't doubt it. I thought your questions about profiling the other days were theoretical. You actually took on a serial killer case?"

"Well… not intentionally. It was just the disappearance of a friend that Pat asked me to look into. But I guess you know now he wasn't the only one to disappear."

"Me, along with the rest of the country. You made the news in a big way. And the fact that you've solved a couple of murders in the last year gives you a bit of credibility."

"I'm not the one who leaked it. That was… unintentional. I wasn't looking for any publicity."

"You've certainly caused some waves. Phone lines are all lit up looking for comments from officers who have had contact with the great Zachary Goldman on other cases."

"No one is going to talk to them, though, right? Just a lot of 'no comments.'"

"That's the official line. I don't know whether they'll be able to wring a quote out of anybody anonymously, but there won't be anything official." She paused. "And then there are people who know that you and I have been seeing each other for the last year and are now confused by the report that you're gay."

Zachary felt himself flush. "You know that's not true."

"Well, it would explain a few things…"

"Kenzie, I just don't want to rush things—"

She was laughing. "After your experience with Bridget, I don't blame you for not wanting to rush things. But then, I wouldn't blame you for going off of women, either…"

"I was at the bar for the investigation. If I'm investigating the disappearance of a gay man, doesn't it make sense to investigate the places he frequented?"

She gave another laugh and let him off the hook. "Okay, okay. Really, I wasn't calling to bust your chops. I just thought I'd check in with you and see how you were doing. So how are you?"

"I'm okay." Zachary considered. "I'm not as anxious about the publicity as you would think."

"That's good, but I was more worried about your trip to the hospital. How badly are you hurt?"

"Bumps and bruises. Nothing broken or ruptured."

"Still, you must be pretty sore. How many were there?"

Zachary thought back. It had all happened so fast. He tried to slow it down in his brain. "Maybe… six. Two guys were holding me, and…"

Kenzie swore. "You're lucky you're still in one piece. How did you manage to get away?"

"A bystander interrupted them."

"Lucky for you."

"Yeah, it was. Could have been a lot worse."

"How are Pat and Lorne handling the publicity? I don't imagine they were expecting to have a spotlight shined on their lives."

"There are reporters camped out outside their house. They're handling it pretty well, but I hope it doesn't go on for too long. Another story will break, and the reporters will have to go somewhere else."

"Serial killers are good copy. They won't give up for a while."

"Thanks."

She chuckled. "Just had to bring a little ray of sunshine into your life. But seriously, you're okay?"

"Yeah. Thanks."

"And I know you probably aren't as far along in the investigation as you were hoping to be, but do you have everything you need on serial killers?"

"I'm going on your advice and trying to match up suspects with opportunity, rather than a psychological profile."

"That will give you the most solid information. You can get a behaviorist to try to create a profile for you, but they're not as accurate as you see on TV. It might help you to focus on a smaller group of suspects, but you wouldn't be able to rely on it like an alibi."

"Motive, means, and opportunity. That's what I'm going to focus on."

"Good. Are there many suspects?"

Zachary thought of the people he had already talked to. None of them had struck him as serial killers, but wasn't that what they always said? *He was the nicest guy. He was so quiet. Always helpful.* And then there were the names he had pulled from the online forums.

"I don't really have a handle on it yet. I'll be looking for connections between the victims. Did they frequent the same places, live in the same area, have mutual friends, that kind of thing?"

"If this guy has been hunting the same waters for a few years... he's going to be hard to spot. Or he would have already been discovered."

"Yeah."

"You should probably just let the police investigate it. They aren't going to want you getting in the way, and you can't exactly hide your investigation from the killer now. I wouldn't want you to be a target."

"I'm just reading files right now. And the police haven't yet opened an investigation, despite what the reporters are saying. They have an investigation open on Jose's disappearance, and on my informant's death, nothing on a serial killer. We're all a bit behind the eight ball. No one was expecting this to go public so soon."

"This informant... that's all a little spooky. He comes to you with this theory, and then he gets murdered within an hour? No one can tell me that's a coincidence."

"I know." Zachary had been trying not to focus on this issue as he worked his way through John's papers. He just kept telling himself how much he appreciated the work that John had done and how lucky he had been to find him.

"You need to be careful, okay? Neo-Nazis and burning cars... you're taking risks."

"I'm at home with Pat and Mr. Peterson. They have a state-of-the art security system. We're surrounded by reporters eager to get a picture of something they can publish. We couldn't be much safer."

"Okay. Well, you be careful. It's really the job of the police department, not you, so let them do their thing."

"I will," Zachary agreed.

CHAPTER TWENTY-ONE

Zachary dialed Philippe's number with the list of possible victims in front of him. Philippe hadn't been around for long, but he might have known the last few people on John's list, since the two of them were acquainted. And he might have the names of some of the other men who would know the earlier victims.

The phone rang immediately through to voicemail. Zachary hung up and looked at his phone.

There was no reason to jump to the conclusion that something had happened to Philippe. If any of the news articles had linked him to Zachary or Jose, he was probably dealing with calls from reporters and, like Zachary, had either turned his phone to airplane mode or turned it off. Or he had seen Zachary's number and sent it to voicemail or had blocked it. There was no reason to think that something had happened to the boy.

He looked up Nando's number and it also went to voicemail. Chances were, the illegals were spooked. Now that Zachary's name had shown up in the news, they wanted nothing to do with him. They didn't want to be caught in any investigation, whether by the police, or Zachary, or news reporters. They knew how to go underground to avoid inquiries.

Zachary went to talk to Pat, and found him busy in the kitchen making sandwiches.

"Be ready in a few minutes," Pat promised.

Zachary wasn't hungry, but he knew Pat was right and he should probably eat soon, so he didn't argue. "I was wondering whether you had talked to your friends."

"What friends, Zach?"

"I asked if I could talk to some of your acquaintances who knew Jose. You said you needed to talk to them first. So I'm wondering whether there's any way I could talk to them now...?"

"All of the publicity complicates things. I don't know how far you'll be able to get with them. But I've got a couple who said yesterday that they would talk to you."

Zachary let out his breath, relieved. "Good. And I have some names I wanted you to look at, when you're not busy..."

Pat glanced at him. "The names of the missing men?"

"Uh, yeah. I wondered whether you knew any of the others."

"There are different social groups in the community, just like with any population. Jose moved between the music scene and some... riskier places. Most of the people Lorne and I do things with are stable older couples or bachelors. Not young pups who are polyamorous. The newspaper articles blurred the last names of the missing men, but I don't think I knew any of the others. Not well enough to know anything about their lives, anyway."

"I'll show you the unmasked list, just to be sure. It might trigger something."

Pat nodded. "Just don't get your hopes up. If this guy has avoided discovery, it's by targeting men who aren't in committed relationships. Otherwise, their partners would have talked to the police."

"Even if they're illegals?"

"Hard to say," Pat admitted, "but I would think some of them would have, considering the number of names on that list."

———

Eric Naylor had agreed to talk to Zachary, but it was obvious he was still leery of the idea. Zachary arrived at his used clothing store at closing time, as Naylor had suggested, and when Naylor got a look at him, Zachary thought he was going to lock him out. The swelling on Zachary's face was going down, but the bruises were setting in and the split cheek and lip were still livid. Despite the fact that he looked like a victim rather than a goon,

Naylor still looked hesitant about letting him in. Eventually, he steeled himself and opened the door wide for Zachary, then closed it and locked it behind him, turning the sign over to 'closed.'

Naylor was an older man, probably in his sixties, slim and neat and expensively dressed. He had long, tapering fingers and a prissy manner.

"I appreciate you agreeing to see me," Zachary told him. "I know you probably aren't too eager to talk about what might have happened to Jose, especially in light of all of the stuff in the news today."

"I think, actually, that seeing it in the news made it seem more real. When Pat said that he was afraid something had happened to Jose, I didn't think it was anything. He could have just gone away without telling anybody. But seeing all of those names... if this really is a serial killer..."

"We don't know yet. But we'd like to catch the guy if it is. Before he hurts anyone else."

Naylor nodded. He busied himself with tidying up the store as he talked to Zachary, his fingers always moving.

"Do you recognize the names of anyone else on this list?" Zachary handed him the printed page.

Naylor's eyes went over it, working their way down the page. "I don't think so," he said. "Sometimes you know someone's first name and not their last, but I don't recognize anyone."

"Okay, thanks. So you were part of the group that hung out sometimes with Pat and Lorne? And Jose?"

"Yeah. We like our music," Naylor made an abbreviated motion in the air, as if he were leading a band. "When there was someone good playing or singing, we made sure we were there."

"In mixed groups, or just LGBT venues?"

"Mostly LGBT. That's where we can fit in and not have to worry about being harassed. But if there was something we just had to see at a bigger venue, we would."

"Were you and Jose close?"

Naylor flashed him a look. "Is that what Pat told you?"

"He didn't say anything. I'm wondering."

"We were friendly. We did things with the group."

"You never saw each other outside of the group?"

"We didn't date."

Zachary filed that away for future reference. "What did you talk about?"

"Music. Other things. Small-talk. Work."

"Did he talk to you about his job?"

"No. He asked about the shop sometimes, I'd tell him anything interesting that had happened. You know, interesting customers, estate sales, bell-bottoms."

"Sure." Zachary looked around the store. It was higher than thrift-store quality. Vintage or designer, mostly. An upper-class used closing store. "You look like you carry some good stuff."

Naylor smiled, looking around his shop. He nodded. "It's a good place. I enjoy the work."

"You must not be here by yourself."

"Right now, yes. But not during the day. I have several employees. I close up on my own, spend time on administrative tasks. Things like that."

"Did you ever consider hiring Jose or any of the other immigrants?"

"Uh… no… I liked Jose, but I wouldn't hire illegals. I don't want to get in trouble with the feds. That's a good way to ruin a business."

"They're cheap labor, if you don't get caught. Better margins."

"Not worth the risk."

"What did Jose talk about? His family back home? What his plans were for the future?"

"Not much. He would mention them in passing, but we were… in a different space than all of that. It was an escape. He could be himself instead of a family man, someone who was responsible for others… he could relax."

"Makes sense. Did he ever talk to you about his other friends? People he saw outside of your group?"

Another sideways look. Naylor made a show of trying to remember any such conversation, then shook his head. "No, I don't think he ever did."

Zachary let the silence draw out for a few seconds. He raised a brow at Naylor. "I don't get the feeling you're being completely honest with me."

"What do you mean? I'm answering your questions."

"Yeah. What I mean is, whenever I ask you something about your personal relationship with Jose, I get the feeling you're lying or avoiding the question."

"I don't know what you're talking about."

"You're lying to me about something."

"What did Pat tell you? I am not in a relationship with Jose."

"I don't think *anyone* is in a relationship with Jose anymore. This has nothing to do with Pat. I just asked him for names of other people in your circle of friends who would talk to me about Jose. He didn't say anything about your relationship. But your body language whenever you talk about him… is wrong."

Naylor just stared at him challengingly, not changing his tune.

Zachary leaned on one of the clothing racks, studying Naylor's expression. He watched for any change. "One of Jose's partners told me that he had bruises on his throat one day. Like someone had choked him."

Naylor's eyes got wide.

"Was that you?" Zachary asked.

"No, it certainly was not!" Naylor's tone was heated. His voice had a satisfying ring of truth. He did not like hearing about Jose getting hurt. Or he didn't like hearing about one of Jose's other partners.

"Did he tell you who it was? Or did you already know?"

"I didn't know anything about it."

"You must know some of the men that he's gone with. He talks with you. He must mention his social life sometimes."

"There are rules. You don't talk about people's other partners."

"Ah." Zachary nodded at the confirmation that they *had* been seeing each other. "That's one of the rules. And it never gets broken? It would be easy to slip up now and then, or maybe someone didn't like the rule and wanted to talk about others."

"No." Naylor shook his head. "No, we follow the rules."

"Who else was Jose with?"

"I don't know."

"Just because you didn't talk about it, that doesn't mean you don't know."

Naylor's eyes narrowed. He looked down at the floor, worried.

"Jose is gone. I don't know if he's alive anymore or not," Zachary said. "After more than a week… probably not. Don't you want to find out who did this to him? Don't you want to know who it is that's taking other men in the community? You can't just turn a blind eye to it and pretend it's not happening." Zachary paused, analyzing Naylor's expression. "Or maybe you don't care, as long as he doesn't come after you. You're not dark-skinned like the others. You're tall and fair. Not the same physical type at all. So maybe you don't care about any killer, as long as he doesn't come after you. You and the rest of the community will just stay quiet and let him prey on immigrants, because they don't count."

"Of course they count!" Naylor said hotly. "They are people just like anyone else. Being from another country or being dark-skinned or dark-haired doesn't make you less of a person. They matter just as much as anyone."

"Then help me. Lying to me isn't going to help Jose. It isn't going to help the other men. If you tell me the truth, you might be able to protect others in the future. Maybe other current partners. How many of the men that you are seeing now meet that type?"

"I'm not here to talk about my personal life," Naylor said stubbornly.

"So you don't really care about saving anyone else's life. You're just worried about your own reputation."

"I… I am a business owner. I can't have people looking at me as if I'm just a… I am a mature, responsible member of this community."

"I don't see what your personal practices have to do with any of that. And I'm not going to tell anyone what you tell me now. I'm just trying to find out what happened to Jose. I want to know who it is that's taking these men. It's been going on for years. Maybe you don't care if it keeps going on. What's another five or ten years? Twenty to sixty men. Your community will tolerate that kind of loss. There are always new immigrants, and new couples moving in because of the marriage laws. They refresh the pool."

"You can't talk about them like that, as if they're just playing pieces and don't matter!"

"That's how you're treating them. Like your reputation is worth more than they are."

Naylor slammed his hand down on an accessories table, sending a number of small pieces flying. "You don't have any right to talk to me like that!"

"Then tell the truth. How hard is it to admit that you and Jose were together?"

"Yes, okay. We were together. Sometimes. Privately. Not in public."

"That's fine. I don't care if you never went out with him in public. I want to know who was seeing him and what you know about it. You know that the person most likely to harm him is an intimate partner, don't you? Statistically speaking, the person most likely to kill him is a lover."

"I did not kill him."

"Maybe not, but who else might have known where he was or might have had reason to be jealous of him? Who were his enemies? Ex-lovers? Did his wife know he was seeing men while she was waiting for him to bring her here?"

"I don't know who else he was seeing."

"I thought you were going to start telling me the truth."

"I am."

"Who else?"

Naylor growled. "Philippe. You already knew that. John Mwangi. Honore Santiago. Others. I didn't always find out if it was just a one-time encounter. Even if you don't talk about it... you get a feel after a while. Suspicions. The way people react around each other."

"And do you know who choked him?"

"No."

Zachary believed it. "Did you ask him about it?"

"He said it was off-limits," Naylor's tone was sullen.

"Philippe still talked to him about it. Demanded to know who it was."

"Philippe is a boy. He doesn't always follow the rules." Naylor gave Zachary an appraising look. "What did Jose tell Philippe?"

"He suggested it was consensual."

Naylor frowned, shaking his head.

"You don't think so?" Zachary asked.

"I don't know. It was... out of character."

"Do you think he was lying?"

"I thought..." Naylor fiddled with the clothing in a rack closer to Zachary, adjusting the spacing between the garments. "I thought he was afraid."

"And what did you think of that? What did you do?"

"I wanted to know what had happened, how he had gotten hurt, but he wouldn't talk to me about it. He said it was off-limits, but I thought he was just saying that to make me stop asking."

"So what did you do?"

"I stopped asking." Naylor gave a shrug. "What was I supposed to do? I wanted to spend the time with him. I didn't want a fight. So I figured he could take care of himself. He was an adult. If there was trouble, he could handle it." Naylor shook his head, eyes glassy. "Would it have made any difference if I had done something? What? Tell him to go to the police?

Force him to tell me who it was and confronted them? There wasn't anything I could do if he didn't want to talk about it."

Zachary nodded. "I don't know what you could have done. He wouldn't go to the police because he was illegal."

Naylor sighed. "It makes them so vulnerable. How would you like to be invisible? Disposable? He didn't have any rights."

Zachary did know what it was like to be invisible and disposable. "It must have been very difficult." Zachary waited a few seconds, watching Naylor's face, curious about whether he would let the tears fall or force them back. Naylor looked away. "How long was this before he disappeared?"

"A week, maybe two. Long enough to put it out of my mind. I don't think it could have been related."

"What did you think happened when he disappeared?"

"I thought… he was gone. He must have taken off. Immigration caught wind of him or he decided to move on somewhere else."

"Did he ever talk about going somewhere else? Was there somewhere he would have liked to have gone?"

Naylor gave a little laugh. "Somewhere warmer. Hawaii. He never talked about it seriously. Just one of those things you fantasize about. What you would do if you had the money and the means. Retire somewhere warm and live the good life. It wasn't something that was ever going to happen to him."

"And there wasn't anywhere else, somewhere he might really go? Somewhere there was better work? A friend or relative who could help him?"

"No. Not that we ever talked about."

"It didn't occur to you to go to the police when he disappeared?"

"No. He wouldn't want that."

"But you didn't say anything to Pat when he went to the police?"

"He didn't ask *my* permission. I didn't know he was doing it. I would have told him not to bother, but that's all."

"He didn't know about the two of you?"

"Not that he ever said. But he and I didn't discuss personal relationships. I knew that he and Lorne were happy together and weren't looking for anyone else. When we got together as a group, it was just as friends, and Jose and I never showed any special affection in public."

"Do you think that there is someone out there who is killing these men? Or do you think that they just disappeared by their own choice?"

Naylor fiddled with the buttons on the front of a jacket on display. "I don't know. There are rumors. People say not to go out alone. To make sure you have someone to walk you to your car. I always thought it was a little bit 'Big Bad Wolf.' Something that people said to make sure you didn't go wandering in the woods alone. Not a real threat. Something to keep people alert and avoid encounters with skinheads and other gay-bashers."

Zachary ignored the subtle jab. His eyes were following Naylor's fingers, distracted by his fidgeting. He looked at the jacket, trying to capture the thought nagging in the back of his brain. He concentrated.

In the picture Pat had given him, Jose had been dressed up. When Zachary had seen Jose's possessions in the rented apartment with Nando, there had been no sign of formal clothing. Not on Jose's bed, and nothing hanging in the closets.

CHAPTER TWENTY-TWO

"**I**s that Jose's jacket?"

Naylor stiffened. He turned his head and looked at Zachary.

"He might have worn it once or twice." He ran his hand down the jacket nostalgically, as if remembering it lying over Jose's chest. He looked back at Zachary again. "With a store like this, do you think I'd let him show up at La Rouge in a t-shirt? He always came here before we went out."

Zachary looked around the store with new eyes. Serial killers sometimes kept trophies. Was it possible that any of the clothes on display had belonged to or been worn by any of the other missing men? How would anyone ever know? Though, if Naylor were keeping trophies, surely he wouldn't have them out front where other people could buy them. Maybe on a special rack in the back of the store, carefully protected in garment bags. Or was it a game for him, watching to see who would buy them? Maybe getting to know the men who bought them.

It was a morbid thought, and Zachary knew he was letting his imagination run wild. He needed to focus on the evidence. What could be proven. Not flights of fancy.

"Did you date—or *see*—any of the other missing men?" He'd already asked Naylor if he knew any of the other men on the list, but wanted to touch on it again, now that Naylor had admitted his relationship with Jose.

Naylor shook his head. "No. I don't know many of the immigrants. Jose was… special."

"Have you dated any men who disappeared who are not on the list?"

"People come and go… go in and out of circulation… but I don't think so."

"If you did, you should tell me now. It wouldn't be good if it came up later," Zachary warned.

"You think I have something to do with these men disappearing? That's ridiculous. Whoever it is, if there is a serial killer, it's not me. He's not anything like me. There are plenty of people out there bashing gays. You should be looking at them, not at me."

Zachary tended to agree with him. Naylor's name had not popped up in any of John's papers or with any of the people Zachary had questioned at the club. There was no reason to suspect him of having anything to do with the disappearances.

"I just want to be sure. We don't want there to be any confusion over who you knew and who you didn't." He used 'we' as a reminder that he wouldn't be the only one asking questions about the missing men. The police too would want those answers, and if they got a different answer from him than from Zachary, it would bring up more questions and suspicions.

"I don't remember meeting any of them. Maybe we ran into each other at some social event. I can't say I was never in the same room as any of them or talked to them. But I didn't have a relationship with any of them. Only Jose."

———

Unlike Naylor, Honore Santiago, rival for Jose's affections, didn't want to meet Zachary at his place of business or at home. He wanted neutral ground. Neutral turned out to be La Rouge, the gay lounge that Naylor had mentioned, so it wasn't nearly as neutral as Zachary would have liked. So close on the heels of the attack by the skinheads, it was about the last place he wanted to be seen. Maybe that had been Santiago's hope when he suggested it.

Climbing right back into the saddle was probably the best thing for Zachary. It meant he didn't have the time to develop a phobia of gay venues. He would go, nothing bad would happen to him, and his brain would learn that it wasn't an innately dangerous place to be. If Mr. Peterson and Pat ever wanted to take him to some show they loved, he would want to be able to go and not to be held back by unwarranted fears.

He planned to do the opposite of what he had done at the bar, having his car valet-parked so that he would be able to step right out the front door and not walk along lonely streets to get to it.

He hadn't expected to run into any issues. He had gotten into the bar without any problems; it had looked just like any other bar and people had walked by it on the street without another look. La Rouge was a different story. There were all kinds of people up and down the sidewalks in front of and beside the lounge. Not patrons, but protesters and reporters.

There probably wouldn't have been reporters there if not for the news of the serial killer. They wouldn't be hanging around La Rouge waiting for something to happen or to get pictures of gay celebs. But the word was that there was a serial killer targeting gay men in the state, and where else would such a killer go? Obviously he would go somewhere gay men hung out. La Rouge might not be quite the kind of place that the MSM immigrant men hung out, but the reporters wanted photo ops, and La Rouge was big and flashy and recognizable.

Apparently, it was also where the gay bashers had gone to make their voices heard. As Zachary got closer, he could see some of their signs citing scripture and sin and burning in hell. There were women there with children. It was the last place that Zachary would have brought children, especially at night. He supposed the protesters thought that they would be less likely to be arrested if they had children with them, since the police wouldn't want to have to deal with screaming children and figuring out what to do with them while their parents were arrested. Or maybe the children were supposed to make the gay men feel guilty in some way. Embarrassed to be seen at such a wicked place by innocent children. Or sad that they could not have biological children as a gay couple. They must have had some logical reason to bring children there, other than their entertainment.

The traffic slowed to a crawl, which gave Zachary time to reconsider meeting there. He could call Santiago back and suggest that they meet somewhere else, since it was such a circus at La Rouge. He didn't even have to use the reporters or protesters as a reason not to go. He could just say that he had run into traffic, or that something had come up.

But he didn't want to give himself an excuse to avoid the lounge and to reinforce to his brain that it was a dangerous place to be. By confronting it head on, he would teach himself that it was nothing to be afraid of. So he stayed in the lane inching toward La Rouge, texting Santiago that he was going to be late but would be there as soon as traffic allowed.

Giving his car to the valet meant that he had to get out right in front of the reporters. There was no easy way to avoid them. He hadn't planned for a trip to La Rouge; he didn't have a tux or a black suit or any kind of fancy dress. He had a button-up shirt and a jacket, and had borrowed a tie from Pat, so he was dressed decently, but his face attracted immediate attention. Zachary heard a collective gasp when he got out of the car and handed the valet his keys, as people saw his bruised face and then started to talk to each other, pointing him out. It wasn't long before he was hearing his name in their comments. They had clearly made the connection between his beaten and bruised face and the man in the news.

A wave of reporters surged forward as he got close to the front doors, shouting their questions and holding up cameras. Security was already on hand and did their best to restrain and subdue the intruders, and one of them was quickly at Zachary's side, sweeping him inside.

"Sorry about that, sir. We don't usually have this much trouble. Everyone is going crazy over the articles in the news today, about the possibility of a serial killer, did you hear?"

He looked at Zachary and his eyes widened at the condition of Zachary's face.

"Uh… you look like you've already experienced worse than being harassed by reporters and Bible thumpers! Are you all right?"

"Yeah, thanks. Sorry for all of the disruption."

"It's not your fault." The security guard passed him off to the maître d', with a murmur of "Welcome to La Rouge, sir."

The maître d' was skinny like a greyhound, with the same alert, quivering-with-expectation look. The guy was going to have a stroke by the time he was forty if he didn't chill.

"Welcome, sir, welcome. Are you meeting another party here today, or are you alone?"

"I'm meeting someone. Santiago?"

"Monsieur Santiago…" The maître d' looked down at his appointment book and nodded vigorously. "Of course. You have a private dining room. I think you will find that quite acceptable. This way, sir."

Zachary followed the greyhound through the busy lounge until he came to a series of small, private dining areas. Each one had a room name beside the door, and the maître d' stopped beside one labeled 'Presidential.' He knocked lightly on the door, waited two seconds, and then opened it a crack. He peered in through the crack, then swung the door wide for Zachary, giving a grand gesture. "There you go, sir."

CHAPTER TWENTY-THREE

Zachary entered the small, dark-paneled room. The lighting was dimmer than he had expected, but it wasn't dark. There was a dining table, a sideboard with drinks, and various paintings and plaques on the wall. The man standing at the sideboard pouring himself a drink was, he assumed, Honore Santiago. He was a tall man, darker than the Hispanics but not as black as John. He was luxuriously dressed in clothing that Zachary was sure had designer names he wouldn't even recognize. The thread count was probably higher than he could count, and it had all been hand-woven by children in some third-world country with twig-thin fingers. He was slender, but not whippet-thin like the maître d'.

"Mr. Goldman," Santiago said. "It is a pleasure."

He offered his hand to Zachary, but when Zachary held his hand out to shake, the tall black man instead grasped it with one hand and brought the other hand in to caress the back of Zachary's hand, holding his sandwiched between them. Zachary jerked reflexively to pull away, but the older man held on, giving him a wide, bright smile and pressing Zachary's hand between his own firmly. Zachary nodded, gave a little squeeze, and then managed to extricate himself from the man's grip.

"Nice to meet you too, Mr. Santiago. But you can just call me Zachary."

"Delighted. Won't you have a drink?"

"I can't mix it with my medications," Zachary said, indicating the bruises on his face. "Just something fizzy, no alcohol."

"Of course! Coke with a twist? Or do you prefer sparkling water?"

"Coke is great."

He stood near Santiago's elbow, not sure whether he was supposed to sit down, prepare his own drink, or stand there while Santiago prepared it. Apparently, the third was acceptable, and he took the cold glass from Santiago once it was prepared. Santiago then motioned to the table set with sparkling china and silverware.

"Won't you have a seat, my good man. I don't imagine it's good for you to be on your feet for too long after what you have been through."

"I'm fine, really. It's worse than it looks."

"Not according to my sources. You're lucky you didn't have internal bleeding or a ruptured spleen or kidney. You're supposed to be taking it easy."

Zachary sat down where Santiago had indicated and put the Coke by his plate. "I am taking it easy. I'm sitting down."

"You're running all over town pursuing a serial killer. That's not exactly taking it easy."

Zachary didn't point out that the reason he was running around town was because of where Santiago wanted to meet with him. "I'm sitting down to talk with you. That's all. Then I'll go home and hit the hay before midnight."

"Ah, we'll see about that. You really should stay and take in the floor show. At least part of it. I don't know how many chances you will get to see the divine group that is playing today. The next time you hear of them, they'll probably be on a world tour, sold out before it even starts."

Zachary shrugged. He didn't have that much interest in music, or theater, or cabaret or whatever La Rouge was showing that night.

"We really don't need to do dinner," Zachary said, gesturing to the plates. "I don't have much appetite. I just thought we would have a discussion and then I'll be on my way. You don't need to entertain me or to feed me. Really."

"Nonsense. How could I not?" Santiago sat down and put down his old-fashioned glass. He leaned forward in his seat, lacing his fingers together with his elbows on the table. "Now, where has that naughty Pat been hiding you? You are the most fascinating person! He should have told us about you *ages* ago."

Zachary tried to ignore Santiago's dramatic, flamboyant manner and just talk to him as if they were businessmen having a routine discussion. He didn't want to get wound up by all of Santiago's nervous energy and enthusiasm. If he did, he would either be exhausted once the night was over, or bouncing off the walls so hard that he wouldn't be able to sleep for a week. He took a couple of deep breaths, mentally coaching himself before speaking.

"I've known Pat for more than twenty years. He is my foster father's partner."

"Ah, so Lorne...? I didn't know that he fostered."

"It was a long time ago. While he was still married to... his wife. I was only with him for a little while, but we kept in touch, and I met Pat later on... when they moved in together. It was all a little shocking at the time."

"Back then? It would have been," Santiago agreed. "And foster parenting. I don't imagine his agency was too happy about that. Allowing homosexual men around children was a big no-no. Hard for them to be approved even now. People still have that prejudice that we're all attracted to little boys and just won't be able to help ourselves. Really." He rolled his eyes. "As if we have no self-control whatever."

Zachary nodded wordlessly, unable to think of any response to this.

"Tell me," Santiago said in a confidential tone. "In foster care, in your experience, did you never run into any predators? You were never abused?"

Zachary caught his breath. He stared at Santiago, waiting for him to realize what an inappropriate question it was. Santiago waited. Zachary tried not to think about any of the men, women, and older children that he'd had to deal with during his growing-up years, defending himself against their abuse when he was far too small and weak and outclassed to succeed. He didn't need to go back to any of those places in his memory and he certainly didn't need to detail them to Santiago.

"I would expect that anyone who spent any length of time in foster care has run into that kind of thing," he said flatly, as if it were not an emotional topic at all.

"Exactly," Santiago agreed. "And were they gay men? Any of them?"

Zachary shrugged. He had never put himself into the heads of those predators. He didn't know what turned them on, whether it had anything to do with his gender or just his helplessness. He didn't know whether it was a physical attraction or the desire to bully and control someone, to torture him and own him completely.

"No. I don't know."

"That's right. They think that by keeping gay men from becoming foster parents that they are protecting the children? When you look at their track record over the last hundred years or however long the foster care system has been around it should become blazingly obvious that it isn't gay men who are perpetrating the crime."

"No," Zachary agreed. "Now if we could get on to the topic at hand…"

"Oh, I didn't mean to take us so far off-track. It's just so interesting that you got to know Pat and Lorne as father figures. That's just so fascinating to me. I've never seen them that way. It's a whole different perspective that I had never considered."

Zachary nodded, hoping to move things alone. "They've both always been great examples. Even though they weren't the ones taking care of me, they were so kind and patient and caring… to each other and to me. I suppose it would have been different if I had been their foster child. I wasn't easy to get along with, and they probably would have had too much of me before very long. But as it was, just having them around when I needed some help or someone to talk to… They've been very good to me."

"What was your biological father like? How well did you know him?"

"I was with him until I was ten. Him and my mom."

Santiago nodded encouragingly.

"He was… physically abusive. Didn't have much use for kids. We pretty much just tried to stay out of the way when he was home."

"Nothing like Pat and Lorne."

"No. I don't know that I've ever heard either one of them raise his voice, much less his hand, in anger."

Santiago smiled and nodded, looking happy with that comment. "I've always thought they were a very nice couple. Never a cross word to each other. Almost too good to be true."

Zachary shrugged. He knew that Mr. Peterson and Pat still got on each other's nerves just like any heterosexual couple. They weren't perfect and were sometimes irritable and cross. One of them might be stubborn and the other hurt, but in the end, they always made up, and they never had to apologize for physical harm or to try to take back cruel, hurtful words.

"Why don't you tell me about Jose?" he pressed Santiago, trying to get back on topic. "Tell me what your relationship with him was like."

"Oh, you're rushing me. This should be an after-dinner discussion, not something that we're rushing through now."

Zachary knew that no one had promised Santiago that Zachary would have dinner with him, and he should just make that point and get on with it. He took a breath. "I'm not here to eat. Why don't we—"

"You must have something. What's the point of my booking a private dining room if I have to eat by myself? You have to at least allow me that."

"I'm not up for much. My stomach really isn't recovered yet from yesterday." Zachary touched his side with an exaggerated wince.

"We'll just get a couple of appetizers, then. That's not a problem."

Santiago pressed a button recessed in the table, and in a moment, a waiter opened the door and entered.

"Gentlemen, you are ready to order?"

"Just some light fare," Santiago said. "A variety of canapés and amuse-bouches. If you would."

"Certainly, sir. Anything specific for either of you?"

"No," Santiago shook his head and looked at Zachary. "Escargot? Caviar?"

"Nothing rich," Zachary protested. "Just… crackers, fruit…"

Santiago rolled his eyes. "A cheese platter too, then, and some berry parfaits, bowls of grapes…"

The waiter nodded. "It will be just a few minutes then," he agreed. He scribbled down his notes and withdrew from the room.

"You really should have thought of something more challenging," Santiago said. "I'm always trying to stump the chef." He laughed. "It's so much fun."

Zachary nodded. He was starting to understand that they were not going to get to the topic of Jose and Santiago's relationship until Santiago was good and ready. If he said they would have to eat first, then Zachary would have to wait until the various canapés and amuse-bouches arrived. Then they'd get down to brass tacks.

"So what is it you do?" he asked. "I didn't ask Pat about your background."

"I'm sure you would have been very amused if you had! Yes, I'm a bit of a black sheep around here." He indicated his cheek to point out his skin tone, in case Zachary didn't notice the pun. "There are really not enough non-whites in circulation. It can be a little frustrating if your tastes run to dark meat. But I digress. I am an entrepreneur. A business owner. I have my own little kingdom, with hundreds of men under me."

"Oh…? What is it you do?"

Santiago grinned, showing off his brilliantly white teeth again. "I own and run the Peaceful Retreat Funeral Home and Cemetery."

Zachary stared at him, slowly processing the words. It was so unexpected; his brain was puttering along behind him and hadn't caught up. He stared at Santiago. "A… cemetery? You run a…"

"I run a cemetery. A graveyard. A boneyard. Yes, sir. That's me. I have many men *under* me. You see?"

Zachary barely refrained from groaning. But even though his brain seemed to be running on super slow speed, it was still generating all kinds of possibilities.

A cemetery? A funeral home? What better way to dispose of men you never wanted found again? He could dispose of the remains so completely that no one would ever find them. If the funeral home also had a crematorium, he could burn up all of the evidence, and then bury the ashes in the graveyard. How could anyone ever find any sign of them again?

Even without a crematorium, how easy would it be to dump a body in a grave and bury it? Who would ever know the difference?

Santiago was chuckling to himself, pleased at having surprised Zachary.

CHAPTER TWENTY-FOUR

Santiago was still laughing when the appetizers arrived. He helped himself, and Zachary put a few on his plate. They didn't actually look too bad. He wasn't hungry, but the little bites looked interesting and tasty and he wouldn't be required to get down a full meal. He popped one little canapé in his mouth and chewed, nodding at Santiago.

"It's good."

He didn't ask what it was. After Santiago's suggestion of escargot or caviar, he didn't want to know what he was eating. The fruit that accompanied the other platters was cool and fresh and he popped a couple of grapes into his mouth.

"So, tell me about Jose," he suggested.

Santiago sighed. He stretched and leaned on the table plucking up various different fruits and canapés throughout the conversation.

"Jose was a very pleasant companion to pass the time with," he said. "I'm sure you've heard from others that he was easy to get along with, friendly, a good conversationalist. He spoke English well and blended easily with most company. He was... open to new experiences, to trying new things. Enjoyed music, food, nice clothing, and jewelry. For a working-class illegal immigrant, he was surprisingly well-educated and up on the latest news and trends. He didn't come across like a farmer or a janitor."

Zachary nodded. "And how long had the two of you been seeing each other?"

"Some months. I really couldn't put a date on it… between six and ten, maybe?" He shook his head. "I'm not always good with timelines."

"You knew that he had other partners."

"Oh, of course." Santiago waved the question away as if it were of no concern. "No one expected him to be exclusive. Nor am I."

Santiago was not part of Pat and Lorne's circle of friends, though obviously Santiago was familiar enough to comment on their character. Pat had said that most of their group of friends were stable couples. Unsurprisingly, Santiago didn't fit in as part of that group. What was surprising was that Jose did, when it was apparent that he had multiple partners and no interest in settling down.

"Was there anyone that he was seeing that… concerned you? Maybe you thought they weren't right for each other, or that he might be in danger?"

"No. I wouldn't have interfered with his social life. He could see who he wanted. I wasn't jealous, if that's what you are getting at."

"Was anyone else? Maybe someone who *did* want to be exclusive?"

"I didn't get involved in his other relationships. We didn't discuss it."

Not quite Naylor's 'off-limits,' but close enough.

"And you don't think there was anyone who was interested in him who might have been resentful because they were rejected or had broken up?"

"I can't think of anyone. I don't know who his exes are. When we were together… it was just the two of us. Not all of those other relationships. We just focused on one another."

Zachary doubted that their relationship had been quite as ideal as Santiago made out, but he let it go.

"Do you know if any of Jose's other partners ever hurt him?"

"Hurt him?" Santiago shook his head. "No."

"You never saw him with bruises, like someone hit him or choked him?"

Santiago showed no reaction to this. "No."

"Others have said that they saw bruises on his throat. Like someone had choked him."

Santiago shrugged. "Different strokes. That's the whole point of having multiple partners. Different people go for different things."

"I have a list of names that I'd like you to look at."

Santiago shrugged and picked up another canapé. Zachary handed the list across the table and Santiago looked at it while he continued to pick at the food. "Yes, I know some of these names…" His eyebrows went up. "Oh, I had forgotten…" He shook his head. "It's funny just how quickly one can forget. These men were part of our lives, part of our community, and then… they were gone. Without a word. We moved on, but there they all are… there are so many when you see all of their names together."

"How many did you know?"

"Mmm…" Santiago's eyes went over the list. "I would say maybe half. That doesn't mean that I had anything with them, just that we knew each other. Could sit and talk at a bar or a show."

"How many *did* you have relationships with?"

Santiago looked up at Zachary for a moment, his eyes calculating, then back down at the list again. "Maybe… half a dozen." He flicked the paper back over to Zachary. "And don't bother asking me when I knew them and when the last time I saw them was. I told you I have difficulty with time-lines. You know, I've never really felt like I move linearly through time…"

Zachary wasn't about to tackle that one. He picked up the paper and put it back into his folder. Santiago was definitely on the suspect list. He was the first one to admit to knowing so many of the missing men. Though why Santiago would want to hurt Jose or any of the others was beyond Zachary.

"Who else would have known a lot of the men on that list?" Zachary asked. "So far, everyone I talk to says they don't recognize them. But you knew half of them. Who else ran in the same circles and might have known more of them?"

Santiago had a swallow of his drink. "You don't want to go back to The Night Scene," he indicated the bruises on Zachary's face, "but I imagine if you were to try there or The Blue Goose, you would find that they were familiar to those crowds. Didn't anyone at The Night Scene say they knew them?"

"I didn't have the list when I was there. Just Jose's name. Didn't get the others until after."

"Ah, well there you go. You have to go the right places if you're going to find people who knew them."

"Yeah. So they all tended to circulate at The Night Scene or The Blue Goose?"

Santiago drained his glass and again pressed the button on the table. "Those that I *knew*," he said pedantically. "I don't remember everyone on the list."

"But those that you remember, you would have seen them there?"

"Yes. That's right."

"And is there anywhere you don't go where they might have circulated? Maybe The Night Scene one day, and The Blue Goose another day, and then... where...?"

The waiter appeared and Santiago handed him the glass, motioning to the sideboard. "Fill me up."

The waiter took the glass from him and nodded, going to the sideboard to prepare another drink. Santiago leaned on the table, helping himself to some cheese and some of the fruit. He wrinkled his nose at the grapes, like maybe one of them was sour. He waited until he had his drink to wash the taste away and the waiter was out of the room before answering.

"There are a few other places they might have hung out. I prefer to hit places with a little more class," he gestured to indicate their surroundings, "but some people's tastes run to... grittier establishments."

"Grittier?"

"My boy, The Night Scene is one thing. Despite your experience upon leaving there, it is a pretty safe environment. Mainstream. There are other places where people who are interested in other sorts of encounters might hang out."

"Meaning what?"

"You'll find that the people who come to places like La Rouge are more interested in the arts, in good food, in long-term relationships where you know each other and respect each other's boundaries. At a bar like The Night Scene, you're still going to see a lot of dating couples. People who are getting together and getting to know each other and see how they get along together. More casual. You could go there with someone, or to meet someone new, have a few drinks together, and see how you got on. But there are other places where you wouldn't be looking for a regular date. You might never even know the other person's name."

"Just a one-night hookup?"

Santiago nodded. "Yes... or something anonymous. Someone you saw occasionally, but didn't have a relationship with. There are all sorts. In the straight community as well as the gay."

"Sure, of course," Zachary agreed. As a private detective, he was often hired to follow cheating spouses, and some of the venues that he had walked into made him not only want to wash the residue of the place off of his skin, but to strip off the first layer of skin altogether. He gave an involuntary shudder. He'd seen places that catered to all sorts of unusual and taboo tastes. Zachary could envision a predator trolling places like that, looking for his next victim. "Did Jose go places like that?"

"I wouldn't know. We never discussed them. But Jose was exploring, seeking out new experiences. I wouldn't be surprised if he explored some of the seamier elements. He wanted to have a... full range of experiences."

"Where are these places? Are they public? Do they have names?"

Santiago's eyes glittered with interest. He obviously hadn't expected Zachary to be aware of how things operated on the underbelly. "I'm sure your police friends would know some of the places to look. If they're really interested in finding a serial killer, they should look under a few rocks. It's always of great interest to see what crawls out of dark places."

CHAPTER TWENTY-FIVE

Zachary finally managed to extricate himself from the dinner with Santiago. It had been a very long day, and he had already decided there was no way he was going to one of the seedier bars to ask after the missing men. He'd had enough excitement at the 'classier' joints and would leave that job to the police, as Santiago had suggested. People might not be as quick to provide a policeman with the information as they would to a friend of a friend, but the cops would be safer there than Zachary.

He made his way back out to the main entrance, aware that people turned and watched him the whole way, curious about his battered appearance or recognizing him from the news articles. He'd been in the news with previous cases, but usually it wasn't until the end after everything was sorted out, when publicity wouldn't have an effect on the investigation.

He handed his valet ticket to the attendant who appeared beside him.

"We'll have you just wait here, sir, until your vehicle pulls up outside the door. We're having a little trouble tonight. Not usually like this."

"Thanks."

After a short wait, his car pulled under the canopy in front of the door. Zachary nodded to the attendant and went outside. As before, it was only seconds before people recognized him and surged forward, waving their signs or holding out their mikes and shouting at him. Zachary held up his hand to ward them off, indicating that he wasn't answering any questions.

"Are you assisting the police in their investigation?"

"Are you making any progress in finding the serial killer?"

"The holy scriptures say that God shall strike the sinners dead! It is the wrath of God!"

Zachary turned toward the religious nut. There were a lot of serial killers who had claimed to be doing the will of God by killing gays or prostitutes. He couldn't afford to ignore a credible threat.

A man in blue jeans and a t-shirt with more religious rantings stenciled on it waved his sign at Zachary, pressing against the guard who held him back. His already wide eyes popped when he saw Zachary was looking at him.

"They shall all be stricken with a plague!" the nut shouted, thrusting his sign forward. "They shall all die!"

"Do you know something about the men who disappeared?" Zachary demanded.

"Just keep moving, sir," the valet told Zachary, pressing his keys into his hand. "Don't give these guys any attention."

"I want the police called. They need to talk to him."

"Police can't do anything about protesters. They'll just tell them to stay behind the line, unless there's violence going on when they arrive."

"This guy is a suspect in the serial killer case. They need to talk to him."

The valet gave him a look. "A suspect? He's just a nut job."

"He thinks God should strike all gay men dead. You think he wouldn't take that into his own hands himself?"

"No. He's just a screamer. You ignore them, eventually they go away."

"You didn't hear about that policeman in Russia? How many was he convicted of killing? Seventy women? Because he decided they were loose women and God wanted them dead."

"I doubt he announced it in public." The valet hooked a thumb at the protester, who was released after he'd been pushed back behind the property line.

"He was quite willing to confess everything to the police when he was caught. Who knows whether he told anyone else before that? You really do need to get the police here."

"Not up to me. I'll pass it up the line, but don't hold your breath. You have a nice night, sir."

He was clearly waiting for Zachary to get into his car so he could go and get the next car in line. Zachary looked back at the protester. He was just one of many. How could they tell the ones who were dangerous from the ones who were just kooks? The valet was right that serial killers, while they might enjoy the spotlight, didn't generally announce their intentions to the public. They picked out a cop or news reporter and started feeding them little clues, getting a kick out of how much smarter they were.

The valet touched his cap, again saying goodbye to Zachary and trying to get him on his way. Zachary got into his car. The valet shut the door firmly, again wishing Zachary a nice evening. Zachary pulled out and headed back to Mr. Peterson's house, moving slowly past the protesters and reporters.

———

Zachary didn't even turn on the radio on the way home, needing the silent space of the car to unwind. The verbal repartee with Santiago, the shouting protesters and reporters, and the valet who refused to listen all sucked the energy out of him. He knew he was going to have to spend some time visiting with Mr. Peterson and Pat when he got back, letting them know how the investigation was going and that he was making progress. If he was. He did have a couple more places for the police to look, some suspects for them to check up on, and the protesters at La Rouge. He still couldn't point to one suspect and say that he was the killer, or even prove that the missing men had been murdered. But maybe what he had found out would help to lead the police to the solution.

At least the police were being forced to take Jose's disappearance seriously.

Zachary pulled into Mr. Peterson's street. Even before he turned the corner, he could see red and blue lights bouncing off the houses. He hit the brake, almost coming to a complete stop, as he looked at the squad cars stopped in front of Mr. Peterson's house. His mind flashed back to a similar scene at Bridget's house when she had been kidnapped. Marked cars and unmarked cars parked in front of the house and pulled up on the lawn, all of them with lights flashing.

He took his foot off the brake and hit the gas, shooting down the street and then hitting the brakes again hard with a screech of tires when he reached the house. He threw the car into park and bailed out, rushing the door.

He should have known that the police wouldn't let anyone go belting into the house like that without first verifying his identity, but he wasn't thinking logically. He was just reacting to the police presence and the memory of what had happened to Bridget.

He had almost been too late for Bridget.

"Whoa, stop right there!" Hands grabbed him and he was pushed to the side, the impetus of his run for the door redirected to slam him into the side of one of the police cars. They pinned him, feeling for weapons. Zachary struggled to break free of them.

"No, let me go! What's happened to them? Let me see! Let go!"

"Zachary. Zachary, it's okay." Mr. Peterson made an appearance on the front step, speaking urgently over the shouting. "We're okay, Zach. We're both fine."

Zachary stopped fighting and slumped against the car, hitting the bottom of his chin. The policemen finished frisking him, and by the time they were done, Dougan was on the step with Mr. Peterson, telling them to let him go.

Zachary hurried to the door, where Lorne pulled him in for a hug. "It's okay, Zachary. Everybody's fine."

Zachary gripped him tightly, trying to convince himself it was true, and looked past Mr. Peterson into the house.

"Where's Pat?"

"He's inside. Let's go in." Mr. Peterson released him and they entered the house together, both squeezing through the doorway at the same time. Pat stepped into Zachary's line of sight.

"You okay, Zach? We tried to call you. We didn't want you coming home to this unexpectedly."

Zachary gave him a quick hug as well, relieved that neither one of them had been kidnapped or killed. His heart was still thundering, but he knew they were both okay.

"What happened? Why are all the police here?"

"It's just the protesters. Things got out of hand. Damage to the property. A rock through the window." Pat gestured and Zachary saw the window-pane with a piece of cardboard taped over it. "We'll get it fixed in the morning. Nothing permanent, just a nuisance."

"Was there... a note with the rock?"

That was the way it was done on TV. A rock through the window with a threatening note attached to it. That was the way it always started, before escalating to gunshots or Molotov cocktails.

At the thought of flaming bottles being thrown into the house, Zachary swayed on his feet. He tried to focus on Pat, on the fact that neither of them had been hurt, instead of the idea of the house going up in flames.

"Come sit," Pat insisted, pulling him a couple more steps over to the couch. Zachary sat down and tried to control his breathing. Dougan had already been privy to one flashback, Zachary didn't want to break down when they were face-to-face.

"There was a note," Mr. Peterson admitted, drawing Zachary's attention back to the present rather than letting him focus on what could happen or what had happened in the past. "Nasty bit of hate mail."

"I need to see it."

"You don't want to, Zachary. No one wants to be reading that garbage. Leave it to the police."

"Let me see."

They exchanged looks with each other, weighing the possible consequences of allowing Zachary to see the note against refusing to. Eventually, Mr. Peterson nodded at Dougan, who said a few words to one of the other cops traveling in and out of the house, and the note was brought to Zachary, pressed flat in a plastic page protector.

Zachary swallowed and looked down at it. The messy writing spidered across the page in wandering lines. It was difficult to read, which made it an excellent distraction. Zachary worked through it a bit at a time, then nodded and pushed it away. It wasn't a mocking note from the serial killer. It wasn't a threat that he had to get off the case and keep quiet, or else. It was just a horrific bit of hate mail aimed against homosexual men.

"There were eggs earlier in the day," Pat sighed, and it took a moment for Zachary to realize he was talking about vandalism, not what he'd made for dinner. "Cleaned that up... the reporters were gone by dark... the alarm went off a couple of times, but we couldn't see anyone. Then the rock through the window."

"I'm sorry... I feel so bad that this investigation leaked out and ended up causing you trouble like this. It's been such a nice neighborhood, and now..."

"It will go back to normal as the story dies down," Mr. Peterson assured them. "It's just a temporary disruption. It isn't from our friends and neighbors, it's from strangers. They think they can vent all of their crap and stay anonymous. That's nothing new."

Zachary took a deep breath in and let it out. He rubbed his eyes, careful of his bruised, tender face, and looked around.

"You came because of the vandalism?" he asked Dougan. It seemed like it was a little out of his purview. Why would he be assigned to look into such a minor charge?

"The vandalism, making sure that everyone was safe, talking to each of you again about Jose, and whatever else you've been stirring up."

"I haven't been making any trouble," Zachary protested. He had been gathering information that might be useful to the police, not interfering with their inquiries. He hadn't cause them any extra trouble.

"Then why did I get a call from La Rouge about protesters over there?"

Zachary blinked. The valet had done as he said he would and passed the information along the line, and the management had actually decided to do as Zachary said and call the police department.

"I didn't think they would. There was one guy over there who was spouting all of this stuff about how they deserved to die... I just... wasn't comfortable with just ignoring it, pretending he couldn't possibly be serious."

"Well, I sent someone to pick him up, so if he is guilty of something, we'll find out. The good thing about these nut jobs is, they're perfectly happy to tell you everything they have done. They're not calling for lawyers and asserting their rights, they're begging to tell you everything they know."

"I don't know if he's dangerous, but he rubbed me the wrong way."

Dougan nodded, not looking upset about it. Pat and Mr. Peterson sat down and everybody got comfortable. Zachary shifted. "Could I take a break? I need to check my voicemails and... just catch my breath."

The police officer seemed unperturbed. "Go ahead. I have some questions for your two friends, and it's probably best if they feel like they can talk freely."

Zachary opened his mouth to point out that Mr. Peterson and Pat had talked to him voluntarily and wouldn't feel like they needed to hide anything from him, but Dougan beat him to the punch.

"I know, you're all open and talk about these things; it's just good practice. If I have to ask anything awkward, they can answer knowing that it won't get back to you. They can figure out whether to share it with you later."

Zachary shrugged and shook his head as he walked away. There was no point in arguing about it, since he'd been granted the time he needed to check his messages and get himself back together again emotionally.

He went to the bathroom first, looking at the horror show that was his face before taking a painkiller. He had a new bruise and cut on the bottom of his chin from being pushed up against the side of the police car. There was only a trickle of blood, so he pressed a wad of toilet paper to it and waited for it to stop.

CHAPTER TWENTY-SIX

With his bedroom door shut, Zachary sat down on the bed and played his voicemails.

The news of his investigation had been nationwide, and it hadn't taken people long to connect his name up and start calling him. He'd had the call from Kenzie right at the beginning, and had pretty much ignored the voicemails he had been getting since then, other than taking a quick glance at the name or number attached to each one to make sure that there weren't any from Philippe or other witnesses who he needed to talk to. Others could wait.

Rhys Salter's grandmother, Vera, had left a halting message. Zachary had investigated the death of her daughter, Robyn, and had made friends with Rhys, an emotionally broken and usually nonspeaking teen during the case and kept in touch with him afterward. Zachary hadn't received any messages from Rhys recently, which he hoped meant that Rhys was just living his life and getting through one day at a time and didn't need to check in with Zachary.

Vera hadn't called to say that Rhys needed Zachary or that there was anything to be concerned about. Instead, she was worried about the publicity. "I don't think you'd better be seen anywhere with Rhys," she said in a near whisper. "I didn't know that you were gay, and it doesn't matter to me, but you can see how people are going to talk about a gay white man taking out a teenage black boy, especially with all of the teasing Rhys has to put up with for being mute and his momma being in prison. He doesn't need that. So I would appreciate it if you don't meet with Rhys without talking to me first. You can message with him, I know he enjoys that, but please don't offer to take him anywhere."

If she were there, Zachary would have explained to her that he wasn't gay, but that he understood how it could be harmful to Rhys's reputation, so he wouldn't do anything that could be misconstrued as an inappropriate relationship with the boy. But she wasn't there, and maybe by the time he saw her again, the whole thing would have blown over and there would be no need to even mention it. He deleted the message and went on to the next.

A short greeting from Kenzie, just checking in to make sure he was okay. "Give me a call sometime to let me know you're still alive," she joked. Zachary smiled and went on to the next.

There were several hang-ups. Probably reporters. Then a couple of reporters who had left long detailed messages urging him to call and get his story out there as soon as he could.

He was really hoping that one of the numbers he didn't recognize would be from Philippe, but so far none of them had been.

There was a call from Campbell, a more senior cop back home. Zachary hadn't expected to hear from him, but he supposed Campbell had seen the news coverage like everyone else and was curious about it or wanted to razz Zachary about the inaccuracies in the articles.

"Zachary," Joshua Campbell's voice boomed even on the small phone speaker. "Helluva life you're living these days. I gather you're down south rather than here, but give me a call when you've got a few minutes. I got a call from a Thurlow Dougan down there, and he's asking a lot of questions. I've told him you're okay, of course, but call me to talk things over. You know the number."

Zachary made a couple of notes to himself so he wouldn't forget who he needed to call. So Dougan had checked up on him. Called home to see how the locals felt about him. Zachary hoped that he had been satisfied with the answers.

There was a brief, teasing call from Tyrrell. An attempt to be light-hearted, but Zachary heard real concern behind his words. They had just been reunited, and Tyrrell wasn't sure how to take his big brother being splashed all over the national news. And he probably didn't know how to take the conflicting information he was reading about Zachary. It was a pretty confusing way to get to know a long-lost sibling.

More junk calls. Hang-ups and nut jobs. He shouldn't have made his phone number quite so easy to find.

Then there were the calls that Pat had said they made to warn him about the police circus at the house. Pat first: "Everything is fine, Zachary. Just a heads-up to make sure you're not worried if there are still police cars here when you get home. We've just had some damage to the property. We're both okay."

And then later, Mr. Peterson's carefully measured tone, "Just checking to see when you're planning to be home, Zach. Give me a call when you're on your way."

The call from Bridget had come early on, but he had left it until last, pretending to himself that it was because he didn't want to hear what she had to say, when the opposite was true. He wanted to listen to her last, just like he left the cherry on a sundae for last, as one final treat to savor.

"I guess you know why I'm calling, Zachary," she said in a disapproving tone. "I couldn't very well help seeing all of the coverage. I just wanted to say that I am not one who subscribes to the theory that all publicity is good publicity. This coverage, with all of its inaccuracies, could really be damaging to your reputation as a private investigator. I know it's none of my business and I don't have any right to advise you on these things... it's just a bug in your ear. Something to think about. I have a friend who is a publicist, if you want some help in dealing with this."

She hung up. Zachary sat there, listening to her voice in his head. Even when she called him to criticize, he still longed to be with her again. But she had made it clear. That wasn't going to happen. He needed to accept it.

He'd believe it if she ever stopped calling. Then he'd know it was really over.

He sat for a few more minutes, trying to get himself into the right frame of mind to talk to Dougan, then took out his notebook and went back out to the living room.

The living room discussion between the three men being conducted in low voices stopped when Zachary stepped into the room, and they all looked up at him. He sat down on the couch, and the discussion didn't resume.

"Okay, then, Zachary?" Mr. Peterson asked with a reassuring smile.

"Yeah, all good. Thanks for leaving those messages for me... sorry I didn't pick them up before coming back."

"I'm sorry you didn't. We didn't want you to come home to police cars and panic. But..." He gave a shrug. "All things considered, you didn't do too badly."

Meaning at least Zachary hadn't ended up a heap on the sidewalk in a full-blown meltdown. Lorne had seen worse reactions from Zachary before. Zachary's response to finding the house surrounded by police cars had been pretty normal, just like any man coming home and worrying what had happened to his family might have.

Zachary shrugged and didn't look at the pane of the window that had been covered with cardboard. He looked at Detective Dougan. For an instant, his own words came back to him, about the cop in Russia who had been convicted of dozens of murders. *He decided they were loose women and God wanted them dead.* Zachary had no doubt that the Russian officer's bosses and colleagues had had no idea what kind of a monster he really was inside. He'd had a wife and kid, helped the homeless, donated money for his daughter's dead teacher's funeral—a woman, as it turned out, he had killed. He was a man everybody had thought was safe. No one had suspected what was really going on in his head.

Zachary pushed these thoughts out of the way. He knew that Dougan was a good cop. He was looking into Jose's death and hadn't had a stroke when Zachary had given him all of the information about the missing men. If he had not been what he appeared, it would have been easy enough for him to set up a meeting with Zachary in some remote location and then to make *him* disappear. He wouldn't have shown up at Mr. Peterson's house when he heard about the rock through the window.

"Where do you want to start? Do you want me to tell you about my most recent interviews?"

Dougan sat back, putting his notepad on his knee, one leg crossed over the other. "It's as good a place to start as any. Tell me about who you talked to."

Zachary told him about Naylor and his shop and finding clothes there that Jose had worn. Pat leaned forward as he listened, his eyes wide.

"Eric Naylor and Jose were seeing each other?"

Dougan's eyes flicked over to him. "You didn't know?"

"No. They never acted like it when we were out as a group. I had no idea that they had a relationship outside of what we all did together."

"How much do you know about Naylor's relationships?"

"Well, nothing... he comes to our group as a bachelor. He's never brought a date. I assumed that he saw people, but never anyone in our group."

"And you didn't know that Jose's clothes came from Naylor's shop?"

"No. I suppose... I should have wondered where Jose got his clothes. He couldn't have been making much mowing lawns and moving bricks for A.L. He sent whatever he could home. He was always nicely presented. I never even thought..."

Dougan chewed on the end of his pencil. "It would be a jump to assume he was keeping clothes as trophies, especially if he has them out on the sales floor. But I would like to get my hands on that one outfit, just to make sure there is no blood spatter or anything suspicious on it."

Zachary nodded. "Do you have enough to get a warrant?"

"Don't need one if I can just walk in there and buy it off the rack."

"Oh. I guess not."

"Describe to me where it was and what it looked like."

Zachary did the best he could, and Dougan took down the details.

"And is that it? No, you went on to La Rouge after that."

"Yes. One of the men that Naylor had mentioned was seeing Jose was there and agreed to see me. Honore Santiago."

Dougan looked at Pat questioningly. Pat shook his head. "Not part of our group. I know who he is, but he didn't hang out with us."

"And you?" Dougan looked at Mr. Peterson.

"He doesn't see anyone else—" Zachary protested.

"Zachary," Mr. Peterson said quietly. "Hush. I can answer for myself."

"But you don't—" Zachary forced himself to stop. He looked down at his feet, waiting for Mr. Peterson to answer.

"I don't know him well either," Mr. Peterson confirmed. "As Zachary will no doubt tell you, Honore has a long string of dalliances, and while we might run into him occasionally at La Rouge or other venues, he's far too... capricious for our tastes."

"Does he date the type of men who are missing?"

Loren and Pat looked at each other.

"Yes," Pat confirmed. "Younger men, usually of color. That same sort of body type." He indicated Zachary. "Smaller, wiry... Zach would be very much his type, aside from his white skin."

Remembering how flirty Santiago had acted with him, Zachary felt his cheeks heat. He hoped that at least the bruises covered his embarrassment. Mr. Peterson chuckled.

"I wouldn't recommend you take up with Honore, Zachary."

"You think he's dangerous?" Dougan asked.

"I don't think he's a serial killer. But he's not... stable."

"If Jose was unfaithful, do you think Santiago would have reacted violently?"

"Well... it's hard to be unfaithful if there's no expectation of being faithful," Mr. Peterson explained.

"They were both seeing other people," Zachary said. "Santiago said so."

Dougan nodded. "Doesn't mean he couldn't have changed his mind and decided he didn't like Jose seeing other people. I've seen it happen before. People start with grand ideas of how an open relationship works for everyone, and then they find out they actually have feelings and want the person all for themselves."

Zachary hesitated. "Do you know what he does?"

Dougan looked at the notes he had made. "What he does? No. What does he do?"

"He owns a funeral home and cemetery."

Dougan frowned. His mind obviously followed the same scenarios as Zachary had already considered. He nodded slowly. "It's something to think about. But we won't be able to get a warrant, and I don't think he's going to invite us over to dig up any graves and troll for extra bodies."

"He admits that he knew a lot of the men who disappeared, and was involved with some of them. It's possible that he was responsible for *those* disappearances, and the others were just men who disappeared on purpose, like you thought to begin with," Zachary said.

"Why would he admit to being involved with them, though?" Mr. Peterson challenged. "Wouldn't he deny it?"

"Some serial killers like to brag and point out how smart they are. Some almost seem to get caught on purpose so they can tell how many people they killed without getting caught."

Dougan flipped a page over in his notepad. "Besides, we would have found him out if he lied. People would have seen them together. Did your Mr. Santiago know Philippe?"

"I don't know... he didn't mention him, but I would guess so. If he liked younger immigrant men. He and Philippe were both seeing Jose. Even if they didn't date each other, they must have known about each other."

"I went over to see Philippe to ask him a few questions."

Zachary nodded. Maybe that was why Philippe hadn't called him back. He was talking to Dougan or he was irritated with Zachary for pointing Dougan in his direction. He didn't want to talk to the police.

"I wasn't able to make contact with him," Dougan said.

"He was probably working."

"I checked with his work. He didn't show up today."

"And he wasn't at home?"

Dougan studied Zachary, his eyes sharp. "No, he wasn't at home. Nobody was at home."

Zachary thought about the number of men who were living there and was surprised. He would have expected there to be at least one person there at all times. They wouldn't all have the same shifts. Someone would always be around.

"Nobody?" he repeated, thinking that maybe Dougan just meant Philippe wasn't home. Or Philippe and Nando.

"It had been cleared out," Dougan said. "Not a matchstick left in the place."

Zachary sat there with this mouth open. They had all moved out in the middle of the month. They'd packed up all of their stuff and abandoned the apartment.

"There were a lot of people living there. I can't believe they're all gone."

"When was the last time you talked to Philippe?"

"Tuesday. He called me when he couldn't get John on the phone. Before I called you. I tried to get him, but his phone just kept going to voicemail."

"You don't think anything has happened to him?"

"I'm hoping it's just that he's mad at me, so he's rejecting the calls. With everything that was in the papers, Nando might have figured out about Philippe and Jose seeing each other."

"Why is that significant?"

"Nando is Philippe's uncle. Phillipe is living with him so that Nando can make sure he doesn't get into any trouble. I don't suppose he'll be too happy to find out that Philippe was seeing a man who is now missing. That doesn't sound safe to me."

"I would guess not. And you think that they've all just gone underground. To avoid having to talk to me and you."

Zachary nodded. But what if the killer were Santiago, or someone else in the same circles? What if one of them had known about Philippe and decided that he knew too much or had seen something he shouldn't have?

"If it was the serial killer, then they wouldn't *all* be gone. Just Philippe. He couldn't make that many men disappear that fast."

"No, probably not. That would be quite an undertaking. But if Philippe disappeared, what would Nando and the others do? Go to the police?" Dougan directed the question at Mr. Peterson.

"No. Definitely not. I guess they'd disappear."

Dougan nodded. "Any indication that someone was watching them or investigating them, and they would disappear."

Zachary looked through his notepad, thinking about it. It made perfect sense that the men had all disappeared, but Zachary didn't like it. Why hadn't Philippe called? Why didn't he at least called to tell Zachary not to look for them? If he wanted to find Jose's killer, why didn't he answer Zachary's calls?

"I'll keep calling. He'll answer sooner or later."

Dougan shook his head, but didn't speak his doubt out loud. "If you manage to reach him, let me know. I need to talk with him. It's pretty hard to put a case together if the witnesses keep disappearing. He's the one person we know John Mwangi talked to about the missing men. He may know things that were not in the papers. If Mwangi had suspicions about who was involved, he might not have written it down, but he might have talked to a sympathetic listener."

Zachary nodded. "I'll let you know."

He tried to push down the growing dread that something had happened to Philippe, that the killer had reached him.

It made sense that Philippe and the others had just gone underground because of the publicity.

That had to be why.

CHAPTER TWENTY-SEVEN

"Zachary, you're looking pretty rough," Pat observed. "Is it time for you to take another painkiller?"

Zachary's head pounded and every part of his body throbbed or protested when he moved. "Yeah." Zachary blinked his eyes. His lids were getting heavy and the pages in his notebook were starting to blur. "And I think I'd better be heading to bed."

"The doctor told you to take it easy. This isn't exactly taking it easy," Pat chided. He got up and went into the kitchen, returning with a glass of juice and one of Zachary's pills.

"Have you had any more contact with Dimitri?" Dougan asked, ignoring the fact that Zachary had said he was ready to go to bed.

Zachary rubbed his temples. *Dimitri?* Then he remembered the younger man who had been with Teddy at The Night Scene. Teddy, the big teddy bear and Dimitri, his date, who had wanted to talk to Zachary about Jose. About their broken date and the cell phone that went to voicemail.

"Oh, yeah. Dimitri. With Teddy. No, I haven't heard anything else from him."

"He did have a number of phone exchanges with Jose's number before Jose's phone went offline."

"You got his phone logs." Zachary tried to smother a yawn. "So that helps pinpoint when he disappeared. Or when his phone stopped taking calls."

Dougan nodded. "It verifies what we already knew. So who is Teddy? Where does he fall into all of this?"

"I don't really know. Ran into him at The Night Scene. He was kind of hitting on me at the bar, but then he had a date there." Zachary shook his head. "I don't really understand the rules in a place like that. Or maybe I'm just seeing men's behavior from a different perspective than I ever have before."

"Teddy Archuro? He's been a fixture at The Night Scene for a long time," Pat contributed. "I know him from way back."

"You wouldn't have any concerns about him?"

"No." Pat looked at Mr. Peterson and they both shook their heads. "He's been around for a long time and I've never heard anyone complain about him. Other than maybe to say that he's too friendly." Pat made a gesture to indicate Zachary and what he had just contributed. "But no, he's harmless."

"He's not harmless unless I say he is," Dougan said sharply. He closed his notepad and sat up. "If you have more contact with Dimitri, encourage him to talk to me. With half the witnesses disappearing and the other half refusing to make a statement, it's difficult to conduct an investigation."

Zachary nodded tiredly. "I'll do what I can."

———

Before going to bed, Zachary took one of the prescription painkillers and a sleeping pill. In spite of how exhausted he was, he knew that he wasn't going to be able to shut off his brain and stop analyzing the case and the discussion with Dougan if he didn't. Having a case debrief right before bed wasn't the best idea. But Dougan was there at his own initiative and Zachary couldn't very well brush him off.

He checked the security alarm settings before going to bed. Twice. There was no one visible outside when he looked out the window, other than one police car that had stayed to keep an eye on things for a few hours. Zachary knew what it was like to sit surveillance in a cold, dark car at night, and considered taking a cup of coffee out to the officer, but in the end he decided not to. To do so would mean disabling the door alarm and then re-enabling it when he returned to the house. Chances were, the cop already had a thermos of coffee in the car with him, which he would have to ration strictly to avoid inconvenient interruptions.

Zachary looked once more at the settings on the security system. There were footsteps in the hall and he looked up to see Mr. Peterson taking a last run to the bathroom before bed. When he returned, he gave Zachary a knowing smile.

"Everything is properly armed. Between you and Pat, it's probably been checked a dozen times. You want a warm milk before bed?"

"No. I'm fine."

"You need your sleep. You look like a zombie."

Zachary nodded and headed back to the guest bedroom. "I'm sorry to still be underfoot. Depending on what happens tomorrow, maybe I'll go home for a few days. Keep up by phone and email."

It was a good thing he had kept an emergency bag with clothes and necessities in the car, since he hadn't initially been planning to stay overnight, let alone for several days. But he needed to get fresh clothes or launder what he had, and he longed for his own space.

"It sounds like Dougan and his men are talking to people. You probably don't want to get in his way. But don't feel like you have to go home on our accounts. We're happy to have you here."

"You guys don't need me kicking around here. If I can get the rest of the interviews done that I want to tomorrow… I'll leave it to Dougan to check out these other places where Jose might have hung out. I wish Philippe would respond. I know he's just gone quiet because he and the others don't want any attention, but it still bothers me." Zachary sighed. He knew his attention was bouncing from one piece of the case to another, and if he let himself, he would just keep babbling on.

"Maybe he'll call you tomorrow. Or maybe by the weekend, he'll decide that they're safe and he can respond to calls. I'm sure the media attention just has him spooked. But that will die down as they don't find anything new to report on."

"Yeah. Okay, I'm going to bed for real now."

"Get a good rest. You won't make any progress on the case if you're too tired to think straight. You'll do better after a solid night's sleep."

Zachary nodded. He went back to his room, swallowed a couple of pills, one for anxiety and one to help him sleep. He stripped down and slid into bed, waiting for sleep to come.

CHAPTER TWENTY-EIGHT

He was groggy when he awoke. Someone was shaking him by the arm and he didn't know why. He just wanted to return to the darkness and sleep. His body needed rest. His sleep was often restless and disrupted, but he was so deep in the well that he couldn't open his eyes.

The shaking persisted. Zachary tried to push the hand away. A foster mom or group home worker trying to get him up for school? He was too tired. He was sick or it was too early in the morning. The middle of the night. Why would they try to get him up in the middle of the night?

"Zachary. Come on. Talk to me."

Zachary groaned, trying to protest.

"Try to sit him up. See if that helps."

Zachary tried to fight back against the manhandling, but that just woke him up further, when he wanted to return to the darkness.

"Zachary. Wake up."

He hurt all over. He felt bruised down to his bones and his head was thudding, feeling huge and ungainly like a lead balloon. He tried to hold it still, as it was making him nauseated whenever it flopped one direction or the other. He put his hands up to his face to brace it and help hold it still.

"Are you awake? Zach?"

"Why?" Zachary groaned. "Why won't you let me sleep?"

"It's late. You're always an early riser."

He was aware of fingers on his wrist, pressing over the pulse point. He tried to remember. Was he in the hospital? Had he been in an accident? That would explain why his body hurt so much, but not why they were trying to wake him up. At the hospital, they let him sleep, unless there was some test or procedure they had to do.

Zachary managed to get his eyes open a crack. At first, he couldn't comprehend his surroundings and figure out where he was. He frowned and blinked and tried to clear the blurriness from his eyes and sort out the inputs.

"Lorne?"

"Yes. Are you okay?"

Zachary tried to rub away the pain in his head, but his face and head were too tender.

"What's wrong?" Zachary asked, trying to focus. "Did something happen?"

"You scared the hell out of us, Zach." Pat's voice was nearby, but Zachary didn't want to turn his head to look at him, still too woozy. "How many pills did you take?"

How many pills? Zachary rubbed his tender eyes and looked around, at the side table and at Pat, then all the way back to Mr. Peterson, studying him closely.

There were several pill bottles beside the bed. Pills he always took. He didn't remember being depressed the night before and trying to overdose. None of the bottles appeared to be empty, though his eyes still weren't focusing properly. He tried to remember. Painkillers, anti-anxiety, sleeping pills. He'd been feeling pretty rough before bed. The long day and his physical injuries must just have caught up with him. His body had just been more exhausted than usual, so he had slept heavily once his brain had let him.

"I was just really tired."

"It's almost eleven o'clock," Mr. Peterson said.

Eleven? For someone who was used to waking before six, that was very late. It was no wonder they had been concerned.

"I think... I just did too much yesterday. Can I get one of those pain pills? My head is killing me. And my side..." He tried to readjust the way he was sitting. It must have been Pat who had pulled him into a sitting position. Zachary's bruised ribs had flared up in protest.

Neither man answered him right away.

"I don't think that's a good idea," Pat said. "You were really deep under. You shouldn't be taking anything that could depress your system."

"Just a pain pill. Just one."

"I'll get you a Tylenol."

Zachary looked at the pill bottles on the table. He *would* just get one himself. But he would have to move, and they seemed very far away. He knew that Tylenol wasn't going to even begin to address the pain.

He let his eyes close again. "Then get me two Tylenol. The strongest you got."

Pat left the room and Mr. Peterson stayed there with him. He sat down on the edge of the mattress, rocking the bed and making Zachary seasick. Pat returned a couple of minutes later with two red pills and a glass of water. He helped Zachary take them, supporting the glass so he wouldn't drench himself.

"Are you okay?" Mr. Peterson asked.

"I'm just tired. I need more sleep."

"I knew you weren't getting enough rest. But this is more than being tired. Being tired doesn't depress your breathing."

Zachary didn't have an answer for that. He was listing to the side and tried to make himself comfortable, his consciousness already starting to drift.

"Gather up the pill bottles," Pat said. "We won't leave them in here. I'll call the pharmacist, go over the doses and the possible interactions. We'll make sure he doesn't take too many tonight."

Zachary remembered fleetingly that he was going to go back home, so they would have to give him his pills back. But then he was asleep again.

———

When the fog started to lighten and the pain broke through, Zachary tossed and turned for some time before finally waking up. He was curled up in a ball on top of his pillows in a distinctly uncomfortable position. Very slowly, he eased his body into a straight line and put his head on one of the pillows. But his restlessness was starting to assert itself, his brain working on the problem of the missing men. What he could remember of Mr. Peterson and Pat waking him earlier in the day niggled at the back of his brain.

He rolled slowly over, waited until his brain stopped sloshing around in his skull, and stretched his arm out until his fingers touched his phone. He pulled it toward himself. He held it in front of his face, squinting at the screen. It was mid-afternoon.

Zachary swore softly. He couldn't remember the last time he'd slept that late. Maybe never. Maybe when they'd been adjusting his meds, when he was off of his antidepressants and couldn't get out of bed. He'd been in the hospital, but he couldn't remember the details, his brain still refusing to work the way it was supposed to.

He pushed himself slowly up until he was sitting, hunched over and waiting for the world to stop spinning. He might have fallen asleep sitting there for a short time, but sitting up told his brain that he was supposed to be awake, and he gradually felt more alert.

Progress was slow, but he managed to pull his clothes on and start the long trek to the bathroom.

"Well, look who's up," Pat greeted. "Need a hand there, granny?"

Zachary grunted at him and continued his way down the hall.

He used the john, and splashed cold water on his face, and leaned with both hands on the counter, breathing and trying to work up the where-withal to make it back to the bedroom again.

"Come to the kitchen," Mr. Peterson told him, when he opened the door.

Zachary knew that if he went back to the bedroom he was probably going to go back to sleep, so he followed Lorne into the kitchen, bright with afternoon sunshine.

Zachary squinted in the light and managed to make it into one of the kitchen chairs.

"Good to see you on your feet again."

"Yeah. Sorry about that. Guess I really crashed."

"That was more than just being tired."

Zachary cleared his throat. Mr. Peterson put a glass of water in front of him, along with one of the pain pills. Not Tylenol, but his prescription. Zachary took it gratefully with several long swallows of the cold water, thirsty after his long hibernation.

"I didn't overdose. I was just tired from doing so much."

"I believe you that you didn't *intentionally* overdose." Mr. Peterson waited until Zachary looked at him. He raised his eyebrows and spoke with emphasis. "But you *did* overdose. The pharmacist Pat talked to said that if you took a few of those pain pills along with a few sleeping pills, it could be very dangerous. Even if you're used to taking the sleeping pills."

Zachary shook his head. "I didn't. I just took one pain pill before bed and one sleeping pill. They said that was safe."

"Well, we're going to have to watch you closely to see how you react if you plan to do that again. You remember how when we first started you on meds, you had a couple of bad reactions."

It was a long time in the past. Zachary remembered throwing up at school from his day meds, and then Mr. Peterson having to take him to the hospital after his night meds. He'd started too many prescriptions at once and the ER doctor had been pretty annoyed that the Petersons hadn't introduced them individually to monitor for adverse reactions.

"Yeah… I remember that. But they didn't make me sleepy."

"You can have different reactions to different meds. I don't know if you've been on these painkillers before, or if you've combined them with this same cocktail."

Zachary wanted to protest, but he couldn't find a way to counter what Mr. Peterson was saying. He felt like a kid again, being lectured for a mistake that he'd made at school. Mr. Peterson wasn't saying it in a critical way, but it was almost worse for him to be so patient and understanding about it. Zachary didn't want any pity.

"Have you ever had a reaction like this? Where you couldn't wake up or were breathing so slowly?"

"I don't know." Zachary took another drink of the water. "Maybe." He had the shadow of a memory from long ago of the police trying to wake him up, back when he was eleven or twelve. But what would they have been trying to wake him up for? He couldn't pin the memory down properly. More clear was the outraged voice of Mrs. Pratt, his social worker in his head: *You were so doped up you couldn't keep your eyes open.*

He frowned, trying to remember, but he couldn't quite grasp it.

"Maybe once, in foster care. I can't remember."

Mr. Peterson put a cup of coffee and a slice of toast on a plate in front of Zachary. Being late in the afternoon, it wasn't really breakfast time, but it was Zachary's first meal of the day. He nibbled the toast without objecting.

———

He felt out of sorts getting started so late in the day. But once he'd had his coffee and the pain meds had started to work, he was at least feeling like himself again. He went through his notes from the day before, adding in other thoughts as they came to him, trying to work through everything he had learned from each person he had talked to, including Dougan.

He had promised Dougan that he would do what he could to encourage Dimitri to talk to the police, so he searched out Dimitri's number on his phone and called him. There was no answer. Zachary hung up when he got the voicemail message, thinking about it. It shouldn't surprise him that so many of the numbers he called just went through to voicemail. People had call display. They either ignored the unknown number or knew it was Zachary and didn't feel like having to talk to him. Dimitri was sure to know who he was now, after having seen all of the news coverage. He would know that Zachary wasn't a personal friend of Jose's, but had been asking his questions under cover. He wouldn't have the same motivation to talk to Zachary on the phone as he had to talk to him when he had viewed Zachary as the friend of a friend, and maybe a potential date.

He tapped his finger on the phone for a few minutes, then decided to text Dimitri, encouraging him to talk to Dougan to potentially help the police find the serial killer who had been running rampant in their community for years.

There was no immediate response. Zachary wasn't surprised. Even when texting with a friend or acquaintance, there often was not an immediate response. People were driving, in meetings, or doing other things. Dimitri would need time to review the message and decide whether he wanted to respond.

He checked his email and social media direct messages and put the phone down to continue to go through John's papers again, looking for patterns and how the players he had met so far fit into the picture. He was getting a better feeling for the shape of Jose's life. He stopped to text Philippe, again suggesting that they meet to discuss developments.

He shuffled through the papers, reassembling them in a different order.

His phone buzzed with a return text. Zachary picked it up.

Meet me tonight to talk. I have something to tell you.

Zachary started to compose a reply. His gaze strayed up to the top of the screen and he realized that the text had come from Dimitri, not Philippe.

"Well, well…"

What did Dimitri know? Had he only told Zachary half of the story when he'd thought him a curious friend? Did he know more, and wanted to share it now that he knew that Zachary and the police were trying to track down a serial killer? Things might have been different, now that he knew that Jose had not just hooked up with some other man, but was more than likely a victim of violence?

He texted back to Dimitri to arrange the time and place for their meeting. He remembered Dimitri's falsetto voice, his dramatic manner. Underneath that playfulness, he had real feelings for Jose. He wanted to know what had happened to his partner.

CHAPTER TWENTY-NINE

Zachary called Detective Dougan once he had things set up with Dimitri.

"Goldman," Dougan acknowledged when he picked up the phone. "What's up?"

"You asked if I could do anything to get Dimitri to talk to you."

"Yes." Dougan's voice was brusque, as if he had other, more important cases to deal with.

"I called and texted him to encourage him to talk to you, and he texted me back. He wants to meet with me to tell me something about Jose's case."

"He does. Did he say what?"

"No. But I have a time and place set up, if you want to come along."

The was a silent pause. "Did you tell him I would be coming?"

"No, I thought it would be easier to explain and convince him to tell you about it once we saw him in person."

"Yeah, you're probably right. What are the details?"

Zachary relayed them to him.

"All right. I'll see you then. I'll hang back to begin with, let him see you and get comfortable. Then I'll move in and we'll get him to spill what he knows."

"Okay." Zachary's heart was pounding faster as he thought about the meeting with Dimitri. It would be his job to keep Dimitri calm and on track so they could find out what he knew. It wouldn't be easy to do; Dimitri was obviously a highly-excitable person.

But it could be just the break they needed. If he could help break the serial killer case, it would be quite the feather in his cap. That would show the doubters.

————

"Do you want us to come with you?" Pat asked as Zachary got ready to go to his meeting with Dimitri.

"No, it's fine. Dougan is going to meet me there. I don't really want to show up with a whole crew for this meeting."

"He knows us, though. It wouldn't be like we were all strangers ganging up on him. I just don't like the idea of you meeting him alone at night."

"I won't be alone. Couldn't be much more safe than having a policeman along with me. You don't need to worry about it."

Pat sighed, nodding. "I'm sorry… I'm all nerves. You're very calm about the whole thing."

Zachary might have looked calm on the exterior, but inside he was just as on edge as Pat. His heart was going a mile a minute and his stomach was tied in knots. He didn't know whether Dimitri would be the break in the case that they needed, or if it was just a ruse to see Zachary again. He did not look forward to Dougan finding out that it had all been a line, if Dimitri didn't come up with anything.

He made sure that all of his papers were put away properly. He left his nearly-full notepad and took a new one with him instead. He needed to be sure that all of his records were kept safe. He should have been taking pictures of his notepad to upload to the cloud so that he had a backup, but it was too late to worry about doing it before the meeting.

He had one more cup of coffee and put on his jacket. "I don't know how long I'll be," he told Mr. Peterson. "Don't wait up. If Dougan ends up taking Dimitri in for questioning, I could be most of the night."

"Well then, it's a good thing you got in a good sleep last night," Lorne said lightly. "We'll see you tomorrow."

————

Zachary slowed and looked around. He had arrived early, wanting to be able to scope out the unfamiliar area before Dimitri arrived. He didn't want to be taken off-guard by an ambush, however unlikely that might seem. Whoever was killing the men must be feeling the pressure of the investigation and the media attention. It wasn't easy to work in the dark when a spotlight was being shone on you.

The streets were deserted. It was a residential area with some light commercial development; strip malls, convenience stores, coffee shops, and schools. There might be a few people out walking their dogs, but after dinner things were pretty quiet in the neighborhood.

Zachary drove in widening circles, looking for anything out of place. Why had Dimitri chosen the area? Was it his own neighborhood? Or maybe he worked close by? People didn't choose places they were unfamiliar with for meetings.

His phone buzzed in his pocket. Zachary pulled over and fished it out. On the screen was another message from Dimitri.

Are you alone?

Zachary hesitated, uneasy. Of course Dimitri expected him to be alone, but asking if he was implied that Dimitri had something to hide. Eventually, Zachary texted back confirmation that he was by himself.

Good. You can't trust that cop Dougan.

Zachary stared down at the screen. *Dougan?* Dougan had done all of the appropriate things. He'd made inquiries into Jose's disappearance, though he hadn't done any more than he had to, glossing over with routine inquiries only. He had asked for John's files in order to review the possibility of a serial killer, though he hadn't yet opened a file on the serial killer or organized a task force. He had ordered the logs on Jose's phone when Zachary provided it to him and cross-referenced Dimitri's phone number. He hadn't asked Zachary for anyone else's numbers, but it was possible that he already had access to a database of all of the numbers he needed. He had even gone back to Philippe's apartment when the young man had not answered his phone.

Zachary shifted, his brain working through the possibilities. Remembering the cop in Russia. Seventy dead women. Seventy that he had admitted to and described, more that he had lost track of. A loving father and husband. A decorated cop. And one of the worst serial killers the world had ever known.

Why can't I trust Dougan?

His text back went unanswered. Had that been enough to scare Dimitri off? Was he sure now that Zachary was in league with Dougan, sitting in the dark, waiting to ambush him when he showed up for the meeting?

Zachary wasn't sure where Dougan was. He had said that he would wait until Zachary had met with Dimitri before moving in. Zachary hadn't seen him during his reconnaissance of the neighborhood, so as far as he knew, Dougan wasn't there yet. But he could be sitting in a darkened car somewhere, watching Zachary drive by and waiting for Dimitri to make an appearance.

Zachary waited, but there was no further text. It was still early for the meeting with Dimitri. Zachary put his phone back in his pocket and pulled the car out onto the street to continue familiarizing himself with the area. If Dimitri decided not to show, then he wouldn't show. Zachary had to assume he would, and he'd be ready.

There was a wooded area up ahead. Zachary squinted at it through the darkness. A park? It seemed like a strange place for one. He drove closer and saw a decorated archway leading into the park, the name of the park inlaid within the wrought iron frame: "Peaceful Retreat Cemetery."

Zachary stared at it, making the connection to Honore Santiago. He was sure it was the name of Santiago's cemetery. But why would Dimitri want to meet Zachary there?

CHAPTER THIRTY

Santiago was one of Jose's partners. So was Dimitri. They had to know each other, to know about each other. Were they somehow acting together? Were they involved with each other as well?

He wanted to contact Dougan, to give him a heads-up that it might be an ambush. They might be dealing with two men rather than just one. There might be something going on that Zachary hadn't yet been able to wrap his mind around.

But the seeds of doubt that Dimitri had sown about Dougan were sprouting and twining around his brain and he couldn't be one hundred percent sure that the cop was clean. Dimitri could be right. He might be the one who held all of the answers, and he said that Dougan couldn't be trusted.

Zachary sat in the car, looking at the words in the arch over the entrance. Eventually, he had to satisfy himself that there was no one lurking in the cemetery, and he drove in.

He turned his brights on, casting long, dark shadows of tombstones and trees over the smooth, even turf. He watched for any movement, fresh graves, equipment out of place, or anything else that might be suspicious. He saw movement through the trees and dimmed his lights. He drove the rest of the way around a loop in the other direction and drove out of the cemetery.

If he were lucky, then whoever was in the cemetery would think that he was just someone who had made a wrong turn. He drove far enough away that anyone inside the cemetery would not be able to see the vehicle, parked it, and got out. He hesitated, weighing his options.

He took out his phone and texted Dougan.

———

Zachary walked back into the cemetery, slowly and as quietly as possible. He didn't use his flashlight, but let his eyes adjust to the dark. He could hear the man before he could see him, the sound of heavy equipment.

Looking through the trees, Zachary could see a small excavator at work. He probably didn't need to be tiptoeing around with the racket the engine was making. He kept behind trees as much as possible as he approached, not wanting to attract attention with his movement.

He couldn't see the operator of the excavator. The headlights and the lights that would normally have been lighting up the cab had been turned off so that he had to rely on the moonlight for illumination. He could only vaguely see the shape in the operator's seat, not well enough to discern if it was Santiago.

He was pretty sure that gravediggers didn't normally work at night, even if it were still early evening. If there were an interment in the morning, they would have been sure to get the work done earlier in the day. The man was working without lights for a reason. He didn't want people calling in the unusual nighttime activity to the police.

Thinking about the police, Zachary looked over his shoulder the way he had come, but still didn't see anyone else. If Dougan were there, he was keeping carefully hidden, like Zachary.

The excavator backed up and clattered to a stop. Zachary froze where he was and watched the figure climb out of the equipment. He had on a bulky coat so it was still impossible to make him out.

The man walked away from the excavator and the hole he had been digging, his footsteps crunching through the gravel. Zachary watched him until he was out of sight and his footsteps were no longer audible.

He crept closer. He decided he really didn't like cemeteries in the dark. It was one thing during the day when the sun was shining and there were people around, but night was another thing altogether. There was good cover most of the way to the freshly-dug grave. Zachary looked around, checking for any sign of the shadowy figure, but he seemed to be alone.

He stood there for a few more minutes, his own skin dimly illuminated by the moonlight. There wasn't really anything to see. A rectangular hole in the ground. The excavator, its engine ticking as it cooled down. A tarp and some hand tools beside the grave; shovel and pick for finishing off the edges of the grave. He supposed that the man had gone to get the other equipment needed to stage the grave. The rails and strap system that Zachary had seen used at graveside ceremonies to hold the casket and then lower it into the grave when everything was done. Maybe it was just a worker who had not managed to get everything done that he was supposed to during the day. Maybe Zachary had jumped to conclusions, spooked by the idea of tracking a serial killer.

He blinked a few times, focusing in on the smaller details of the gravesite. There was a headstone moved to the side, which suggested that the grave being dug was previously occupied. Zachary knew that sometimes a grave was used for a second body, perhaps a spouse. So it wasn't that unusual. If somebody were disposing of a body illegally, then they surely would have picked a more isolated spot, not an existing grave that had been dug up again. A visitor might notice that and find it suspicious. Zachary stepped closer to have a peek at the tombstone.

He knew he was stepping out from the cover of the trees, but he would hear anyone coming down the gravel path again, and no one would be able to see him unless they were past the break in the trees.

It was too dark to see the name and dates on the stone. He didn't know whether it was just the dark or whether the stone was older and worn, the letters blurred in the dim moonlight. His toe bumped against the tarp. Just a little nudge, not hard enough to dislodge it. He looked down at it, his brain registering the fact that it wasn't just a rolled-up tarp, but had some heft to it. It hadn't been weighted down with tools or rocks, but had something wrapped up inside. And of course he knew what it was going to be without looking.

He bent down anyway and touched the tarp. It was cold to the touch as if it had been outside for a long time. It hadn't just been pulled from a warm vehicle.

The smell that Zachary detected wasn't just the newly-turned earth from the grave. And it wasn't whoever was in that grave, probably buried years before and contained in a sealed casket. The stink of decomposition so close to the tarp was almost overwhelming. Zachary felt for the edge of the tarp. It was rolled neatly, with the seam on the underside.

He could wait. He could go back and hide in the trees and let the police deal with it when they arrived. He knew that was what he should do. But if Dougan were not on his way, or worse, if he were involved in the crime, then Zachary needed to find out everything he could before the return of the man trying to conceal the evidence. Breathing through his mouth instead of his nose, Zachary tried to get a purchase on the bundle to roll it over.

His body protested, his muscles and his bruised ribs throbbing with the pain of the effort to roll the heavy burden over. He closed his eyes, held his breath, and heaved. He managed to roll it one hundred and eighty degrees, revealing the edge of the tarp so that he could begin the unwrapping process.

Zachary had his winter gloves on already so, sure he wasn't going to leave any evidence behind, he started to work the edge free and pull it up. It wasn't a quick process. He didn't want to destroy any evidence the killer might have left behind or to spread the already-nauseating smell. If he were on a detective show on TV, the reveal would have been almost instant, with the fictional private eye or cop pulling back a corner of the tarp, which would be directly over the victim's face, to reveal his identity.

The wind had picked up, rattling the now-loose half of the tarp noisily, making it whip into Zachary's face. He was sure it wasn't clean and didn't want any fluids or pathogens, however microscopic, being sprayed into his face. He held his breath again, hoping that the next flip of the bundle would be the last.

He pulled back the tarp again, finally freeing it from the dark shape that had pinned it down. Though his eyes had adjusted to the moonlight, he still couldn't get a clear view of what was now undeniably a body, lying face down on the tarp.

His brain worked through the different possibilities. Jose? Philippe? He knew it wasn't John, who had been burned and was at the medical examiner's office or somewhere further along in his journey. He wore a suit. So probably not Philippe. Zachary swallowed hard and moved up to the head, holding his breath one more time and bending down to peer into the face of the badly-bloated corpse.

It wasn't Jose or Philippe.

It was Dimitri.

CHAPTER THIRTY-ONE

Zachary jumped back, shocked.

How could it be Dimitri? They had just been texting each other.

He scrabbled for his phone, not sure what he was going to do with it when he pulled it out. Call Dougan again? Take a picture? Re-read the texts he had exchanged with Dimitri?

He managed to work it out of his pants pocket before a heavy blow landed on the back of his head and neck, dropping him onto the corpse.

CHAPTER THIRTY-TWO

I t was another groggy awakening, and at first Zachary thought he was still asleep at Mr. Peterson's house. His head throbbed. He needed another pain pill. It was dark, not light, so they had been wrong about him sleeping in. It was still night time. If he could force himself to move, he could take another pain pill, and maybe another sleeping pill, and go back to sleep until he was feeling better.

But he wasn't in Mr. Peterson's house. Wherever he was, it was dark and cold. He wasn't in a nice, soft bed. Zachary groaned and tried to move. He couldn't remember everything that had happened, but it was like there was another self in the back of his brain, yelling at him that Dimitri was dead and Zachary was in danger. He couldn't remember how he knew that, but it was the truth. He tried again to get up, fighting against the throbbing pain and vertigo. He couldn't move his hands to get them beneath him.

"Zachary Goldman."

He froze at the whisper. The room was dark, but the whisper gave him something to focus on and, staring into the black space, he thought he could make out the outline of the man.

There was a flare of light, and then a glow. An old-fashioned oil lamp, the wick lit by a match. Zachary swallowed and tried to lick his lips, but his mouth was so dry it didn't help.

The lamp was bright after the blackness of the night. The room around him was rustic. A cabin or shack, crudely furnished. The large shape put down the lamp and moved toward him.

Teddy.

Zachary immediately remembered Pat's reassurance that Teddy was safe. They'd known him for years.

And the serial killer had been operating for years, right under their noses, suspected by no one.

Teddy was a big man. Looming up in the darkness, he was even bigger than Zachary remembered, tall and broad, casting his shadow all the way across the room.

Zachary tried to move. He thrashed to escape, but it was no use. His hands were cuffed in front of him. He was on the floor and his leg was shackled to the iron frame of the bed beside him.

"Thought you were smart, didn't you, Zachary? You thought you could just waltz in and catch yourself a killer. Well, it isn't that easy, is it? Not when the killer is smarter than you are, always a couple of steps ahead."

The noise of the tarp had covered the footsteps of the returning killer, Zachary realized, his mind shooting off on a tangent instead of staying focused on the man standing before him. Teddy had probably returned walking through the grass rather than on the gravel pathway, and the wind and the flapping tarp had kept Zachary from hearing his approach. He should have been more aware. He should have been looking around, keeping a better lookout.

He should have waited for Dougan's arrival.

Zachary looked around the room, trying to figure out where he was. Was he still in the cemetery, in a crypt or an equipment shed? Had Teddy hauled him off somewhere even more remote?

He was trying not to focus on the fact that Teddy was getting closer to him. He denied the possibility that he could be in even worse danger, that Teddy was there to kill him.

Why hadn't Teddy just rolled Zachary and Dimitri both into the grave and covered them up?

Zachary looked at the bed. At least Teddy hadn't brought Dimitri's corpse back with him. How much time had passed, then? If he had stopped to bury Dimitri, that must have taken at least half an hour. Where was Dougan? Had he decided not to show up after all? Were he and Teddy partners in crime? Or had Teddy done him in too?

Teddy reached down for Zachary's leg and Zachary felt a sharp pain jab into his thigh. He let out a hoarse shout and his heart raced. He was sure that Teddy had neatly nicked an artery and Zachary was about to bleed out. He tried to reach for the wound, but the combination of the handcuffs and his woozy head prevented him from being able to sit up and put pressure on it.

"There now," Teddy crooned. "Just relax for a few minutes and let that take effect. Nothing to be concerned about. You'll feel much better."

"No…"

Teddy tousled Zachary's head like he was a little boy, then gripped him under the chin, holding him tightly to prevent him from turning away. "You're not a bad-looking boy. At least, you weren't before they messed your face up like that."

Zachary tried to pull away, but his muscle responses were sluggish and he was starting to feel light-headed. Not light-headed, exactly, but removed. As if he weren't the one in control of his body anymore. Whatever drug Teddy had injected him with was taking effect swiftly.

He stopped trying to pull away from Teddy.

Teddy smiled. The expression was ghoulish in the lamplight. "You see how much better this is? Why don't we get you more comfortable?"

He ran his hand slowly down Zachary's leg to the shackle. Producing a key, he unlocked it. Zachary thought he should take the opportunity to kick Teddy. A well-aimed kick to the temple or crushing his nose would disable him, and then Zachary could make his escape.

But he didn't kick Teddy. Teddy bent over and picked Zachary up with one arm under his knees and one under his neck, like a sleeping child. He lay Zachary down on the bed.

Zachary tried to protest. "No…"

"Don't you worry. I've never had anyone complain, when it was all over." Teddy chuckled to himself.

CHAPTER THIRTY-THREE

Zachary was far away when the cavalry finally rolled in.

Without any warning to Teddy, the cops came crashing in through the door of the shack, flashbangs tossed in ahead of them to stun their quarry. Teddy didn't have a gun. He froze with the knife in his hand, too startled to do anything but turn toward the door with his mouth open.

In the seemingly chaotic entry, Teddy was disarmed and thrown to the ground. He clearly had nowhere to hide any additional weapons. They handcuffed him, shouting charges and a Miranda warning. They wrapped a blanket around him and hauled him out of the shack, Teddy grinning like he was having the time of his life.

It was Dougan who bent over Zachary on the bed, feeling his pulse and calling his name, but Zachary himself was far from the scene, watching it all from a distance, time and space morphing into shapes he hadn't known existed. He remembered Santiago's words, 'I've never really felt like I move linearly through time…' It hadn't made sense to him before, but now he understood.

He watched without emotion as Dougan took a series of pictures and then pulled the single sheet of the bed over Zachary's body.

"Need paramedics in here!" Dougan barked. "Where are they?"

They must have arrived and assembled with the cops before the breach, because they were right on hand, pushing their way in the door as soon as Dougan called for them.

"Preserve all the evidence you can," Dougan ordered. "Make sure they take blood as soon as he gets to the hospital. Swabs of everything. Full forensic kit. Act as if this is the one and only thing we can get Mr. Archuro for. I want it to be ironclad. Is that understood?"

"Not our first rodeo," one of the paramedics growled, bending over Zachary's body to shine a light in his eyes and check his pulse.

"I don't care about your hurt feelings. This monster needs to be locked up."

"We'll take care of it," the other paramedic, a woman, reassured Dougan.

———

The drugs were wearing off and Zachary was more in control of his faculties a few hours later when he heard Mr. Peterson and Pat arrive. The ordeal of the forensic examination was finally over. He could hear the doctor talking to them before they were allowed to see him.

"Is he all right?" Pat demanded. "I want to know what that bastard did to him."

"Under patient privacy laws, I really can't give you any specifics. I'm sorry. If Mr. Goldman wishes that information to be shared, I can talk with you later. But right now, I have to assume that he wishes it to be kept private."

"Is he awake?" Mr. Peterson asked.

"He may be in and out. And he may appear to be conscious of what's going on around him and be able to answer questions, but then later wake up and have no recollection of it. His memories of the past few hours and the next few may be patchy or even totally lost. Don't worry if he asks you the same questions over and over. It will probably be a while before he's really back with us."

"He was drugged, then."

"I can't answer that. Let's see how he feels about sharing that information once he's feeling like himself again."

There were a few more murmurs, and then the two men were escorted to Zachary's gurney. There were curtains pulled around the bed. Zachary knew by the noise on the other side that he wasn't in a private room yet. He was still in the emergency room examination area.

"Zachary." Mr. Peterson was the first to his side, reaching out to touch him and reassure him. "Zach, how are you?"

Zachary shied away from his hand, his body convulsing with sudden panic.

"Whoa." Mr. Peterson pulled back slowly. "It's okay. I'm sorry. Too fast."

Zachary let his body melt back into the mattress again, breathing through his open mouth and watching the two of them uneasily.

Mr. Peterson leaned in slightly, trying to meet Zachary's eyes and evaluate his state. "Pretty rough night, huh?"

Zachary breathed in and out a couple of times and nodded. "Yeah."

"Oh, Zach," Pat's face was lined with grief. "I'm so sorry this happened to you. All because I had to involve you in Jose's disappearance."

"No. Not your fault. I shouldn't have gone on without Dougan."

"Why did you?" Mr. Peterson asked. "You said you weren't going to meet with Dimitri alone. Why didn't you wait?"

"I wanted to make sure... I was afraid of losing the evidence. That by the time Dougan got there, it would be gone and he wouldn't be able to get a warrant. And I wasn't sure... I didn't even know, at first, if what was going on in the cemetery was related. It could have just been a coincidence, someone in the cemetery right before I was supposed to be meeting Dimitri. I didn't know if it was anything related, I just wanted to check."

"You took a real risk."

Zachary nodded. "Poor impulse control," he reminded Mr. Peterson with an embarrassed shrug. "It's always been at the top of my psychological profile."

"Yes, it has. Of course, we had hoped you would outgrow it."

"Not yet."

Mr. Peterson gave him a warm smile. "I think you turned out pretty good. I just worry about you. If the police hadn't gotten there when they did..."

Zachary swallowed. He had no doubt whatsoever how it would have ended. Teddy had been explicit in his descriptions of what he planned to do, and he hadn't planned for Zachary to be found when it was all over. Teddy had plenty of places close at hand in which to hide a dead body, where he could continue to visit it for years to come.

"The police got there," he said. "I'm okay."

"Are you?" Mr. Peterson's eyes moved down Zachary's body and back up again. With Zachary wearing a hospital johnny and a sheet pulled up over him, Mr. Peterson couldn't see the things Teddy had done. The most he could do was guess. Zachary wasn't going to divulge any details.

"I'm just sore," he said. "Nothing a few pain pills won't cure." He closed his eyes, resting, thinking about sleep. As removed as he still felt from himself, he wondered whether he would ever sleep again. Maybe he would always float above himself, watching his sleeping body from a safe distance. "You won't have to worry about me taking my pills tonight," he said, nodding toward the IV bag.

Mr. Peterson lowered himself into a chair. He kept his hand near Zachary's head, as if wanting to comfort him, but worried about Zachary's reaction. "I'd rather be worrying about your pills tonight."

There were strange lights and colors behind Zachary's lids when he closed his eyes. He opened them again. "I'm sorry about that. About taking too many. I'm usually very careful."

"I know you are. I think that's one of the reasons it scared us so much. You're more likely to not take something you ought to than you are to take too much. When you weren't up and I went into your room and found you so pale and your breathing so shallow... I was afraid at first..." He didn't finish the thought.

Zachary knew what he'd been afraid of. Mr. Peterson knew that Zachary had attempted suicide in the past. That he might not have made it past the previous Christmas if he had been left alone.

"I'm sorry," he said again.

Some time passed without any of them saying anything.

"Where's Dougan? Did he come to the hospital?" Zachary asked.

"He's got his hands full right now," Mr. Peterson advised. "He said he would check in when he could, but he's got a body and a serial killer on his hands, and that's way above his pay grade. He will be passing everything on to whoever is heading up the investigation into Teddy Archuro."

"Teddy," Pat repeated, putting his hands over his eyes and shaking his head. "Can you believe it? I can't. He never seemed... he was normal, just like anyone else. I never saw anything weird..."

Zachary thought about how Teddy had zeroed in on him at The Night Scene. Zachary had attracted Teddy's interest as someone new. He remembered how Teddy had suggested a shorter, more intense relationship. Just how short and intense, Zachary had not guessed. Teddy had been a predator, on the prowl for fresh meat.

"I think I'll go to sleep now," he said. "I want to be awake when Dougan gets here later."

Both men nodded. Mr. Peterson touched Zachary's shoulder very lightly, the weight of a butterfly. "Do you want someone to stay with you? In case you wake up and don't know where you are or need someone to talk to?"

"No."

Zachary was too enervated to explain. He wanted them to just go home and leave him alone.

CHAPTER THIRTY-FOUR

He knew that Dougan would come when he was able, to discuss the case and tell Zachary what their findings had been so far. He lay awake into the morning, staring at the tiles on the ceiling, knowing that despite what the doctor had said, he wasn't going to fall asleep.

Nurses checked on him periodically, usually expressing surprise at finding him wide awake. An orderly showed up to take him to the room he'd been assigned. He entertained Zachary with a Caribbean-accented monologue as he wheeled Zachary's gurney through the hallways and elevators to find his new home.

Zachary couldn't help evaluating the orderly as he'd been evaluating everyone the last few days. An immigrant, obviously. But not an illegal or he wouldn't be working in the hospital. He didn't match the body type of the immigrants who had disappeared. He had a big, well-padded body rather than the small, wiry frame Teddy seemed to prefer. That meant that Zachary could relax. The orderly was just the man taking Zachary to his room, away from the constant din of the emergency room, where he would be able to sleep.

Except he knew he wouldn't.

Eventually, Dougan did come see him. His face was tired and drawn. He looked like he had aged ten years since Zachary had first met him. But he gave Zachary an encouraging smile and nod.

"We've got him. We've got him wrapped up nice and tight. He'll never see the outside of a cell again."

Zachary waited for the relief, but it didn't come. The world went on, whether Teddy was in jail or out. He was hardly a blip on most people's radar. Others like him would continue to operate in the dark long after Dougan and Zachary had shuffled off their mortal frames.

"How did you find him?" After the words were out, Zachary knew he should have said 'me' or 'us.' But he didn't correct himself. Dougan flopped into a chair and leaned back, arms and head draped over the sides and back like a long-legged spider.

"You led us to the cemetery, where, as you probably guessed, we found Dimitri's body. It was obvious by the state of the body that he'd been dead for some time. Not just an hour or two, but probably since you first talked to him. That threw suspicion squarely onto Teddy. We put all of our resources into finding him. APB out on him and his vehicles, warrants to track his phone, Dimitri's, and yours, searched title records for any proper-ties he owned, got dogs to try to track his vehicle where it had been parked at the cemetery, everything we could think of."

Zachary nodded.

"The land titles got him. It wasn't just a place he had found, that shack in the woods. It was on land that he owned. There were fresh tire tracks on the road and we had a helicopter with thermal imaging fly over, which told us that there were, in fact, two men inside. With that, we went in hot on the basis of imminent danger."

Zachary stared at the tiles on the ceiling.

"He's talking," Dougan advised. "Just like you said, these guys love to talk once you catch them. They want to show you how clever they are and how they managed to avoid suspicion for years. All of the close calls that they had when a traffic cop pulled them over with a dead body in the trunk or some guy drugged and unconscious in the passenger seat." Dougan shook his head indignantly. "They're just so damn charming they get away with anything."

"When I met him at the bar..."

"What did you think? Did you suspect him?"

"I thought... he was *off*. He made me uncomfortable, but I thought it was just... because he was coming on to me. He thought I was gay, so he treated me like a possible conquest."

Dougan considered this, nodding. "I suppose it's lucky he was interested in you. If he'd been smart, he would have killed you and disposed of your body right away instead of just capturing you."

Zachary swallowed. "Did he say... why he didn't?"

Not that Zachary didn't know. That had been clear from the start. Zachary just wanted to know if *they* knew.

Dougan hesitated. "He's like a cat... likes to play with his food before he kills it. He didn't figure we were right on his tail. Thought he had plenty of time to stash you in the cabin and then go back to finish burying the body before anyone found it. Who would be tramping through the cemetery in the middle of the night?" Dougan cleared his throat. He didn't look at Zachary. "Then he could go back to the cabin and take his time. From what he's confessed, it takes him a few days to get through all of his usual rituals."

Zachary concentrated hard on the white tiled ceiling and the sounds and smells of the hospital around him. He would not acknowledge what had happened to him. He would simply deny the memories. They were not a part of him.

"What about Philippe? I didn't see any sign of him. If he wasn't at the cemetery and wasn't at the cabin... did Teddy have other places? Would he ever have several quarries at the same time?"

Dougan's head turned toward him, but Zachary continued to look at the ceiling, not responding to Dougan's attempt to make eye contact. Dougan shifted in his seat and looked back away from Zachary.

"He says he didn't have anything to do with Philippe's disappearance, and I'm inclined to believe him. He was skilled enough that he would have been able to take Philippe without tipping the others off. But Philippe and Nando Gonzalez and all of the rest of them? He couldn't be responsible for all of them disappearing."

"Unless Nando was freaked out when Philippe disappeared and got everyone out of there before the police could come looking for another missing man."

"Could be," Dougan allowed, "but I'm inclined to believe what Teddy Archuro says. I think if he'd taken Philippe, he would have been happy to admit it. That seems to be his response on all of his other accomplishments."

Zachary breathed a sigh of relief. That was one thing, anyway. He hadn't pushed Teddy into eliminating Philippe. He didn't know how he would forgive himself if his investigation had caused the boy's death.

CHAPTER THIRTY-FIVE

"I want to go home."

Mr. Peterson had been surprised to find Zachary sitting up, waiting for the clothes that he had requested, eager to get out of the hospital.

"I don't know if that's a good idea. You need some recovery time."

"Not here. I don't want to be here; I want to go home."

"Well, I suppose we can keep an eye on you there…"

"No. Back to my apartment."

He saw the hurt in his former foster father's face and knew that he'd said the wrong thing, or said it the wrong way.

"It's not because of you," he assured Lorne, "I just want… the reason I was here was to find Jose, or to find out what had happened to him. I've done that. I need to go back to my other work. I don't want… everything that has happened here. I don't want to be reminded about it every time I turn around."

"I can understand that. But I'm concerned. You're still hurt. A lot has happened. I think you need some support."

"I have a therapist and friends, and I can still call you. Pat can set up Skype and we can talk face-to-face, just like if I was still there."

"That would be nice. I'd like to hear from you more than I do." Mr.

206

Peterson's mouth thinned into a straight line. "Zach… do you want to talk about it? I don't think we should… pretend that nothing happened."

"No."

"You should talk to someone. It doesn't have to be me, if that would be uncomfortable. But you need to work it out. Get some counseling, a support group."

"I will."

He saw that he had answered too quickly. Mr. Peterson didn't believe it. Zachary motioned to Mr. Peterson's bag.

"I need to get changed."

Without a word, his old friend handed the bag over. Zachary couldn't help flinching when Mr. Peterson's hand moved toward him with it. An alarmed tightening of all of his muscles. He swallowed and took the bag.

"Thanks. Be right back."

In the small hospital bathroom, he leaned for a minute on the sink, taking long, even breaths and pushing the panic away. There was no reason to be anxious. He was going home, where he could be alone and relax. He could catch up on the routine investigative work that he had let slide while he had been looking into Jose's disappearance.

Zachary made himself move. He pulled on the clothes, relieved to have his body properly covered again. The loose, thin hospital johnny had made him feel too much like he was still naked. He felt more secure dressed like a real person. Like he could go back to his former life without a hitch.

CHAPTER THIRTY-SIX

His phone was ringing yet again. Zachary had been turning it off for a couple of hours at a time in order to give himself time to focus on work, but he didn't want to miss calls from new clients, who weren't likely to leave messages.

The number was unfamiliar. Not one of the reporters who had been calling him repeatedly, wheedling and cajoling for the inside story. But he was getting a lot of calls from kooks too. It was getting easier to pick up the phone and just terminate the call when it wasn't someone he wanted to talk to. He no longer felt bad about hanging up on people. So much for the phone etiquette lessons painstakingly instilled by a series of foster mothers and group homes. They hadn't anticipated a situation like the one Zachary was in.

He tapped the speaker button without picking up the phone. "Goldman Investigations. Zachary."

A few seconds of staticky silence ticked by.

"Hello?" Zachary prompted, finger above the red 'end' button.

"Zachary?"

It wasn't a good line, static and background traffic noise making the voice difficult to recognize.

"This is Zachary."

"It's Philippe."

Zachary turned off the speaker and put the phone to his ear, relief flooding through him. "Philippe! You're okay."

"Yes, I am fine."

"When you wouldn't answer any calls and then disappeared... I was worried. I didn't know if *he* had gotten to you."

"Teddy Archuro," Philippe said in a voice that was still stunned. "I knew him."

"He didn't—you didn't date him?"

"I hung out with him a couple of times. Not a date, just casual... getting to know him."

Zachary drew in his breath in a whistle. Philippe could have been Teddy's next victim. In spite of what Zachary had been through, he could take comfort in the fact that he had prevented Philippe from being tortured and murdered.

"The news reports said that the police were looking for remains. Do you know...?"

"They haven't released anything official, but they have recovered some... I think they probably found Jose, but the medical examiner hasn't confirmed identities yet."

"Where?"

"He was using Honore Santiago's cemetery some of the time. And there are graves out at his property in the woods, where he had a cabin. I don't know if there was anywhere else; they're not giving me much information."

"Honore was not involved, though...?"

Zachary's heart gave an extra beat. Was Philippe involved with Santiago too? "No, I don't think so. If they have found any connection other than the cemetery, they haven't told me. But please... be careful."

"Honore is a nice man. Very generous."

"I'm sure he is. But he still had connections with a lot of the missing men. I just want you to be careful. Teddy wasn't the only predator out there."

———

At the knock on the door, Zachary got up and walked through the kitchen to look through the wide-view peephole. He opened the door, giving Kenzie a forced smile. "Hi, Kenz."

"How's it going, Zachary? I'm hoping you don't have too much going on tonight…"

"Come on in." He opened the door wider.

She walked in and looked around. Zachary gave the apartment a quick scan. He had been hard at work and hadn't had much time for cleaning or other chores. But he had picked up groceries and there wasn't a sink full of dirty dishes. He didn't think Kenzie would find anything of concern.

"I'm glad to have you home," she remarked. "Though you look like hell."

"No worse than most of the stiffs you work with," he teased.

"Actually, most of the remains look better than you do," Kenzie countered, hands on hips. "You could give most zombies a run for their money."

"That's just because it's healing. Bruises always look worse as they get older and change color."

Kenzie gave a nod of agreement. She opened the fridge and helped herself to a soft drink. "You want anything?"

"I'm good."

They both drifted into the living room. Zachary straightened up the papers he had been working on and piled them carefully in his tray. He closed his computer lid and sat down on the couch next to Kenzie. She looked at him for a minute, then leaned back and took a sip of her drink.

"I missed you."

"I was only gone for a few days."

She stretched her arm behind him. "But I still missed you. You hardly even called." She stroked the back of his neck.

Zachary jolted at her touch. He pulled back from her, feeling suddenly crowded.

"Wow." Kenzie stared at him. "What was that? I didn't hurt you…"

Zachary took several deep breaths. "No. Sorry. You just startled me."

She shifted her body a little closer to him, watching his face. Zachary couldn't help squirming, overwhelmed by her closeness.

"Seriously, are you okay?" Kenzie persisted.

"Yeah, fine."

She withdrew slightly and took several swallows of her soft drink. Zachary tried to calm down and relax his muscles.

"There weren't a lot of details in the news stories about how this Teddy guy was arrested," she observed.

"It was a good arrest. He's talking. He's never going to be out on the street again." He said it as much for his own sake as much as for hers. Reminding himself that Teddy would never be able to hurt anyone ever again.

"That's not what I meant," Kenzie said. "I'm not worried about whether it was a good arrest. I'm just wondering… about your part in it. They kind of glossed over the part about you being 'briefly captured' by this guy. Like it was just a few minutes… a standoff or something like that."

Zachary nodded.

"Is that what it was?"

He swallowed. "No."

"What happened?"

Zachary shook his head emphatically. "I'm not ready to talk about it."

"Okay…"

But he could see she was not ready to let it go. She was still looking at him analytically, trying to think of another way to get the story from him. Zachary picked up the TV remote and turned on the television. Not only did he not want to talk to her about it, he didn't even want to think about it. "You want to watch a movie?"

"If you want," Kenzie said. "I thought we'd visit."

"I just need time to unwind."

"Sure. You've had quite a week. Your body obviously needs healing time. Maybe your mind too."

He nodded. "It's been pretty taxing."

"I'm here. Whenever you're ready to talk…"

He nodded. "I know. But… I might not want to talk about it."

"I guess that's up to you."

He switched channels on the TV. Kenzie reached out, and he steeled himself not to react. She put her hand on his knee and he jerked it away. It was beyond his control, a reflex. His heart raced and he felt like he wasn't getting enough air.

"It's okay, Zachary."

"I'm fine," he assured her, even though it took everything he had to talk in a calm, even voice.

She offered her hand to him. Zachary took it in his. He held it between the two of them as he flipped channels with the other hand to find a movie they would both enjoy. He didn't cuddle up to her.

And he didn't pick a romance.

HE WAS NOT THERE

Zachary Goldman Mysteries #6

That those who have been hurt may find healing.

CHAPTER ONE

Zachary was glad that Tyrrell had called. He had needed a reason to get away from Kenzie for a while. Their relationship, which had begun more than a year ago, had gotten more complicated since Zachary had been attacked, and he needed a reason to take a break from Kenzie's ministrations. He didn't want to tell her to leave him alone and give him some space, but he wasn't sure how else to get her out of his apartment when she came over for a visit.

But his brother Tyrrell's call had given him an excuse to say that he was busy and needed to deal with a family emergency.

Not that Tyrrell had said it was an emergency. He and Heather were perfectly willing to wait until a convenient time for Zachary, but for Zachary that was a good enough excuse to tell Kenzie that he needed to take care of family stuff and would have to see her later.

"Do you want me to drive you somewhere?" Kenzie offered, still happy to do whatever he needed her to.

"I'm fine to drive."

"I know, it's just that..." she trailed off, apparently unable to find an excuse for taking care of him. He hadn't been drinking. He hadn't been having a particularly upsetting evening. She just wanted to know that everything was okay. She wanted to keep an eye on him. Zachary appreciated it, but he didn't want the attention.

"I'm fine," he repeated, getting his jacket on to signal to her that it was time to go.

Kenzie reluctantly got her coat on as well. She pulled the hood on over her dark, short curls and gave him a brief kiss with her bright-red-lipsticked lips, holding on to him more tightly and longer than was necessary for a goodbye. He gave her a squeeze of acknowledgment and headed to the door. Kenzie walked out ahead of him and watched as he locked up.

"What's going on with Tyrrell?"

"I don't know. I need to see him to find out."

"Is something wrong? Is there anything I could help with?"

"No, I don't think so. I'll let you know."

Kenzie nodded. "Okay."

They took the elevator down together, and Zachary sketched a little wave as they separated in the parking lot. "We'll talk later," he said. "Thanks for coming by."

He would have suggested that the next time, he would come by her place, just so that he had some control over the timing, but she had never invited him to her apartment, so it was out of bounds. She needed her own space and privacy. He just wished that he could have some of his back too.

———

As he headed to the meeting with Tyrrell, he thought about his relationship with Kenzie, the medical examiner's assistant. The relationship had transformed over the months they had known each other. Kenzie had changed from a girl who was just interested in having some fun to a woman who was really interested in him and in taking their relationship further, to one who was in his space a little too often and felt like she needed to take care of him.

It had never been like that with Bridget. He had always felt warm and rewarded when she wanted to do something for him or showed her concern. His ex-wife had more often been angry and critical when he went through a crisis, upset with him for taking too much from the relationship.

He had tried to take care of Bridget too. He had tried not to let it be a one-sided relationship, to put as much into the marriage as he took out of it, but she had never seen it that way. She had only seen him sucking the energy out of her, taking time away from her parties and social events. He'd never felt smothered by Bridget. Like with his relationship with his mother before he was put into foster care, he'd felt like he had to earn every bit of attention and every smile and kindness she might bestow upon him.

It was good that his younger brother Tyrrell was back in his life. Zachary hadn't had any contact with biological family for thirty years and it felt good to see him again. And he was going to meet Heather. He hadn't seen any of the others since the fire. He could remember the scrappy little blond tomboy Heather had been. His second sister, a couple of years older than he was, she had been one of his little surrogate mothers. One of the two big sisters who tried to keep the younger children out of trouble and out from underfoot to avoid any unnecessary problems with their mother or father. To him, they had seemed so much older and more mature at the time. He had only been ten and they had almost seemed like adults to him.

He hadn't expected to meet any of the other kids. Even Tyrrell had said that he hadn't met Heather face-to-face since they had found each other. They talked on Skype or FaceTime, but hadn't actually gotten together. What could have happened that had changed that? Was it just the natural progression of their relationship, or was there something wrong? Tyrrell had sounded concerned on the phone. Then relieved when Zachary said they could meet right away instead of trying to put it off and schedule something in the future. But maybe he was reading too much into it.

They had set up a time and place, allowing them both to meet halfway so that neither one had to drive halfway across Vermont to see each other. Zachary wasn't sure where Heather lived. Even though he was a private detective, he had never tried to find any of his siblings. They had a right to live their own lives without having to deal with him, especially since he was the reason that the family had been broken up.

Whatever reason Heather had for wanting to meet with him, Tyrrell had sounded pretty serious. Zachary pushed back the worry that it might be just to give him a piece of her mind about the problems he had caused in her life and the way he had ripped apart their family.

———

They had agreed to meet at a coffee shop. Clintock was a small town, so it didn't take long to find the little store. In a world that seemed to have been taken over by Starbucks, it was nice to see some independent shops were still alive and well. Zachary sat in his parked car for a few minutes, suddenly anxious about going inside. He knew Tyrrell didn't hold any resentments about what had happened to their family. But Heather was an unknown. Zachary had tried hard to please his big sisters when he was young. With his ADHD and their family problems, it had been an impossible proposition. One of them would go off on him for some stupid, impulsive mistake he had made, and he would get that knot in his stomach, that feeling that he had again come up short. And the worry that he always would.

Now she wanted him back in her life again. Why? What if he couldn't meet her expectations? He spent too much of his life with that lump in his stomach, worrying that he would never measure up to expectations. His clients, Bridget, Kenzie, the police officers that he worked with, his doctor and therapist, his surrogate fathers Lorne and Pat. They all had expectations, and he was only too aware of his failings.

The longer he stayed in the car, the harder it was going to be to actually break free of his fears and go in there and see what Tyrrell and Heather wanted, so in spite of his anxiety, he forced his body to climb out of the car, lock the doors, and walk toward the coffee shop. He clicked the lock button on his key remote a couple more times just to be sure, then stood at the door of the coffee shop, staring inside.

He saw them before they saw him. They were sitting at a table in the back. The coffee shop tables were almost deserted. People lined up at the counter to order and pick up their drinks, but they didn't stay to consume them, taking them 'to go' and carrying on with their busy lives. Tyrrell looked much the same as Zachary, but his dark hair was cut longer and shaggier than Zachary's buzz-cut. They both had dark eyes and a narrow build. Tyrrell was taller than Zachary was, not having spent as many years in a home where the food was inadequate or on meds that stunted his growth. He didn't have the hollows in his cheek that Zachary attempted to hide with a few days' growth of beard.

Zachary always lost weight before Christmas, and he hadn't been able to get back to a healthy weight before the assault. Since that incident, he'd been lucky if he could keep his weight stable. He told himself it was just a side effect of the meds, not admitting how much of his day was spent thinking about what Teddy had done to him and of other assaults in the years before he aged out of foster care. He didn't want those experiences to be a part of his life. He wanted to forget them.

Heather's appearance was quite different from Zachary's and Tyrrell's. She was blond, with a full figure. Not overweight, but a look that suggested she was a mother, having borne and nourished a few children, giving her wider hips and a silhouette that was no longer girlish, but mature. Her face looked worn and a little sad. She talked to Tyrrell earnestly, but her manner was hesitant, not animated.

She didn't look angry. Yet.

As Zachary entered the coffee shop, a two-tone electronic chime sounded, and Heather and Tyrrell looked up and turned toward the door. Tyrrell said something to Heather, probably 'there he is,' and got up to greet Zachary.

Tyrrell was always cheerful and enthusiastic when he saw Zachary, as if he really were happy to see him. Zachary's doubts always built up when he hadn't seen Tyrrell for a while, thinking his brother wouldn't really want to see him. But when he saw Tyrrell's face wreathed in smiles, and the way he reached out his hand to shake Zachary's and then pulled him in for a hug, he couldn't doubt it. Tyrrell slapped Zachary on the back and then pulled back to look at him.

"How are you, Zach? Doing okay?"

It was the first time Tyrrell had seen Zachary face-to-face since the assault, so he looked Zachary over searchingly, wanting to verify for himself that Zachary wasn't horribly mutilated.

"I'm fine," Zachary assured him. He looked past Tyrrell to Heather, who had remained sitting and didn't rush forward to be reunited with Zachary. She watched the two of them, her expression pensive.

Tyrrell turned and looked toward Heather. "Come and meet her."

They walked over to the table. Heather gazed up at Zachary and still didn't stand up to hug him or shake his hand. He sat down and she nodded to him.

"Hi."

"Hi, Heather."

Her eyes moved over him, taking everything in and finally stopping on his face. "Wow. You know, you look just the same."

"Really?" He thought of himself as almost a completely different person from who he had been before the fire. He'd only been ten years old, how could he look the same as an adult?

But he remembered recognizing Tyrrell's eyes. How they danced just the way they had when he was five. It didn't matter if the rest of him had grown up, Zachary had still seen his little brother in those eyes.

Heather nodded. Zachary fumbled for something to say. "You... grew up."

She gave a little smile. "Yeah. That's the way it works."

He didn't see it yet. He couldn't find the little girl's face he remembered in this grown-up woman.

"So, how are you? Tyrrell said that you are married with a couple of kids?"

"Yeah. They're grown up now, but I have a boy and a girl. And Grant."

"Grant is your husband?"

"Yeah."

"You're still married after the kids moved out? How many years is that?"

"Twenty-four."

"Wow. Coming up on the big one. That's really something. Not a lot of people make it that far anymore."

Of course, his perspective was slightly skewed, spending hours following unfaithful spouses during or before divorces. But lasting twenty-four years was still a big accomplishment.

"We've had our ups and downs," Heather said. "But... I never really considered leaving him over any of our issues. We just pressed on through them. You're not married?"

"No... divorced. We managed about two years. Doesn't measure up too well to your twenty-four years, does it?"

"Living with someone else can be hard." Heather's voice was toneless, she sounded as if she were far away. "If there are things that you can't come to terms with..."

Zachary nodded. "I guess... we were just too different. We wanted different things."

But it wasn't really their philosophical differences that had precipitated the divorce. The truth was far more painful than that. Zachary didn't see the need to bare his soul to Heather yet. They hardly knew each other. He had the feeling she had come to him in some kind of trouble. She needed him for something. There was no point in telling her all of his problems when she was looking for help.

Heather nodded and had a sip of her coffee. Zachary realized that he hadn't ordered, and probably should have. He had to decide whether it would make Heather more uncomfortable for him to be sitting there without a drink or for him to take a break to go get one. On balance, he thought it was probably better to stay where he was. Heather seemed like she would spook at the slightest provocation. He glanced at Tyrrell to see what he thought of the situation. Tyrrell gave him a quick nod of encouragement. But Zachary didn't know where to go with the conversation.

"So… are you in contact with any of the others? Other than Tyrrell, I mean?"

"Me and Joss have kept in touch pretty well. There were times when we couldn't, but as adults… we reconnected and have kept up with each other."

"You and Joss didn't stay together?"

"No. We were put in the same home to start out with, but… well, they said they couldn't handle both of us, and that it was interfering with their discipline to have us both there because we always got in the way. You know, if one person was getting crap, the other one was always jumping in. So they said that one of us had to go, and I was the troublemaker, so…"

"You were a troublemaker?" Zachary repeated. He could remember how Heather used to get after him when he had screwed up. He had always thought she was next to perfect. She and Joss were always trying to help their mother by taking care of the younger kids and whatever they could around the house. They were nearly adults, as far as Zachary was concerned. They couldn't have been more than twelve and fourteen when they were separated. That was awfully young to be taking care of all of the other kids. And Joss and Heather had been trying to drag up the rest of the children since they were much younger than that, probably nine or ten.

He couldn't believe that Heather would have been identified as a troublemaker. Zachary had always been a disciplinary problem, but not the girls.

"Sure," Heather gave him the corner of a grin, looking engaged for the first time. "You don't remember all the stuff I used to do? I was always getting in trouble for leading the rest of you into trouble. If everyone was into something, it was always me who had started it. I had brilliant ideas of fun things to do to entertain ourselves and they didn't always turn out well."

Zachary smiled. He did remember that Heather had been the more fun of his older sisters. She had been better at thinking up things to do and keeping the younger kids engaged and involved in a game or project. He didn't remember them ending badly because of Heather. He was so often in trouble himself, he just assumed that he had been to blame for whatever trouble they got into. "You used to make up great games. Imaginary zoos or trips. Going on an adventure. Cops and robbers."

"Yeah. We were all pretty good at pretending." Her expression grew distant again. "Maybe too good."

"What else were we going to do? It wasn't like we had electronics or the latest toys. We had ourselves, whatever we could find outside. Rocks, sticks, stuff we scavenged from other people's garbage. We had to do something."

"It was really different raising my children. They expected to have all of the things that their friends did. To be able to do all of the same things. I was always trying to get them involved in imaginary games, role playing, stuff like that, and they just wanted to watch TV or play video games. We never had that choice. We had to use our imaginations."

Zachary nodded his agreement. Tyrrell gave a bit of a nod, but he wouldn't remember much. He had only been five or six when they had been separated. He wouldn't have much memory of those lean times and how much they had lacked that other kids had. Not having the latest and greatest toys had not been their worry. They had been more concerned with getting enough to eat, and avoiding the back of one parent's hand or the other's. Or worse.

"So they moved you out how long after we were separated?" Zachary asked. "Was it right away? They never gave me an update on how either one of you was doing. I used to ask Mrs. Pratt, but she would just give me the brush-off, like she didn't even know. I knew she knew. She just didn't want to tell me."

"I don't know how long we were together. Maybe a few months or a year. Then they decided I needed to go somewhere else."

"Did you get moved a lot?"

"No, not too much. I was mostly with one family, the Astors. They weren't too bad."

Zachary nodded slowly. It was good if she'd managed to stay in one place. Not like him, jumping from one family to another so quickly that sometimes he couldn't remember where to go home after school. And institutions and group homes in between, when his behavior or anxiety was too much for a family to handle.

"I was there until I was sixteen, almost seventeen," Heather offered. "Then... mostly groups homes and shelters until I aged out. I figured I'd better get myself straightened out and either get a husband or a job, or I wasn't going to be able to last on the streets."

"Yeah." Zachary too had been driven to find a way to support himself right away. Mr. Peterson—Lorne—was the one who had suggested putting his photography skills to use in a way that would bring in some money. Art obviously didn't make anything, but private investigator work had brought in enough to pay the rent most of the time. "So what did you get into?"

"Into?" she repeated vaguely. "Oh... I didn't ever really find a job that would make me anything. I was in and out of a few relationships before I found Grant. Since then... he's a good supporter. I didn't have to work when the kids were little. Then once they were gone... he said there wasn't any reason for me to be rushing out to find a job just because they were old enough to look after themselves. So... I didn't. I just stayed at home. Kept house. Kept myself busy."

"Yeah? Good for you. I bet you were a really good mom. You were so good with us when we were kids."

"I don't think I was too bad at it. But... I don't think I ever really excelled at anything, including being a mother." She shook her head and made a face, as if he'd tried to feed her something bitter. "I didn't come here to talk about small-talk and get caught up on each other's lives."

Her words were clipped and abrupt. Zachary blinked at her. He thought that he'd been putting her at ease so that she would be able to share whatever it was she had come to him about. If it wasn't about the family and reuniting, then what was it?

Heather opened her mouth, but she seemed uncertain of herself, no longer able to speak. She looked at Tyrrell as if he might help her.

Tyrrell hesitated for a moment before venturing, "Heather saw reports of what happened with Teddy Archuro."

So had everyone else in the country. Even on the international stage. Teddy Archuro had been big news. A serial killer who, for so many years, had flown under the police radar, primarily because the men that he used and killed were illegal immigrants whose status as missing persons was never reported to the police department. No missing persons meant no investigation, and he was able to keep torturing and killing men until Zachary had investigated the missing Jose Flores. Then everything had changed.

"Uh-huh," Zachary waited for Tyrrell to finish the thought and explain why Heather wanted to contact him after the announcement of his involvement with the capture of serial killer Teddy Archuro.

Tyrrell looked at Heather to see if she would explain it to Zachary, but she said nothing, chewing on the inside of her lip.

"Heather wants to know if you would investigate an old case for her. Something that happened a long time ago."

Zachary looked at Heather. "What kind of case?"

She stared down at her coffee. Zachary again regretted that he hadn't gotten one for himself as soon as he walked into the coffee shop, but he seemed to have missed the opportunity. He waited, not pressing Heather to answer. She would get to it faster if he waited than if he tried to force her. He'd learned at least that much from his investigations and interrogations as a private detective. The hard-hitting style of the noir private eye didn't work. At least, not for him.

"It happened a long time ago," she said. "I don't know whether there is anything you can even do now. Cold cases are... I know a lot of them never get solved."

"Some of them do get solved," Zachary assured her. "Especially as new technologies come into existence. There are a lot of cases that have been solved recently solely on forensic evidence where the technology to use it just wasn't there ten or twenty years ago, but now they can go back and test the materials that they already have."

Heather nodded. "I know... I think about that... whenever I see one of those cases..."

"You never know until you try it. What kind of case was it?" Most of his high-profile cases had been murder. With Heather approaching him due to his appearance on the national news scene, he was anxious about whether it was another murder case. What kind of murder could Heather have been involved in years before?

"I saw on the news, about that serial killer, how he would... *abuse* the men he kidnapped before he killed them."

"Yes," Zachary agreed. He focused on the pulse pounding in his head. He didn't want to go back there. He didn't need to replay what had happened to him. He had been rescued, and everything that had happened between being kidnapped and being rescued was like it had happened to someone else. He didn't need to integrate it as his own memory.

"Zachary?"

He didn't even hear Heather or Tyrrell trying to call him back to earth. He just saw and heard and felt the things that had been done to him. He was in the grip of the memory, trying to pull away from what happened to his body. Trying to separate from it. He didn't want to allow it to become part of his consciousness.

"Zachary." Tyrrell's hand on his arm made Zachary jerk back instantly. He looked at Tyrrell in panic, then looked at Heather, rising an inch or two off of his seat, before he realized that he wasn't in any danger and plopped back down.

"Sorry." He swallowed. He looked at Heather. "What happened?"

"I… I was just telling you… about how… I didn't know whether…" she looked back at Tyrrell for help. He didn't offer anything, just looking from her to Zachary. "They said that he had captured you. They said it like it was just a few minutes. Was it… just a few minutes?"

It might have been only a few minutes or it might have been hours. Zachary had no way to measure the time that had passed. Teddy had given Zachary drugs so that he could act without any resistance. Zachary had been so doped up, there had been no chance of escape from the sadist who worked him over, doing whatever his twisted little brain could come up with. And yet, he'd been conscious the whole time.

"I don't know," he told Heather honestly. "It seemed like a long time."

Heather nodded, and he saw understanding in her eyes. Not just a surface emotion, but something that told him that she too understood that disassociation and time distortion. As if she, too, had been through a similar experience. He looked at her, hesitating to ask.

"What happened to you?"

CHAPTER TWO

She resisted, not answering his query. "That man. What did he do to you? Did he...?"

Zachary looked at Tyrrell, self-conscious. Then back at Heather. "I don't really want to talk about it, Heather. I don't... I don't even know you. My foster father wanted to know. My girlfriend wanted to know. But I can't... I don't want to talk about it to anyone."

She nodded. "Then he did, didn't he? He hurt you and you couldn't do anything to stop it."

He shrugged. She had read the news articles. She had read about the conditions of the bodies that they had discovered. She could read between the lines. She knew that he hadn't just been held as a hostage, but that Teddy had centered his time and attention on Zachary. He had exercised the power he had over Zachary to take whatever pleasure he wanted.

Heather looked away again, breaking eye contact. She swallowed and looked at the surface of her coffee.

"I was raped when I was fourteen," she said baldly. "They never figured out who it was, and I want you to find out. I want to know that he's been punished and been stopped from doing it to anyone else."

"These guys... like the guy that held me. They don't stop after one. If he assaulted you, you can bet that he assaulted other girls as well. It wasn't the first time. They don't stop unless they are behind bars."

"Yeah, I know," she admitted, still looking down. "That's why I want to put him there. If he's not already. And to make sure that he's not getting out again."

"Thirty years ago. It's not going to be easy to find him, unless you have a really good memory or some evidence. If he was thirty or forty at the time he hurt you... then he's sixty or seventy now. Hopefully, not a threat anymore."

Teddy had not been a young man. He was probably sixty. But he had still been strong and virile and able to do all kinds of unthinkable damage. He'd had plenty of experience and lots of time to experiment over the years. There was no way he would stop being a predator just because he was sixty or seventy. He would be one of the men who was always going to victimize people around him. He would always take on a new victim, as long as he had the ability.

"No. I think... unless he's lost his drive... he's going to just keep going on and on as long as they let him."

Heather nodded.

Zachary looked down at his hands, focusing on a freckle near the webbing of his first finger and thumb.

"Would you help me?" Heather prompted.

"I should," Zachary said, which he knew wasn't any kind of answer. "I don't know... how much evidence was kept? What do you remember?"

"Are you going to find him? Are you going to put him behind bars?" Heather pressed, not satisfied with his non-answer.

"I don't know. I'll start out... doing what I can to help. But I don't know how far I'll be able to get with it. I don't want to promise you results when.... there might not be anything I can do."

He took a glance in her direction. She was looking at him angrily, wanting to insist that he put her attacker behind bars. But he couldn't promise anything on a case, especially one that he hadn't been given any information on. She had undoubtedly been told before that no one could promise her anything, but that didn't stop her from wanting it. From needing it so badly.

Heather put her hands over her face and bowed, leaning her elbows on the table. "I need someone to do something about it."

"I'll try. If you'll give me the information you have now, I'll do every-thing I possibly can... but I don't know what to say. If there aren't some pretty good leads, I can't very well promise results. Did the police look into it at the time? Did you report it?"

Heather nodded. "Mrs. Astor took me to the police and made an official report. I had to go to the hospital, get a rape kit." She swallowed hard and tried to keep her composure. She looked at Tyrrell instead of Zachary, explaining it to him. "It was... almost worse than the rape itself. It took hours and hours... having to describe everything, them processing my clothes, my skin, every part of my body. Everything. You have no clue what it's like. When they talk about it on TV, it's like, they just do a cheek swab and clip your fingernails. But what it's like... it's like being assaulted all over again. It's like they don't even care what happened to you. They examine every inch of your body. Every... orifice."

Tyrrell nodded, his face pale. It was probably more than he wanted to know, and it was certainly more than Zachary wanted to hear, having been through a forensic exam himself much too recently. He stared away from Heather and Tyrrell, looking out one of the side windows of the coffee shop into the parking lot. He didn't have to remember anything he didn't want to. In his earlier years, he'd been able to just forget about what they did to him and go on with his life, since otherwise, there was no way he could carry on.

There was silence from both Heather and Tyrrell. Eventually he turned back toward them. Heather looked at him for an instant, the raw pain in her own eyes. How could it be so raw after so many years? Zachary cleared his throat, wishing that he at least had a drink of water in front of him, and spoke as unemotionally as he could.

"It's good that they opened an investigation and did a kit," he said brusquely. "That means that there is a cold case file somewhere with information in it that we can access, and evidence that we can have retested. You never know. With today's technology, they may be able to get a hit."

Heather nodded.

"I'll need the details of what police department it was reported to and it will probably take me a few days at least to track down the file and get it pulled from storage. Pray there were no black mold infestations. It would be good if you could come in with me to talk to them, because they'll be more likely to put the time and effort into it if they can put a face to the victim and understand that you're still waiting for justice than if it's just some annoying little PI demanding answers."

Heather gave a little smile at his words, but shook her head. "I don't know if I can do that," she said. "I'm not… very good with people and with talking about it. I haven't talked about it since it happened. I just… never told anyone else about it."

"What about your husband?"

She shook her head. "I didn't think… there wasn't any point in having to relive it and get all emotional. It wasn't like there was anything he could do. Knowing wouldn't make either of us feel any better, so I just didn't talk about it."

Zachary couldn't imagine her having a relationship with someone for so long and not talking about the things that had affected her so intimately.

Or maybe he could, since he had pushed his own memories away and had never discussed them with Bridget. But she would have been over-whelmed if he had told her everything that had ever happened to him. She was overwhelmed enough by just dealing with him on a daily basis.

For something to do, Zachary pulled out his notepad and flipped through it to find a blank page. He smoothed the paper. "What's he like? Your husband."

She eyed his pencil and paper. "He doesn't have anything to do with this. It happened long before he was ever in the picture. And he doesn't even know about it."

"I know. I'm not looking at him as a suspect or even as a witness. I'm just looking for something easy to talk about. To get warmed up before we get into anything that might be painful."

She looked doubtful. "I don't know how that's going to help. Grant is… he's a good guy. Bookkeeper. He's always been a good supporter for the family. Hasn't ever been out of work. He's changed jobs a few times, but he always has something new lined up before he gives up on the old job. He has a lot of friends. Likes to get out and do things. I don't know… what else you want to know about him? He's a good father. Loves the kids. He wasn't ever one of these dads who came home and read the paper and didn't want anyone to make any noise until he'd had his smoke and his dinner. He'd come home and want to know all about what they'd been doing that day, how things were going at school, he'd help them with homework or *ooh* and *ah* over projects that they brought home."

Zachary smiled, nodding. "He sounds like a really good guy."

"He is. Nothing like some of the dads you run into…" she didn't finish the sentence, but he assumed she was going to say 'in foster care.' There were a lot of good dads in foster care too. It was just that some of the others, the dads who didn't want anything to do with the kids, or who were violent, or who wanted too much contact of the wrong sort, ruined it for everyone. Spend time in one home with a dad like that, and it felt like he represented every other home.

"One of the foster dads I had," Zachary told her, "he was like that. He was really great. Always interested in hearing about what had happened during the day. He introduced me to photography, and even though I wasn't in the home anymore, he still helped me to develop my film over the years after that. I'm still in touch with him, even though I was only in the home for a couple of weeks. He's the only one who I would consider... a parent."

"Really?" Heather cocked her head, thinking about it. "That's really cool. I'm glad you found someone like that. There *are* some really great parents in foster care."

"It's just that those bad apples make it a miserable experience for everyone," Zachary agreed.

"Is that your Mr. Peterson?" Tyrrell asked. "Lorne?"

Zachary nodded. Of course it was. "Yeah."

"I had dinner with him and his partner," Tyrrell informed Heather. "Zachary invited me over to dinner. And Lorne and Pat are really great. You'd never guess that they weren't Zachary's foster dads for years."

"They were in the articles, weren't they? The ones about the serial killer? They were involved?"

"They weren't *involved* in anything," Zachary said quickly. "They knew one of the victims, and that's how I got the case. I offered to look into Jose's disappearance for Pat. They were really close and Pat wanted to find out what had happened to him. Didn't believe that he had just gone back home to El Salvador or was somewhere else, hiding from Immigration. They knew... that something must have happened to him for him to have disappeared suddenly like that."

"But nobody else did?"

"Other people might have doubted it. But the police didn't really think there was anything to it. And that's the trouble... because they were immigrants, no one ever took it seriously. Immigrant men disappear without a trace all the time. On purpose."

"But you were right."

"Pat was right," Zachary corrected. "I wasn't the one who thought anything. I was just following the evidence and making inquiries. He was the one who knew that something was wrong."

"Zachary really is a great investigator," Tyrrell told Heather. "He cares about people and he is good at tracking down details and noticing the things that other people don't. I was telling you about the other cases that he's solved recently—"

"I know," Heather agreed. "The paper talked about some of those cases as well. But those are all murder, right? What about something else? What about rape? Do you have any experience with that?"

Zachary looked away, swallowing. "I haven't had a lot of cases that I've investigated, no. But I've worked with other police departments and I'm good at following the clues. I have a friend who helps me with some of the forensics." He didn't tell her that Kenzie was with the medical examiner's office. That might freak Heather out. "So I have all the bases covered. Whatever I don't know, I can contract help on. I doubt there will be much I'll need to go to outside consultants on in a case like this. It sounds pretty straightforward."

"Does it?" When he looked back at her, she leveled her gaze at him. "I haven't told you anything about it."

"I just mean that you dealt with the police on it, so things are straightforward from there. We need to reexamine any data that they have, see if we can figure anything else out… identify suspects…"

"How can you do that? How can you find a suspect when they couldn't all those years ago? You can't talk to people anymore. You don't know who might have seen something or been close by. You don't know who was living in the area. You don't know anything that would help you to identify who it was in those woods all those years ago."

"I'll follow the evidence that the police have on file. I'll get your statement. You may remember more than you think you do. A lot of attacks by strangers, they aren't really strangers. It was probably someone who lived in your neighborhood. They might have seen you coming and going to school or other places. Even if you don't know who it was, the chances that it was someone who just randomly drove into the neighborhood and attacked you are pretty slim."

"Look at Elizabeth Smart. That's what happened to her."

"Even with her, they did have some contact with her father. They had been around the neighborhood and seen her before they targeted her. The police in your case would have canvassed the neighborhood. They would have talked to people they thought were suspicious. They might have talked to the perpetrator and not known it. Or they might have suspected him, but then not been able to prove it. I'll find out what I can."

She nodded slowly, studying him. He waited for her to make her decision. Finally, Heather nodded.

"Okay… I'll tell you what happened. You can talk to the cops, see what they can tell you about the investigation back then." She paused. "I don't think they did much. I never heard about any suspects and they never called me back to ask me anything else."

"They probably wouldn't have told you very much about the investigation, especially since you were a minor. And I don't know how much we'll be able to find of the original file and evidence. Sometimes there isn't a lot. We'll cross our fingers…"

"How much do you charge?" Heather asked, shifting and pulling out her purse to find her checkbook. "I assume you'll need a retainer."

Zachary shook his head and held up his hand. "Oh, no. You're family. I wouldn't charge you…"

"You're trying to make a living, aren't you? If you're working on my case, I want it to get your full attention, not just be something you're doing on the side between paying gigs."

He wanted to tell her that he would give it his full attention whether she paid him or not, but he couldn't quite say that truthfully. Not when he had done Pat's case pro bono. He needed to get a cash injection. He had plenty of small jobs, the bread and butter jobs that would pay his daily bills, but they also filled up his day. If he were going to put in the effort Heather's case deserved, he would have to put some of the others on hold for a few days or weeks.

"So how much?" Heather repeated, pen poised above her checkbook.

CHAPTER THREE

Zachary's mind wouldn't let go of Heather's story as he tried to calm himself down enough to find sleep. He tried to distract himself by thinking about other cases, mundane tasks. It was like counting sheep.

He had been sleeping better since he'd gotten home from the hospital. Not because he was on any different sleep aids. The reason, instead, was that he wanted to shut everything off. The more the stresses built up in his head, the more he just wanted to sleep to shut them off. That had never been the case before. He'd had problems getting to sleep for as long as he could remember.

But since the attack, he was sleeping more and more. He would find himself in bed halfway through the afternoon, unable to cope with the images pressing in on him. He would close his eyes to escape into the nothingness. More than once, he had slept through supper, had slept through Kenzie calling him or knocking on his door, and had wakened long after his usual pre-dawn rising to wonder what the heck had happened to the rest of the hours of the day.

Talking to Heather about her experience decades before had not calmed the beast. Focusing on someone else's experience instead of his own had not distracted him from his own distress. Instead, Heather's recollection had been added to his own; the images pressed in on him, mixing with his own experiences, adding their own weight and insistence.

He pressed his face into the pillow, seeking the darkness of sleep, but when it came it was not silent and quiet.

He dreamed he was walking in the woods. Going home from school, cutting through a green park area. He was enjoying the green of the trees and the birdsong and the rustling of squirrels in the leaves, letting the pressures of the day go. Technically, it was out of bounds, but the space called to him and he couldn't avoid it. What was wrong with walking through a public park on the way home from school? It wasn't like he was damaging property. He always just walked quietly through and didn't break branches, cut his initials into the trees, or litter.

Then he became aware of another presence in the woods with him. Not a squirrel or a bird. Something menacing. There was a presence in the woods with him. He could feel someone watching him.

He turned and looked back the way he had come, weighing whether he ought to retreat and go around the park like he was supposed to. He was past the halfway mark, so it was faster to just keep going through the park. If there were someone else there, it was probably just someone else from school, and they wouldn't want to be caught either. If he actually saw someone threatening, he could run. It wasn't that much farther. He would soon be out the other side of the park and there would be other people around who could help if he needed assistance.

He shifted the backpack on his back, running his thumbs under the shoulder straps. He looked around for any sign of anyone else around him. He looked back behind him once more to make sure he wasn't being followed. He couldn't rid himself of the feeling.

Instead of continuing in a straight line, he stepped off the worn trail and ducked behind a tree. For a minute, he just stayed there, frozen, listening for someone else's footsteps. But he couldn't hear anyone. Just the birds in the trees and the rustling of the leaves. There was another way out of the woods, a twistier path, less traveled. If someone else were in the woods with him, they would continue to follow the well-traveled path. Zachary could take the quieter path and remain unseen.

He took a few tentative steps through the grass and leaves, stopped and listened, and then took a few more, until he reached the faint trail that led through the darker, denser trees.

He had looked back so many times, not expecting the danger to come from ahead of him. And instead of avoiding trouble, he had walked right into it. A dark shape stepped out of the trees and, before he could turn and run, grabbed him.

Zachary let out a shout and jerked back, trying to pull away. But the man held him tightly.

He towered over Zachary, much taller than he was, face covered with a black balaclava that was a sharp contrast to the warm spring weather. The eyes were blue, fringed with eyelashes that were long and dark, almost feminine.

"Let go!" Zachary croaked, trying to pull away.

But the intruder didn't let go. With a glistening knife held at Zachary's throat, he pulled Zachary deeper into the woods. He looked around, making sure that they were alone and no one else who followed the trails through the park would be able to see them.

CHAPTER FOUR

Zachary's own scream woke him up. He thrashed around, trying to get loose of the blankets, sure that the man was still holding on to him. He could still feel the man's weight pinning him down. His heart thudded hard and he fought back against the images of Archuro admiring his knife, laughing at Zachary's inability to get loose from him, the drugs preventing Zachary from being able to control his body properly. Archuro could see the panic in his expression and drank it in, high on Zachary's terror. He talked to him in a low, pleasant voice, talking about the things he would do to Zachary, all of the delightful tortures he had in store. He had honed his craft on the many men who had come before Zachary and looked forward to the rituals he had developed.

Zachary stumbled out of bed, needing to prove to himself that he had control over his own body and wasn't still lying in bed to be victimized again. His limbs were clumsy and his head spun, but he was able to control his body enough to stumble and crash his way into the bathroom to turn on the light and look at himself.

His face was slick with sweat, his eyes and hair wild. But the bruises and cuts that had been on his face were gone, what remained blending in with the other scars from the past.

He was not the one who had been attacked cutting through the woods on the way home from school. His experiences had been different. That was not his memory.

With shaking hands, he filled a glass with water and raised it to his lips. His mouth was as dry as a desert. Maybe a side effect of his meds, rather than the terror of the dream. His throat hurt from screaming. He wondered how long he had been yelling before he had woken himself up. He wouldn't like to be one of his own neighbors, wondering what the heck the weirdo next door was screaming about again. Maybe they thought he watched horror movies late at night.

He sat down on the lid of the toilet, breathing and trying to get his body calmed down. He was still fully dressed. He squinted at the bedroom clock, trying to read the time. Two in the morning. He should go back to bed and try to sleep more, but he didn't want to fall back into that dream. He'd been sleeping enough lately that being short on sleep one night wouldn't be a problem. He was used to being chronically short on sleep.

For a while, he just sat there, hands on his face, elbows on his knees, and sought equilibrium. He focused on other images; happier times with Kenzie, Bridget, Tyrrell, Lorne Peterson. The amazing fact that he'd met another of his siblings. That was a highlight in his life, not something to be upset about. He knew two of his siblings now. In the future, maybe there would be more. Maybe eventually, he would have contact with all of them.

They might get together for some holiday reunion and talk and share memories together. Good memories of the games they had played and other things they had done together. Not the fire and the break-up of the family.

Zachary got up, letting out a long, calming breath. He combed his hair and had another drink of water. He splashed cold water on his face and bloodshot eyes. Then he went to his computer.

———

He worked through reports that he hadn't completed and made sure that he got final billings out to all of the clients he had finished the work for. He wanted to clear the decks of as much as he could before diving into Heather's case, and to make sure that he had billed everyone he could so that the household bills would be covered even if Heather's case took longer than usual. He had to stay on top of the money if he wanted to stay in business. He hated accounting and hated asking people to pay up, even though he knew he was providing a valuable service and that he should expect to get paid for it. It sometimes felt like making money off of someone else's painful experience was unethical.

He did some research into cold cases and what police were solving with new technology. He was going to need to know what to look for and what to ask for as he went over Heather's case. It wouldn't get him anywhere if some file clerk just gave it a cursory scan to make sure that nothing new had popped up on the case. He needed to stay on top of it and to ask the right questions.

There were a lot of advancements in forensics. Back when Heather had been attacked, there would not have been much for the forensics guys to do when they got her evidence. They needed something to compare it against before they could provide any useful information. There weren't the same databases and computer matching abilities as there were thirty years later. Technology had blown up. As long as they had stored Heather's evidence properly, the police might be able to use it to find a DNA match to her attacker and get him put behind bars or, if he were already there, to keep him there.

Light had crept in through the windows until the whole apartment was bright, and Zachary looked at the system clock and decided it was time to take a break. He wasn't hungry, but he forced himself to go to the fridge and pick something for breakfast. His stomach just didn't appreciate food first thing in the morning, and later on, his appetite would be low because of his meds. A lot of the time he was nauseated, and that didn't help when he was supposed to be putting weight back on so that his doctor and Kenzie would stop getting on his case about how he looked like a skeleton or a scarecrow. He picked up a cup of cherry yogurt and put it on the table beside a granola bar. The kind with chocolate chips. It was his way of bribing himself to eat breakfast.

He got out a clean spoon and sat down, staring at the food, which, in spite of the sugar levels, seemed incredibly unappetizing. He removed the wrapper from the granola bar and the lid from the yogurt and sat looking at them, smelling them and waiting for his mouth to start watering in antici-pation. But of course, he had no such luck. He slid his spoon into the yogurt and managed to finish it off in a few quick swallows. He took the granola bar with him to the computer, even though he was usually disciplined about not eating around the electronics. He would nibble at it while he was checking his social networks and email, and it would be gone before he knew it.

CHAPTER FIVE

couple of hours later, he decided it was time to make the call to the Clintock police department, where Heather's rape case had been reported. The day shift would be in and would hopefully have had their coffees and have cleared all of the morning emergencies out of the way. He dialed the main number and prepared himself to have to tell his story to several people as they transferred him around and tried to figure out who would talk to him about getting Heather's file and evidence pulled for a new review. Police tended not to like it when people started inquiring about old cold cases. They preferred to let sleeping cases lie, or to let someone else do the footwork. He waited for the formal greeting from the duty officer, stating her name and the department and asking how she could help him.

"My sister asked me if I would call about an old case of hers to see if anything can be done to move it forward," he explained. "I'm not sure who to ask for, whether I need to talk to someone in archives, or in sex crimes, or whether there is a department that reviews cold cases regularly…"

She made an irritated noise in the back of her throat. "How old is this case?"

"Thirty years."

"Oh, good grief. It won't even be here anymore."

"I imagine it's in a warehouse somewhere," Zachary agreed. "But it is a rape, and there's no statute of limitations, right? So it stays open as a cold case indefinitely."

"I suppose so. Is there new evidence to be considered?"

"No new evidence," Zachary admitted. "But there is the old evidence to be considered. There is a lot more they can do with the forensics that they collected back then. You never know, we might just get a hit on CODIS."

"It happens," the woman allowed. "But you don't know what evidence might have been collected that long ago. Whose file is this?"

"My sister's. She's asked me to look into it and see if I can find anything out. We'll need to pull the file and the evidence before we know if there is anything that can be pursued."

"Maybe she should just let it go. It was a long time ago. She should go on and live her life."

Zachary could find nothing to say to that. He sat with his mouth open, waiting for the words to come, but he couldn't think of an appropriate answer. Would the policewoman have said the same thing if it were a murder or kidnapping? Just go on with your life and don't worry about it? Maybe she would have. Maybe she didn't understand that a violent crime could leave a black hole in the middle of a person's life, pulling everything into it, swallowing up all of the light and goodness that was created anywhere else and leaving nothing but a bare crater behind. Someone who hadn't personally experienced a crime like rape or murder... maybe she just didn't understand how it consumed a person's whole life.

"Are you still there?" the duty officer asked eventually.

"Yes."

"I guess you'd better give me her name and any other information you have. The year of the offense. If you have a file number or the name of the officer who opened it. Anything else."

Zachary dutifully gave her Heather's name and birthdate, and the date of the assault. "She didn't have the file number or the name of the officer. She was only fourteen at the time. It would have been her foster mother that had that information."

"Poor kid. Well, this will be enough to start, but it may take a while for us to find the file and evidence and get it back here. Are you in town?"

"No, but I'm in Vermont. I'll come in once you find it."

"Don't expect a lot," she warned again.

"I know. I've told Heather not to get her hopes up. But if there is anything… I have to at least try. See if I can bring her some kind of peace. If we can get the guy who did this to her behind bars, or keep him behind bars…"

"If it was investigated at the time, they would have run down all of the leads. It could have been someone who lived out of town, even out of the state. And if there is any evidence left, it might be completely degraded by now. You don't know if it will be usable."

"Yeah."

There was the tapping of keys and Zachary didn't know whether he should say goodbye and get off of the line, or wait for her to say something else.

"I am getting a hit on our archives catalog," the duty officer offered. "So we do have something at the warehouse. That's good news. That means that at least you called the right police department. You wouldn't believe the number of times when people don't even know what police department a file was opened with. We spend hours looking for a 'lost' case, only to find out that it was opened in another county. Or even another state."

"Memories are faulty," Zachary acknowledged. "Especially if it's someone like Heather, who was only a child at the time. I don't remember the details of a lot of the homes that I was in. If they move a kid to another city to get away from a bad influence, he might not even remember a year or two later."

"Mmm-hmm." Her voice was distant, as if she weren't really listening to him.

"So, you'll put in a request for that file and then let me know? And I'll come in to talk to whatever officer it's assigned to and we can work through what evidence there is and if there are any other leads to pursue?"

"Yes, that's right. *Who* exactly are you?"

Her tone made it sound like she had suddenly discovered he had told her a lie or was trying to pull something over on her.

"Uh. My name is Zachary Goldman. Heather is my sister…"

"But who are you? You're not a reporter…?"

"No. I…" he wondered if she recognized his name from the news and was trying to place it. "I'm a private investigator, actually. That's why Heather thought I might be able to help. Find a lead that hadn't been considered before."

"Oh, you're a PI. Well, that changes things."

"I don't see how. I'm just helping my sister out, like I said."

"Our department doesn't work with private investigators."

"I'm looking into it for my sister. I'll bring her along when the officer is ready, if I can, but she's traumatized. I don't know whether I'll be able to get her in. If I can't, do you need her to fill out an authorization or something to talk to the officer?"

"We'll definitely need her written authorization. And I don't know if they'll accept it if it's for a private investigator. Like I said, we don't deal with PIs."

"I'll deal with whatever forms you need me to. I'm Heather's brother." It was obviously going to be a tricky situation, and he was actually grateful that the duty officer had tipped him off to it before he had to deal with the officer who would be in charge of the file when it was brought out of storage. He wouldn't mention to them that he was a private investigator, just Heather's brother.

––––––

Zachary had been checking his social networks when an alert came up on his computer and he saw that he had an incoming video call. It was Lorne Peterson, his former foster father and probably his best friend, so he couldn't turn down the call without a good reason. If he were in the middle of something important or a conference with a client, that was one thing, but he had just been taking a break to look at his email and social networks, and Lorne had probably seen that he was online in a status line. Zachary let it ring for a minute while his mind jumped ahead, trying to script the call. He clicked to answer it.

He would have turned off the video and just done a voice call, except that the whole reason Mr. Peterson was calling using video chat was so that they could talk face-to-face. Zachary had promised that they could see each other more often that way so that he didn't have to make the two-hour drive to see Lorne and Pat for them to see that he was okay. So he let the video load, and in a minute was looking at the round face and fringe of white hair that was so familiar and important to him. He couldn't help smiling at Mr. Peterson's cheerful smile.

"Hi."

"Zachary! Believe it or not, I actually set up the call myself this time."

He gave a self-satisfied nod, as if he had conquered a difficult task. "I'll get the hang of this yet!"

"Great job." Zachary rubbed his face and scratched at his stubbly skin, looking at himself in the smaller picture in the corner of his screen. "I don't actually look as bad as this video makes me look, trust me."

"It's just good to see you. You don't have to get all dressed up for me."

"Yeah, but I could have at least combed my hair and washed my face." Zachary rubbed his slightly-bleary eyes. At least with the buzz cut, he didn't really have to do anything to take care of his hair. And he had splashed water on his face; that had to count for something.

"So tell me what's new. I can't believe how fast the time goes by. It seems like you were just here, but it's been weeks."

They had, at least, talked in that time, so Zachary didn't have to feel guilty about not having gone to visit Lorne and Pat during that time. "I saw Tyrrell yesterday. He says 'hi.'"

"Oh, I'm glad to hear that you got together. He's such a nice young man. Tell him 'hi' from me too. How is he doing?"

"Seems to be doing pretty well. He actually called me because one of my sisters wanted to meet me. Heather."

"Really? Zach, that's fantastic. How was it?"

"It was nice to see her again. She's… a lot older."

Mr. Peterson laughed. "I would guess so!"

There was movement behind him on the screen and, in a moment, Pat was leaning over Lorne's shoulder to look at Zachary. "Hi, Zachary! How's it going?" Pat was younger than Lorne. Not a young man anymore, looking more distinguished with some gray at his temples, but still vigorous and fit.

"Good, Pat. How about you?"

"Can't complain. I'll leave you two alone. I just wanted to make sure that Lorne hadn't run into any problem and that I got to say 'hi.'"

"Thanks!"

Pat withdrew again. Mr. Peterson watched him leave, smiling fondly. "Okay, where were we? Oh, your sister. Which one?"

"Heather. Second-oldest."

"Right. How did that go? Did you have a good visit?"

"Well, it wasn't really much catching up… she had T contact me so that she could talk to me about a cold case she wanted me to look into."

"Oh." Mr. Peterson's eyebrows climbed upward. "What kind of a case?"

"She was assaulted as a teenager. They never caught the guy who did it, and she's thinking that now with the technological advances, maybe they'll be able to, and she can rest a little easier knowing that he's off the streets."

"The poor girl. Do you think you'll be able to help her? It's been so long."

"I know it's been a long time, but with DNA testing and some of the other forensics they can do now, I think there's at least a good chance that they'll be able to make some kind of break on the case. It's worth looking at, anyway. And there might be other leads on the file that I can follow up on. Sometimes just a fresh pair of eyes on a case…"

"Well, I hope it works out. After this long, I'm sure she'd be glad to get a little justice. But it was a long time ago…"

"Yeah. We're all trying not to get our hopes up about everything just falling into place and being able to pin it on someone."

CHAPTER SIX

Zachary gave it a few days before calling the police department of Clintock again, hoping that they would call him back and let him know that the file had arrived. But there was no word, so eventually, he called again to find out if they had made any progress. Sometimes he just didn't hear from people until he started to make some noise. There was a different officer on duty on the main phone number, and he muttered under his breath while he tapped information into the computer, trying to get the system to spit out the status of the case that Zachary had requested. Not complaining about Zachary, just a steady stream of search terms, talking to the computer, and cursing the makers of the software and computer for making it so difficult to find what it was he was looking for.

"Okay... Heather Goldman, is that what you said?"

"Yes. That's right."

"Looks like there was a request to pull the file. I just have to jump over to another database to see where it is in the system..." More muttering. "Looks like we got it. It should have been assigned to an officer. Why isn't it showing up on the damn system?" The duty officer pounded the keys, frustrated and trying to beat an answer out of the computer. "There's the file in the log, so whose desk did it end up on? Just a minute. Can you hold?"

Before Zachary could answer, the man was gone and he was listening to some easy listening version of U2. Zachary rolled his eyes and put down his phone, switching it to speaker phone so he could keep himself occupied while the officer tried to track down the file. Several songs played, and he was getting sick of whatever station they had it tuned to. It had to qualify as some kind of torture to have to listen to that music for more than a minute. Zachary checked his email and went through the next few bits of spam and responses on other files. It would be ironic if he got an email from the officer who had been charged with Heather's case while the duty officer was trying to track down that information. But no such luck.

"Hello? Are you there?"

"Oh, hi." Zachary tapped the phone off of speaker mode and picked it back up. "I'm here. Were you able to track it down?"

"I was able, and he is Able."

"What?"

"It's been assigned to Detective Able. I'll put you through. Do you want his number in case you have to call back later?"

"Yes, please."

The Duty Officer read the number off to him and Zachary jotted it down. Then he was ringing through to Detective Able without another word. Zachary didn't know whether the Duty Officer had already talked to Detective Able to give him a warning that he was putting a call through or not, so he again prepared to start from the beginning.

"Able."

"Uh… hi, Detective Able. I don't know if anyone told you, but I'm Zachary Goldman and I'm calling about a file that has apparently been assigned to you. A cold case for my sister, Heather Goldman."

"Yeah, I saw that. Goldman…" He made a noise for Zachary to wait while he apparently looked through his inbox or a stack of files that had ended up on his desk. "Yeah, here it is. Heather Goldman. This is a dusty one!" Able sneezed. "Nineteen eighty-nine. Really?"

"Yes, really. She was only fourteen at the time. It would be nice if we could find something that would help her to move on."

"Who's going to find something after this long?"

Zachary hoped that he wasn't assigned too many cold cases to review, if that was his approach.

"You never know. There have been a lot of advancements in technology," Zachary started again, "There might be—"

"Technology isn't going to be able to help us much in this case." There was the sound of turning pages as Able looked over the file.

"What do you mean?"

"I mean that all I've got here is paper. Maybe there is a police sketch or something that they could age-advance, but other than that, about the only technology that's going to be used in this case is eyes on paper."

"You didn't get the physical evidence? Maybe it was transferred to your medical examiner or forensic department...?"

"No physical evidence here," Able agreed. "If they transferred evidence to another department for testing, there should at least be a sticky on the file, and I don't see anything. There is no physical evidence on this file."

"But a rape kit was done."

"No, it doesn't look like it."

"I think Heather knows whether there was a rape kit done or not. They take several hours and she has a very clear recollection of it."

"Witness recall is often faulty. She might have had to go to the hospital for some follow up and thought that they did a kit. But there wasn't anything sent back with the file."

CHAPTER SEVEN

Zachary went to Clintock without Heather. He wasn't about to drag her all that way just to find out that they hadn't managed to find the forensic evidence that had been collected all of those years ago. She had been as traumatized with the collection of the evidence as she had been by the assault itself, and he understood better than anyone how it would feel for all of that evidence to be lost after the ordeal it had been to collect it in the first place. He'd wait until he had something concrete to tell her.

The town brought back memories. He had lived there for most of his growing-up years. The shape of the place had changed; there were new buildings and broader streets and other indications of the progress of time, but he recognized a lot of what he saw. The hospital, the skyline, though it was much more crowded now. The residential streets that he had walked or been taken over by bus or social workers or foster parents. He passed one of his old schools, and tried hard not to be sucked into the memories. He had been at a lot of different schools, and he didn't remember specifically anything that had happened at that one, but that just meant a flood of unfiltered memories rose up around him, threatening to drown him in flashbacks. He kept driving, refusing to be distracted, trying to keep them all at bay.

Because of Heather's case and the time he had spent thinking about it, memories of school bullies and foster families who had threatened or assaulted him were at the forefront, pressing for him to remember what he had worked so hard to forget. He stared at the road and reviewed his route to the police station in his mind, trying to keep everything else out. How was it going to help Heather for him to remember what had happened to him as a kid? He might be able to be sympathetic to her, but that didn't help to solve her case.

It was a little better once the school was out of sight again, and he pressed forward, finding the police station and looking for the public parking.

It was a building that he knew. He hadn't been there as Heather had, reporting the assault that had happened to her. Instead, he was pretty sure it was the station he had been taken to that first December after the fire. With the first anniversary of the fire looming large ahead of him, he had run away, and had, for a day at least, joined up with a group of older, more experienced street kids and learned some of the ropes of street life.

It was cold and he'd left home without the clothing he would need to get through the bitter nights on the street. He had worn the coat that he would wear to get from the climate-controlled house to the warm car, not the kind of gear he would need to keep warm all day and all night outside. Unfortunately, he and his partner in crime had been caught shoplifting warmer clothes, and he had been taken to the police station where his social worker had picked him up.

He could clearly remember sitting there on a bench with older criminals around him, waiting for Mrs. Pratt to pick him up, unsure where he would go or what he would do once she arrived.

As it turned out, he hadn't been able to handle it when she took him back to his foster family, and she had eventually taken him to Bonnie Brown, the children's secure care facility, where they could keep him safe for the next couple of weeks until he could get past the anniversary. It had been a relief to get away from the Christmas tree, candles, and wood-frame house and to know that he wasn't going to be caught in another fire on Christmas Eve. But unlike Scrooge's Christmas Eve visitors, those ghosts had continued to haunt him all through his life, whenever the anniversary approached again.

Zachary swallowed and had a drink of his cold coffee. He got out of the car and went to the front doors of the police station. He wasn't a child anymore. He was a grown man and no one there would have any idea of his past history. Not that they would care, even if they knew. He wasn't a master criminal. He was just a guy who'd had a troubled childhood.

He waited at the front desk and then introduced himself, explaining that he'd set up an appointment with Detective Able.

———

Detective Able called Zachary's name and motioned him to follow. He was an older cop, maybe riding a desk until retirement. He had dark hair with plenty of gray. He was a little too heavy, not in the same shape he'd been as a patrol officer on the streets.

"Nice to meet you," he said to Zachary, not meeting his eye or paying any attention to see if he answered or not. He led Zachary through a number of corridors to a small meeting room. It was furnished with a wood conference table and soft chairs, not the spare, sturdier furniture of an inter-rogation room. A room intended for meetings with families and victims, not violent offender interviews.

There was an old, yellowing folder on the table. Maybe half an inch thick, with an archival bar code on the front and Heather's name neatly printed in black felt pen on the tab. Able motioned for Zachary to have a seat on the side of the table, not the head where the folder was.

"So Heather is your sister?"

"Yes."

Able stared at him. Zachary worked his wallet out of his back pocket and produced his driver's license. He also unfolded the authorization note Heather had written and smoothed it out on the table while Able examined his license and compared the picture to Zachary's face. He'd lost weight since the picture had been taken, but it was still a good enough likeness. Able glanced at the authorization letter but didn't read it, pick it up, or make a copy. He sat down in front of the folder.

"So you remember when she was attacked? You were how old?"

"I would have been twelve."

"So you probably weren't told much."

"I was in a different foster home. We were only recently reunited, I didn't hear about it at the time."

"And what has she told you?"

"The basics. A stranger attack when she was walking home from school through a wooded area." Zachary swallowed and tried to keep his voice unemotional. "She was dragged to an isolated area and assaulted at knife point, then released. She told her foster mom and that started the whole investigation."

Able nodded. He opened the file. Zachary could see the edges of the yellowing pages, all trued up at the top and inserted into a two-prong fastener. There were brown, heat-transfer fax reports that were probably completely unreadable if they hadn't been copied onto regular paper. Some colored forms. Heather's sad story, all reduced to a small sheaf of papers. Just like Zachary's experience with Archuro, all summarized in bald, unfeeling description by someone removed from the experience. But it was good that it was all reduced to words on paper. That meant that it was recorded for anyone who needed to know the details and he could forget about it. He didn't have to think about being trapped in the dark, dirty shack, too drugged to do anything to stop a man who wanted nothing more than to control and degrade him.

"Sir...?"

Zachary caught his breath, startled. He looked at Able and tried to relax his body. This interview wasn't about him. It was about Heather. Helping her to find the man who had hurt her and to put him behind bars or somehow assure her that he wouldn't be able to hurt anyone else again.

He cleared his throat. "It doesn't look like there's a whole lot to go on there."

Able looked down at it again. "They investigated what they could. But Miss Goldman was not able to provide them with any kind of description of her attacker. Average height and build, white, wearing a mask. No identifying features. Nothing that she noticed about him. You would think that she could have at least given eye color, but maybe not. Maybe it was too dark or her eyes were shut or she was just too panicked to notice."

"So what did they do? Canvassed the neighborhood to see if anyone had seen anything? Check registered sex offenders in the area?"

"No sex offender registry until 1996. They checked anyone known to police. But without a description, there wasn't much they could do."

"What about the rape kit?"

Able looked down at the folder, fiddling with one of the corners. He flipped through a few pages as if looking it up, but Zachary knew from his body language that he already knew what he was going to tell Zachary, and it wasn't good news. Able searched for a form and held the other pages in place so they wouldn't flop back down over it.

"She was taken to the hospital and a forensic sexual assault kit was performed that day, as well as treating her injuries." He looked up at Zachary. "He beat her up pretty good. Her foster mother couldn't have helped but see that something had happened to her."

Zachary nodded. Heather hadn't told him those details, but he wasn't surprised. Rape wasn't about love or sex. It was about violence and control. Depravity.

"So what were they able to discover from the forensics at the time?"

"Not a lot. The technology wasn't where it is now. There were dark hairs recovered. Straight. They should have done blood typing, but I don't see any on the file. It was too long ago for any kind of DNA testing."

"But that can be done now, if the samples were preserved."

Able didn't look at him. Zachary waited. The duty officer had told him that there wasn't any physical evidence. He wasn't sure how they could have done a rape kit and then lost it, but it was decades before. Things went astray. Got mis-cataloged. It happened.

"The rape kit was destroyed," Able said finally.

"Destroyed. By accident?"

"No. It wasn't the same as it is now… They couldn't use it to develop a profile. They could only test it against suspects, compare samples. If there were no suspects, and the case wasn't going anywhere… they had a policy."

"A policy on what?"

"On retention of rape kit evidence. They were only retained for two years."

"Two years? But there's no statute of limitations on rape."

Able scratched his ear. "There's no statute of limitations on *aggravated* sexual assault. Sexual assault has a six-year limitation. But back at the beginning of eighty-nine, before your sister's case… aggravated was six years and sexual assault was three years."

"But if they destroyed the evidence at two years…"

"That was just the policy at the time. In some jurisdictions, it was as little as six months. Or if it didn't look like there was any chance of solving the case… it might be ditched within a few weeks. They never anticipated

that we'd be able to do anything with it decades later. It was beyond imagination."

Zachary sat back in his chair, head spinning. After all that Heather had
gone through, the rape, the kit, and the decades of emotional trauma that
followed her everywhere she went, she was going to have to face the fact
that all of the hard evidence in the case had been destroyed, and with it, any
chance of identifying the unknown man.

He would still go through the motions of following up on every lead
and trying to solve the crime, but the chances that the police who had
initially investigated it had overlooked some obvious clue that was still
usable thirty years later were slim to none. Without the evidence, they were
up the creek.

"Sorry," Able said without looking at him. "Wish I had some better
news for you. But maybe… this is a sign that it's time for her to just move
on, and give up on the case ever being solved."

Like the duty officer Zachary had talked to the first day, Able didn't
seem to have any comprehension of just how impossible that was. He had
no doubt that Heather had tried to move on. She had gone on to get
married and have a family. But she hadn't been able to leave it behind and
had finally turned to Zachary for help. He hated the fact that he was going
to have to tell her that it wasn't going to work.

"Well…" Able closed the file and started to heft himself up from the
table. "I'll show you out."

"I still want to look at the file," Zachary said, not getting up.

"Why would you want to do that? There's nothing in there. I'm telling
you. I've read through it. They did everything they could, and they weren't
able to find the perp. Being able to find a stranger without any forensics is
hard enough when it just happened. But decades later? There's no way. It
can't be done."

Zachary nodded. "I know. But I need to do this for her."

Able stared at him, waiting for him to reconsider and come to his
senses.

Zachary bit his lip. He shook his head. "I've been where she is. I know
what she's going through. I have to do what I can. Maybe I can't do
anything for her, but I have to try. This is all my fault. I have to try to make
it right."

"Your fault?" Able questioned, not sitting back down, but towering over

Zachary and making him feel ten years old all over again. "You said that you weren't even in the same home as her. So how could any of this be your fault?"

"It was because of me that she was there, in that home. It's my fault that we all got separated and had to go into foster care. Because of the stuff that I did. If I hadn't… then we would both have still been home with our biological parents, and this wouldn't have happened to her."

"I'm not exactly a fatalist, but I don't think it's that simple. I think some stuff is going to happen, no matter what, we can't stop it. If it didn't happen in that foster home when she was fourteen… then maybe in another when she was sixteen. Do you know how many women are sexually assaulted at some point in their lifetime? Yeah, kids in foster care are a big target group, girls and boys, but outside of foster care, a high percentage of women still get assaulted. And some women are just natural targets, no matter what they might do to try to protect themselves." He shrugged his thick shoulders. "You can't put that all on yourself."

"The only reason she got in contact with me again was because she thought that maybe I might be able to help her out with this. That maybe there was someone who could understand what she had been through and who cared enough to try to get her justice."

Zachary reached for the file.

"It's a small file. It won't take that long for me to read through. I can make my own notes, right? I can make notes, just not photocopy it?"

Able stood there looking at him. "She's lucky to have you, but you're an idiot. Go ahead. Read the file. You're just putting yourself through extra emotional trauma that you don't have to. Cops have to face this stuff and deal with the emotional fallout that comes from seeing the world's depravity. You don't have to."

Zachary pulled the file over to himself and opened it up. He said nothing, just looked at the first page in the file, which was the last page chronologically, and skimmed over it.

Able paused in the doorway. "I'm just across the hall. Give me a shout if you have any questions. Check out at the front desk when you leave. Leave the file and everything in it here."

He left the conference room, shutting the door much harder than he needed to.

CHAPTER EIGHT

Z achary looked at the first page of the file after Able was gone. It was a densely handwritten form, and he knew from experience that he wasn't going to be able to get through the whole file or to absorb everything he read. He was better at reading than he had been in school, but he'd also taught himself some tricks. One of them was to use the tools at hand and to give himself lots of time to go over things repeatedly, getting another layer of knowledge each time.

Able wasn't there directly supervising him and, as far as Zachary knew, the video surveillance inside the room hadn't been turned on either, so he pulled out his phone and went to work. He opened up the two-prong fastener so that he could lay each page flat and work with one at a time instead of trying to hold the file open like Able had. He took a quick photo of each page, and the camera straightened and squared them and started processing them in the background. It wouldn't be able to interpret the handwriting, but it would be able to OCR the typewritten information so that he could search it for keywords later. And he would have all the time he needed to read and re-read each page of the file.

He skimmed each page as he took his photos, reading the form headings and phrases on the typewritten statements and reports. Incident report. Evidence logs. Who had been questioned, what streets had been canvassed. He would go through it all and make sure that no lead had been left unfollowed. Did she have classmates who knew what was going on? Had other girls been assaulted? Had there been any eyewitnesses who saw the man in the mask or someone dressed in dark colors as he had been? He could put together a profile. They could find *something* out. Even if it didn't lead anywhere, at least he could show her that he had done everything he could to help her out.

He stopped when he got to the pictures.

Long, spindly arms and legs. Unruly or uncombed blond hair pulled back into a messy ponytail. Bruises all over her body. He had cut her throat a couple of times, minor lacerations. He hadn't drugged her. He'd used force and violence to keep her under control.

Zachary laid the pictures out one at a time and snapped photos of them. Her eyes had been blocked out, and in some of the pictures, the more intimate parts of her body, but they had taken close-ups of those areas as well, showing the bruising and tearing. He felt nauseated, but went on, working his way mechanically through the stack. Maybe Kenzie would be able to tell something from the photos. Something that they now knew on a visual inspection that they wouldn't have known back then.

He was relieved when he got through the small stack of photos and got back to statements and questions. There was commentary on what Heather had been wearing at the time. Where she had been and the time of day. All pointing toward the authorities thinking that she'd gotten herself into the situation by being careless. Or worse, that she'd been asking for it. That had been the culture at the time. Victim blaming. Shaming. Rather than being kind and gentle in their questions, they would attack her with their words, trying to break her. Trying to get her to admit that it had all been her fault or that she had made it all up.

Zachary himself had known, even at a very young age, that he couldn't go to the authorities with complaints about the abuse that he received. He had known that they would blame him. Didn't he get blamed for everything else? Didn't they always tell him that it was his own fault when he got hurt? He was too impulsive, he made stupid decisions, he took risks. He never stopped to think about what he was doing or what the consequences could be.

Going to anyone to report sexual abuse would just be admitting that he wasn't big enough, strong enough, or man enough. That kind of thing didn't happen to *real* men. And Zachary, always small for his age, always skinny with twigs for arms, did not need to be told how unmanly he was.

———

When he got back home, he wanted nothing more than to just lie down and go to sleep again and shut out the rest of the world, especially all that he'd just seen of what had befallen Heather.

First, Heather had been attacked. Then she'd had to endure the questioning at the hands of the policemen who wanted to find out whether it had really been an attack, or whether she had somehow consented or asked for it. They should have known, looking at her bruises, just as her foster mother had known, that there was no issue of whether consent had been given. Heather had obviously been attacked. It hadn't been some kind of frat party mistake. It hadn't been a date. Even if she had arranged to meet with someone—and Zachary believed her when she said she hadn't—that person had been there only to victimize Heather.

Had her foster mother not known what kind of culture they would face if she took Heather in? Maybe she was a militant mom, wanting to change the world and make things better for her foster kids, even at their own expense. Zachary remembered then that she hadn't had a lot of foster kids. Heather said that she had two older sons and had wanted to take in a girl. So Heather wasn't one of many, as Zachary had usually been when he was placed in a new family, but just one girl, maybe their only foster. Maybe her mother hadn't known what kind of a world was out there for a teenage girl who was just trying to find her way in the world and hadn't known the kind of rape culture that they lived in.

Zachary was thinking longingly of his bed from at least ten miles away. But when he got up to his apartment door, he could see that someone had been there. There was a sticky note at eye level, beside the peephole.

I'm here. K

Kenzie. She knew better than to surprise him by being in his apartment unannounced. Even though he had given her a key, she still didn't usually go into the apartment if he weren't there. She knew that he had previously called the police on Bridget when he had thought there was an intruder in his apartment. Best not to startle him or to have the police on the scene because of a visit from his girlfriend.

Zachary pulled the note off of the door and turned the handle. Without the note, he would have noticed that the door was unlocked, and that would have set off all kinds of alarm bells. He closed and locked the door behind him and walked through the kitchen into the living room.

"Hey." He gave Kenzie a smile and held up the note. "Thanks for letting me know."

"I figured it was better not to give you a heart attack."

"Yeah. Much appreciated."

She knew how jumpy he had been since the attack. It wouldn't be hard to send him into a flashback.

"Long day?" Kenzie asked, looking him over.

Zachary rubbed his eyes with the pads of his fingers. "Yeah, a little rough."

"Come sit down." She patted the couch cushion next to him. "Get yourself a drink and come relax and tell me about it."

He went to the fridge for a soft drink and returned.

"I'm working on a new case." He elected not to tell her that it was Heather. She could be more objective if she didn't know that it was his sister. And he wasn't sure how comfortable he was sharing Heather's story with anyone without her express permission. "It's a cold case. Really cold. Thirty years ago."

"A murder?"

"Aggravated sexual assault."

She cocked her head. "Do you really think that's wise?"

"Why?"

"I just think... you've been having such a hard time since... you know... Archuro... I didn't think you'd want to be reminded about what happened to you."

Not that he'd told her anything about what Teddy had done. But she wasn't stupid.

"I'm just fine." He popped the top of his can and wiggled closer to her, cuddling up to show her that he was over what had happened with Teddy Archuro and she didn't need to worry about dealing with a head-case. No more than usual.

"Okay. If you're sure. I wouldn't want it to set you off."

He thought about his nightmares the night before and didn't admit to her or himself that she might be right. He was over it. He was completely okay dealing with Heather's case.

"Anyway… I had to drive out to look at the police file today and see what we had to go on."

"I gather from your tone that it wasn't very much."

"No. The file is pretty small, and it looks like they pretty much blamed her for what had happened. Why was a young woman walking through the park on her own, you know? And even though she had a sexual assault kit done… the evidence was all destroyed. There's nothing left to test."

"Ouch. That's not very helpful. I had heard that a lot of kits had been destroyed. Or else stored but never tested."

"I'd understand if it was never tested. They didn't have the ability to do it back then, and they can't have every kit that was ever taken tested all at once. There has to be some kind of decision made as to priority, and then it takes time. But destroying it… I just can't fathom how they thought that was a good idea at the time. The statute of limitations wasn't even up. How could they ever prosecute anyone if they destroyed all of the evidence?"

"I guess they didn't think there was any way they'd ever be bringing anyone to trial."

"Exactly. A stranger attack, no one to try to match it against… so they just decided it was worthless." Zachary shook his head. "Tell me that wouldn't happen with today's protocols and procedures. Tell me that there are no destruction polices for hard evidence in a murder or aggravated assault."

"Most of the police departments have pretty strict retention policies now. Which causes other difficulties, like finding enough warehouse space."

Zachary sipped his cold drink, savoring the sweetness at the end of a long, hard day. Of course, a beer would be even better, but he intentionally didn't keep any alcohol in the apartment.

"So it was a wasted trip?"

"I'm still going to find out what I can. See if I can pick up on any leads or avenues they might have left unexplored. But I'm not really hopeful of finding anything like that… much less the rapist. It was just too long ago. We can't go back and question people who were in the area at the time."

"There might still be some old residents. But after thirty years, you're not going to have a whole lot of luck that way. Either people weren't there that long ago, or if they were old enough to observe anything and know that there was a problem, they are getting on in years now and aren't reliable as witnesses."

"Yeah. We might be able to find a nosy neighbor, if we're lucky, but the chances that the neighbor would have a lead that was never followed up on..."

"Not great," Kenzie agreed.

"I have some pictures. Do you want to look at them?"

Kenzie shrugged. "If you want. How bad are they?"

"She was pretty battered. But I'm sure you've seen worse."

"I probably have, but sexual assault is always a difficult one to deal with."

"Worse than murdered children?"

Kenzie just had a sip of her drink and didn't answer.

Zachary grabbed his tablet and pulled up his photo stream to look at the pictures of the file photos. He made sure they were not labeled on the front with Heather's name, then passed the tablet over to Kenzie to allow her to examine them. Kenzie put her drink down on the coffee table and slowly swiped through the photos. A couple of times she panned or zoomed the pictures, taking a closer look.

"Poor girl. He must have been pretty strong."

"That's what I figured." There had been a lot of bruising. Her arms where he had held her down. Her battered face. Her ribs and her thighs. She had fought back, but he had overwhelmed her with force.

"I think these are bite marks," Kenzie said, pointing to one of the bruises, outlining a semicircle shape. "We can compare those to the guy's teeth, if you get a suspect. Teeth do change over time, they might have drifted or he might even have had braces to straighten them later in life. He could have implants or dentures now. But if you're lucky, he's still got his permanent teeth and hasn't done anything with them, and we'll still be able to compare the positions against the bruises."

Zachary nodded eagerly. At least it was something. It wouldn't help him to find a suspect, but if he had one, they might be able to rule him in or out. "That would be good."

"If it was modern-day, they would have swabbed those for saliva, and have a DNA profile."

He was quiet while she continued to look through the pictures.

"A lot of sexual assault victims don't have any visible injuries," Kenzie said. "But it's pretty obvious in this case. Scratches and gouges and restraint injuries on her arms. Back abrasions. The genital bruising and tears. The level of violence… there shouldn't have been any doubt that this was non-consensual, even disregarding her age, which I would put at thirteen to fifteen?"

Zachary nodded. "Fourteen."

Kenzie sighed, shaking her head. "And they never found the guy?"

"No. No suspects. It was a stranger and she couldn't describe him."

"What else did they find? Did they log any fingerprints? Hairs? Plant matter and soil? Footprints?"

"They got some hairs. Dark and straight. They were destroyed along with everything else. Not much else. There is some fingerprint evidence; I have to look through it. Not sure what I'm going to find. Just partials. Nothing that they could match at the time, but the officer has agreed to run them through the system and see if they have anything now. Back then, they didn't have a properly automated system and weren't connected to other states."

Kenzie handed the tablet back to him. "I hope you can find something. Because I don't see much here that could be used to identify the perp now. Other than the bite marks. Possibly."

Zachary nodded and put the tablet on the side table.

———

"So," Kenzie settled against him, pulling his arm around her shoulders, "how are you doing?"

"I'm fine."

"Yeah? This hasn't bothered you at all?" She indicated the tablet. "You aren't triggered by it?"

Zachary shook his head, aware that he was not being completely truthful. While he was trying not to let Heather's experience affect his life, it had triggered nightmares and at times he had trouble untangling his experiences from hers. But Kenzie didn't need to know that. He wasn't melting down over the details of Heather's assault. He wasn't constantly fighting flashbacks. It was bothersome, yes, but probably no more than it would be for a normal person. He had a hard time judging exactly what impact it would have on Kenzie.

"Good." Kenzie snuggled close and warm against his body.

Zachary breathed slowly, trying to relax all of his muscles so that she'd know he was enjoying himself and not overreacting to her proximity.

"What do you want to do tonight?" Kenzie asked. "Have you eaten?"

"Uh… I've had some food." But mostly, he'd been thinking more about getting the documents on the file digitized and getting home to go over them, and he hadn't stopped for anything nutritious along the way. Not a real meal, like she would have expected him to have.

"*Some food* meaning a cup of coffee and something else from the gas station?" Kenzie suggested.

"Well… yeah, something like that."

She laughed. "At least you're telling me the truth. Should we order in? Pizza? Chinese? Or you want to go out?"

"I don't want to go out," he said immediately. He was glad to be home and didn't have any desire to leave again so soon. "Whatever you want to eat is fine."

"Well, let's just go with a pizza. I've been behaving myself lately, so I deserve a treat."

"Why don't you go ahead and order. And I could… find something on TV for us?"

"Sure. But no more thrillers. How about something a little more romantic tonight?"

She gave him a look that told him she wasn't just talking about the movie. He quickly analyzed whether that meant she was looking for some attention before the pizza came, or whether she would want to wait until after the movie was finished. They had only recently become intimate. They had taken their relationship slowly, and she'd been pushing for more romance before Christmas, but he hadn't been able to do anything about it then, too mired in depression.

It wasn't until he had gotten home after the serial killer case that they had actually taken the next step. Not because Zachary felt like he was ready or Kenzie had pushed harder, but because he wanted to prove that he hadn't been affected by Teddy. He'd wanted to prove it to Kenzie so that she would stop asking questions and telling him that he needed more therapy. By showing her that he was in full working order, she could stop worrying about him and they could just enjoy their relationship and the increased closeness.

"Zachary?"

He looked at Kenzie. She had her phone to her ear, and at first he wasn't sure whether she had spoken to him or to the pizza place.

She said his name again and he smiled cheerfully. "Just thinking about a movie. Let's see what's on."

She watched him like a hawk while he turned the TV on and browsed through what was available.

"How about an old classic?"

She looked at the Bogart he had selected. "A bit *too* slow for my tastes. A little bit of action is fine."

"Uh, sure." He continued to scroll through. Kenzie turned her attention back to the phone to finish the transaction, then hung up.

"Okay, dinner and a movie, and then a little action of our own."

He loved her laughing eyes and wildly curly dark hair. She was fun to be with and supportive in spite of his many shortcomings and issues. He counted himself lucky to have her as a girlfriend. He just wished sometimes for the space to decompress by himself and not to have to worry about putting on a mask for her.

CHAPTER NINE

Zachary awoke to someone touching him. He instantly clenched every muscle in a full-body flinch, pulling back and gasping for air, trying to figure out where he was and who was threatening him. It only took a split-second to recognize his own bedroom, and another second or two to focus on Kenzie beside him.

"Oh. Sorry. You startled me."

She laid her hand back on his shoulder, warm and firm. "Your phone."

"Huh?"

"Your phone is ringing," she pointed out. "I didn't know if it was anything important or whether you would just want to let it go...?"

"Oh." Zachary rolled over away from her and felt for the phone on the side table. He managed to pick it up and fumbled for the on-screen answer button before he processed the name on the screen.

Bridget.

He couldn't exactly talk to his ex-wife with his girlfriend in bed with him. Zachary looked around for something to put on so he could at least go into the other room. Kenzie would assume that it was a confidential client call. She wouldn't know it was Bridget.

But he had already touched the answer button and he could hear Bridget's tinny voice coming out of the speaker. He hoped it wasn't loud enough for Kenzie to hear, because she seemed to be rousing herself and looking at the time. It was early, but not as early as Zachary used to wake up before the attack. Zachary scrubbed at his eyes with a fist as he hurried out of the bedroom.

He put the phone to his ear as he sat down on the couch. He grabbed one of the cozy blankets on the couch that Kenzie liked to cuddle up with and wrapped it around his waist.

"Hello?"

"Zachary? What happened, did you drop the phone? I was asking you—"

"Is everything okay?"

"Yes, everything is fine," she enunciated as if she were talking to someone who didn't know English well. "I was calling to make sure that everything was okay with you."

Zachary shook his head, wondering what it really was that she wanted to know. She didn't just call him to ask him how he was without a reason. There was always something. Some ulterior motive or favor. Or because she knew that he really was in bad shape. But he wasn't. He was doing very well for himself.

"Yeah, sure. Everything is good with me."

"Everything? Because I was worried, you know, about how you were doing after that horrible case. I can't imagine how difficult that must have been for you."

If anyone could understand what he had been through, it was Bridget. Because she too had been kidnapped. She hadn't been tortured, but she had not been given the necessities of life, and when he had finally found her, she had been at death's door. She knew what it was like to suffer at the hands of someone who was not in their right mind.

"It wasn't fun," Zachary agreed, "but I'm over it. Everything is back to normal and I've got plenty of cases to take care of, so everything is moving forward at a pretty brisk pace."

"Okay. As long as you're sure. I don't want you pretending to me that everything is perfectly okay when it isn't."

That hadn't been the way it was when they were married. She could afford to say it now when they weren't living in the same house and she didn't have to deal with his depression and anxiety and flashbacks. She just dealt with the public Zachary, the one who was doing his best to show everybody else that he was perfectly competent.

When they had been together, it had been different. She railed at him to quit acting like such a loser and man up. She had hated the cases that he 'wasted his time' on—surveillance of cheating couples, insurance work, accident recon-struction, skip tracing, all of the things that brought in money on a regular basis. He couldn't afford to do nothing while he waited around for the 'right' job, but that was what she had wanted him to do. Just take the cases that really sounded like they were important, that he could get good money. The real money.

She no longer had to see the way that he lived. It was ironic that he didn't get any of the really big jobs that had gotten his name on TV until after they had broken up. She had never gotten to be a part of that lifestyle. She would have liked it. The name recognition. The people who saw him at the store and stopped and stared for a minute, trying to figure out where they knew him from, and then were too awkward to approach him to talk to him about it. She would have loved that.

But being a big name wasn't necessarily good for a private investigator. He didn't want people to recognize him when he was out on surveillance or reconnaissance.

"It must have been hard for you," Bridget pressed.

"Yes, but I'm fine now."

"Okay." She sounded uncertain, which wasn't like Bridget. "That's good, then."

He waited but she didn't seem to have anything else to say. "Did you need something?"

"No. No, that was all, really. I just wanted to make sure that you were taking care of yourself."

"Okay. Talk to you later, then."

He hung up. For a few minutes, he just sat there, blinking his bleary eyes and trying to finish waking up. He wanted to go back to sleep, but he knew he should be working on client files, not lazing around in bed. It was early, but Bridget knew his usual schedule and would have assumed that he'd been up for a couple of hours already.

A movement caught his eye and he realized that Kenzie was standing there looking at him. Her hair was tousled from sleep. He wasn't sure how long she had been there, great detective that he was.

"Was that bloody Bridget?" Kenzie demanded, clearly pissed.

Not sure how much she had heard or guessed from his body language, Zachary decided it was best not to lie.

"Uh… yes."

"What is she calling you about? She'd better not be trying to get you to do another job for her!"

"No. Just checking to see how I am."

"Checking to see how you are? Bull."

"That's what she said."

"Really?" Her tone was suspicious. "Have you been over there lately? Are you tracking her again?"

Zachary's face heated. He shook his head. "No. I haven't even been near her neighborhood. And I'm not tracking her. I'm behaving myself."

It sounded juvenile, but she was the one treating him like a teenager. He hadn't done anything. Just answered a call from his ex-wife. She might have been sick or in need of his help. He couldn't just ignore her.

"You need to tell her to take a hike," Kenzie told him. "Block her calls. She's got Gordon now. She doesn't need to be trying to reel you back in."

Zachary stood up, gathering the blanket around him. "She's not getting anyone back."

She paused, considering whether to go on with her tirade or to back off. "Yeah?" She asked in a softer voice.

"Who's here with me? You or her?"

"Me."

"Then she's not getting me, is she?"

Kenzie gave a little smile. "No."

In the beginning, Kenzie had been entertained by the post-divorce animosity from Bridget. Far from feeling threatened, Kenzie had even asked Bridget to check in on Zachary once when he was very low and she was worried for his safety but couldn't get there herself.

But Kenzie's amusement had faded as Bridget's anger toward Zachary waned and she had asked him to take on a case for her. Kenzie had not been impressed by Zachary's immediate agreement and his hopes that it signaled a healing of the rift between them and maybe, just maybe, there was still hope of them getting back together again.

Kenzie no longer thought Bridget was one bit funny.

"Do you have work today?" Zachary looked at his phone, trying to remember what day of the week it was.

"No, I'm free all day. But you'll have work to do. This new case."

"Old case," Zachary corrected. "If you're not in a hurry, then why don't we go back to bed and see if we can forget about Bridget calling?"

Kenzie gave him a warm smile.

CHAPTER TEN

The fridge whirred to life as Zachary looked inside it, then closed the door without taking anything out. Zachary stood in the kitchen and looked at the time again. The day was getting away from him, marching on before he'd managed to get anything done. Kenzie was in the shower and had been in there for much longer than her normal splash-and-dash. He didn't know whether to put on coffee and toast, or to wait until she got out of the bathroom, or if it were too late to worry about breakfast and he should just use the quiet time to blast through a few emails.

Eventually, he turned on the coffee maker and drifted over to his desk and booted up the computer.

By the time Kenzie got out of the shower, the whole apartment was feeling humid and sticky. Zachary turned his head as she left the bathroom to get dressed, but she didn't say anything to him or poke her head in, so he just left her to get ready for the day on her own. She didn't need him hovering over her while she dressed.

Eventually, she made her way out, crossed behind him into the kitchen, and returned with a mug of coffee. She sat down on the couch. He could feel her watching him. He looked in her direction.

"What's up?"

"Can we talk for a minute?"

Up until then, Zachary had been feeling pretty good about himself. But a serious talk meant that he had done something wrong. And if he were to judge by the length of her shower, it wasn't a minor detail.

Was she still upset about Bridget's call? He shouldn't have answered it. He shouldn't have left the room to talk to her. He should have just done like Kenzie said and told her to shove off.

"I'm sorry."

She quirked an eyebrow at him. "Sorry for what?"

It was a foster mom's favorite trick to find out if he really understood what it was that he had done wrong. Foster dads were almost always happy if he just said he was sorry. There might still be a punishment, but they were happy to just dispense with arguments and lectures and get on with it. Women were different.

"I'm sorry about Bridget's call. I shouldn't have taken it, you're right. I should just block her."

"Oh." She waved the subject away as if it were nothing. "That's not what I wanted to talk about."

He shifted to find a comfortable position. He swallowed and tried to force himself to sit absolutely still and not fidget.

"Zachary… I'm not even sure how to say this."

It sounded like the beginning of a breakup talk. How could she be breaking up with him when they had just started sleeping together? Was that the culmination of their relationship, and now that she'd reached the peak, she was on her way out the door?

"Just… say what you're thinking," he encouraged, hoping he wouldn't regret it.

She still didn't speak right away, looking for the words. She eventually started haltingly. "When we're *together*… something happens to you. You go away. You're going through the motions, but your head… you just aren't there. You check out."

Zachary looked at her, trying to think of an argument to counter what she said. Bridget had never said that. Bridget had always said the opposite— that he was excessive in lovemaking. Immoderate.

He just sat there with his mouth open, unable to marshal any defenses.

"I'm sorry," Kenzie shook her head and took a drink of the coffee. It had been sitting on the burner throughout her marathon shower, and she winced, but drank it anyway.

"No... that's my fault, not yours. I... I'll try to do better."

"Do you even know you're doing it? What are you feeling when that happens?"

He shook his head, trying to make sense of what she said. He had done everything he could to convince her that he was okay, that he wasn't damaged. He didn't pull away when she touched him or cuddled. He never told her no, or that he was too tired or too anxious. He initiated intimacy, just as he had that morning. But it still wasn't enough for her. She still thought that there was something missing.

Him. He wasn't there.

When he thought back to what had happened that morning, he could remember everything they had said and done, up to a point. And then, as she had said, it was like he had left the room. While one part of his brain stayed behind to keep everything running, the part that was really him left. He was vaguely aware of what had happened after that point, but it was behind a heavy veil. He had no longer been a participant.

Zachary stared down at his hands, embarrassed, his skin warming as he tried to figure out what to say and how to fix it.

"I guess I feel... overwhelmed. I don't know."

"I feel like you don't want to be with me. Like you're thinking of Bridget or someone else and I'm not even there."

"No! No, I don't want to be with anyone else. I wasn't thinking of Bridget."

Her eyes were intense as she studied his face. He hoped she could see the truth there. He hadn't ever used Kenzie as a surrogate. He was with her because he wanted to be with her, not someone else.

"Then what's going on?" There was a long, awkward pause. "Do you know what dissociation is?"

"Yes, of course."

But he hadn't thought of it that way before. He had flashbacks. He had anxiety attacks. But he hadn't felt separate from what he was doing. Not until Teddy had drugged him to be free to do what he pleased. Since then... it had returned a number of times, without his really being aware of it.

"Have you ever had a psychiatrist diagnose you with dissociation?" Kenzie asked.

"No."

"If you're having dissociative episodes, you need to talk to someone about it. You've experienced a trauma and your brain and your body are trying to deal with it."

He lifted his hands helplessly. She knew that he saw several different doctors and a therapist and was also going to support groups sporadically. He didn't know what more she expected him to do to fix himself.

"Have you talked to anyone about being kidnapped? I'm not saying you have to tell me about it, but… you need to work through it. It *was* traumatic and you *haven't* fully recovered."

"I don't want to talk about it."

"Do you want to keep dissociating every time we make love? Because I'd kind of like it if you were around for that part."

"I will be," he promised. "I'll work on it. I'll try harder."

She sighed and had another sip of her coffee.

CHAPTER ELEVEN

Zachary brought up the documents contained in Heather's police file on the screen of his computer so that he could focus on them and gather everything he could from what had been recorded thirty years before. He tried to forget that it was Heather, his big sister, and just to concentrate on the details in the reports.

It had been a warm spring day. She was cutting through the park on her way home from school in the afternoon, something the students were not supposed to do. Zachary didn't find any explanation as to why it was out of bounds, whether there had been attacks there before or whether students had misbehaved, littering or breaking tree branches, or if there was another problem like drug dealing or prostitution going on in the shadows of the trees. Whatever the reason, Heather had known the rule against going through the park and had chosen to disobey it.

Zachary could remember a conversation he'd had with a psychologist when he first went to the Petersons. The psychologist had wanted to know why Zachary had disobeyed the rules at his school. The upshot of the conversation was that Zachary often disobeyed the rules when they were a barrier to what he wanted. He felt the rules were unfair, or that the adults didn't really understand the situation, or that he was an exception to the rule for one reason or another, and went ahead and did what he wanted to.

Of course, everyone did that at some time or another, justifying speeding because they were late, taking towels from hotels or hospitals because they felt they had been overcharged, or breaking curfew because they really wanted to attend a concert or party. But Zachary had broken rules with serious consequences, first and foremost the fire on Christmas Eve. The psychologist wanted to curb his impulsive rule-breaking to prevent further catastrophes.

Like Zachary, Heather had been quick to bend or break a rule that she felt unfair, and had done so that day in cutting through the park. According to the police report, she had been provocatively dressed, in short-shorts and a halter top. He didn't know if she had gone to school in an outfit like that. From what he remembered of the various schools he had gone to around that time, the students were not allowed to wear anything above the knee or that bared the shoulders or showed cleavage. Students who showed up in inappropriate dress were sent to the home economics room to alter their clothing, outfitted from the lost and found, or sent home to change. Maybe she had changed into a cooler outfit after school let out, wanting to be comfortable in the summer heat.

It had been a daylight attack. Because the park was off limits for the students, it had been isolated and it had been easy for the perp to grab her and drag her off where no one would see or hear her, a knife at her throat to quell any protests.

Zachary couldn't find any indication that the police had identified the exact spot she had been assaulted. There were no footprints taken or notes made of litter that might have been nearby that could have been analyzed in case he had dropped something and left his fingerprints behind. And of course they hadn't been looking for DNA. It would seem that they had simply noted the park as the place of the crime and had not made a direct examination of the scene.

There were notes that Heather was distressed and didn't want to talk, and that her foster mother had insisted a report be filed despite Heather's protests.

She had changed her clothes after the attack, but there was no indication that the police had asked for the clothes she had been wearing at the time or gone to her house to retrieve them. She had been interrogated for some hours before the police were convinced that it had, in fact, been rape and that she hadn't just gone for a tumble with some boyfriend and was trying to cover the fact up so she wouldn't be in trouble at home.

Zachary looked at the pictures of her and couldn't believe that the police could entertain the idea it was anything other than an aggravated sexual assault.

After that determination had been made, they had sent Heather to the hospital for treatment and the collection of the forensic sexual assault kit. Heather's foster mother had not taken her to the hospital for any treatment before taking her to the police station. While Zachary was glad she was so determined that the assault be properly reported and documented with the police, he wondered at the heart of a mother who was more concerned about the police report than the possibility of broken bones, concussion, internal bleeding, or any other injuries her foster daughter might have been suffering. Was she more concerned about establishing that the child had not been assaulted in her own house than she was in having her treated?

He took a break from the forms, putting his hands over his aching eyes. He knew he had been sitting at his desk staring at the screen without blinking for much too long. Kenzie had once suggested that he should set a timer to remind himself to get up and walk around and rest his eyes every fifteen or twenty minutes, but Zachary didn't like being pulled away from a job once he was focused on it. If he had been interrupted every fifteen minutes, he'd have to reestablish his focus over and over again, and that just wasn't the way his brain worked. He could hyperfocus for long periods of time, but if he were interrupted, it was hard to get back into it. He wouldn't have been nearly as effective.

He got up and poured himself a cup of coffee, even though it had been sitting on the warming burner for some hours. He put a cold cloth over his eyes for a minute or two and attempted to get some hydrating eyedrops into them, which was always a challenge because his eyes were determined to blink to avoid the drops no matter how he positioned the bottle or tried to keep his lids pinned open with his other hand.

He returned to the file, took a deep breath, and dove back in again. After the initial report, there had been some investigation. As Able had said, they called on the sexual predators that they knew, which would have been only a very small percentage of those who were actually living in the area. The police would only know of those with multiple convictions, those who were on parole, or who had warnings out on them that they were expected to reoffend. People who hadn't been caught for some time or since moving into the neighborhood would be unidentifiable. Zachary studied the names and descriptions of the various sexual predators they had talked to, memorizing their names and trying to see whether any of them could actually be ruled out.

Heather's vague description of a man who was of average height and build eliminated only a couple of them. There were a few with ironclad alibis—namely the ones who had been in court or jail at the time of the assault. The others' whereabouts were harder to verify. They had been with friends, home alone, or at the bar. The police had nothing that would rule them out, but also no reason to suspect them other than that they were known sex offenders. All of them had, of course, claimed to be reformed. The police had tentatively eliminated those who had a preference for boys or for prepubescent girls, since Heather was too well-developed for someone looking for a child's physique.

That still left way too many options. They hadn't been able to narrow the pool down to two or three solid suspects. And, of course, the perpetrator might not have been a known sex offender. He might have been someone who was just trawling the area at random, who had never been convicted before, or who had moved into the area without their knowing about it.

There was no mention in the file of similar assaults in the area, so the man had apparently not established a recognizable pattern. Maybe Heather had been his first victim. Zachary doubted it, but it was possible. Offenders usually worked up to an attack like that. The rapist first behaved inappropriately with girls he knew personally. He groped strangers or was caught peeping. He had questionable encounters at parties and bars, until he reached the point where he had to do something bigger and more audacious to satisfy his drive. Then there were a couple of bumbling, abortive attempts before he managed to close the deal.

The attack on Heather felt experienced. Maybe even someone that the school was aware of, hence the prohibition on walking through the woods. It hadn't been his first attempt, Zachary was sure of that.

———

Before making the call, Zachary reviewed the list of notes and questions he had made as he reviewed the file. He called Tyrrell's number first.

"Zachary! Hey, how's it going?"

"Good. Everything is fine. Uh, I wasn't sure…"

"Mmm…?"

"Whether I should contact Heather directly, or whether I should go through you. Because she went to you initially, she might not be comfortable talking to me directly."

"No, you should call her. The whole reason that she thought you might be a good person to investigate it is because of what you went through. She drew her own conclusions from what was in the news. She and I talk sometimes, but she never discussed anything personal like that with me."

Zachary knew there was a question behind Tyrrell's words. Zachary hadn't told him, or Kenzie, or the nagging reporters what had happened during his imprisonment by Archuro. The police had carefully worded any of their releases or interviews with the press to leave the question open, trying to give Zachary his privacy, but when word had spread about the details of what the man had done to his other victims before finally killing them, people easily drew a line to Zachary and made the assumption that he had been a victim of similar depravity. Tyrrell would never ask him directly, but Zachary knew the question was there every time Tyrrell mentioned the kidnapping.

"Great," he said, without giving Tyrrell any more details than he already had. "I'll call her, then."

"Sounds good. And you and I should get together for supper again before too long… maybe take in a game."R.

Zachary nodded automatically. "Sure, that sounds like a good idea," he agreed. But he didn't suggest a date.

"Okay… I'll call you, then. We'll talk about it another time."

CHAPTER TWELVE

Zachary was more nervous about calling Heather's number. It wasn't going to be an easy call, and he wondered if he should meet her in person to make sure that she was okay and didn't go off the rails. If it had been Zachary, he was pretty sure he would have gone off the rails. He couldn't imagine how devastating it would be if he got a call from the police saying that because of some glitch or technicality they would not be able to prosecute Archuro for what he had done.

But in the end, he was too much of a chicken to go to her house and see her face-to-face. Maybe it would be easier for her if she could just hang up and go cry into her pillow.

He dialed the number and it rang a number of times before Heather picked up. She probably didn't recognize his number, being so new to her. Her answer was tentative. "Hello?"

"Heather, it's Zachary." There was no response, and he tried again. "Zachary, your brother."

"Uh… hi. I guess I wasn't really expecting to hear from you."

"Would there be a better time for me to call?"

"No. Best to just get it over with, I guess, like ripping off a bandage. You didn't find anything?"

"I'm not actually done yet, but I don't have a lot of leads. I just wondered if I could ask you a few questions."

"Uh, yeah. Okay."

"You changed when you got home. You were in different clothes when you went to the police station. Did you take the clothes to the police? Or did they go to your house to pick them up?"

"No. They never asked for them. I never gave those clothes to them."

"Did you keep them?"

He couldn't think of a reason why she would keep such a morbid reminder, but he had to ask.

"No. Why would I?"

"I can't think of any reason you would. I was just hoping… that you might have something with the perp's DNA on it."

"Does that mean they couldn't use what was in the rape kit? I thought that kind of thing took weeks to analyze it."

Zachary tried to keep his voice steady. "Unfortunately, the kit was destroyed. It was a long time ago, and at the time, they didn't keep evidence like that indefinitely."

He thought that had a nice sound to it. Not that they had destroyed it in two years because that was their policy, or that they destroyed evidence when they didn't think there was ever any hope of catching the guilty party. Just that it had been a long time ago, and that during that time, the decision had been made to destroy the rape kit.

"Oh." Heather's voice was low and rough. "I was hoping they'd be able to do something with it now and maybe catch the guy."

"I know. Me too. You don't have anything else from that day? A necklace, something that he might have touched or rubbed against? Maybe something that you discovered afterward that you hadn't mentioned to the police?"

"No. I threw out anything that reminded me of what happened. I didn't want to think about it."

Zachary could relate to that. He too had tried to get rid of anything that reminded him of Archuro. He tried to avoid any possible memory triggers. When he couldn't do that, he disassociated. In time, he would forget it completely, if he worked at it hard enough.

"I have some other questions that might be hard for you to answer."

She was silent for a few seconds. He heard her draw in her breath and let it out in a long whistle. "Okay. I'll… I'll try."

He tried to start off easy, with questions that wouldn't be too personal or triggering.

"The park was out of bounds for students. Why? What had happened in the past that made them institute that rule?"

"I don't know… it was the rule for as long as I went to that school."

"Was it because of something that the students had done—vandalism or being rowdy and disturbing other people—or was it because of something that had happened to students?"

She considered. She cleared her throat. "I thought it was because of the students. But I don't know if anyone told me that."

"Did you ever run into other people when you cut through there? Students or not?"

"Yeah. It wasn't completely isolated. There were usually people coming and going. I would see one or two people each day."

"So did you start to recognize some of the ones you saw regularly? Somebody who walked their dog at the same time every day? Joggers? Other kids who broke the rule?"

"I guess so. Yeah."

"Can you give me the descriptions of the ones you remember?"

"Zachary… that was thirty years ago. I don't remember."

"You don't have to do it right now. Take some time to think about it. You might be able to recall some of the people you saw there regularly."

"Do you even remember all of the kids you were in foster care with?" she challenged.

"Uh… no."

"If you can't even remember the faces of everyone that you lived with, how can you expect me to remember people that I didn't even talk to, I just saw them in the park now and then?"

"I know it's a long shot. But if there isn't any physical evidence and the police can't give me any leads, then we need to go by what you remember. Your brain might have stored some of those people. If you were walking through that park every day, those images might have ended up in your long-term memory."

"I can't remember them," she said flatly.

"Would you consider being hypnotized?"

"What?"

"Hypnotism might help you to access some of those memories. Even though you can't remember them consciously."

"I'm not letting anyone mess with my brain and implant false memories. No way."

"I can get someone who is a professional. Someone who has been properly trained so that that won't happen."

"No. There are more things about the brain that scientists still don't understand than there are things they do. There's no way I'm taking the chance of having some satanic ritual being planted in my brain."

Even though Zachary knew it was probably the only way she'd ever be able to remember what she had seen way back then, he had to agree. He wouldn't have done it either. It was too risky. He already had too much horrific stuff in his head.

"Okay. I get it. If you change your mind or you remember something that you didn't before, just let me know. I don't want to bug you about it, so just give me a call, okay? If you don't want to talk about it, you can text or email me."

"Okay." She sounded relieved that he hadn't pushed it any further. "Is that everything?"

"Sorry, not yet."

She sighed.

"Do you remember hearing about anyone else who was assaulted around that time, either before or after you? Even if the circumstances were different. Anything at school or in the neighborhood or in the news?"

"Probably." Heather made a humming noise as she considered. "I don't know. There was a girl at school. Maybe a couple. Not like me, but date rape. The boys always laughing and saying they must have been asking for it. Saying that they were sluts."

"Yeah. Do you remember who any of the girls or the boys were?"

"I might... I can look in my yearbook and see if I can put some names to them. But I can't promise you results."

"No. Whatever you can remember is fine. Don't try to force it. Looking at the yearbook is a good idea. How about before that? Or in the neighborhood? Any reports of assaults or rape?"

She didn't answer. He gave it a minute.

"Someone who the girls said was a pervert? A Peeping Tom or someone who looked down their shirts?" he suggested.

Heather gave a grunt. "How about every man in the neighborhood. Seriously, I couldn't count the number of times I got leered at, whistled at, or had some jerk making comments about my body. I was fourteen years old!" she said in outrage. "I've raised a fourteen-year-old girl! They aren't sluts if they wear halter tops. They aren't asking for it. And if a girl is promiscuous—and I wasn't—then it's probably because she's been abused."

"Yeah."

"What did you ask? Oh, about men in the neighborhood who made comments or groped me."

Zachary didn't correct her, but waited to see what she thought.

"It's been so long," Heather said. "And I've tried not to think about it. I've tried not to think of anything that happened around then, or anything that might trigger memories of... the rape."

"I know," Zachary agreed in a low voice.

"I'm glad I had Tyrrell call you."

Zachary smiled, feeling warm toward Heather for her words. "Why?"

"I needed someone who could understand. I couldn't just go to a private investigator or to one of the Clintock cops. I had to have someone who was on my side and understood what I was talking about."

They were both silent for a minute.

"What happened to you in foster care, Zachary? I told you about me. I was with that first family, and then with the Astors for most of the time. But that wasn't what it was like for you."

"No. I was with a lot of different families. I got moved every few months, usually. And I couldn't manage being with a family around Christmas, so I usually went to Bonnie Brown, or ended up in hospital. And then... somewhere else when I got out. Some new program or therapeutic home or institution."

"So you never really had a family. Anyone who really felt like a parent."

"I had Mr. Peterson. Tyrrell told you about him."

"Yeah. He was really impressed that someone would keep in touch for all of those years, and how close the two of you are. But you were only with him in foster care for a few months?"

"A few weeks. But that's not what mattered."

"I guess not. And Bonnie Brown..." Heather trailed off, hesitating. "I never had to go there. But I know what their reputation was like. That's where they sent the intractable kids that foster families couldn't manage. It couldn't have been much fun there."

"I didn't go there because it was fun. I went because... it didn't feel like a home, where something awful could happen and the whole thing could go up in smoke in a few minutes. It was sturdy. Concrete. I wasn't ever very good with rules, but I felt better knowing what the rules and routine were and that they didn't change. There were guards, so any violence... didn't usually last long. Though some of the guards... if they thought I was being insolent and not showing the proper respect... if I stepped over the line..." Zachary gripped the arms of his chair, steadying himself and holding himself stiff and still, as if by doing so he could physically prevent himself from sliding into a flashback of Berens or one of the other guards whaling the hell out of him.

"Zachary," Heather crooned. "Oh, my baby Zach. I'm so sorry."

It was a different kind of flashback. Zachary remembering his little mother. How she held and comforted him when he was hurt or in trouble with their parents. How he felt warm and safe in her arms, protected even though she too was so young that she would not have been able to save him from a beating. She was only a couple of years his senior, but there was a vast difference between a frightened eight-year-old boy and a fiercely protective ten-year-old mama bear.

He felt warm and tingly and found tears brimming in his eyes. He had not heard that voice for thirty years, but it was so tender and familiar, it filled him all the way up.

"I'm okay," he told her hoarsely. "Thanks."

"So many different families. You must have had a lot of bad stuff happen."

"Like you said... I did my best to just forget about it. Move on and pretend that nothing had happened."

"Could you tell me everybody that ever touched you?"

He cleared his throat. "No."

"I'll do my best to remember names, or what I can... but the culture at the time... there weren't the same boundaries as there are now. It's better now, I think, even though people complain about political correctness and about having to get explicit consent. I think it's better if people are more cautious about what they say and do, even if it is only because they are afraid of getting publicly shamed."

"Yeah."

"Back then, people just did what they liked, and you weren't supposed to complain about it. If you did, they shamed *you*."

"It's better now," Zachary agreed.

"If we just had the DNA," Heather grumbled. "I can't believe they would just destroy all of that evidence. After what I had to go through, they could at least have saved it. There were so many changes in science and technology, couldn't they have guessed that in the future we'd have better ways to analyze it?"

"I guess they just didn't have the foresight. And there were shorter statutes of limitation. Sometimes really short."

"Is that everything you wanted to know? I'll think about it and get back to you."

"Did you keep a diary? Something that might help you to remember? Or do you have a photo album? Anything?"

"If I had anything like that as a foster kid—and I don't think I did—I lost it when I was on the street. There just wasn't any way to keep many personal possessions."

CHAPTER THIRTEEN

His next call was to Able. He didn't really want to talk to the cop again, and knew that Able wouldn't really want to have anything to do with him. The cop had made it clear that he didn't think Zachary was going to find anything helpful in the file and that he considered it a waste of his time to have to hold Zachary's hand through the process.

It wasn't Zachary's fault that Able had been assigned to the file. He was actually glad that it hadn't been assigned to some rookie just learning the ropes. Able had the policing history to know how things had been handled back when Heather was assaulted. He knew about the laws and about how the forensic evidence had been handled. He knew the kind of police work that had been done at the time and he knew what the culture had been. Those were all insights that he was able to share with Zachary, so that neither of them had to go look them up or to speculate on what the atmosphere had been at the time.

"You again?" Able complained when he picked up the phone. Probably not the way he had been trained to deal with the public. But Zachary preferred his openness to someone who would smile and pretend to be helpful when he just wanted Zachary to get lost.

"I have a few questions for you," Zachary said, ignoring the sentiment and barreling along.

"Yeah, what?"

"I don't have any experience on what it was like policing back then, about all of the legwork that you guys had to do. So all of this might sound annoying, but I just want to get a clear picture."

"Okay. What?"

"You interviewed the people that you knew were sex offenders at the time. Checked alibis the best you could, tried to rule out anyone that you could."

"That's the way it was done, yeah. That's police work. No shortcuts then like there are now with DNA that can lead you straight to the perp. It was all legwork and police procedure."

"What about other sexual assaults that might have taken place in town that were unsolved? Would you have done a survey of other cases? Tried to match up anything that was consistent between them?"

"Yeah, of course. But it wasn't like it is now, with everything automated and computerized. You talked to people, called other precincts, checked newspaper articles. There wasn't any internet or centralized database where the computer would do all of the work and spit it out for you. Lots of time on the phones, lots of time talking to people."

"And I didn't see a report of any canvass of the neighborhood. Would they have gone door-to-door asking if people had seen anything or thought that they knew anything about it?"

"Normally, yeah. But if there wasn't anything on the file… it might have been that they didn't think it would be productive. She was in an isolated area, there weren't a lot of neighbors around working in their gardens or looking out the windows. Canvassing hundreds of neighbors in the hopes of finding one person who might have seen a man leaving the park at that time… I can see why they would decide that it wasn't worth the manpower."

"What about rumors about anyone in the neighborhood? Creepers that might not have any record, but that people were suspicious of. Or people who had been convicted of peeping or… I don't know, some kind of harassment. Somebody that everyone thought was just 'off.'"

"If there were rumors, we would have followed them up. Sure. There was plenty of paperwork in that file of people who police had talked to. But there wasn't anyone that stood out, one person that they had reason to suspect more than anyone else."

"Were there any other unsolved sexual assaults around that time?"

"I'm sure there were."

"Is there any way to match them up now? To pull out any other cases of sexual assaults that year…?"

"That's asking a lot. It's not digitized, so every file would have to be pulled and gone through manually. All of the details are not on the computer. Just the very basics."

"Could we start with a general list and gradually whittle it down?"

"Like I say, a lot of man hours for something that isn't likely to provide results. Do you really think that you're going to find the perpetrator thirty years later? When you don't even have any physical evidence?"

"It happens. People do it."

"It happens in cases that were not investigated properly. Where there were holes in the information. I'm not seeing that in this case. Everything seems to have been properly followed up on at the time."

"Except for the physical evidence being destroyed."

"Yes, aside from that. But there's nothing we can to to reverse that and bring the evidence back now."

"Could you look into it? Just see if you can pull a list of the unsolved sexual assaults from that year?"

"I'll see if I have the time."

———

Getting together for dinner with both Kenzie and his siblings was not something that Zachary had come up with on his own. Kenzie had met Tyrrell already, and Zachary couldn't keep from her for long that he had met one of his older sisters as well.

"That's fantastic," Kenzie said, gushing a little. "I'm glad that you're getting a chance to meet everyone. What was she like?"

Zachary paused as he thought about it. Not because he didn't want to tell Kenzie about Heather, but because he was having trouble sorting out for himself what kind of person she was and how he felt about meeting her again.

"She's changed. I guess that shouldn't surprise me. I've changed too. It's been a long time, and we were just kids at the time. We've been through all kinds of stuff since then."

"I would guess so. She's had a rough life?"

"Yeah... but not the same way as me. She was mostly with one foster family. She and Joss were together to start with, but they got separated. When we were little kids, before the fire, Heather was... sort of a tomboy, I guess. A bit mischievous. Daring. Joss was the oldest, so she was the perfectionist and the one who tried to keep us all in line. Heather was supposed to help take care of us too, and she did, but sometimes she got us into trouble."

"And she's not quite the same as she was back then? She's matured, married, had kids of her own?"

"Yeah. But she's not... she is so introverted and shy now. Doesn't want to rock the boat... afraid to speak up for herself."

Their show had returned from a commercial break on the TV, and Kenzie eyed it, but didn't unmute it.

"Is that because she was abused by her foster family?"

"I don't know. Not that she's said. She was the victim of an aggravated sexual assault when she was fourteen, and maybe that's what changed her."

"Something like that could have a profound effect on a person," Kenzie agreed. She picked up her glass of water and watched Zachary over the rim as she sipped it. She didn't bring up Archuro, but she didn't have to. Zachary already knew she was thinking it. Of course he was affected by the attack, but it hadn't changed his personality. He was still the same person as he had been before. The change in Heather was jarring to him.

"I'd really like to meet them," Kenzie said after putting her glass back down on the coffee table by her knee. She cuddled up against Zachary.

He forced his muscles to relax and put his arm around her, focusing on the warmth of her body and how good it felt to have her close.

"Maybe we could get together sometime."

"When?"

"I don't know about doing it right away. Heather might need some time to get used to the idea... we just barely met."

"Why? If she's interested in reuniting with her family, why wouldn't she want to go out to dinner with you and meet your girlfriend? And I'd like to see Tyrrell again too. He's a nice guy."

Tyrrell was like a less-damaged version of Zachary. He hadn't had to live with the same abuse as Zachary had and he hadn't had to deal with the guilt that Zachary did, knowing that he was the one who had set the fire that night that resulted in the breakdown of his family.

Kenzie's eyes narrowed and the corner or her mouth lifted. "Is that jealousy I see? I'm not interested in him *romantically*, Zach. I'd like to get to know your family better. That's all."

It occurred to Zachary that he hadn't met any of Kenzie's family. He knew about them; she had two parents, both living, divorced, and she was an only child. But it had never occurred to him to ask if he could meet her parents. But maybe now that they were so close to each other, he should be considering it. Sooner or later, her family was going to want to meet him and find out what kind of a guy she was with.

"I'll ask them," Zachary said finally. "But like I said… Heather is pretty shy. I don't know whether she'll want to do it."

———

But Heather had agreed. Fairly quickly, and without any apparent reservations. Maybe she was only careful of men. So they arranged a place, a Chinese restaurant that each of them could get to in under an hour's drive. It was quiet, but not too quiet. A good place to talk without feeling awkward or having people eavesdrop on the conversation.

Kenzie and Heather seemed to click pretty well from the start, talking to each other comfortably and able to maintain small-talk seemingly without effort, in a way that Zachary had never been able to. Both women ordered wine, and there was a noticeable relaxation of the lines around Heather's eyes.

Zachary hadn't told Kenzie that the cold case he was investigating was Heather's, but it hadn't taken Kenzie any time to figure it out, and Heather seemed willing to talk about it with her. Zachary expected Heather probably didn't have a lot of chances to talk about it with sympathetic female friends. It didn't seem like she had much of a support network.

"What was probably hardest was raising my daughter," Heather was confiding in Kenzie. "It's so hard to raise a daughter to be cautious and to make her understand how dangerous it can be out there without sounding like a hysterical nut job or else making her too scared to do anything."

"Teaching her to take precautions," Kenzie contributed, nodding.

"Men don't understand," Heather's glance flicked to each of her brothers before going back to Kenzie. "They don't know the lengths that women have to go to to try to avoid being victimized. Grant was totally clueless about the dangers; he always thought I was being too strict with Nicole when I would get after her for thinking she could dress provocatively without any consequences or for being late and not keeping me informed about where she was."

"I would expect him to be more understanding, knowing what you had been through," Kenzie commented.

Heather splashed more wine into her glass from the bottle on the table. "I never told him about it."

Zachary paused with his fork held right in front of his mouth, remembering she had mentioned that before. "You didn't tell your husband anything about the assault?"

"I didn't talk about it with anyone. After the trauma of having to tell my mom and what happened at the police station and the hospital... I completely shut down. I can barely even remember the next ten months."

Zachary put his fork down. He looked at Kenzie for her reaction. He could see that, like he, she was struck by this comment. She looked back at him with wide eyes. Neither said anything. Tyrrell was murmuring something to Heather about being sorry for what she had gone through. Heather looked back at Kenzie and caught her expression.

"What?"

"Did you get pregnant?"

Heather looked unsure of how to answer. She looked at the three of them and fiddled anxiously with her wine glass. Finally, she gave a little nod and answered quietly. "Yes."

At first, Zachary just saw red. He was furious with the rapist and in spite of Zachary's normally nonviolent demeanor, had the man been in front of him at that moment, Zachary didn't know what he would have done. Not only had the scumbag raped Heather, but he'd gotten her pregnant, so she had to go through that physical ordeal for months, and then all of the feelings of guilt and heartbreak that she must have suffered through in giving the baby up.

Kenzie put her hand over Zachary's on the table. He struggled to get his rage under control and to mask it, so that Heather wouldn't have to deal with his anger on top of everything else. He had a sip of his soft drink and looked away for a minute. He looked back at Heather, more calm.

"You gave the baby up for adoption?" he asked.

He knew the ages of her children with Grant. She had obviously not made the choice to raise the baby conceived by the assault.

"Yes. What else was I going to do? I was fourteen. It wasn't like it is now when they practically pin a medal on a teenager for having a baby. Mom said she'd never give me permissions to have an abortion, and I didn't know that I could go ahead and have one anyway. So I did what they told me to."

Zachary sat back, his dinner forgotten, his head buzzing with the possibilities. The conversation went on around him, but he didn't hear anything else that was said.

"Do you know who adopted the baby?"

Everyone stopped talking and looked at him. Zachary realized that he had spoken out of turn and interrupted the conversation which had continued to go on without him, his question no longer seeming relevant. His face heated a little in his embarrassment, but he looked at Heather, waiting for an answer.

"No. How would I? They just took it away. Took *him* away. The birthmother didn't get any input back then. I could tell them I wanted a Christian home or something like that, and they would consider it, but it didn't really matter what I said. They would just go ahead and do what they wanted. I didn't have any rights."

"You did, but they wouldn't tell you that."

"No. They didn't. They just overrode everything I said, decided what they wanted done with me. I didn't have anyone on my side telling me I could have made a different choice. I don't know that I could have, but it would have been nice to know I had other options."

"You didn't get put in a home?"

"No. The Astors 'let' me stay with them. Told the school I had mono. They acted like it was my fault I got pregnant. Like they didn't know that I'd been assaulted." Her voice shook with outrage. "It wasn't my fault."

"No, of course it wasn't," Kenzie agreed, rubbing Heather's shoulder soothingly. "It's horrible that you had to go through that. I hope the world has improved since then. That they aren't so ignorant and narrow-minded."

"There are still plenty of ignorant people around," Tyrrell contributed.

"Who would know what family the baby went to?" Zachary persisted, not to be distracted from the track he was on. "Did your foster parents? Your social worker?"

"I don't know." Heather shook her head. "Why does it matter? It was supposed to be a secret, no one was supposed to know. That's how it worked back then. They didn't have open adoptions."

"It matters because the baby carries his DNA."

CHAPTER FOURTEEN

There was silence around the table. Everyone stared at Zachary. He shifted uncomfortably and leaned forward, resting his elbows on the table.

"Half of that baby's DNA is Heather's, and half is *his*. If we can get the baby's DNA, we might be able to get a match on the system."

"I don't know if the technology is that far advanced," Kenzie disagreed. "I see where you're going with this, but I don't think they'd be able to do anything like that. The database isn't set up that way. You need the perpetrator's DNA, not his child's"

"Why not? If they can test a child and test a man and prove whether he is the father, why can't they do that in this case? Why can't they prove who the rapist is by proving who the father is?"

"I don't know. You have to have a sample to test against. You can't just run the baby's DNA against everyone in CODIS to find a paternity match."

"Why not?"

She shook her head. "It's not set up to do that!"

"It doesn't matter anyway," Heather said. "Because there's no way to figure out who adopted that baby."

"They do it all the time. They have TV shows where they reunite biological families. People put posts up on Facebook with their birth information on it. There are times you can get the records unsealed. There are databases to register in if you want to be connected with a child or parent."

"Or you could hire a private investigator," Tyrrell said wryly.

Zachary had never been asked to trace an adopted child, but he knew a lot of ways to track down people who changed their names and didn't want to be found. He'd done all kinds of tracing in his career. He was sure he could track Heather's baby down, given enough time.

Heather's eyes were wide. She shook her head. "I don't want you doing that, Zachary. Don't look for him."

"But this could work. It could find the slimeball who hurt you."

"Kenzie's right, they aren't going to search CODIS to look for the father. Even if they did, they'd only get a hit if he was in the system. He probably isn't. You said it was a long shot and not to get my hopes up."

He stared at her, not understanding her sudden reluctance. Just when he hit on something that might help them to track her attacker down, she backed out of it? If she wanted to find him, then she needed to be open to all channels. Unless she had entered into the prospect knowing it was a wild goose chase and hoping to get some closure by running into a nice solid dead end. Maybe she didn't really want to find the guy; she was just hoping for some kind of confirmation that there was nothing more they could do.

Heather looked away, her eyes brimming with tears. Zachary forced himself to look down at his plate and take another bite of the Chinese food. It was good food, but he just didn't have the appetite, and had no interest in it with his brain zooming off down the paths that he could take to find his quarry. He took a deep breath, and managed to force down a few more bites while letting Heather relax and hoping Kenzie would start the conversation up again. He glanced over at Tyrrell to see what he thought. Tyrrell gave him a tiny shake of the head, which Zachary interpreted as 'just let it be for now.'

Maybe when Heather had had a chance to think about it, she would change her mind. He had sprung it on her too suddenly, and she needed time to catch up and mull over the idea. Once she'd had a few days to consider, she would change her mind.

He put down his fork, unable to eat anything else. Kenzie looked over at him, but didn't make any comment. She and Tyrrell both knew that he didn't have much appetite because of his meds, and could only force himself to eat so much.

Heather wiped at her eyes. "I'm sorry. I'm being such a spoilsport. We got together to visit and have a good time, and I'm crying all over everything."

Zachary raised his brows and shook his head. "You're allowed to have feelings about it. How could you not? It's unhealthy to just stuff them."

He caught Kenzie's amused glint.

"Or so I'm told," he added.

"I know, but this isn't the place. I'm out in public. I should be a grown-up and stay in control of myself."

"Is that what they told you?"

She got a faraway look. Zachary poked at his food, pretending he was still eating, and waited for a response. After a minute, Heather nodded. "Yeah... I guess that's where I got that from. They hated me being emotional. After the attack... I cried about everything. I cried at school, at home over dinner, when I got up in the morning... the least thing would set me off."

"You went through a very traumatic experience," Kenzie said. "And not only that, but you were hormonal as well. It's much harder to control your emotions when you're pregnant."

It was Zachary who looked at her this time.

"Or so I've heard," Kenzie said.

Heather gave a little laugh. "Yeah, I remember with my other kids... I was just a wreck. I would go into the bedroom to set up the nursery for the baby, and just lose it. Blubbering all over everything. Because of something... I don't know, a teddy bear or a cloud, and I'd just be off to the races. Grant would come home and find me with bloodshot eyes and a red blotchy face and have no idea what to do. He'd think that he'd done something wrong, but of course, he hadn't. It was just hormones."

"And you think your foster parents should have freaked out over them? Told you not to have feelings? To button them up and get them under control?"

"No." Heather picked up a napkin and wiped her nose with it. "I never told my daughter that. Not that she was pregnant, but when she was hormonal as a teenager. I never told her that she was wrong to feel something or that she shouldn't let other people see it."

"When she does get pregnant, and calls you for advice and breaks down blubbering over the phone? Or when you take her out to a nice dinner that she doesn't have to make and she bursts into tears at the restaurant, are you going to tell her it's time to grow up and not show her emotions in front of other people? Are you going to tell her that she's embarrassing you with her tears?"

Heather shook her head again. "No. I would never do that."

"You went through a lot more than just being pregnant," Tyrrell contributed. "You went through a very traumatic experience, and then you were pregnant on top of it. You felt alone and abandoned."

Heather gulped. She picked up her glass of wine and drained it. "Yeah. No one had the right to treat me that way."

Zachary stared at his plate, lost in thought.

CHAPTER FIFTEEN

Zachary started his day with a number of phone calls and web searches as he tried to figure out his next step, which fully depended on Heather and what she decided. If she didn't want him to search for her baby... well, he still could, he didn't need her permission— but he didn't think he would. If she didn't want him to, if she really wanted him to just drop the case, he'd do what she wanted him to. He didn't want to wreck his relationship with his sister by not heeding her wishes.

But he really wanted to find that baby. He was the key to everything. With him, they might have a chance of finding the rapist. Without him, Zachary didn't see many other options. He could go back to Heather's old neighborhood and canvass homes, see if he could find anyone who had lived there thirty years before, but even if he found someone who had lived there that long, the chances that they'd have anything that could help him to break the case were doubtful.

He would search through the file again for any other leads that had been missed, but he wasn't hopeful that he'd be able to find any other avenues of investigation, other than talking a news magazine show into investigating it and blasting it all over TV. If they got some publicity, maybe they would have a chance of finding a witness that the police hadn't found. But even that was a long shot.

Still, he wanted to have all of his ducks in a row for when Heather came back with her answer, if she changed her mind. He would be all ready to put his plan into action.

He made a call to Mr. Peterson. Not a Skype call, because he didn't think that Lorne would be at his computer. Zachary also didn't want Lorne to see his face, when he still wasn't looking any better and would attract more comments about how he needed to be taking care of himself and eating properly. He would preempt a video call from Mr. Peterson by making it clear he wanted to keep in touch, even if he were having issues.

"Zachary! Hey, I'm glad you called!"

"How are you doing?"

"You know me. Still above ground. We're as happy as clams."

Zachary chuckled. "Just what makes clams happy, anyway?"

"Warm water, I assume," Lorne laughed. "So how about you, what makes you happy?"

"I had dinner with Tyrrell, Heather, and Kenzie last night."

"All three of them together. How did that go?"

"Really well. I wasn't sure about how Heather would handle it, but she and Kenzie got along."

"Your Kenzie is pretty good at putting people at ease. I'm not surprised."

"I'm still trying to get a handle on Heather... she's so different from how I remember her. But every now and then, I see the old Heather, for just a second."

"A lot has happened since you knew her. And a lot has happened to you. The two of you are coming from two completely different backgrounds, even if you started out in the same place."

"Yeah, I know."

"It's good that you're getting together and getting to know each other. You'll find each other again."

"Yeah." Zachary hesitated, not sure what he could or should share with his foster father. He didn't want to break any confidences, but he wanted to talk to Lorne about Heather. "We were talking about her case last night and she said she never even told her husband about it. They've been married for twenty-four years and she's never talked to him about it."

"Wow." Mr. Peterson thought about it. "It sounds like maybe she's tried to suppress it. To pretend it never happened."

"Yeah, I think so."

"Sort of like you're doing."

"I didn't say that," Zachary said quickly.

"You don't have to. I already know."

Zachary didn't know what to say to that. He cleared his throat and looked for a segue into another topic that would be more comfortable.

"You should be talking about it to your therapist, even if you don't want to talk to anyone else about it," Mr. Peterson advised.

"That's what everyone keeps telling me."

"We want the best for you. We want you to be healthy and happy."

"I'm doing okay." Zachary looked back at his computer. "I just thought I'd call you in between a little computer work, but I should probably be getting back at it."

"You don't need to run away. I won't harass you about it."

"It's not that. I just have a lot to do."

"We can talk for a couple more minutes. Nothing is going to blow up if you take a ten-minute call."

Zachary conceded. "How's Pat?"

"He's doing well."

But Zachary sensed a hesitation before the answer. It felt incomplete, as if there were something else that Mr. Peterson wanted to say, but had stopped himself from saying. Why? Because he wanted to protect Pat's privacy, or because there was something he didn't want to get Zachary involved in? Was it bad?

"Is he... I guess he's probably still having trouble with Jose's death," Zachary suggested.

"It takes time to process a thing like that. Not just losing someone close to you, but having them taken away so suddenly and in such a violent way. We know that Jose's last few days on earth... were not happy ones. It's not like when someone goes peacefully in their sleep, or even unexpectedly with a brain aneurysm or car accident. It's... it's very hard to work through, and Pat was closer to Jose than I was. It's hit him harder."

"Is there anything I can do?"

There was a long pause as Mr. Peterson considered it. "I don't think so, Zach. I try to talk to him about it, but we just keep going in circles. Because there's no way to explain why it happened or say it was for the better or that something good will come of it. It's just something that we have to accept."

"Is he getting any counseling? That cop, Dougan, he said that he could recommend some victim services and support groups or therapists."

"He's gone to a couple of meetings. I think that's good. But it's still very raw, and I don't know if rehashing it with this group is any better than going in circles with me. Too early to tell. I just have to be more patient and see what comes of it."

Zachary knew that it hadn't been a long time since Jose's death, but it seemed like his murder and Zachary's experience with Archuro had happened in another lifetime. And that was how he wanted it to be. He wanted it to be far away, somewhere he didn't have to think about it.

"They say time heals…"

"Yes. I'm sure that it will help. It will be less painful over time. You know Pat; it's not like him to let things get him down. He's always so cheerful, trying to make everyone else feel better."

"Well… give him a hug for me. Tell him that I'm thinking about him." Zachary stopped short of saying, "Tell him I'm here if he wants to talk," because he didn't want Pat or anyone else talking to him about what had happened.

"I will. Thanks for that, Zachary. Things will get better, I'm sure."

"Well… let me know if they don't. If you're worried about him…"

"I know you could help out with some advice and direction. I don't think that things are going to get to a crisis point, but if they do… you'll be the first one I talk to."

"Okay. Sounds good." Zachary felt a little buoyed up by the possibility that his own struggles with loss and depression might help someone else, especially someone who was so deserving as Pat was. Zachary wasn't usually the go-to guy for emotional support, but he definitely had the experience if they wanted to talk to someone about depression and mental health services.

"Okay. I'll let you go get back to your computer work. But call me anytime. Tell Tyrrell and Heather and Kenzie 'hi' for me, when you see them again."

After saying his goodbyes, Zachary ended the call and looked back at his computer. He didn't really have anything else to do while he waited for Heather to make her decision. Not on her case, anyway. As usual, there was a big pile of skip traces and other work for him to do. If it took any length of time for Heather to get back to him, he could take up a few smaller cases. There were a number of people who were looking for surveillance of employees or cheating spouses, and those kinds of jobs rarely went over a few days.

But he'd just wait a little while and see if Heather changed her mind.

———

The next call that he got was from Rhys's grandmother, Vera. Rhys Salter was a black teenager that Zachary had met on a previous case and liked to keep in touch with. He felt a little responsible for Rhys's mother having been sent to prison as a result of his investigation and he had a connection with the boy, who had selective mutism. They seemed to hit it off in spite of their differences in age, race, and backgrounds. Rhys had been institutionalized for some time as a child after his grandfather's murder. Institutionalization was an experience Zachary shared with Rhys that not many other people did.

"Mr. Goldman, it's Vera Salter."

"Mrs. Salter," Zachary prompted formally, trying to nudge her out of calling him Mr. Goldman again. They had been on a first name basis, but it had been a while since they had talked. Zachary never went by Mr. Goldman.

"Oh, it's Vera!" she insisted immediately. "Zachary."

"That's better. How are things going?"

"Well, they could always be worse. I have to remember what we were going through last year around this time," Zachary could almost hear her shake her head. "It was a very difficult time, with Robin suffering so badly with her cancer… a very difficult time."

"Are things not going well with Rhys? Or is it your health?"

"I'm okay. But I do think our Rhys could use a little extra support. He can be so isolated, I worry about him, about how he has no one to talk to. I mean, there's only so much you can tell an ancient old gramma like me."

Zachary liked that she said 'talk' for Rhys's communication, even though he rarely spoke more than a word or two in an entire conversation. He used gestures and text and pictures on his phone to communicate his meaning. A conversation with him could be exhausting, but it was also like playing a game or solving a puzzle. Zachary found a certain amount of satisfaction in being able to communicate with Rhys, even though most of it was non-spoken.

"Should I set something up with him? You had said that you didn't want me doing that…"

"I said you could still see the boy, but I would like it to be here. With all of the stuff about you in the media, I don't want him getting teased for being homosexual or something. I just want to protect him."

"That's fine with me. I don't want to cause him any grief. He has enough to deal with without having that on his plate too."

"Yes, that's exactly what I mean. You know how cruel teenagers can be. Even though it seems like everyone or his dog is LGB-whatever these days. I don't want him getting bullied or beaten up for his friendship with you."

Zachary nodded his silent agreement. "So shall I set something up with him next week?"

"Well…" she sounded suddenly hesitant.

Zachary frowned. She was the one who had contacted him saying that Rhys needed someone to visit with him. Why was she suddenly waffling about it?

"You don't think you could find some time today, do you?"

"Oh. Sure. I can pop by after school today. Would that work?"

"That would be wonderful. And you would be welcome to stay for supper. Is there anything you can't eat?"

"You know me. I don't eat a lot, but anything goes." Growing up in a home where they sometimes didn't have enough to eat and then in foster care where he had been faced with all different kinds of food, good and bad, and institutional food at Bonnie Brown and in the hospital, Zachary had learned to eat whatever was put in front of him. Which had served him well when Bridget had taken him to fancy events where they had all manner of fish eggs and sea creatures.

"Great," Vera declared. "We'll see you after school, then."

CHAPTER SIXTEEN

Zachary was glad to have somewhere to go later in the day when Heather still hadn't called him back and he couldn't face the pile of skip traces in his inbox anymore. He enjoyed visiting with Rhys and with his grandmother but hadn't seen either of them for some time. It had been too long. He had neglected the relationship. But he had felt put out the last time Vera had called, in the middle of the serial murder investigation, because she didn't like the way that Zachary was being presented in the media. He had been shy of calling again after that, even when life was getting back to normal again.

He made sure he gave Rhys enough time to get home after school before he showed up on the doorstep and rang the bell. Vera was there quickly, greeting him like an old friend and inviting him into the spotless living room. Roast chicken and other food smells emanated from the kitchen, making Zachary hungry in spite of his usual nausea and lack of appetite.

"Why don't you go on in to see Rhys, and I'll call you boys when dinner is ready," Vera suggested.

"Sounds good," Zachary agreed. He headed to Rhys's room.

Rhys's room looked like the typical teen boy's room. Definitely not up to Vera's standards for the rest of the house, but she had apparently accepted the fact and simply cleared out the worst of the detritus or closed the door when he was not home. Rhys was lying on the bed with his phone. Texting or playing a game, Zachary wasn't sure which. Usually when Rhys texted, he communicated in images rather than words, though he did throw in a word or two here and there, the same as in a face-to-face conversation.

Zachary knocked on the open door to warn Rhys he was there.

Rhys looked up from his phone and smiled. He sat up and gestured for Zachary to enter.

"Hey, Rhys. How's it going? I'm sorry I haven't been around much lately."

Rhys reached for his hand and gave it a strong shake, clapping Zachary on the shoulder with the other hand. He released his grip and drew his hands apart in a questioning gesture, then pointed to Zachary. *How about you?*

"I'm doing all right," Zachary said, shrugging off the question. He was more concerned with how Rhys was faring. He looked for a place to sit down, but Rhys didn't have a chair and sitting on the floor was not going to allow them to communicate properly, besides which it was covered with shoes, sports equipment, books, and whatever else Rhys could fit in his room. Rhys motioned to his bed for Zachary to sit.

He hesitated. He didn't want Rhys to feel uncomfortable or like he was invading his privacy. He remembered how he had felt as a teenager when a house parent or social worker would sit down on his bed to talk to him. He always felt threatened, his space invaded, and he always worried about what the next step would be. Whether they wanted to be on his bed just to test out how close they could get to him, if they could desensitize him to inappropriate contact. Rhys widened his eyes and pointed again to the end of his bed insistently.

"You sure?" Zachary asked. "We could go out to the living room or something."

Rhys pointed again. Zachary sat down and tried to look comfortable.

"So, what's been going on with you lately? How is school?"

Rhys indicated a backpack on the floor, the size of a small boulder and probably just as heavy. Rhys rolled his eyes and shook his head.

"That's a lot of work," Zachary observed. "Can you really get through that much?"

Rhys shook his head. Then he shrugged and indicated his phone.

Zachary hazarded a guess at his meaning. "Not when you're spending too much time online talking with friends?"

Rhys pointed a finger at him, making a shooting-a-gun motion. *Exactly.*

"I don't imagine Grandma thinks much of that. She doesn't threaten to take away your phone?"

Rhys nodded and gave a grin. He bent over to look under the bed, clinging to it upside-down and eventually coming back up for air with a small laptop in his hand. He showed it to Zachary. It had a sticker with the school's name and logo on it, along with a warning that it was for homework only and that any student-installed programs would be deleted.

"Nice. And I'm sure you only use it for homework, like it says."

Rhys grinned again.

"I don't imagine you can do your homework without a computer and online access these days. Back in the stone ages, we didn't even have computers."

Rhys shook his head in silent disbelief.

"So, other than getting a crap-load of schoolwork, how is it going?"

Rhys pressed his lips together in a slight grimace and shrugged. *Okay.*

"You involved in any after-school sports?"

Despite the various bits and pieces of sports equipment scattered around on the floor, Rhys shook his head. He didn't seem saddened by the fact that he wasn't on any of the school teams. It was something that had never particularly bothered Zachary either. He had been more concerned with survival than with being on a team. He had been small and awkward and always was one of the last to be picked for anything when his gym classes had been forced to split into teams. Rhys was a lot taller than Zachary had been, already an inch or two taller than Zachary's adult height. Zachary suspected from the way that he walked and moved that he had at least basic skills in the sports that he played. He had a certain grace in the way he moved.

"Any girlfriends?" Zachary didn't have any doubt that there would be girls interested in Rhys. He wasn't bad looking, was black in a population that was largely white, and his mutism gave him the sympathetic appeal of a lost puppy. There would definitely be girls who wanted to make him feel better.

Rhys shook his head and made a straight line gesture with both hands. *No way.*

"That's probably a good thing," Zachary said. "If there's one thing more distracting than social media, it's girls."

Rhys nodded and laughed silently. Zachary cast around for something else to comment on or another safe topic of conversation. Rhys reached over and touched his wrist, a signal that Rhys had something else to say and wanted Zachary to focus on the message. Zachary watched carefully, meeting Rhys's eyes briefly and waiting.

Rhys pointed at Zachary, and spread his hands wide. A typical *how are you?* But made significantly slow and with plenty of eye contact and an eyebrow that stayed raised, demanding more than just a quick social *fine*.

Zachary hadn't seen Rhys since Archuro's arrest. It had been in the news and Rhys had doubtless seen online chatter that Vera might not even have been aware of, speculation on what had happened that the police weren't talking about. What had happened during the time that Archuro held Zachary, before the police were able to track them down and effect an arrest and rescue. Like Zachary's other close friends and family members, Rhys wanted to know how Zachary was *really* doing following the traumatic events.

"I am doing okay. Really. It was all pretty crazy, but I'm managing. Moving on and working on other cases."

Rhys cocked his head, considering. He didn't seem to have anything else to say, but waited, looking for more.

"It was hard," Zachary said, "but I'd rather not even think about it. I want to put it behind me."

Rhys still didn't seem satisfied with this. He considered Zachary for a few more long seconds. Zachary couldn't think of what else to say to him.

Rhys lifted his phone and powered the screen on. He tapped around for a minute, and then turned the face toward Zachary.

He saw a picture of himself. One that he had seen a few times, since it had been plastered all over news sites for days after the ordeal had ended. It was a picture of Zachary as he left the hospital—earlier than the hospital or any of his friends had wanted him to—and it clearly showed the bruises on his face. The bruises were not from Archuro, but from a group of neo-Nazis who had attacked him earlier in the investigation. But no one reading the article would know that. In the picture, Zachary's eyes were dark shadows, his face almost skull-like in appearance. He was wearing his own clothes, which he had asked Lorne to bring to the hospital, but they hung loosely on his frame.

He looked awkward and uncomfortable, and if Rhys had seen the accompanying video footage, he would have seen how gingerly Zachary had been moving. No one could see the damage that Teddy had inflicted, but it was there, under Zachary's intentionally loose clothing and deep beneath the surface.

Zachary touched Rhys's hand holding the phone, as if to steady his hand from shaking so that he could see the picture more clearly. But that wasn't the reason he felt the need to touch Rhys.

"I know it looks bad," he said. "But I look better now, don't I?"

Rhys's gaze was piercing, looking not just at Zachary's healed face and his lean body, still not quite up to what the doctor had set as a target weight. Rhys looked much more deeply into Zachary's face, seeking the truth.

Zachary looked away, avoiding the close scrutiny. "I'm doing okay," he promised.

Rhys tapped some more on his phone, and turned it around again to show Zachary a gif of a cartoon character sinking underwater, his fingers held up in a three-two-one count with a bye-bye wave before disappearing below the surface. Certainly apropos of how Zachary sometimes felt.

"Not right now. If I need to… I'll get help. If it gets that bad, I'll check myself in."

Rhys gave him one more keen look, then nodded. As he slid his phone into his pocket, he raised his eyebrows and made a kissing sound. Zachary knew it was an inquiry into Kenzie and how things were going with her, and couldn't prevent the blush that rose to his cheeks. Rhys laughed in delight, the sound giving Zachary an unexpected rush of joy in response. He scratched his nose to hide the grin he couldn't suppress.

"Kenzie is good. I'll have to bring her by to see you again one day."

Rhys made a louder kissing sound, both eyebrows up.

"None of your business!" Zachary's cheeks grew even hotter.

Rhys mimed two hands joining, and then burping a baby on his shoulder.

"Getting married and having a baby? That might be rushing things a bit!"

Rhys indicated heads at descending heights.

"Lots of babies?" Zachary laughed. "You'd better talk to Kenzie about that." He smiled, relaxed. It was nice to think of his relationship with Kenzie and to wonder if it might someday lead to marriage and children.

That was still a long way off, and he needed to sort out the issue of remaining present and not dissociating when they were together. But maybe someday...

He hoped that Kenzie wanted children. Bridget had not. She had told him that from the beginning, but he had assumed she would change her mind. Kenzie had never offered her thoughts on the matter, and it seemed like asking her would be presuming too much. Their relationship was stable, and they were seeing each other exclusively—at least, he assumed that they both were—but he didn't want to scare her off by getting too serious and talking about having babies together. While he badly wanted children of his own, he worried Kenzie might have doubts about his fitness as a father.

He looked back at Rhys, who was waiting for Zachary's attention to return. Seeing that Zachary was once again focused on him, Rhys continued the burping-a-baby mime, followed by acting out throwing up and then gingerly handling a stinky diaper.

Zachary shrugged widely. "You have babies, you have to be prepared to deal with all of the messy stuff," he agreed. He'd cared for and changed younger siblings. It had never bothered him. It made him feel grown up and responsible.

Rhys gagged.

"Then you'd better not mess around," Zachary advised.

Rhys crossed his arms in an X, then pushed them forward and out in a definitive *no way*.

Vera called them to the dinner table.

CHAPTER SEVENTEEN

He was more relaxed when he got home. For once, he felt like he could enjoy the evening instead of needing to crawl straight into bed. Maybe it had been thinking about the future of his relationship with Kenzie, or maybe just seeing Rhys and reminding himself that things could be a lot worse.

He surfed his social media and TV for a while, sent an email note to Kenzie to pass on the greetings from Rhys and to thank her for being so supportive. That was one of the things that he found much easier to say in an email than face-to-face. It could be hard to get the words out when the person was right in front of him and emotions were running high. He could empathize with Rhys in that respect.

Gradually, the night noises of the building started to bother him. It was too quiet, even with the TV left on, and each of the creaks and groans of the building or footsteps in the distance made him flinch or tense further. He decided it was time for a sleeping pill and bed so that he could shut it all out.

He fell asleep quickly, but had restless dreams, his brain obviously processing his concerns with Heather's case and his discussions with Rhys. He dreamed of finding Heather's baby, not a grown man but still an infant, and trying to get Heather to take him. Heather refused, and the baby was sobbing and squirming and threw up on his shirt. Heather still wouldn't take the baby, even to let Zachary get cleaned up, claiming that he'd gotten himself into the mess, it was up to him to get himself out.

The baby became a toddler, crying Zachary's name and pinching his arm. It was his baby brother Vincent, who he hadn't seen since the day of the fire. Zachary tried to kiss his cheek and settle him down, but Vinny continued to call his name and pinch him, jab his finger into the center of Zachary's chest and to slap him on the cheek. He couldn't figure out what was bothering Vinny.

Zachary's eyes opened and he was abruptly awake. He tried to clutch at Vinny, to hold him close and not lose him to the dream, but his arms were empty and he was left puffing, out of breath, trying to reorient himself in time and space.

"Zachary." It wasn't Vinny's voice, but Kenzie's, coming from the dark shadow beside him. He startled violently.

"What? Kenzie?" He sat up, trying to blink her into focus. "What are you doing here? Is everything okay?"

"Oh, thank goodness." She was sniffling.

Zachary fumbled around until he managed to find the lamp on the bedside table and turn it on. Her eyes were shadowed, but he could see tears on her face.

"Kenzie!" He hugged her, trying to comfort her, even though he didn't know what was wrong. She must have had bad news, and she'd needed someone to talk to, so she came to him. "What is it? What's wrong?"

She wiped her tears on his t-shirt, giving a shuddering sob as she tried to stop and talk to him. She swore. "I thought you'd done something. I got your email and it scared me, and when I tried to call you, there was no answer. Then you wouldn't wake up... I was afraid..."

"What?" He squeezed her and then pulled back so that he could see her face. "How did my email scare you? I just wanted to send you a note..."

She wiped her face again. He hoped she wasn't planning to blow her nose on his shirt too. "It sounded like a goodbye. I thought... you'd decided..."

He shook his head. "No!" Zachary was baffled. He grabbed his phone and pulled it off of the charge cord to look at the email he had sent Kenzie, which he could immediately see that she had written several replies to in a row. Without stopping to read them, he opened the original message. His eyes raced over the lines, and he stopped, lowering the phone to look at her.

"I was just being nice!"

"'Thanks for being such a good friend and supporting me all this time'?" Kenzie returned, "That doesn't sound like 'thanks and so long' to you? You scared the hell out of me!"

Zachary allowed a chuckle. "I just wanted you to know how much I appreciate you." He swallowed, trying to keep the lump in his throat from turning into tears. He had a feeling she wouldn't let him wipe *his* tears on *her* shirt. "It wasn't goodbye. I just... it's hard to say out loud, so I thought..."

"Sheesh, Zach." She snuffled, the mucus thick in her throat. "If you're going to say something like that in an email, you'd better at least answer your phone."

He looked at the call log, embarrassed. "I was just asleep. This new one doesn't vibrate very loudly, I didn't hear it."

She leaned with her face against his chest, cuddled up, her body relaxing. He liked the way it felt to hold her close and comfort her. Like when he used to comfort Tyrrell or one of the other littles.

He stroked Kenzie's hair, thinking back to before he had awakened. "I was having a dream. About Vinny."

"Vinny?" She didn't look up at him and her voice was muffled against his body.

"One of my little brothers. Younger than T. I was dreaming about him right before I woke up."

"Yeah? A good dream or a bad one?"

"Good." He held her, rocking slightly. "Except for when he started pinching me."

Kenzie laughed. "Sorry about that. You were hard to wake up. I was worried that you had overdosed, I didn't know whether to keep trying to wake you up or to call for an ambulance."

"I didn't overdose. I took one pill. I just didn't want to wake up from that dream."

"Okay."

He shifted so that they could both lie down together, pulling her legs up onto the bed and spooning against her. Kenzie sighed, warm and soft in his arms. He kissed the top of her head. "I'm sorry for scaring you. I never meant to do that."

"It's okay. It's not like you said 'this is the end' or 'if you're reading this I must be dead.' It just hit me the wrong way, with the trouble you've been having lately... when you said 'thank you for always supporting me,' I just immediately thought it was goodbye. It's not your fault."

"Still. I'm sorry. Next time I'll say 'thank you and I'm not going to kill myself.'"

"Yeah, that would be better," she agreed, her body shaking slightly with a silent laugh.

Zachary fell back asleep holding her.

———

In the morning, he was awake early, like he used to be, and didn't know what to do with himself. He wasn't sure whether he should try to get more sleep, because he'd been sleeping so much recently, or whether he should get up and attack his day, assuming that he was finished sleeping and ready for the day.

What would it be like to have a body that only slept when he needed to sleep and woke up when he'd had enough sleep, instead of trying to analyze it and force his body into some kind of reasonable facsimile of a circadian rhythm? He tossed and turned for a while, but then decided he didn't want to keep Kenzie awake and got out of bed.

"I'll just be a few minutes," Kenzie murmured.

"It's still early. Go back to sleep."

There was no response. She was probably already fast asleep again. Zachary went to his computer and checked his email, again feeling guilty as he deleted Kenzie's increasingly frantic replies to his email. He never would have guessed in a million years that she would misinterpret his intent and panic over something like that. Communication and relationships were complex systems. Miss one signal, and it could throw everything off the rails.

He was glad that Kenzie had just come over and had not panicked and called the police or stayed awake all night worrying about him. And he was glad she had been able to get to sleep after she had found out that he was okay. They would both laugh about it again when she got up. It was a work day, so she wouldn't be in bed too late. But it was still too early for decent people to be out of bed.

He checked social networks and his business emails, routing and sorting what had come in overnight.

There was an email from Heather telling him to call her.

If he hadn't gone to sleep so early, he would have been able to connect with her the night before, and wouldn't have to wait for an answer. But he couldn't call her back so early in the morning and would have to wait until the sun was up and the birds were chirping before calling to see if she had changed her mind about finding the baby.

CHAPTER EIGHTEEN

Eventually, he heard Kenzie stirring. When she got up to use the bathroom, he put the coffee on and checked the cupboards and fridge to see if he had any breakfast foods that might appeal to her. There were some bagels in the freezer, so he took a couple of them out and put them in the toaster oven. She had a quick shower, and then was out, had changed into a spare set of clothes that she kept at his apartment, and joined him in the kitchen.

"Sorry about busting in on you last night."

"No, it's okay. If something had happened, then I would want you to be able to get in." He paused, thinking about what he had just said. What he meant was if some accident befell him. He would want to know that Kenzie was able to get in. But he would not want her coming to the apartment and discovering his body if he intentionally overdosed. It wasn't something he had ever thought about before, and it made him stop buttering the bagels to consider it for a moment. "If something happened to me, I mean," he said. "Not if I…"

"If you intentionally overdosed. Or did something else. That's probably something you should think about, Zachary, because I'm the one who is going to have to deal with it if you do something like that."

Zachary shook his head and resumed buttering the bagels. "I'm not going to do anything. I'm not suicidal right now. You don't need to worry about it."

"I *always* worry about it. Just because you're feeling good right now, that doesn't mean you're not going to have a setback next week. I'm always watching you for signs. Hoping that you'd tell me if you started to feel worse. Worrying because you won't talk about what happened with Archuro. And even when you're acting cheerful, I worry that it's that last little energy boost people get when they've made the decision to kill themselves."

"I've never understood that," Zachary confessed. "I never had that."

She took the bagel that he had buttered and put it on a plate, and then the plate on the table. She got a jar of jam out of the fridge. "Have you ever actually…" she stopped, mouth closing, unable to go on. She looked at the bagel he was buttering, then looked at his face. "Of course you have. I've seen the scars on your arms. You're telling me that when you made that decision, you didn't get a mood elevation?"

"Nope. I've heard that it can be one of the red flags. If you know someone who is depressed and they have an abrupt mood change for the better, that it might actually be an indicator that they are going to make an attempt. But I never had that. I felt kind of ripped off about that."

"That you didn't feel better?"

"Yeah. They say you'll feel better after you make that choice, so that's what you think. But for me, it never happened."

"Huh. Then maybe I can stop worrying when your mood picks up."

He nodded his agreement. He'd never realized before that she worried when he started to feel better. She must feel like she was on tenterhooks all the time. He sat down at the table with her and the second bagel. He watched her eat hers, not really hungry. She looked at him and raised an eyebrow. He took a small bite of the bagel.

"So, what are your plans for the day?" Kenzie asked.

Zachary looked at his watch. "After you go, I'm going to give Heather a call. She emailed me last night to call her back, but I figured it was too early to call her yet. I don't want to wake her up."

"You're probably right. She should be up any time now. Though she doesn't work, so who knows what kind of a schedule she keeps."

"Do you know what she's calling about? Did she say if she thought of something? Remembered a name or another clue?"

"No. Probably not. I want her to have changed her mind about tracing the baby, because I think that's the one thing that could really help. But she really didn't want to the other night. I don't know if that's just because she was afraid and it was too sudden…"

Kenzie nodded and sipped her coffee. "Let me know how it goes. I'm interested in if she'll go for it. I don't know of any cases where they've done that kind of DNA matching for a criminal case."

Zachary leaned toward her. "They have, actually. I've been doing a bunch of research so that I'll be ready if she decides to go ahead, and there are a number of cases where a DNA search has pulled up familial matches, and they've been able to use it as a starting point to identify suspects and build a case. They still need a direct DNA match eventually, but it's a lot easier if you just have one or two suspects to follow around and retrieve their used coffee cups or cigarette butts to make a match. Then once you know you've got the guy, you can start building a case."

"They've used familial matches?"

"Sure," Zachary nodded vigorously. "They do a search on CODIS and find out that they've got the guy's brother in prison. Or there have even been cases where they have used GENEmatch, a public database, to find several relatives of the perp, and then have used genealogical research to find out the relationships between those people to find out who is related to all of them."

Kenzie pursed her lips, thinking about it. "That's pretty smart."

"Yeah. The technology is really amazing."

"I knew DNA profiling was maturing, but I really had no idea we were to that point."

———

When Kenzie headed off to work, Zachary sat down with his computer notes in front of him and dialed Heather's number. He was worried that he would wake her up or that there would be no answer, but in a few rings, she picked up.

"Hi, Zachary."

"I got your email. You wanted to talk about something?"

"I just wanted to thank you for all of your work on this case. I'm sorry that there wasn't enough evidence to lead anywhere…"

Zachary immediately heard Kenzie's 'thank you and goodbye,' and understood why she had been so worried about his email. It did sound like a terminal statement.

"You're welcome. I'm not done, though. I can still canvass the neighborhood, try to make contact with the policeman who initially investigated it, maybe even call your old foster parents to see if they have any insight—"

"No."

"No?" Zachary echoed back, even though he had understood her statement perfectly.

"No. You can't contact the Astors. I don't want you to talk to them."

"They might have a recollection of other assaults that could be related, there might have been certain men they were suspicious of, but there was never any evidence to go on so it didn't make it to the police file... they might not have said anything to you because they didn't want to upset you."

"No. I mean it."

"Okay... well... like I said. There are neighbors. The cops who investigated it."

"I think I made a mistake in asking you to look at the file. I thought that I was ready to know more and to put this guy away, but I was wrong. I can't sleep at night. I just keep dreaming about the assault. I can't think about anything else. Grant wants to know what's wrong. I just want to let it go. Put it back to bed."

Zachary thought about holding Kenzie until she fell back asleep. About doing the same with his siblings when they had cried and had trouble sleeping. The dream of Vinny throwing up the night before and Rhys's miming of Zachary having to take care of baby messes.

"Heather." He interrupted her apologetic goodbyes, cutting right across her. "Maybe there's another way. Did you keep anything from your hospital stay? A memento of the baby?"

"Why would I keep a memento when I was supposed to forget about him?"

"Maybe you didn't want to completely forget. Did you take care of him at the hospital before they took him? Did you hold him and feed him?"

"Why?" she demanded, her voice irritated.

"It's just that... if you have anything that the baby wore or spit up on... we might be able to retrieve his DNA from it."

Heather gave a sharp intake of breath. She didn't answer the question, breathing in his ear and considering the question.

CHAPTER NINETEEN

He arrived at Heather's house a couple of hours later. Zachary wasn't sure what kind of shape he was going to find Heather in when he got there. Would she be angry at him? Would she break down? Would she be emotionless behind a mask? She had to be going through all kinds of turmoil he could only imagine.

He looked at her house for a moment before getting out of the car. A nondescript single-family bungalow in a nondescript, middle class neighborhood. A community where the adults came and went to work every day, the children came and went to school, each family with two cars in a heated garage, a basketball net mounted on the outside so the children could play in the driveway close to mom's watchful eye, and everyone pretended that they were happy with their lives.

Maybe some of them were.

But for Heather, it was all just a masquerade. She pretended to live a normal, happy life while inside she was broken and bleeding. Years ago, not only had she been brutally assaulted, but the people who should have protected, comforted, and avenged her had failed to show any empathy for what she had gone through.

Eventually, he got out of the car and made his way up the sidewalk. He thought that she would open the door as he walked up to the house, having been watching for his arrival, but she didn't. Nor did she open within seconds of his ringing the doorbell. Instead, Zachary was left standing on the front steps, waiting as the seconds ticked by, listening for her footsteps or some other sound from inside. He finally rang the bell again, and knocked hard for good measure. Maybe the doorbell didn't work. Maybe she had been downstairs or had been flushing the toilet or some other sound had drowned it out.

He began to worry that something had happened to her during the time he had taken to get to her house. Had the despair gotten to be too much for her and she had done herself harm? Or had she gone into a dissociative fugue, unaware of the world around her, maybe even wandering off to end up on the street somewhere with no recollection of who she was or where she had come from? All sorts of scenarios ran through his mind.

"Heather?" He pounded on the door again. "Heather, are you there? I want to make sure you're okay. Heather!"

Finally, he heard the sound of the locks being turned and the door made a little suctioning sound as the handle was turned, but it was still a few seconds before she gathered up her courage to open the door completely.

Her eyes were red and swollen, but her expression gave away nothing. She had been hiding behind a mask for decades, and that mask was firmly in place. She wasn't going to let him see her distress. Maybe she felt she had already revealed too much to him. It hurt him to see his big sister in such bad shape. He wanted to give her a hug and comfort her, but he didn't know her well enough. He didn't know how she might respond.

"Do you want to do this?" he asked. "I'm sorry for pushing. If you've changed your mind, I'll leave."

She looked at him for a long moment, emotionless. Then she shook her head, stepped back, and motioned him in.

The house was as quiet as a mausoleum. Zachary imagined it when her children had still lived there, playing and fighting when they were home, coming and going to school, bringing friends home and playing loud music. All of the chaos covering up what Heather was feeling and giving her a sense of normality. Since they had gone, did she feel the silence pressing in on her every day when Grant went to work?

Or was it only oppressive to Zachary and his imagination, and she was actually quite happy with her quiet existence? She could have turned on music or the TV. She could have had friends over, coffee, sewing parties, book club, whatever it was she was into. She could have found a job, or volunteered at the school or some other facility. She didn't have to stay home all day listening to the silence and reliving her assault, her confinement, and handing over the baby she had never planned and couldn't care for.

She didn't stop in the living room, but Zachary paused, not sure what he should do. She must expect him to stop and sit down there on the couch and wait for her return once she had calmed herself or retrieved whatever she had kept all of those years. But Heather looked back at him for an instant, clearly indicating that she expected him to follow.

All the way to the master bedroom. Zachary looked around uncomfortably, feeling like he was intruding on an intimate place. Like the rest of the house, the bedroom was tidy, neat as a pin, immaculately decorated with every picture straight, not a wrinkle in the bedspread, and each pillow artistically placed. It looked like a show home, not somewhere someone actually lived. What did she do with herself all day? He could picture her out in the garage sitting at a potter's wheel as she formed one perfect clay pot after another, opera playing quietly in the background. She must have somewhere she could escape to. Some activity that gave her a sense of peace in the silent, artificial shell.

"Sit down," Heather advised.

Like in Rhys's room, there was no chair. Nowhere to sit besides the bed. And again he felt that feeling of intruding on her space, of being somewhere he wasn't supposed to be. He had pushed past her defenses and into a private place, a violation. When he didn't move, she motioned to the bed.

Eventually, Zachary sat at the end, barely perched on the bed, his feet on the floor, in a position of readiness. He imagined her husband coming home and wondering what the hell this man was doing in his bedroom. Or maybe he and Heather slept separately, Grant in a spare room or a man cave, to give each other their own space. Maybe Grant snored, so they used it as an excuse for their distance, and they lived separate lives, side-by-side in the fake happy home.

Heather went to the closet. She glanced at Zachary. Not nervous about him being there, just checking to make sure that he was settled, that he was watching her. She didn't attempt any conversation. It wasn't the time for small-talk. He was surprised, as he watched her slow, robotic movements, that she wasn't crying anymore. He had expected the tears to start again.

She reached into the closet and pulled out a box. Everything in the closet matched. It wasn't filled with odds and ends of cardboard boxes like Zachary's closet. Instead, they were all in graduated sizes with matching decorative print exteriors. Small flowers on a medium smoky blue background. All the same, lined up on the upper shelves, the whole closet furnished with wire shelves and rods of enamel white.

She placed the one box, larger than a shoebox, but maybe the size of one that would be used for snow boots, and removed the lid.

It was a time capsule of her childhood. There was a bedraggled teddy bear, no bigger than her hand, the backpack that had served her as she had moved between group homes and shelters before she aged out of foster care, a worn shirt that might have had a rock band logo on it, folded so that he couldn't see it. A couple of other trinkets and bits of costume jewelry that looked like Cracker Jack prizes.

"I don't believe it," he said, looking at the teddy bear, "it's George the Bunny."

He couldn't remember why it had been George the Bunny. One of the younger kids must have named it. Maybe Tyrrell. Zachary had never imagined any of their possessions escaping the fire. Heather had slept with George the Bunny clutched to her every night, even as a twelve-year-old, and she must have been holding on to him tightly when the firefighters had rescued her that fateful night.

Heather smoothed one of the bear's round ears with her index finger. "Bunnies have long ears, Zachy," she said softly. He heard the echo of her words over the intervening years. He must have been the one who had named the bear decades before. He hadn't remembered that.

"Joss held on to Mindy and got her out of the house," Heather said. "I held on to my teddy bear. That tells you what kind of mother instinct I have. Rescuing my bear instead of my sister."

"Joss already had Mindy. You couldn't both take her. And the boys were in the other bedroom."

"It was so hot and there was so much smoke. I wanted to go out the door, but it was hot. When we used to have safety presentations at school, and the emergency responders would come and hand out coloring books, they always said to feel the door and if it's hot, you're not supposed to open it. You're supposed to stay low and go out another way."

Zachary breathed shallowly. He stared at the bear, focusing on not sliding back into the memories. His experience hadn't been the same as hers.

He hadn't been in a bedroom, away from the fire. He'd been right in the midst of the blaze.

Heather must have noticed a shift in his body language, because she reached over and grabbed his hand, squeezing it. Trying to hold him in the present.

"I was so relieved when they brought you out. You had been screaming, waking everybody up and telling us to get out of the house. We couldn't get the window open, but the firefighters broke it and got us out. Mom and Dad were out. The firemen brought out everybody except you. I couldn't hear you screaming anymore and I thought you were dead." She swallowed. Her eyes were distant, focused on the memories of that day. "I was so relieved when one of them finally brought you out. We couldn't see you. They took you straight to the ambulance stretcher and the paramedics, so we never got to see if you were okay. But I knew they wouldn't be working on you and giving you oxygen if you were dead."

Zachary nodded. He hadn't seen any of them that night. When the fireman had carried him out of the burning living room, his eyes had been shut, blinded by the smoke, and after they laid him down and started to treat him, he had been surrounded by a wall of people and had never seen his family watching from a distance. He hadn't seen any of them again until the day that he opened Mr. Peterson's door and saw Tyrrell on the doorstep.

"Tyrrell said that you have scars," Heather said. "The social worker told us you were okay. She never said how badly you were burned. You don't have scars on your face."

He had scars on his face, but no burn scars from that fire. Nothing that was too grotesque. "I covered my face," he explained. "Tried to protect it and to breathe…"

With reluctance, he took off his jacket, pushed his sleeves back and displayed his arms to her, turning them to show her the worst of the burn scars on his arms.

"On my legs too, and some on my back."

She studied them, integrating their experiences. She had escaped with George the Bunny and no injuries, and he had been burned badly enough to require skin grafts and still have scars. But most of the time he didn't even think of the burns. Thanks to plenty of PT, there had been no permanent physical disability. The emotional scars ran much deeper.

He saw Heather's eyes shift to his scarred wrists, and he pulled his jacket back on. She made no comment. Zachary looked back at the box from the closet, wondering why she had brought him there. He didn't see any mementos of the baby she had borne.

Heather turned back to it. She gently lifted George the bunny out of the box and laid him on the bed. She lifted out the backpack and felt inside its various pockets. On the third attempt, she grasped something and pulled it out. She opened her hand and displayed it to Zachary. A pacifier in a zipped plastic bag. It was so small he wondered whether it was for a preemie baby. There was a little Donald Duck painted on the front.

She had kept it all those years. He knew how hard it was to hang on to personal items in foster care and group homes. He had kept his camera strapped around his neck all the time, even when he was sleeping. He still lost specialty lenses, even when nobody else in the home had a camera to put them on. Somehow Heather had kept the small memento all of those years, hiding it and guarding it carefully. If any other children had found her hanging on to a baby soother, she would have been teased mercilessly about it. Worse than for a teddy bear.

Zachary didn't take it from her. He wanted it to be her own decision and her own initiative. She could take her time. She'd been pushed around enough by everyone else who had ever touched the case.

CHAPTER TWENTY

Heather sat down on the bed beside him. She didn't look at him, but stared down at the pacifier held in her lap.

"I don't really know why I kept it. Everyone kept telling me that I needed to make a clean break. I had to have the baby, but then I had to give him up. I couldn't raise him. A fourteen-year-old didn't have the resources to keep a baby back then. I would have been on the street. They said that I shouldn't look at him, or hold him, or name him. The doctor would just pass him to the nurses, and they would take him to the nursery, and that would be the end of that. The adoptive parents would get him when he was released from the hospital."

"Things were different back then. But you had other ideas?"

Heather nodded. "I thought at the beginning that I was just going to do what they said. But in the delivery room, after he was born... I couldn't. I couldn't hear him cry and not hold him. I had to see him, to touch him and know that he was real and that he existed. I was so young, Zachary, and I knew I couldn't raise him, but I wanted to see him."

Zachary nodded. He put his hand on her back, then rubbed it when she didn't object to his touch. "None of it was your fault. Not getting attacked and not getting pregnant. And not having to give him up for adoption."

"I told them to give him to me, even though Mrs. Astor said no, and the doctor listened to me." She shook her head. "I'm lucky he did. I've heard of other cases where they wouldn't listen to anything the teen mom said. Like she didn't matter. Like she didn't even exist. But he overrode Mrs. Astor and told the nurses to let me hold him when he was cleaned up."

They were both silent for a few minutes. Zachary let her decide where she wanted to go with the conversation.

"Do you remember what it was like, Zachary? When Vinny was born? Or Mindy? You remember what it's like to look into a brand-new baby's face and hold him in your arms?"

Zachary nodded. They had all been responsible for the children younger than they were. They had taken as much of the load as they had been able to, feeding and changing the babies, taking them for walks in the afternoon after school, going to the park. Trying to keep all of the children out of the house as much as possible. There had still been too much of a burden on their mother. Six children were just too many, especially with their poverty, and when you threw into the mix a child who couldn't moderate his behavior, who was always getting into trouble at school and raising havoc at home... no woman could have been expected to handle it.

"Yes," he whispered to Heather. "New and innocent and... like angels from heaven." He didn't believe in God or heaven. Not really. But he couldn't think of any other way to describe the awe that he felt on holding one of his newborn siblings. He ached to have children of his own and to feel that again. To be responsible for them and to be a good father and raise them to a happier life than he had enjoyed.

Heather looked at him briefly, and nodded. "And he was. Even with everything that came before... I didn't blame him. He was innocent. I imagined him growing up and the things he would do with his life and how lovely he would be."

There was another period of silence.

"I held him as much as I could for the next couple of days. I gave him bottles and changed his diapers and just held him and rocked him and told him how perfect he was. I didn't nurse him. I was afraid it would hurt too much when they had to take him away. They gave me drugs to help to dry up my milk. Then it was time for me to go home and for him to go to his. But I kept this." She looked down at the soother. "Nobody knew. I hid it. I never let anybody see."

Zachary nodded. She looked at him for a moment, pushed her hand into the backpack again, and pulled out another little bag with teeny tiny flannel mittens in it.

"And these." She smoothed the plastic over the mittens, flattening them out. "I was always afraid that someone would find them and take them. So for a long time, I kept them inside my bra." She gave a laugh at Zachary's expression. "In the bag. But that way... I knew no one could see them or get them while I was away from the house. The binky was too awkward to keep with me all the time. I kept it in my school bag, but if I was somewhere else... I couldn't always carry a backpack with me."

Zachary looked down at the two treasures. "That's amazing. I can't believe you managed to hang on to them and keep them a secret for that long. And... were they always in the plastic bag? Did you ever take them out to touch them or wash them or anything?"

"No. I just kept them in the bags. Like they had to be kept in mint condition."

Zachary wondered how many skin cells the baby would have needed to shed inside the mittens for a lab to pull enough DNA to test and how long he would have had to have them on. The soother was a better prospect. It would be coated in the baby's saliva.

"Would you be okay about giving the binky to the police to test for DNA?"

"Would I get it back?"

"I don't know. Maybe not."

She looked at it for a long time. Finally, she sighed and nodded. "Yes. I guess." She swallowed. "Let me take a couple of pictures of it, at least."

"Sure. Of course. And you should probably be the one to hand it to the police. To preserve the chain of evidence. You're the one who can testify that it was in your baby's mouth. That you're the only one who has ever had it in your possession."

"I don't want to talk to the police."

"I'll set up a meeting with Able. He won't accuse you of anything. He's not going to treat you like a suspect. He's not one of the officers who initially investigated it. They're long gone."

"I thought you would do it."

"I'll come with you. I'll do the talking. Everything except actually handing it over."

She drew back. "Maybe. I'll have to think about it. I don't know."

"You've held on to it for thirty years. You can think about it for a few more days."

"Yeah."

"This could catch him, Heather. I've been reading about other cases that have been solved with DNA testing recently, and this could really work."

She raised her eyes to him. "Do you really think so?"

"Yeah. We can't go very far on physical descriptions or people's memories three decades later. But if there is surviving DNA that they can test and search, the chances of getting some kind of hit are really good. A stranger assault way back then, there wasn't much they could do. With your rape kit being destroyed, I didn't think there was any chance at all of finding a stranger. But with this, it's a definite possibility."

"Okay. Give me some more time. I'll think about it. Try to prepare myself."

"Good. I know it can't be easy for you. I know... I wouldn't want to have to relive any of my experiences. And I wouldn't want to have to face the police about them. But if this could end up putting the guy behind bars... it would be good for you to know that he wasn't out there anymore. That someone actually was punished for it."

"Yeah." She touched his face gently, looking into his eyes. She ran her finger down his stubbly chin. He should have shaved before going to see her. Made himself more presentable. "It's so good to see you again, Zachary. I never thought I'd see you again. When they separated us, I thought that was the end of it. That social worker always said she'd let us visit each other, but the longer it went... I knew she never intended to. She thought it was better if we just went on and lived our new lives and didn't think about the past."

"As if that was possible."

She put both of her hands on his face, framing it, staring at his face as if she might never see it again. She ran her fingers over his features like a blind person. Normally, having someone that close to him, intruding on his space would have made him anxious and uncomfortable. But he didn't feel that way with Heather. He took advantage of her closeness to examine her face as well, looking for signs of the little girl he had known. She had a sprinkling of freckles over her nose and cheeks that were familiar. He remembered how freckled she would get in the summer, remembered her blond hair pulled back into tatty pigtails and pictured her laughing, caught up in a game with her siblings. It had been a long time since he had seen that girl.

"It really is me," he told her.

"Yes. I can see." She released his face and sat back again, holding the baby things in her lap. "I don't know how they could have given us up. I know that the social worker said it was voluntary, that they hadn't apprehended us. She said that Mom just couldn't take care of us anymore, but they'd try to change her mind. Maybe after she'd had some time to get some rest, some of us would be able to go back home. But I never thought that was going to happen. I couldn't understand why she gave us up in the first place. I know... it was hard, and she... I don't think she liked being a mom. But I never thought she'd just give us away, like unwanted kittens."

"It was my fault."

"No, it wasn't. The fire might have hurried her decision along, but I think it would have happened sooner or later anyway."

"She said that I was incorrigible. That I was the worst and she would never be our mother again."

Heather frowned. "She didn't. The social worker never said anything like that. Why would she tell you something like that?"

"It wasn't Mrs. Pratt who told me. It was Mom. She told me to my face. At the hospital."

Heather gaped. Her eyes and her mouth were round circles. "How could that happen? The social worker took her to the hospital and let her say that to your face?"

"I think... she thought that when Mom saw me there, when she saw me, she would realize I was just... a hurt little kid and that she would want to take care of me. But she didn't. She said she would never take us back again, especially not me."

"You didn't set that fire on purpose."

He shrugged helplessly. "No. But I did cause it. She's right about that. And if she'd taken us back, who knows what other crap I would have pulled. The house could have burned down with everyone in it. I could have been responsible for all of your deaths, not just for the family being split up."

She put her arm around his shoulders and squeezed him tightly. "You're not the reason the family split up."

"I started the fire and the fire split up the family."

"It would have happened sooner or later anyway. After that night...

how much longer do you think they would have stayed together, even without the fire? Do you think Mom and Dad would have made up and been able to be a happy family after that? Tyrrell doesn't remember how it was, but I know you do. You remember how they would fight. Not just arguing, not just yelling, but hitting and shoving each other around. I thought they'd kill each other one day. It's probably a good thing that they broke up when they did, because I don't think they would both have survived otherwise."

Zachary had seen enough domestic abuse and infidelity cases since then to agree. Couples who fought didn't just stop hitting each other one day. They didn't quit until one of them was killed or had the sense to get out of the situation. Too often, it ended up tragically with one partner or one or all of the children in the morgue. Whenever he heard of one of those cases in the media where one of the parents had killed the children, he thought about his family, and about how lucky he was to have been pulled out of such an explosive and abusive home before it had happened to them.

Or on his darker days, how unlucky.

Zachary gave Heather's knee a squeeze. She used to have such knobby little knees and stick-thin legs. But she'd grown into a woman. "You take whatever time you need to make a decision. And maybe… it might be time to tell your husband about what happened. I think he'd want to know and you need the support."

"Did you tell Kenzie what happened with that sicko serial killer?"

She knew before he shook his head that he hadn't. She'd known it when she had met Kenzie. Probably as soon as she had met Zachary.

"And have you told her about everything that happened when you were a kid?" Heather persisted.

"I don't think I could remember everything that happened when I was a kid."

"Have you told her any of it?"

"She knows generalities. About what happened to the family and me being in foster care. Some of what that was like."

"And did you tell her about any of the sexual abuse?"

Zachary's throat was dry. He swallowed. "No."

"Exactly. Then don't be a hypocrite and tell me I should tell Grant."

He nodded in agreement. It was easy to look at someone else's life and say what they should do, and to repeat what he had heard other people say to him so many times. She should talk openly to her husband, get counseling, go into some kind of support group.

All of the things that Kenzie and Mr. Peterson said would help Zachary to heal.

It was easy to give advice. Not so easy to follow it.

CHAPTER TWENTY-ONE

He went home empty-handed and without Heather's agreement to turn the pacifier over to Able. He thought that she would agree in time, but he understood her not wanting to face another cop over her rape. The cops who had further traumatized her during the investigation had made sure of that.

His phone buzzed and he looked down at it. Kenzie. He answered it hands-free, staring out at the highway ahead of him.

"I'm on my way back. Should be about half an hour. Are you off?"

"Just cleaning up," she confirmed. "You did get out to see Heather, then?"

"Yeah. And after I left there, I went back to the scene... the neighborhood she lived in. The park is still there. Looks like most of the original homes are still there, though a few have been knocked down and replaced. I didn't canvass any homes, but it looks mostly like younger families now, not the people who would have been there thirty years ago. I asked at the library about the old newspapers, and they have an archives room. I didn't have enough time to go through it today, but maybe... I can look through the papers and see if there were any other assaults reported around the same time. Heather said that hers never made it to the paper, so maybe there won't be. Maybe they didn't report on stuff like that."

He was just running through a stream-of-consciousness report of what had happened that day, trying to clarify and order everything in his own mind. He stopped, giving Kenzie a chance to contribute.

"That's good. But...? Did Heather change her mind about tracking the baby down?"

"Oh! I didn't catch you up... we went another direction. I asked her whether she had anything from the baby, anything that might have spit-up or any of the baby's DNA on it."

"And...?"

"She has a pacifier and little mittens. That she's kept in plastic bags all this time and never told anyone about."

"Are you getting them tested?" Kenzie's tone went up, excited about the new lead.

"Maybe. She doesn't want to go to the police herself, but I don't want to break the chain of evidence. So she's going to think about it. I think she will. I'm pretty sure."

"That's great! The pacifier especially should have enough DNA on it to test. Maybe there is a way to catch this guy after all."

"We might just get lucky."

———

Checking the gas gauge as he reentered city limits, Zachary decided he'd better fill up. There was an independent gas station nearby that often priced its gas a few cents cheaper than its competitors, so he thought he might as well go there rather than the station nearer his house.

He and Bridget used to gas up there all the time. It was close to their old apartment. He pulled up to a free pump, his mind flooded with memories. Was it silly to have romantic memories of filling the car with gas? Those first few months after they were married had been happy. They did lots of things together. Went to a lot of events, which required filling up the tank pretty often.

There was a yellow VW parked at one of the other pumps, which set his heart racing. It looked just like Bridget's car. The owner was inside the convenience store, so he allowed himself to fantasize for a moment that it was Bridget's car and they were both there together again. It was hard to stay focused on filling his own car with the yellow VW there.

His brain immediately went back to the days after the divorce when he had been tracking her movements. It wasn't creepy, it wasn't to threaten her or to show up places where she was. It was just… comforting to know where she was and what she was up to. Even as he pumped his gas, it was difficult to tamp down his impulse to meander past the yellow VW and see if he could unobtrusively slide a tracker under her bumper. He could crouch down to tie a shoe, make sure that no one was looking, and put it into place. Then once again, he'd be able to follow her on his phone and to know where she was at all times.

And she would find it again, and she would get a restraining order. And he could end up in jail.

He looked away from the car to the numbers on his pump as the tank was nearing full.

He looked back at the convenience store as a blond woman walked out and headed toward the yellow VW.

It *was* Bridget. He had to blink his eyes several times and shake his head before he was convinced that it really was her and not a flashback or hallucination. It really was her car. It really was Bridget.

He should have been thrilled at the unplanned sighting, but Bridget seemed pale. Maybe it was just the fluorescent lighting underneath the canopy. She opened her door and then stood there for a moment, her hand going to her pelvic area as if she were bloated or in pain. That was all it took for a kaleidoscope of memories to flood back of Bridget before and in the early days after her diagnosis. Before their relationship had blown apart and he had been excised from her life. As if she needed to surgically remove him before the cancer.

He stared at her, and as if his gaze were so intense that she could feel it, she turned and looked at him. Zachary swallowed. He immediately looked for an excuse to be there, a way to explain to him why he was in the same place as she was. Bridget slammed the door of the VW closed and marched over to him, her eyes blazing.

"Zachary. What are you doing here?"

He looked at the gas pump, where the numbers had quit moving. "I was out of town. I was just filling up. I remembered it was cheaper here."

She looked at the gas pump. It was obvious that his tank had been low. He wasn't just pretending that he needed gas while he stalked her. "Are you following me?"

"No. I haven't done that for—" he choked, his voice betraying his emotion, "—it's been months. I swear."

"If you put anything on my car, I'll find it! I'll go straight to a mechanic and have him put it up on a lift, and he'll find whatever you put on there!"

"I didn't. I was just filling up. I didn't realize it was your car until you came out."

"Excuse me," Bridget used a loud voice to address the potential witnesses, who were in their own worlds gassing up their cars or picking up snacks. She pointed at the VW. "Has this man been near my car? Did anyone see him walk up to my car or touch it or look in the windows?"

They looked around at each other, not liking being pulled into some kind of dispute. But everyone shook their heads, looking at Bridget with wide eyes.

"I've just been here, I didn't get close to it," Zachary insisted.

"Don't try telling me you wouldn't rather be over there, touching my car, looking through my stuff, putting a bug on it." Bridget's voice was harsh as she turned back to him.

Zachary shook his head, unable to find his voice. He was electrified by her proximity, his heart racing at being so close to her. Was it possible that she could stand there, just inches away from him, and not feel the chemistry between them? Kenzie insisted that the vitriol Bridget aimed at him was proof that she was still attracted to him, that it was just camouflage for what she was really feeling.

Being so close to her, Zachary just wanted to hold her and comfort her, to tell her that he was sorry and that they could get back together again. It was a complete betrayal of the relationship he had with Kenzie, but he couldn't help the desire he felt whenever he was close to Bridget. He wanted to recapture those first happy days together.

Bridget stopped talking. She just stood there looking at him, breathing heavily. Her paleness was more than just the bluish lighting of the gas station. Her eyes rolled up as if she were going to faint and he released the gas nozzle and reached out for her, trying to catch her before she could collapse to the ground. She recovered and slapped his hands away, not letting him touch her.

"What is it?" Zachary asked. "Are you okay? Bridge?"

"Don't touch me. I don't need your help."

His heart was beating so fast he was only a hair's breadth away from a panic attack. But he had to hold it together for her. Despite her words, he was sure that she needed him. She was clearly sick.

Was the cancer back? He remembered how she had been in the days before and immediately after the diagnosis, before she had started treatment. Pale, nauseated, making frequent trips to the bathroom. They had both mistaken the early signs for pregnancy.

Zachary had been overjoyed at a positive home pregnancy test.

She had not been.

Not overjoyed and not pregnant.

"I didn't follow you here. I didn't know you were here. That it was your car here. Bridget, you're sick. Let me help. Does Gordon know…?"

He reached toward her again, wanting to escort her back to her car, to settle her in and make sure she was safe to get home. Maybe he should call Gordon to pick her up, to avoid her having to drive when she was sick.

"Just leave me alone, Zachary. Don't touch me. And if I see you near me or my car again…!" She didn't voice the threat. "I'm going to get it checked out, and if you have put some kind of tracker or bug on it, I swear, I'll have you in court for stalking."

"I didn't. I haven't been anywhere near it." He gestured at the people who had spoken up for him, the people who had agreed he hadn't been close to the car.

"Maybe you didn't now. Maybe it was earlier in the week, and you followed your tracker here so you could just *happen* to be where I was. I'm going to have it checked out."

"Is it back?" He had to know. "Your cancer? Please tell if it is."

Her look softened only slightly. "No. It's not. Now just stay away from me and leave me alone."

CHAPTER TWENTY-TWO

Kenzie was at the apartment went he got there, as they had agreed. Zachary had forgotten between the time that they talked and the time that he got home that she was coming. He brushed it off irritably as ADHD distraction. He'd just had his mind on the case. Of course she was there.

Kenzie greeted him with a brief hug and kiss, then studied his face. "What is it?"

"What? Nothing."

She touched the worry lines between his eyes. "Something is bothering you."

"Just thinking about the case."

"What is it? You sounded happy on the phone with the way things were progressing."

"I am. I'm glad that we might have a way to find the guy who hurt Heather. Really glad." He didn't want to tell her about running into Bridget at the gas station, and about his concerns with her health. What if Bridget were lying and the cancer was back? Or she didn't know that it was back yet? He knew Kenzie wouldn't like him worrying about it, but how could he not be upset when his ex-wife was in danger of her life? "No, I'm just worried about her."

"About Heather?"

Zachary brought his thoughts back to the conversation. "Heather. Yes."

"What are you worried about?"

They wandered together into the living room and sat down. Zachary looked around. Kenzie had ordered in, but he wasn't hungry. His insides were still twisting around as he worried about Bridget.

"Just… I don't know. Heather is dealing with something really traumatic… but she doesn't have a support system. Her husband doesn't even know about it. When she came to the door… it took a really long time and I was worried that she might have done something. And then, it was obvious she had been crying, but she didn't show any emotion. The whole time I was there… she was keeping so much bottled up. I kept waiting for her to start crying, but she just withdrew. Put up a wall."

Kenzie nodded, a hint of a smile on her face.

"I know I'm a hypocrite for thinking she'd be better off if she would talk about it and get some support," Zachary admitted. "She told me that."

"Yeah. You see what it's like now to deal with someone who is holding so much inside, and you just can't… reach them."

"Uh-huh. I'm sorry for being that way, but… it's just… when we were kids, the attitude was just to forget it and go on. It was best to just put bad experiences behind you."

"Are you talking about the fire," she asked carefully, "or something else?"

He wasn't going to talk about Teddy.

"About everything. As a foster kid, they know you're damaged. They know you're not going to like things about the home they put you in. That you're going to have trouble adjusting to a new school. That there are going to be personality clashes, especially with other foster kids or 'troubled' youth. And the attitude is—or at least, was—just shut up and deal with it. They don't want to hear the complaints. The family is doing the best they can to deal with your physical needs, and they know it's never going to be perfect. If you're going through a rocky patch… you just push through. Whatever kind of crap you might have to deal with… you just try to survive."

"I can understand that for little things. You're not going to have all the toys and clothes other kids have, and you're going to have to get used to new foods and rules and bedtimes. But for the more serious stuff… they wouldn't tell you to just shut up, would they?"

"If they don't listen to you about the little stuff, why would you talk to them about the big stuff? You don't have…" Zachary searched for a way to put it into words, "you don't have any trust. They haven't given you any reason to think that they would fix it. If they can't fix little things, and they don't believe you or they blame you for things when you complain… you know they'd just do the same about other stuff. Look at the way Heather was treated when she was attacked. The cops told her it was her fault. Her parents and social worker told her that she had to give the baby up and never think about him again. They all knew she'd been raped. But it was inconvenient for them. They told her to just forget about it and move on. So that's what we learned to do."

Kenzie stroked his arm with the tip of her finger as she thought about it. "That makes me so sad, Zachary. For her and for all of you. You know, you see these movies on TV about foster care… about those inspiring cases where they took in a foster child and made him part of the family and everything worked out so wonderfully. Like Anne of Green Gables or The Blind Side. But what you've told me about your experiences, and what I've gathered from what Tyrrell and Heather have said… it's far from a fairy-tale ending."

Zachary nodded. He caught her hand and held it for a minute against his face, so warm and strong. She wanted to be there for him. And he didn't want to shut her out. Not really.

"Everybody has stuff happen in foster care. People know they can get away with abuse because you've been trained not to complain."

She looked at him and he tried not to look away. "You want to talk about it?"

"No. But maybe I do need to."

───

It was three long days before Heather called. Zachary worked hard on other jobs to try to forget about her case, and to forget about the rest of the mess broiling in the back of his brain. He slept a lot, sometimes even in the middle of the day, and was irritable when anyone woke him up, though he refused to tell them that he'd been sleeping. He didn't want anyone to know how much of his day he was spending just avoiding life.

He'd been dozing in front of his computer, trying to decide whether to lie down on the couch and actually get an hour of sleep, when the phone vibrating jolted him back into consciousness. He pulled it out, already scowling about whoever was waking him up, when he saw by the caller ID that it was Heather.

"Hey, Feathers."

There was a sharp intake of breath and then she laughed. "Do you know how long it's been since I heard that name, Zachy? Oh, my. I forgot!"

He smiled at the real pleasure in her voice. They'd had good times together. He wanted her to remember that. She had been a fun big sister. He wished he could still see some of that carefree bluster in her.

She gave another laugh and continued. "So I called to say… go ahead and set something up with the cop. I'll give him the baby's binky to test."

"Great. I'll give him a call. Is there a specific time that you want to meet? Or a time that doesn't work for you?"

"No, I can do it pretty much any time. There's no one here to tell me when I can or can't do anything."

"Okay. I'll let you know when I've got it set up. And don't worry, it's going to be okay. It's not going to be like it was back then."

"I'm tough," she said breezily, as if she had no concerns about it. Apparently, it was easier for her to mask her feelings over the phone. "Whatever. I don't care what he says."

CHAPTER TWENTY-THREE

Zachary had a meeting set up with Able and was on his way to meet the two of them within half an hour. The highway driving didn't bother him. He always found it meditative, easy to get into a zen state. He'd had several therapists who had suggested meditation as a way to deal with his PTSD and ADHD, but none of them had ever suggested highway driving as a way to get into that mindset.

He met with Heather in the foyer of the police station. She was noticeably jittery, her eyes flicking around, trying to take everything in, hands tapping at the sides of her legs and worry lines between her eyebrows. He tried to be supportive and reassuring without treating her like a child or making promises he couldn't keep.

"It shouldn't take too long. Able is an old hand at this. He wants to solve the case, he just hasn't had any evidence to go on. He'll be happy to get DNA to test."

Heather nodded. Her eyes were so wide that he could see the whites all around her iris. He tapped the thumb and fingertips of one hand together, trying not to get wound up by her anxiety.

"It's lucky that you kept those things from the baby. Not lucky, I mean. Smart. You couldn't have known back then that they would ever be useful in the assault case, but you kept them, and you made sure they were safe, and that's why we can move this case forward."

"I just… wanted something to remember him by. I didn't want to be forced by the social worker and everybody else. I wanted to make the decision myself."

"Would you still have given him up if you'd had the choice? If it had been all up to you and you knew that you could have supports?"

She looked at him for a minute, the frown lines getting deeper, then they smoothed out. "No, probably not. I was just a kid myself. I wasn't ready to be a mom. I was trying to keep myself alive. Being in charge of another person would have been too much for me. I was just trying to make it from one day to the next."

"Yeah. But it still would have been nice if they had let you make that decision."

Heather grunted in agreement.

Zachary saw Able approaching. Able looked around the lobby and gave Zachary a wave. "This way, folks."

He led them again to a meeting room. A different one from where he had met Zachary before, he thought. Smaller. But maybe that was just Zachary's anxiety and having more people in the room than when they had met the first time.

"This is Heather Goldman, my sister," Zachary introduced. "Heather, this is Detective Able."

Heather nodded. She folded her arms, not putting her hand out to shake. She looked thin and cold and Zachary could almost see her as she had been back then, a gawky adolescent, hurt and scared to death by what had happened to her and what was going to happen next. She probably hadn't known the ordeal she was going to go through, but she knew enough to recognize that it wasn't going to be good.

"Why don't you have a seat," Able suggested. He pulled out one of the chairs and sat down himself, not waiting to see if they would. Heather paused for a moment, then pulled out the next chair and sat down. Zachary pulled out the chair around the corner on her right and sat down with her. He gave her leg a reassuring pat and looked at her face to see if she wanted to say anything.

"We've come across some evidence that the police didn't have at the time of the original investigation," he told Able.

Able raised his eyebrows. He scratched the back of his neck and waited for more information. He hadn't brought the file with him. Zachary had said that they had something to show him, not that they wanted to look at the file again.

"What they didn't know at the time of the investigation was that Heather got pregnant by her attacker," Zachary said, enunciating the words quickly and getting them out of the way. Like ripping off a bandage. "She had the baby and gave him up for adoption."

Able tapped on the table with the end of a pen. "That's very interesting. Even if they'd known it at the time, though, there wouldn't have been anything they could do with it. Paternity tests wouldn't be available for a number of years, and even then, they would need a sample to compare it against."

"But now they can."

"Do you know the location and identity of the baby you gave up?" Able directed his question at Heather.

But Zachary had promised her that she wouldn't have to talk, and he jumped in to make good on his word. "She doesn't know where he is and was never told who adopted him. But when I asked her if she had kept anything from when she was in hospital with the baby, she did."

Zachary nodded to Heather, and she carefully put the baby pacifier in the plastic bag down on the table. Able stared at it, fascinated.

"A soother. The baby used this?"

"Yes," Zachary agreed. "He used it for several days and it wasn't washed. She put it into the plastic bag and she kept it hidden until now. It hasn't been taken out of the bag."

Able looked at Heather. "If we match it to something, you might have to testify in court. Could you testify to that? That the baby was the only one who used it and that you kept it protected from the time you took it out of his mouth until now?"

Heather nodded. "I never took it out of the bag. And no one else has ever touched it. Just me and the baby."

"Well, there's no telling how much the DNA might have degraded and if it will still be usable, but we can try."

Zachary breathed out a long sigh of relief. "You'll have the lab test it and run it through CODIS and any other databases the police department has access to? You'll find out if the father has ever been convicted of a crime?"

Able nodded. "Best if I have a swab of the mother too. Will you give a sample?"

Heather nodded without the hesitation Zachary had seen in her previously.

"Thank you," she said softly.

"Don't thank me. You're the one who is doing this. It never even occurred to me that there might be a baby or DNA that hadn't been destroyed. I'm going to ask you some questions. This is for the record, it's just procedure. Don't take them personally, okay?"

Heather nodded. She looked at Zachary with dread in her eyes. Under the table, he caught her hand and held it tightly.

"Are you one hundred percent sure that your attacker was the baby's father?"

She breathed out. "Yes."

"Was there anyone else that you had sexual contact with?"

"No."

"Before or after the assault. Anyone at all."

"No."

"Did you have a boyfriend at school?"

"No."

"Anyone that you messed around with? Kissed under the bleachers or in a lonely hallway?"

"No."

"What about in your foster home? Did Mr. Astor ever molest you?"

She shook her head. Zachary could see her withdrawing, shriveling up into herself. He squeezed her hand again.

"Never? He didn't come into your room at night? He didn't touch you? Ever?"

"No."

He studied her, looking for the truth. "There were other boys in the home. Two older boys."

"Yes."

"What about them? Did you go out with either of them? Experiment? Did either one of them show you unwanted attention?"

"No." She held tightly to Zachary's hand. He could see her breathing, rapid and shallow. The little freckles stood out on a sheet-white face.

"And there was no one else who you were intimate with? No one at all?"

She shook her head.

"So you're one hundred percent sure that this baby was conceived in the assault."

"Yes," she whispered.

"What day was he born?"

Heather gave his date of birth. Able's lips moved as he calculated the weeks between the two dates.

"A couple of weeks preterm."

"Yes."

"And his weight?"

"Six pounds."

Able was checking all of the boxes. If the baby were weeks premature and weighed ten pounds, that would be a problem.

"Whose names were on the birth certificate?"

"Mine. And unknown."

"If I tracked down the Astors or your social worker, they would tell me that you didn't have any boyfriends?"

Heather looked terrified. "You're not going to call them?"

"If we end up prosecuting the case, these questions are going to come up. They're going to want to question your foster family and the social worker. And anyone else they deem appropriate. They'll want as many first-hand witnesses as possible."

"I didn't have a boyfriend."

"They would corroborate that?"

Heather nodded. "I haven't seen them in years, though," she said. "I don't know where they are."

"You leave that to me. If necessary, we can track them down. First, we'll see if we can get a hit on this sample."

She blinked, looking at it. "I just want to be able to move on."

"Have you had counseling? We have victim services. I can give you some numbers."

"I couldn't talk to anyone about it."

"But you have now. You're stronger than you think."

Heather looked up at him in surprise.

He met her gaze. "You *are* strong. You look at what you went through. If you want, I can bring the file in here and show you the pictures. The little girl that went through that hell was tougher than any of the cops who questioned her. Tougher than the foster mom or the social worker. Strong enough to stand up for herself and tell what happened to her. And to carry a baby and bring it into the world."

Heather swallowed. "And to give him away."

He nodded. "And to give him away. You have carried a heavy burden for decades. By yourself, without telling anyone about it. And you're strong enough to share that burden with someone now and lighten the load a little."

CHAPTER TWENTY-FOUR

Heather's step seemed a little lighter when they left the police station. Zachary didn't know if she was going to call any of the numbers that Able had given her, but she had accepted them, folding them carefully and putting them into her purse. She was quiet as Zachary walked her to her car, a dark blue four-door. She stopped with her door open before getting in.

"Thanks."

"He's right, you know. You're strong."

"Strong enough to let it go?"

"I think so."

"What about you?"

Zachary didn't answer. His hand was on her car door, and she stroked the scar on one of his wrists that showed with his sleeve riding up a couple of inches.

"You're strong too."

Zachary didn't believe it. He was a train wreck. Bridget had taunted him for being a coward, for running away from conflict, for having a panic attack when faced with his worst fears. Group home leaders and professionals who had been tasked with caring for him had bullied him relentlessly for his dysfunctional ADHD and PTSD behaviors.

Even those who tried to help him; Mr. Peterson, Kenzie, Mario

Bowman, they pitied him for his weakness and tried to protect him from the stresses of the world because they knew he couldn't handle it himself.

He forced a smile and nodded at Heather. "Sure."

She looked at him for another minute, then climbed into her car. "He said it would be a couple of weeks for the lab to do their work."

"Yup."

"And you'll come in with me when he calls?"

"Of course."

———

Zachary had, without Kenzie or anyone else in his support network knowing, been skipping his appointments with his therapist ever since getting back after breaking the Teddy Archuro serial killer case. He would call his therapist's office a day or two before an appointment or even the day of, and announce that he wouldn't be able to attend due to some work or family emergency. They would dutifully reschedule, and he'd have a couple more weeks before he had to do it again.

After all of the talks with Kenzie and Heather, he decided it was time to tough it out and actually go to his appointment. So he sat in the upholstered chair in front of Dr. Boyle's desk and waited for her to begin the session. She wrote down the date at the top of the page at the front of his file, then flipped back to look at the last session notes. She flipped through a few pages, frowning.

"Has it actually been that long since you've been in, or are we missing some session notes?"

Zachary cleared his throat. "It's been quite a while," he admitted. "I've rescheduled... a few times."

"A few? What's been going on?"

He sat there looking down at his hands. If he wanted to get help, then he needed to be truthful with her. He knew all of the things he would tell Heather. He would tell her that she needed to be fully open and honest if she wanted to get the benefits of the therapy session. That there was no way for the doctor to know what she had been through if she didn't explain it. But he wasn't sure how to start.

"Zachary? How about you tell me what's happened with you since the last time you were in for a session?"

"I had a case."

"A case of what?" She didn't look up from the file.

"A missing person case. Someone I was supposed to track down."

"Oh. Of course. And how did that go? Did you find him?"

"I was…" Zachary was a little baffled that she didn't seem to be aware of anything that had been reported in the media. "You didn't see any of it on TV or the internet? About the serial killer they arrested?"

She looked up, frowning. "Yes, I heard the buzz about that, of course."

"That was my case. That's what it turned into. The missing man was one of his victims."

"You broke *that* case?" Dr. Boyle looked astonished.

"They didn't even know there was a serial killer before I started. I was the one who had to convince them that they were looking for someone who had been killing gay illegal immigrants for years."

"And you tracked down who it was."

"I sort of… walked into his net. Not the best way to track a killer."

"No," she studied him, "probably not the best." She swiveled her chair toward her computer. "Do you mind? My recollection of the articles that I saw is really vague. I don't know how I didn't connect that you were involved in the case."

She brought up a browser window and tapped in her search. Her screen immediately filled up with hits, and she opened one of the top links, the comprehensive story by one of the big national syndicates. Zachary saw Teddy Archuro's handsome face. She scrolled down too fast to actually be reading the article, but maybe skimming the headings as she moved down the page. She paused at a picture of Zachary, the one Rhys had of Zachary leaving the hospital. She stared at it for a long minute.

"I never would have even recognized you. I'm sorry, I never clued in that this was you." She was silent as she read the next portion of the report. Then she clicked to minimize the browser and turned to him, her expression grave.

"If I'd realized… I would have made sure my office manager knew not to reschedule you."

Zachary shifted uncomfortably. "Sorry."

"You should have been in here for extra sessions, not skipping out."

"I just didn't feel like I could handle it. I wasn't ready."

"Well, now it's time to pay the piper." She sat back in her chair, giving him her full attention. "Let's talk."

———

Zachary awoke to the ringing of his phone. He had given up on leaving it on vibrate, sleeping through too many important client calls. He had selected the loudest, most annoying ring he could find, and kept the sound on whenever he was at home. When he left the house, he could turn it back to vibrate so that he could drive or meet with clients without interruption, but when he was at home, he needed to know when people were calling him.

He picked it up and looked at the face. Heather.

"Hi, Feathers."

She gave a little laugh, not so surprised by this greeting as she had been the first time. "Hi, Zachy. How are you doing?"

"Fine. What's up?" He tried to figure out what day it was and to count back to when they had given Able the DNA sample. He was pretty sure that it was too soon to have any results back yet, even if they had put a rush on it.

"I told Grant."

"Told him what?"

"Everything. Well…" she trailed off a little. "I couldn't tell him every-thing at once, that's just too much, but I told him the main points. About… the assault and the baby, and giving him away. And about you, and opening up the case again. And the DNA."

"That's a lot. How did he handle it?"

"Really well." Her voice was warm. He could hear the relief in it. In spite of everything that they had all told her, she had still been afraid that he would reject her when he heard the truth. He would consider her damaged goods, or think it was her fault, or would be angry at her for keeping it a secret for so many years. But that hadn't happened and Zachary was grateful to the man that he'd never met. He'd shown Heather the respect that she deserved, and that would go a long way to helping Heather to talk more about the details and to start the healing process.

"I'm glad. That's really good."

"And you know… he actually wasn't that surprised. I always thought I'd done a pretty good job of hiding my past and acting like nothing had happened. But he'd suspected for a long time. He said he knew that someone had hurt me that way. He knew that I had issues that I'd been trying to cover up all these years."

"Didn't he ever ask you about it?"

"Well… little things, now and then. He never pushed hard, and I was never ready to tell him anything about it, so he'd just let it go."

"Patient guy."

She laughed. "Yeah, he is. Waiting all this time, through pregnancy and kids and being empty-nesters, before I finally told him what had happened."

"I'm glad you did it. You sound… less burdened."

"Yeah. That's how I feel, too. Lighter. It's been really hard all of these years, to wear a mask the whole time. Or at least the whole time that I was with other people. Being here alone in the house, sometimes I could let go, and cry or scream into a pillow. I didn't even always know what was bothering me. Just that everything was too much. That I was unhappy all the time, even though nobody was doing anything to make me feel that way and I could choose to do whatever I wanted to… I just couldn't find anything that would make me happy. I didn't have anything I wanted to do. Except maybe sleep. Grant and the kids used to joke about how I needed afternoon naps more than the kids did. I would just…"

"Hibernate," Zachary contributed. "Shut it all out and not have to think about anything."

"Yeah. Exactly."

They were both quiet for a bit.

"How about you, Zachary?"

"What?"

"How are you doing with everything? When I came to you, it was because of that guy. Because I knew that you had gone through what I had gone through, so you would be able to understand. I'm just wondering… how you're managing."

He sighed and stared off into space. Heather was one of the people who wouldn't accept that he was just fine and had gotten over his experience with Teddy Archuro. She knew that even if he were doing everything he could for his mental health, it was going to take time, and that his mind would need time to heal just like his body did. And it would take longer.

"I went back to my therapist. I couldn't tell her much, but she knows now, and she's modified up my schedule, so that I'm seeing her more often. I'm still… not really ready to talk about what happened."

"Yeah. That's okay. You don't need to rush it. Work around the edges."

"Uh-huh. Are you seeing someone?"

"Yeah. I called some of the numbers that Able gave me. So I've got a therapist, and a doctor who has put me on a few meds to see if they will help with my focus and depression, and I'm going to a couple of support group meetings a week now, while I try to sort it out."

"That sounds like a lot. It must keep you busy."

"Not really. But I'm trying to get out to other places too. Going for walks. I might do some volunteering. I've never really worked, so I don't know if I'll get a job, but I can at least help out at a shelter or soup kitchen. Do something for other people. Think about other people who are going through troubles too, instead of just myself. It might help."

He thought about her sleeping the days away, like he had been, blocking out the memories, not just for days but for decades. He didn't want to live that way. He didn't like it when he couldn't sleep, either. It seemed like there should be a happy medium somewhere between not getting any sleep and having to sleep all the time, but he couldn't seem to find it.

"I could teach you some stuff about skip tracing and some other basic detective work. If that's something you'd be interested in."

"Really? You think I'd be any good at that?"

"There's a lot of stuff that you can just do on your computer. Finding people, doing background, scouting out surveillance locations, that kind of thing. It wouldn't be anything dangerous. It's not like on TV. I don't carry a gun and end up in firefights with suspects. I don't even own a gun."

"No, but you have gotten yourself into some trouble," she pointed out.

"Well… that's not stuff you'd have to do, though. Kenzie says these things wouldn't happen to me if I just thought things through and made better decisions." He paused. "Just like every school teacher and foster mother always told me. Being a private investigator doesn't mean that you have to put yourself in harm's way. And you don't even have to have a license to do a lot of the stuff that I do. If you're interested…"

"Yes!" She surprised him with her vehemence. "I'd love to learn about what you do. I don't know if I'd like it or not, but since you're offering… yeah, I'd like to give it a try."

CHAPTER TWENTY-FIVE

enzie had been working long hours for a couple of weeks, staying late and putting in so much overtime that a lot of the time she didn't even have time to talk to Zachary on the phone. Surprisingly, that was okay with him. He felt like he needed some time to himself and that he hadn't had any since he had returned home from the Archuro investigation. Kenzie had been there too much, attentive, watching him, trying to keep him on track, and it had been suffocating him. It was good that she had to pull back and focus on her work more.

Dr. Boyle said that Zachary needed to talk to Kenzie and get things sorted out with her, but he was content that for a couple of weeks anyway, he had a good excuse not to. She had too much on her plate as it was. She didn't need a needy, damaged boyfriend trying to split her attention.

But she had put away the big case that she and the rest of the medical examiner's office had been working on, and had arranged for a celebratory dinner at their favorite buffet. She claimed she was going to take a full week off and just sleep the whole time. That sounded like paradise to Zachary, but he knew she wouldn't actually do it, and that even if he tried to sleep for a solid week, he would still have to get up and think about his life and deal with his career and relationships and face the world. There wasn't any way he could just turn off for a week or two.

Back at the apartment after dinner, Kenzie waved away Zachary's suggestion of a movie and popcorn.

"I want to spend some time with you," she insisted. "It's been crazy hectic and you're important. I know it hasn't felt like it lately, and I want to make up for it."

"We would be watching together. We could cuddle. I could rub your feet."

Kenzie shook her head and gave his hand a little tug to urge him toward the bedroom. "Real time. Not screen time. Just you and me. That foot rub is not a bad idea. And maybe a back rub. Maybe a full-body massage. And whatever else we need to do to get totally relaxed." She grinned and waggled her eyebrows at him in a Groucho Marx impression.

Zachary followed her without objection, but his mind was going a mile a minute. Kenzie sat down on the edge of the bed, and patted the center of it. "Come on. Come here. Let's just enjoy each other's company."

He did as he was told. Kenzie kissed him, pushed him down, and embraced, putting her weight on him. Zachary put his hands on her shoulders, stopping her. Kenzie rolled onto her side and looked at him, curious but not upset. Looking at him to see what he wanted.

Zachary swallowed. He looked past her, but then realized he was shutting her out and tried to focus on her face. He looked at the bridge of her nose rather than into her eyes. "I've had a few appointments with my therapist."

She cocked her head. "Yeah... but you've been doing that forever, haven't you? For at least the last year."

"No." He pressed his lips together, biting them inside and trying not to feel like the little boy who had been caught shoplifting. "I've been skipping out. Avoiding it. Ever since... you know."

She leaned back onto one of the pillows, fluffed it up and repositioned it, and continued to look at him. She was relaxed. Not jumping all over him. He'd been expecting a Bridget-scale explosion, demanding to know why he hadn't been going to his appointments and how he could have lied to her and told her that he was. He wasn't sure he had ever lied to Kenzie about it straight out, but he had certainly obfuscated and never intended for her to know that he was skipping them.

"And now you've started going again," Kenzie prompted.

"Yeah. I'm sorry..."

"No. Go on. I'm glad you started going back to him."

"Her."

"What?"

"Her. My therapist is a woman."

"Why did I think it was a man?"

He shrugged uneasily. "I might have let you think that."

"Why? Did you think I would be jealous? Or think it was inappropriate?"

"I don't know. I just didn't want you to think I was spending time with another woman, I guess. Or telling another woman things about myself and our relationship."

She shook her head, smiling and bemused. "I don't know why you think that would bother me."

"Just being silly, I guess... Bridget might have minded."

"Might have, or did?"

"I don't know. I wasn't really seeing anyone while I was with her. Just whoever I needed to see to get my meds. Bridget never liked me talking to other women..."

"She's one crazy broad."

"She's not crazy," Zachary protested. "If anyone was crazy... it was obviously me."

Kenzie chuckled. "Well, I'm not going to argue with that part. You're kind of veering off topic though. You're seeing your therapist again. That's where this started. So tell me about that."

Zachary hesitated. He shifted around on the bed, trying to find a position where he was comfortable and didn't feel vulnerable. It was difficult talking about intimacy when he was on the bed with her and feeling so exposed.

"I talked a little about us, and about dissociation..."

"Good." She nodded. "I'm glad you talked about that. What did she have to say?"

He felt a little more confident going on. "She talked about grounding and anchoring. Ways to help me to stay present when I have a flashback or something starts bothering me. And she said that we—you and I—should try to find things that are less triggering, and get gradually more comfortable before... moving into things that are more triggering."

"Okay."

"The trouble is…" Zachary gave a helpless shrug and his face heated. "Pretty much anything is triggering right now, so I don't know what to do about that."

"We could talk about it."

"Isn't that what we're doing?"

"No… I don't mean talking about it as a concept. I mean, talking about it in the moment. Talk about how it feels. When she's talking about anchoring, is she talking about noticing concrete things in your environment? Five things you see, five things you hear, stuff like that?"

Zachary shouldn't have been surprised that she would know the technique, but he was. He nodded and rubbed his short whiskers. Kenzie was in the medical profession, so why would he be surprised? She was the one who had brought up his dissociation, so she had probably researched it on her own, looking for ways to help him or fix their relationship.

"Yeah. That's what she was saying."

"So you can talk to me about what you're seeing and feeling, right? That will help you not to dissociate. And if something bothers you too much, I'll know right away and can back off. It's not that different from telling your partner when something feels good or you want them to do something differently, is it?"

Zachary's scalp prickled as his embarrassment grew. He gave a quick nod.

"I'm cool with talking. Are you?" Kenzie asked.

"Uh… maybe. I'll try."

"Okay." She reached out and cupped the side of his face in her hand, and ran her thumb down his jawline. "Since we're talking about what feels good and what doesn't, why don't you go shave so I don't get whisker burns all over the place? That will give you a few minutes to calm down, and then we can start over."

Zachary agreed and retreated to the bathroom. He was glad to shut the door and to be able to breathe in his own space for a few minutes. He didn't understand why his throat was so tight and the tears were so close to the surface. He cupped both hands over his eyes for a few minutes, breathing deeply and trying to calm his roller coaster emotions. There was nothing to be upset about. Kenzie had been perfectly understanding and agreeable. She hadn't criticized him for skipping his appointments or for bringing up his therapy right when she had been ready to engage. There had been no yelling, no recriminations. Maybe that was why he felt so raw and exposed. He'd fully expected an explosion, and she'd reacted with a calm and informed attitude. It was more than he could have expected.

He ran the tap and first splashed cold water on his eyes and face to head off any tears, then ran the hot water to prepare for a shave.

———

She was right, and after Zachary had finished the ritual of shaving, he was feeling a lot more calm and relaxed. He went back to the bedroom and found her on the bed with a housecoat wrapped around her, reading something on her phone. She put it down, smiling at him. "That looks better. And I love the smell of the shaving cream. Come here."

He slid in beside her and she wrapped her arms around him and buried her face in the soft skin below his ear, breathing the smell of the shaving cream in deeply and making him break out in goosebumps.

"Hey!"

She snuffled against the sensitive skin, laughing. "Does this bother you?"

"No. It tickles!"

Her body pressed up against his, warm and soft. He held her close, closing his eyes. She started to kiss him.

"Just let me hold you for a minute," Zachary whispered.

She stopped and snuggled in his arms, molding her body against his. "That feels good, huh?"

"Yeah."

He wasn't sure how far he was going to be able to get before he started to flash back or dissociate. In the weeks immediately following the encounter with Teddy, he had been unable to tolerate her touch or even to let her see his body. Knowing how uncomfortable he was, she hadn't asked him, once he had been able to let his guard down, about the pink, healing scars on his body. She hadn't asked him exactly what Teddy had said or done to him.

Zachary had worked hard to overcome any negative reactions to her advances, which resulted in the natural progression of their physical relationship, but at the expense of Zachary's mental participation.

It was going to take time to fix his problems.

CHAPTER TWENTY-SIX

"Zachary?" Heather's voice was in his ear before he could even greet her on the phone. "Detective Able called to say that they got the DNA results back and we should go in. Would you come?"

"Sure, of course," Zachary agreed. He looked over the paperwork on his desk. He had been planning on doing surveillance for a few days, but if he had to put it off for one more day, it wouldn't hurt anything. He took out his phone and looked at the calendar to assure himself that he hadn't forgotten about any appointments. "Today?"

"Yeah. I know it's a long way to come just to go with me to the police station, but I don't think that I can do it by myself."

"It's not that far. I don't mind a little drive. I'll head over right away. You want me to meet you there?"

"Yes."

"I'll call you when I hit city limits, then we should both get there about the same time. Okay?"

"Okay." Her voice was a little calmer with a plan in place. "And do you mind if Grant is there? He wanted to come along too."

Zachary frowned at the phone. He wasn't sure why she needed him there if her husband was going along. She wasn't exactly going to be alone. But he didn't know very much about Grant. Maybe Heather would find it harder with him there, instead of easier. Maybe he was the kind who asked too many questions, or was too boisterous, or something else that sucked the energy from her or made it harder for her to deal with the policeman. Maybe it was because of Grant that she needed Zachary there, as some kind of a buffer or to handle the questions when she couldn't think of what she needed to say. In which case, he'd better be prepared with his questions and not let himself be distracted by her husband.

"Of course. Bring whoever you want. It's good that he wants to be involved."

"Yeah. It's just kind of weird. He hasn't had anything to do with it before."

"It will be okay," he assured her.

"I hope so."

———

They arrived at the police station at just about the same time. Heather's husband had driven her. Zachary eyed him as the two of them got out of the car. Grant was tall and had probably been lean in his earlier years when he and Heather had first met and gotten married. He had put on some weight in his later years, around his neck and stomach, but still moved like a younger man. He was outgoing, immediately approaching Zachary and putting out his hand in greeting. "You must be Zachary. It's wonderful to meet someone from Heather's family! I knew that she had siblings, but I never really thought that I would get the chance to meet any of them."

Zachary looked at Heather. Didn't he know that she'd been in contact with Tyrrell for some time? Or that she was in contact with their eldest sister, Joss? Didn't he think that sooner or later he would meet them in person?

But Heather didn't speak up. Maybe she hadn't shared those things with him yet. There had been a lot to tell him, and the information about the progress on the cold case was obviously more urgent than a few Skype calls she had while he was at work during the day.

"Good to meet you, Grant," Zachary said, taking Grant's hand and giving him a friendly nod as they shook hands.

"You don't look like her at all," Grant marveled, studying Zachary's face.

"I thought I would at least be able to see a bit of a family connection, but the two of you couldn't be less like each other."

Zachary looked at Heather. "Well, we could be," he pointed out. "We have the same skin color."

Grant laughed quite a bit more loudly than Zachary thought was warranted. If their parents had been mixed-race, the children could have a variety of skin colors. Or if they were foster or adopted siblings... but they weren't, and Grant was probably right. With two white parents, he and Heather couldn't have been much more different. Heather was blond and fair, Zachary was dark-haired, his face lean and hollow where Heather's was filled in. Not round, but pleasant. And she had those pretty freckles that he remembered from their early summers.

"Zachary and I are a lot more alike than you would think," Heather said, touching Zachary's arm fleetingly as they moved toward the police station together. Zachary smiled and nodded. It wasn't what was outside that counted. It was what was inside, their shared experience and genetics, the personalities that had been shaped in their early years.

Able didn't keep them waiting very long. He seemed surprised to see one more person joining the meeting, and nodded to Grant. "Mr.... er..."

"Garrity," Grant offered, and Zachary realized that he'd been introducing Heather as Heather Goldman the whole time, and had never even asked her if she went by her married name.

"Mr. Garrity. Nice to meet you. Follow me."

He led them to a meeting room and they all sat down, the room seeming closer and more claustrophobic than ever.

Able didn't have the file with him, just a single sheet of paper, and Zachary couldn't read it from where he sat. Able settled into his chair with a noisy sigh, and wriggled around to get comfortable, something Zachary didn't remember him doing on previous occasions. Why was he so uncomfortable?

"It turns out," Able said, his eyes down, "that in Vermont, the police are prohibited from using partial DNA matches obtained from database searches."

They all looked at each other. Heather's face was blank. Grant's was confused. Zachary couldn't see his own expression, but he could barely control himself. Fury rose up inside him that Able would lead them along for weeks and then announce that he was unable to do what they had asked him to.

"You can't even search it?" Grant demanded. "I understand that you'd have to get a direct match to prosecute someone, but you can't even use it as an investigative tool?"

"Vermont's current policy is such that we are prevented from doing so."

"You can use a partial license plate, why can't you use a partial DNA match?"

"I'm sorry, sir, that's just what the state legislators have determined."

"So you can't give us anything," Zachary said flatly.

Able looked at him. There was a gleam in his eye. Zachary tried to understand what Able looked so smug about. That he was telling Zachary what he had told him weeks before; there was nowhere to go with the case and he shouldn't bother investigating it? Was Able happy that he hadn't been able to get anywhere? Had it just been a ruse to get them off his back?

"Why didn't you tell us before that you wouldn't be able to do a partial match? You knew we weren't looking for the baby in CODIS."

"With all of the advances in technology, it can be difficult to keep track of what the policies are and what's allowed or not allowed," Able said slowly. "Sometimes, for instance, a policeman might put a DNA profile into the system before he's told that he isn't allowed to use a partial match. Most states allow a partial match, so CODIS is set up to allow it."

Zachary raised his eyebrows. He looked down at the paper in front of Able.

"So you ran the DNA and *then* were told it wasn't allowed?"

Able nodded.

"Was there a hit?"

Able shook his head. "He was not there. No partial matches."

Zachary smacked his palm down on the table, making everyone jump. "There's nothing? You called us in just to tell us that there was nothing?"

"*Nothing* is still a result," Able pointed out. "It means this guy has not been convicted of any other felony. Not since all felons have been required to give a DNA sample, anyway."

"That doesn't help us at all!"

"I can't give you what I don't have," Able said reasonably.

Zachary's blood was boiling. He had put all of his hopes on this one piece of evidence. He had been sure that the baby's father would be in CODIS.

Heather put her hand on Zachary's arm. "It's okay, Zachary. We knew it was a long shot."

Zachary shook her off, irritated. In his brain, the wheels spun, unable to find purchase. After all of the research he had done, there had to be something more they could do.

"What about public DNA profile repositories like GENEmatch?"

"Did you not understand what I told you? Vermont cops are prohibited from using partial matches. In CODIS or any other database. The only thing we could use in GENEmatch is a direct match to the donor, but we don't have the perp's DNA."

Zachary was stymied. He looked at Heather. He did not want to let her down. There had to be a way for him to pursue it further and get more information. According to what he had read, there was a twenty-five percent chance that submitting the DNA to GENEmatch would link the DNA profile to relatives. Those relatives could help them triangulate a single branch of the family tree, isolating two or three suspects.

"Since you can't use the pacifier, can we get it back so we can test it?"

"It's already booked as evidence. It won't be released."

"Can your lab give us the raw genome data, or transfer it to another lab?"

"No."

Zachary stared at Able. The man had acted like he was being helpful, but he had just destroyed what chance they had of matching the DNA in GENEmatch. He should have told them to start with that he couldn't use a partial DNA match. Then they could have tested it privately and used the results.

"Zach... we still have the mittens," Heather pointed out.

But were the mittens going to have enough DNA on them to test? Skin cells on the inside, but how much? Maybe the baby had sucked on his hands while he had the mittens on, but as far as Zachary could remember, babies didn't find their own hands and feet to suck on until they were older.

"The reason they put them on is because he was scratching his face," Heather said, as if she could see the inner workings of Zachary's brain.

Maybe he got blood and skin under his sharp little nails. Maybe that tissue was transferred to the inside of the mittens. Maybe he'd drooled on them or spit up. There were a number of different ways the baby could have contributed DNA to the mittens. And hopefully, no one else had. It wasn't as good a source as the pacifier, but it would have to do.

"If you have another source, that's your best bet," Able confirmed. "There's only so much we can do."

Zachary shot him a look, but didn't say any of the things he was thinking.

CHAPTER TWENTY-SEVEN

Zachary was still angry and was exhausted by his anger by the time he got home. He had talked with Heather and Grant as calmly as he was able after leaving the police conference room, telling them that he would send Heather the information for the private DNA lab he had come across during his research, and she could send the mittens there. He would contact them ahead of time to explain the situation, and they would give him the raw genome data to upload to GENEmatch once they had done the gathering, preparation, and sequencing.

He drove home too fast, zipping past commuters on the highway. When he returned to his apartment, he slammed the door, not caring if everybody on his floor heard it. Luckily, Kenzie wasn't there, so he was free to kick doors and furniture, smack the counter, and handle the dishes for his supper as loudly and recklessly as he liked.

He felt a little calmer after having something to eat. Mr. Peterson had tried to reach him during the day, when Zachary hadn't been in any mood to talk, so once he'd had a bit of time to unwind and to regain his composure, he called back.

"Zach, how are you doing?" Mr. Peterson greeted cheerfully.

Zachary let out a long breath, trying to stay calm and centered. He didn't need to dump on Mr. Peterson. He was having a hard time even understanding where all of the anger was coming from, but it certainly wasn't Lorne's fault. He forced a smile, knowing that Mr. Peterson would be able to hear it in his voice.

"It's been a frustrating day. But I'm okay."

"Oh, what's going on?"

"Heather's case. We ran into a brick wall with the police. Which he could have told us about three weeks ago, but didn't bother to do."

"I can see how that would be annoying. I know how pleased you were that they were going to run the DNA and maybe be able to identify Heather's attacker."

"Yeah. Would have been helpful if they had told me that they wouldn't actually do that. Apparently even though it's allowed all over the country, Vermont won't allow the police to do partial matches."

"Ouch. Why didn't he tell you that, then?"

"I guess he decided to go ahead and run it anyway and get forgiveness later. But… there was no match in the database."

"So it doesn't really matter that it's against their policy. He wasn't there anyway."

"But that meant he logged the soother and used the DNA and the police won't share the data. So we're stuck trying to test another piece of evidence, and I don't know whether we'll be able to get enough DNA from it to use for our own purposes."

"What would you test it against, if he's not in the police database? Is there some super-secret private investigator database?"

Zachary had to laugh, as angry as he was. "No, there's a public database. People upload their DNA onto it for genealogical research. Anyone can access the shared data. If there's a match there, we can trace the family trees and narrow down what family the perpetrator came from."

"Really?" Lorne whistled. "That's amazing. People share that information publicly? Why would someone who had committed a felony voluntarily post their DNA to a public site?"

"It's not necessarily the criminal who does it. It might be his second cousin, or his aunt, or several different people, which allows you to really narrow down who it is, sometimes to just one or two people. Then you get direct DNA from them, and see if there's a match, and presto… you have something to build a case on."

"Isn't that automatically enough to convict?"

"It depends on the source of the DNA. People can leave DNA wherever they go, and it can be picked up by someone else and transported to a new scene. So I could leave hair or skin cells on a doorknob at the coffee shop, and then the next person could transfer it to… their boyfriend's apartment. The police could pick it up there and put me at the scene, even though I had never been there."

"But in this case, where you're testing the baby's DNA, then you know for sure that whoever the father is, he's the one who assaulted her."

"It's only a partial match, because we don't have his DNA from the rape kit. We only have half of his DNA from a baby that he fathered. They can determine paternity to a certain percentage, but it isn't ever going to be one hundred percent. And they still have to prove the circumstances, that he and Heather didn't have consensual sex at some point. She says the only person she had intercourse with was the rapist, but a jury would have to believe her. The defense would do whatever they could to prove that they might have had consensual sex at some other time."

"Ah. That makes sense, Zachary. I guess I wasn't thinking about it that way. You believe Heather, and so do I, so it didn't occur to me that someone else might not believe her story. We know she was attacked violently."

"But that doesn't mean she'd never had any other contact with anyone else and that the baby was definitely conceived in the attack. The timing is right, but…"

"Yeah. Poor Heather, she must be frustrated too."

"I think she took it better than I did, actually. Maybe it will hit her when she gets home. But at least she's got someone with her. She's not alone."

"Good. I worry about you being alone. At least Kenzie is there more often now."

"I'm fine." The words came too loudly, and he was worried that Mr. Peterson would think he was angry at him. "Sorry. I'm just… frustrated and irritable."

"Understandable. You had quite a disappointment over the case. Have you eaten?"

"Uh…" Zachary had to stop and think about it. "I'm not sure." He looked around him and saw the used dishes. "Yes. I ate." Provided the plates weren't from the previous day. He usually remembered to wash them.

"Is that Zachary?" He heard Pat's voice in the background. "Say 'hi' for me."

"Tell him 'hi' back," Zachary responded.

"He heard you. He says 'hi,'" Mr. Peterson passed the message along.

Pat said something else, his voice lower, and then he was apparently gone. Mr. Peterson didn't return to the conversation immediately.

"How is he doing?" Zachary asked.

"He's really having trouble with Jose's murder. And even more than that, with you getting… injured."

"I'm fine. Tell him everything is okay. I'm keeping busy with work, all healed. Nothing to keep worrying about."

"He blames himself for you getting hurt. You never would have gotten involved if it hadn't been for him."

"It's my own fault for not thinking about the consequences. Being too impulsive. I was supposed to wait until I met up with Dougan. I didn't do that and I walked right into Teddy's operation. I should have realized it was too dangerous."

"The two of you," Mr. Peterson sighed. "It wasn't Pat's fault and it wasn't yours. It was Teddy's. He's the one who hurt you. He's the one who killed Jose. He's the one who chose to break the law and to hurt people. Neither of you wanted anyone to get hurt. It was *Teddy's* fault."

Zachary shrugged to himself. He knew what had happened. He knew that if he'd made other choices, he wouldn't have gotten himself hurt. He might not have 'asked for it,' but he certainly could have been smarter.

"Pat knows that it was more than just physical injuries," Mr. Peterson said slowly. "He knows that even though the physical injuries have healed, you're still suffering from the emotional fallout. And that your relationship with Kenzie…"

The knot in Zachary's stomach tightened. His chest hurt. "What?"

"We've all noticed how it's affected you."

Zachary thought about it, the seconds passing.

"Zachary?" Mr. Peterson prompted. "You there? Are you okay?"

"Kenzie."

"What about Kenzie?"

"You *all* know that Kenzie and I are having personal problems."

Mr. Peterson didn't reply.

"How would you know that? Because I didn't tell you we were having any issues."

"I've talked to Kenzie," Mr. Peterson admitted after an awkward pause.

"You've been talking to my girlfriend behind my back."

"Don't think of it that way. That's not how it was. Kenzie is worried about you. We're worried about you. We talk to each other…"

"Did she call you?"

Lorne didn't answer, obviously weighing his response. He didn't want Zachary to think that he'd been invading his privacy. But he also didn't want to get Kenzie in trouble.

"Did Kenzie call you?" Zachary repeated.

"Yes."

"Kenzie called you to discuss our private relationship."

"It wasn't like that. She called because I know your history. As much of it as anyone. She called for advice."

"How to deal with our relationship."

"Yes… but that's not a bad thing, Zachary. She didn't dump you. She didn't tell you that you had to change to suit her. She called to ask about the best way to… stay with you."

"It's not bad for my girlfriend to call you to discuss what's wrong with our sex life?" He could barely keep his voice under control.

"I wish I could explain… that's not how it was."

"We have a good relationship," Zachary said hotly. "I've done everything she wanted. I don't ignore her or push her away. I started going back to therapy. We're working through the stuff between us. Why would she have to call you?"

"I guess… she needed someone to bounce ideas off of. How to handle the problems you were having. She wanted to know if I knew about… previous problems. What would you want her to do? Call Bridget?"

Bridget.

Darkness bloomed in Zachary's brain. He felt himself falling down a deep dark hole. A black hole.

"Zachary?" Mr. Peterson prompted, trying to bring him back.

"This is about Bridget?"

"No. It's not about Bridget. She wasn't calling about Bridget. I was just saying, who else would she go to? Who else knows anything about you and your previous relationships?"

"Bridget…"

"I told you, it's not about Bridget."

Zachary swallowed. He didn't know what to say or do. He was used to being able to talk to Mr. Peterson without any problems. Lorne was next to perfect in his eyes, always supportive and compassionate. He let Zachary have his privacy and had never gone behind his back, as far as Zachary knew, with either Bridget or Kenzie. And other than Bridget and Kenzie… there hadn't been anyone else in Zachary's life. No one serious. No one that he had introduced to Mr. Peterson and Pat.

"What did you tell Kenzie?"

"I… I just said she should be patient, give you time to work it out. Bring it up with you directly."

"But she wanted to know about my past."

"To know how much of this was new, and how much… might have already existed before Teddy."

"And what did you tell her?"

There was an uncomfortable pause. It was the point at which Mr. Peterson was going to have to admit that he had given Kenzie personal, private information about Zachary without his permission.

"Zach… it's not something that you and I have ever talked about…"

"Yeah. So…?"

"I told her that… you had probably been abused in foster care. That I didn't know any details, but with the number of different homes and institutions you had been in, it was probable. That there were red flags."

Zachary swallowed. What else could Mr. Peterson have said? He hadn't been there. He couldn't give Kenzie any details. He was just confirming the suspicions that Kenzie already had.

"And Bridget never came up?"

"She asked about Bridget, sure. Whether… either of you had ever mentioned anything about your relationship."

"Our sex life."

"Yes."

"And…?"

"You never said anything to me. That's not the kind of relationship that we have. And Bridget…"

Zachary could just see Bridget ranting to Lorne about Zachary's failings.

She had no filter when it came to complaining about Zachary's inadequacies in other areas of his life. Why not the bedroom as well? Zachary covered his eyes with his hand, as if that could block out whatever Mr. Peterson was about to say.

"And Bridget?" he repeated.

"Zach… you know I would never say anything negative to you about Bridget. I know how much you loved her and how hard it has been to let her go. But… your relationship with her was toxic. Things might have seemed idyllic back in the beginning, but I was never comfortable with her. You weren't yourself with her. And she treated you like a project, something she was going to fix. It was never a partnership."

"What did she say to you?"

Mr. Peterson's voice was strong. "I never let Bridget run you down in front of me. Not with you there and not when you were out of the room. Whatever she had to say about your private life, she didn't say it to me. And that's what I told Kenzie. I don't know whether you had intimacy issues with Bridget and I preferred not to hear about them from Kenzie either."

Zachary chuckled. He could see Mr. Peterson telling her that and could see Kenzie's frustration at being told that it wasn't appropriate. Zachary had never wanted to know any details of Mr. Peterson's and Pat's intimate life, and Mr. Peterson had never asked for any details about Zachary's.

Lorne sighed. "I'm sorry. Maybe I should have said something to you at the time… but it was just a brief discussion, pretty much me telling her that her guess was as good as mine and if she wanted to know, she should ask you."

"Yeah."

"And you two *have* been talking, haven't you…?"

"Yeah. Sorry if I overreacted. I just… this stuff is…"

"Personal."

"And really hard. I don't understand my own reactions. I don't *want* to react the way I do, but I can't help it."

"How could your experience with Teddy *not* affect you? Would you expect Heather's assault not to color her future experiences? It's not a matter of choice."

"But before… I could shut it out before. I thought that was all in the past."

"It's stirred up some old memories?"

"Yeah."

"You said you're going back to therapy."

"I thought… it was time. If I want to be able to get over these problems with Kenzie… ignoring it wasn't making it go away."

"You guys will work it out. Give it time."

CHAPTER TWENTY-EIGHT

Zachary kept busy over the next few weeks as they waited for the results of the second DNA test. The lab assured Zachary that they had retrieved enough DNA from the tiny mittens to run a profile, and after that it was just a matter of waiting while it worked its way through the system.

Zachary didn't tell Kenzie that he knew about her going to Mr. Peterson behind his back. He knew she wouldn't see it that way; she thought she was totally justified in digging into his past life to gain some insight into dealing with Zachary's anxiety and dissociative episodes. But he found excuses not to be with her and to put her off most of the time when she wanted to get together. He spent almost a full week on night surveillance, which eliminated any time they could get together that week other than lunch hours, which they took close to the morgue rather than at the apartment.

Then he needed a week to organize and write the reports and to train Heather on some of the basics of investigative work. Since she was available during the day, he relegated his report writing to the evening, and the rest of the time he slept.

He was starting to run out of excuses not to see Kenzie, but he was also expecting the DNA results back from the lab any day. He would upload the results to GENEmatch, and it would spit out the names they needed, and he already had the name of a genealogist on hand who would help them make sense of the relationships and home in on the suspects.

———

Ella Day, the professional genealogist, was a small woman with thick blond, curly hair. She had a bright red lipstick smile and greeted Heather and Zachary warmly. He had the sort of feeling meeting her that he might have had in meeting with a medium or fortune teller. What she could do with DNA and genealogical information would have seemed like magic just ten years before. If Zachary hadn't thoroughly checked out her background and references, he would have taken her for a scammer for sure.

She welcomed them and had them sit down in her comfy living room. She offered coffee and tea or cold beverages. Grant had not been able to make it due to a work commitment, so it was just Zachary and Heather for the meeting.

Zachary was all edges, worried about whether they were going to get any information or whether it would just be another report of 'he was not there.' They needed to find the guy for Heather's sake. Zachary knew how important it was in his own case to know who it was who had hurt him, to be able to put a face and a personality to dark shadow who had spoken to him and tortured him that night. When he allowed himself to think of what had happened, he wanted to know that it wasn't some faceless bogeyman, but a real person. A person who was behind bars and would not hurt him or anyone else again.

Ella set down the drinks on the coffee table, smiling sweetly at Heather and Zachary. She still seemed to be emitting some sort of vague, other-worldly vibe, and Zachary didn't know why. What she did was science-based. It was genetics, not ethereal vibrations or listening to ghostly voices. She was not an artist, but a kind of a scientist.

"Tell me about your story," Ella told Heather, as she sat down and smoothed her skirt. Maybe it was the flowered skirt that was giving Zachary such a weird vibe. She should have been wearing neatly-pressed slacks or faded bluejeans, depending on whether she liked to present a professional appearance or a geeky one. The flowery skirt didn't fit either image.

"What do you want to know?" Heather asked, guarded.

"This is your baby, right? You're trying to track him down?"

"Well… no, not exactly. We're trying to track down his biological father."

"You lost track of each other, want to reunite? Or does your son want to meet him?"

"We want to put him in prison," Zachary said, wanting to put a quick end to Ella's fairy-tale notions. "This was no love affair. It was a brutal assault. We want to track the guy down, lock him up, and throw away the key."

"Oh." Ella nodded. "I'm sorry. I see."

"You can help, right?" Heather asked.

"You've already uploaded it to GENEmatch and got some hits?"

Zachary pulled out the USB key and held it up.

"Great. Why don't I get that loaded while the two of you relax for a bit? I'll see what pops up."

"Will you be able to do it today? Identify the biological father?" Zachary asked.

"There's no guarantee. I'll need to work the family trees and see if I can identify who the potential father is. It can take a few hours to a few weeks, but sometimes it is only a few minutes' worth of work. You just don't know ahead of time. But I'll take a preliminary look at the results, and then I'll have a better idea of the timeline for you."

Zachary and Heather nodded together. Ella retreated to her computer on the other side of the room and sat down. Zachary watched her out of the corner of his eye for the first few minutes, saw her put the USB key in and start tapping away, waiting, mousing here and there, clicking, mousing some more. He couldn't really tell what she was up to, and in a few minutes returned his attention to Heather, who was doing the same thing, looking away from Heather and back at Zachary. They both gave a little laugh.

"Leave her to it, I guess," Heather said.

"Yeah. Hard to do. I keep expecting her to jump up and shout 'eureka!'"

"At least we know it was good DNA and that there were matches."

"The lab said they got a good DNA profile."

"I was terrified of cross-contamination. That it would end up being the DNA from someone's cat."

"If it had been cat DNA, I think they would have told us before they sequenced it."

"I know." Heather bounced her legs up and down, sneaking another look at Ella. "I just feel like it is all going to go wrong. If I get my hopes up, I'm just going to end up being disappointed."

"We can't predict the results. All we can do is pursue every lead."

"Well, you've done that. You're really good at this."

"I want to help you."

Heather nodded. Her cup rattled on the saucer when she picked it up. Zachary wished that Ella had just served their drinks in regular mugs. He felt like he was going to smash something. Heather steadied her cup using both hands and took a little sip. She made a face and Zachary thought she probably wasn't usually a tea drinker. It wasn't his preference either, but he often had it with clients who were nervous, because it helped them to calm down, when coffee just make them more jittery. That was why he had suggested it to Heather when Ella had offered. Heather set her cup down again with a clink.

"How is Grant?" Zachary asked. "Your kids? What have you been up to lately?"

She rolled her eyes, recognizing that he was forcing small-talk, but she answered anyway, needing the distraction.

"Things have been really good with Grant. It's like... talking about this has opened things up for us. It's like we're newlyweds again, just learning about each other and exploring new sides of each other that we'd never seen before."

"You too? I mean... are there things that Grant has told you about him that you didn't know before?"

"Yes... because he didn't share. He knew that I was holding back on my history, and that I didn't want to talk about anything to do with sex, so we just never did. We had a relationship... but it was just an outward, physical thing, without much passion or imagination."

"Going through the motions," Zachary said, remembering Kenzie's words.

"Yeah. Like that. Going through the motions. I had two kids, so obviously we had a physical dimension to our marriage. But it was never emotionally fulfilling. Just... an appetite to be satisfied."

"And that changed when you told him about what had happened to you?" Zachary tried to wrap his mind around that. He would have expected the opposite. That Grant would push back, not wanting to do anything that might make Heather feel bad. Or he would not want to have anything to do with someone who had been spoiled before they ever met. He hadn't expected that it would have helped them to grow closer physically. Emotionally, maybe, but he had expected it to put a wedge between them as far as physical intimacy went.

Heather made some answer, but Zachary didn't hear what it was. Ella's typing suddenly got louder and sharper, like the final percussions in an anthem. They both looked over at her, looking for a change in her expression.

"*Yes*," Ella said. "We can narrow it down to one family tree."

Heather sat straight up in her seat. "Who?" she asked. "What is the family name?"

Despite the fact that her attacker had been masked, it could still have been someone that Heather knew. Someone who was afraid that she would recognize him. It was thirty years later, but she might still remember the name and be able to match it to a face or role in the neighborhood.

"Reid-Clark," Ella said, staring intently at her screen, clicking with her mouse and tapping in various searches or commands. "Looks like a union between Reid-Clark and Astor…"

It took Zachary a few seconds to compute this. He looked at Heather. Heather was looking at Ella, her face blank and expressionless.

"Heather…? The family you were living with was the Astors. Was there someone who was related to them?" Zachary asked.

"No," she said flatly.

"Your foster mother was in the delivery room with you. Was she the one who put the mittens on the baby? Is it possible that she got her DNA in the mittens when she put them on?"

Heather shook her head.

Ella looked up from her computer at Zachary with an irritated expression. "Don't confuse things," she said sharply. "This is male DNA, not female. And Mrs. Astor would not actually be an Astor if that was her married name. It has to be her husband or someone from his line."

"Heather…?"

Heather was blank. Silent. Her eyes didn't move. Her knees no longer bounced up and down with nervous anticipation.

"Heather, was Mr. Astor at the hospital? Did he handle the mittens?"

"No."

Zachary looked back at Ella, trying to connect with her to get more information and her read on the situation. She was staring at her computer screen and paid him no attention.

"Feathers," Zachary tried her nickname to pull Heather out of the trance. He knew what it was like to get so wrapped up in his brain and his feelings that he couldn't escape the thoughts. "We're here together, Feathers. It's Zachary. We're having tea with Ella. Do you smell the tea?"

There was a flicker of life in her face. In a moment, she looked down at the cup of tea in front of her. She picked it up, took a sip, and again gave a grimace at the taste.

"Do you want some sugar or cream in that?" Zachary looked at the tray Ella had placed on the table. "Some honey? Lemon?"

Despite the fact that she didn't respond, he reached over and squeezed one of the lemon wedges over his own tea, squeezing the rind hard to spray the pungent oils into the air. "Do you want some lemon in yours?"

Heather shook her head. She reached out and touched the outside of the rind as he put it down. She licked the oil off of her finger and wrinkled her nose at the bitterness.

"Heather." He put his hand on her arm. "What do you remember? You told Able that the Astors didn't molest you."

"No, they didn't."

"The story about you being attacked in the woods… was that what they told you happened? Did you remember that, or did they plant it?"

"You think I don't know what happened to me?"

"I think memories can be manipulated. If you're told something enough times and in enough detail, then that's what you remember. Especially if you were in a vulnerable state. You were traumatized. If you were given drugs or alcohol and given their version of what happened, that's what you would remember."

"No. It's not a fake memory. They didn't tell me what happened, I told them."

Zachary thought about the police file, about the things that Heather had said in her statement, the mother being the one to take her to the police, the pictures of what had been done to her. He remembered the scrapes on her back from the rough ground, the leaves and grass tangled in her hair. That hadn't been staged.

"The man who attacked you wore a mask. Could it have been your foster father or one of the sons?"

Heather stood up abruptly. "I have to go."

"You want me to take you home?" Zachary had picked her up from her house. He'd been worried that she would be too emotionally overwrought after the visit to the genealogist, and he was not happy to have been right. He hadn't been expecting the revelation.

"I want to go home," Heather echoed.

There were still no tears, no raised voice. Ella was watching them, a little M frown line appearing above the bridge of her nose.

"I'll be in touch," Zachary told her. "I'm sorry this is so abrupt. I'll call you."

She nodded and didn't try to stop them from going. Zachary wondered if her clients always got so emotional. Maybe that was the reason for the soothing atmosphere and the tea. It wasn't a show, she knew it would be an emotionally taxing visit, even if Heather had just been there to try to track down her child.

Zachary took Heather by the arm, leading her out to the car like she was a frail old woman. She walked like a sleepwalker, not looking at him, not looking to the right or to the left. Zachary unlocked the car, opened her door for her, and warned her not to bump her head as he guided her into the seat. He shut her door and returned to the driver's side. She automatically pulled her seatbelt across, and Zachary made sure that it clicked into place.

"Do you want something on the radio? Do you want to talk?"

She didn't answer.

Zachary pondered as he drove her home. It was a shame that Grant hadn't been able to go to the meeting with her. He didn't like to take her back to an empty house with whatever emotions she was going through, finding out that her attacker that day had not been a stranger, but one of the men living under her own roof.

Heather started to rock forward and back. There were still no tears. Zachary tried to keep up a running description to her of the things he was seeing, hearing, and smelling around them, hoping to keep her anchored in the physical world, not stuck in flashbacks of the assault.

How could someone she had lived with not only rape her, but also beat her up so badly? Someone who was supposed to be caring for her and being a loving and kind father or brother? He had lain in wait for her, obviously knowing that she broke the school rule and walked through the park every day. He had worn a mask so she wouldn't be able to identify him, had brutally assaulted her, and then he had lived with her afterward, watching her growing large with his child.

She had to feel devastated. Betrayed. The police had told her that it was her own fault, and now she knew it had been her own foster father or brother.

"Can we call Grant? I'll stay with you until he can come home."

"He'll be home soon. Maybe even before we get back."

Her voice was so calm and measured that someone who didn't know her or the effect that shock could have would have thought that she was unconcerned and feeling no distress over the revelation of her attacker's identity. Zachary understood that the opposite was true. She was so overwhelmed by the news that it had pushed her over the edge. Past being able to feel it or express it.

"Do you want to call your therapist? Or a hotline? Do you have tranquilizers?"

"I'll talk to Grant. It will be okay."

Zachary kept talking to her, kept trying to keep her engaged. When he parked at the curb in front of her house, Zachary pulled his key out of the ignition and released his seatbelt to walk her into the house. She reached for her door handle.

"It's fine, Zachary." She indicated the blue car in the driveway. "Grant is home."

"I'll just walk you in, make sure he knows what happened."

"No," she insisted. "Let me speak for myself."

Back when it had happened, she hadn't been allowed to speak for herself. She'd done what her foster mother and social worker had told her to and had not been allowed to make her own decisions. Zachary had to allow her the chance to have her own voice.

"You're sure you'll be okay?"

"I'll be fine."

"Heather." He stopped her one last time before she could walk away.

"What?"

"Do you know which one it was?"

She stared at him for a long moment, her expression still completely blank and unreadable.

"Thank you for your help today, Zach. And for all the rest. I don't know how I could have done it without you."

CHAPTER TWENTY-NINE

He didn't feel good about leaving Heather alone after receiving such shattering news. But he had to keep reminding himself that she wasn't alone. Her husband was there. He had been fully supportive of her since she had told him about what had happened to her as a child, and he would be there for her now, giving her whatever comfort she needed.

But he didn't get all the way home before finally breaking down and calling her to make sure she was okay. There was no answer. She was probably working it through with Grant, hugging, crying, letting out all of the emotion she had been stuffing down for thirty years. It wasn't a good time to talk to Zachary. She needed to be with her husband, not her brother.

He called again when he got back to his apartment. Again, no answer. Zachary was getting uneasy. She must know how worried he would be. Couldn't she at least answer to say that she was okay? She must be finished crying. He hung up and tried again immediately. He anxiously checked for text messages, emails, or messages in social networking platforms. She hadn't sent him anything. There was nothing to reassure him.

What if it hadn't been Grant's car in the driveway? What if she'd lied to him about someone else being home and had planned to harm herself once he was out of the way? She could already have bled out, or her respiration

384

could be getting too slow after taking pills. Or she could have chosen another way to exit the life that she couldn't bear anymore.

He concentrated, trying to remember his previous visit to her house. Had the car been in the driveway? What had she driven when she met him at the police station? The dark blue car? Uneasy, he called her again.

When there was no answer, he changed tactics. Firing up his browser, he started searching for Grant Garrity. Luckily, the man had an electronic trail a mile wide and it only took Zachary a few minutes to find his phone number.

"Hello?" Grant's voice rang in Zachary's ear, too cheerful to have been comforting his wife for the last hour. Zachary's stomach knotted.

"Grant, this is Zachary Goldman."

"Oh, hi, Zach. Is Heather with you, then?"

"No. I dropped her off at home. She said you were there already."

"I just got here," Grant said, confirming what Zachary had feared. "She's not home."

Zachary swore under his breath. He didn't want to panic Grant, but he was starting to panic himself.

"She said that you were home. She's not answering her phone and I'm worried about her. If she lied to me about you being home… you're sure she's not there? In the bedroom or bathroom? I'm worried… she might have done something."

All cheer had left Grant's voice. Zachary could picture him, his face ashen. "No… I just called out. She didn't answer. I didn't think…"

Zachary could hear him pounding up the stairs. He could hear doors opening and closing. After a few minutes, he was back. "I don't know where she is, but she's definitely not home. Her car is gone. What happened? Why would she…?"

"You know that we were meeting with the genealogist today to see if we could get a hit in the GENEmatch database."

There was a moment of silence from Grant. "No. She didn't tell me that was today."

"She said you were busy at work and couldn't come."

"I had work, but I could have gotten off to come with her. Why would she say that?"

Zachary's brain was spinning. Had Heather known, consciously or unconsciously, what she was going to find? Had part of her brain known all that time who it was that had assaulted her in the park? She might have recognized him by something other than his face. His aftershave. The way he moved. A ring on his finger, belt buckle, shoes. Heather might have been subconsciously repressing it all along.

"I don't know why she wouldn't have told you. Maybe she was confused and thought you had something else going on today. Did she leave you a note? Send you a message or leave a voicemail?"

"No... I don't think so. I don't see anything. She's usually here when I get home from work."

"Does she know how to reach her old foster family? The Astors?"

"No." This answer, after all of his uncertain and hesitant replies, was immediate and strong. "She didn't keep in contact with them. I always thought it was a little strange that she wouldn't have anything to do with them, after living with them for a couple of years. But after hearing what she went through when she was there... well, I can understand it a bit better. I'm sure they were only trying to help her and do the right thing when they forced her to give the baby up, but I think she felt like... it was adding insult to injury."

"You don't have any idea where they are now?"

"Why...? I don't know where they are. I don't know if she ever heard anything, but it wasn't like they moved in the same circles."

"Okay. I'll see what I can find."

"I'll have her give you a call back when she gets home," Grant said, acting as if Zachary were just making a social call.

"Grant." Zachary stopped him from hanging up.

"Yes?"

"Do either of you own a gun?"

"Yes, of course. Heather was always afraid of getting mugged when she was out with the kids or by herself. She's carried one for years. I never really knew why until now, but I felt better knowing she could protect herself if she needed to. You think she's going to need it? What's going on?"

"Grant... the man who raped and beat Heather was one of the Astors."

Grant swallowed his curse, making it impossible for Zachary to tell for sure what he had said. "And you think... she's gone after them?"

"That's why I asked if she knew where they lived."

"But she doesn't. I'm sure of it."

"She might have had some idea... and I've been teaching her how to skip trace. Do you have any sense of which one of them it would be? Did she ever say anything that would have put one of them higher on your list than another?"

"She never talked about them. About any of them."

"Even when she was telling you about what happened to her? It might have been very brief, even just a sense that she was afraid of men of a certain age. Would she react more to a forty-year-old or a teen?"

"I don't know... if I had to pick one, I would say a forty-year-old. But she never mentioned them. I don't even know their names."

Zachary flipped through the file on his desk. He had printed out all of the documents he had taken pictures of, the ones that had originally resided in the police file. "Hang on a second. Their names. That could be an important piece of information."

Grant waited. Zachary skimmed the pages, looking for the original reports that had been made, which listed household members. "Okay. Kevin, Mark, and Robert."

"Uh... Robert... I suggested it as a name for our son. My grandfather was named Robert. But she wasn't having it. She said there was no way our son was going to be named Robert."

"No objection to Mark or Kevin?"

"I don't remember either of them ever coming up. We have a family friend named Mark... I have a nephew named Kevin... she's never said anything about the names bothering her or not wanting to be around them. Just Robert. That she'd never allow her son to be named Robert."

"Okay, that's a pretty good guess, then." Zachary checked the file. Robert was the father. Heather's foster father, likely her attacker. He couldn't believe it.

"What are you going to do?" Grant asked.

"I'm going to track him down. Find out where he is now. And get over there."

"Can I come? I can help. I know Heather better than anyone."

Except that he hadn't even known her secret. Not for thirty years. "I'll call you when I know something," he promised. "I don't know where he is yet and I don't want to put you in any danger."

"Call me as soon as you know."

Zachary said a quick goodbye and hung up. He sat staring at the papers in the file for a long minute, then he navigated to Able's number on his phone and turned to his browser to start typing in searches as he waited for it to ring through. It continued to ring. He waited for voicemail to answer, trying to compose a script in his head. Where was Able? Was he away from his phone or on another call? Or had he decided he'd had enough of Zachary and didn't want anything else to do with him? Should he try getting through the police switchboard, explaining that it was urgent? Or just hang up and call 9-1-1? The trouble was, he didn't yet have any information to give to 9-1-1 and they would probably just write him off as a kook.

"Able."

Zachary looked away from his computer. He waited for the rest of Able's recorded voicemail greeting, but it didn't come. He had answered in person.

"Detective Able. It's Zachary Goldman. We've got a problem."

"We? You and Heather?"

"No. You and me. Heather and I met with a genealogist today to see whether we could match the baby's partial DNA to a father using GENE-match. Or to a family tree where we could identify suspects."

"Okay."

"It turns out it wasn't a stranger. It was one of the Astors. My money is on the father."

He swore. "You couldn't tell which?"

"Not until we get direct DNA and paternity testing for each of them. Heather… she didn't exactly freak out. More like… shut down. She said she wanted to go home, so I drove her home. She said her husband was there and she wouldn't be alone. But she lied. He wasn't home. She took the car and left."

"You think she's going to hurt herself?"

"I think she might… but I think she might also go after him. Or all of them."

"Has she kept in touch?"

"No. Her husband doesn't think that she knew where they were anymore."

"Then we've got some time to track them down and head her off. You don't know where she's gone?"

"Well, that's the thing." Zachary tapped another search into his browser, quickly opening tabs and scanning through the information he found as he talked on the phone with Able. "In the past few weeks, while we've been waiting for the DNA results, I've been helping Heather out. She wanted to change the way she was living. Do volunteer work or develop some marketable skill. So I've been helping her."

"With what?" Able's voice was gruff, and Zachary figured he'd already figured it out.

"With basic detecting. Skip tracing. Finding missing people."

Able swore again. "How much of a head start does she have?"

"A couple of hours. But she is a beginner, it might have taken her a while to find him with only internet search capabilities. She's not hooked into all of the databases that I am, or that you have access to. Can you check DMV for current address?"

He heard Able start to tap computer keys on his end. "What's the name?"

"Robert Astor. Age seventy-two. Do you need his social?"

"You got DOB?"

Zachary gave it to him. Able typed the information in. "Got it. Thanks for the heads-up. I'll get someone sent right over on a welfare check. But I don't think Mrs. Garrity presents much of a threat."

Zachary was about to ask who Mrs. Garrity was, before he remembered that was Heather. Even though they hadn't seen each other for such a long time, it seemed incongruous that she should have a different last name from his. But they could all have different last names. Any of the children could have married or been adopted or just taken on the name of a foster family or started life with a new identity when they had aged out of foster care.

"Heather carries a gun."

"She what?"

"I asked her husband. She's a former victim. She wanted to be able to protect herself from an attack."

"Great. Okay. I'll give them a heads-up that this might be more than just a welfare check, then. I don't want cops getting killed."

"Give me the address. I'll head over there too. I might be able to talk her down."

"You think I'm going to give you that information? I don't want you interfering. I'll call you back when everything has been sorted. That's the most I can do."

Zachary looked at the address on the screen in front of him. He read it aloud to Able. "Is that it? Is that the address on his operator's license?"

Able's muttered curse gave him the answer. "Stay out of this, Mr. Goldman."

"I don't want her getting shot by some jumpy policeman, either. She's my sister. She's more of a danger to herself right now than to anybody else. I'm going."

"Give the police department some credit. We can manage this."

"I'm a ways out. If it's handled by the time I get there, then there won't be anything for me to do when I arrive. If it's not, you might very well be looking for someone who can talk to her."

Zachary hung up before Able could make any further objection. He jammed the phone into his pocket, sent the information on his screen to himself, and grabbed his keys. He was back in his car in no time, headed back to the highway. He ignored the calls coming into his phone from a blocked ID. That would be Able, and he didn't want to talk to Able. After Able gave up and stopped dialing him every two minutes, Zachary called Grant back.

"I've got an address for Robert Astor. The police are sending someone over there. I'm on my way. But I'm going to be a while, even speeding on the highway."

"Where is he?"

Zachary tapped his phone to bring the address back up again, and read it out to Grant.

"Don't go in if the police aren't there yet. Wait for them. Tell them that you can talk to her, there's no need to go in guns blazing. I'll be there as soon as I can. We need to give her some time to cool off. We don't know what kind of shape she's going to be in."

"Heather wouldn't hurt anyone. She's never hurt a fly."

"He hurt her. And if he triggers her, there's no telling what she'll do with a gun in her hands to protect herself this time."

CHAPTER THIRTY

I t was a good thing that Kenzie wasn't in the car with Zachary, because he was going much faster than she would have tolerated on the highway. Having driven with her before in an emergency, he knew she would have been freaking out.

But he was a good driver, and his ADHD meant that he could hyperfocus and react quickly if something unexpected happened. That wouldn't necessarily help him if a cop happened to see him, but he hoped that the traffic gods would be on his side and there wouldn't be any police on his way there.

It was possible he would beat Grant there, but he didn't expect to, not unless Grant was a real old-lady driver. If he stepped on the gas and ran a few lights or stop signs, he'd get there ahead of Zachary. The police would be there too. Zachary hoped that Able had activated whatever tactical team or hostage negotiator that he had to, and that they knew enough to approach the house quietly and not just rush in. He wanted Heather to see her way out of there. He didn't want her to be a headline on the next day's news, another statistic in police-involved shootings for the year. He prayed that they set up a perimeter and took it slow.

And that Heather hadn't already killed the sicko.

He had let his mind wander as he thought through the possibilities, and he almost missed his exit, which would have been bad because there weren't a lot of places to get turned around and get going in the right direction again. He'd miss the whole town or have to wind his way through tiny streets at a crawl, watching for children and elderly pedestrians.

When he pulled onto the block, he knew he had the right place. Lots of police cars. A nice wide perimeter around the house in question. It probably looked almost normal from the inside of the house. But past the house's viewlines, activity buzzed and everybody was working on their particular jobs, keeping the public back where it was safe and letting the experts work out what they were going to do.

Zachary left his car behind the barricades and walked in. He was looking around for whoever was in charge, not sure whether Able would be there, and if he was, what kind of authority he would have over the operation. Zachary didn't try to breach the barrier, but walked up to one of the cops keeping the public at bay.

"That's my sister in there. I'm the one who called it in."

"That's nice, sir, but there's nothing you can do at this point. Just stay back out of the way and let the police do their jobs."

"Is Detective Able here? Who is in charge?"

"Not Able."

"Is there a hostage negotiator? What's the plan here?"

The cop looked irritated. "Buddy. You got no special standing here. You're going to have to wait and see what happens, just like everybody else."

Zachary looked over the faces of the police inside the taped-off area. "Is her husband here yet? Grant?"

The cop's eyes went to the side, and Zachary identified a small knot of people that must have included Grant Garrity. He walked along the outside of the perimeter toward them, pulling out his phone and dialing Grant's number. Grant jumped when the phone rang, and pulled it hurriedly out.

"Yeah? Zachary?"

"I'm behind you. Can you talk to whoever is in charge about letting me inside?"

Grant turned and looked, then waved at Zachary. He spoke to one of the cops, turning and pointing Zachary out. A couple of times. Until the cop finally nodded and spoke into his radio, and in a moment, there was a hulking big uniform in front of Zachary, looking him over like he was some kind of bug.

"You're Zachary Goldman?"

"Yeah. Are they going to let me talk to her?"

"Talk to her?" the big ape repeated. "I doubt that!" He laughed.

But he led Zachary into the perimeter, and he was allowed to go over to Grant to talk to him.

"Have they verified that Heather is inside?" Zachary asked. "That we guessed right?"

Grant nodded slowly. He seemed distracted, like he wasn't sure what to think of his wife being inside, the subject instead of the victim. He'd probably never even thought about her that way before.

"They put listening devices on the windows. So they can hear what's being said inside. Heather is there."

"Doing what? Talking to him? Threatening him?"

"They won't really tell me anything other than to just be quiet and wait for them to do their thing."

"Who is in charge?"

Grant scanned the various worker bees, shaking his head a little as if he were lost. He pointed to a long truck on the other side of the perimeter, some kind of mobile command center. "I don't know his name, but he's in there. Or they are. I don't know if it's one guy or if there are different departments or what."

Zachary moved toward the truck. He was stopped by one of the apes. Either the same one as had escorted him through the barrier, or another very similar. Zachary hadn't been paying any attention to their faces.

"You can't go in there."

"I'm Heather's brother. I need to talk to her. They're the only guys who are going to have any say in whether I can talk to her or not."

"You can't talk to them."

"Just let me go talk to them. They'll want to deal with someone with a clear head. Someone who knows Heather."

The big cop didn't like it, but he shook his head and escorted Zachary over to the bus. He knocked on the door with loud bangs, and eventually, someone pushed the door open. "What is it?"

"This is apparently the perp's brother?" the cop said it as a question, and shrugged. "He said you might want to talk to him? I don't know."

The other cop looked at Zachary for a minute, then motioned him up the three stairs into the bus.

"Come on, come on," he urged.

Inside the bus, Zachary took a look around. Lots of electronics and people wearing headphones. Talking to each other, talking to someone off the scene, coordinating whatever plan they were setting up.

"I thought the husband was here," commented the man who had let him in. "I'm Jones."

"Jones. Uh. I'm Zachary Goldman. I'm Heather's brother. I was with her earlier today when she… got some disturbing news about Robert Astor. If I could talk to her, I think I could help."

"Her husband is out there. What makes you think you're in a better position to talk to her than he is?"

"Because… she initially came to me about it. She talked to me about it before she talked to him. Because… we've both had some similar experiences. Some experiences that help me to understand what it is she's going through in there."

"She's not going through anything. She's the one putting someone else through pain and distress. She may have been the victim before, but she's not now."

"She still is. At least in her mind. So let me talk to her. What's it going to hurt?"

"Having the wrong person talk to her, or the right person say the wrong thing, and she could go nuclear. No one wants that. We're just going to take this slowly, one step at a time."

"Exactly." Zachary nodded. "That's exactly right. Nice and slowly. Has she talked to anyone? Does she know you're here?"

"Oh, she's knows we're here. We've had some contact."

"What did she say?"

"She doesn't have any demands. She just wants to kill the guy. But she hasn't done it yet, and that's a good sign."

"How long has she been in there?"

Jones looked at his watch. He had dark hair and bright, intelligent eyes. Every movement looked like it was choreographed. "Thirty-five minutes."

Zachary had been right, it had taken her a good amount of time to track down his address and get there. They had caught up to her quickly. And maybe that meant she wasn't too invested yet in killing him or being killed herself.

"How long have the police been here?"

"Twenty, give or take. The phone contact was… ten minutes ago, maybe. She's doing well; she didn't drop him as soon as she arrived, and she didn't do it when we got there. So far, she's kept her cool."

Zachary shook his head. Cool, Heather was not. She might come across that way, but she was traumatized and Zachary knew that she wasn't feeling calm and collected at all. She felt like the whole world was coming down around her and she didn't know what to do.

"I want to talk to her. I have my cell phone, does she have hers? If I call her, she'll pick up."

"No unauthorized contact. That's just playing with fire."

"I can talk to her. I know I can."

"You're not a trained negotiator. And you may think you know your sister, but in a case like this, you have no idea what's going on in her head."

"She came to me to help her to find out who hurt her. I need to finish it. I understand what's going on in her head. He hurt her and she wants to hurt him. He ruined her life and she wants to ruin his too. It's not enough to just shoot him. She needs him to be just as afraid of her as she was of him. Physically, it doesn't really matter how badly he's hurt. She wants him to hurt on the inside. To be as broken and terrified as she was."

Jones looked at Zachary in silence, chewing on his gum, considering. Finally, he nodded. "Give me your phone."

Zachary handed it over uncertainly, expecting Jones to dial Heather's number on it. But Jones slid it away in his own pocket. He motioned to one of the techs. "Get Mr. Goldman a headset."

In short order, one was placed over Zachary's head. He looked at Jones. "What do I do with this?" There was no keypad, no way he could see to dial out.

Jones smiled. "Just keep it on. We'll do all the work. Understand that we can cut you off at any time. We can also whisper prompts in your ear. Our job here is to deescalate. Get her calmed down and hopefully she will come out of there of her own free will, without any guns and without any harm done to Mr. Astor."

"Right."

Though Zachary himself would have liked to have been left alone with Mr. Astor for a few minutes. He was not a violent person, and had never been the instigator of a fight in his life. But he would have liked to hurt Mr. Astor. Just like he would have liked to hurt Teddy.

CHAPTER THIRTY-ONE

There was a ringing on his headset, and everybody in the bus was suddenly silent, listening in. Zachary rubbed his clammy hands down his pants. He waited to see whether Heather would pick up. Maybe she was too far gone. But they were monitoring her through the windows. They would know if she had already killed Mr. Astor.

"What?" Heather demanded.

Zachary took another breath. He forced a smile, which he hoped would make his voice sound cheerful and unstrained. "Hi, Feathers."

"Zachary?"

"I guess I should have walked you in."

She grunted. "You weren't going to get in my way."

"How are you doing in there?"

"Things aren't going quite the way I expected," she growled.

"It's a little harder than they make it look on TV, isn't it?"

There was a lengthy silence. Zachary wondered if he had said the wrong thing. But she wasn't shooting Mr. Astor to bits, so he supposed it could have been worse.

"I thought… I could come here and talk to him and he'd admit what he did. I'd tell him that I had proof he was the baby's father and he'd admit what he did."

"But he's not budging?"

"He's… weird."

"What does that mean? Weird how?"

"He's smaller than I remember. He was all… authoritative when I was a kid. He was… like God."

"And now, he's just a regular man. A regular man who isn't as big and scary as you remember him."

"Yeah."

"What did he say about the assault?"

"He said… he couldn't believe I thought he had anything to do with it. That there must be a mistake. Someone screwed up the DNA samples."

Zachary's first reaction had been that the mittens had been cross-contaminated and that it wasn't the baby's DNA that they had ended up testing. But Heather swore that Mr. Astor had never touched the mittens. So how could his DNA end up being on them? Or the DNA of one of the boys?

Zachary had told Mr. Peterson about DNA transfer. Heather could unwittingly have transferred the DNA. She would have touched other things that had the Astors' DNA on them at home. Then she could have transferred it to the mittens herself. Maybe it wasn't the baby's DNA at all. Maybe it was one of the other boys'.

"Do you think that's true?" he asked Heather. "What do you remember about your attacker? You lived with Mr. Astor every day. He couldn't fool you just by wearing a mask."

Zachary jumped when he heard Jones's voice in his ear. "We're trying to settle her down, Mr. Goldman. Not make her more angry toward the victim. If she has doubts about him being her attacker, that's a good thing."

He looked over to Jones, then away again, trying to stay focused on Heather. He couldn't talk to her if he was being interrupted by someone else's thoughts. But he remembered Jones's warning that they could shut down the call any time they wanted to.

"I know it was him," Heather confirmed. "As soon as that lady said it was from one of the Astors, I knew."

"Because of the way he behaved toward you? Had he… been inappropriate before?"

"No." Her tone was confused. "He was always really strict. He wasn't creepy. He didn't sit on my bed or touch me when he talked or anything like that. He never tried to be the only one in the house with me, and when he was… nothing ever happened."

"So he never gave you any sign that he had designs on you?"

Heather sighed. "He ignored me most of the time. It was Mrs. Astor who was the parent. He would go off to his office and just work on stuff there. I never even knew what it was he did. He just wasn't even there most of the time."

Zachary shook his head. He touched the earphone over his ear uncomfortably. He didn't like over-the-ear models. He liked the ones that fit inside his ear. That was what he used for his phone. They were distracting him from the conversation.

"So he kept to himself. Whatever he was thinking, he just kept it inside. You didn't have any way of knowing what he was up to. You couldn't have known."

"Yeah. No warning," Heather agreed.

Would it have been better if she had known his inner thoughts? Or would that just have drawn the torture out?

"He knew that was the way you came home from school?"

"It's the only way I ever came home. He knew. I had fights with Mrs. Astor about it all the time. She'd get calls or notes from the school. Then she'd get after me, tell me I had to obey the rules and go around the park like everyone else. Because that was the rule. But... I didn't like going around. I didn't want to be out on the road, with all of the traffic. Why should we have to avoid the park? It was a public park, it was meant to be enjoyed. I like being in nature. At least, back then I did."

He wondered how she enjoyed nature now. Did she still go out for walks in the park? Or did she stay at home, where she felt more safe?

"Could I come in, Heather?"

Jones spoke in Zachary's ear again. "You are not allowed to go in there. No one is allowed to go in."

He put his hand around his mike to muffle it, not sure if he had a mute button somewhere. "If she wants me to go in, I can go in and help to calm her down. I can keep her from shooting Mr. freaking Astor. As much as he deserves it."

"It's against policy. We can't send more potential victims in there. Especially civilians."

Zachary grunted. He looked for a way around the rule. There was always a way around. He was an inveterate rule-breaker. "What if I go sit on the doorstep. Can I do that?"

"No."

"She could come out to talk to me. I wouldn't have to go in. You want her out of there, don't you?"

"You would still be putting yourself in the line of fire."

Zachary shook his head. He took his hand off of the mike to talk to Heather. "Never mind. They won't let me come in there."

"That's probably a good thing."

"Do you think it's time to come out?" he suggested.

"I need to do this."

"I don't think you can. Can you?"

"I can. I just need to get my courage up. It would help if he wasn't such a weaselly little snot. That isn't what he was like when I was little. He was the dad. I was so used to… you know what our dad was like. You didn't disobey him, or he was likely to take your head off. We all knew that. When I went to the Astors, I just thought… he was the dad. He had to be obeyed like that. He was the authority."

"Yeah. It's always different when you're at another home, the rules change, the roles change, it takes forever to figure out the way things work. And for me, by the time I figured things out, I was always on my way somewhere else. You know?"

"You changed families way more than I did. I just had the Astors."

There was a voice in the background that Zachary couldn't make out. Then Heather's voice shouting directly into his ear. "You shut up!"

Zachary waited for the ringing in his ears to stop. He glanced around the command center at the others listening in on the call and saw that a number of them had pulled the earpieces away from their ears momentarily.

"Hey, Heather. What's going on there?"

"I don't want him to speak!"

"Okay. Gotcha. Is he… physically okay?"

"Have I hurt him?"

"Have you?"

"Why do you care? You know about people like him. You know what he did to you."

Zachary noticed her pronoun confusion and tried to let it float over him. Mr. Astor hadn't done anything to Zachary. It had been Archuro who had hurt him. But Archuro wasn't in there. Zachary wasn't with him. He breathed through his brain's attempts to sweep him back in time.

"I'm just wondering," he said casually. "The cops are wondering. Whether he's tied up, or injured, or you've got your gun pointed at him. You know. They want the whole picture."

"He banged up his face a bit. I told him to take his clothes off to humiliate him, but I can't stand looking at his body, so the joke's on me. He's sitting here in his tighty-whities looking like some dead fish the dog drug in. But he *won't shut up!*" She shouted the last few words again.

Jones was looking anxious, but Zachary shook his head at him. It was good for Heather to be getting her frustration out by yelling. She had said a couple of times that she was trying to work herself up to killing Astor, but Zachary thought that if he kept bleeding off her anger safely, he could bring her down.

"What's he saying?" Zachary asked.

"I don't know. He's saying that he'd never hurt anyone. But he did! You know what he did to me."

"I know. He should have to pay for that. He should have to go to prison."

Zachary motioned to Jones for his phone, but it took a few mimed requests before Jones got it out and handed it to him, frowning. Zachary thumbed through the photos, turning to one that just showed teenage Heather's face, battered and bruised, which he turned around and showed to Jones.

Jones's lips tightened as he looked at the young teen's injuries. He shook his head slowly. "I hate it when we have to protect scum like that," he said in Zachary's ear, "but it's part of the job."

Zachary nodded his agreement. "You want him to go to prison, don't you, Feathers?"

"Yes." Her voice sounded teary and sullen.

"If you want him to go to prison, then you need to let the police arrest him. You need to let them in there."

"But he has to say what he did! They won't arrest him if he doesn't admit it."

"He'll admit it. He's just scared right now. Once he gets out of there and gets a lawyer, he's going to be trying to get a plea. That's what his lawyer will tell him to do. They'll know that we have him dead to rights and they'll tell him to plead it out."

"I don't want him to plead!"

There was a loud crash. Zachary pulled his earpieces away from his ears, looking anxiously at the other people in the command center. No one seemed to be panicking or ramping up a response to the next level, so the loud noise had been something other than a gunshot.

"What was that?" Zachary asked.

"His chair fell over," she said more calmly.

There were a couple of muffled laughs inside the bus.

"He peed himself," Heather said, disgust in her voice. "How could I have been so scared of this little rat? I spent every day of my life worrying that the man who raped me was going to come back and do it again. I was afraid to go out of the house, to take my kids to the playground. I thought he was a big, scary monster."

"But he's just a man. And not even as big as you remember him being."

"He barely even had to raise his voice and I'd start shaking. I never let anyone see it, I always put on a front, but you know what it was like. They were all bigger than we were. The grown-ups who controlled our lives."

Zachary could taste the fear when she talked about it. He remembered how his heart would freeze as soon as one of his parents raised their voices. He put on a brave face for the younger kids, telling them how everything would be okay and that he would take care of them, but he still felt it.

He still knew that bowel-loosening terror that one of his parents was going to kill the other, or that they would turn on one of the children. All of the kids had been in the hospital at one time or another after suffering an 'accident' at home. Falling off a ladder, jumping a bike off a ramp, climbing up a dresser or bookshelf and pulling it over onto himself; he and the others could all be very inventive explaining their injuries to the authorities.

They had taken that fear with them to all of the families they went to. They still carried it with them.

"I know," he whispered, unable to raise his voice as the memories flooded his brain. As if one of his parents might hear him and fly into a rage. "I know, Feathers. But it's okay now. He's not going to hurt you anymore. None of them are."

The specters of their parents would never be gone. They would continue to taint every relationship he had. Even Mr. Peterson, who had always remained calm and had never raised his voice to Zachary, could still set Zachary off by touching him when he didn't expect it.

Heather's foster father had done more than accidentally triggering her. He had betrayed her trust and taken something precious from her.

Zachary realized that Heather was crying. He tried to swallow the lump in his own throat and to comfort her.

"Grant is out here. He doesn't want anything to happen to you. And I just met you again. I want to get to know you and the strong, loving woman you became. Don't give that scumbag another thought. He's not worth all of the time and agony you've wasted on him. He's in the past now. You have so much to look forward to."

She tried to answer, but her words were scrambled and he could only hear her crying.

"Put the gun down. You don't need it anymore. You're free of that fear now. Come on out. You have so much more to look forward to now."

Zachary was aware that the others in the bus were watching him, everyone so silent they would hear a pin drop, waiting for Heather's response.

"She's on the move," someone said in Zachary's headset. He didn't know if they could see her through the window or were watching her heat signature through the side of the house. He waited, holding his breath. "Subject is moving away from the hostage."

He hated that they referred to Mr. Astor as the hostage. He was the one who had held Heather hostage for three decades. But they didn't care about the history. Only about whether she was going to shoot him or not.

There was a dial tone in his headset for a brief moment before it was cut out by whoever was managing the audio.

"Subject has terminated the call."

Zachary headed for the door of the command center.

"Stay here, Mr. Goldman."

"I need to go out and meet her."

"Stay inside where it's safe. They will need to secure the sub—your sister —before you can see her."

"I can at least be out there so she can see me, see that I'm there for her."

"She already knows that, you've just been on the phone with her."

Ignoring him, Zachary stepped more quickly and got out of the bus without any of the cops grabbing him. Outside the command center, it was another story. He immediately ran into a wall of cops, most of whom were watching the house, listening to their earbuds, radios, and headsets. But a few of them were alert enough of their surroundings to immediately identify Zachary as a civilian who shouldn't have the run of the secured area, and a couple of them grabbed him to prevent him from going any farther.

"Sir!"

Zachary could at least see the door of the house from his position, so he didn't fight their hands, but stood still, watching. On cue, the door swung open. Heather stood framed by the door, her hands held up, empty. No attempt at suicide by cop; she was surrendering. Zachary breathed a sigh of relief.

She was swarmed by a black-suited tactical squad. They took her to the ground, but they didn't throw her down. They weren't yelling or hitting her, but had to frisk her to make sure she didn't still have the gun or any other weapons. Zachary tried not to react to the sight of her being frisked and handcuffed. Just because she was being taken into custody, that didn't mean they were going to charge her with kidnapping or assault.

There were extenuating circumstances. Once the authorities understood what had happened, they would go easy on her. She could plead down to minor charges, maybe not have to serve any time. Some community service, a suspended sentence, probation…

"Now let me go see her," he told the cops holding on to him, once Heather was in handcuffs and on her feet again. They looked around for someone to give them directions. Jones was standing behind them, in the doorway of the bus. He nodded.

"Go ahead. But escort him over, I don't want chaos."

Zachary allowed the two big cops to walk him toward the house. Heather was back on her feet and a group of them were moving her toward a vehicle. Zachary hastened his step.

"Heather. Wait. Please let me see her."

They were talking in loud, clipped voices, but Zachary managed to make himself heard. They turned to him.

"Just let me see her. Let me talk for a minute."

Heather turned to him. Her eyes were sunken and her face streaked with tears. That morning, she had looked so fresh and bright and neatly-pressed, but the day had taken its toll on her.

"Heather. It's okay. He's going to be arrested and you're going to be all right. It's okay."

"I wanted to hear him say it. I wanted him to admit what he'd done."

"He still will. And he'll say it without a gun to his head."

He wanted to give her a hug, but didn't figure the cops were going to let him get that close to her. He sniffled back tears of his own. "You need to let her see her husband too. Let him know where you're taking her so he can pick her up."

The head of the tactical team looked at him. "She's not going to be going home."

"You just watch. When the media and the judge see the pictures of how she looked after he raped and beat her, she'll be going home."

They turned her away from him and continued getting her into a car for transport.

CHAPTER THIRTY-TWO

Zachary was exhausted. Jones caught up with him after Heather was given a chance to speak to Grant and then transported from the scene. Zachary was watching the house, waiting for the men who had gone in to escort Robert Astor out. He wanted a good look at the man who had hurt his sister.

"You're a private eye?" Jones asked. He'd obviously talked to someone. Zachary's face and name had been in the media a lot over the past months and somebody had recognized him.

Zachary nodded. "Yeah. Zachary Goldman. Goldman Investigations."

"What do you have by way of proof that Astor was the one who assaulted your sister?"

"Besides her word?"

Jones shifted uncomfortably. He nodded. "Besides her word."

"We have the DNA profile of the baby she conceived as a result. It leads back to the Astors. You do a paternity test, and it will verify that he is the father. She was fourteen."

"We'll need a sample to test for ourselves."

"It's already in the hands of the PD. Talk to Detective Able. He should be around here somewhere, he's the one who called this in."

Jones gazed around, then nodded. He put his hands in his pockets, trying, Zachary thought, to look casual and relaxed. "You did a good job talking her down. A little irregular, but it worked."

"Yeah. I'm glad she didn't kill him. I was afraid she might before we got here…"

"He's a lucky man."

"Are you going to arrest him?"

"We're going to… invite him in for questioning. And if he doesn't give a DNA swab voluntarily, we'll get a warrant."

Zachary looked toward the door again. "I don't think you'll need a warrant."

"You think he'll give it voluntarily?"

"I think Heather already saw to that. Is he in there changing out of wet underpants?"

Jones's nose wrinkled in distaste.

"Bag them up and test them," Zachary advised. "Then you can confront him with the evidence."

———

Eventually, Zachary saw the door open, and several uniformed policemen escorted Robert Astor down the sidewalk to a waiting car. He wasn't hand-cuffed like Heather had been, but Zachary knew that he was going to have to face some pretty tough questioning anyway. There wouldn't be any way for the police to look the other direction and say that she was just some crackpot making wild accusations. After causing such a big circus, they were going to have to show either that she was right or that she was wrong. There would be no waffling about it. She wasn't going to be relegated to a quiet corner somewhere.

Astor was not a big man, as Heather had observed. Taller and heavier than Zachary, but that wasn't saying much. Zachary had always been the smallest in his school classes. Astor was in his early seventies, so he no longer looked like the man that Heather had respected and feared as a father figure. He was slightly stooped, had brown spots on his skin, and had hair that was more gray than its original dark brown. He didn't have a lot of wrinkles, so his face probably still looked pretty similar to what it had when he had been Heather's foster father. For the moment, he looked beaten-down and fright-ened. Zachary didn't know if that would last, or if he would be yelling about his rights and insisting that they release him once he'd had a chance to recover from the encounter with Heather. At least things had ended pretty quickly. He hadn't been locked in the house with Heather for hours on end. Some standoffs went on for hours or days.

After he was directed into the car and was sitting in the back seat, a woman was escorted over to see him. His wife, Zachary assumed. Her hair was a somewhat unnatural shade of red, gray at the roots, and she had a sad face with more wrinkles than her husband. She looked like she had lived a hard life.

She talked animatedly with the police officers around the car, obviously arguing to have her husband released or to let her talk to someone in authority, or whatever other concessions she could get. She didn't like the idea of them taking Astor in for questioning. She kept shaking her head, looking at her husband waiting in the car, and shaking her head again. Zachary drifted closer, hoping to be able to hear some of what she was saying. He caught Jones watching him, but Jones didn't stop him from getting closer, and neither did any of the other cops or authorities present. He listened carefully, trying to read her lips to catch the portions that he couldn't hear.

"I don't understand why you think he's done anything," she said. "How is it that the victim of violence gets blamed for what happened? You can't take him in to the station. If you want to talk to him, you can talk to him here. And you can wait until he's feeling better. This... this doesn't make any sense. This isn't how you treat a victim."

"The subject in this case made a lot of allegations. We'd like to get everything cleared up."

"What allegations? I don't know this person. Heather Garrity? Is she just some random person? She's crazy. She just picked this house out because it reminded her of something from her past. There's no way she knew what she was talking about."

Zachary frowned. For someone who didn't even know what accusations had been made against her husband, she had made an awful lot of defensive statements.

The cop who was trying to handle Mrs. Astor looked around and saw Jones watching. "Boss, you want to talk to this lady? Explain to her what's going on...?"

"I thought you were doing a fine job all by yourself, Walton."

"Boss..." Walton made a gesture toward her, frustrated, not wanting to deal with the disgruntled woman. He just wanted to get Astor in to the police station. Hopefully, he wasn't the one who had been tasked in questioning him, and someone who had a little more training would be trying to get a confession out of Astor. Maybe Jones himself. Maybe a woman detective who knew how to handle scumbags like Astor.

"You're Mrs. Astor?" Jones asked gently, looking at her.

"Yes. And I don't see why my husband is being detained when he was the victim here! It's ridiculous. Why should people who have been targeted be victimized all over again by the police like this?"

Why indeed? She had seen it happen to Heather. Was she remembering that, or was she only concerned about her husband?

"Your husband has been asked to come in to answer some questions about Mrs. Garrity and his history with her. I'm sure he can fill you in on it later."

"My husband? How would my husband know anything about her?"

In the car, Mr. Astor put his face in his hands. As if that could shut out his wife's argument and her voice.

"Robert? You tell him. You tell him that you don't know what they're talking about. Who is this person? She's not anyone that we know."

"Margaret..."

"What? You don't know her, so you can't answer any questions about her. This is ridiculous. They shouldn't be allowed to just interrogate anybody they want. There is a limit. And you don't have to agree to talk. You can refuse and they can't do anything about it."

"Margaret!" he said in exasperation.

She looked at him. "What?"

"It was Heather, Margaret. Not some stranger. Heather, our foster daughter."

"Heather," she repeated, her face suddenly going slack. "What would she be doing here? She hasn't lived here for years and years. And she never lived in this house. What did she want? Robert, you told her to leave, didn't you? Someone can't just go into your house and start threatening!"

"Margaret, please... shut up."

She stared at him, unable to believe he would talk to her that way. Zachary took another step forward, watching with interest. Heather had said that she was afraid of Astor, that he was authoritarian, but Zachary wasn't seeing a man who asserted his own position and bullied his wife. Zachary watched them both for the minutest tells.

Margaret Astor regained her composure, and deferred to her husband rather than making further accusations.

"What is this, then?" she asked. "I don't understand."

"She's accused your husband of aggravated sexual assault," Jones told her.

"Him?" Margaret's voice was scathing, and Zachary expected her to run down her husband's manhood right there. "He's an old man. Why would he chase after some girl from the past? Heather Goldman was never any great beauty as a girl. She was knock-kneed and pimply and I don't imagine she turned out to be much of anything. We did everything we could for that girl, officer, but she was sullen and ungrateful and it didn't matter what we did for her, she never appreciated it. In the end, she left us and ended up in a group home for girls like her."

Zachary clenched his fists. He would have liked to have clocked her one for running down his sister after all that she had gone through at their hands. They thought that they had done everything for her? All they had done was to damage and traumatize her further.

"Not recently," Jones said, once he could get a word in edgewise. "She says that your husband assaulted her when she was fourteen. When she was living with you."

Mrs. Astor's mouth snapped shut like a trap. She looked at her husband but didn't say anything to him. She didn't immediately jump to his defense, which Zachary found interesting. She was not afraid to speak her mind, but one thing that she hadn't said yet was that Robert Astor had been a saint and that he had never done anything to hurt anyone. She didn't immediately protest that he hadn't raped Heather. That he couldn't have.

"Trust that little minx to come up with something like that," she snapped, and shook her head. "I don't know what happened in the woods that day, Mr. Jones, but my husband was at work, not at home or in the park. He could not have done that to her." Her mouth closed, and her lips formed a long, thin, straight line. She glared at Jones, but she couldn't keep quiet about the injustice being perpetrated on her husband.

"The police investigated it at the time. If there had been any reason to suspect my husband, they would have arrested him at the time. She's just making things up, and why she's doing it now, thirty years later, I don't know. The woman's off her rocker. That's obvious from what happened here today, isn't it?"

"She was highly agitated," Jones agreed.

"Probably off her meds. Those kids were damaged. All of the children in that family. I used to hear about their exploits sometimes from the social worker or the other foster parents. They were uncontrollable. Lighting fires, starting fights, running away. Our little Heather was quiet by comparison. But that didn't mean she didn't get in any trouble. Never thought she had to follow anyone else's rules, that one. Did she think that they were told to stay out of the park because the school had nothing better to do than to think up unnecessary rules? But no, little Miss Delinquent had to do it anyway. And you look at what happened to her when she did."

Zachary swallowed. So there *had* been a history around the park. Maybe Robert Astor saw it as his own personal playground. And it hadn't mattered to him that one of the girls was his own foster daughter. He wasn't afraid of it being too close to home. After all, he wore a mask. No one could identify him.

"We went to the police at the time," Margaret insisted again. "Heather didn't want to go to the police. She didn't want to report it. But I did the right thing. I took her in. They questioned her and they gathered all of the evidence they could. None of it ever pointed at my husband. He was never a suspect in her case."

Jones took all of this in with equanimity. He nodded understandingly, making Mrs. Astor feel like he was on her side. "I understand there was a *baby*," he said, as if this were a shocking secret, something that pointed at Heather's delinquency.

"Yes, there was," Mrs. Astor said with relish. She appeared to be perfectly happy to dish up the details on every detail of Heather's ordeal. "She was terribly sick with morning sickness. I had hoped to leave her in school until later on in the pregnancy, but she was so sick all of the time that we had to pull her out. Said that she had mono and would be back the next year." Mrs. Astor leaned toward Jones to confide in him. "There was no talk of abortion and no talk of her keeping the baby. It wasn't like that then. She only had one choice, and that was to have the baby and put it up for adoption." She straightened up and shrugged her bony shoulders. "I hoped that she'd miscarry and not have to carry it all the way to term, but in spite of the morning sickness, she was healthy enough. When the baby came, we wrapped everything up lickety-split and had that baby to his adoptive parents within a couple of days. That's the way it should be done. Not all of this nonsense they have now."

"We have a sample of the baby's DNA. We will be able to identify your husband as the baby's father or rule him out. That should settle the question of whether he was the one who assaulted her once and for all."

Mrs. Astor went still again. She looked at Jones, and looked at her husband. Zachary wondered whether she had known or suspected back then. Surely she wouldn't have insisted on Heather going to the police station and having a rape kit done if Mrs. Astor had any suspicion that her husband had been Heather's rapist.

But she didn't say anything further and neither did Robert Astor.

CHAPTER THIRTY-THREE

Zachary eventually sat in his car, eyes closed, going over the events of the day. He was beyond tired. Exhaustion had come and gone several hours before. Everyone was at the police station, but he hadn't been invited. In fact, Jones had made a particular point of non-inviting him, telling him to go home and not to show up at the police station.

"You leave it to us now. You've done your part. It's our turn to tie it all together and see if we can build a case that will stick."

"You'll take care of my sister? Don't let her talk to that woman or to him. Make sure that she's comfortable, and that she sees a judge as soon as she can...?"

"The wheels of justice move slowly, as I'm sure you know. They won't be too quick to release an armed gunman. But I think things will play out, if you're patient. She'll be able to see her husband at the police station for a few minutes. Probably best if you aren't working the case."

"Okay. But if she needs anything... call me."

As Zachary sat in the car by himself, reviewing it all in his head, his phone did ring. He worked it out of his pocket and looked at it. Tyrrell. Zachary looked out his window at the floodlights that had been set up around the house. There had been plenty of news reporters there to comment on the hostage-taking and the rumors surrounding what had happened there. Zachary had been sorely tempted to put in a few words of his own, but he hadn't. He needed to let justice take its course, as Jones had suggested. Zachary didn't need to be in the spotlight yet again.

Zachary answered the call. "Hi, T."

"Zachary? Was that Heather on the news? What's going on? What happened?"

"Sorry I didn't call… things have been moving pretty fast."

"It was Heather?"

"It was Heather."

"But who did she go after? You found the rapist? After all this time?"

"Yeah. It was the foster father all along. She went a little crazy when she found out it was him. But she remembered enough to know that it was true."

Tyrrell swore. "Poor Feathers. Is she okay?"

"She's safe. Her husband is with her at the police station. It might be a few days before they release her, but when the media gets wind of the story behind the hostage-taking… they won't let her stay in jail for long."

"I hope not." Tyrrell swore again. "At least she knows who it was, now. I think that was probably the worst part for her, not knowing who it was. At least if she knows, she has a direction to aim her anger. Without that, it's just everything. Never knowing where he might be, if it's the guy standing next to her in line. She could never start the healing process."

"Yeah." Zachary knew which way to aim his anger, but he was far from healing. He hoped it wouldn't be thirty years before he was able to face what had happened to him. He knew who the perpetrator was, and despite what he had told the police who had interviewed him, he remembered everything that had been done to him. But being able to move on… that was still too far in the distance to even see a pinprick of light at the other end of the tunnel.

"Zach."

"Yeah?"

"You okay?"

"Yeah."

"You want company tonight? You want to stay over here?"

"No. Thanks. I need my own space."

"Okay, man. But if you need to talk, just give me a call. Even in the middle of the night. I'm good at middle-of-the-night calls."

———

He didn't call Tyrrell in the middle of the night. He didn't call Kenzie either, and she didn't call him, though he was sure that, like Tyrrell, she must have seen the coverage on the TV and internet and known what it was all about. She kept her distance, waiting for him to acknowledge that he needed her. That was for the best. There were messages on his phone and in his email from Mr. Peterson, Mario Bowman, and a few other acquaintances as more details became available and they wanted whatever tidbits they could get from him.

He knew he wasn't being fair. They were people who, for the most part, really did care about him and wanted to know how he was more than just gathering juicy gossip they could share online. But he felt like they were vultures circling his dead carcass.

Or watching his dying body for his last breath, when they would swoop in and start the feast.

———

There was a message from Rhys. Not a voicemail message, of course, which would have been too difficult for him, but one of his gifs, sent over a messenger app, waiting for Zachary to open it.

He mentally prepared himself to interpret Rhys's intention.

Sometimes Rhys was more cryptic than others. Zachary didn't know whether he was intentionally vague or symbolic when he could have been more clear, or if that was just the way that Rhys's brain worked after the traumas he had been through.

The gif was not at all hard to interpret. It was the same one as Rhys had shown him the last time they had visited face-to-face. The drowning man, giving the three-two-one count and waving bye-bye.

Two meanings. Either Rhys was feeling worse and reaching out for help, or he was worried that Zachary would be feeling low and needing extra help. Despite the late hour, Zachary called Rhys's grandma.

"Vera. It's Zachary."

"Oh, Zachary. It's good to hear your voice. I'll go get Rhys."

"No, wait. Is he okay?"

She paused. "Is Rhys okay? Yes… why?"

"He sent me a message. I wasn't sure whether he needed help…"

"Or whether you do?"

Zachary laughed, a little embarrassed. "Well, yes."

"He saw you on TV again. He's always impressed when he sees you on TV. But he always worries, especially if he can't reach you."

"He's very intuitive."

"That he is," Vera agreed. "Now hold on and let me get him. It will only be a minute, you know he doesn't chatter on like some of us."

Zachary waited while she walked to Rhys's room. He heard her knock on the door to announce herself and then open the door.

"It's Zachary, Rhys."

Zachary closed his eyes, envisioning Rhys lying on his bed with his computer or his own phone, and tried to imagine how he would communicate what he wanted to say. Facial expression, body language, simple signs and gestures, and maybe a word or a picture displayed on Rhys's phone.

"Are you at home, Zachary?" Vera asked, after a few minutes of silence.

"Yeah. I'm home."

"Is Kenzie there?"

"No… I'm by myself."

"You should go to the hospital." Vera paused and double-checked with Rhys. "Is that right, Rhys? You think he should go to the hospital?"

Zachary sighed. He had told Rhys that he would check himself in if he was feeling any worse. And in the stillness of his apartment, isolated from the people who cared about him, wondering whether Kenzie was gone for good, what was going to happen to Heather, and stuck in a morass of his own memories, the darkness weighed him down inside and out.

———

He texted Rhys a selfie or himself in the hospital waiting room as he waited for his name to be called so that Rhys would know that he had followed through. Rhys texted him back a thumbs-up and a sad emoticon. Zachary didn't make any attempt to carry on a further conversation with Rhys. He powered off his phone and sat there waiting. His elbows on his knees and his head in his hands, he stared down at the floor.

He knew he should have sought help sooner. Everyone had known that he was shattered after Archuro. They had all told him that he had checked himself out of the hospital too soon. When he had finally gone back to his therapist, she too had suggested that at the very least, he needed a med review, and that he should seriously consider a couple of weeks at the hospital to get stabilized.

But like Heather, he was stubborn, and he figured he could just tough it out on his own. Checking himself into psychiatric always made him feel like a failure. The kid who couldn't control himself. A lunatic. No different from the homeless schizophrenics he saw wandering downtown in the city, mumbling or even yelling at their hallucinations.

"Mr. Goldman?"

He looked up to see a nurse hovering a few feet away from him, clipboard in hand.

"Would you come with me, please?"

CHAPTER THIRTY-FOUR

Tyrrell visited him. Mr. Peterson visited him. Kenzie did not. Zachary didn't get any calls or messages from her. The staff in the unit didn't mention any inquiries from her. Zachary knew he should call her, but he couldn't bring himself to do it. As long as he didn't talk to her, it wasn't officially over. He could pretend that she was too busy, like he was, and that when life settled down for both of them, they would again be cuddling on the couch to watch an old Phillip Marlowe flick with a big bowl of popcorn resting on both of their laps.

And Heather came. Grant was with her, but he stayed in the background, letting her visit with Zachary.

"Hey, Feathers," Zachary awkwardly gave her a hug around the shoulders. "How are you doing?"

She looked around the unit. "Glad it's you here and not me." She laughed. "I guess that's a pretty tactless thing to say, isn't it? I guess I mean I'm lucky they didn't commit me involuntarily. After what I did... they certainly could have said that I was a danger to others and needed to be evaluated."

Zachary nodded. He wasn't offended by her saying that she didn't want to be there. "So is everything going to work out? Did they... do the DNA test against Astor?"

"It could drive a person crazy how long it takes to get results back, even when they are rushing it. But I know what it's going to say."

She sounded certain of herself. And she was calm about it. She didn't set any alarm bells ringing for Zachary. She sat down with him and held his hand for a minute. Her touch was reassuring, and in his mind's eye he could see the little mother he had known. A blond, scraggle-haired gamine with freckles sprinkled across her nose, taking him in hand to teach him life lessons and to try to keep him from running wild or attracting the attention of their parents. She gave his hand a squeeze, and he suspected that she was thinking of a short, spindly-legged boy with buzzed dark hair and the attention span of a gnat.

"I got a call from Ella."

He frowned. He took a minute to recall who Ella was. Ella Day, the genealogist who had worked on the genetic family tree. She had probably been concerned about Heather and wondered whether she wanted any further details of the baby's heritage. He wondered whether she had been able to pin down the father as Robert Astor from the GENEmatch database, or whether she'd only been able to isolate that branch of the tree.

"What did she have to say?"

"There are different flags that can be set in the GENEmatch database, for privacy and contact information. How much you want to reveal to the public if someone ends up being a close hit."

He nodded. "Uh-huh."

"When she uploaded the DNA profile, it triggered another match that wasn't public information. But I guess the person who uploaded his information got an email notification about it, so that he had the option of seeing what had been posted and making contact."

Zachary looked into Heather's eyes, and saw happiness rather than fear. "Was it...?"

"My son." Her eyes teared up. She looked at the ceiling and dabbed at the corners of her eyes. "The baby that I gave up."

"Did you meet him?"

"Yes. It was..." She closed her eyes, searching for the words. "It was such a comfort." She opened her eyes again. "He has a wonderful family. It wasn't like us, being raised in foster care. He had a stable, loving family and he's very attached to them. It's what I wanted for him."

"And now he knows who his biological mother is too."

She nodded. "He's going to keep in contact."

"That's cool." Zachary smiled. "Awesome."

"Thank you so much for helping me. Not just for solving a cold case that everybody said was impossible, but for helping me to find him too. I was afraid that I would resent him, or see Mr. Astor in him. But he's okay. I can look at him and just see Mikey, my son, and not anyone else. And know that he turned out okay."

———

Zachary walked out of the hospital to wait for his cab. It felt good to be out in the fresh air. He wasn't one hundred percent okay, but when was the last time he had been?

He'd been through some intensive therapy, another overhaul of his meds, and had been kept under observation for a couple of weeks to ensure that he was sleeping properly and wasn't being overwhelmed by suicidal thoughts. Healing would be an ongoing process, as it always was.

He did a double-take and blinked at the figure at the end of the sidewalk outside of the hospital entrance. The man turned and saw Zachary at the same time.

"Oh." He looked awkward. "Zachary. Hello."

Zachary approached Gordon hesitantly. His brain went spinning wildly with speculations of why Bridget's partner would be at the hospital. Bridget had been ill. She had said that the cancer wasn't back, but maybe she just hadn't known yet. Something had obviously been wrong. Gordon wasn't there for himself.

Gordon nodded to the cigarette in his hand, holding it away from himself as if it belonged to someone else. "Filthy habit. Just when you think you have it licked, some stressor kicks in and you're out on the sidewalk smoking again, everybody coughing and glaring at you as they walk by."

"Is everything okay?"

"Yes, she's fine," Gordon said immediately. "Just getting dehydrated. Can't keep anything down and we needed to get some fluids into her."

Zachary swallowed. Bridget must be on chemo again. Why had she lied to him? She'd said right to his face that the cancer wasn't back. He knew that a second appearance of the cancer so soon did not bode well for her chances of survival. Every time it came back, her odds went down significantly.

"Why didn't you tell me?"

Gordon didn't owe him any explanation. There was no rule that said Bridget had to report a recurrence of her cancer to her ex, or that Gordon should. Zachary was supposed to be living his own life, not always getting wrapped up in hers.

Gordon looked at him blankly. "Bridget said she had seen you. She didn't tell you?"

"I asked her, she said the cancer wasn't back."

"Oh, no." Gordon agreed. He touched Zachary's forearm briefly. "Heavens, not that." He searched Zachary's eyes. "She's pregnant."

CHAPTER THIRTY-FIVE

Zachary was still reeling when he got back home. He busied himself with housekeeping details, putting on the coffee machine and taking out the garbage that he had neglected to dispose of before going to the hospital and which smelled to high heaven. He filled the sink to soak the dishes with petrified food cemented to them.

He didn't realize that he'd left the door open when he took the garbage out until he looked up and saw Kenzie standing there.

"Oh. I didn't hear you come in."

"Yeah, you seem a little distracted."

Zachary didn't know what to say to her.

"Lorne said that you were getting out today," Kenzie explained. She stepped into the kitchen and wrinkled her nose at the smell of the garbage that still lingered there. "I figured it would be a good time to stop by and get my things."

"Kenzie, I…"

"I pride myself on being able to take a hint, Zachary. You've been avoiding me. Pushing me away. I get it."

"I just…" He didn't know what to say to her. He didn't know what he wanted. He had hoped that once he was ready, she would come back, and they would be able to resume where they had left off. But he had screwed up by not talking to her about it. He had instead been a coward and avoided talking to her. What was she supposed to think?

He didn't want her to take her things. He didn't want her to be angry and disappointed in him. He'd never thought that she would just give up on him.

She faced him, her face pink. "Lorne told me that you were upset about me talking to him about our relationship."

"Well… yeah, sort of…"

"No 'sort of' about it. Be honest with me, Zachary. You can at least do that."

He looked down at his hands, anxious and embarrassed. He hadn't wanted to make a big deal of it. But it *had* bothered him. He forgave her for it; he knew that she was only trying to sort things out and figure out how to have a relationship with him, or if she even could.

"I was upset," he admitted.

"I shouldn't have talked to him. Not without your permission. I should have talked more to you about it, or asked if we could see your therapist together to discuss it. I just thought that Lorne might have some insight. He's known you longer than anyone else, saw you as a kid, and single, and with Bridget, so I just thought… he could help me to understand what you were going through and weren't ready to talk about. I knew that whatever happened with Archuro had triggered some really bad stuff. But I didn't know if it was all Teddy, or if it went deeper than that."

"I guess… it's deeper," he admitted. Too little, too late.

"I guess so," Kenzie agreed.

She headed toward the bedroom to gather up her belongings. Zachary followed her. He watched as she went through the drawers and closet and the little bathroom to search out anything that was hers.

"Kenzie, can we still—"

"Oh, don't give me the 'can we still be friends' speech. Show me a little respect."

He stood there, tapping his fingers to the sides of his legs, unable to be still.

"You should know that I talked to Bridget too," Kenzie said, without turning around to face him.

"What?"

"I know. It was stupid. I was desperate. You were so… it was obvious how badly you were hurting. And then when we started to get more intimate and it was obvious that you were just… totally checking out, I wanted to know if it had always been that way. And there was only one person I could think to ask."

Zachary remembered how Bridget had called him out of the blue, saying that she wanted to check on him. Had that been after she had talked to Kenzie? Kenzie had acted so indignant that Bridget had called. Was that to cover up the fact that she had spoken to Bridget herself? How could she expect Zachary to go on with his life and forget about Bridget, when she herself had involved Bridget again? How was Zachary supposed to move on?

"She's pregnant," he told Kenzie.

Kenzie had just picked up a bottle of pills and it fell to the floor of the bathroom with a loud clatter. She turned and looked at him.

"What?"

At least Bridget hadn't told Kenzie and refused to tell Zachary.

"I just ran into Gordon at the hospital. She's been admitted because she's dehydrated. Throwing up too much."

"And he told you she's pregnant? Not that she's sick, but she's *pregnant?* He said that?"

He was glad she found it just as shocking as Zachary did. He had told Kenzie their history. How Bridget had said that she never wanted children. The pregnancy scare that turned out to be cancer. Zachary remembered how the doctor had suggested Bridget have the eggs in her cancer-free ovary frozen before they started treatment, to bank them for later. Bridget hadn't even wanted to. She'd said she wasn't ever going to use them.

Apparently, she had changed her mind after meeting Gordon.

He nodded in answer to Kenzie's question. "He thought she had told me. But she hadn't. I was so worried that the cancer was back."

She looked at Zachary for a minute, shaking her head in disbelief. He wished that she would walk up to him and give him a hug and tell him that it was all going to be okay. Zachary would be just fine without Bridget. Bridget could have babies with Gordon, and Zachary would be just fine.

But she didn't.

She bent over and picked up the dropped pill bottle and readjusted her grip on the items she had collected.

"I should have brought a suitcase. I didn't realize how much stuff I had left here. Do you have a bag I could use?"

He went back to the kitchen for a couple of the plastic shopping bags under the sink that he never got around to recycling. He handed one to Kenzie and helped to fill the other, his eyes burning and a lump in his throat.

"I'm sorry about Bridget," Kenzie said. "I know that must be very difficult for you." She took both bags and let out a deep sigh. "Good luck. I hope you can be happy."

Zachary nodded, not trusting his voice.

She walked out of his apartment without another word.

HER WORK WAS EVERYTHING

Zachary Goldman Mysteries #7

To those who know that work is not everything

CHAPTER ONE

Zachary had heard about the death of Lauren Barclay in the news before he was contacted by Barbara Lee. It seemed like such a tragic waste. A promising young investment banker, she had been tragically killed in a slip-and-fall accident in her home. It wasn't particularly newsworthy, except for the fact that she had been an attractive, brilliant young woman, and that played well in the press on a slow news day. There were a lot of quotes from family and friends about how awful it was and what a wonderful person she had been. There would be a lot of mourners at her funeral.

But he hadn't really given it anything more than a passing thought. He had that little twinge of regret that he got when he read about a tragic death, but since he hadn't known her and there didn't seem to be anything unusual about her death, he had just given himself a second to feel bad for her and her family, and then moved on with his day.

Barbara Lee had told him that she wanted to meet about the death of a friend, but it wasn't until they sat down together for coffee that Zachary found out the friend was Lauren Barclay.

"I just can't believe it." Barbara sniffled and wiped at the corner of her eye. "She was so brilliant, so full of life, I can't believe she's gone. It just isn't fair. She was so young!"

Zachary nodded. "I read a little bit about it... there wasn't any hint in the news that there was foul play, though. They said it was an accident. She slipped in the tub?"

"I can't believe that. You don't think that's really what happened, do you?"

He looked into her bloodshot eyes. She was probably an attractive woman when she wasn't a complete mess. Her eyes were red, her face was blotchy; it looked like her hair had been put up into a partial bun at some point, but she had wisps of hair going in every direction and she might have slept on it once or twice since she had put it up. She smelled of sweat.

"I don't know anything about it, so I wouldn't venture a guess," he said. "Why don't you tell me what you know about it? Why don't you think she slipped?"

Barbara rummaged in her handbag for a tissue and wiped her red nose. "I didn't even know she was home. She worked all hours, she was always at the office. I hadn't seen her for days. Then I got home... it was the middle of the day, and I could tell that she'd been there. I called out to her, but she didn't answer. I figured she probably came home to change and then had left again. Or maybe she'd fallen into bed and was catching a few winks before she had to go back. But she wasn't usually home during the day, so I didn't expect... to find her..."

Zachary thought he should touch her arm or make some other comforting gesture, but he wouldn't want it to be taken the wrong way. She might not think he was professional and decide not to hire him.

"I'm so sorry... you were the one who found her?"

Barbara nodded, giving another sob. A bubble of snot blew out her nose and she wiped it away. If she had been the one to find her friend's body, it was no wonder she was such a mess. He couldn't imagine what that would have been like for her.

"Take your time," he told her. "You don't need to rush into this."

"I just want... to get it all out. Everybody wants to know, but nobody wants to hear about it. They all think that they want to hear the details, but... it isn't like watching a murder mystery on TV. It's something that... it's so unreal. I didn't know what to do. It was such a shock finding her, I felt like she was a mannequin or it was a prank, I just didn't want to believe it. I couldn't touch her. I called 9-1-1. And then... the police came, and the paramedics, and they all wanted me to tell them about finding her. I had to keep repeating it over and over again."

She stopped talking to wipe and blow again. Her nose was red and raw.

"But they didn't think there was any foul play?" Zachary prompted.

"No. But they didn't ask if there was anyone who wanted her dead or if she had a boyfriend that was violent or she had just broken up with, or anything like that. Not like on a cop show or in a mystery book. They just asked about... when I'd been home last, what time I had found her, when she would have gotten home. The paramedics asked if she had a history of epilepsy or fainting spells. Just... like it was an accident."

Zachary nodded. He sipped his coffee, which was still a bit too hot, but he wanted to give her time to think and to calm down a little. He would get more out of her if she were relaxed and composed than if she got all wound up and couldn't think straight.

"So what was the timing? You said she wasn't usually home during the day?"

"No. She worked really long hours. They were supposed to be at the office before their boss got in, so like six-thirty or seven at the latest. And she would work past dark. She would come home late, sleep for a few hours, and then be back at the office before I even had breakfast. Her hours were crazy."

"How long could she keep up like that? She must have had to take breaks on the weekend at least. Did she get a day off? Sunday?"

"She worked every day. It wasn't a rule that they had to work on weekends, but everybody did. It was so competitive. If the other interns were there on the weekend, then Lauren *had* to be there on the weekend. Otherwise, people would think that she wasn't as dedicated, and when her internship was up, they would just say goodbye and she'd have to find something else. No other investment banking firm was going to take her if she failed her internship there. She'd be... damaged goods. She'd have to find a job in something else, and she really wanted to be in finance. She really did."

"Why was it so cutthroat? Is that normal?"

"For investment banking, I guess it is. They're all like that. And Chase Gold is just a small firm, so if she couldn't make it there, there's no way that some Wall Street or Japanese company would look at her. She had to get a permanent position with Chase and work there for three years before she could go on to look for something else. No one would look at her otherwise."

Zachary shook his head. "Why would anyone want to work like that?"

Barbara pushed tendrils of hair away from her face, making a half-hearted attempt to push them back into the bun. "Lots of professions are like that, not just finance. Look at doctors and nurses. They're the same way. Long-distance trucking. Cab drivers."

"They all have rules now about not being able to work more than a certain number of hours in a row to prevent people from falling asleep at the wheel or cutting off the wrong leg."

"I guess. But this isn't that kind of place. I don't think there are any rules about not being able to work that long. She always worked for hours and hours. She slept at the office on the floor sometimes. Or didn't sleep at all for two or three days. You can't even imagine how bad it was."

Zachary thought about that. He pulled out his notepad and jotted down a few notes to himself. Avenues to pursue. Things not to forget. Barbara's eyes tracked his pencil as he scratched out the lines.

"You look like you've never held a pen before," she commented.

Zachary's cheeks heated. He looked down at his awkward grip on his pencil. Many teachers had tried to correct it during school. He'd moved among a lot of different schools, classrooms, and institutions, and the first thing they always tried to do was correct his grip.

"I have dysgraphia," he said. "That's the only way I can write. I know it looks bad to you, but it's the only thing that feels right to me. It's the only way I can see what I'm doing and form the letters."

She shook her head and didn't make any comment on his chicken scratch. He *could* write neatly. He did when he was filling out forms or writing something down for someone else. But it took two or three times as long if he wanted to make it tidy. When he was writing for himself, he could scrawl it however he wanted to. He could still read it. Usually. Sometimes. He could normally figure out what he had meant, even if he couldn't read every word.

"Lauren had beautiful handwriting," Barbara said, tears starting to make their way down her cheeks. "She should have been a schoolteacher, it looked like something out of a handwriting textbook. But..." she sniffled, "of course, teachers don't make anything, and Lauren wanted to make a lot of money. A lot of money."

CHAPTER TWO

"I don't really know what an investment banker does," Zachary said, "but I know it *is* something that I associate with making a lot of money. She was pretty wealthy, then?" He was thinking about motives. If there were anything to Barbara's fears—and he had to assume for the purposes of his investigation that there was—then whoever had killed her needed a motive. And money was always a good motive.

"No, not yet," Barbara said. "She was just starting out, so she wasn't making a whole lot. We rented an apartment together, and it's a nice one, not some little rat's nest, but neither of us could have afforded it on our own. Maybe we could, but only if we didn't need to eat or pay for heating or internet."

Zachary nodded. "And if she was just starting, then she probably still had school loans to worry about too."

"Yeah. All of that stuff. She wanted to get rich, but she wasn't there yet. We are—were—both making good money for our age, but nothing like it would be if she got to be a permanent employee with a few years under her belt."

"That makes sense. What's the name of the place that she worked?"

"I have to look it up…" She pulled out her phone and fiddled with it. "We always just called it 'Chase Gold,' because it was close to that, and that's really what they were trying to do. Chase after the gold and get as much as they could. For themselves and their clients."

Zachary waited while she tapped through a few screens on her phone, searching for it in her contacts or on an internet browser. He made a couple of other short notes while he waited. Things to look into. Questions to ask. Who would want to kill a young woman who spent all of her time working and was still in debt?

"Yeah, here it is," Barbara offered. "Drake, Chase, Gould." She spelled Gould for him to make sure he got it right. "She was really devoted to her job. And I don't just mean that she liked it or put a lot of hours in. She did, but there was more to it than that. She thought they were the best company to work for, and that they were going to get her everything she wanted. She was always saying how good the management was, how well they took care of their employees, how good the other people she worked with were. She thought they were going right to the top. That they would compete with the Goldman Sachs and Wells Fargos of the world. They just started up a few years ago, and their portfolios were amazing, especially considering how short they had been in business. Or so she told me." Barbara sniffed and rolled her eyes. "Multiple times."

Zachary smiled at that. Nice to hear about someone who liked her job. "That's great."

He leaned back in his seat. The coffee shop didn't have particularly comfortable chairs. He supposed it was to encourage people to have their coffees and to move on, not to just camp there drinking lattes and using the free Wi-Fi all day long. He looked at Barbara.

"So what makes you think it wasn't an accident? Tell me about the things that made you concerned."

"You think I'm just crazy, don't you? Everybody just looks at me like I've got two heads. How could a slip in the bathtub *not* be an accident? It's like being hit by a bus, the classic accident that everyone uses as an example."

Zachary waited. He wasn't the one who was doubting her opinion or sanity. He waited for her to stop defending herself and to fill the silence with her concerns. She would, if he just waited.

"It just doesn't fit that Lauren was even home," Barbara said. "Like I said, she was never home during the day. Between ten in the evening and six in the morning, if she was lucky. That's it. No weekends. No days off. No afternoons going home to have a nap. She just shouldn't have been home."

"What was the time of death?"

Barbara looked at him. She shook her head. "I don't know."

"What time had she gotten home? You were out of the apartment from when until when?"

"I was out with a friend overnight. So I didn't get back until... ten or eleven o'clock. That's when I found her. But she was never home at that time of day."

"But if she had been running a bath at six, and hit her head then, that would make sense."

Barbara sighed. "I know. Everybody says it makes perfect sense. But it doesn't. She was young and healthy. She wouldn't just fall down and die. She wasn't drunk or doing drugs. She didn't have any diseases that would have made her pass out. To just step into the tub and fall down and die...? That doesn't make sense either."

"Sure. I understand that. No one expects something like this to happen. But she could have had the flu, or just wasn't paying attention and slipped."

"She wasn't an old lady. Maybe old ladies slip and fall like that, but Lauren never did. If she slipped, she would have caught herself. If she got hurt, she would have called someone to help her."

Zachary made a couple of notes of questions to pursue. He'd have to talk to the medical examiner's office, and he really didn't want to. He would have to psych himself up for it.

"What was the mechanism of death?"

Barbara frowned. "She... fell...?"

"Yeah. Did she drown? Or did she die from the blow to the head? Brain swelling or bleeding?"

"Drowning, I guess. She did hit her head, but then she went into the water. That's where I found her. I guess... she knocked herself out, and then she didn't know that she was drowning, couldn't do anything about it."

"The medical examiner hasn't made a finding yet?"

"I don't know. I guess that's what they're working on right now."

"Okay. We'll need a copy of their report once there is a finding. I'll put in a requisition for it."

Which meant that he would take the elevator down to the basement level at the police station. He would walk up to the desk and fill out one of the forms in his neatest printing, trying his best to avoid an intensely awkward situation with Kenzie.

He wasn't sure how she was going to react. Things had been pretty quiet since they had broken up. He felt horrible about the way everything had ended, but he hadn't called her and begged for her to come back. He hadn't given her excuses for his behavior or followed her around in his car. He had done his best to just back out of her life and forget about what they had shared together.

But going back there, onto her turf, he didn't know how she was going to treat him. Would she yell at him and call him out the way that Bridget did? Would she go all quiet or ignore him? Or just stare at him with her dark, intense eyes boring into him, hating him for the time she had wasted on him?

"Uh… Mr. Goldman?"

Zachary blinked and refocused on Barbara. It was Barbara he had to talk to and interact with. He needed to stay focused on her. "Sorry, just thinking about something. What was that?"

"If the medical examiner says that it was just an accident, that will be the end of it, won't it? The police won't investigate it as a homicide. They won't hold anyone responsible."

"No. But if I find something, we can get them to open an investigation. I've done it before. I'm assuming you already know that. That's probably why you picked me out, isn't it?"

She gave an embarrassed little shrug and nodded.

"I can't guarantee anything," Zachary said. "I don't know whether it was an accident or something else… but it sounds like it's going to be pretty hard to find evidence that it was anything else. I'll look. I'm just warning you… Don't expect miracles. Just because I've been able to prove that other deaths were homicides, that doesn't mean that I can prove any death was. Some of them are going to be just what they look like."

"I know. But… no matter what anyone else says… I want to do everything I can for Lauren. I can't just close my eyes and say 'oh, what a bizarre accident.' I need to know. I need to do everything I can to bring the responsible party to justice. If there is a responsible party."

"You said before that the police hadn't asked you anything about an exboyfriend or anyone who might have wanted to harm her."

"Yes. I mean no. They didn't. They didn't want to know anything like that."

"Does that mean that she *did* have an ex-boyfriend who might have wanted to harm her?"

Barbara's eyes widened. "Oh, no. I didn't mean to imply anything like that... She did have ex-boyfriends, of course, but no one who was bitter or anything. No one who ever threatened her or stalked her."

"Was there anyone who was abusive while they were together? She might not have told you that he hit her, but was there ever anyone that you suspected... that you thought might have hurt her? Even someone who was verbally or emotionally abusive. Someone you didn't feel comfortable around or were glad that she broke up with him."

"No... I don't think so... everyone that she was with was pretty casual... it isn't like she had any time for a relationship. She would take someone to a firm event, or sometimes she brought someone home from work... but she didn't really have a life outside of the office."

"She dated people from the office?"

"Yes... she went out for a meal with them, maybe brought one or two back to the apartment to..." she shrugged uncomfortably, "...to sleep it off. Just to crash somewhere before they had to go back to the office again in a few hours. There just was so little time, and she was under so much pressure... it didn't leave time for a real relationship."

"Even if it isn't what you would call a relationship... men can still decide that they want what they can't have. They might think that she should have spent more time with them, given them more attention, maybe not gone on to see someone else so soon... if they went out to eat, or he went home with her, then he might have expected more. He might have thought that it was turning into a committed relationship when it wasn't."

"I guess so. I don't know. I never saw anything like that. The guys that I met from Chase Gold always seemed pretty casual. Not like they were pining after her or acting possessive."

"Do you have the names of some of the men that she dated? Maybe an address list?"

"All of her numbers would be on her phone... I guess it's at the apartment. The police didn't take it, I don't think. They just took a quick look at her electronics, but there wasn't anything that didn't look right to them, so they said they didn't need to take anything with them."

"Who is the detective on the case?"

"I don't think there was a detective. Just... whoever comes out to have a look when someone dies suddenly. They're not really investigating it. Just filling out the forms."

"Someone would have been assigned to it. I'll look into it. See if they have any thoughts."

"They aren't going to. They are just going to think that it was an accident, like a million other accidents that happen every day."

CHAPTER THREE

Zachary had made sure that Barbara was able to pay his retainer and understood his fee schedule and then went to work on her case. He still had other cases to work, but they were not time-sensitive. He always had insurance cases, marital infidelities, and skip tracing and other issues to follow up on. The bread and butter that got him from day to day. The big cases were nice when they came along, but he didn't know what he would have from one month to the next, so he couldn't rely on cash flowing from big cases.

Not that Lauren's death investigation was that urgent. It looked like an accident, no matter what feelings of denial Barbara was going through. She didn't have anything concrete to suggest that it was anything other than an accident. Tragic, yes. Untimely, certainly, but there were hundreds of untimely and tragic deaths every day. Chances were, Zachary wouldn't find anything to indicate any kind of foul play. The police would have turned up something in their investigation. They were well-trained, and he was just a self-taught PI.

Still, in a death investigation, it was best to get started as soon as he could. While everything was still fresh in people's minds and the evidence— if there was any physical evidence—had not been destroyed. He'd gotten lucky in Heather's case to be able to put his hands on physical evidence thirty years after the fact, but all of what had been collected by the police had been lost in the intervening years.

He could have started at Lauren's office, but decided he'd better bite the bullet and go to the police station and request a copy of the medical examiner's report. Like swallowing a frog first thing in the morning, nothing worse would happen to him all day.

Most of the personnel on duty knew him. The guard that ran him through the metal detector and made sure he was properly checked in. A police officer or two who stopped to ask and see how he was doing. Zachary was awkward, unsure how many of them knew that he had been dating Kenzie and how many knew that they had recently broken up. And he'd been on the news a bit too much for his liking the previous few months. Good for publicity, not so good for his ego. Not when it exposed his private pain.

He tried to greet everyone warmly and to assume that they didn't know anything about what he had been through recently. It was easier that way.

Pressing the down button for the elevator, he was drawn back to the day, over a year previous, when he had first met Kenzie. She had been pretty, interesting, and had smiled at him and treated him with respect. He'd liked her right from the start. With her wild, dark, curly hair, her deep red lipstick, she was cute and pretty and very unlike Bridget.

That had been important.

But they were no longer together. Now, she knew too much about his rocky past and the emotional issues that he struggled with every day. She was no longer an outsider looking in and curious about what kind of a person he was and if they would make a good couple. Now she knew that they couldn't, and that she had been wasting her time.

Who knew what she might have told Dr. Wiltshire and her other colleagues about the relationship and about Zachary himself? Women liked to talk, and one of the issues he'd had to confront with Kenzie was the fact that she had discussed details of their intimate relationship. He didn't like to think how much she might have told her co-workers about Zachary and his issues.

Before he reached the desk, he could see that Kenzie was on duty, staring at her computer screen as she worked through whatever tests and requests she had to do. She didn't look at him immediately. She liked to concentrate on what she was doing until it was a good time to take a break, and then she would turn her full attention to her visitor.

After a minute of concentration, she looked away from her computer screen to Zachary's face. Her lips tightened. She said nothing.

"I have a new case," Zachary said, wanting to assure her immediately that he wasn't there for personal reasons. He wasn't going to try to talk her into giving him another chance. Kenzie had given him countless chances. He knew that. She had done more than anyone could have been expected to do.

Zachary was too damaged to be able to carry on a normal relationship. He should have learned that from his marriage to Bridget. Kenzie had been so different, he had thought that maybe he had a chance with her. But he had only been fooling himself.

"Could I get the form to request a copy of the medical examiner's report?"

She delved into her drawer and pulled one out. She handed it to him without a word, her eyes sliding to her computer screen so that she could pretend she was still working on something else, too busy to talk to him.

"Sorry," Zachary murmured, unsure of what to say to her.

Kenzie looked at him. Her lips were still pressed tightly together, but her clenched jaw relaxed slightly.

"Nothing to apologize for," she said stiffly. "You have a job to do. Can't help it if that brings you to the medical examiner's office now and then."

Zachary nodded as he started to fill in his name and address. "I know... I just don't want you to think that I'm here to bug you..."

She shrugged and fiddled with a pen. "You've been good about not harassing me," she admitted. "I wasn't sure how you were going to handle it, to tell the truth. After seeing how stalkerish you were with Bridget, I didn't know what to expect."

Zachary swallowed. His mouth was so dry he could hardly speak. "I'm doing better. I mean, different meds, and seeing my therapist and all..."

"I've been watching for it, you know. Any sign that you've been hanging around, messing with my car, following me. I figured..." She trailed off.

He wondered if it had hurt her feelings that he *hadn't* pursued her. Had she hoped that he would protest her leaving, try to talk her into coming back, beg her and follow her? Did she feel like she must not have lived up to Bridget's level in his eyes? That she hadn't meant as much to him?

He wasn't really sure how to compare the two women or his feelings toward them. They were not at all like each other. He had never been head-over-heels in love with Kenzie the way he had been with Bridget. But he'd felt like their relationship had been more equal, and maybe deeper than he'd ever managed with Bridget.

He'd worshiped Bridget. He'd been devoted to her. But after those first few blissful months, her attitude toward him had changed. As she realized that she wasn't going to fix him and that she couldn't just tell him what to feel and how to behave, her attitude toward him had changed completely. And when she'd been diagnosed with cancer… that had been all the impetus needed for her to boot him out of her life. Get rid of toxic relationships. Put all of her energy into recovery.

With Kenzie, it had been different. She hadn't been abusive or looked down on him. She hadn't been a replacement mother figure. She'd just been… Kenzie. A friend first. Things had gone well for them until the Teddy Archuro case had driven the relationship off the rails.

Not just off the rails, but crashing into an abyss.

"I could put a tracker on your car if it would make you feel better," he told Kenzie, forcing a smile that he didn't feel. "As long as you promise not to take out a restraining order against me. Because that would make it impossible for me to fill out these fascinating forms."

Kenzie laughed and shook her head. Her eyes didn't dance like they did when she was having fun and enjoying herself, but the smile was real. His attempt at humor was appreciated.

"No, I think I'm okay on that score, thanks."

Zachary shrugged, meeting her eyes for a second and then turning his gaze back down to his form. It was going to take forever for him to fill out if he kept getting distracted. And while that had been okay in the past, he didn't want to make things more painful for Kenzie by overstaying his welcome.

"What case are you working on?" Kenzie asked.

He couldn't exactly tell her that it was confidential or wasn't any of her business. She was, after all, the one who was going to process the form. She would know as soon as he handed it to her.

"Lauren Barclay."

"Barclay? The slip-and-fall?" Her tone expressed surprise.

"Yes. Dr. Wiltshire hasn't made a finding yet, has he?"

"No, but he will before long. It's a pretty routine case."

"I know. I don't expect to find anything, but as long as I've got a paying client… I'll do what I can to check out all avenues and reassure her that it was just an accident."

"How could it be anything else? I mean, the woman was found alone, floating in her own bathtub. No forced entry, no signs of violence, just fell and cracked her head. Sad, but it could happen to anyone. Who is your client? Family member?"

Kenzie was creeping into the confidential with that question. He didn't need to tell her anything about who had hired him. But he missed talking with her about cases. He enjoyed pulling out medical examiner's reports to discuss over dinner. Not romantic by any stretch of the imagination, but how many other women were there who would be okay with looking at gruesome pictures over dinner?

"Not the family."

"Well, good luck. I don't know how you're going to make any money on the case. How much can you charge for reading the report and talking to the detective?"

"If that's all there is, that's all there is. I'm not trying to pull something over on her. She wants someone to look into the death, so I will. I warned her there might not be much I could do."

"At least you're not the kind of guy who is going to take advantage and rack up the charges."

Zachary nodded his agreement, glad that she recognized he had standards. He was sure there were people who would take advantage of Barbara, but he wasn't one of them. She hadn't balked at his rates and, looking at the address of the apartment she had given him, he saw that even if she'd had to share the rent with Lauren, she couldn't have been hurting too badly. But he wasn't going to take advantage of her wealth.

"Is she pretty?" Kenzie asked, after a period of silence, during which she had been looking at her screen and occasionally scrolling down.

"Lauren Barclay?"

She rolled her eyes and shook her head. "Not Lauren. I've already got a good idea of what she looks like, and it's not pretty. Drowning victims never are."

"Oh. The client." He realized that he had used 'she' when talking about Barbara, so Kenzie knew the client was female. And if she was a friend of

Lauren's rather than family, then probably a young woman of her general social circles. "Uh… hard to say."

"Hard to say? I'm not exactly going to be jealous if you say she's hot."

Zachary's ears burned. He filled out Lauren's name on the form.

"It's not that… she wasn't in very good shape. Disheveled, swollen and blotchy, running nose. I had a hard time judging what she normally looks like."

"Oh. Fair enough." Kenzie scrolled down a couple more times, waiting for Zachary to finish dating and signing the form.

Zachary handed it to her and swallowed. "Thanks, Kenzie."

She dropped it into the wire basket on her desk. "Take care of yourself, Zachary."

CHAPTER FOUR

Making inquiries upstairs, Zachary was advised that the detective assigned to Lauren's case was Detective Robinson. Zachary had seen him before, but had never worked a case that he was on. He was a thin man with very thick glasses. He made Zachary think of a praying mantis peering at him, triangular head cocked slightly, big eyes taking in every movement.

He was unimpressed by Zachary's interest in the case, doing the best he could to get rid of him.

"I'm afraid there's not much to tell you, Mr. Goldman. It was an accidental slip-and-fall, an open-and-shut case. Nobody else around, no suspicious circumstances. Just a home accident, like thousands of others. We're not wasting resources on it."

"No, I wouldn't expect you to," Zachary agreed. "You have cases that require your attention. I'd been hired to look into this case, so I can afford to spend a little time on it. Just look at it from different angles to see if I can find anything concerning."

Detective Robinson peered at him, clearly suspicious that Zachary was being sarcastic. Zachary kept his gaze steady and Robinson decided he was being sincere.

"We can't stop private citizens from asking questions, obviously," he said. "But I don't see how it would be in anyone's best interest to spend time on a case that was so obviously an accident."

"Of course. I understand."

"We have released the scene, so the roommate can show you whatever she wants. We don't have anything to do with it."

"I'll be going over it tomorrow. There wasn't anything that stood out to you? Nothing out of place?"

"Nothing. Young working woman. Neat bedroom. No sign of forced entry or violence. Nothing out of place or suspicious."

"Okay. Would you let me know if anything occurs to you? And do you want me to give you updates, or...?"

"I don't need anything from you. Because you're not going to find anything."

"Okay. Sometimes detectives like regular reports, even if I haven't found anything."

"No. I don't expect to hear from you again."

———

That evening, Zachary bounced around the empty apartment for a while, not sure what to do. He worked through a pile of skip traces and added touches to other client reports, but he missed having Kenzie around and couldn't sit down and watch TV or do something else calming without her there. He needed something to keep him busy, but he'd put in a lot of work hours and he needed to do something quieter before bed if he were going to be able to go to sleep at a decent hour. Recently, his brain couldn't decide whether he should sleep all the time to avoid having to deal with his emotional issues, or whether he should be obsessing over every detail of his life, his past, and his failed relationships to the exclusion of sleep, so he swung back and forth unpredictably between the two.

Dr. Boyle had advised him to keep to a regular schedule whether he felt tired or not. Go to the bed at the same time every day. Get up at the same time every day. His body would become entrained to the schedule and his brain would follow.

Of course, that was assuming he didn't need to do any overnight surveillance jobs. Something like that would throw a wrench into the works.

But so far, he'd been able to avoid any night surveillance while training his body and brain to a reasonable schedule.

It wasn't bedtime, so he needed something to keep him engaged and help him to unwind. After scrolling restlessly through his email and social networks, such as they were, he double-clicked the Skype icon and selected Lorne Peterson's name.

Even though Mr. Peterson—rarely Lorne, even though he'd told Zachary numerous times that he could call him by his first name—was more than twenty years older than Zachary, he was probably Zachary's closest friend. He had been Zachary's foster father for a few weeks after the fire that had destroyed not only Zachary's family home, but also his family structure. His mother and father divorced and relinquished the six children to social services, wanting nothing more to do with them.

Zachary hadn't stayed with the Petersons for long. He'd celebrated his eleventh birthday while there, the first birthday that had ever actually been marked by a cake and a birthday present. But his needs and behavioral issues had been too much for them to handle, and Mrs. Peterson had insisted that he couldn't stay there, possibly putting the other children at risk, any longer. Zachary had gone on to another foster family, and another, and a long series of homes and facilities for the rest of his childhood and adolescence. But he and Mr. Peterson had stayed in touch throughout.

The call rang for a few minutes before it was answered. Then Mr. Peterson's round, cheerful face was centered on the screen. He patted down his fringe of white hair.

"Zachary! Good to see you! How are you doing?"

Zachary relaxed into his seat. Mr. Peterson represented safety and security for him. The only person who had felt like family until his younger brother, Tyrrell had reached out and made contact with him, followed by Heather, his older sister. He hadn't yet had any contact with the remaining three siblings.

"I'm good. Picked up a new case today. How are you and Pat?"

Pat moved into the frame behind Mr. Peterson, wiping his hands on a dishtowel. He bent down to look into the screen and smiled into the video cam. "Hi, Zachary!" He gave a thumbs-up. "We're fine! Good to see you!"

Zachary nodded and smiled. Pat clapped his hand on Mr. Peterson's shoulder and gave it a squeeze, then he moved out of the picture, off to the kitchen or whatever job he was doing next. Zachary kept his smile in place.

"How is he…?"

Mr. Peterson's smile grew strained. He gave a little grimace. "It's been tough, I won't lie to you about that. But we've been seeing a therapist and I think we're making good progress. His mood is better. But that could be the antidepressants."

Zachary felt a stab of guilt. He would have taken away Pat's pain if he could. But he couldn't bring back Pat's friend Jose, who had been killed by a serial killer. And he couldn't wipe out Pat's feelings of responsibility for what had happened to Zachary because he had been investigating Jose's disappearance.

"Well… he'll get through it," Zachary encouraged. "He's got a strong support system."

Mr. Peterson shrugged, getting a little pink.

"Thank you, Zachary. I'm sure you're right, he'll get through it. We're seeing progress."

Zachary nodded. The words made his apartment seem even more empty and hollow. He tried to focus on Mr. Peterson's friendly features. Zachary still had support too. He might not have Kenzie, but she was not the only person in Zachary's support network. Mr. Peterson and Pat were there for him, as well as his therapist, doctors, and support groups. Young Rhys Salter and his grandmother. Mario Bowman and other friends on the police force and consultants who provided other services he used in his PI business. Tyrrell and Heather and Heather's husband. He had received a number of calls, emails, and letters of support from previous strangers after bringing Teddy Archuro to justice, both from people who were grateful or impressed by what he had done and by people who understood the trauma he'd been through and offered their support and encouragement.

He had a big circle of supporters. He didn't need to feel alone.

"New case today?" Mr. Peterson prompted, leaning toward the camera.

"Oh. Yeah. I don't know if you would have seen in the news, a young woman named Lauren Barclay…?"

"The intern at that investment company? Yeah, we saw that. I thought that was an accident."

"No determination has been made yet, but yes, the initial word is that it was an accident. But her friend is not convinced and wants someone to look into it."

"Well, great. That's a good case. High profile."

Zachary nodded. "I doubt it will really go anywhere, but I'll see what I can find out."

"It will at least put her mind at ease to know that it was an accident. Even though it seems unfair… I'm sure she'd rather know that it was an accident than to be worried that there might have been some kind of foul play involved."

"Yes, I think so. And maybe she just needs some time to process. It happened so fast, and she was the one to find the body. That's a shock."

Mr. Peterson emphatically agreed. "The poor girl. She must be devastated."

"I think so."

"So you just started on that today?"

Zachary nodded. "Just getting the initial information processed. Stopped by the medical examiner's office to request a copy of his findings when they are published…"

"Oh," Mr. Peterson understood immediately. He and Pat had met Kenzie. Mr. Peterson cocked his head to the side empathetically. "You saw Kenzie?"

Zachary nodded. "Yeah. It was… weird. She didn't yell or anything, but it was… awkward, I guess."

"Hopefully, some of that will fade. You guys are still going to run into each other, both being involved in crime investigation. You'll keep bumping up against each other. Best if you can be civil, if not friends."

"Yeah. I'd like to still be friends, but she doesn't. Not yet, anyway. I'm trying to … give her the space she needs. Maybe sometime down the road… we can still share a meal together as friends… talk about cases. We don't have to be dating to do that."

"No, of course not. You're probably right about her needing her own space. You don't want to smother her." Mr. Peterson shifted, moving his head the other direction and considering his question carefully before voicing it. "There is no chance of the two of you getting back together again?"

"No… I don't think so. She says not, anyway. I would… I'd like to give it a try. We got together pretty well… I wasn't really ready to break it off."

Mr. Peterson made a noncommittal noise. Zachary looked at the screen and considered the matter. It had been Kenzie who had said that they were over. But he had been avoiding her before that. He had been the one with a problem.

"Or maybe I was," Zachary admitted. "Maybe I knew it wasn't working."

"You need to put work into a relationship," Mr. Peterson said. "It isn't something that just magically happens and is self-perpetuating. Once you're comfortable and committed… things start to chip away at the relationship. Personality conflicts, irritation, other relationships, work… you have to keep building it up to make it work."

Zachary nodded his agreement.

"You have been through a lot. Things that challenged you and your relationship. If you're not willing to put the work into fixing it…"

Zachary opened his mouth to argue that he had been working at fixing it. He had been talking to his therapist, trying to work through his reflex reactions to intimacy since the assault. It had stirred up a lot of old issues, and the avalanche of old memories and emotions had been too much to deal with all at once.

He had been trying. He and Kenzie had been talking about it and trying to work through it together. They'd been making progress.

Until Zachary discovered that Kenzie was talking to Mr. Peterson and Bridget, trying to get details of Zachary's past relationships and abuse. It had been an invasion of his privacy that he couldn't accept. If they were going to have a relationship, then she had to be willing to wait for him to work through his past and share it with her in his own time. For her to go behind his back to talk to his foster father and ex-wife about such intimate issues was beyond the pale.

"I don't know," he said finally. "We were working on it… but I'm just… I'm not what she wanted, Lorne. I can't change what happened to me and I couldn't share it with her… so how could we have the relationship that she wanted?"

To his credit, Mr. Peterson didn't come out with some glib answer or try to sweep away Zachary's feelings. "Maybe not, Zach. It seemed like the two of you were good together. She was a much better fit for you than Bridget ever was. But I can't tell you how to deal with it. I don't mean to imply that you didn't work on the relationship. Just that… when it's the right relationship… it's worth it to forgive and try again. When it's the right relationship —and you're the only one who can decide that. You and her."

Zachary sighed. He had been telling himself that it was all Kenzie's fault. She was the one who had betrayed his trust. She was the one who had then broken it off and didn't want to continue to see each other or be friends. But that was only half of the story. The truth was… he had been struggling and she had been trying to help, in her own way. He had felt betrayed and had shut her out. He had effectively ended the relationship some time before she had come to the apartment to pick up her things. It hadn't been her at all.

"I'll think about it. But I don't think she'd be willing to try again even if I said I wanted to."

"You're the one who knows best. I'm not going to meddle in your relationships."

"Thanks. You've always been really good about accepting whoever I was with, wherever I was."

"And there have been some doozies," Mr. Peterson laughed, and Zachary knew he only meant one—Bridget. "But who am I to say what will work and what won't? A lot of people told me to go back to Lilith. To mend fences and find a way to make it work. But I never would have been happy staying with her. And I never would have met Pat and been able to have the relationship I do with him, if I was still with her."

Zachary swallowed. "Yeah," he agreed, wondering whether Mr. Peterson could see how pink Zachary's face was getting on the camera. Zachary always felt awkward talking about Mr. Peterson's and Pat's relationship. Zachary liked and respected Pat enormously, but he didn't want to know the intimate details of their relationship.

He changed the subject and still didn't tell Mr. Peterson the news about Bridget.

CHAPTER FIVE

Barbara had indicated that Zachary could come to her apartment in order to see the scene of the accident and to pick up Lauren's phone and computer. Then he could get the names of her friends, contacts at Chase Gold, and see whatever else he might need to see in the apartment and her possessions. Not that Zachary expected to find anything, but he'd been surprised before. Most cases, he'd found exactly what he'd expected to. But every now and then, there was one that blew up big, turning out to be something very different from what he'd initially thought.

Barbara opened the door and silently ushered him into the apartment. She stood there, not sure what to do or say at first. Then she took a deep breath.

"I'm going to go out. You can stay here as long as you need, just lock the handle and pull the door shut when you're done. Shoot me a text when you're on your way out. I just—" she looked around the front room of the apartment, "—I really can't be here while you're going through her things or looking at... the accident scene. I don't want to talk to you about it and walk you through it. You already know what happened, between the paper and what I told you. I don't want to relive it."

"I understand. That's fine, as long as you trust me to be here by myself."

"I know how to find you. If something disappeared or I thought you were messing with my stuff, I would go to the police, believe me. But... I do trust you. I'm comfortable around you, and I'm a pretty good judge of character. So I'm just going to go with my feelings, and if I'm wrong... I'll have to deal with it."

"I won't get into your things or make a mess. Just point me at Lauren's room, and I'll proceed from there."

Barbara indicated one of the bedrooms. "That one." She swung her handbag up to her shoulder. "Good luck. I'll talk to you later."

He went to Lauren's bedroom and heard the front door click shut behind her.

He didn't mind the fact that she had left. Far from it; it was easier for him to concentrate without somebody hanging over him. He disliked clients who hovered. With Barbara gone, he'd be able to immerse himself in Lauren's life and learn all he could from her possessions.

———

The bedroom was remarkably sparse. He'd seen students' rooms before, and they were usually full of clutter. Posters on walls, bookshelves, boxes that hadn't been unpacked, bags shoved under the bed. But Lauren's room was nothing like that. It was like a hotel room, with hardly any personal furnishings. He looked in the closet. Her clothes were neat and well-cared-for. Not much by way of casual blue jeans and tees; she mostly wore black skirts with white blouses. Some workout clothes in the drawers. He checked the bottoms and backs of the drawers and didn't find anything racy hidden away.

Her drug supply consisted mostly of headache pills of various sorts, caffeine and herbal remedies for alertness and mental acuity. No narcotics, no coke, no pot. No seizure medications or insulin. Though insulin, he remembered, would be in the fridge. He'd have to double-check that for his report.

She had a few pictures. Parents and a sister, it looked like. No cuddly fiance photos or groups of young people out partying.

There were books and notebooks full of scribbled notes on her computer desk. Flipping through them, they were much more complex math than Zachary was qualified to analyze. If he hit a dead end, he might have to find someone who could interpret what she had been working on to see if he should be looking in another direction. Maybe she had discovered some new way of predicting or manipulating markets.

She had a little shower caddy with all of her toiletries in it. Zachary poked through them. Nothing unusual; they all looked like brands he seen at the grocery store or on TV.

He checked all of the usual hiding places. Under the mattress, behind the nondescript artwork on the walls. He unscrewed the plates over the light switch and wall outlets. In the closet, he searched for any hidden panels or safe, checked the pockets of the clothes hanging in the closet—why did women have so few pockets?—and the purses that hung neatly on hooks inside the closet. The purses contained only the usual miscellany. Combs, cosmetics, and feminine supplies, together with coins, gum, tissues, and crumpled receipts.

He went through the room one more time for hiding places. Her computer and phone were on the desk waiting for him, as well as a music player. He left them all there and went to the bathroom.

The scene of the accident.

There was nothing to indicate what had happened there. No blood, no fingerprints blackened with powder. No flower memorials. Just a scrubbed-clean bathroom, like he would find in any other apartment in the building. Probably cleaner than any others. He suspected Barbara had spent several hours cleaning it after the police and paramedics were gone, wiping out every trace of the horrible accident her friend had suffered.

Zachary looked at himself briefly in the mirror. He didn't like to look in the mirror. He was a small man, dark-haired, not particularly attractive, with various scars on his face from childhood accidents and abuse growing up in foster care and institutions. He had shaved for his initial meeting with Barbara, but not since, so dark stubble shaded his jaw.

He pictured Lauren standing there. A pretty girl, as evidenced by her pictures in the news articles and the family pictures in the bedroom. Hair the color of dark honey, tall and slim, probably athletic in high school. But from Barbara's description, Lauren had been wearing thin. She probably had bags under her eyes, hidden as best she could by the miracle of modern make-up, and lines of fatigue at the corners of her eyes and across her fore-head. She had probably stood there, wondering how much longer she could continue to go at that pace.

Shower or bath? If it had been him, he would have been worried about falling asleep in a bath. He would have had a shower. A cold one to wake him up, not a hot one that would make him more drowsy. But she'd drowned in the water in the bathtub, so she'd made the opposite choice. Getting ready for work in the morning, knowing she had to get there before her boss, instead of starting the shower and jumping in and out in two minutes, she had drawn the bath to have a soak.

He stepped into the tub. Of course, any evidence of the accident had already been cleaned away. But he wanted to take a closer look anyway.

There were no anti-slip decals, but the bathmat should have prevented a slip-and-fall. It seemed to be in good shape. The tub was larger than the one in Zachary's apartment, and jetted. Not a huge soaker tub, but big for an apartment. Those jets probably felt great on sore muscles and feet at the end of a long day at the office. But she'd had a bath in the morning, not on coming home from work. Or so Barbara had assumed. He'd need confirmation of time of death to be sure.

He looked at the faucet and handles for any tiny spatters of blood, but found nothing, not even hard water spots. No dents. No cracks in the plastic tub surround. He couldn't tell by looking at it what Lauren had hit her head on.

———

Back in the bedroom, Zachary opened the lid on Lauren's computer. He looked through the papers on the desk and found one with ten-character strings of random characters carefully noted. He typed the last one in the password field and the lock screen disappeared, revealing the desktop and windows behind it.

No biometrics, luckily. Nothing that would require a computer hacker to break. He looked at the apps running along the bottom of the screen, then started the task manager to see how long they had been running and which ones had downloaded the most data packets. He started with the top ones and worked his way down the list, opening all of the "recently opened" documents in each program. Most of it was Greek to him. High finance was not his wheelhouse. He found one app that appeared to be corporate software that pulled Lauren's various social networks and team workspaces and calendars into one program, all neatly tabbed across the top and side.

Zachary browsed through Lauren's internet history and email. He felt a twinge of guilt reading through her corporate email, knowing that it probably contained confidential information that the firm wouldn't want outsiders to see. But most of it he couldn't even follow. He wasn't going to be passing any tips on. He was more interested in the personalities of the people she worked with: bosses, the other interns, human resources, receptionists, and others. Even if he didn't understand the financial jargon, he could glean the attitudes and personalities of Lauren and the others that she corresponded with on a daily basis.

He was amazed at the hours she worked. He had taken Barbara's outline of Lauren's schedule with a grain of salt, but looking at her archived and sent mail, he could see that she was sending out emails regularly, all hours of the day and night. It was rare to see an interval of more than two hours between emails. She had been keeping a brutal schedule. And it was apparent that the other interns were too.

He glanced over at her laundry basket, where he could see colorful workout clothes waiting to be washed. How had she found the time and energy to follow any kind of exercise routine? He couldn't imagine her finding the energy to walk home, let alone for a stationary bike or aerobics.

Zachary browsed through the last few emails that had come into Lauren's inbox following her death which had not, of course, been dealt with. The first few were just routine emails, giving her information she had asked for or giving her instructions on files. Then there were a number of emails with increasingly stern or frantic tones wanting to know where she was and why she hadn't returned to the office. He wrote down the names of those who had been looking for her. He made a short notation as to which ones were concerned, which were angry or bullying, and which were routine or frivolous. If Lauren's death had been something other than an accident, then the person involved could have sent her an email during that interval to establish an alibi. *I didn't know she was dead, see? I was sending her emails at the time.*

After he had checked out the initial things he wanted to look at on her laptop, he did the same thing with her phone—which luckily Barbara had known the unlock code for—making notes as he went through the calls, text messages, and notifications in any other apps. He wrote down her calendar schedule both before and after she had died. Her task list was enough to make him sick. He thought he had a lot to do running his own business and keeping up with medical appointments and the various different cases he was working on? He had nothing on Lauren, whose lists of tasks to be done was dizzyingly long. How could one person be expected to do so much?

He jotted notes about the files she had and the types of tasks that populated her list, rather than trying to write them all down. It would have been easier to print them all out, but there was no printer on the desk. He would take it back to his apartment and print it out there, but in the meantime, he wanted a short synopsis that he could read and ponder on later. The big picture, not all of the little bits.

Zachary hit the play button on Lauren's music player to occupy the part of his brain that was trying to distract him from writing, seeking more interesting input elsewhere. He expected music. Pop or classical would be his top guesses.

But it wasn't music at all, it was a man speaking. He was reciting market information which, Zachary suspected, was now several days out of date. He looked at the LCD screen and scrolled through her playlist. It was all podcasts. And nothing light. No fiction or entertainment. All financial stuff, dry as a bone.

He felt sorry for Lauren, who apparently found ways to work every minute of the day, listening to financial reports while she worked out, commuted, maybe even while she slept. She hadn't ever been able to leave it behind.

CHAPTER SIX

Zachary wasn't sure how the folks at Chase Gold were going to feel about his nosing around and asking questions about Lauren, her last few days, and whether anyone had thought there was anything suspicious about her death. Since the medical examiner had not yet published his findings, Zachary could at least hide behind the pretense of a police investigation—implying that he was with the police department without actually saying so—and no one would be able to say, 'but a ruling of accidental death was already made on that.' But just how far would he be able to investigate at the firm?

He decided to go about it sideways, and when he walked up to the woman in the plush reception area, he didn't try to get into Lauren's office or to talk to her bosses or the principals of the company, but instead asked for Mandy, one of the interns who seemed to have been close to Lauren.

"Will she know what it's about?" the receptionist asked, raising one eyebrow at Zachary as if she guessed that he wasn't one of their usual high-class clients and didn't have any excuse to be there.

"No," Zachary said. "It's a personal matter. I'll discuss that with her."

She eyed him, but she didn't threaten to call security and, after a few seconds' silence, she punched a few buttons on the phone keypad and informed Mandy in a doubtful tone that there was someone waiting for her.

She nodded to the seating area and Zachary obediently picked out a chair and sat to wait. There were magazines and newspapers arranged on the coffee tables. No Cosmopolitan or Reader's Digest for Chase Gold. Not even People. Chase Gold was the center of the financial community—or at least wanted to be—so all of the reading material was high finance. Zachary stared at the abstract landscape painting in muted pinks and grays on the opposite wall, wondering if it was an original work, or whether the things were mass produced for somber reception areas all over the world.

A young woman with a pencil poking into her messy bun sidled up to the receptionist and looked at her questioningly. The receptionist pointed to Zachary, looking as if something in the room did not smell very good.

Mandy tiptoed over to Zachary, smiling pleasantly, with a frown line across her forehead that clearly communicated she had no idea who he was.

"You wanted to see me?"

"Is there somewhere we could talk privately?"

"Uh… yes…" She looked back around at the receptionist and pointed to one of the glassed-in meeting rooms visible from the waiting area. The receptionist rolled her eyes and nodded, reaching for a reservations sheet to write Mandy's name down.

"Come right this way… sir." She was still fishing for his name and why he wanted her. But Zachary waited until they were in the meeting room and Mandy reluctantly shut the door and turned to him. She was taller than he was, in her early twenties, on the slim side without being skinny.

"Miss Pryor. I appreciate you agreeing to talk to me. My name is Zachary Goldman, and I'm investigating the death of Lauren Barclay."

"Oh." Her face turned to a mask, shocked and not sure what emotion to show. She looked at him, at the table, at the door, and tried to think of how to handle the surprise interview. "You're investigating Lauren's death?"

"Yes. I'm sorry I didn't say something sooner, but I didn't know if you would want me to say something out there…"

"Oh, of course. No, it's alright. Everybody here knows about Lauren… but I don't really understand. It was an accident, she fell down in her tub, so why would anyone be asking questions and investigating it?"

"That's what we do."

Mandy bit her lip, nodding quickly. "Of course. I'm sorry, it's just a bit of a shock. We were all so shocked when we heard about her accident. And that she died… just a freak accident like that… it's really kind of scary."

Zachary nodded understandingly. He sat down on one of the big padded chairs and motioned for Mandy to take one of the others so they could talk to each other at the same level.

"It is so shocking when someone close to you dies so suddenly and unexpectedly. It seems... unfair and arbitrary. You can hardly believe that it's really true."

"Yes," Mandy nodded vigorously. "Yes, exactly. I think we're all still in a state of shock, to tell the truth. We're all trying to go on and work, but it's very difficult. It's hard to concentrate on your job when you're dealing with something like that."

"Does your company offer any counseling? Maybe something outsourced, if they don't have someone in house?"

"Of course. They've offered; there's someone we can talk to if we need to. But it's not... I don't know. It doesn't seem like the thing to do. We should be... taking a few days off, talking to each other, grieving properly, going to her funeral. Right? You don't go to therapy just because someone dies. Everybody dies sooner or later, and it wasn't like she was shot or murdered. She just... slipped and fell. It's tragic, but not traumatizing."

"You could take a day or two off, I'm sure..."

Her lips tightened and she shook her head in a definite 'no,' even while saying, "Yes, I suppose I could..."

"I gather that you and Lauren were pretty close."

"Well... we were friends, yes, if that's what you mean. We didn't know each other before we started working with the company. We just started at the same time and we had similar personalities. Helped each other out a bit, joked around together."

Zachary raised his brows. He looked around, making a wide gesture to indicate their surroundings. "Joked around? Here?"

Mandy gave a little laugh. "I know, right? Pretty serious place. But you've got to let off steam every now and then. We would all be having nervous breakdowns if we didn't have a way to... express our frustrations now and then."

"Sounds like a healthy attitude."

"They're really big on employee health around here. Like, we all have to get in a certain number of hours of exercise every week. There's an on-site gym, so that we can take a break and do it whenever we need to. Clears your head, gives you an energy boost without caffeine. You know how many studies there are on how dangerous it is to be sitting at a desk all day. So they make sure that we get up and take care of our bodies."

"Ah. I noticed Lauren had workout clothes and wondered how she managed to fit it in."

"There's so much work to do, it's really hard to break away to do it, but you feel so much better when you do. Better health, better wealth!"

"That's good to see. I wondered, when I heard how many hours Lauren was putting in, if the company cared about their employees' health at all."

"It's only while we're interns. Once we have our permanent positions, it won't be as many hours. Right now... it's kind of like a competition. This is our Everest. If we can get over the top... then it gets easier."

Zachary wondered if she knew how many people died on Everest.

"That's good. So you don't feel like they work you too hard here?"

Mandy's eyes went to the side, like she was afraid someone might be listening. She put on a brighter smile. "No, of course not," she assured him earnestly. "Sure, you'll catch us complaining about the hours, but it really isn't that bad. I pulled all-nighters in college all the time and it didn't hurt me. One or two now... it's nothing to worry about."

"So most nights, you don't sleep under your desk."

"Oh, no way. That would be so against company policy. Sometimes... maybe you put in a few extra hours to get a project done that you need for the morning, but nobody is allowed to sleep here. You have to go home and get a good rest."

What Zachary had read in Lauren's private email suggested otherwise. As had Barbara. But he imagined there was an official company policy that said it wasn't to be done, and an unofficial policy that said if you had to, go ahead, but don't advertise the fact. Sometimes it might not even be safe for an employee to leave if they were overtired or it was too late to be out on the street. A person could always get a cab, but even that could be tempting fate for a young woman alone.

He took out his notepad to make some notes, but it was really a ploy to allow Mandy a few moments of distraction, an unguarded moment when she could relax and not worry about what he was going to ask her next. When she looked away, toward the door they had come in, he could see that her eyes were bloodshot, the skin around her eyes pale and stretched-looking. Grief or exhaustion? He couldn't be sure.

He scribbled a few notes about corporate exercise and sleep.

"What is the company's policy on overtime? Are you paid hourly? Do you get more if you work longer hours?"

"No, we're all monthly salaries. Doesn't matter how many hours we put in. Officially, we're supposed to work nine to five, but…" Mandy laughed once. "Believe me, I've never put in a nine-to-five day. Lauren either."

"Yeah. I got that impression."

"But we're just banking it for the future. You know, once we're permanent employees, we won't have to put in those kinds of hours. It will be a lot better."

Zachary opened his mouth to answer her. A man had walked up to the door, and he opened it, sticking his head in. "Mandy, do you know if Jack —" He cut himself off, eyes going to Zachary. "Sorry, I didn't know you were—" Then his eyes got wide. "Zachary?"

CHAPTER SEVEN

Zachary stared at Gordon Drake. He scrambled to his feet.

"Gordon? What are you doing here?"

"What am I doing here?" Gordon stared at him and gave a slight head-shake. "My name *is* on the doors."

Drake, Chase, Gould.

Gordon Drake.

Zachary was still flabbergasted. He stood there staring at Gordon. Bridget's new partner. The man who had replaced Zachary in her life. He opened and closed his mouth like a fish.

With everyone calling the company 'Chase Gold' as a joke, he hadn't even focused on the Drake. He didn't know a lot of Drakes. In fact, he only knew one Drake. Gordon Drake.

Gordon pushed the door open the rest of the way and stepped in. Zachary tensed as the man came toward him, ready for an explosion. Ready for a fist swung straight for his nose. He didn't know what Gordon would think of him being there; he might not be too happy about it.

But Gordon thrust out his hand instead, open, reaching to shake Zachary's. Zachary gave it to him mechanically, not understanding what was going on.

"Good to see you, Zachary. You're looking a lot better."

The last time he had seen Zachary was when Zachary was leaving the hospital after a psychiatric admission. Not the best time for him. Better than he had been before the stay, on his way to better health, but still a bit wobbly on his new legs.

And before that… Gordon had probably seen him on TV after his encounter with Teddy, both eyes blackened, his body beaten and degraded. And before that was when Zachary had gone to see Bridget at the hospital, at which time she had told him thank you very much for helping to catch her kidnapper and to make it clear that she never wanted to see him again. As Kenzie had warned him, Bridget had brought Zachary back into her life only to use him and then to throw him away again.

Gordon pumped his hand. "So to what do we owe the pleasure of your company here today?"

Zachary swallowed. He had intended to visit Lauren's office covertly, to talk to her friends and coworkers on the quiet before the management could figure out what was going on. He hadn't counted on one of the owners of the company knowing him on sight.

Zachary slowly pulled his hand out of Gordon's grip, nodding and clearing his throat. "Uh… well… I'm investigating Lauren Barclay's death."

Gordon didn't freeze or go pale. Nothing to indicate any guilt or complicity in Lauren's death. He nodded gravely and patted Zachary on the side of the shoulder, as if to comfort a fellow mourner.

"Lauren Barclay. So tragic. It was such a shock for all of us here, wasn't it, Mandy?"

Mandy nodded. "Yes. That's what I told Mr. Goldman. I just couldn't believe it."

"Lauren's death has left a great hole in our company," Gordon said, and his prose didn't sound at all fake or insincere. "We are all going to miss her smiling face and can-do attitude."

There were a few seconds of silence. Zachary wasn't sure what to say about the investigation or Lauren's death. He licked his lips uncertainly.

"You feel free to talk to whoever you need to," Gordon told him without prompting. "I know you'll be discreet and won't upset people. Unfortunately, there is a lot of work that must be done, so we must all go on even in Lauren's absence. And her work will have to be divided up among the other interns." He raised his brows at Mandy in good humor. "Like you don't already have enough."

Mandy gave a little laugh. "I'm sure we can handle Lauren's work between us, sir. There's a lot to do, but we'll take up the slack, sir."

"Good girl," he said approvingly. And such praise from Gordon never came across as patronizing. Zachary himself had felt warm and appreciated when Gordon had told him 'good man' in the past. Mandy smiled and looked a little embarrassed.

"I appreciate you letting me talk to people," Zachary said. "I really didn't even realize this was your company, or I would have come to you first."

Gordon laughed. "Somehow, people always seem to leave my name out. I'm never sure quite what to think of the habit. I can assure you that I am by no means a silent partner. If you need anything, you feel free to come to me. I'll help you out any way I can, in order to put this matter of Lauren's death to rest. Such a lovely young lady. Very smart and a hard worker."

"I'm impressed that you knew her so well, when she was just an intern."

"Just an intern? They are the lifeblood of this company. We couldn't do anything without all of the hard work they put into it. It's too bad that we can't hire them all on after their initial term is up... unfortunately it is a very competitive business, and if we are going to continue to forge ahead as we have been, we need to be a little bit hard-nosed about it, recognize the realities of the situation. I know every employee in this company. Right down to part-time file clerks. I'm a hands-on leader. No sitting behind a desk drinking my tea and letting everyone else do the work. I'm out there like everyone else, closing the deals."

"Well... very good. I'll let you know if there is anything I need from you. You might be able to give me a little bit of background... the corporate culture, your philosophy here at Drake, Chase, Gould. If you can think about anything about Lauren or her work here that you think I should know about."

"Come by my office when you're done. Say..." Gordon looked at his watch. "Five o'clock? Maybe you won't be here that late. I need to leave at six for dinner with a very important woman you and I both know, but any time before then. If I'm not in my office, my assistant will be able to track me down."

———

When Gordon left, Zachary turned his attention back to Mandy, trying to determine his best course of action.

"I'd like to meet with the other interns that worked with you and Lauren," he said slowly. "It would be best if I could meet with them one-on-one, I guess… There's no need to take everyone away from their work at the same time or to disrupt things with a big meeting. People will find it easier to talk about things one at a time, I think…"

Mandy shrugged and looked out through the glass wall. "I should be getting back to work. I don't like to lose too much time, especially when we're going to be expected to absorb Lauren's work." She sighed.

"If it's too much, you should have told Gordon that, shouldn't you? He doesn't have any way of knowing how much of a burden it is if you don't tell him."

Her eyes widened. "I would never tell Mr. Drake no."

"He's a reasonable man, he wouldn't fire you for saying that you had too much on your plate."

"Maybe not, but one of the VPs or managers might, once word got around. I don't want to put my job in jeopardy."

"But you need to protect your health too. If you put yourself in hospital or end up on long-term disability, you're not going to achieve your goals either."

"I'm not going to end up in hospital." She stood and drew herself up as tall as possible. "It's been nice to meet you, Mr. Goldman. I guess you have to investigate and ask all of these questions if it's your job, but you're not going to find anything out. Lauren just had an accident. It wasn't anything to do with anyone here at the office. She was at home, alone. That's what happened."

He nodded and shook her hand in thanks. "Would you have one of the other interns come and see me…"

She looked like she would say no, but looking in the direction Gordon had gone, she nodded grudgingly. "Yeah. Sure."

"I appreciate it."

CHAPTER EIGHT

Most of the interns were men. The one who came to the boardroom next was Aaron Morgan. Zachary saw him stop for a moment outside the door and wipe both hands on his pants. When he entered and approached Zachary to shake his hand, Zachary could still see lines of fatigue around his eyes. His complexion was pale, but it was possible that he was just fair-skinned.

"Aaron Morgan," the intern announced, and gave Zachary's hand a perfunctory pump.

"Zachary Goldman. Thanks for agreeing to meet with me."

Aaron shrugged with one shoulder. "I was under the impression it was required."

Zachary let that go, keeping a friendly smile pasted to his face. "Why don't you have a seat? I expect you're pretty tired."

Aaron sat. "Why?"

"Why what?"

"Why do you think I'm tired?"

"You are all working long hours, and I don't imagine that's going to be shortened by Lauren's death."

"Yeah. Doesn't sound like they're going to be hiring someone to replace her."

"How many hours have you been working?"

Aaron looked at him, blinking and either trying to decide whether to answer truthfully or calculating the number of hours. "I guess... fifty-something straight. I had a report that had to be presented this morning."

"Are you presenting it?"

"No, one of the VPs. I just do the grunt work, I'm not worthy of client interactions."

"I'll bet you'll be the one taking the heat if there is anything wrong with the report."

Aaron gave a short bark of laughter. "You don't have to tell me that."

"So now that your report is prepared and handed in, are you going to go home to take a well-deserved rest?"

Aaron shook his head and yawned at the thought.

"No, can't go home during office hours. That would be a big problem. I'll just have to push through until tonight. Then I guess... get a few hours of shuteye, if I can still remember how."

Zachary nodded. "You must be exhausted. I can't imagine staying up that long on purpose."

"Well, people do it for medical tests or all kinds of other things, right? So I can handle it. It's not the first time."

"What makes it worth that kind of effort? You must feel like crap."

"Yeah? Try going seventy-two hours straight."

"Have you done that?"

Aaron started to answer, then shook his head. "I don't see what this has to do with anything. I thought you were here asking about Lauren."

"I'm wondering what kind of physical shape she was in... seeing you and Mandy, I have to wonder how many hours she had put in before she died. If she was that tired, it could have had an impact on what happened."

Aaron shook his head firmly. "I saw her when she left here. She was just fine. She wasn't a zombie. She was just going to go home to catch a few winks and a shower, and then come back."

"But then she never did."

Aaron nodded his agreement, shrugging. "We all got here in the morning, and she was nowhere to be seen. Mandy started calling her after a while, but there was no answer. Eventually, we just gave up. And then we heard after that how she had died in her bathtub. I thought... what a waste. All of that work for nothing."

Zachary thought Aaron meant that all of the work Lauren had done had been for nothing, because she died before she ever saw the benefits of it, but his supposition was dispelled by Aaron's next words. "All of the effort spent competing with her, trying to beat her out... and then she ends up eliminating herself. Unbelievable."

Zachary raised an eyebrow. He wrote a few words in his notepad. "Is it that cutthroat?"

"We're all competing for the same position or two. They do it intentionally, getting more interns than they need, so that we have to win the right to stay on. And in the meantime, they've squeezed all kinds of work out of us. Good for their bottom line."

"I assume you must track your hours."

"Yeah, we have to."

"So they know that you're putting in several days in a row, without any kind of rest in between."

"Well..." Aaron made a face and tried to come up with an answer. "I guess they know what kind of hours we're putting in, because they see us here at work."

"Sure. So... how well did you know Lauren? I know that she and Mandy were close, I imagine because they were the only two female interns. How did the rest of you get along? Did you do things together, or were you too competitive to socialize with each other?"

"There wasn't time to socialize."

"But you need to eat, joke around to break the stress and tension. There must have been times when you were just too brain-dead to continue working on a project and had to put it to the side until you were fresh again."

"Yeah... we did do some of that. Buy pizza and everybody would dive in, take a few minutes to pig out before getting back to our projects. Or sometimes after a big deal closed, go out to the bar and just wipe away the cobwebs. Not very often, but sometimes."

"So you must have known Lauren pretty well."

"No. Just to talk to. Like, I know that she lives in an apartment with another girl to pay the rent. I know she was good with numbers and was the top of all of her classes—but we were all the top of our classes. She had a sense of humor, I guess. She and Mandy would giggle together about things."

"You didn't go out with her?"

"Like a date? No."

"Like anything. Did the two of you go out for a drink together, just the two of you? Or a bite to eat? Or crashing at her apartment because it was closer than yours?"

Aaron clearly didn't like Zachary's line of questioning.

"If you think that I went back there with her one day and drowned her, you're crazy. Why would I do that? I knew I was going to beat her out. She wasn't my most serious competition."

"Oh. Who was your most serious competition?"

"Well, it had to be the men, right? It wasn't like the partners were going to pick a girl over us."

Zachary let the words hang in the air for a few minutes, thinking about them.

"Why is that a 'given'?"

"Because girls... women... they get distracted. Just when they hit the top of their career, the biological clock starts clicking and they have to have babies. And then they've got to stay home to take care of them, for like a year. For each one. And then if they ever get back into the workforce, they've lost their position, and they can't get to the top again. They'd have to intern all over again, and who would hire a thirty- or forty-year-old intern? No one wants someone that old."

"Is that really the way they see it?"

"Of course. They have to take on women interns, but they're never going to get the top positions, because they have the whole biological imperative."

"There must be female investment bankers. It's not all just a men's profession."

"Sure, there are a few. Even here at Chase Gold, there are a couple. But they don't last and everybody knows it. So they hire someone they can downsize a few months or years down the line. Get what they can out of them and then let them go."

"Did Lauren know this?"

"Sure. Everyone knows it. Lauren was talking about getting her tubes tied so that she couldn't have any kids. That would show them she was really serious about working for the company."

Zachary couldn't believe anyone would give up the opportunity to have children just to work at a place that was so demanding. Barbara had said

Lauren wanted to be wealthy. Did she want it badly enough to give up any chance of having children?

Of course, tubal ligations could usually be reversed. And people could adopt. Or foster. Or end up getting custody of a deceased relative's children. Would Chase Gold really only have accepted Lauren on equal footing with a man if she had opted for sterilization?

"Wow. That's pretty dedicated. She really wanted to get a permanent position here."

"Yeah, she did."

"It didn't worry you, this talk of getting her tubes tied? Did that put her ahead of you in the competition?"

Aaron clenched his jaw. "I would still have been ahead of her," he insisted. But Zachary had a feeling that the young man was, in fact, pretty worried about the possibility. And what would he have been willing to do to protect his position?

"So, I didn't catch whether you had ever been out with Lauren, or to her house."

"We didn't date."

"No. But did you ever go out anywhere together?"

"With the group, maybe."

"Ever by yourself?"

Aaron hesitated.

"Come on," Zachary gave Aaron a conspiratorial grin. "Are you telling me that the two of you never spent any time alone together? She was a nice-looking girl. She didn't have anyone else. She didn't have time for any real dating. All she could do was flirt a bit with the men at the office. Maybe go out together for drinks. I can ask Barbara; she said that Lauren sometimes saw men from the office, maybe even brought them home."

"Okay, maybe once or twice," Aaron admitted grudgingly. "It wasn't dating. It wasn't anything serious. It was just letting off steam at the end of a long day, or a long week."

"You've been to her apartment?"

He again hesitated, but Zachary waited him out this time, and Aaron conceded. "Yeah. A couple of times. She was close by, like you said. Going back to my place would have added an hour of commuting time. And going back to the office and sleeping on the floor... that wasn't any way to live. Not when I could just stay at her place and be comfortable in a bed."

"Sure."

"But I'm telling, you, it wasn't anything serious, and it was only once or twice. And I wasn't with her the day that she died. I didn't go home with her. We didn't do drinks or anything that night."

"Did anyone else?"

"What?"

"Did anyone else go home with her that night? Just because you didn't, that doesn't mean no one in the office did."

"No… I don't think so. No one left with her."

"Nobody left at the same time? Followed her out a few minutes later? It could have been covert."

"No." Aaron frowned and shook his head. "A few people went home, but… no, I'm sure no one left with her."

"Okay. Just thought I'd check. She didn't have any health problems that you knew about?"

"No. She would never have made it here if she was sick. You gotta be able to work all the time. Even through a cold or the flu. If it was something worse than that… no way. They'd have her out of here. We aren't permanent employees yet; they can terminate us at any time for any reason. If she was a risk because she was sick, they could just boot her."

"What about substance issues? Did she drink? Abuse pills? Something to help her stay mentally alert?"

"Well, everybody has caffeine. Like, all the time. We're drinking coffee and energy drinks like there's no tomorrow. And NoDoz."

Zachary nodded. "Lauren too?"

"Sure. As much as any of us."

"What about coke? Meth? Adderall?"

"I don't know anything about that. Not around me."

"What about you? It's out there, right?"

"It's out there. I don't know who does what. I don't do any prescription drugs or anything hardcore. Just the caffeine, to help stay awake on a day like this. Perfectly legal."

"Not necessarily safe, though, if you abuse it. You can still do some real damage."

"Nah. We're young and healthy and it's not like we're shooting the stuff. A drink to pick you up when you start to get sleepy. That's all. People all over the world drink it every day."

"They do," Zachary agreed. "I'm just saying, it can still be dangerous."

"Anything can be dangerous. We're trying to make a life for ourselves here. If you had the last twenty years to do over, what would you do? Would you try something more daring? If you knew you could be where you wanted to be right now instead of..." He wobbled his hand back and forth, expressing his opinion of Zachary's job. "What are you, detective? If you could put in a few years at a higher-octane level, and instead of being that, you could be... private security or something else you liked, making ten times the money? Come on, you'd do it, wouldn't you?"

Zachary smiled blandly and didn't give Aaron any information that he didn't already have. He'd found it useful in the past to have people underestimate him.

"Maybe I would," he said noncommittally.

"Yeah, exactly. I'm putting in my time now so that I don't have to be stuck in a dead-end job later. No offense. I have my life planned out. I know where I'm going and what I have to do to get there."

CHAPTER NINE

Blair Bieberstein was a little man who made Zachary think of a hyperactive squirrel. And as a small, ADHD man himself, that was saying something. Bieberstein seemed so hyped up and on edge that Zachary assumed he'd either just drunk every energy drink in the fridge, or he was dipping into the illegal stuff. He looked Zachary up and down and stood back, gazing at him, his whole body vibrating.

"So it's you, huh? You're the one investigating Lauren's death? This is just so crazy. I never thought that anything would happen to Lauren. She was always so grounded, so down to earth, you know? I never expected her to die like that. And then to have the police investigating it. You have to do that with accidents? Because no one was there when it happened? Is that why?"

"I was asked to look into it," Zachary started, keeping his voice pitched low and slow, trying to bring Bieberstein down. But the man didn't give him time to even start an explanation. He just nodded vigorously, as if he knew the whole story, and started to shift his feet back and forth. Zachary didn't know whether he had to go to the bathroom, or to pace, or if it was some kind of tic. Or a combination of all three. Bieberstein seemed like exactly the sort of person who was wound so tightly he was just going to spring apart at the slightest provocation. He was not the type of person Zachary would have pictured as an investment banker. He seemed way too out-of-control to be any kind of financial planner or to be able to plan anything ahead of time. They must have had a reason to hire him, but Zachary wasn't sure what it was. Maybe he was related to somebody. An idiot nephew that Chase or Gould had to give a chance to in order to get his sister off his back.

"I don't think I know anything that could be of any use to you," Bieberstein said, shaking his head rapidly. "Lauren and I weren't close or anything. We never went out together or snuck into the storeroom together, like some of the guys around here might have done. She wasn't my type. Or I wasn't hers. Doesn't really matter, because none of us have any time to be messing around while we're working here anyway. I don't need any more distractions in my life."

Zachary could see that. He could just see Bieberstein racing off down some rabbit trail when he was supposed to be preparing a report. His manager would find him days later, curled up under his desk with three laptops, typing and laughing maniacally.

"If we could just sit down for a minute to go over things, I'm sure it won't take very long."

Bieberstein looked at the chairs and the boardroom table. "I don't sit. I have a standing desk. I pace. I have a lot of nervous energy. I don't sit."

"Well..." Zachary was prepared to argue that he must sit down at some point, even if it were just to eat, but that really wasn't the point. Bieberstein probably didn't sit down to eat, either. He hovered over the computers, devouring Danishes, getting crumbs between all of the keyboard keys. He must be a menace to work with. "Okay, then," he said. There was no point in a battle of wills or trying to force Bieberstein to sit down.

Even if he were to succeed, Bieberstein would not be able to talk or focus once he was forced to sit still. Much like Zachary had felt as a kid when he was told he had to sit at his desk to do all of his schoolwork or homework. He wanted to get up and move around and think about it, work things through with his body. Once he sat still, everything fled from his brain and he couldn't explain why.

At least he was better than that now. He could—and frequently did—sit at the computer for hours to do research or compile reports, working through the puzzles that he had been tasked with solving. Sitting at the computer was, he knew, bad for his eyes, his heart, his posture, and everything else, but once he got into a project, it was hard to break off to do anything else, like getting up to walk around and give his eyes and body a break.

"Did you and Lauren work on any projects together?"

"Yeah, of course. I work with all of the other interns on their files. If they need research on markets, or need some numbers crunched, or whatever, I'm your man. Their man, I mean. That's my thing. I don't do my own files or projects, I'm a resource for others."

"Oh. So does that mean that you're not in competition with the others for a permanent position?"

Blair rocked back and forth and twisted his head around, thinking about it. He gave a wide shrug. "I don't know. Who really cares? I don't think so. I'm pretty sure that no matter who else they pick to go full-time permanent, I'll still have a place here. I don't think they're going to be getting rid of me anytime soon."

Zachary pondered. Although the others had not said anything about Bieberstein getting one of the permanent positions, they had made it sound like there was only one opening for them to fight over. So maybe Bieberstein did have a locked-in position, and it was everyone else who was trying to get that last chance. If they already knew that somebody had one space, it would make them all the more desperate to get the last one.

Bieberstein started to pace. He drummed his fingers against his legs and looked up at the ceiling, but he obviously wasn't counting ceiling tiles or avoiding Zachary's questions. His mind was busy on something else. Something that was far away and totally separate from what was going on in the boardroom.

Bieberstein had heavy, bristly whiskers, as if he hadn't shaved for three days. Maybe he hadn't, or maybe he was just one of those men who grew facial hair really quickly. He had the same bloodshot eyeballs and dark bags under his eyes as the others, clearly working the same brutally demanding schedule. Zachary wasn't sure how Drake, Chase, Gould could get away with working them for so many hours. There had to be laws against it. Was there any regulation of investment bankers or other office types? There had to be laws in place to prevent them from getting used as slave labor, as the interns clearly were.

"When was the last time you saw Lauren?" he ventured.

"Two days ago, ten thirty-five," Bieberstein said crisply, not even looking at him.

Zachary hesitated a moment, wondering if he was joking. But he didn't appear to be. "Morning or night?"

"Night. She went home. Had to get some rest so that she could work on a project Mr. Drake had given her the next day. So she went home to sleep. Then she never came back. You should have seen, everybody was going absolutely nuts around here trying to call and text her and find out what had happened to her, how she could have just stayed home and not come back in like she was supposed to. I wondered if she was dead. I wasn't surprised when the police came around and said that she was."

"You weren't surprised?"

"No. Why else wouldn't she answer anything? Even if she was sick, she would have at least sent a text back explaining that. But not a word…? No communication at all? That's just not the way we work. That's not the way Lauren was. She was always sending emails and texts out at all hours. That was how she got as far ahead as she did."

"I suppose so. I just didn't think that anyone would have thought 'maybe she's dead.'"

"Maybe not, but I don't always think the same way as other people do."

That much was clear.

"What did you think of Lauren as a person?"

"She was nice. She wasn't rude to me. She'd tell me to push off sometimes, but sometimes I need to be told that. That's okay, there's always something else to do around here."

"And what do you think happened? How do you think she died?"

"You already know how she died, don't you?" Bieberstein challenged. "She just fell and hit her head, drowned in the bathtub. That's what they're telling us. Unless everyone is lying and something else happened."

"Let's say something else happened. What are the possibilities?"

Bieberstein seemed unperturbed at being asked this. His chin jutted up toward the ceiling as he tipped his head way back and ran through scenarios. "She slipped in the bathtub. She stepped on something in the bathtub. She slipped or tripped on something outside the bathtub and fell into it. Someone pushed her and made her hit her head. Someone hit her over the head. Someone forced her into the tub and held her head under the water."

Zachary swallowed. That was a pretty good list of possibilities. And Bieberstein clearly wasn't concerned that anyone might think that he was the party who could have hit Lauren or held her head under the water. He wasn't connecting the possibilities to the dead girl personally, she was just a variable he was trying to solve for.

"If someone hurt her, who would you suspect?"

"If someone hurt her? But someone didn't hurt her. The police said that she slipped and hit her head. If someone hurt her…" He paced across the room, head back down, thinking, then walked back across the room again, backward this time, but avoiding the chairs and the corner of the side table without looking to see where they were. "It could be any of the interns. Everyone left at the same time. All of them wanted the job and knew she was probably the first in line for it. Most of the rest of the staff was gone, but there were still a few people around. Mr. Drake was still here, I know, because he'd just given Lauren the new assignment. I don't think any of the other partners were in. Receptionist goes home at six. Night security man was on, but he wouldn't have followed her home; he has to stay here to make sure that no one tries to break in. Or it could be someone who we don't know. Just a random burglar or junkie. There's nothing to indicate that it's anyone from work. It could be someone from her family, too; I don't know how close she was to them. Then there's that roommate. Is she really telling the truth? Or is she the one that knocked Lauren out and drowned her, and then just called in a report to say that she had found her, to throw suspicion off of herself? Nine times out of ten, it's the lover, a family member, or the person who reported it. Most fatal accidents occur in the home, so that was the best place to set something like that up. Lauren had to go home sooner or later. At most, her roommate would just have had to wait a couple of days."

Zachary felt like he was stuck in the middle of a whirlwind. He liked Bieberstein. He liked the way that he thought and that he didn't care whether Zachary thought he was crazy or guilty or just weird. He liked that Bieberstein didn't hold back, but just poured everything out, where they could both look at it and analyze it.

———

An older man poked his head into the boardroom. It was the second time that someone had done this to interrupt one of Zachary's interviews. It was irritating. The more senior members of the firm obviously felt like it was their domain and they could interrupt a meeting whenever they wanted.

Gordon had been gracious about it and had been happy to see Zachary. But having another man stick his head in and act like whatever Zachary was doing was unimportant got his back up.

"Biebs. Hey. I need you. You done in here?"

"Yeah," Bieberstein nodded, switching directions to leave the boardroom. "What do you need?"

"Hey—we weren't done yet," Zachary protested. "Can't it wait for a few minutes?"

"I don't have anything else to tell you," Bieberstein said. "I don't know anything about it and I've told you everything I could to help. Maybe one of the others will be able to give you some more insight. I'm not really good with people. I'm better at numbers."

"Maybe we could meet again later and finish up…"

"I don't think I have anything else to contribute," Bieberstein said dismissively.

The man who had come to fetch him nodded his head in agreement. "It was just an accident. What's anyone here going to know about it? None of us know anything."

"Who are you?" Zachary asked, holding up his hand for the older man to wait.

"Not part of your investigation. I have work to do. I'll see you around."

He left, taking Bieberstein with him.

CHAPTER TEN

"I know you're trying to talk to everyone," Kelly Pierce, one of the supervisors of the interns said. "They're just all busy right now. You can wait until their time frees up, but they're all working on vital projects right now. Maybe you could make an appointment and come back later when things are quieter."

Zachary studied him. "If I can't see any of the other interns, maybe I could talk to someone in human resources. Do you have a Manager of Human Resources I could follow up with?"

"We do… I don't know if she'll be busy right now…"

Zachary waited, and eventually the supervisor realized that there wasn't anything he could do other than make a phone call and ask. Zachary wasn't going to go away and wasn't going to offer any easy outs. Pierce rolled his eyes and pulled out his cell phone. He searched his contacts and found the person he was looking for. Obviously not someone who was on his favorites list.

"Bev… hey, we've got a bit of a situation here that I wonder if you can help with. I don't know if you've heard, but we've got this detective up here who's looking into the Lauren Barclay accident… yeah… and he wants to talk to someone in Human Resources. I guess that's you, so… tag, you're it! Do you want to come upstairs to the boardroom, or do you want me to send him down there?"

He spoke for a couple more minutes, mostly just listening to Bev on the other end, watching Zachary and looking around the room restlessly. "Yes… yes… I know. But we've been told to cooperate."

More commentary from Bev in human resources, with Pierce nodding and uh-huh'ing, waiting for her to finish.

"So… you want me to send him down?"

He was finally able to hang up the call and rolled his eyes at Zachary. "Just be warned you're going to have to hear all of that for yourself when you get down there."

Zachary chuckled. "Okay. Thanks for the heads-up. Where do I go from here?"

"I'll walk you down," Pierce sighed.

"I can find my way."

"We have to be careful of security. The door down there is locked. She said she would let you in, but…"

"Well, I appreciate you looking after me."

They headed out to the lobby and onto the elevator.

"Everybody seems to get along pretty well here," Zachary commented. "I expected the interns to be a lot more… antagonistic toward each other."

It surprised Zachary how close-knit the employees seemed. Since they were competing against each other, he would have thought that they would have shown animosity toward each other, have talked behind each other's backs and made accusations or tried to direct him against their enemies. But everyone seemed to consider themselves part of the team.

Pierce raised his brows and nodded. "We try to foster a strong corporate identity. A unified, supportive culture. It's important in a place like this. People have to work so hard, and if there isn't any kind of intrinsic reward —and monetary reward just doesn't cut it—then people are just going to burn out and leave. If you want to reach people, you need to… inspire them."

"How do you do that?"

"Bev can fill you in on that kind of thing. That's one of the jobs of Human Resources."

"Okay. You like it here?"

"Of course I do, I wouldn't stay here otherwise. Like I said, money isn't the be-all and end-all. You have to get something deeper out of it. Something more… spiritual."

Zachary couldn't help the skepticism that entered into his tone. "Spiritual?"

"That's maybe not the right word, but I'm not sure what word to use. Fulfillment. Satisfaction. Wholeness."

"Out of an investment banking company?"

"You can find your zen anywhere. We happened to find it at Drake, Chase, Gould."

"Okay. Well… good for you. That's pretty amazing."

They got off on a lower floor, and Pierce led Zachary over to a plain brown door. Closed and, as he had said, locked. They both stood there for a moment, looking at it. Pierce sighed and pulled out his phone again. He tapped the number and stared up at the ceiling as he waited for Bev to answer.

"We're here, Bev. Yes, already. Waiting for you."

He hung up again, shaking his head.

"You don't have a key?" Zachary asked.

"I'm not part of the department, I'm not supposed to be letting people in and out without approval. Gotta make sure we know who is where and have some kind of security."

Zachary nodded. They waited a few more minutes, and eventually, the door opened.

Bev was a tall woman, black hair pulled back, liberally streaked with gray. She towered over both of them. Her face was smooth and unwrinkled in contrast to her hair. Maybe the hair was colored. Though Zachary didn't know why a young woman would want to color her hair gray.

"So you are…"

"Zachary Goldman." He held his hand out to her, and she hesitated for a few seconds, then offered her hand and let him squeeze it, offering no firmness in response. The quintessential dead fish.

"Come this way, I suppose. Thank you, Kelly."

Pierce nodded and made a little gesture to Zachary that he interpreted as, 'you asked for it, and now you got it.' He went back to the elevator to ascend to his own floor, and Zachary followed the tall, stern woman. She took him, not to a meeting room, but back to her own office. It wasn't big. The walls were lined with metal file cabinets, a few paintings on the walls, some inspirational posters and awards. Stacks of paper on her desk and on the visitor chair, which she had to remove with a sigh before Zachary could sit.

"Thanks so much for agreeing to see me," Zachary said. "I know it's inconvenient…"

"It is," Bev agreed. "And there's no reason for it. I don't understand why the police are investigating Lauren's death. It was obviously an accident. Why would you waste your resources on this?"

"I was asked to," Zachary said simply, not correcting her impression that he was with the police. If she knew that he was a private investigator, he had a feeling that she wouldn't help him, even with the instruction coming down from Gordon Drake that they were to help Zachary.

Zachary flipped a few random pages in his notebook, thinking.

"Pierce said you could tell me about the corporate culture you have here at Drake, Chase, Gould. It seems like you have a really close-knit community. I thought it would be… cutthroat. But people seem to get along with each other, for the most part."

Bev studied him, the lines of her face softening a little. Starting with a compliment always went a long way to getting some cooperation.

"Yes, we've worked very hard to develop a real community. A team where people help each other out, rather than trying to steal files from each other or to talk each other down. Kind of unusual in this industry. But it's something that we've consciously worked on."

"Do you have some literature on the company? And can you tell me about some of the stuff that you have done to build it up that way?"

Bev looked at him for a moment as if to make sure that he was really serious. Then she bent down and opened a drawer, where she went through a number of folders, taking one item out of each to put on the desk in front of him. A company handbook, pamphlet on their health and welfare program, some glossy brochures on retreats and team-building volunteer days, various items that they had put together showing what a wonderful company new employees were coming to work for.

Zachary picked up the handbook and opened it up to one of the first pages, reading the big, bold headlines.

Drake, Chase, Gould
Building wealth, building community
A world leader in investment banking.

He didn't spend a lot of time browsing through the handbook, just reading a section heading here and there throughout the book and looking at the pictures of happy employees doing various things. He'd spend more time on the handbook later, when he had the time to read it without someone hovering over him.

"This looks really good, thank you."

He turned to the health and welfare brochure, and saw that it outlined information about the company gym and their activity program, as well as a few other headings about counseling for substance abuse issues, benefits for things like massage therapy and acupuncture, and a corporate dietician to help employees work through meal planning, weight loss, and other issues.

"One of the interns mentioned your gym," he said. "I think it's great that you have something on-site where employees can go to get their workouts. When you've got people working as hard as your employees do, it's such a great idea to have something right on-site so that they can take a break whenever they need it, get their workout, and go back to work fresh."

"That's right." Bev nodded vigorously. "Exercise is absolutely vital for employee health. And we've gone one step further. Not only are they allowed to take breaks to go get some exercise, it's actually prescribed. They have to log a certain number of exercise hours a week at our gym. And not all on a Saturday or Sunday, either. They have to be working out regularly throughout the week. We want to make sure that people are getting the exercise they need, that they're getting away from their desks and actually doing something physical."

"You track their workout hours?"

"Absolutely. And if they are not putting in the hours they need to in order to maintain peak health, then their supervisor is going to be talking to them. It's very important to us."

"Wow. That really is forward-thinking. I've never heard of a company doing that."

"Our employees are important to us. If we don't take care of their health, then we're going to end up losing a lot of hours that they could have been working dealing with sick leave and disability. We don't want to have to deal with downtime. We schedule workout time so that they have the best possible chance of maintaining peak health."

"Do you require a physical when they start? They always say that you have to consult a doctor before beginning a new exercise program. I mean, what if you had someone who had a bad heart and they got on the tread-mill, and…"

She chuckled. "Well, we don't want to have to deal with that kind of liability. So, yes, we do have employee physicals, both before they begin working here and annually, so that we are up-to-date on those kinds of issues and can head off problems before they really become an issue. If you can see a problem developing and refer the person to the corporate dietician to get them back on track, why wouldn't you do that? So much easier to deal with it at the beginning than once it becomes entrenched."

"So everybody would have a physical before they start working here."

She nodded her agreement.

"I'd like to see the report on Lauren's physical, if I could."

Bev stared at him. She didn't move. She didn't get up to go to one of the banks of file cabinets and pull out Lauren's personnel file or a file on employee physicals.

"We don't have one for Lauren."

"Not for Lauren? Why not?"

"She wasn't a permanent employee, she was just an intern. If she had stayed on with us, we would have had a physical done then. But we don't do them for interns. Why would you waste your time and money on a handful of employees who are not going to stay with the company? Once they've been put on-track as permanent employees, then we do the physicals."

"But they were required to go to the gym."

Bev's mouth twisted into different shapes as she tried to find a way to explain this discrepancy. "Well… an intern isn't actually required to attend at the gym, but they do have access to it. It's at their own discretion. They are allowed to, but they don't have to."

Zachary frowned, thinking about that. He made a note to go back to it later.

"That makes perfect sense," he told Bev. Her face relaxed, relief showing through. "Why would you spend money on temporary employees who were only going to be here for a few months and then move on to something else?"

She nodded her agreement.

"So what do you do when an employee has heart problems or high blood pressure or some other issue that precludes them from exercising?"

"You'd be surprised. There aren't really a lot of conditions that would bar someone from exercising. They might have to start off easy, limit what kinds of exercise they did at the start, but most people can do some kind of exercise. It's just a matter of finding out what it is and starting slowly."

"Okay. Sure. That makes sense."

"We have a portable v-fib machine in the gym," she said proudly. "And we have staff who are trained in how to use it and in CPR and first aid. All that kind of thing. They are on-site to handle any issues, from a sprained ankle to heart attack. We're investing in our employees' futures."

It sounded like another slogan. Zachary looked down at the brochures and saw the same tagline written across the front of the health and welfare brochure. *We're investing in our employees' futures.*

"That really sounds good. I wish other companies would do that." He fidgeted with the edges of the brochure, running his eyes over the headlines again. "Do you have a lot of issues with substance abuse? I would imagine you must have a few employees who… abuse caffeine… maybe drink too much on weekends when they get away from the grind."

"There are issues in any company. I don't think we have any more than is normal in any other company. And we are dealing with it right away, with counseling and keeping track of employees through their annual physicals. I don't think you could say the same about most companies. That's just not normally done. We're way ahead of the curve there."

"And how about overwork? It seems like your interns especially are racking up some crazy hours…"

"No, certainly not. We have policies on how many hours they're allowed to work. We know that the type of people who become investment bankers tend to have those type A personalities and really get into their work. So we have policies to guide them on how long it's reasonable to work, and then they need to go home and get some sleep. These self-starters, they will run themselves into the ground if you let them. You have to be strict and say they aren't allowed to work more than a certain number of hours in a day or a week."

"Really. Do you have a written policy?"

She went to her drawer again, and pulled a single sheet out of a folder. Zachary looked it over. It was an infographic with numbers and graphs and little pictograms showing how employees needed to log their hours and ensure that they weren't working too many days or hours per month. On the back was a daily time log that could be photocopied. As well as an internet URL showing where they could download a tracking app on their phones or computers.

"So they actually have to clock in and out."

Bev nodded.

"Could I get a copy of Lauren's logs? And the other interns' that she worked with?"

"That's private employee information. I really can't share that with you."

"I'm going to need to see it," he said firmly. He pressed a little harder, working on her assumption that he was a police officer. "Am I going to have to come back here with a warrant? Gordon told me that I would have the company's full cooperation."

"Well, of course I am cooperating, but this information is private..."

"I see." He wrote 'warrant' slowly and deliberately in his notepad. He didn't know how well she could follow his pencil movements and tell what he was writing down, but he figured that even someone who had no talent for cryptography could tell that the word started with a W.

Bev was looking distinctly uncomfortable. Zachary looked down at his page, and wrote down 'call Gordon' in his slow, awkward printing. She shifted in her seat. Her forehead was creased with frown lines. Finally, she decided to cooperate with him.

"Okay, okay, you don't have to do that. I'll get you Lauren's log."

Zachary sat back and waited. She looked back at him. She clearly expected him to go on with the interview, and she would track down and send him Lauren's work log later. Or not at all, hoping that he would forget to follow up on it. He just looked at her, waiting for her to produce the log.

Bev finally turned her attention to her computer and tapped on the keys, logging into their time tracking program and searching up the employee and report that she wanted. She printed it off and handed it over to Zachary, her nose wrinkling like Zachary smelled bad.

"I really don't like this. I don't think I should be compelled to give you confidential employee records..."

Zachary looked over the columns of numbers. He would have to study it at home later, when he could really focus and see whether Lauren had been working the hours that her roommate claimed, or whether that had been untrue.

"And the other interns' logs?" he pressed. He had waited until he had

Lauren's log in his hand, not wanting her to backtrack and end up hiding the information because he'd asked for too much.

"It's one thing to give you Lauren's. She is dead and you are investigating her death, but the other employees... I really don't think that I can justify that. I might have to talk to our lawyer..."

"I see." Zachary put down Lauren's time log and sat back in his seat. He looked at the other handouts that Bev had given him. "Why don't you tell me about the employee retreats?"

CHAPTER ELEVEN

"I'm sure you've seen or been to corporate team-building events before," Bev said, looking over at the flyers she had handed to Zachary. "Inspiring speakers, building trusting relationships, working together for a unified goal, camp type situations where everybody eats together, sleeps in communal cabins or cottages. We work on visioning, corporate cheers, personal goal-setting, or dream-mapping. We're really invested in developing a sense of community and loyalty to each other. Not just to the company brand, but to their coworkers and the company's vision."

"Well, from what I've seen, it's working."

Bev nodded her agreement. Zachary didn't point out that she was the only one so far who had resisted being a team player, trying to get out of talking to him. While the lower-level workers were loyal to the company, he wasn't sure that management had the same attitude.

"You don't ever get anyone who refuses to participate or comes back with a bad attitude? Maybe mocking the whole team-building process? Because it seems like you always have the one guy..."

She rolled her eyes. "One clown who has to mock everything and act like he's above it. Yes. We have had one or two of those. But you know what? If they don't come around in a session like that... your best course of action is to get rid of them. Give them notice when they get back to the office and have them out of there in two weeks or sooner. You don't need rabble-rousers like that who aren't going to fall into line."

"So I assume you never got that kind of attitude from Lauren."

"Heavens, no. And not from any of the other interns either. They all know that if they want to stay with the company, they'd better show us what they're made of. There's no skepticism tolerated with the interns. Fall in line or you can go home. Everybody else is working their butts off to earn a place here."

"How many intern positions are open?"

"Two or three, depending on the needs of the company. It does change a bit from one season to the next."

"The current batch of interns? How many are they fighting over?"

"Two."

"Blair Bieberstein seemed to think he has one of them tied up."

Bev pressed her lips together.

"Would that be accurate?" Zachary asked. "Is Bieberstein already picked for one of them?"

"I don't know that I would put it in quite those terms… but he is a serious contender."

"You haven't been told that he's been picked already?"

"There's been talk. But policy says that they don't get finalized for another month."

"So maybe he's an unofficial pick?"

Bev shrugged. "Call it what you like."

"Was Lauren at the top of the list for the other one?"

Bev shook her head. "I don't think I could say that. She was definitely up there, but we have some extremely capable and hard-working interns. It is going to be a close race."

"Would she be picked for the other slot, being a woman? I got the feeling that male interns are preferred, because they don't have the inconvenience of childbearing to worry about."

She tapped the end of her pen on the desk, considering what to say.

"It's a tough world out there for women," she finally said. "Men don't really understand what it's like to have avenues closed because of the fact that they might become parents. For women, it is a reality. Even if you keep working right up until you go into labor, and return as soon as you can be on your feet, there is still a prejudice that you are going to miss a lot of work with baby illnesses and when your childcare falls through, or school gets out for a snow day. For the next ten to twenty years, you have another priority. And if you keep having children... even worse."

"Is that a consideration here?"

"It is everywhere, whether they will admit it or not. Women of child-bearing or child-rearing years are second class. Whether they are married or single. Even if they tell you that they don't plan on having children. Everyone has been burned at some point by a woman going on mat leave."

"Lauren was talking about getting her tubes tied. Would that have made her a better candidate?"

"It would certainly help, not only in showing that she wouldn't accidentally get pregnant, but also that she was willing to put the company before family. Definitely a step in the right direction. The board had been getting pressure because of the gender inequality in the company. You get one woman on the board, and suddenly you have to address why there aren't women everywhere in the company, on an equal basis with men. Why aren't we hiring more women? Why are their salaries smaller? We need to be proactive in putting women before men until the inequality is evened out. It's one thing to have women as secretaries or in human resources," she indicated herself, "but that's not the same as having them as investment bankers or vice presidents."

"So you were actually under pressure to hire a woman rather than a man."

Bev shrugged and didn't confirm it in so many words.

"So the male interns didn't really have much of a chance of getting a position once Bieberstein and Lauren were locked into place. Unless one of them... dropped out for some reason."

"That's probably overstating the situation. There was still plenty of competition for those positions. Nothing was—or is—set in stone. It's still an open audition."

"But a little less competitive than it was a few days ago."

"Of course. But I don't think anyone is going to go through all of our interns, knocking them off until there are only two left. No one did anything to Lauren. She slipped in her tub."

"Perhaps. Or maybe she had a little help."

"You don't have any proof of that," Bev challenged, leaning forward in her chair. "I really don't understand what's going on here. The girl didn't die under suspicious circumstances. Everything I read and heard said it was an accident. I don't know why there's any investigation going on at all. It doesn't make sense."

"We want to know what happened. What really happened. Don't you?"

"Of course I do. Lauren seemed like a nice girl. But to imagine that there was anything... suspicious going on is ridiculous. There wasn't anything going on."

"Will Mandy Pryor get the position, since Lauren isn't in the running any longer? Because she's the only other woman?"

Bev's nose wrinkled, clearly projecting her feelings. "I don't think Mandy has what it takes. Not like Lauren did. She's a good, capable candidate... but she doesn't have that extra luster. And I don't think she'd ever promise not to have children. With someone like that, who would eventually leave you in the lurch... it's better to say no now than to pick her up and then be scrambling to fill her position another year down the line. We would go back to that original pool of interns to replace her. Why not just replace her before it ever becomes a problem?"

"By not hiring her in the first place."

"Yes."

"So much for equality in the workplace."

"I wish I could say it wasn't true. But society has a long way to go before we get to the point where women are not held back by childbearing and childcare. Maybe like one of those dystopian books where the children are all grown in vitro and then raised and trained by the state instead of their parents..."

Having spent much of his youth in the care of the state, Zachary didn't have much confidence in the government's ability to raise all of the children without the interference of loving parents. They would all turn out to be psychopaths.

"I really need to get back to work," Bev said, looking at her watch.

"I appreciate you spending the time with me. Before I go, would you mind getting me those time reports for the other interns?"

She froze. "I told you, that isn't going to be possible right now."

"You want to talk to a lawyer."

"I don't want to, but sometimes you have to. I can't just give you confidential company information."

Zachary worked his phone out of his pocket. "Do you have Gordon Drake's direct line?"

She stared at him without responding. Zachary waited, and she still didn't offer any help. Zachary turned his attention to his phone and found a web listing for Drake, Chase, Gould. He reached the receptionist and asked for Gordon.

"It's Zachary Goldman. He asked me to be put through to him directly."

"I don't know if Mr. Drake is in his office right now."

"Give it a try. He said his assistant would help if he wasn't in the office."

Bev stared at him as he waited for the receptionist to put him through to Gordon. Her eyes moved back and forth around the room as she tried to come up with a strategy to deal with him, and probably to figure out whether he was really calling Gordon directly to overrule her or whether he was just bluffing. Zachary gave her a pleasant smile while he waited. The receptionist put him on hold, which was a combination of easy listening music and commercials for the firm. He'd heard the same commercial about five times when the receptionist finally came back on the line.

"I'll put you through to Mr. Drake now," she said in a tone that pretended to be pleasant, but she was clearly not happy with this outsider who could just call any time he liked and get put directly through to the big boss.

There were a couple of rings, and then Gordon picked up.

"Ah, Zachary. How is it going? Are you getting everything you need?"

"Everybody has been very cooperative," Zachary assured him. His eyes were on the human resources director, her complexion pale as she looked at him. "There's just one issue. Your human resources department has concerns about releasing information to me."

"What information? We do have to protect employee privacy of course. We'd be in trouble if we just released confidential information to you. As much as I want to help you, you're not the police, and there are no court orders compelling us to turn information over to them."

"I'm looking for the time logs for the interns."

"Time logs?"

"When they clocked in and out. How many hours they were putting in. What time everyone got off the night before Lauren's accident."

"I don't see a problem with that. Give me to Beverly."

Zachary offered Bev the phone. She took it from him, her eyes wide, handling it like it was a live snake. One that might whip around and bite her at any moment. She put it up to her ear.

"Hello?" She listened for a moment to Gordon on the other end. Zachary couldn't hear that part of the conversation. "Yes, sir, everything is fine. I've been doing everything I can to help. Though I really can't understand why..."

She stopped talking and listened some more.

"Yes, sir. If you really think that's okay, but isn't that breach of confidential information? I wouldn't want to have to defend against a lawsuit for disclosing private employee information... Yes, sir. Okay. Yes. I'll see to it. Okay."

Eventually, she pulled the phone away from her ear, and after checking to make sure the call had ended, handed it back to Zachary. She swallowed and looked at him.

"It may take me a few minutes to get you everything you need. You just want the few days before Lauren died? And just the interns?"

"If I could get all of the time they've logged since they started here. It's only been a couple of months, right?"

"Yes."

"Give it all to me, then, if you could. That way I can track patterns."

"It will take me some time." She looked at her watch. "Do you want to come back after lunch, and I'll have it ready for you then?"

Zachary thought about this. He hadn't expected it to take her more than a couple of minutes to tell the computer which employees she wanted to see the timesheets for and what dates she wanted to cover. Why would she need an hour to print that out? She obviously wanted time to review the information to make sure that there was nothing that would show the company in a bad light.

"I thought you just had to tell the computer... like you did for Lauren's..."

"I know, but going back through previous pay periods is stupid on this computer. They've already been paid out for those months, so the information all gets archived, and you have to query in a different database and..." She searched for further explanation. Zachary shook his head. He was a private investigator. He knew the way that computers worked, and none of the mainstream payroll programs were going to make it complicated to print timesheets. There was no special procedure to go through to get the previous months, other than to tell it the dates you wanted and that you wanted already billed information. Whatever else she wanted to do, she wanted him out of her office for a while.

He weighed whether he should go back to Gordon again, but didn't want to press his luck. She would complain and give him a sob story about how Zachary was asking her for things that couldn't be done, that he was going beyond what he needed to for the investigation, that he was being rude or unreasonable in his demands. Zachary didn't want to risk getting on the wrong side of Gordon. For more than one reason. The investigation into Lauren's death was only part of it. Gordon had always been pleasant to Zachary and treated him with respect, trying to keep Bridget calm when she got angry with Zachary.

Gordon had been the one to call Zachary when Bridget had been kidnapped. Had called him even before the police. He had made sure that Zachary was involved in the investigation, no matter what anyone else had to say about it. He trusted that Zachary would be able to find Bridget, and Zachary had. He'd tracked her down and he'd saved her. Another day, and they wouldn't have been so lucky. Even a few more minutes... Zachary knew that the kidnapper had been trying to give her an injection before abandoning her in the remote shack in the woods. Zachary didn't have any doubt that it hadn't been a vitamin shot.

Gordon had been open and honest with the police investigator who was in charge of investigating Bridget's disappearance, protesting when the police had suspected Zachary of being complicit. He had told them that Bridget and Zachary's rocky relationship and bitter divorce had not been Zachary's fault, but Bridget's, putting the blame squarely on his own partner.

And Gordon would be the one who either kept Zachary up-to-date on Bridget's pregnancy or blocked him out. Since it was really none of Zachary's business how Bridget was doing, the only way he was going to hear anything was if Gordon had positive feelings toward him.

He got up and left Bev to whatever subterfuge she was up to, giving her a friendly nod. "I'll be back after lunch, then."

CHAPTER TWELVE

Zachary decided to have a look around the more public areas of Drake, Chase, Gould to glean what he could of the corporate culture and what other issues might be present that he wasn't aware of yet. People would be gossiping about Lauren, and gossip could provide valuable information about whether her death had merely been an accident or there was someone in particular—one of the interns or someone else altogether—who might have wanted to see Lauren dead.

There was an employee cafeteria, which no one had mentioned in their interviews. Zachary suspected that most of them probably ate at their desks, whether they bought their food in the cafeteria or somewhere else. He just hoped that the food wasn't so bad that nobody bought it there, and that was why they hadn't mentioned it.

There was no guard at the door to make sure that only employees of the company could eat there, no security passes required to get into the lines, so Zachary took a look over the offerings and got himself a small soup and a sandwich.

Far from being the bland, over-processed foods that he would see in a hospital cafeteria, the Drake, Chase, Gould cafeteria seemed to focus mostly on fresh, unprocessed foods. Lots of fresh salads, sandwiches, soups, beans, and stir fries. There were a few more processed offerings such as Jell-O dessert and Rice Krispies squares, but that was to be expected. There were also baskets of ripe fruit, granola bars, and other easy-to-grab snack foods.

Zachary looked around for a place to sit down to eat. There were lots of available seats, but he couldn't see any of the interns he had already talked to. He was pretty sure that they were still at their desks, whether they had popped downstairs for something to eat or not. Working the long, arduous hours they did, they wouldn't be willing to give up an hour, or even half an hour of wasted time sitting in the cafeteria doing nothing.

He sat at a table that had several empty chairs so that he wouldn't be sitting too close to anyone else or, hopefully, taking anyone's favorite seat without leaving an acceptable alternative. He took the lid off of the soup and was peeling the plastic wrap off of his sandwich when someone sat down beside him.

"That doesn't look like a very satisfying meal," the man said, putting down a large, well-stuffed hamburger, a carton of chocolate milk, and a chocolate pudding for dessert. The hamburger was surrounded with thick-cut fries and he had a small cup of gravy to dip them in or to pour over them. Zachary raised his eyebrows.

"I don't think I could get all of that down," he said, turning his eyes to the owner of the voice and the burger. To his surprise, it wasn't a big, over-muscled body builder, but a slim, almost skinny man with a pencil mustache.

"I can pack it away with the best of them," the man said, laughing.

Zachary shook his head. "You must have a hollow leg."

"Or two."

Zachary chuckled. "You must."

The man sat down and inhaled the fragrant steam coming off of his burger and fries. "So you're the detective who's asking questions about Lauren Barclay's death."

"Yes. Word gets around fast."

"Corporate grapevine. Faster than a speeding bullet."

Zachary took a bite of his sandwich. "Did you know Lauren?"

"Sure. Worked with her on a number of projects. She was one of the interns that I managed."

Zachary held his hand out to him. "Zachary Goldman."

"Oh, sorry. Daniel Service." Daniel shook hands with him, then dug into his meal.

"So how was she as an employee? Everybody seems to agree that she was a hard worker. Maybe at the top of the list for a permanent position."

Daniel nodded his agreement. "She was really driven, that one. And that's a good thing around here. It's a tough atmosphere for anyone who wants to take it slow or needs a long time to ramp up. Lauren got into the swing of things right away and had what it took. Very impressive."

"How are the other interns? Anyone else that measures up to her?"

Daniel ate a couple of french fries, swirling them in the cup of gravy first and then chewing them slowly.

"Maybe not quite," he admitted. "I mean, there's Bieber, and he's absolutely unmatched. No way we would want him going to another company. The others are good, don't get me wrong, they're just not... outstanding. It won't be easy to decide which of them is going to stay and which will have to go." He shrugged. "At least they've had the experience of working for Drake, Chase, Gould. I really believe there's nothing like it in the industry. It's going to be a world leader within a couple of years. Really, it is now, people just haven't recognized it."

"You think so?" Zachary thought about what he knew about the company. "I mean, it's a big company for a town like this, but on a world scale? How are you going to compete with Goldman Sachs and JP Morgan? They have thousands of employees worldwide."

"And we will too. What we're doing here is scalable. Everything is done with expansion in mind. The program the interns are in, company policies, infrastructure, communications, the health and welfare program, everything. You could take this office and replicate it in any city around the world. You could have a new office set up in days and up and running efficiently within a couple of weeks. It's brilliant."

Zachary took out his notepad and put it beside his plate, making a couple of notes.

"What can you tell me about the health and welfare program?" he asked. "Obviously, it's a huge step forward to have your employees working out in the company gym and eating in a cafeteria with its focus on healthy foods like this." He made a gesture to indicate the room and the people around them. "What else is involved? And how do these high-finance types react to being told that they have to work out a certain number of hours a week?"

Daniel chuckled. "I'm not one for organized exercise myself. It's not easy to get into the mindset that whatever you do during the day, walking to work or running back and forth all day long, isn't enough, and that you need to log a certain number of workout hours on top of that. I like to incorporate my exercise into my life, but you can't log that. But… yeah, I know it's good for me, so I do it, and I try not to whine too much about it. Some of the managers and VPs, they really think they should be excused from the workout requirements, but Mr. Drake says they knew what they were getting into when they signed on, and if they didn't like it, they shouldn't have joined the company."

"Ouch."

"Maybe they thought they would be able to get away with not working out, that it was just a throwaway clause and no one would be tracking them. But it is included in everyone's contracts, which means that Chase Gold can enforce it. Do what you promised to do, or you're out the door."

"Do you think it has made a difference in absentee rates? Is there a noticeable reduction in sick days or in people having major health problems?"

"You'd have to talk to human resources to find out what our rates are like compared against the industry. I don't know… we still have our fair share of people with high blood pressure, heart disease, and all that. We had a VP who had a stroke a few months back. Went down right at his desk in the middle of a big deal. That really refocused management on making sure that people were logging their workouts and getting to their annual physicals. And if there was a major problem observed in their physical, they have to be seeing their regular doctor or specialist every month and bring in a signed note confirming that they have."

"And people don't complain about that?"

"Oh, they complain about it. But would you rather have people complaining or going down at their desks? Management is of the opinion that it's more important to be sure people are seeing their doctors, taking their meds, and getting in their exercise than worrying about whether they like it. You have to do what's best for the company. And for the machine to work, you need to make sure that all parts are running efficiently."

Zachary nodded. He sipped a couple of spoonfuls of soup, which was surprisingly good.

"And these retreats and team-building days that are part of the health and welfare program, what do you think of those? Is it a waste to take time away from the office? Or is it worth it?"

Daniel didn't take long to consider it. "A corporate community is very important. If you've got a bunch of politics to deal with, people who won't work with others, employees who haven't bought into the company's policies and procedures, that damages productivity. It cripples communication. If you can get everybody onside, that's worth a day or a weekend or a few days for a retreat."

"You're able to make changes like that in a day or two?"

"We're always working on it when we're here at the office too. It's not like that's the only time we're working on company productivity. But a retreat is a lot more intensive, you can make more headway with difficult cases in that setting."

Zachary had a couple more bites of his sandwich and soup, but he was about finished. He didn't have a good appetite with the meds he was on. He had to make an effort to eat enough to get back up to what his doctor would consider a healthy weight.

"You like working here?"

Daniel gave him a broad smile. "There's nowhere like Drake, Chase, Gould. It's a privilege to work here."

He'd only spent a few minutes of the hour Bev had asked for in the cafeteria, and Zachary was interested in seeing a little more of the employees away from their desks. He found his way to the on-site gym. While he wasn't exactly inconspicuous, with everyone else in their workout gear, he tried to look natural and relaxed. He had been given permission by one of the owners of the company to go where he wanted to and ask the questions he needed to. There was no reason for him to feel like he was doing something sneaky.

The gym was not big. There were no running track or squash courts, but there were plenty of stationary bikes and ellipticals, treadmills, weight machines, and some free weights at the ends of the room. Everything the employees needed to stay in shape. Not every machine was occupied, but it was a busy place over the lunch hour.

The music that was being piped into the room, with a quick, pounding beat, was interrupted momentarily by a recorded message, praising the employees for being there to take care of their health, giving a short message about getting good nutrition and sleep, and ending with the phrase 'better health…' which the employees responded to with 'better wealth!' It was an automatic response, not emphatic, but also not with eye-rolling and a groan. The way they answered immediately, in unison, reminded Zachary of some of the church services that he'd been forced to attend growing up, living with foster families who were devout, or who dragged him along for a funeral or Easter Mass. Never Christmas, because he was usually at Bonnie Brown or the hospital Christmas Eve. He couldn't face Christmas Eve with a family since the fire that had devastated his life, and he certainly couldn't have gone to a service with lighted candles.

But the services that had required certain responses from the congregation always fascinated him. He tried to predict when they were going to prompt a response and to memorize the appropriate replies. He'd never had any particularly spiritual feelings about the practice, he just found it immensely satisfying to be part of a group and to know what response was expected of him. There were few other times when his behavior was explicitly scripted so that he knew exactly what he was supposed to say or do. He always felt like he was doing the wrong thing and was going to be caught and punished for it. Probably because all too often, that was the case.

The music started up again, and Zachary just watched the employees for a few minutes, their legs and arms moving with the beat of the music, faces shining with sweat, focused and intent on what they were doing.

"It's Detective Zachary again," a voice observed.

He looked over to the nearest treadmill and saw Blair Bieberstein, in all his hyperactive squirrel glory, knobby knees showing under long shiny shorts.

"Oh. Mr. Bieberstein. Good to see you again."

"Are you here to work out? No, probably not, because you're not an employee and you're not dressed for a workout. You know that the rest of us have to put in workout time every day? They want to keep us healthy and happy." He kept up a brisk walk on the treadmill, not quite running, but definitely hustling.

"Yes, I heard about that. How do you feel about being forced to work out?"

"It's good. It shows that the company cares about us and our health.

They don't want us to just have a heart attack or stroke one day. They're trying to keep everyone in good shape. Healthy employees mean a healthy bottom line."

"Better health…"

"Better wealth," Bieberstein chimed in, and grinned. "You got it. And I'm all for better wealth, aren't you?"

"I am…" Zachary said slowly, "but I wouldn't want to give up my life-style for it. Working the crazy hours you guys are… I don't think I could ever do that."

"You give up some time on the front end so that you can enjoy yourself more later in life." Bieberstein shrugged. "Either way, you want to be healthy to enjoy it, right?"

Zachary looked at a few of the other employees working out, then returned his eyes to Bieberstein. "But are you?" he asked. "You look… exhausted. Pale like you haven't seen the sun in a month, and your eyes are red and have bags under them. I know you're competing for the permanent positions but are you sure you're not pushing it a little too hard?"

"Best shape I've ever been in," Bieberstein declared. "Never did any sports or exercise before. Exercise is better than sleep. Refreshes your brain and gets it revved back up again when you start to get tired."

"Do you take anything to help you stay awake? Caffeine? Energy drinks?"

"Sure. Everybody around here does."

"Did Lauren?"

"As much as anyone else, yeah. Everybody has to do something to stay awake. It's like being in the army. When they had to stay awake for long periods of time and still be alert, then they gave them amphetamines. Tried out different drugs on them to see what worked best. Where do you think meth came from?"

"Meth?"

"It was developed by the army to help keep troops alert and focused when they couldn't sleep. That's what it's for."

"You use meth?"

Bieberstein gave him a grin. "I didn't say that."

"Would you consider it?"

"Maybe. Under the right circumstances. Using it the right way, like a prescription. Why shouldn't we use every tool at our disposal?"

"Because it's illegal and dangerous."

Bieberstein kept up his brisk pace. "Did you find everything you were looking for?"

"I wondered… everyone seems to act like this is a pretty good place to work. You talk about them in positive ways. You seem to like your coworkers alright. Here's this company that has a great health care program… but what about the other side of the coin?"

"The seamy underbelly?" Bieberstein asked in a joking voice.

"Well… *is* it the perfect place to work? Would you recommend it to all of your friends? What do you really think of it?"

Bieberstein walked, his feet pounding in time with the music. He shook his head. "It's no utopia," he admitted. "But when you apply to work at a place like this, you've got to know that. The high finance community is known for being pretty harsh. It would be like applying to be an air traffic controller and thinking it wouldn't be stressful. Or like training to be a doctor and thinking that you could just keep whatever office hours you felt like, right from the start. You know what you're getting into."

"So tell me a little about that side of it," Zachary suggested, finding a spot where he could lean against the wall to talk to Bieberstein, and be out of the way of other employees coming and going.

Bieberstein considered, looking up at the ceiling, but miraculously not losing his stride. "Where to start… there's a lot of egos here. Everybody thinks they're the best. You got managers and other bosses who think that you only work for them, and if you don't get something done on their arbitrary schedule, look out. I don't think I've ever been anywhere that I've been cussed out so much. I've had grown men totally lose control and full-out scream at me, red-faced, trying to shame me in front of everybody else. Just because of some arbitrary deadline, or because they didn't like my conclusion—even though it was right."

"Yikes. I think that would be it for me. I'd be out the door."

"I'm a pretty hard guy to offend. I look at idiots like that and think, 'what a schmuck,' and then go on and do my own thing. But the girls, and some of the other interns, I've seen them break down. Tears, talking about quitting, harming themselves, everything. I hate seeing girls cry, I really do."

Zachary nodded. It was something he couldn't bear either. He never knew what to do. And he had a lot of women cry around him. Not because he was nasty to them, but because they came to him with their stories of heartbreak and loss, asking for his help when they were at their most vulnerable. Like Barbara, crying while she told him about finding Lauren dead in the bathtub.

"Sometimes, I think they actually do it on purpose. Like they want to break us down before they build us up. Like they're seriously trying to hurt us as much as possible. Completely destroy everyone's egos, and then you have something to work with. Once you've reduced someone to mush, then you can sculpt them into what you want."

Zachary frowned, thinking about it. Knowing Gordon as he did, he couldn't imagine him approving of anything like that going on in his company. Did he know about it? He had always been calm around Zachary, even with the problems that he and Bridget had, and Gordon had always been the first to give a compliment or register approval. He had welcomed Zachary at Chase Gold, hadn't he? He wouldn't have done such a thing if he thought that Zachary might discover abusive behavior toward employees.

"I'm used to people not liking me," Bieberstein said conversationally. "I get on people's nerves. But you know, I don't care. I would rather be in a place like this, where they can use my talents and I can spend my days playing with numbers than in any other place where they are nice but expect good social behavior in return. I can't be bothered."

Zachary nodded, chuckling a little. Bieberstein was nothing, if not unfiltered. He would always be someone who would attract criticism for his hyperactive, in-your-face communication style.

"And then there's the hazing."

"Oh? What kind of hazing?"

"Same kind of thing that goes on in any closed society," Bieberstein said with a shrug. He hit a button on the treadmill console to check his progress, and kept going. "They want you to earn your position. You'll be loyal to the society if you had to work to get into it. And if you know things about other people and they know things about you. Shared secrets, ordeals, proving yourself. You know."

"I know what hazing is… but it isn't usually something you see in corporate culture. Usually military or college. I don't think I've ever heard of it in a company like this."

"It's the same thing, though."

"So you went through hazing? What did you have to do?"

"Lots of drinking involved. Running messages from one place to another. Doing stupid, dangerous stuff just because it's on a list of things to do. Like a scavenger hunt."

"What kind of dangerous stuff?"

Bieberstein looked sideways at him. "That's the kind of stuff that you promise never to tell. You have to keep other people's secrets, and they have to keep yours. You show that you're willing to go above and beyond what would be considered reasonable. You make them believe that your soul is theirs and you would never tell."

"So you're not going to give me an example?"

"You don't need an example. You said you know what hazing is. So you already know the kinds of things I'm talking about."

"And was this... who was in charge of this hazing? Do the owners know about it? Is it just one department or the whole company? Does everyone go through this? Or just the interns?"

"Ah." Bieberstein raised one finger. "I neglected to say, there were masks, hoods, and blindfolds involved. So you couldn't identify who was there and who wasn't. You don't know who you can talk to, because they might be watching you, reporting on your activities."

Zachary let out his breath. Hazing? Was Bieberstein pulling his leg, or was it the truth? Had he been pranked by some of his fellow interns? Did the bullying come from his direct manager or someone else? Bieberstein's expression was open and unconcerned, untroubled by what had happened or by the fact that he had revealed so much to Zachary.

The treadmill gave a beep, and Bieberstein leaned on the handrails as he read the display, relaxing his posture so that Zachary saw how exhausted he was. He might comply with the company policies and declare that the exercise gave him the energy and clear mind that he needed for his work, but he didn't look alert and refreshed after his powerwalk. He looked like he was ready to pass out.

Bieberstein punched a few buttons on the console and, as it started to slow, held on to the bars and let out a deep sigh. Then suddenly he clenched his hands tightly around the bars and let out an animal-like howl. Zachary took a step away from him, startled and confused. Bieberstein's feet stopped moving on the treadmill, and that meant that the treadmill, still moving, pulled the lower part of his body toward the end of the treadmill while his upper body remained anchored by his clenched hands to the handrails.

Zachary couldn't do anything, had no idea what was going on and what

Bieberstein was trying to do. Was this some kind of ritual? A bizarre dismount?

For a moment, Bieberstein's body was suspended over the treadmill, supported by his hands, while his feet dragged to the end of the treadmill, and then his arms sagged and he fell face-down onto the treadmill.

CHAPTER THIRTEEN

Zachary tried to pull Bieberstein off of the treadmill when his brain processed the fact that Bieber had passed out, but his body was slow, his feet not responding to his brain's directive to jump in and help. In the time it took for him to get into a position where he could grab Bieberstein and try to pull him off of the machinery, Bieber had been pulled to the side and got a nasty gash on his head as it collided more than once with the side of the treadmill. He hadn't been wearing the emergency shut-off clip that would automatically stop the treadmill as soon as he fell, so the machine continued to run through its cool-down routine.

Zachary managed to grab one of Bieberstein's elbows and jerk him off of the running treadmill. It was a good thing that Bieberstein was a small man. Zachary had a hard time wrenching the dead weight off of the machine.

There were shouts and exclamations around him, people gasping and asking what had happened. Zachary tried to move Bieberstein into a natural position on his back so that he could be examined. He expected Bieberstein's eyes to open, confused by his momentary loss of consciousness, but instead Bieberstein's body was rigid and started to shake wildly while Zachary tried to get him into position. A full-on tonic-clonic seizure.

"Someone should call an ambulance," Zachary said, releasing his grip on Bieberstein and hoping that he wouldn't hit his head on anything else while in the midst of the seizure. Someone reached over and shut off the treadmill so that it wouldn't present a further hazard. People gathered around, talking and making suggestions. One man brought over a small suitcase and opened it up, and Zachary saw the small v-fib machine that Bev had mentioned.

"I don't think you need that," Zachary said. "It's a seizure, not a heart attack."

"You don't know that. Are you a doctor?"

"Uh… no."

"I've been trained on this thing. It will tell us if he needs to be shocked or not. We just have to stick the pads on him."

"But he's…" Zachary motioned to Bieberstein, at a loss for words. How exactly were they going to do anything while he was in the midst of the seizure?

The other man moved in and attempted to pull Bieberstein's shirt up over his head, which did not work with him thrashing around, and Zachary wasn't about to try to hold his arms still to assist with the operation.

"We need scissors," the other man said, "so that we can cut his shirt off. I need to be able to put the sticky pads on his skin."

"You're not getting close to him with scissors while he's having a seizure," Zachary warned, prepared to defend his position. He might not be a doctor or have much experience with seizures, but he knew the recommended approach—leave the person alone other than trying to make sure he couldn't hurt himself while seizing. No forcing a spoon into his mouth or using sharp implements to cut off his shirt.

There were noises of agreement from the rest of the employees gathering around. The man looked angry.

"I'm the one who's been trained in first aid. How many of the rest of you have been certified?"

A number of them raised their hands, taking a bit of the wind out of his sails.

"Has someone called 9-1-1?" Zachary asked, looking around at them. Some of them had their phones out to video the episode or were tapping away, maybe tweeting the moment, but not one had his phone to his ear talking to an emergency dispatcher. Zachary pointed at a woman with a bright blue halter top. "You. Please call 9-1-1."

She rolled her eyes, looking put out.

"It's just Bieberstein," one of the onlookers joked. There was a ripple of laughter, but then the disapproval that was leveled at the jokester made everyone sober up.

The woman tapped on her phone and held it up to her ear. Zachary turned his attention back to Bieberstein and left her to the call, watching for any sign that the seizure was slackening. His head wound was bleeding, the movement of his seizure spreading the blood around grotesquely, making it look much worse than it was. Zachary had seen enough childhood mishaps to know that scalp wounds always bled profusely. He wasn't going to be able to press anything over the wound until the seizure stopped.

"They're on their way," the woman informed Zachary. "They shouldn't be too long. We're pretty close to the fire station."

Every second that ticked past seemed to take forever. By the time the paramedics got there, the seizure had stopped and Zachary was pressing a towel over Bieberstein's head wound. Once the seizure stopped, he could see that there was something wrong with Bieberstein's arm too. It was bent where it shouldn't be bent, and while there was no bone sticking out through the skin, it was pretty obvious that it was broken. Zachary breathed deeply, trying to slow the wild beating of his heart. He was feeling nauseated, regretting that he'd just eaten. Seizures, blood, and broken bones were not exactly his forte. He preferred to stay out of the way and let other people step in when something like that happened, but he wasn't about to let the determined first aider bully his way in and end up cutting something other than Bieberstein's shirt with a pair of scissors.

Bieberstein's breathing was even and when Zachary had felt ineptly for a pulse, he'd been able to feel the beats of Bieberstein's heart racing away under his fingertips. No need for CPR or the v-fib machine.

"Make some room," one of the paramedics advised, motioning the crowd back. "Who here saw what happened?"

Zachary made a motion with his free hand. "I was talking to him."

"Great, why don't you walk us through it?"

Zachary did the best he could to describe each movement, not wanting to miss anything that might require special treatment. The paramedics could see that Bieberstein was bleeding, had at least one broken bone, and was no longer seizing. What else they could tell on a quick visual examination, Zachary wasn't sure. He moved out of the way so that one of the paramedics could get in to sneak a look under the towel. He grunted and nodded, and the two of them worked through an examination of Bieberstein.

"Anyone know if he has epilepsy?"

There were head shakes from the crowd. No one offered anything. The paramedics looked for a medical bracelet or necklace, but didn't find anything. One of them took a few long seconds to examine Bieberstein's arms, and Zachary realized after a delay that they were checking for needle marks.

"Has he taken any drugs? Does anyone know if he takes anything?"

More head shakes. Zachary spoke in a low voice, not wanting to spread Bieberstein's business to all of the spectators.

"Caffeine for sure. He was acting really jacked up earlier. I don't know if he was on anything, or just hyperactive. He's probably short on sleep, I don't know if he might have taken anything else... he was talking about meth, but he didn't say that he took any, he was just saying... that it was intended for mental alertness, and wasn't dangerous if it was taken like a prescription, like they would use for soldiers..."

"Then it could be an overdose. We'd better get him in and have his blood levels checked. We'll need the heart monitor," the man told his partner, who nodded agreement.

"I don't know that he *did* take anything," Zachary warned, not wanting to mislead them. "I'm just saying we were talking about it..."

"That's good enough for me. We'll take him in. Does someone here want to come along? Know who to contact in case of an emergency?"

No one volunteered. The paramedic looked at Zachary.

"I just met him today," Zachary said, his face heating. "This was only our second conversation."

"Fair enough. We'll see if he has an ICE contact on his phone." The paramedics looked around. Someone found a phone on the floor beside the treadmill and handed it over to them. There was a crack in the screen, but it still appeared to be operable. The paramedic did a couple of clicks and swipes to bring up Bieberstein's emergency ID screen. "Okay, thanks for your help. We'd better get him in to get checked out."

Zachary had been hoping that Bieberstein would wake up before the paramedics took him away, just to reassure him that he was going to be okay, and that he hadn't just had a seizure and slipped into a coma, from which he would never awake.

Everybody watched the paramedics get Bieberstein onto a gurney and remove him from the gym, murmuring quietly to each other. No one jumped immediately back into their workouts. One of the health and welfare commercials played, and while a couple of people said 'better wealth' at the appropriate juncture, no one seemed to have much enthusiasm for it.

———

When Zachary checked the time on his own phone, he saw that more than an hour had elapsed since he had seen Bev, so hopefully she'd had enough time to get the timesheets for the rest of the interns printed off for him. He went back to the human resources floor and knocked, but that didn't raise any response. He called the main switchboard number again, and got the receptionist to put him through to Bev. Her line rang a number of times before going to voicemail.

He muttered to himself and left her a message. But he didn't have any appetite for standing there in the elevator lobby waiting for her to pick up his message and let him in. She knew when he was supposed to be getting back, and she should have been ready for his call. If she had decided to go off for a late lunch while he hung around waiting for the information that he had requested…

Zachary went back up to the main reception desk. The receptionist gave him a wary look. Zachary did his best to paste a friendly smile on his face.

"Hi. I'm trying to track down Bev in human resources. She doesn't seem to be answering her phone. She was expecting me."

"You'll have to wait until she can get back to you. I can't do anything from here to make her answer her phone. I know that we did have a medical emergency, and she's probably dealing with getting in contact with family members or providing medical records. You'll just have to wait."

"I know there was a medical emergency, I was there when it happened—"

"Then you know that I'm not just trying to put you off. You'll have to wait until it's been dealt with." Her tone was stern, brooking no argument, and Zachary couldn't argue that it was unreasonable to make him wait while they dealt with Bieberstein's care and his family.

He went over to the reception chair he had waited in that morning and sat down once more.

CHAPTER FOURTEEN

Zachary decided it was a good time for him to check on his email messages and go over the notes he had made so far in his notebook. There were a few inquiries in his email that would need to be followed up on. There were always more cases to look into and work to be done. He immersed himself in the notes he had been making about Drake, Chase, Gould and Lauren's death.

Was he getting distracted by the work environment at Chase Gold? Was it really relevant to his investigation?

If Lauren had simply slipped and hit her head in the tub, then it had nothing to do with the company. Was it even remotely likely that one of the other interns had gone to her apartment and killed her because they were fighting over the same permanent position? He felt their desperation to get one of those coveted spots, to beat each other out to get the one remaining opening. Was it a matter of life and death for them? Would they really go so far as to harm the other competitors in order to get it?

Of course, with Bieberstein's accident, maybe they were back to two openings again. A seizure wasn't usually fatal, he knew, and even though Bieberstein hadn't woken up before the ambulance had taken him to the hospital, he would probably wake up with only the concerns of his broken arm and lacerated scalp to worry about, and everything else would go back to normal. Unless the management decided that, like a woman who might get pregnant at any moment, someone who had seizures was too much of a risk for the company to hire. They wouldn't have to fire him for his medical disability. They wouldn't have to put him on leave. He was only there in a temporary position, so all they had to do was to make the decision not to hire him; he was too much of a risk.

That would be good luck for the other interns.

But was it just luck? Was it possible that someone had drugged him or done something to cause the seizure?

Who would kill off all of the competition for a permanent job opening? There were jobs to be had at other companies. And no one could just keep eliminating the other interns in the competition without making everybody suspicious. Two of the interns had now fallen victim to accidents. Any more, and people would start to get suspicious. Two could just be bad luck. Three would arouse suspicions.

So who was the next in line for those positions? If two positions had now opened up, then the next two remaining interns could get in. He couldn't picture Mandy Pryor as a murderer. He knew that you couldn't tell by looking at a person whether or not they had what it took to kill some-one. Or multiple someones. The serial killers were always charming, easy to make friends with, seemingly harmless.

He resisted the urge to think of Teddy Archuro. Of Pat's words that he would never do anything. *He's been around for a long time. He's harmless.*

But Archuro hadn't been safe. He'd been around for years and he had been killing for years, managing to stay below the radar. Everyone thought him charming, a perfectly nice guy. Entirely trustworthy.

Zachary felt himself sliding back into darkness. Seeing Archuro looming over him. Feeling the drugs take hold of him so that he couldn't fight back. Teddy Archuro's greedy eyes and crooning voice as he began his sadistic ritu-als, telling Zachary what he was going to do, wielding his weapons while Zachary lay there lifeless, but conscious, unable to even protest.

"Zachary?"

He heard the voice, but couldn't believe that it was real. How had he slid from flashing back to the assault by Teddy to hearing Bridget's voice? What did *she* have to do with the memory? There was no connection other than that Bridget too had been abducted. They had both had to face oppo-nents who had been intent on killing them.

"Zachary!"

He jolted at the second call, looking up from his notebook to see Bridget standing there staring at him. One hand was over her lower abdomen. He couldn't tell by looking at her that she was pregnant, but for some reason her unconscious reaction to seeing him was to cover the baby bump, to hide her pregnancy from him or protect her baby from his eyes.

She looked better than she had the last time he had seen her. She had been so nauseated that she had looked like she was on chemo again. Her color was back. The shape of her body had not yet changed and her slim form still fit into the stylish professional dress she wore. She didn't look happy to see him there, but when was the last time she had been happy to see him?

Other than when he had rescued her from certain death, of course.

"What are you doing here?" Bridget demanded.

"Oh… uh… Bridget."

She looked around, as if expecting someone to jump in and explain to her what her ex-husband was doing sitting there in the lobby of her current partner's company. Or was she looking for an audience? Or making sure that there were no witnesses?

There was no one else sitting in the waiting area. Only the receptionist looking up from her work to see what was going on.

"I asked you what you're doing here! I can't believe this. You said that you would stop. You said that you wouldn't track me, wouldn't show up in the places I go to. First I see you at the gas station, and now here! At Gordon's work! And don't try telling me you're interviewing for a job or something stupid like that. I'm going to call the police and report you for stalking. This is just too much!"

She pulled out her phone and tapped the screen, glaring at him, just daring him to fight back. Zachary supposed she expected him to leave, to run away from Gordon's office and never return. But he had a legitimate reason to be there. There was no restraining order against him, so Bridget couldn't claim that he was breaking the law by being there. She would just have to accept that he had the right to live in the same town as she did and to occasionally bump into her around town.

So he just looked at her, waiting for her to make the next move. Bridget put her phone to her ear, looking at him, her expression pinched and sour. Zachary leaned back in his chair, trying to look comfortable and unmoved by her threats. He looked back down at his notebook, trying to pick up his earlier thread.

Not Mandy. Statistically speaking, serial killers were hardly ever women.

Though poisoners were more often women than men. Maybe she hadn't meant to kill. Maybe she only intended to disable the competition. Maybe Lauren was only supposed to sleep too long, riling her bosses by not getting back to the office when she was due. And Bieberstein hadn't died. It might be dangerous for him to have a seizure while walking on a treadmill, but no one could have foreseen that that was where he would be when the attack hit him. Or maybe they could. Maybe he was on that treadmill every day at the same time. People like Bieberstein often had strict routines, so it wasn't a stretch that he would have insisted on doing the same workout at the same time every day.

Maybe neither one was intended to die, but only to be removed from the running for the permanent positions.

And what about the other interns? If it were one of them, would Zachary be able to figure out which? They all had the same motive. They all had opportunity, working closely together in the same office. He hadn't seen their desks, but he knew from experience that students and interns were likely all jammed like cattle into small cubicles. They would have access to each other's water bottles. Someone took a run to the restroom or the coffee machine, and their bottle could be spiked. Or one intern could bring coffee to the others, spiking one of them in the kitchen. Or he could be poisoning all of them by degrees, and Lauren and Bieberstein were merely the first to succumb, due to lower body weight or faster metabolism.

What could they have been poisoned with? A sedative? Something known to cause seizures? Was it intended to kill or only to make the other interns less productive and competent?

"Gordon?"

Zachary looked up from his notepad as Bridget's call apparently connected. Her face was flushed. She did not appreciate the fact that Zachary was unconcerned by her phone call.

"Zachary is here! He's in the reception area."

She listened to his response, her mouth tightening and going white around the edges. She was still staring daggers at Zachary, angry that he was there in her domain and furious that he wasn't cowed by her appearance. If he were there just to spot her or to stalk Gordon, then he would have been worried by her discovering him there. He would have protested and given excuses and run away. But for once Zachary didn't feel the need to justify himself.

"He can't do that. He's not supposed to be here. He's not supposed to be anywhere around me. You need to get rid of him."

Zachary couldn't hear Gordon's responses, but he could imagine them. Reassuring her that Zachary wasn't there because of anything to do with Bridget. That he wasn't there because he was harassing Gordon. He wasn't there trying to talk Gordon into stepping aside and giving Zachary the chance to woo Bridget once more.

Zachary would have loved that. It wasn't going to happen, of course, but if Gordon had been frightened off by Bridget getting pregnant, if he were the type who didn't want to be responsible for a child, Zachary would have been only too happy to step back in and take care of Bridget and her child. It didn't matter to him that the baby wasn't his. He would go back to her in a second.

Bridget pulled the phone away from her ear and turned it off, her thumb tightening convulsively over the hardware button. She didn't tell Zachary what Gordon had said to her. She didn't walk away or try again to bully him into leaving. She just stood there looking at him.

CHAPTER FIFTEEN

Gordon walked into the reception area. He gave Bridget a squeeze around the shoulders. "Hello, my dear. Why don't we all go to my office where we can have this discussion privately?"

"I don't care who hears it," Bridget snapped.

When Zachary and Bridget had been together, Bridget had always kept her fights private, or confined to certain close friends. She dropped caustic comments to Zachary with a vicious smile he came to dread, but kept anything further private. But once they had separated, the gloves came off. The more witnesses to her disparagement, the better.

"This is my office. A certain level of decorum would be appreciated," Gordon told her.

Bridget didn't argue with that. Gordon twitched his head at Zachary to follow, and they all took the short walk down the corridor to Gordon's large, bright, corner office. He ushered them in and shut the door.

Rather than sitting behind his desk with the two of them standing or sitting in front of it, Gordon motioned to a small grouping of chairs and a couch on the opposite end of his office. He sat down with Bridget on the couch and Zachary sank down into an upholstered chair.

"He is not allowed to be here," Bridget insisted.

"As I said, he is here with my permission. He is investigating the death

517

of a young woman who worked here as an intern." Gordon's face was appropriately sober.

"You hired him?"

"No, I did not. But I do not object to him looking into it. We have nothing to hide. Let him reassure her family and friends that there was nothing they could have done to prevent it and that it was, in fact, just a tragic accident."

"What else would it be?" Bridget looked at Zachary, sneering, "You think it was murder?"

"Bridget," Gordon reprimanded gently. "Who did you go to when you thought there was something suspicious about Robin's death?"

She pressed her lips together as if she didn't want to remember a moment of weakness.

"And who did I go to when you disappeared?" Gordon went on. "Zachary is a good investigator. I wasn't expecting you to come by today or for him to be in the lobby, or I would have called to warn you ahead of time. I'm sorry for any distress this has caused you."

Bridget was silent.

"Why were you sitting in the lobby?" Gordon asked Zachary curiously. "You weren't waiting to see me, were you?"

"No. I'm still waiting for those reports from human resources. Bev said it would take an hour to get them together, but now she's not available, so I'm just waiting for her to get everything sorted out."

"Bev is 'not available'?"

Zachary shrugged. "There was an accident in the gym over the lunch hour. I'm told that she's dealing with the hospital or his family on that, which of course takes precedence over handing over the reports to me."

"An accident. I'm afraid I've been out of pocket. What accident?"

"Blair Bieberstein. He had a seizure while working out on the treadmill. Fell on the machine while it was still running, cut open his scalp and broke his arm."

"Good heavens. Is he okay?"

"He didn't wake up before the paramedics took him away, so I don't know any more than that. I imagine Bev will be able to give you an update."

"Just a moment." Gordon walked over to his desk and hit a button on the phone. He gave instructions to his assistant to put Bev straight through if she happened to call, then returned to the couch to sit down by Bridget.

He patted her knee absently, frowning. "You were there?" he asked Zachary.

"Yes. I was talking to him when he went down."

Gordon shook his head. "What a bizarre accident. I wasn't aware that he had a seizure disorder."

Zachary shrugged. "It didn't come up in our conversation," he said lightly. "I got the impression from talking to him that he is... neurodiverse... and people who are wired differently are more likely to have seizure disorders. But I don't know anything about his health. Bev said that your company does employee physicals before hiring anyone permanently, but not the temporary positions like interns. So there wouldn't have been any reason for it to come up, unless he happened to talk to someone about it."

"Well, it sounds like that is a policy that needs to be revisited. I will bring it up, once we know how Blair is doing."

"If he does have a seizure disorder, would that stop you from hiring him for the full-time position?"

"Oh, no. If he has the skills that we need, an occasional health problem like epilepsy shouldn't come into it."

Zachary would withhold judgment on that. While Gordon seemed as open and generous as ever, Zachary was beginning to have some concerns about Drake, Chase, Gould, and he doubted that Gordon could be unaware of all of the bullying, hazing, or overtime issues.

"If you don't have anything you want to discuss with me, I guess I'll let you go back to waiting for Bev," Gordon told Zachary. "Or if that's the only thing you're waiting for, she could certainly email them to you when she gets back to her office. You don't need to wait around for them."

"I'll give it a bit longer." Zachary stood up. "And there may be issues that I need to pursue after today..."

"Really? Well, whatever you need, of course. Just let me know. Do you have my cell number?"

"No."

Gordon got up to get a business card from his desk for Zachary. He clapped Zachary on the shoulder in a friendly goodbye.

"Zachary *is* investigating this matter," he told Bridget in a calm, detached voice. "I am sorry that you ran into each other accidentally, but I'm sure it won't be an ongoing problem. You wanted to see me, my dear?"

Bridget wasn't quite willing to let it go at that. "You know what he's going to do, don't you? He's going to dig up anything he can that throws you or your company in a bad light, and then he's going to publicize it far and wide. He's trying to destroy the company you've built, all out of petty jealousy."

Gordon spread his hands wide. "I have nothing to hide. I am not the least bit concerned about what he might find in the course of the investigation."

CHAPTER SIXTEEN

Zachary eventually left the building without the additional timesheets for the interns. He didn't know where Bev had disappeared to, but he eventually got tired of waiting and left her a message before heading home. It had been an interesting day and he needed to ponder on what he had heard before he was sure what to think of it.

Once settled at home, he called Heather, his older sister. They had only recently been reunited and he was still building a relationship with her. It was a strange feeling, knowing someone and yet not knowing them. He knew her and her personality from when he was little, before the family was split up, but he hadn't been in contact with her during all of the intervening decades, and she had grown up and had experiences that had changed her. Every now and then, he caught a glimpse of the old Heather, like the sun coming out from behind the clouds. But then the moment would pass, and he'd be looking at a stranger again.

But he was trying, and so was she.

"Hi, Zachary."

"Hi. How's it going?" He forced himself to start with an inquiry about her health and some small talk, rather than launching directly into the reason he had called. She wasn't just some contractor he had hired; she was his sister, and he needed to take the time.

"Really good. When am I going to see you again?"

"Uh… I don't know right now. We'll have to set something up."

"Yeah. I'd really like to see you again."

"Maybe… next weekend, if I'm not too busy with this case?"

"You got a big new case?"

"Well… I don't know whether it's going anywhere, but it will take some time before I know. Maybe something, maybe nothing."

"What kind of case?"

"Accidental death."

"An insurance case? Are you doing accident reconstruction?"

"No. Someone who thinks… maybe it wasn't so accidental."

"Hmm. One of those. What do you think?"

"Too early to tell."

"Okay." She obviously recognized that he wasn't going to give her any details. It was still confidential; he didn't want word of the investigation getting out to Lauren's family or the media. It needed to stay under wraps until he had a better idea of what he was dealing with. "So what else is going on in your life?" she inquired. "Anything interesting?"

He thought fleetingly of Bridget and her pregnancy and running into her at Gordon's office. And Gordon's connection with his current case. So far, he hadn't told anyone else about those details. Other than Kenzie. He had told Kenzie about Bridget's pregnancy the day they had broken up. He'd been so shocked with the news that he'd had to tell someone.

"Well, I've had a few things come into my inbox, and I was wondering whether you wanted to help with some skip traces."

"Sure!" Heather's voice was warm and eager. Zachary had been training her on some of the basic detecting skills he had learned over the years, and she was enjoying it. She hadn't had a hobby or a job in all of the time that she'd been married, and she needed something to keep herself occupied now that she was an empty-nester and was recovering from events that had kept her a near-recluse for so many years.

"Great. I'll send you some names and details, and you can see what you can find. That would be a real help. Keep track of your time and bill me."

"It really doesn't seem like I should get paid for it. I'm just playing at being a detective."

"You're not playing, you're doing actual detective work. So you should get paid for it. If you were working for any of my competitors, you'd get paid for it. I don't want you leaving me to go to someone who gives you a better deal."

Heather laughed. Zachary knew she wouldn't even consider it. But maybe in a few years, she'd have the confidence to go somewhere else. And if she did, that was good for her. He'd be happy. Until then, he was happy to use her for some of his overflow work. He could take on more than he could otherwise, and help her out while he was at it. A win-win.

"Well, feel free to shoot them my way. I'll see what I can track down."

Zachary nodded to himself. That would clear out some of the work in his inbox. "That's a big help to me. Let me know if you need any help with getting your license, right?"

"I will. So far, it's just paperwork. I keep worrying someone is going to show up at my door and ask me who I think I'm kidding. Me, a private investigator? Whoever would have thought?"

"You'll make a good investigator. You relate well to people. You're interested in solving puzzles. That's all you need. It isn't like on TV, you don't need to carry a gun and drink hard and challenge organized crime figures. A lot of it is just computer work. Knowing where to look for the information you need."

"I suppose. Have you talked to Tyrrell lately?"

"Uh… no. It's been a little bit. I'll have to get to him soon. Maybe we should invite him for next weekend."

"That would be nice."

"I could bring some doughnuts?"

"Sure. Of course."

Zachary wasn't sure if she planned to bring Grant. Zachary and Tyrrell wouldn't be bringing along dates, but it would be rude to ask her to leave her husband at home. Especially when they were growing so much closer to each other than they had been in the previous years of their marriage. Grant was a nice guy and Zachary got along with him okay.

Maybe one day, he would have a girlfriend to bring to dinner with his siblings. And Tyrrell should be dating. Zachary couldn't see any reason for him to be holding back.

One day, maybe they would all have happy families.

He thought longingly of Bridget and her unborn child. The child that he had hoped for while they had been together. And of Kenzie, giving up on him. It wasn't her fault. He had driven her away. He had pushed her until she had finally given in.

But someday. Maybe.

———

He had another call to make, and he knew it wouldn't go as well as the call with Heather. He kept putting it off, telling himself that he had other things he had to get done before that. But he knew that he was just procrastinating because he didn't like the job at hand.

Eventually, he forced himself to stop puttering around with less important tasks and called Kenzie's number. One of the only numbers that he knew without looking it up or using his phone directory.

It rang a few times, and he wondered if she was just going to let it go to voicemail. She probably didn't want to talk to him. Not now, when she was out of his life. He wasn't sure if he should leave her a voicemail. Probably, if he ever wanted to get an answer. Or send her an email, but that might just end up in her spam folder.

"Zachary." Kenzie sighed.

"Uh, hi. I'm sorry to bother you, but—"

"I'll call you when I have anything to tell you. I do know your number. And if I didn't, it's on the form."

"No, it wasn't about that. I know you'll get me the information when it's released. This is completely unrelated, and you're the only one I could think of to call. I don't really know any medical doctors…"

"Aside from the ones who prescribe you your meds?"

Zachary winced at her sarcastic tone. "Uh… right, I guess so. But I don't know if they would have any insight into this…"

"Well, you've got me on the phone, so you might as well ask. What is it?"

"I had a request come in from a doctor who does organ transplants. He wants someone to investigate potential recipients. Weed out the ones who are a bad risk for transplants. You know, alcoholics who are waiting for a liver transplant. People who engage in high-risk sports. Things like that."

She was silent. Zachary gave her some time to think about it before prompting her. "Kenzie?"

"Why would you ask me about that?"

"Uh… I don't know. I just figured that being with the Medical Examiner's office, you would have some insight into things like organ transplant and risk management. Your education is recent, so you could maybe tell me what you think of the ethics of something like this that an older doctor wouldn't be up to speed on…"

There was another silence. At least she wasn't railing on him like Bridget would if he asked her something that was out of line, but because she said nothing, Zachary wasn't sure what the problem was or how to fix it.

"Is there someone else I should talk to?" he asked. "Maybe you know a doctor or professor who would be interested in talking to me?"

"I just want to know why you picked *me* to ask about it."

"Just… what I said. I figured you'd know something about it."

"Is this something to do with my dad?"

Zachary was floored. He sat there with his mouth open, trying to formulate an answer. Kenzie rarely even mentioned her parents. He knew that they were both still living, but she didn't spend much time with her family, even on holidays, and didn't like to talk about them. He didn't think that she'd had a bad childhood, but for some reason, she just wasn't in close contact with her parents.

"I don't know anything about your dad," he assured her. "Is he waiting for a transplant? I didn't know. I'm sorry if I hit a sore spot. I didn't have any idea."

"No, he's not waiting for a transplant," she snapped.

"Um… okay. So I'll find someone else to talk to about it. I really didn't mean to say anything to upset you. It was just a random inquiry. I don't want to accept the case if it is unethical."

"Yeah, why don't you ask someone else about it?" she agreed. "Call up one of your own doctors, or call the Medical Board and ask for the Ethics Committee."

"Okay. I'll do that. Thanks for pointing me in the right direction."

"Sure. Happy to help," she snapped. But she clearly did not want him to repeat the blunder. He was not to call her and ask her something like that again. He didn't know why transplants were a sore subject for her, but he was kicking himself for bringing it up.

"I'll let you know when Lauren Barclay's results are in," Kenzie said.

She hung up. Zachary gazed at the phone as he set it down on his computer desk. He didn't know who Kenzie's father was, but he was itching to do a little investigating to find out. Would it be crossing a line if it were just for his own information, so that he wouldn't make that same mistake again?

———

Zachary looked through the fridge for something edible. He needed to be able to show some increase in his weight, no matter how slight, before he saw his doctor again. He always lost weight before Christmas and then had to gain it back again over the following months. It was a familiar pattern. But the last Christmas had been particularly bad, and the trauma of his encounter with Teddy Archuro afterward had not helped matters. He didn't want Dr. Carter threatening to refer him to a feeding program, so he had to make eating a priority.

He had a few microwave dinners left, so he put one into the microwave and set the timer, then went and sat down in front of his computer again. Trying to keep his mind off of Kenzie's reaction to his call, he pulled out Lauren's timesheet. He ran his eyes down the columns of numbers, and frowned.

He was better at math than most other subjects, but he had to be reading the timesheets wrong, because they didn't make any sense. He got out a highlighter and read each column heading carefully. He highlighted alternating columns to make sure he was following the columns down properly and not drifting from one to the next without realizing it. He looked down the left-hand side, translating the numbers into dates. He looked at the heading at the top to make sure that it was Lauren's timesheet and not one for the receptionist or another member of the staff.

He had Lauren's computer, so he opened the lid, tapped in the password, and pulled up her email. He started with the day before she died, and worked his way backward, comparing the times of her emails against the hours that the timesheet said she had worked. It didn't take long to confirm that the timesheet was a complete fiction.

CHAPTER SEVENTEEN

Zachary didn't need to keep comparing the emails against the timesheets. He knew they were wrong, and likewise he knew that the timesheets he was going to get for the other interns were going to be wrong. But who was falsifying them? The interns themselves? Their supervisors? Human resources? He had no idea what level they were being changed at. The interns clearly worked long hours, far longer than could be expected of any employee, and probably longer than any labor laws would allow. So the company just changed the timesheets and then they were in compliance. The computer clearly showed that Lauren had been working all hours of the day, with only a few hours off here and there for sleep.

He started browsing through the subject lines and contents of the emails for more information. Anything that looked like it was a specific client project, he didn't open, or if he had opened it to preview the contents, he quickly closed it again and went on to the next one. He was looking instead for personal emails. Communications between Lauren and the other interns, or her supervisor, or the human resources department. He wasn't interested in the projects that she was working on, but on what else she had to say.

There were a couple of emails with her manager, Daniel Service, asking about time off for a family event or a break. But it soon became obvious that Daniel had no intention of giving her any time off for such frivolous activities. No one had died. She could fit her family events into her own personal time. Even if she didn't have any. Exactly when was she supposed to get together with them, at two o'clock in the morning?

She had communicated with human resources regarding a note from her doctor saying that she had been ill and needed time to rest and recover. The request was quashed. She was to get back to the office as soon as she was physically able and, in the meantime, to do what she could from home. If she wanted more time off than that, she was going to need to submit test results that showed that she had some disease or disability that required treatment.

Obviously, being exhausted or having the flu were not on the list of approved reasons for missing work.

Lauren wrote to Mandy about her problems, how tired she was and how run down her body was getting.

"I can't even run on the treadmill anymore. I'm so tired I can barely do anything but walk. I feel like I'm going to pass out any minute. I keep falling asleep in the middle of eating, because that's the only time that I stop and relax. How can anyone keep up this pace?"

Mandy had commiserated, but she was going through the same thing too, and however she was handling it, she didn't give Lauren any tips. Was she constantly taking caffeine? Another performance enhancer? Was she taking the opportunity to sleep at her desk when she was supposed to be working? Zachary had fallen asleep at his own computer numerous times. It really wasn't that hard to sleep sitting up if you were really tired. Lauren was trying not to fall asleep on the job, but maybe the answer was in falling asleep wherever and whenever she could. Could Mandy appear to be working, but hide the fact that she was sleeping covertly? Working so closely with the other interns, would she be able to keep it from them?

Zachary scribbled down a few thoughts and continued to look for more personal mails.

There was a desperation in Lauren's emails. She was obviously at the end of her rope, fighting illness constantly as her body's immune system was defeated by stress, too tired for the physical activity she was supposed to be logging, trying to remain alert and on top of her files and keep the information flowing to her supervisor and the other employees she was doing work for.

But the human resources department continued to block any attempts to take time off. She was expected to be there the hours she had agreed to, and unless her doctor could provide something other than that Lauren was tired or fighting a virus, there was no way for Lauren to get approval to take a few days off.

There were a few personal emails with her family or friends as she dashed off quick notes to them to let them know that she couldn't make it to some planned event or that she was okay, or promising she'd be able to spend more time with them once she had a permanent position.

"It's just too risky right now," she explained to her mother. "I'm pretty sure that it will be Blair and me, and then once I've got it, I can schedule some down time. But right now, if I slack off, they'll say that the other interns are more productive and I won't be able to get in."

That confirmed Zachary's suspicion that she and Bieberstein were lined up for the permanent positions. Had someone intentionally caused their accidents, hoping to clear one or both of those positions to allow him—or her—the chance at one of them? Was it really that important for them to get the jobs they were fighting for?

There were some general emails from the company. Newsletters and notices of policies, days that the building would be washing windows or carpets, and other routine administrative matters that every company sent out. Zachary skimmed through them, not expecting to find anything important there.

He opened one email that was apparently from the company's legal department. He wasn't sure at first why an investment banking firm would need a legal department, but it soon became apparent. There were updates on a number of pending matters; some files where clients had sued the company claiming that they had been given bad advice and lost money. And one that appeared to be the firm suing a former employee, Cody Russo. Zachary tracked the spare sentences across the screen. He frowned, trying to parse their meaning. The company was reporting their success in the lawsuit against Russo for breaking the confidentiality clauses of his contract, revealing the company's trade secrets and making defamatory statements about it.

He thought about what that might mean, and came to the conclusion that Russo might be a whistleblower. Someone who had tried to speak out about what the company was doing to its employees. Or maybe some other practice. And for being courageous and telling what he knew,

Drake, Chase, Gould had retaliated by suing him for talking about the company.

Could they do that? Could they sue him if what he said was true?

First, he would have to prove that it was true, and then he'd have to prove that he was not revealing confidential information about the company. If he really did have a confidentiality agreement that said he couldn't talk about the way things were run at Drake, Chase, Gould, that would be pretty difficult. Zachary wrote down the name of the defendant. He could order the court documents and see what it was that the employee had revealed, and then read through the company's defense.

But aside from whatever had happened, he got the feeling that the reason the legal department had circulated the memo about the lawsuit was not to reassure the employees that all was well and the company was defending itself. They had circulated the memo as a warning to anyone else who had thoughts about talking about the company. If you talk about Drake, Chase, Gould, you will be sued. Whether the allegations were true or not didn't really matter. What really mattered was that they could crush anyone who got in the way of the firm. It wasn't going to be David versus Goliath. It was a human being stomping on a bug or slapping a mosquito. The rest of the mosquitoes had better watch out.

When he went into the kitchen to get a glass of water, he could smell the remains of his dinner hanging in the air. He looked at the sink, but there were no dirty dishes in the sink. He took a peek under the sink and there was no recently-opened microwave tub discarded in the garbage. He stepped toward the living room and looked around to see if he had eaten his dinner in front of the TV or left it on his computer desk.

Nothing.

He ran the water and filled a glass of water, frowning. Finally, he reached over to the microwave and popped it open.

What a detective. There was a freezer meal, sitting in the middle of the microwave turntable. He touched it, and it was room temperature. Not cold from the freezer, not warm from heating it up. It had obviously been sitting there for long enough to either thaw out or cool off.

As he took it out and dumped it into the garbage, he tried to remember when he had heated it up. It didn't smell like it was going bad, so it had probably been in the past twenty-four hours. He had left dishes in the microwave until they started to go rotten before, so he knew what that smelled like.

He needed a new microwave. One that kept beeping to remind him that there was something in it so that he didn't forget to eat what he had heated up.

CHAPTER EIGHTEEN

Zachary was directed by a receptionist to the unit and room that Blair Bieberstein was in, and found his way through the maze of corridors at the hospital. It was never as easy as it seemed it should be, almost always resulting in some backtracking to correct wrong turns, even though he thought he knew the hospital fairly well.

He knocked lightly on the open door before entering to let Bieberstein and whoever else was in the same room know he was there.

The first bed was occupied by a large, red-faced man who looked at Zachary like he was invading his private space. Zachary nodded hurriedly and went past the privacy curtain to the second bed. Bieberstein was there, sitting cross-legged in the middle of the bed, staring up at the ceiling and snapping his fingers.

"Hey, how are you doing?" Zachary greeted.

Bieberstein didn't look at him.

"Bored to death. Ready to get out of here, but the doctor doesn't want me to go yet. Wants me to have a bunch of tests. Wants me to talk to their counselors and to get therapy or something. I don't need to do any of that. But I'm in the hospital and they're saying not to leave, so I may as well take advantage of it and get a bit of a break. Catch a few winks and get away from exercising for a day or two. Sounds good, huh?"

"I never feel exactly comfortable in the hospital. I'm almost always jonesing to get out before they want to release me."

Bieberstein nodded. "Yeah. Not exactly a restful resort vacation. Always noisy. People coming in and poking me and wanting to know my vitals and pain level and why I'm not sleeping and all of that. I'd sleep better at home. But once I'm home, I need to go back to the office, and that wouldn't be restful."

"Did you ever talk to Lauren about that? It sounds like she had been sick a lot lately and wanted to take some time off, but human resources said no, she couldn't get it off, even with a note from her doctor."

"Well, Lauren didn't have a seizure, a lacerated scalp, and three broken bones."

"Three?"

Bieberstein nodded. "Two in the arm, and one rib," he explained, tapping each in turn. He pulled his gaze away from the ceiling and looked at Zachary. "So what are you doing here? You got everything you needed from me, didn't you?"

"I guess so... but I wanted to see how you were doing. Make sure you were okay. Seeing you fall down and have a seizure like that was kind of a shock... I've been worrying about you."

Bieberstein laughed. "No need to worry about me! I'm just fine. Hunky-dory. Better than fine." He gave Zachary a slightly-loopy smile.

"What have they got you on? Painkillers?"

"Maybe a few. I should be sleeping. But I'm not. Been awake since they brought me in."

"You have? I can see why the nurses keep telling you that you should be asleep. Aren't you exhausted?"

"They think maybe I'm having a paradoxical reaction to the painkillers. Normally they are sedating, but in my case, they seem to be hyping me up."

"I hope you can get some sleep soon. That must be frustrating."

"Frustrating is having nothing to do. I asked Aaron if he would bring me my laptop from work, but so far, he hasn't shown up. Doing his own work, I suppose. But I need that computer. I need to be working on something."

"Do you have a seizure disorder? Have you had this happen before?"

"If I had a seizure disorder, they wouldn't be keeping me here saying that they just needed to do one more test. And one more after that. And another one after that."

"They're testing for epilepsy?"

"Epilepsy. Sleep disorder. Toxins in my blood. Maybe I've been licking lead paint or something. But I haven't."

"No. You do seem pretty hyped up. Are you taking meth?"

"They already tested me for that," Bieberstein said, waving the question away with his non-injured arm. "They would know if that was the problem. Of course, my caffeine levels are off the charts, but what do you expect with Drake, Chase, Gould?"

"So could that have caused your seizure?"

"Maybe. They haven't said they think so and keep looking into other things so it might be a contributing factor, but they seem to be looking for something else."

"You said that they were looking for toxins, so I assume they would know if you'd been poisoned...?"

"Poisoned?" Bieberstein shook his head at Zachary. "Why would I poison myself?"

"No, I don't mean you poisoned yourself, I mean... what if someone put something into your water bottle or coffee cup at work? What if someone wanted you out of the way so that they had a better chance at getting a permanent position? Or maybe someone had a grudge against you for some other reason. Have they checked for any poisons?"

"No," Bieberstein shook his head quickly, irritated. "They haven't checked for poisons. Other than... whatever else they test for in their blood tests. I don't know all of what they were looking for. What would cause seizures?"

"Whatever caused Lauren to fall down and not wake up. Or maybe something different, so that it wouldn't be too suspicious."

"You think that someone tried to kill both of us off? That would be a pretty bold move."

"You don't think it could be a possibility?"

Bieberstein considered it only briefly. He shook his head.

"Why don't you think so? The competition at Chase Gold seems to be pretty fierce."

"But I wasn't really competing against the others. I was... my talents are totally different than any of them. None of them could really outplay me."

"Exactly. So how else would they get you out of the way and open up the position for one of them?"

That made Bieberstein think for a little longer. He shrugged uncomfortably. "Someone trying to kill me at the office? That's just ridiculous. Pushing me in front of a speeding car, maybe, but spiking my drinks? I don't see how anyone could do that. If they hated me for being there, or hated the work that I was doing, thinking I was showing them up... it would have made more sense to have me just disappear. Or to start undercutting me by telling stories about me. Stories that aren't true," he was quick to tell Zachary. "But they could make up anything about lifestyle or what I thought of them, or that I was selling company secrets behind their backs. That would get me out of there a lot faster than poisoning."

"Not if you'd died right away. Or had been too injured to get back to work right away."

"Hmmph." Bieberstein still didn't seem to think it was likely. "What were the chances that I would have died from it? Whatever it is? I had a seizure... hit my head... woke up in the hospital. That didn't even come close to killing me."

"But it could have, with you being on the exercise equipment. If you'd been going faster... or maybe it was supposed to do something to your heart when you were in the middle of your exercise routine." Zachary thought of the man who had wanted to use the portable v-fib machine on Bieberstein, when he didn't have any reason to think that there was anything wrong with Bieberstein's heart. *Or had he?* Had he known what Bieberstein had been given? Was it supposed to stop his heart? Mimic a heart attack?

"Maybe you just didn't get enough," Zachary suggested. "Maybe there wasn't enough in your drink, or it's something that is supposed to work on you over time. Who knows? It could be something slower-acting, so they're hoping that you won't notice any symptoms, and then by the time you realize that you really are sick... it's too late." He thought about all of the health issues that Lauren had been complaining of. "Have you had anything lately? Flu symptoms? Headaches? Malaise?"

"You mean like being tired?" Bieberstein laughed. "Everybody is tired."

"But they could have been giving you something over time that took away your energy. If it's something they wouldn't normally test for..."

Robin Salter, Bridget's friend in the cancer ward, had been poisoned with an iron overdose by her own sister. And no one would ever have known if Zachary hadn't taken on the case at Bridget's request. They all would have laid Robin at rest, thinking that she had just died from her cancer or from the chemo treatments. No one would have known that she'd been poisoned with iron.

"Nobody has been poisoning me," Bieberstein said firmly. "I would know."

CHAPTER NINETEEN

There were noises in the hall. Zachary and Bieberstein both stopped talking and looked toward the door, trying to decipher the voices. There was an increase in volume, a female giggle, and then it sounded like they were grouped outside of Bieberstein's door. Zachary and Bieberstein both looked toward the door, waiting.

Zachary was alert for trouble, but he knew he probably didn't have to worry, since the voices had not sounded threatening, and the woman had giggled. But bad things could still follow when people were laughing and in a good mood. Sometimes, bullying or pranking someone was the funniest thing in the world. If someone had evil designs on Bieberstein, they could be planning something that would hurt or humiliate him.

Zachary's muscles tensed, listening to the quiet, whispery voices outside the door and waiting for the arrival of the visitors. Maybe they weren't even there to see Bieberstein. Maybe they were there to see the dour man in the other bed. Or they were checking names outside the doors looking for the person they actually wanted to visit. It might be nothing at all to do with Bieberstein.

At least Zachary wasn't worried that they were targeting him. No one had known he was planning to see Bieberstein.

After a few expectant seconds, the visitors finally entered, streaming into the hospital room. Mandy and the other interns from Drake, Chase, Gould.

Other faces that he didn't recognize. Bev. And, of course, Gordon. Gordon Drake himself, main owner of the firm, had deigned to come and visit Bieberstein, following through on his comment that the interns were the lifeblood of the company, that he knew everyone by name, that they were all important to him.

Bieberstein's eyes were wide. He looked from one person to another, his body language tense, movements jerky.

"We came to tell you to get better soon," Mandy told him in a high-pitched voice. She handed him an oversized card. Bieberstein took it from her, and looked at the other visitors warily, as if expecting one of them to jump out and assault him. Zachary knew the feeling. He didn't like crowds, and he didn't like this crowd in particular. It all seemed too phony. These were people who worked hard for hours, who couldn't take time off for their own sickness or family events, but they could all get time off at the same time to visit a lowly intern? Someone that most of them probably didn't even like, hyper and annoying, socially indifferent.

Bieberstein opened the card awkwardly, the cast on his arm keeping his elbow at the wrong angle. He tore the envelope and pulled out the card. He barely looked at the cartoon picture on the outside, the punny greeting on the inside, or the scribbled get well soon messages that everyone had penned inside. It had obviously moved from desk to desk at the office, everyone required to put some happy, encouraging message on the inside for him. Some of the signatures overflowed onto the back. It was crowded with their well-wishes.

Bieberstein looked back at the mob of people. "This is really nice," he said. "Thank you. I'll be back to the office as soon as I can. I don't like to miss…"

"Oh, this is for you," Aaron said, reaching out with Bieberstein's slim, silver laptop in his hand.

"Now that, I need," Bieberstein said eagerly, lunging a little to grab it from him, as if fearful that he might pull it back again at the last moment. He gripped it in both hands, clearly precious to him.

"We wanted to tell you how much we miss you," one of the other employees, who Zachary didn't recognize, told Bieberstein. "You're very important to the company and we're sorry that you got hurt. We want you to get better again soon."

"Yeah, thanks," Bieberstein said with a quick nod.

"You're one of the smartest people that I know," Aaron said. "How you manage to do what you do with numbers... in your head... it absolutely amazes me. You're brilliant."

"We're going to be very happy to have you on permanently," Bev said, giving him a quirky smile. "If you are one of the ones to get the position, of course." But her words left little doubt that he had, in fact, earned one of the full-time positions.

Bieberstein grinned. "You're not going to be sorry," he said. "Drake, Chase, Gould is one of the up-and-coming investment banking firms, and they're going to be able to compete with the biggest and most elite firms in the world. I'm going to make sure of that."

"Yes, you will," Gordon agreed, beaming his beneficent smile on Bieberstein and then on everyone else. "It is people like you who will make Drake, Chase, Gould a household name. When they are writing biographies fifty years from now on the most influential men of the century, your name will undoubtedly be one of those on the list."

"Yours too," Bieberstein said, looking uncomfortable.

"Well, if I'm lucky, but I'm not counting on it. I'll more likely be one of the men behind the scenes who saw which way things were going and got on the train before it was fully up to speed. I'll be there, but I don't know that I'll be one of the influencers. It is minds like yours that will be counted when all of the votes are in."

Bieberstein was getting red. Zachary worried a little that his emotion over Gordon's praise might throw him into another seizure, but nothing untoward happened. He just clutched his laptop to himself and stared up over their heads.

"That's really nice," he said, "I don't know if it's true, but thank you."

The visitors started to talk to each other instead of Bieberstein, taking some of the pressure off of him and leaving him to get his equilibrium back. Zachary watched him covertly, not wanting him to feel like he was under the microscope, but concerned.

Someone offered to tape the 'get well' card to the wall for him, as if there were going to be a lot of cards on display there. Zachary supposed that he should have brought one as well, but it hadn't even occurred to him. Someone else had a bunch of flowers, someone else a vase, so they filled the vase with water and added the flowers, displaying them on the small shelf that acted as a bedside table.

Mandy sat on the edge of Bieberstein's mattress and made jokes to him, most of which seemed to fall flat, either because Bieberstein didn't get them or because her nervousness was making her muff the punchlines. Zachary didn't actually get most of them. He would have been worried if they hadn't been financially-themed jokes.

After a while, he caught Bieberstein's eye. "I'm going to sneak out," he said, motioning to the door.

Bieberstein nodded. "Okay. Thanks for coming by."

"Let me know if you think of anything… if you want to discuss anything," Zachary said. He didn't want to say too much in front of all of Bieberstein's coworkers. "If you get anything back in the results…"

"Yeah. I'll let you know."

Zachary met his eye to make sure he realized that it could be important. If someone were trying to kick him out of the running, they were obviously going to have to try harder. Gordon and the others who were in charge over at Drake, Chase, Gould were not going to just drop him because he'd been put in the hospital for a couple of days. They obviously thought a lot of him.

Bieberstein wasn't going anywhere.

———

After leaving the hospital, Zachary ran a few personal errands. He needed more groceries. Gas in the tank. All of the grown-up, adult things he was supposed to be doing to take care of himself. At the store, he had to stop himself from buying the things he normally got for Kenzie. She wasn't there anymore. There was no point in filling the fridge with the things that she liked if he wasn't going to consume them himself.

He was still thinking about her when he got home and shoved the newest frozen dinners into the freezer. When the phone rang, he knew without looking at it that it was going to be her. He didn't think the medical examiner's report would be in yet, so he didn't know why she would call him when they were broken up. It probably wasn't her. He just thought of her when it rang because he'd already been missing her.

He pulled out his phone and looked at the screen. It *was* Kenzie. And from her cell phone, not the office. Zachary closed his eyes and took a couple of breaths before answering it.

"Kenzie, hi!" He tried not to sound too eager. Or like her call was unexpected. He had wanted to stay friends with her, and friends called each other now and then. He couldn't expect too much from it. Even so, he wished he *had* bought the treats that she enjoyed from the grocery store, so he could tell her that they were there waiting for her now, whenever she was ready to come over.

"Zachary. Yeah, hi." She sounded down. Depressed? Or just tired after a long day? "Uh… listen… I was a little harsh with you yesterday. More than harsh. That was unwarranted. I'm sorry. You didn't do anything wrong, you just called to ask me a medical question and I jumped to conclusions."

"I am sorry," Zachary said. "If I had a medical ethics question, then I should have just gone to the Ethics Committee to start with. I don't know why I didn't. I didn't need to bother you with something like that."

"I don't want you to think that you can't still talk to me and ask me for advice. Really. We're not together anymore, but that doesn't mean that we can't ever talk to each other again."

"That's good. I wouldn't want that."

"My family is sort of a sore spot with me. Especially my dad. So when you were talking about transplants, I just automatically got defensive."

Zachary didn't say anything. If it was a sore spot, then asking her *why* would probably not be the right thing to do. She needed to know that he could just accept that it was off-limits.

"My dad… our family has some history with transplants, and he and I don't see eye-to-eye. He thought that after I finished my medical degree, I would agree that he was right about everything, but… well… I don't."

"Okay. I won't ask you about it again. I didn't mean to trigger any bad feelings. Sorry about that."

"Not your fault. You'd think that I'd be able to handle it better by now. But those feelings are still raw. I try not to hold it against him, but…"

"Do you want to come over tonight?" Zachary offered. "Just to relax and hang out?"

There were a few seconds of silence during which he thought Kenzie might actually be considering it. Or maybe she was just startled by his asking and how inappropriate it was.

"No, Zachary," she said with a sigh. "I think that would just be asking for trouble. We both need to move on. Try out some other relationships. We just don't work together."

"I think that we could. I've just been going through some stuff… you know with my therapy… everything that I've been dealing with lately…"

"I don't see things getting better anytime soon. I can't keep putting my energy into a relationship and not getting anything back."

That stung. Zachary had put a lot of effort into the relationship too. Kenzie didn't have any idea how hard he had tried, how far he had gone out of his comfort zone to do things for her. Even as far as going back into therapy to try to deal with their relationship. That had all been for her.

Kenzie had done a lot for him and had stood by him through some very tough times. But he had been working on it too. He had thought that she was getting something out of it.

CHAPTER TWENTY

H e was still thinking about the call with Kenzie when he went to his therapy session that afternoon. It rankled. He kept making the arguments in his head, but had no way to get them out and see how they resonated with her. With Bridget, at least he'd been able to make his arguments. She might have screamed at him and mocked his arguments and dismissed his feelings, but at least he'd been able to tell her, to try to talk her into getting back together again.

With Kenzie, she didn't even want to hear his arguments. She didn't scream. She was calm and reasonable, but she didn't want to hear what he had to say and he was left arguing with himself and imagining what Kenzie would say to him in response.

Of course, even in his head, she didn't agree with him, and he could still hear her repeating herself in that calm, reasonable voice. "We're just not good together."

But they *had* been good together. He had enjoyed having her as a friend and someone to bounce ideas off of and to discuss any medical issues he was trying to sort out with her. They had moved slowly to a more intimate relationship, and he had felt good about it. Until Teddy. That had blown everything all to hell.

"You're not looking too happy today," Dr. Boyle commented as he sat down and shifted around in the chair, trying to get comfortable.

Zachary didn't have a naturally happy face, so he must have really been scowling for her to notice the difference. He rubbed his forehead, not wanting to overwhelm her with the avalanche of words that threatened to come out, burying her beneath their weight.

"I guess… I'm just having trouble getting used to being alone. To not being with Kenzie anymore."

"It is hard to get over a relationship like that. The two of you had been together for a long time. You were close friends and cared about each other."

Zachary nodded. Dr. B waited, watching him. She knew there was more to come out and she was not afraid to use silence to draw him out. She got paid the same amount whether he spent it talking or brooding in silence. He was the one who would get less out of it if he didn't address the issues.

"She called me today."

"Uh-huh?"

"Not because she wanted to get together, nothing like that."

"Why did she call, then?"

"She called to apologize. I called her the other day about a medical question and it made her upset. So she called to say sorry for snapping at me."

"That was nice of her. It can be hard to admit that you were in the wrong, especially when you're dealing with emotional issues."

"Yeah. It was nice of her. But… I asked her if she wanted to come over."

"Did she give you some sort of sign that she would be interested in coming over?"

Zachary thought about it. He was a good observer of human behavior and he was good at reading people. Body language and tone of voice told him a lot. It was a skill that he had honed through his years in foster care and as a private investigator.

"No… I guess not. She said that she still wanted to be friends and to be able to talk to me, that it was okay if I called her about things that I had questions on. So I just… I guess I jumped ahead and thought that maybe it would be okay if she came over and we just hung out… watched a movie or had a chat. I didn't mean that we had to jump right back into being a couple again. Just that we could… be friends… spend some time together."

"And she probably saw it as something more. She knows your history, that you might have trouble letting go."

"I just don't understand… why she left. She just gave up on us. I was having problems, and she decided that she'd had enough."

"Do you think that she should have put up with your issues for longer? Or handled them differently?"

"I..." Zachary thought about all that had happened. Kenzie had stayed by him through all of it. He had thought that they could weather any problem together. She had seen him through injuries and depression, through the initial aftermath of the attack. She had put up with a lot of things that he hadn't really had a right to expect that she would. "I don't know. I guess she couldn't keep doing it forever, when she wasn't getting anything out of the relationship."

He said the words with a bitter edge. Dr. Boyle studied him, waiting.

"I thought she was. I thought I was giving her something too. But she said that she didn't get anything out of the relationship."

"Does her saying it mean that it's true? Is it a fact or a feeling?"

"I guess... maybe it's a feeling?"

"What do you think? This is your relationship. I don't know Kenzie."

"It *isn't* a relationship. She made that clear."

"She made it clear that it's not a romantic relationship. She said that you could still talk to her, that you could still be friends. Do you think that's true, or was that just words to make the two of you feel better?"

"I don't know."

"If she's willing to still be friends and to talk about your investigations and medical matters with her, then obviously those are things that were important to her. She was getting something out of the relationship, or she would not have been willing to continue those things."

"But she wasn't getting anything out of our romantic relationship?"

"Maybe not. What do you think?"

"I was trying. I was working it through, talking to you about it, talking to her about it."

"And...?"

"I think... I think we were both getting something out of it."

"Then why did it have to end?"

"I didn't end it, she did."

Dr. Boyle was silent.

"I contributed," Zachary admitted, "But she was the one to call it off. She was the one who decided that it was over."

"Did she decide it was over? Or did you?"

"She did. That's what she said."

"You hadn't pushed her away? We've talked about this before."

"I… yes, I was trying to work through her talking to Mr. Peterson and Bridget about our relationship. She was trying to dig into my past. Talking about intimate things with other people. Things I wasn't ready to share. How would you feel if you found out that your husband had been talking about your sex life with his friends? Or not with his friends—with your friends!"

"That would put me in a very difficult position. But I think you need to consider her intent. Was she talking to your family about your intimate relationship because she wanted to brag? Or because she wanted to put you down? I understand you being embarrassed and worried about what details she might have revealed to them. But you need to consider her intent."

Zachary put his hands over his face, cupping his eyes. "I know she was doing it because she wanted to work things out. I know that she meant well. But she shouldn't have done that. She shouldn't have gone to them, asking them about my past relationships. She went behind my back."

Dr. Boyle made an encouraging noise.

"I would have talked to her about it and gotten it smoothed out eventually," Zachary said. "I just needed to work it out in my brain first. I was going through a bad spell."

"When would you have gotten to it, do you think? How long would she have to wait in limbo while you worked it out and figured out how to talk to her about it? And would you have decided that it was okay for her to go to alternate sources when you couldn't talk to her about these issues, or would you have decided that it was wrong?"

"It was still wrong. But… I just got out of the hospital. I could have used another day or two to get settled back into my life. Then we could have discussed it."

"Until then, she was just supposed to sit back and wait for you to work it out and decide to talk to her again."

"I think she could have waited a few more days."

"I'm sure she could have. But she didn't know how long it would be. A few more days, or would it be weeks or months? And in the meantime, was she still in a relationship with you, or were you on a break? How long should she wait until you were ready to talk? And would you make that move on your own, or would she have to prompt you and talk you into it?"

"I don't know. Because she didn't give me that chance."

"How long did she wait?"

Zachary scratched at a seam in the upholstery of the chair he was sitting in. "What do you mean?"

"I mean, how long had she already been waiting when she decided that the two of you were done?"

"Uh…" Zachary considered, trying to construct the timeline in his head. The time between when he had learned that Kenzie had been talking to Mr. Peterson about the relationship until he had gotten out of the hospital and she had come by the apartment to clear out her things. "It was… a few weeks, I guess. A couple of weeks before I was admitted, and then a couple while I was in the hospital."

"So probably a month…?"

"Yeah. Something like that."

"A month without you talking to her at all?"

Zachary cleared his throat. He looked down at the carpet. "We talked a few times… just to say… that I was busy and couldn't get together. She was busy too, I wasn't the only one. We had lunch… a couple times…"

"But a month with no significant contact or time together."

"Yeah."

"Do you think she should have waited more than a month? Maybe two?"

"A month is a pretty long time."

"Yes, it is."

"She would have waited if I was away on vacation or a work trip for a month."

"More than likely, yes. But that's something that you would have defined. And during your vacation, you would have kept in touch with her. The two of you would have talked to each other, shared what you were doing, even if it was only once a week. Don't you think?"

"So you're saying she was justified. That she should have split up with me because I didn't talk to her while I was going through a crisis."

Dr. Boyle gave him a tolerant smile. Zachary knew that he was dramatizing, that he was just trying to get her on his side. He wanted to be told that he was right, not that he had screwed up.

CHAPTER TWENTY-ONE

Zachary returned to the offices of Drake, Chase, Gould to pick up the timesheets for the other interns, even though he knew that when he looked at them, he would find the same thing as he had looking at Lauren's timesheet. That it was completely untrue. He took the reports from Bev and put them away in his bag before challenging her about them.

"I suppose these have been sanitized, just like Lauren's?"

"What are you talking about?"

"That Lauren was working eighteen- or twenty-four-hour days. And her timesheets show that she was working a regular nine-to-five job, with occasional hours of overtime at either end. You know that isn't true, and that her computer records would show that they are lies."

Bev stared at him.

"I assume there are laws that you have to follow in the way that you treat your employees. You can't let them—or force them to—work for twenty-four, forty-eight, or seventy-two hours straight. You can't deny them medical leave when the doctor says that they need it. You can't deny them the ability to take an evening or weekend off or to do other things."

"I don't know what you're talking about."

"I've seen her computer and her emails. I know she was working all hours of the day, just like her roommate says. I know that you denied her any time off, even for medical reasons."

"Lauren didn't have any medical issues. She was a perfectly healthy young adult, and if I had allowed her to take time off every time she had a cough or a sniffle, then pretty soon all of the interns would be faking sick after the weekend. Or whenever they wanted time off to mess around with friends, go on dates, or have dinner with their favorite aunts. We needed them to show that they could be dependable and do what they had promised to. Lauren was very smart and got along well with her superiors and coworkers. But she had a problem with putting in the time. She was always looking for a way out."

"She put in the time. I can see it from her computer."

"You're misinterpreting what you see. Are you making an arrest? You think that I went to her house and pushed her down in the tub and held her underwater?"

"I'm not making any arrests. I'm asking you whether these records are true, or whether you were just making them up."

"I resent the suggestion that we would do anything unethical or illegal. We cared for these interns like they were our own kids. If they put in timesheets for too much time... we would correct them. Nobody wants to get into trouble with labor policies because they don't know how to fill out their timesheets."

"How were they supposed to fill out their timesheets?"

She motioned to the reports that she had given Zachary. "Like those. You can't fill out a sheet alleging that you have been working for twenty-four hours at a time. That's just going to get people in trouble. And they weren't working for that whole time. They would take breaks for meals, exercise, or gossiping. They would nap at their desks. They weren't working for that long. So we would correct them to the time they were actually working."

"I see."

So she admitted that she, or someone in her department, had been involved in making the changes to the timesheets.

"What other records do you change?"

"What do you mean?"

"I mean... you change the timesheets to bring them into alignment with your policies. Did you find it necessary to change other records as well?

Are there other things that they would get wrong? Because they didn't know what they were doing? Because they were new to the employment world and didn't know the right way to fill them out?"

"I don't appreciate your implications…"

"I'm asking a question. Did you change other records as well?"

"If they were wrong, yes, of course we changed them. If someone put down the wrong address, birthdate, or social, wouldn't you fix them?"

"Sure. If they were wrong."

"It's the same with the rest of their human resources records."

"If they made a mistake, you would fix them."

"If they were wrong," Bev agreed. "That would be our responsibility."

———

When Zachary left the human resources department, he saw an atrium where several people sat around looking at their phones or typing on their computers, on benches surrounded by cobblestone pathways and lush plants. Obviously, another part of the "health and wellness" programs offered at Drake, Chase, Gould. He wouldn't be surprised to find a spa somewhere, just another way of ensuring that the employees were in the peak of health. The trouble was, everything was being counteracted by an environment where the employees were expected to work long, arduous hours, where there were bosses who were alternately abusive and approving, and where their needs were actually being subverted in the name of productivity.

He remembered the reading he had done when he'd been investigating the ABA programs at the Summit Learning Center. How being angry and abusive toward a child and then later showing love and approval, you could bond the child to you and get better compliance. The same way that spouses convinced their partners and children to stay in abusive relationships. The same way that gangs initiated their members and cults controlled theirs.

He'd heard from Bieberstein the way that the interns were abused and humiliated about their work, and how they hazed the new employees. He'd seen the love-bombing of Bieberstein at the hospital, how emotional and appreciative he became at the excessive praise. He had been overwhelmed, as anyone would have been, at Gordon's praise. They had gushed over how much they loved him and handed him his computer. *We appreciate you and get back to work.*

Zachary sat down on an unoccupied bench in the atrium. He kept his eyes down, looking at his phone and then at his notepad as he checked his email and jotted down some of his thoughts. He was watching the employees who were enjoying the atmosphere of the atrium out the corners of his eyes.

One of the men balanced a laptop on his knees and stared unblinkingly at the screen, intent on whatever it was he was doing. He pecked with the index finger, middle finger, and thumb of his right hand. His left hand was beside his leg, and he plucked at his pant leg as he read through whatever he was reading. Pluck, pluck, pluck, in a steady rhythm. Zachary looked away, studying the next employee.

While he had expected the employees other than the interns to look better, less tired and well-rested, he didn't find that to be the case. The receptionist looked okay and Bieberstein had declared that she left at six o'clock every day. So she was one person who wasn't expected to work the ridiculous overtime hours that everyone else was, and she had looked fresh and well-rested. The face of the company, it was probably important that she not look like a zombie. The other employees, even those who were sitting in the paradisiacal setting of the atrium, looked fatigued. They had red eyes and heavy lids. Some were falling asleep where they sat, eyes slowly closing and heads nodding, losing the battle with the work they were trying to get done.

One man was holding a heavy, thick binder and, as he drifted off, it slipped from his grip and fell onto the flagstones below him with a crash that sounded like a gunshot.

Everybody in the atrium was instantly awake and alert, eyes wide as they looked around for the source of the noise. The man sitting on the next bench to Zachary's right leaped to his feet, his face a picture of panic.

"What the hell was that?" he shouted. Looking around, he spotted the binder and the owner picking it up, red-faced. "What are you doing? Don't you have any consideration for anyone around you? This is supposed to be a quiet place to study, not a war zone!"

The woman sitting between them muttered under her breath. "You're the one making this a war zone," and in a louder voice, "Just chill, Chris."

But Chris was just getting ramped up. "Why should I chill? He's the one causing a disturbance. Can't you be quiet?"

"He made a mistake. He dropped something. People make mistakes sometimes. Just go back to your work."

Chris took a few steps toward the man who had dropped the book and Zachary shifted anxiously, worried that it was going to escalate into a physical fight. This was what constant stress did to people. Lack of sleep and the pressure to produce made them so anxious and hypersensitive that they couldn't respond in a logical, reasonable way. Chris was acting like he *was* in a war zone ready to take down the enemy, instead of in a quiet atrium.

"I'm sorry," the other man said. "It just slipped out of my hand. I didn't mean to startle anyone."

"People think it's so funny to scare others. So funny to see how they react," Chris snarled.

Zachary could remember bullies at school or Bonnie Brown who had thought it was hilarious to make him jump. He was so tightly-strung, so hypervigilant, that they were guaranteed a really good reaction. Zachary couldn't help it. He would be running or fighting to protect himself before he had any idea what was going on.

He had once hit a teacher who had decided to wake him up when he had fallen asleep at his desk by slapping the ruler down on the desk next to his head. He had been terrified upon realizing what he had done, fleeing the room and hiding in a toilet stall until they had managed to find him. That had been while he was at the Petersons', and Mrs. Peterson had been ready to send him on his way that day. It had taken Mrs. Pratt a long time to talk her down, and she only succeeded in getting Zachary a few more days there while she looked for another home to transfer him to. It had been the last straw for Mrs. Peterson. Any boy who would hit a teacher was not a safe person to have in her home. Not with other children to consider. She wouldn't take the chance that he could hurt one of them if they happened to startle him.

"It wasn't on purpose," the man with the binder said again. "Really. I'm not laughing. I don't think it is funny to scare anybody. Hell, *I* just about wet my pants!"

Chris stared at him, then finally was able to give a little smile, nodding his head. He forced a chuckle. "Yeah, okay," he said finally, his voice shaking a little. "Sorry to overreact. I just… I don't like being scared like that. I don't know what I thought was happening, but it scared the crap out of me."

His opponent nodded eagerly. "I know, I know. I'm sorry. Guess I'd better head back to my desk. Reading in here wasn't such a good idea after all."

They gave each other space to maneuver, and both ended up leaving, the atrium falling into silence once more. Zachary took a few breaths, long and even, trying to calm his own body back down. No need to get anxious about a little accident.

Holding his phone in front of his face so that it would look like he was reading something, Zachary looked around at the others who had stayed behind. Everyone was looking pretty shaken. It was incredible that the stress level in the building could be so high, especially in a calming environment like the atrium. The plants and the sounds of a waterfall in the distance should have made it a paradise of peace, but all it took was one mistake for everyone to turn on each other.

———

Zachary put a frozen dinner into the microwave, mentally prompting himself not to forget it was there this time. After considering for a moment, he told his phone to set an alarm for him, then went to his computer to do a quick email check while the dinner was heating up.

He had cleared a few items out of his inbox when his phone rang. At first, he assumed it was the alarm for his dinner, even though he hadn't heard the microwave beep. That wouldn't be unusual; he often tuned out noises like that when he was concentrating on something on the computer. That was why he had set the alarm on his phone. But when he reached for it to turn off the alarm, he realized it was a phone call from Heather. He sank back into his seat and touched the green answer button.

"Hi, Feathers."

"Hi, Zachy," she returned, laughing a little at the use of their childhood nicknames. "Though I'm not so sure I should be calling my boss Zachy."

"I don't think anyone else could get away with it, but I don't mind it coming from you. What's up?"

"I have results on some of those skip traces for you."

"Oh, good." Zachary reached for his notepad. "Will you email them to me?"

"Sure. I did run into problems with one, though. I wondered if you could think of anywhere else I should look."

"Okay, shoot."

She outlined what she had found for the man, and the various databases and searches she had tried. Zachary's phone vibrated in his hand and beeped, and he dismissed the alert, focusing on Heather's skip and what she might have missed or any creative ways he might have tried to find the man.

"You might want to check with unions," he suggested. "Tradesmen are usually registered with unions, no matter where they go and who they work for. He'll want to keep his membership active so he can use them if he runs into any trouble. There are also some job boards you might try out. If he hasn't landed a full-time job, he might be doing short contracts on one of them."

"Oh, good idea," Heather agreed. He could tell by the way she was drawing out her words that she was writing it down, so he waited until she indicated she was ready before moving on to anything else.

"If we can't find anything else, we might try courthouse searches. If he's disappeared because he owes child support or was found liable in some traffic accident, it would be nice to know that. If there are any court cases, his lawyer might have a current address, or family members to check with."

"Good. Okay. I'll do those too, if nothing else shows up."

"Sometimes people are just very careful not to leave a footprint, but chances are, he won't be able to avoid it, and we'll find him somewhere."

"I'll do my best. How is your accident case going?"

"I'm starting to wonder if there was foul play... there are several people trying to get the same job, and two of them have had accidents in the last week. I don't know if someone is trying to clear their way to one of those positions, or if it's just a coincidence. Or if it's because with how hard the company is working them, they're just dropping from exhaustion."

"Where are they working? Some sweatshop?"

Zachary chuckled. "The modern-day equivalent, maybe. They certainly seem to be taken advantage of. I don't know how you could expect anyone to work that hard."

"More immigrants?"

"No. An investment banking firm, Drake, Chase, Gould. That's in confidence, though, don't go repeating it to anyone. I'd really like to know if any of the other interns bought any poison lately... but so far, as far as I know, any toxicology screens have come up negative, so I could just be trying to find foul play where there isn't any."

"I doubt it. You seem to have a pretty good sense of these things."

"Well, so far I'm not sure that it's anything. Just a possibility at this point."

"If there's anything to find, you'll find it."

He liked her confidence. He wasn't sure that she actually had anything to be confident about, but he appreciated it. He'd had a few cases where he'd made lucky finds. Maybe Lauren's death would be another.

And maybe it was just what it looked like. A woman slipping in the tub and hitting her head. Accidents like that happened every day.

CHAPTER TWENTY-TWO

A s Zachary thought about the information he had gathered in Lauren's case so far, he thought back to Bev and her admission that they would change whatever records they needed in order to get them to fit the company's reality. By now, Bev had probably realized that that had been a stupid thing to admit to Zachary. And while Zachary had the proof on Lauren's laptop that the timesheets were a lie and that Lauren had repeatedly been refused time off, that information resided in a corporate mailbox, and if they decided to shut down and erase that mailbox, Zachary could lose what information he had.

To preserve it, he would have to be sure not to let Lauren's computer connect to the internet. He had connected to it once via his Wi-Fi router, so to prevent it from connecting again, he delved into the network settings and deleted the Wi-Fi profile. The computer wouldn't be able to connect again unless Zachary gave it the password. After deleting the connection information, Zachary watched it search for another connection and find an open Guest network somewhere in the building. He looked for the settings that would prevent it from searching automatically for networks.

He shut off everything he could, including the Wi-Fi radio. The Bluetooth indicator pulsed, and he saw Lauren's phone wake up. Of course, sometime in the past, Lauren had tethered the laptop to her phone, and it had remembered the connection information. He deleted that profile, telling it to forget the device, and also shut down the Bluetooth radio.

He watched the screen for any other activity. With Wi-Fi shut off and Bluetooth shut off, it shouldn't be able to connect to the internet unless he plugged a network cable into the port. But he was still half-expecting it to find some other way to connect to the internet. The computer was desperate to find a connection and start downloading new information. Lauren had been connected to the information superhighway night and day, always looking for the most recent market information.

There were no more connection icons on the screen. Zachary went to the browser and tried connecting to a couple of sites, but just kept getting 404 errors, and the computer didn't find an alternate route to the internet.

Sure that the company could no longer remotely delete the information already in the computer's mailbox, Zachary again opened the application and browsed through the mail. There were a few more routine mail pieces that had arrived while he had been trying to keep the computer from reconnecting, but nothing unusual and, as far as he could tell, none of the already-downloaded emails had been deleted.

He went to the sent mail and did a screen print of the first page of emails so that he could save the evidence of the times that Lauren had been sending out emails. The printer icon flashed warnings at him and nothing came off on the printer. Zachary looked at it. No connection to printer. Of course he couldn't print anything over Wi-Fi if he had prevented the computer from connecting to Wi-Fi. He could plug it into his network with a cable, but then it would have internet access as well, and he only wanted it to talk to the printer. Which meant he needed a printer cable. Something that he had not purchased since setting up his new system.

Zachary took a look at the connectors on the printer and on the computer, then looked through the USB cables he had on hand. He had charge cables for various devices, or to connect his phone or tablet to the computer, but they used specialized connections that the printer didn't. He was going to have to get a new cable to connect the computer to the printer to memorialize the information that was currently on it. Unless he could plug into his router but not let the router connect to the internet. Zachary examined the router, tracing the cables visually.

He should also have cloned the hard drive before he'd done anything else. Gerry, his technology consultant, had tried to drill the importance of this into him on more than one occasion. Gerry had given him the hardware he needed to do it. Any time he touched a computer that was not his own, he was supposed to clone the drive before even attempting to log in. Gerry would not be impressed that Zachary had not only logged in without cloning it, but was now worried about losing the information stored on the hard drive and was resorting to printing hard copies to save it.

Clone the hard drive, bonehead.

———

Zachary didn't know how long he had been working on Lauren's computer and emails when the phone rang. He knew that his eyes were getting sore and gritty, which probably meant that it was late and he'd been spending too much time staring at the screen.

He looked over at his phone laying on the desk to his right. He wasn't sure whose number it was, but it appeared to be local, and it was too late at night to be a telemarketer. He picked it up and answered the call.

"Zachary here."

"Is this Detective Goldman?"

Zachary squirmed a little at not correcting the fiction. "This is Zachary Goldman. Who's calling?"

"It's Blair."

Zachary drew a blank.

"Blair Bieberstein."

"Oh, Blair. Sorry, my brain was somewhere else. How are you feeling?"

"I want to know if you really think that someone could be trying to kill me."

"Well... I don't know. I don't want to scare you, but at the same time... Lauren is dead and you did have a pretty serious accident. If someone was trying to get one of the permanent positions, they could go to great lengths to get what they wanted. So... let's say it's a possibility. But it's also possible that it was just someone who wants the company to see you as a risk, they don't really want to kill you. Or it could just be an accident. A strange coincidence."

"So you think someone is trying to kill me."

"Uh… yes, maybe."

"The hospital said that everything was fine in my bloodwork. There was no reason to think that anyone had poisoned me."

"That's good news."

"You know they don't routinely check for poisons, and there are so many poisons out there, they would have to know which one they were looking for. They don't just assume that anyone who comes in with a seizure has been poisoned."

"I realize that."

"Then why are you trying to scare me? No one is trying to hurt me."

"Okay."

"Okay?" Bieberstein repeated, his voice rising in tone. "It's not okay! What's happening to me? Why did I pass out?"

"I don't know. You haven't ever had that happen before?"

"No, never."

"What did the doctors say?"

"Maybe I'm fighting a virus. Most people who have a seizure never have another one, so it's really nothing to worry about unless I start having more of them. They don't know what's going on, and they don't really care about finding out."

"Are you still at the hospital?"

"No. Checked myself out of there. Too many people watching me. Didn't want to stay there."

"So you went home?"

"I can't go home. Lauren died at her apartment. I don't want them to get me."

"Them?"

"Whoever killed Lauren. Whoever poisoned my water bottle. I don't want them getting me."

Zachary gripped the phone more tightly. "Have you had any sleep, Blair? Where are you?"

"I'm at the office. Can't sleep. Need to stay on top of things."

"I think they can do without you for a day or two until you start feeling better. If you don't get any sleep, you are not going to be able to do your job anyway."

"I'm just fine. As long as I don't let them catch up to me."

"But if they poisoned you at work, wouldn't it be safer to go home?" Zachary reasoned, hoping to be able to get Bieberstein to go home and get the sleep he needed. Who knew how long he'd been awake before his accident, and if the medication they'd given him at the hospital had kept him awake since then, Bieberstein could be putting his health at serious risk.

"No, they got Lauren at home," Bieberstein reiterated. "I just need to make sure nobody can put anything else into my water bottle. That's the trick. I'll keep it with me. Won't let anyone near it."

Zachary heard him take a pull on his water bottle and chug down several gulps of water.

"You're not taking anything, are you?" he checked. "You know that if you take meth or something else to keep you awake, you're going to damage your health further. You need to find somewhere quiet and have a nap."

"Yeah, yeah," Bieberstein said impatiently. "When are you coming back here again?"

"I don't know. I don't have anything else to pursue there right now. I can't just hang out there without something specific to do."

"You need to arrest them so that it's safe for the rest of us."

"Do you know who it is?"

"It's *them*. You told me that. Why won't you do something about it?"

"I'll do something when I have the proof, Blair. If you know anything, you need to tell me. Give me the proof so I can do something."

Bieberstein muttered something in an angry tone and ended the call.

Zachary set his phone back down, pondering the call and what he should do about it. The hospital hadn't found anything wrong with Bieberstein, but that wasn't unexpected. As Bieberstein said, they needed to know what to look for, and it wasn't that unusual to have a seizure without ever discovering the cause.

If Bieberstein were home and resting, that would be one thing, but trying to continue to work at Drake, Chase, Gould while he was in such rough shape was not a good idea. He was sounding paranoid, which he hadn't been when Zachary had talked to him earlier. That could be a sign that his sleep deprivation was getting really serious.

He looked at the time on his phone. It was too late to be calling anyone. If any of the interns were still at Drake, Chase, Gould, they would already know that Bieberstein was having issues. He doubted any of the supervisors would be working there so late, and he didn't have any of their personal cell numbers.

Except for one.

But was it really appropriate to call the owner of the firm about a low-level employee?

CHAPTER TWENTY-THREE

Zachary dithered for a while. He didn't know whether to leave Bieberstein alone and just let the other interns deal with him if they were still there, or whether to get involved.

But if his theory of the poisoning was true, which Bieberstein now believed, then the interns would be working against him.

After considerable mental back-and-forth, Zachary finally decided to just bite the bullet. What was the worst that could happen? Gordon would tell him off and say not to call him again. Zachary tapped in the number Gordon had given him, and waited.

He had to allow several rings for it to actually connect, and then there would be a few more before Gordon woke up. Even more, if his phone was on vibrate and he was a heavy sleeper, in which case it might just keep ringing until his voicemail picked up.

"Zachary? What's wrong?"

Gordon's voice was sharp and alert, not like he'd just been awakened from a sound sleep. Zachary looked at the time again to confirm to himself that it was the middle of the night; he hadn't just been confused or misread it.

"Uh, Gordon..."

"Yes. What is it?"

"I just had a call from Blair Bieberstein, and I'm a little concerned..."

"Blair? What was he calling you about in the middle of the night?"

"He's checked himself out of the hospital and he's at the office, working."

"At three o'clock in the morning? What's he doing?"

"I don't know. But he hasn't been able to sleep since he was admitted, something they gave him kept him awake. And who knows how many hours he was awake before that. These interns put in wicked hours."

"We have rules about how long employees can work. We don't want people working themselves to death."

Zachary paused, considering. "We'll have to talk about that," he told Gordon. "But to get straight to the heart of this… I think Blair is having a breakdown. He's paranoid. He hasn't been sleeping. He's afraid to go home."

"You think he could be violent?"

"Violent? Well, no… I'm worried about his state of mind. That he might be harming his health. You wouldn't want any more bad press."

He knew that big corporate types worried about how their organizations were portrayed in the media. What people thought of them. They didn't want people to boycott their services.

"You really think that he's at the office and having a breakdown?"

"Yes."

"Okay." There was a period of silence. Zachary pictured Gordon wiping his eyes and trying to get his brain and body woken up and operating properly. "Thanks for letting me know that, Zachary. I'll see if there is anything I can do."

———

Zachary decided that it was time for him to go to bed if he didn't want to end up in the same shape as Bieberstein. He wasn't operating on very much sleep himself and he'd been sitting in front of the computer for far too long.

So he did a quick toilet before bed and climbed in under his blankets.

As he tried to settle himself to sleep, he longed to hear Kenzie's voice or to have her in the bed with him, her body stretched out warm along his. He slept better with her there, in spite of any kicking or blanket hogging. It was comforting to have someone there with him when anxiety or nightmares struck.

But he wasn't going to call her at three o'clock in the morning. She was a lot scarier than Gordon and she wouldn't put up with such nonsense.

He had hoped that his tired eyes and headache would mean he could fall asleep quickly for once, but he tossed and turned and couldn't find a comfortable position. He was too hot and too cold and too restless and too exhausted. After an hour, he got up and went to the medicine cabinet for a sleeping pill. Maybe just half of one. He needed something that was just strong enough to take the edge off. He'd been reluctant to take any kind of sleep aid since accidentally overdosing at Mr. Peterson's house during the serial killer investigation. He had been taking painkillers he wasn't accustomed to and had apparently managed to take several pain pills and sleeping pills before falling asleep. The resulting nap had lasted most of the next day.

When he opened the medicine cabinet, he saw Kenzie's note still taped to the back of the medicine cabinet door with the stern instruction to "Call somebody!" with her number, Bridget's, Mario's, and several hotlines or emergency operators. But that was only for when he was contemplating suicide, not when he was just having trouble sleeping.

He took an herbal sleep aid rather than the stronger prescription pills. He would need to be up in just a few hours and he didn't want to be groggy.

————

Zachary woke up as dawn started to peek in through the windows. He lay in bed for a few minutes, thinking he might fall back asleep again, but he knew that he wouldn't. When he was extra stressed or anxious about something, he could shut down and sleep through the day, but in his normal state, he couldn't sleep more than a few hours at night and then his body and brain were too restless to stay asleep.

He got up, made some coffee, and tidied up the kitchen and any stray dishes while he waited for it to perk. He realized that there were barely any dirty dishes. There should have been more if he had eaten the day before. He checked the garbage for microwave dinner wrappers, and closed the cupboard again slowly. He looked over at the microwave and didn't open the door. He knew he had eaten supper the night before. He had set an alarm so he wouldn't forget that there was something warming in the microwave. He had obviously just laid the box down somewhere he shouldn't have.

He went into the living room and checked the garbage by his desk. He checked under the edge of the couch and any other places he might have put down the remains of his meal and not picked them back up again. He returned to the kitchen as the coffee started to drip into his travel mug, and looked on top of the fridge and behind the garbage in case he had somehow missed the garbage bin.

He impatiently watched the coffee dribble into his mug. He still refused to open the microwave door. He knew that he had taken his supper out of the microwave the night before. He had made sure he wouldn't forget.

Zachary picked up his coffee mug and went to his computer to check his email and read through his handwritten notes. After a few sips, he put the spill-proof travel mug far away from his computer and keyboard. Remembering his discussions with Gerry about making sure that all of his work was properly digitized and stored in the cloud, he took a few minutes to snap pictures of the pages of his notebook and save the resulting files where they would automatically sync to the cloud. Having lost all of his work product once before, he wasn't willing to let that happen again.

The phone rang. Zachary leaned back tiredly in his chair and picked it up. Heather's face was on the screen. He tapped it and smiled at her, holding the phone in front of him.

"Hi, Heather."

"Good morning, Zach!" Her voice was chipper. She shook her head at him. Zachary hadn't shaved or even combed his hair yet, but if she were going to video call him in the early morning, she was going to have to take what she got. "You don't look like you've been up for long."

"Not long, no, but you didn't wake me up."

"That's good. You're sleeping better?"

"I'm sleeping… more regularly." His sleep schedule after the assault had been unpredictable, but since he'd been seeing his therapist like he was supposed to, he was doing better. Not a lot of sleep, but he at least had some idea of when he would be asleep and didn't have to worry about missing client calls in the middle of the day because he'd passed out.

"Good," Heather approved. Zachary didn't imagine he looked well-rested. He tended to have bags under his eyes and to look like a homeless person if he hadn't cleaned himself up, but Heather had seen him enough mornings to know that was just his usual morning face. "So… I don't know if you'll approve or not, but I did a bit of extra investigating that you didn't exactly ask for."

"On the skips?"

"No, on your company. Drake, Chase, Gould."

"Oh." Zachary blinked, thinking about that. He hadn't asked Heather to do anything regarding the case, had just bounced a few ideas off of her, but he didn't mind her taking the initiative. She'd obviously found something of interest, or she wouldn't be calling him. "Okay. What kind of investigating did you do? What did you find?"

"They've had a few weird stories in the media lately. This thing with Lauren wasn't the first time that something has happened to one of their employees."

"What else?"

Heather propped her phone on a stand and pulled out a file to refer to the printouts. "Okay, how about this one? A local homeless outreach program picks up a woman who claims to have amnesia. She doesn't know who she is or where she came from."

"Uh-huh…"

"And when the woman's picture runs in the news, they find out that she was an executive at Chase Gould."

"Really? What was her name? What department was she in?"

"Shelby Matters. And she was working in something called foreign futures. Don't ask me what that is. I think I'd need an entire college degree to understand what exactly it is that Chase Gould does. But apparently one thing that they do is drive their employees past the brink of sanity."

Zachary thought of Bieberstein. "Yeah. I've been a little concerned about that myself. So what happened to this Shelby woman? Did she get hit on the head? Was she drugged or sick?"

"She seemed to be in good health. The doctors said that she appeared to have been living on the street for only a few days, and nobody had reported her missing, so she couldn't have been gone for too long. No head injury. No emotional or physical trauma that anyone was aware of."

"Did they do a tox screen? Look for drugs or poisons?"

"They checked for drugs, but they said she wasn't on anything when she was brought in. No one knows why she would suddenly develop amnesia."

Zachary might have seen the reports in the news, but at the time he hadn't known anything about Drake, Chase, Gould so, while it was an interesting story, it hadn't rung any alarm bells for him. But now, thinking about Lauren hitting her head and drowning in her bathtub and Bieberstein passing out on the treadmill, he had to wonder if it was a pattern. But Shelby Matters wasn't an intern. It sounded like she worked in a completely different department. And if it was a few months back, then that had been before the current crop of interns had even started.

"Zachary...?"

He focused back on Heather's image on the phone screen. "Just thinking through the possibilities. Sorry. What else?"

"You're going to need to prepare yourself for this one," she warned.

Zachary looked at her, trying to anticipate what she meant. What had happened that she was worried was going to trigger a bad reaction for him? Another sexual assault?

CHAPTER TWENTY-FOUR

"Telling me to be prepared doesn't really help me, Feathers," Zachary said, shaking his head. "What are you talking about? How is this going to bother me?"

"You told me before that you have flashbacks. And Tyrrell said that he's seen a couple of smaller ones. I just don't want to jump into this and have you panic."

Zachary took a few deep breaths. He didn't know what else to do to prepare himself. He'd gone through ideas of how to get himself grounded with his therapist and with Kenzie. Focusing on the things that he could see and hear and smell in real life to keep the flashbacks at bay. But he didn't usually know ahead of time that something was going to trigger him, and he wasn't sure how to prepare for that. His heart rate was rising just worrying about what it was Heather was going to say.

"It was a house fire."

Zachary swallowed. Yes. That was one of his triggers, alright. Anything to do with fire or candles was bad, but a house fire... that was enough to bring on the worst of his memories. He tried to keep his breathing nice and deep, but found himself gasping in between the longer breaths.

"Okay," he said, his voice strangled, "what about a house fire?"

"They had an employee, or a former employee, who had a fire. She was apparently writing some kind of tell-all book about her life in the investment banking industry in general, and Drake, Chase, Gould in particular."

"And all of her work was destroyed in the fire."

"You got it."

He nodded and breathed and waited for Heather to go on with a more casual topic, something that wasn't going to set off more flashbacks.

"She ran back into the house," Heather said, a little apologetically. "She tried to go back in to get the manuscript or her computer."

Zachary felt the burning flames. He could hardly draw in breath, because the air was superheated from the fire. Paper burned faster and hotter than anything else. She had no chance of being able to go back into the house to save her papers. And her computer… a better chance, but…

He felt himself on the floor, crawling, feeling for safety, for somewhere to hide. The flames roared all around him, sounding like a wild beast, like some living demon that had come to destroy him.

"Zachary. Zachary, it's okay. She got out. She only had very minor burns. No grafts. The firefighters were mad at her for rushing back into the house and putting the first responders who were trying to keep her safe at risk, but none of them were injured. Everyone was okay. Zachy. Zachary!"

Zachary nodded, trying to find his way out of the avalanche of sensations. He tried to do what he'd been taught. He tried to focus on Heather's voice, the smell of his coffee, anything that he could actually see or touch. The flames started to recede.

"It's okay, Zachary. You're safe. Nothing is going to hurt you."

He nodded again.

Heather started singing a silly song, her voice strained and unsure to start with. "Great, green gobs of greasy, grimy gopher guts…"

Zachary laughed. He saw her as she had been before the fire. Sunburned and freckled from many hours spent outdoors trying to keep the kids out of their parents' hair. Her blond hair bleached in the sun, tangled and stringy. Scrapes on her knees and holes in her pants. How had she managed to ruin another pair of pants? He could hear his mother's voice, reprimanding her for being so careless.

Clothes cost money, you know! You're going to have to wear clothes with holes in them to school!

Heather's elfin laugh. She continued to sing the song. The words came to Zachary's lips and he tried to sing them too. They finished together and Zachary looked at her in the small phone screen.

"Thank you."

She smiled. "You always liked that one."

"Yeah, I did. The grosser the better!"

How many times had he sung it at school or the dinner table or somewhere else it would get him in trouble? It just wormed its way into his head and he couldn't get it out, couldn't stop himself from humming or singing it.

"You okay now?"

"Sure." He took another sip of his coffee, which was starting to cool. He looked at the time, tried to get reoriented in the physical world. "Yeah. You're right. That's... a bad one for me."

"Anyway, she was an ex-employee of Drake, Chase, Gould. They said that she had signed a confidentiality agreement and wasn't allowed to reveal anything about the company to the public, but she said that was only limited to trade secrets and client confidential information, and that she could talk about the company and how they operated and the things they were doing if she wanted to. They didn't agree."

"Did they take her to court?"

"You got it. How did you know?"

"Because I know of another case where they took a whistleblower to court. How can they do that? How can they keep saying that people aren't allowed to talk about the company? Just because people are disaffected, that's not enough reason to quash them, is it? How bad is what they are doing?"

"You've been investigating them, so you're the one who probably knows best. What do you think they're trying to hide?"

"Well..." Zach considered. "I know they're hiding how many hours they are forcing the interns to work. They've got this health and wellness program that's supposed to be so wonderful... but if it is, then why are all of these things happening? Why do they have people breaking down and complaining about the way the company treated them? If they really were so perfect, they wouldn't have all of these problems, would they?"

"I don't know. Are they that much worse than any other company in the industry? Comparable in size? I have no idea if they have sued more ex-employees than any of their competitors, or if they've had more employees with mental illness concerns. I don't know if they're doing anything any differently than any other company."

"But they must. You don't hear about this kind of thing with the other companies."

"Well, I don't think that's absolutely true. I came across a few other stories when I was investigating. An intern who stepped off a building. Another who died of a cocaine overdose. There are lots of stories about how hard they work their employees in this industry."

"So maybe it's considered normal? I'm glad I'm not an investment banker."

"You and me both," Heather agreed, nodding her head and putting her papers back in the file. "You and me both."

CHAPTER TWENTY-FIVE

Zachary had called Barbara to update her on where he was in his investigation, even though he hadn't come to any kind of landing on what had happened to Lauren. He didn't have anything that could definitively point to murder or to accident. He was pretty sure that the medical examiner's report was going to come back as 'accident.' He hadn't been able to find anything yet that would have convinced them otherwise, even though Dr. Wiltshire had believed Zachary in the past. He couldn't abuse that past trust, or the next time he was sure that an 'accident' needed to be reinvestigated or looked at more carefully, they wouldn't do it. It was a fine balance.

Happy that he had called, Barbara had asked if they could meet in person once again.

"I have been talking to Deidre, Lauren's sister, and she really wants to talk to you. She has been wondering how it could have happened too, and... she just wants to talk to you. Would that be okay? Could we all meet together?"

Zachary usually liked to meet with the family, so he was glad for an opening. It could be awkward approaching the family on his own if they didn't know that Barbara had opened up an investigation. It would be hard for them to understand why he was looking into it. He also didn't want them calling Detective Robinson demanding to know why Zachary was investigating it when the police weren't. He wanted to keep his relations with the police department as good as possible.

"Sure," he agreed. "I would be happy to meet with her. Can we meet at your apartment or at her place? It would be easier, I think, if it wasn't in a public setting."

He had met with Barbara in public because it was more comfortable that way. A woman by herself wouldn't want to meet at the apartment of a man that she didn't know, and even meeting at her place could be awkward if she were alone. But with there being two women, and Barbara having already met him, he didn't think Barbara would mind a private meeting so much. It was easier to express emotion without everybody in a coffee shop watching you and speculating about why you were blubbering all over the place.

"I guess... if you wanted to come to the apartment," Barbara agreed. There was hesitation in her voice, and Zachary waited for her to decide whether it was really okay with her or not. If she didn't want to talk about what she had seen that day in the setting where it had happened, she could suggest somewhere else to meet. "Yes," Barbara said eventually, in a stronger voice. "I'd be okay with that, but I'll have to check with Deidre. I don't know if she'll want to be here... where it happened, you know. I do want to get some of Lauren's things out of here, so I can see about getting another roommate. I don't really want to move, even with what happened. Though who is going to want to move into the room of someone who just died? I just don't know."

"You might not want to include that fact on Craig's List," Zachary said.

She gave a little laugh. "No, you're right. I think I might leave that part out. If I can avoid them finding out until after they are moved in, that would be better."

Zachary nodded, even though she couldn't see him. "Okay, then, why don't you give Deidre a call and see if she's up for it, and settle on a time and place. My schedule is pretty open. I can see you today, if you like. Just give me a call back when you've worked it out."

So that was how Zachary had ended up back at Barbara's apartment, sitting on her couch and letting his eyes travel around the room, looking for the imprint that Lauren had left on the room and any stray clues he might have missed the first time he had visited the apartment. Barbara had been packing Lauren's things up for her family, but it appeared that pretty much everything in the living room had been Barbara's, since there were no obvious holes left by the removal of Lauren's items.

Barbara was watching him.

"She didn't spend a lot of time here," she told Zachary, repeating what she had said before. "Most of her things were just in her bedroom. We were roommates, equals, but she was really more like a tenant, just keeping things in her own room. I told her that we could decorate together, she could come furniture shopping with me, all of that... but she was so wrapped up with her work chasing gold that she could never find the time. So it was up to me."

"She had changed," Deidre said softly. She had similar features to Lauren's but a little softer, more blurred around the edges. She sat with her hands folded in her lap, looking calm and sedate, but exuding an aura of sadness. Her blond hair was down, just brushing the tops of her shoulders. She didn't have red-rimmed, baggy eyes, but Zachary sensed that she was in mourning just the same. Not everybody was as free with the waterworks as Barbara. "I don't understand how she could have changed so much in the time that she was with that company. It was like they had a hold over her. Not a threat, I don't mean. But a... like they had sucked her into something. Instead of being our Lauren, with all of her interests and plans, she became part of Chase Gold. A dedicated part of their machine."

"She had changed a lot?" Zachary asked, thumbing the pages in his notebook to find a clean page. He looked over at Barbara, who hadn't suggested this when she had talked about Lauren.

"She had," Deidre said. "Before that company, she was Lauren, part of our family, with all kinds of dreams for the future, all of the ways she wanted to change the world, to make a fulfilling life. She wanted a family, a social life, volunteering to do projects overseas, that kind of thing. She was such a warm person, she wanted to make a difference in the world. But once she was there at Drake, Chase, Gould, we just lost her. She stopped seeing the family, cut herself off. She would talk about *the-company-this* and *the-company-that*. Her supervisor said this, the health and welfare program said that, the slimy owner of the company said whatever. Everything that came out of her mouth... came from *them*, instead of from inside her."

Zachary frowned, scratching down a few words to remind himself of the points he wanted to follow up on later. He looked over at Barbara again, raising his brows.

"You didn't notice any change?" he asked her.

"Well... no. Honestly. But she was already working at the company when she moved in here. I didn't know her before Chase Gold, so I wouldn't see a difference, would I? Deidre is right, she did talk a lot about what the company's philosophy was on different aspects of her life. And she didn't talk about her family or do things with them. Just like she didn't do things with me. She would say that it would be fun to go shopping for furniture together but then she didn't have time, and would say that her supervisor needed her to put in some more hours on this project or that she just needed to work a bit longer on something... her work was her life."

"And it wasn't before," Deidre said earnestly. "She was normal before. When she was in school, she was on sports teams. She went to clubs and meetups. She did things with friends. She had dinner with the family, at least on weekends. She'd find the time. She had a more balanced life."

"Did you know she was talking about having her tubes tied? To make herself more attractive to the company for the remaining permanent position?"

Deidre's jaw dropped. She caught her breath and for a minute seemed unable to control the emotions that welled up. She closed her eyes, swallowed, and breathed deeply for a minute. "No," she said unnecessarily. "I didn't know that." She shook her head, eyes welling with tears. "It surprises me and it doesn't." She took a few seconds to try to get her composure again. "That's just what she was like after she started at that company. Before she started working there, she always wanted a family. She always talked about finding the right guy and having a couple of kids. She loved babies, and she loved all of the little cousins in our family. She was always the first one to reach out to hold a new baby or comfort a crying child. Even before the mother could get there. She wanted that life, to have everything, family and friends and all kinds of different experiences. But after she started working there, she was different. She was a corporate woman. She was... I don't want to say cold, but that's how I felt around her. Like they had just frozen all of her feelings. Everything that wasn't in alignment with succeeding at her job. Like freezing off warts."

Zachary pondered the change in Lauren. To go from loving children and wanting them in her life to talking about having her tubes tied so that children would never complicate her corporate life was so very drastic. He couldn't see a person making that kind of turnaround in just a few weeks. It wasn't natural. Had she just been playing for the company? Telling them what she thought they wanted to hear in order to get the job? But what would she do once she had the job and they expected her to follow through? Would she stay that new corporate woman, willing to give herself fully to the company? Or would she try to get her old life back, to let the old Lauren personality seep back in again?

He took a deep breath, looking at the page of the notebook in front of him and addressed the next problem.

"You called the owner of the company slimy. Who did you mean?"

"The top guy. Drake. He was a piece of work. I hated him."

"Gordon Drake?" Zachary tried not to let the surprise enter into his voice. "He seemed like a nice enough guy to me."

"Nice. Yeah. He likes to give that impression, doesn't he? He's the perfect gentleman. The face of the company. He's the one who talks to the media about his wonderful organization and all of the wonderful things they are doing. He's the one that handles all of that public relations stuff and shows everyone how wonderful the company really is. It doesn't matter that people are dying at Chase Gold. It doesn't matter that they are turning workers into drones and zombies. All that matters is that the company gets to be as big internationally as all of the other investment banking firms. He believes that they can take over the world, honestly. He's got this ego that's bigger than anything you've ever seen before. Like… a god complex. He is the master of the company, and when the company is the biggest investment banking firm in the world, he will control the economy of countries. He'll control the economics of the world."

"Really. Wow. I never really got that from him."

Deidre shook her head. "The guy rubs me the wrong way. He always pretends that he cares about his employees. If you saw him on any of the news spots after Lauren died… He's mugging for the camera. He's practically crying, he cares so much. Everything he says and does is calculated to make him and his company look good."

Zachary thought about Gordon's words about the interns being the lifeblood of the company. About him reassuring Bieberstein at the hospital about how important he was and how much he meant to the company. He really did put on a good show. He *seemed* to mean the things that he said. But was Zachary just seeing what he expected to? Was he seeing Gordon in a good light because he had been kind to Zachary in the past? Because he had hired Zachary to find Bridget when she had been kidnapped, had defended him in front of the police, had admitted to the police that Bridget had been the aggressor in their dysfunctional marriage and not the other way around?

Gordon had always treated Zachary with friendliness and respect, rather than as a rival for Bridget's affections. Zachary had always assumed that it was because Gordon believed that he had Bridget for himself and she would never consider going back to Zachary. And he was right, Bridget had a relationship with Gordon that was totally different from what she'd had with Zachary. Gordon was an equal, a partner, someone that she looked up to and respected. With Zachary, it had been different. She had been half mother and half nurse. Trying to fix him and show him off to her friends. They had been besotted with each other in the beginning, but that had ended when she realized that she couldn't change him. She couldn't tell him how to behave and transform him into someone she could take with her to gala events and not have him embarrass her. She couldn't tell him to stop being depressed or having flashbacks.

And Gordon had somehow talked Bridget into getting pregnant. Her pregnancy could not have been an accident. Not when Bridget would have to use the eggs that she'd had frozen before her treatment for ovarian cancer. She had been resistant to freezing her eggs, insisting that she never wanted children. It had only been at the doctor's insistence that she had gone ahead with it. If Gordon could talk Bridget into having children with him, then how hard would it have been for him to talk Lauren out of having a family, and dedicating her life instead to Drake, Chase, Gould?

"Uh, Zachary...?"

Zachary looked at Barbara. He looked back at Deidre.

"He had me fooled," he admitted. "I'm supposed to be a good detective, but I never saw him that way."

"I bet if you looked into his background, you'd find all kinds of bodies," Deidre said. "Not literal bodies, I mean, but all of the people and companies that he stepped on to get to where he is now. He doesn't care who he hurts in his climb to the top. He's like Hitler. He doesn't believe that other people have feelings or purpose. He is bound and determined to rule the world someday, and he manipulates whatever and whoever he has to." Her mouth twisted into a bitter scowl. "He's not what he appears to be."

The thing was, Zachary *had* checked out Gordon's background. Before

577

he'd ever started with the investigation at Drake, Chase, Gould, he had checked Gordon out, looking for dirt, looking for anything to indicate that he wasn't the person he appeared to be. He wanted to find something that he could tell Bridget, to convince her that she didn't want to stay with him. Something that he could hold up and say 'Gordon isn't better than me. Just look at what he's done in the past.'

But he hadn't found any dirt. He hadn't found any bodies. When people talked about Gordon, they smiled and spoke warmly. Past employers and coworkers, past intimate partners, everyone. They all agreed that he was what he appeared to be.

When Zachary had been called in to help find Bridget, Gordon could have thrown him under the bus. He could have told the police that Zachary had been a stalker, that he had pursued Bridget long after they had separated. He could have said that Zachary had a checkered past. That he'd grown up in foster care and institutions, and everyone knew the kind of person that bred. He could have talked about Zachary's many failings, both inside and outside of the marriage. But he hadn't. He had supported Zachary and he'd been completely genuine about it. Zachary had no doubt that he had meant what he said.

But then, it wouldn't have helped Gordon for the cops to have put Zachary in jail or arrested him for Bridget's kidnapping. Then Zachary couldn't do what Gordon wanted him to do. He wouldn't have been able to track Bridget down in time and the police would never have gotten to her until it was too late. If they had kept Zachary in custody for another day, Bridget would have been dead by the time they found her. If they found her.

So which man was Gordon? Was he the man that Zachary had seen and secretly admired, the man that he had wanted to be in his marriage to Bridget? Or was he a snake, a persona that was put on for the public, so that he could get what he wanted?

If power corrupted, then Gordon was surely corrupt.

CHAPTER TWENTY-SIX

Zachary saw Kenzie's name on his missed calls when he got out of the meeting with Barbara and Deidre. He had ignored the vibrating of his phone in his pocket, and it was probably a good thing that he had. Getting the autopsy results in the middle of a meeting with the family and client wouldn't have been a good thing. He wanted a chance to review the results and talk things over with Kenzie before he gave the results to Barbara.

Although, maybe talking the results over with Kenzie was no longer an option. It had always been part of the process before, but now that they were no longer together... were they still friends, and was that enough for him to get her ear and a little bit of her time to go through the results?

He got settled in his car and then called her back.

She answered after a minute with a brisk "Medical Examiner's office."

"It's Zachary."

"Oh, hi, Zachary. Sorry, I didn't look at the caller I.D."

"No problem. You have the results?"

"Dr. Wiltshire has made a finding of accidental death, as expected. Combination of blow to the head and drowning. Probably the lack of oxygen killed her before the intercranial bleeding."

Zachary nodded slowly. Pretty much what he had expected. "Do you have time to go over the details, or should I just come down and get the report?"

"I've got a couple of minutes."

"Anything show up in the bloodwork? Drugs, alcohol, medications?"

"Some alcohol. Not enough to have impaired her. Not considered to have contributed to her death."

"Any stimulants?"

"No."

"Any medications? Prescription, over the counter?"

"Nothing that showed up on the usual tests, but you know that we don't test for everything. Was she prescribed something specific you are looking for?"

"No. It's just that… someone else at her office had an accident this week. Passed out on the treadmill and had a seizure. Lacerations and broken bones, but he was okay."

"And you're wondering whether there was any connection between the two accidents?"

"It's an odd coincidence."

"Did the hospital find any reason for his seizure?"

"No. They said it was probably just a one-time thing, maybe he had a virus."

"And did you find anything to indicate they're wrong?"

"No, not yet," he admitted.

She was silent for a few moments. "Did you have any other questions?"

"Was there anything unusual? Any other illness or recent injuries?"

"Iron levels were low, but not drastically. Some indications of stress on the heart. Maybe she'd been sick lately, some virus. The flu."

"Like my seizure victim?"

"Well… yes. People do get the flu. Sometimes it can hit one person harder than expected. Especially if they are already run down or susceptible. And it does circulate through offices."

"What does it mean that there were indications of stress on the heart? Too much exercise? Or is that just from generic stress like being worried about something or being pressured by a deadline?"

"More like overwork. Not just one brutal exercise session or worrying about making a deadline. But a constant level of stress that put an extra strain on the heart."

"Working eighteen-hour days?"

"Well, that could do it. Yes. Was she?"

"Depends who you talk to. According to the date stamps on her emails and computer files, yes. According to her timesheet at work, no."

"Her heart would agree with the computer."

"And low iron, could that be overwork too?"

"Not directly, but if she wasn't eating properly, was drinking, had heavy bleeding, was taking a lot of Aspirin or another medication, some of those things could cause it. It is possible to die from working too hard. It's common enough in Japan that they even have a word for it. *Karoshi.*"

Zachary thought about that for a moment before going on.

"Did she have any injuries? Other than the injury to the head?"

"No. That was the only thing of note. Everybody gets scrapes and bruises from running into a coffee table or doorway or dropping something on their toes, but there wasn't anything to indicate any violence."

"Could someone have held her under the water?"

"You know from Declan's case that that would cause bruising. Unless she was drugged, which according to our tests, she was not. She hadn't had enough alcohol to knock her out."

"What if someone held her face down by the head, where she was already injured? Then you wouldn't be able to tell there was any bruising from his hand."

"But she would probably also have had bruising on the other side. On her nose or chin or some part of her face. Because he would be pressing her face down into the bottom of the bathtub while she fought back."

"What if she didn't fight back, because she was already knocked unconscious by the blow?"

Kenzie paused while she thought this through. "Possibly," she said cautiously. "Depends how bad the damage to her brain was."

"Defensive wounds?"

"Nothing that looked like defensive wounds."

"Broken hyoid?"

"You don't think I would have led with that? No, no broken hyoid or bruising on the neck."

"Do we have a more exact time of death? Anything more specific than between the time she left work and the time she was discovered?"

"That's pretty tricky, since we don't know the temperature of the water.

So we don't know how warm it kept the body or how quickly it cooled it down. We can make estimates, assuming she would have run it slightly above body temperature, but not hot enough to be uncomfortable... but if she ran a cold bath to wake herself up, then we'd be completely wrong."

"Dr. Wiltshire didn't have any reservations at all? Everything pointed to an accident?"

"We didn't have your report of someone else at her company having an accident, so no. With that information, he might have thought about the possibility of foul play, but I still don't think he would have made any other finding."

"You think it's just a coincidence?"

"Sounds like it. Just one of those things. How closely did they work together?"

"Pretty close. They were both working out of the same bullpen, competing for two permanent job positions. In fact, they were the two who were thought to be the best prospects for the permanent positions."

"Huh."

Zachary thought he might sense a grudging admission of the possibility that the two accidents might be related. But she didn't jump right into it.

"It could just be that they both had the flu as it made its rounds of the office. I'll mention it to Dr. Wiltshire. Like I said, he's already made a finding and nothing is likely to change his mind... but I'll at least pass the information on. What he does is up to him."

"Okay. I'm not going to report to my client yet, not until I hear from you one way or the other."

"Fine. I'll let you know, probably by end of day."

CHAPTER TWENTY-SEVEN

Zachary tried calling Bieberstein. He wanted to make sure Bieberstein was okay, but didn't want to be responsible for waking him up if he'd finally gotten to sleep. Hopefully Bieberstein would at least have the sense to turn his phone ringer off if he were going to sleep.

There was no answer. The phone just kept ringing and ringing until it eventually went to voicemail after about fifty rings. Zachary called the main number at Chase Gold and had the receptionist put him through to Mandy. She answered the phone breathlessly after a couple of rings.

"Hello?"

"It's Zachary Goldman, Mandy. I was looking for Blair Bieberstein. Is he around?"

"Biebs? I don't know." There was a pause, as Zachary assumed Mandy looked over the tops of the cubicles to see if the other intern was there. "I don't see him. But I don't know. He works on other projects sometimes. He isn't always even on this floor. They farm him out wherever he is needed. Do you want me to tell him to call you? Or you could leave a message on his phone or send him a text or email."

"Could you ask whether anyone else has seen him? He was acting kind of weird last night, and you know he got hit on the head yesterday. You wouldn't want anything to happen to him."

Mandy covered up the mike on the phone while she talked to the other interns, then eventually returned. "No, no one has seen him around since the hospital yesterday. Well, except Daniel. He says that he saw Bieberstein for a few minutes last night, before he left for the day."

"Before Daniel left or before Bieberstein left?"

"Daniel."

"Can I talk to him?"

Mandy blew an impatient sigh into her phone. "You'll have to call him on his own phone."

"Do you have his number?"

She was silent as she looked it up. Then she read it off to him. "I gotta get back to work now. Good luck."

She hung up without another word. Zachary dialed Daniel's number. Daniel of course knew who it was and answered right away.

"Hello, Mr. Goldman. Or is it Detective?"

"Zachary is fine. Mandy said you saw Bieberstein yesterday?"

"For a few minutes, yes. He was here before I left."

"Was he the only one here? When you left, I mean?"

"The only one I saw. I don't know if there was anyone else here… not in the bullpen, but a VP in his office maybe, I wouldn't know if someone was sitting with their door closed."

"How did he seem to you?"

"Weird," Daniel said. "But he always seems weird to me."

"Was he any different from usual?"

"I don't know. Honestly. Biebs is just Biebs. He's kind of nutty, but he has a brain and knows how to use it!"

"I gather the company finds him invaluable."

"Yeah, a lot of people think he's the best thing since sliced bread. Can't be replaced or improved upon."

"You don't sound like you think so," Zachary ventured, sensing a dismissiveness in Daniel's tone.

"I don't believe there is anyone who can't be replaced. It's the company that matters, not the individuals. If we work together as a company, as one smooth, efficient machine, that's what makes us great. We become something more when we contribute to the success of the company."

"Uh… yeah. That makes sense. So I guess Bieberstein wasn't there when you got in this morning?"

"No."

"Is that unusual? He must have to check in with you. Have you called around to see if he went home?"

"He's one of my interns, but he gets borrowed by other departments. Whoever needs him the most. It's sort of out of my control and I don't always know where he is."

"Have you tried calling him?"

"No."

"I'm worried about him," Zachary said, trying to convey some urgency toward Daniel, who seemed to think there was nothing to be concerned about. "When he called me last night, he was really paranoid. He hadn't slept and he thought that someone was after him, trying to harm him."

A few seconds passed before Daniel spoke. "He thought who was after him? Exactly what was he worried about?"

"He didn't specify who. Just 'them.' I told you, he was paranoid. I think he was going off the deep end and I'm worried something might have happened to him. Do you think you could spend some time and try to track him down?"

Daniel grumbled. "I don't have a lot of time to be babysitting. I'll send out an email blast to the department heads, but I'm not going to be wasting my time trying to track him down by phone. He knows where he's supposed to be. If he skips out on us, he'll get fired."

"I'm not worried about his job. I'm worried about his safety. I don't think he's skipping work. He might have had some kind of dissociative episode or another accident."

"That didn't work for Matters, and it isn't going to work for him. You either show up at work, or you're fired."

"Matters?" Zachary tried to figure out who Daniel was talking about.

"The one who pretended she had amnesia. 'Oh, no, I couldn't come into work, because I didn't know who I was. I forgot all about my job.' If you think that got her her job back, forget about it. She didn't. She could waste her time in a homeless shelter."

"That's pretty heartless."

"I don't have any empathy for someone who betrays the company. After all the time and money that they spend on us, everything they do for us, the prestige, the money, the health care and other benefits? This is an amazing place to work. If someone can't figure that out…?" He snorted. "If they can't see how much the job is worth, they can find something else somewhere else."

"I guess so," Zachary said. He sucked his cheeks in, hesitating. "So you'll send that email, make sure that Bieberstein is just working for another department, and nothing has happened to him?"

"I suppose," Daniel said grudgingly.

"If the company takes care of its employees… well, it can't do that without the employees doing their part. They can't take care of Bieberstein without your help."

"Yeah. You're right. We're all part of the machine. I'll see if I can find him."

————

Zachary checked his email and saw that he had one from Bev. He was surprised that it had taken her that long to come to the realization that he had Lauren's phone and computer, both of which were undoubtedly the property of Drake, Chase, Gould. He had expected her to demand their return a lot earlier.

He had the cloned drive, so he could still review any of the information that was stored on her computer. He still had the proof that she had worked the hours Barbara said she had, that she had been denied time off, that they had not even given her time when she had a signed letter from her doctor. Kenzie didn't seem to think that Lauren's illnesses and anemia had anything to do with her death—or Dr. Wiltshire didn't think so—but they still could have contributed. If she were even more exhausted because she'd had the flu and hadn't been given the time to recover from it, or if she'd fainted because she was sick or because she was weak from the anemia, then the company could be partially responsible for what had happened to her. Maybe nothing that could ever be proven in court or give her family any financial recompense, but at least they would know a little more about how she had died. Maybe it wouldn't make them feel any better, but maybe it would.

He looked one more time at her phone and computer, trying to think of whether there was anything he had missed. He didn't want to go snooping in any corporate secrets, but he did want to make sure he had looked at anything that might have affected her mentally or any sign that there was someone out there who wanted to harm her. He hadn't come across any jealous boyfriends. Jealous coworkers, maybe. People who wanted the position that she appeared to have clinched. But he couldn't find any motive for anyone outside work to have bad feelings toward her.

He brought up her social networks on his own computer, browsing through the timelines for anything weird or suspicious. There were no menacing messages before she'd died or creepy ones afterward. Any memorial messages indicated that she was a nice girl and that they would really miss her. Earlier on the timeline, before her death, he saw more messages from her family than he had noticed when looking at it before. Of course, social networks changed their algorithms all the time, depending on what you were doing and on what the overlords of the social networks wanted to emphasize. They banned or downvoted some topics and posters and upvoted or emphasized others. Something like an election or a plane crash could upend everything. Maybe it was Lauren's death itself, and an outpouring of loving messages among her family members and friends, that had changed the emphasis of certain topics and posters showing up on her timeline.

He brought the same social network up in the app on her laptop, frozen in time because it couldn't read anything else from the internet. It was handy having all of her personal accounts and social networks contained within the one program, so he could quickly switch from one tab to the other. The computer complained about not having internet access, but he could still read what had been downloaded and cached.

There was barely a word on her timeline from her family or close friends. He scrolled through both computers at the same time, trying to find a place in the timeline when the posts were synchronized, or close to it. But whatever he did, he couldn't find the posts from Lauren's family on her computer. It was like she had blocked them there. Had she been worried about having personal information on an office computer?

He looked through the various settings, trying to find some list of who she had blocked or banned. But if they were blocked on her account, they would be blocked in both places. The work laptop could be filtering certain things, but he couldn't find any user-controlled filters either.

Zachary closed his eyes, thinking about it.

CHAPTER TWENTY-EIGHT

"Gerry… I wonder if you could make a rush visit for me. I have a computer that I need to return to the owner, but there's something weird going on with it. I don't want to put them off for too long, so I was hoping you might have some time today…"

"Did you clone the hard drive?" Gerry demanded.

Zachary smiled. "I didn't remember right away, but yeah, I did."

"So if I can't get over there today, we can access all of the information off of the cloned drive."

"Yeah, I suppose. But do you think you might have some time today? I'd like to have some idea of whether this is important or just some rabbit trail."

"Well… yeah, I could spare an hour or two. You think that will be enough?"

"Yeah. Probably not even that long. Just a few minutes."

Gerry chuckled. "Nothing ever takes just a few minutes on a computer. Especially not anything weird."

Zachary had to admit that was probably true. "So when can I expect you? I'd like to tell the owner something, so they know it's on its way and don't sic the cops or some company thugs on me."

"Just what's going on with this computer?"

"I don't know. Maybe something, maybe nothing. But there have been a lot of accidents going on, and these guys have money, so I don't really want to take the risk of upsetting them if I don't have to."

"I'll try to be there in a couple of hours. I'll get there when I can."

"Thanks. I'll be here."

———

Gerry was, in many ways, the typical computer hacker/nerd. Glasses, messy hair, comfortable clothes, and a way of talking to computers that made them purr with delight. He was older than Zachary might have expected a computer nerd to be and he had a pot belly, when Zachary pictured all hackers as being skinny, underdeveloped kids. But Gerry had all of the ingredients necessary to figure out what was going on with Lauren's computer and social networks. Zachary let him sit down and showed him the difference between the information on the two computers. Gerry nodded rapidly, chewing on the top of a pencil.

"Yup. Yup. Sure. Let me look at this…"

He said more, but it was all Greek to Zachary. IP addresses and proxies and certificates. He clicked his tongue as he worked rapidly, moving from one computer to the other, settling on Lauren's computer and digging deep down into the code that was unintelligible to Zachary. Zachary sat on the couch and looked at his own email on his phone and tablet, trying not to hover or look impatient.

"This is pretty sophisticated," Gerry said eventually, turning toward Zachary.

"Yeah? What exactly are they doing?"

"The content that this computer can see is being filtered. Like you noticed, you don't see the same thing on the laptop as you see on your computer when you log into her social networks. At first, I thought it was just the corporate program that they have set up to access the social networks and personal emails. Like, they were trying to filter out any personal stuff so that it was only being used for company work. But it's not quite that. And it's more than that."

"Meaning…?"

"The first level is within the app they're using to log into the social networks. It uses special heuristics to filter out the majority of the posts by family and friends. Not all of it, or the user might realize what's going on, but just enough to keep her... more isolated from her family and friends. You don't see your family's posts, you don't get distracted from your work, I guess. Stuff from more distant friends, and from friends at the company especially, show up. And the stuff from the corporate discussion or project groups she is in. All of that stuff is prioritized. The most important stuff—company stuff—comes to the top of the timeline."

"Do you think the employees are aware of it? That their information is being manipulated?"

"I don't know. It would be hard to spot, unless you're looking at two different computers at the same time, like you were doing. If this is your primary computer, why would you pull it up on any other computer? You've got this one with you all the time, unless they weren't allowed to take them home."

"They were allowed to take them home, and they worked long days, so they were really only home to sleep. This computer would have been the only one she used to do anything. And her phone."

"I'll look at the phone too, but if it's a company phone, I'll bet they've got filters in place there, too."

"But what if she accessed her social networks through the browser instead of the app? Wouldn't she have noticed that something was off then?"

"Only if she was looking at both at the same time. And only if the browser wasn't being filtered as well."

"Was it?"

"They've set up a bunch of private DNS hosting and corporate security certificates to control what the users can see through any program that accesses the internet. Doesn't matter what browser they install, or whether they try an incognito window or to spoof a different IP address. Whatever she did, she couldn't get any access to the internet through this computer that is not controlled."

"So... Google, email, social networks, everything?"

"Everything. As far as this computer is concerned, the internet is a much smaller place than it is on your computer. It only gets a limited window on the world."

"Wait... so..." Zachary tried to keep up with all of the ideas that flooded his brain. He stepped up behind Gerry. "Search Shelby Matters. What does it find?"

Gerry looked at him, eyebrow cocked, then turned back to Lauren's laptop and tried searching the name. He looked at the results. "Have a look."

Zachary leaned in. There were a couple of articles with quotes by Drake, Chase, Gould, and there was a page on the company's website giving details about Shelby Matter's amnesia and how the company would be looking after Matters on long-term disability, but she wouldn't be returning to work. There were links to the company's health and wellness site, how to get counseling and advice if you needed it, and so on. All very orderly and giving the impression that Drake, Chase, Gould had stepped up to help a former employee in distress, far from what Daniel had implied when he had been talking about her.

Gerry turned to Zachary's computer and, without prompting, typed in the same search. There were a lot more articles. There were social media posts and conversations about Matters and what had happened to her, speculating on what had triggered her amnesia and about Drake, Chase, Gould's reputation in the industry. The Drake, Chase, Gould results were there, but much farther down the search results. Drake, Chase, Gould was obviously throttling the information flow to their company computers.

Zachary stood there behind Gerry, trying to process it all. Not only was the company filtering social networks to keep their employees more isolated from their families and involved in their own work groups, but they were controlling their views of the world completely. Assuming that all of the employees had computers that, like Lauren's, were being filtered, the employees didn't get any news that might throw the company in a negative light. Any incidents relating to their employees or the lawsuits against or initiated by Chase Gold would be presented in whatever light the company wanted to show them in. With the company as the hero and the whistle-blowers and victims as being in the wrong.

"Do you think all of the employee computers are like this? Or is it possible that Lauren's is the only one that was tampered with?"

"You'd have to get me another computer to look at. But this is a lot of trouble to go through for just one computer. It's pretty sophisticated stuff. I would speculate that it is company-wide, not just targeted at one person."

Zachary started to pace back and forth, trying to control the flow of information coming into his own CPU and to follow all of the possibilities and conclusions outward. Everything was getting clearer, but he wasn't quite there yet. Knowing that the computer was being controlled by the company and that the employees' view of the world was being manipulated was a key puzzle piece. As were the health and welfare program and the attitudes of the employees that he had talked to. The things that had surprised him throughout the investigation were coming into clearer focus, making more sense, and starting to form a picture.

"Who could do this?" he asked Gerry, who was watching him with interest.

"This isn't just someone fooling around. A project like this, with all of the servers and certificates and redirects, the sophistication of the filtering… it's not plug-and-play. It would need a pretty advanced programmer and a lot of money. This isn't just some prank."

"So the company hired someone to set it all up."

"Undoubtedly. And to maintain it. As different stories hit the news or different things become important or the company wants to emphasize certain values more or less, then they're going to need someone tweaking the filters and algorithms."

"Can they tell what sites employees go to? Where they spend their time? If they're searching for anything in particular?"

"They'll have a record of all of the traffic that goes through their servers and where it came from."

"Is this 'spyware'?"

"This in particular? No. But that doesn't mean that there isn't spyware on this computer." Gerry turned back to it and started to launch different programs and inquiries, pulling up black command prompt windows full of data and system management windows that Zachary had never seen before, moving quickly from one to another. "Yeah, it looks like they've got a few programs monitoring what employees are doing, whether they are in a browser or not. Even one that has camera access." Gerry casually picked up a pad of sticky notes from Zachary's desk, tore one sheet in half, and pasted it over the camera lens at the top of the computer screen. "Late is better than never, I suppose. If anyone is concerned about what you're doing with this computer, they might have been watching us and listening in." He rifled through some miscellany in the small toolkit he had brought with him, and pushed an adapter into the microphone jack.

"Can you…" Zachary's mind jumped ahead like a squirrel leaping from one branch to the other, skipping over the treetops. Gerry waited patiently

"Can you use the information you have found to get back to the corporate server and… um…"

"Hack it?"

"Well… I don't know. I guess. Can you see what's on it? Employees must be able to access files on their server for work, right? An intern like Lauren probably wouldn't have access to everything…"

"What are you looking for?" Gerry turned back to the laptop and started typing.

Zachary looked at the computer, his stomach knotting. Gerry hadn't said that he'd killed the spyware, so Zachary could only assume that everything they typed and anything they looked at would be recorded somewhere. But he couldn't let that prevent him from investigating the situation fully. He couldn't be scared off by some electronic monitoring.

"Employee records. Whatever we can get access to. I already know they're falsifying timesheets. I'd like to see how much they have in their medical records. And if they're monitoring employee computers, I'd like to see when the computers were on and in use."

"You want to know what they were working on?"

Zachary shrugged. "Not exactly. I don't know what projects they were working on. But if I know who was busy the night or morning that Lauren died, I might be able to eliminate some suspects."

Gerry nodded. He first did what Zachary would have, navigating to the network drives and browsing through them. When he was blocked by the network security, he opened another command prompt and inserted a USB drive into the laptop. From there, Zachary was at a loss as to what Gerry was doing.

He moved back again to wait. Gerry muttered and cajoled the computer, and it was only a few minutes before he was nodding his head.

"Yup, I'm in," he confirmed. "I can get access to human resources… medical, time tracking, employee contracts… I don't see the internet access logs there, so maybe they are with… yeah, there's a security department. This is where the internet logs are stored. Webcam pics. You wanted to know who was where when your victim died?"

"Yes. If we can go through the internet access logs, then I can probably tell who was working when. And you can tell whether they were at work or at home, right? It would be able to tell what network it was connected to?"

"Or if you want to know who was here, you can check the security videos."

"They have security cameras?"

"Oh, yeah." Gerry pulled up a 3D model of the building Drake, Chase, Gould was in, the floors they occupied highlighted and marked with numerous red dots. "They've got cameras."

CHAPTER TWENTY-NINE

"This is crazy," Zachary said, looking at the video feeds. "They've got cameras everywhere. Wouldn't this be hugely expensive?"

"Data is getting cheaper all the time. You can store terabytes of information. Unheard of ten years ago. And security cameras—you can get them for your doorbell on your house now. Super cheap if you're buying them in bulk. These don't have to be able to move, they're just stationary cameras pointed at desks or doorways. Because there are so many of them, they don't need to be able to pan."

"Can you find a specific desk for me?"

"Sure. Do you have a name or location?"

"Blair Bieberstein."

Gerry nodded. "Is he your best suspect?"

"I'm afraid he might be another victim."

The live video feed came up on the screen. A camera pointed directly at the bullpen, showing all of the desks clearly. The interns were all there, working busily, except for Blair. "This one must be Blair's."

"Nobody there now," Gerry observed.

"No." Zachary swore under his breath. "There's no way they can say that they didn't know what employees were working what hours. They had cameras on them all day long. They know exactly when they were at their desks and when they weren't. Unless they were away from the office."

"Don't forget the webcams," Gerry reminded him. "If they were on their computers, the company could check up on them. Unless they were away from their desks and away from their computers at a client meeting, the company could see whether they were working or not."

"And then they probably still have some way to track them," Zachary said sarcastically. "Some ankle monitor or microchip."

"It wouldn't be so hard to do. They probably keep their phones with them all the time. If not... give them a step-counter or smartwatch. Then track away."

"Sheesh." Zachary shook his head. And he knew from experience that a phone could be used to eavesdrop even when it did not appear to be active. As long as it had power, it could be getting or sending all kinds of information. "Okay, so can you move back in time to when Bieberstein was at his desk last?"

Gerry started to rewind the video. Zachary watched the other interns walking to and away from their desks backward. They interacted, looked at each other's desks and computers when they were away, put their water bottles down on their desks and walked away, leaving them unattended. Zachary watched as the cubicles cleared out in the early morning, until there were two figures on the screen, Bieberstein and someone standing next to him. Gerry released the controls and let the video play forward at regular speed. The person standing next to Bieberstein was Gordon Drake.

"Back it up a bit more and let me see what happened," Zachary said. He leaned over Gerry, knowing that he was getting too close, but intent on seeing exactly what had happened.

He should have known that Gordon had something to do with it. He had called Gordon to tell him that Bieberstein was having problems. And Gordon had gone to check it out. He hadn't called Zachary back or answered his phone, so Zachary had assumed he was tired of being harassed and didn't want to be involved in Zachary's investigation anymore. He thought about what Deidre had said about Gordon, her angry accusations. Deidre didn't know Gordon personally like Zachary did. Her accusations had been fed by the fact that her sister had died. She wanted someone to blame, and why not the owner of the company that Lauren had become so obsessed with?

Gerry backed up the video until it was only Bieberstein standing there alone, and Gordon was not yet on the scene. Zachary could see Bieberstein was talking on his phone, and wondered if that was when he was talking to Zachary. Bieberstein moved around jerkily, his head lolling out of control like he was drunk. He typed on his computer, picked up his phone, put it down, and searched through the papers on his desk for something. When Gordon walked into the view of the camera, Bieberstein jerked away in surprise. Zachary could see his mouth moving, his expression angry, but he couldn't make out what Bieberstein was saying. Maybe what was coming out didn't even make sense, since Gordon just looked at him blankly.

After a minute, Gordon touched Bieberstein on the arm, saying something to him. There were words exchanged, and Bieberstein seemed to be winding down a little, but was still jerky and unsteady.

"That guy's really impaired," Gerry observed.

"Sleep deprivation."

"Really? He's not drunk?"

"No. Probably not."

They watched as Gordon tugged Bieberstein's arm a little, trying to lead him away from his desk. Bieberstein resisted, looked around, motioned to his desk, and after a moment of discussion, went back to get his computer. He closed it and picked it up to hold it under his arm. More discussion, and then Gordon and Bieberstein walked away from the desk and the camera.

———

Zachary pulled out his phone and tried to call Gordon again. There was no answer on his cell phone. He tried the main reception number at Drake, Chase, Gould, only to be thwarted by the receptionist, who Zachary guessed had instructions not to let anyone through.

He needed to know that Bieberstein was okay. What if Gordon had taken him somewhere? What if he'd harmed him? Gordon would, he was sure, have some reassuring explanation, and Zachary needed to hear it. One side of his brain didn't believe that Gordon could do anything to hurt anyone, but the other side was suspicious as all hell.

Who would have thought that someone like Gordon Drake could be a dangerous criminal? Everyone would think that he was so kind, so focused on growing his company that he wouldn't have the time or inclination to do anything violent. No one believed that rich people, good society people, could do anything wrong. That was for the masses, the lower class. Poverty bred violence. Wealth didn't. Only the lack of wealth. Jealousy and greed and need.

Even though he knew better, he tried Gordon's home number. Which, of course, was Bridget's home number. He hoped that Gordon was home, that he would see the caller I.D., and that he would answer it. But it was not Gordon who answered the phone.

"Zachary?"

Bridget didn't immediately go into a tirade and recriminations, so that was good. Her tone was cautious, as if she were worried that he was bringing her bad news.

"I just wondered if Gordon was there," Zachary said apologetically. "I can't reach him at work or on his cell phone and I thought maybe he was at home."

"No, he's not here. Why would he be at this time of day?"

"I don't know his usual schedule. Or maybe he had an appointment to go to with you. Or was having something delivered to the house. Or he could have been sick."

At least the owner, if he were sick, could get time off. Zachary wondered about Chase and Gould. Did Drake have to report to them? Or did they report to him? Or neither one? Did any of them have to get the permission of the others to make big decisions for the company? Surely not for everyday things, but if the company were to start in a different direction in marketing, employee security, or a health and welfare initiative, did they have to have unanimous agreement? Two out of three? Or did they each have different assigned areas of responsibility?

"Did you hear me, Zachary? He's not here."

"Okay. Sorry to bother you. If you do hear from him… would you tell him that I was trying to get him? I don't want to be a pest, but I'm worried about one of his employees. I'd like to talk to him—"

"Don't you think you did enough last night?"

"Did enough? I just… let him know what was going on. I thought he would want to know. I didn't have the numbers of anyone else at the company."

"You had him up in the middle of the night. Which meant that he woke me up and I couldn't get back to sleep. You know I need my sleep, especially now."

How was she going to get that sleep once she had the baby? Would Gordon look after the baby at night? Were they going to hire a nanny? Bridget had to realize that the baby wasn't going to sleep all night.

"I am sorry. I didn't want to get either of you up, but I didn't know what else to do."

"Just leave him alone. Don't you think it's time to close this case? It's obvious that there isn't anything to it. The poor girl fell in her bathtub. There's no foul play involved in that. It isn't like someone murdered her. The only reason for you to be so involved in Drake, Chase, Gould is to embarrass Gordon. And it's time to back off."

"I'm sorry… it should only be a few more days. Just have Gordon call me, if you hear from him. Please."

She hung up without saying goodbye. Zachary sat looking at his phone.

"That one's a firecracker," Gerry commented.

Zachary rolled his eyes. "That she is," he admitted. Curiously, he didn't feel guilty as he usually did after talking to her. He didn't feel sad or despairing. He was calm and focused and he needed to stay that way.

Somewhere out there, Bieberstein might be in trouble.

CHAPTER THIRTY

"**D**id you want to look at any more videos?" Gerry asked. "You said you wanted to see who was working when your girl was killed, and you haven't done that."

"Uh... yeah." Zachary tried to decide how important that was. If Gordon was the one who had taken Bieberstein, then did that mean he was the one who had possibly poisoned him? And possibly had something to do with Lauren's accident? He wasn't a big, muscly guy. He was not effeminate, but he was refined and cultured. He had tailored clothing and manicured nails. So he wouldn't have likely physically attacked either of them. Poison might have been more his speed. The hospital and the medical examiner hadn't found anything. But that didn't mean there wasn't anything to find, just nothing that showed up on the usual tox screens, which was a very limited list.

If it was Gordon, then he didn't need to look at any of the other interns or anyone else in the department. It would be a waste of time.

But if he was wrong, if it wasn't anything to do with Gordon, then he was letting the real criminal walk around free and Gordon himself could be in danger. Gordon and Bieberstein could both be missing, not because Gordon had done something to Bieberstein, but because someone had done something to both of them.

Gordon had said that he would make himself available to Zachary, so why had he suddenly changed his mind? Why was he suddenly not available at any of his numbers?

"Yeah, I guess I do," Zachary decided aloud. "I'd better check them just to be sure..."

He opened his mouth to give Gerry the names that he needed to look for, but his phone vibrated in his hand and he looked over at it. He had an appointment with his therapist. But he was right in the middle of an investigation. Right at a critical juncture. Gerry grinned.

"You look like someone just took away your cookie."

"Uh... I have to call to cancel an appointment."

"Why don't you just give me the feeds you want to check, and I'll look at them while you're gone. Then you're not hanging over my shoulder waiting for them. It's going to take time to find each camera and check it for... how many hours?"

"From about ten p.m. to ten a.m."

Gerry nodded. "Checking those at a slow enough speed to see how long each person was missing from the frame, and then checking their computer logs to see if they went home and kept working or what, that's going to take a while. How many people do you need to check?"

"About... five or six."

"Write them down," Gerry motioned to a scratch pad on Zachary's desk. "Are they all in the bull pen?"

"No. Most of them should be most of the time, but they might have moved around, and their supervisor and VP wouldn't be in the bullpen. And there's Gordon... we're going to have to see where he was when Lauren died too. He wouldn't have had to be there, it doesn't exactly rule anyone out if they are alibied for the time of the accident, because she could have been given some poison ahead of time..."

"Poison?" Gerry raised his eyebrows.

Zachary thought about the video of the bullpen they had just watched.

"You'll have to watch her water bottle and coffee too, make sure there is no video of anyone putting anything into them."

Gerry nodded. "A slow review of the bullpen, and then a quicker review of any other offices that they might be in," he suggested.

Zachary nodded. "I should really stay here and do it myself. This can wait..." He indicated his phone.

"If I'm not done when you get back, we can double up and you can look on your computer and I can look on this one. But for now, you go ahead and go to your appointment. We'll pick up again afterward."

"Okay." Zachary still wasn't convinced. He looked for an argument. But Gerry was right. And Zachary had promised Dr. Boyle that he wouldn't cancel any more appointments. Even though he had just seen her, she had suggested that he needed an immediate follow-up to make sure he was managing. Zachary had told her previously that he would get there for all of them and put the time and effort into his therapy that he needed to. Just like he told Heather she needed to do. And Heather would check up on him to keep him accountable.

Zachary groaned. He wrote down the names for Gerry to look into and got ready to go.

———

Dr. Boyle sat back in her chair and looked Zachary over. "So, how are you doing today, Zachary? Feeling a little better than yesterday?"

"I'm good. Everything is going pretty well."

She didn't smile. "You seem to be pretty restless. Are you sure that's true?"

"I just... I have other things to do. I was going to cancel today. But I didn't. So... I'm just... distracted by my case."

"I see. Well, we don't want your case to derail your progress here, so you're going to need to rein it in. Can you do that?"

"I don't know." Zachary had never been very good about pulling himself away from something interesting to focus on something less pleasant. He had inappropriate focus. Inability to follow directions. He'd heard it all. "I'll try, but I'm worried about someone. About a couple of people. They could be in danger."

"What makes you think that?"

"I can't get ahold of either of them. I don't know if something happened, or if I'm just following a red herring."

"Have you told the police that you're worried about these people? They could do welfare checks, go by and see if they can make contact with them."

"I've already talked to everyone who should know where they are. They aren't at home. They aren't at work. I don't know where else to go, so I don't know where to tell the police, either."

"They could do their own investigation."

"Based on me thinking that there's something suspicious going on? No."
Zachary shook his head. "I know them better than that. I can follow whatever hunches occur to me, but they have to have due cause. And they're
busy with other cases that they *do* have evidence on. They don't have time
to be chasing rainbows."

Dr. Boyle nodded slowly. "Well then, we'd better do whatever work we
can while you're here, and then you can get back to it. Right?"

"Right."

"Have you spent some time on some inner work regarding your past?"

A knot tightened in his stomach. "Uh... I haven't done very much. I
know I should have, but I've been working on this case."

"You still need to take time for yourself. You can't work all the time.
That's not healthy."

"Tell me about it," Zachary agreed, thinking about Lauren and Bieberstein and the other interns.

She raised her brows. "What?"

"These people, they're working all the time. Forty-eight hours without a
rest. Getting three or four hours of sleep in over four days. It's no wonder
Bieberstein was getting so paranoid, when he hadn't slept in days. They say
that they take care of their employees, that they care about their health and
welfare, but they don't. They are abusing them, just like if they were slaves.
They think that their employees' lives belong to them."

"This is your case again?"

"They're tracking them. Watching them through surveillance cameras
and their computers. They're feeding them information and limiting their
access to the outside world. What does that sound like to you?"

"Brainwashing? Thought conditioning?"

Zachary nodded, warming to the subject. "Exactly. It's like that
syndrome. The one where people fall in love with their kidnappers, because
their kidnappers hold the power of life and death over them and that's the
only way that they can respond if they want to stay alive. They have to do
what their captors want and feel love toward them. Not something that's
faked, but real love, or they'll die."

"Stockholm Syndrome."

"Yeah. That's it. Traumatic bonding. I was thinking about it earlier in
this case, and I lost track of it. But these employees really do love the

company. They really believe that it's the best place for them to work and that the company goes above and beyond to pay them and give them the opportunities they do. They work together well, seem like they have good relationships. Is it all just Stockholm Syndrome? Could it be, when their captor is actually a company?"

"What difference does it make? Does a cult member get attached to the cult as well as to their leader? You bet they do. Even if they can see everything the cult is doing wrong, they still believe in it. They still believe that the cult is the best place for them, that they wouldn't survive or be happy if they were to leave."

"The *cult leader...*" Zachary mused.

"A cult normally has a dynamic, somewhat mystical leader. Someone who is very passionate, magnetic."

"Yeah. That's like Gordon. Sort of."

"You don't sound sure."

Zachary thought about Gordon. He was a nice guy, calm. He was passionate, but not in the way that Zachary thought of a cult leader. He didn't make demands, he didn't shout, he wasn't magical or mystical, he didn't claim to be talking to God. He was really just a good corporate manager. Smooth, pleasant, a good face for PR for the company.

He wondered again about Chase and Gould. Was one of them the voice behind the health and welfare program? Coming up with chants and slogans and company love? Was Gordon just an empty figurehead for the media?

"Maybe. Maybe not. I don't really know." He looked at Dr. Boyle and gave her a little chagrined smile. "I've never been in a cult."

"But you *have* felt attracted to someone who has abused you."

Zachary's stomach did a nosedive. He felt nauseated. When was the last time he'd eaten? He should have planned his meals more carefully.

"Zachary."

He darted a look at Dr. Boyle. "Maybe I should be getting back to my apartment. I don't know how long it will take Gerry to look at all of that footage. I should be there, helping him."

"Why don't we talk about how it felt to you?"

He swallowed. "What?"

"You loved your mother. Even though she was abusive. Even though she abandoned you."

"I was sad that she did that. I still wanted a family. I missed my brothers and sisters."

"And you loved your mother."

He twisted around uncomfortably. What kind of person loved an abuser? It meant he was weak. He knew people who had been in abusive families and had been happy to make a break with them. They left and they never regretted it. They didn't moon around, loving and mourning the person who had abused them. They didn't long to go back to that relationship where they had been abused.

"And you loved Bridget," Dr. Boyle said.

"Bridget wasn't abusive. She gets mad now and yells to blow off steam, but it's healthy to express your feelings. She gets frustrated over how much time we spent together, that she wasted her life with me. She gets upset when I make stupid mistakes or bother her. But that's just expressing her emotions."

"You don't think she was abusive toward you when you were together?"

"I loved her. I would do anything for her. If she wanted me to be different, that wasn't abusive. That was just telling me what she wanted."

"Even if it wasn't something that you could do? Even if what she expected from you was for you *not* to be yourself?"

"She decided that we weren't compatible," Zachary said. "People find that out sometimes. That their marriage just didn't work because they weren't actually compatible with each other."

"Just like your mother decided she didn't want children anymore. That they were too much work and caused too much trouble."

Zachary swallowed. He stared at Dr. Boyle.

"If you want to see your relationships clearly in the future, you need to be able to look at the past without those lenses. You need to be honest with yourself about what happened. Being abused doesn't make you guilty. It doesn't mean that you did something wrong to wreck the relationship. You have deep-seated feelings of guilt and blame yourself for your abandonment and for the failure of your marriage. I don't know about other relationships. Were there other times in your life when you found yourself in a relationship with someone who was abusive? But you wanted to stay with them anyway?"

Zachary was with Dr. Boyle, but not with her. His attention was fractured, split between the point that she was trying to make and being mired in his past and thinking about Lauren's death.

What if the company were the abuser and Lauren the victim? What would that look like? What if the company were the equivalent of a cult? What would have been different about the case? If the member of a cult died suddenly, under suspicious circumstances, how would the police have reacted? How would Zachary have investigated it differently?

"What if it *was* a cult?" Zachary repeated aloud. "What would have been different?"

"Zachary, you're getting distracted."

"No. This is it. That's the question. What if she was strong? What if she decided to stand up to the cult? What if she decided she'd had enough and she wanted out? She'd been abused enough. She was sick, sleep-deprived, she'd thought the company was everything she wanted it to be, but finally realized it was just a trap. That they were using her."

Dr. Boyle was silent.

"What does a cult do then?" Zachary asked. "They don't want her to leave. They don't just let her walk out, do they?"

"I'm afraid I'm not an expert in cult behavior," Dr. Boyle said dryly. "But from what I've seen and read, then no, they wouldn't just let her go. They would do what they could to stop her. Argue with her, put her through some kind of intervention or ordeal, maybe even physically prevent her from leaving them."

"Physically. A cult would try to hold on to her. Tie her up. Go after her with a gun. Threaten to hurt her family."

"Those would all be possibilities with a cult," Dr. Boyle agreed cautiously. "But when you translate that to a corporate environment, I think it would be a stretch. There's only so much that a company can do legally."

"But why would they keep it legal? If the members all believe that what they are doing is right, and that what their leader says to do is scripture, then they can take whatever action they feel they need to, and they are in the right. They can't do the wrong thing if they are protecting the company and its officers."

"But we don't see that happening. A corporate environment isn't the same as a cult."

"She's with them all day every day. She eats with them, exercises with them, wears their uniform, spouts their slogans, sleeps with them. She does whatever they tell her to. It *is* the same."

"It really isn't."

Zachary got up out of his seat, unable to sit still any longer. He paced back and forth across the room. "I think it could be. You don't know the stuff that's been going on. They burned down a house." Zachary said the words quickly to try to keep himself from dwelling on the fire and getting choked in his own memories. "You can't tell me that's typical corporate behavior. None of this is."

"Zachary… have you been taking your meds?"

"Yeah, yeah." Zachary was practically vibrating. He knew that he was right.

All along, he'd been wondering why everyone was so devoted to the company. He'd been trying to connect what happened at the office with Lauren's death without any success, because he was treating it like it was a normal murder. She wasn't murdered because of the jealousy of her co-workers. It wasn't because they were competing for the same jobs.

They had retaliated against her betrayal.

They had thought that she was the perfect corporate drone. They had been able to pull her away from her family, to convince her that the best thing for her would be to devote herself forever to corporate life and to give up her chances of conceiving just so it wouldn't inconvenience them. And then she had turned on them. She'd had an awakening and decided she was going to get out. And that was the point at which someone had—

"Zachary." Dr. Boyle interrupted his thoughts. "I think you're having a break. You're conflating Lauren's situation with your own history. The trauma bonding. Your fear of abandonment. Your… past traumatic experience."

"I'm not making this up. It isn't about my life and my past. These things really did happen. Everybody who spoke out against the company was squashed. No one was allowed to say anything against them. The people who talked in public were sued. Or they had bizarre accidents. It escalated. Lauren wasn't the first, she was just one in a line of employees and ex-employees."

"Is there someone we could call who would come and get you? I'd like you to admit yourself for observation. If you're taking your meds like you're supposed to, you might be reacting to something. Or you might need some other adjustment. You know occasional adjustments are required along the way."

"I don't need a ride," Zachary said, looking at the clock on Dr. Boyle's desk. He knew he was cutting the session short, but he couldn't waste valuable time in finding out which employee or employees had gone after Lauren.

Gerry might already have found something on the video recordings. Zachary had dutifully shut his phone off when entering the doctor's office, which meant he could have missed a call or text.

He pressed the hardware button on the phone, waiting for it to boot back up. "Sorry, I have to go. I have to take care of this. We'll talk next week."

He ignored Dr. Boyle's protests and walked out of the office.

CHAPTER THIRTY-ONE

When his phone finished its startup routine, Zachary was already in the car. He put the phone in its holder on his dashboard and as if in response, a series of text messages popped up on the screen.

An unknown number: *If you don't back off Chase Gold, you're going to die.*

Gerry: *You'd better come back here as soon as you're done.*

Bridget: *Stay out of Gordon's business and just leave this case alone.*

Kenzie: *Call me when you get a chance.*

Talk about stirring up a hornet's nest. His thoughts were racing and for a moment he considered the possibility that they were all working in concert. It took effort to remind himself that most of them were on his side. They might be influenced by an outside source, but they weren't all working for Gordon. He tapped the message from Kenzie and the phone icon as he started the engine and pulled out.

"Medical Examiner—hi, Zachary."

"Hey. Good to hear from you. I was just thinking about the case, and I wanted to run a few things by you."

"I said that I would call you after talking to Dr. Wiltshire about the other employee's accident. While it is an interesting coincidence, he doesn't think that—"

"Given that the other employee who had an accident is now missing, he might want to reconsider that conclusion," Zachary interrupted.

"Missing?"

"He was acting paranoid last night and then he disappeared. Someone might have taken him away from there and harmed him. We might never even know what happened, if there is no body found. And there probably won't be; they've had too much reported in the media lately. They won't want this to be a suspicious death or another tragic accident. Just an employee choosing to leave the company. They'll establish a story. A logical narrative. He'd been working too hard, he had a breakdown, he decided it was time to leave. They'll have a few different employees telling the same story, saying that they've talked to him and he doesn't want to be bothered by anyone, and—"

"Whoa, Zach. Slow it down. You sound like someone changed the RPM on your turntable. You're going to be going chipmunk in a minute."

Zachary took a deep breath and tried to slow himself down. When everything started to click and he saw the whole picture, it was hard to slow himself down to everyone else's speed. He had to remind himself that Kenzie didn't know all of the details of the case. He hadn't kept her up to speed like he normally would, because they had broken up. That needed to change, but he'd have to address it later, after he'd finished tying up the case.

"Look. The blow was to the back of her head. Not the front."

"That doesn't mean anything," Kenzie said. "It's not unusual for someone who slips to fall backward and hit the back of their head."

"In the bathtub? Wouldn't she have fallen out of the tub instead of into the water?"

"You don't know that. She could easily have fallen backward and hit her head on the side of the tub and then sunk down into the water. There's nothing to indicate anyone else's presence on the scene."

"There had been other people in that bathroom. It wasn't only used by her."

"Obviously."

"So there were other fingerprints and forensic evidence in the bathroom."

"Sure."

"But that would all be ignored, because they thought it was an accident. And because she lived with a roommate. Who knows how many other people came and went? You can't match every hair and fingerprint. There will always be unknowns. People who were one-time visitors or whose hair or skin cells were on Lauren or Barbara when they came home from work."

"Exactly. Of course. The evidence of other people doesn't mean that it wasn't an accident."

"I need you to start trying to identify them. You're going to find contributions from people at her office. Some might have just clung to her, but look for larger contributions. Her roommate said that she sometimes brought men home from work with her. I want to know which men. Which ones can we actually put in the apartment because of the larger deposits of physical evidence and their fingerprints on the scene. We're going to need to do a larger analysis of the fingerprints. Identify the ones that weren't identified initially."

"I don't know if forensics or fingerprints were even taken," Kenzie cautioned. "Certainly nothing was ever tested. It was evident on the face of it that this was just an accident. They wouldn't treat it like a homicide. What would be the point in investigating a non-suspicious death like a homicide? It just takes extra man-hours."

"If there's nothing to this but a tragic accident, then why are there so many stories about other past employees of the company? What happened to Bieberstein? And why am I getting death threats?"

There was a moment of silence from Kenzie. "You're getting death threats?"

"Just now. Someone sending me a text message warning me to back off the case or I'm dead. Why would they do that if it was just an accident? Think about it."

"Zachary... are you by yourself?"

"For now, but not for long. I'm headed back to my apartment. Gerry is there. I don't know what he found yet. Maybe it will be something we can use."

"I'm worried about you."

"I'm fine," Zachary assured her. At least there hadn't been a bomb in the car. Nothing had happened when he started the engine. They might be waiting and watching him, but they would have no way of knowing whether he was going to listen to their warning until they saw his resulting behavior. Then they would have to decide what kind of action to take.

"You should talk to Detective Robinson," Kenzie said. "He'll want to know about the progress you've made on the case. He can help you to decide how to deal with this death threat." He could almost hear Kenzie's doubtful thoughts. *If the death threat was real.* Like Dr. Boyle, she was worried that he was having a psychotic break and just imagining it all.

"You know what else?" he asked her. "Why would she be having a bath without taking her bath things into the room? If you were going to have a relaxing bubble bath, wouldn't you actually take it into the bathroom?"

"I don't think she had any bubbles in the bath."

"No, she didn't," Zachary agreed. "All of her bath things were in her bedroom. She had a shower caddy with everything in it."

"Maybe she was just filling the tub and was still going to go back and get it."

"You don't start the tub filling without getting your bath salts or bubble bath or whatever first," Zachary said. He remembered how Bridget had a big ritual about setting up her baths. It was different from how Zachary would jump into the shower to quickly wash away the sweat and dirt from the day. It was an event, like going to the spa.

"She could have forgotten," Kenzie maintained. "You said she was over-tired. You can do a lot of stupid things when you're overtired. Forget the order of things. Not be able to do something that you've done a hundred times before. *You* know how it is when you're not sleeping."

"But she wasn't just filling the tub, she was *in* the tub. She was already undressed and in the tub when she died. She didn't just start the tub running and then realize that she'd forgotten her things and slipped and fell into the tub. She didn't slip on the floor, she slipped in the tub."

"Yes," Kenzie agreed slowly. "But maybe she got into the tub and then realized she'd forgotten her things. She could have fallen because she got up too fast to get them."

"Or," Zachary offered, "someone hit her over the head and then put her body in the tub and filled it up with water to make it look like an accident. But he didn't know that her bathroom things were in the bedroom. He wasn't familiar enough with her to know that."

Zachary's thoughts raced on. It wasn't someone that she took home with her regularly. They would know that her bath things were in her bedroom. She would shower or bathe before going to work in the morning, and he would know that she had to take her caddy from the bedroom to the bathroom first. Unless the guy was totally clueless, he would know her routine.

"I've got to go," he told Kenzie. "I'll try to get you more details when I know them, but in the meantime, if you can get them started on identifying the hair and fibers and fingerprints, that would be really helpful. Even if it's just preliminary stuff, putting them into groups like hair color and curl. That will make it faster to match once I have a name for you."

"Zachary—"

"Don't worry about me. I'll call you back when I've got something."

———

Gerry was the next sender who Zachary knew was on his side. Zachary's apartment wasn't far from Dr. Boyle's office, so he was nearly there by the time he finished the call with Kenzie. He parked quickly and took the elevator up to his apartment, impatient with how slowly it rose to his floor. He practically ran into his apartment.

Gerry jumped and looked around at him, face white. "What the heck, Zachary? You scared the crap out of me."

"Sorry. I just wanted to get here as quickly as I could and make sure that you were okay."

"Why wouldn't I be okay?"

Zachary didn't tell him. Gerry didn't need to know about the death threat. About the accidents and the house fire and the employee with amnesia. The killer could easily have made it to Zachary's apartment before he was able to get there. And he'd obligingly left the door unlocked, not thinking there was any need for any special care.

"You said that you needed me to come back. What's going on?"

Gerry gestured at Lauren's computer screen. "They discovered what I was doing and blocked me," he said regretfully. "I'm sorry. We knew they were surveilling this laptop, but I thought I could get through the video feeds before they figured out what I was doing and how to stop me."

"Did you find anything out before they did?"

Gerry handed Zachary the scratch pad from the desk, where Zachary had written down the names of the people they needed surveillance footage for. Zachary scanned the list.

As the witnesses had told him, most of them left around the same time as Lauren had. It was bad for someone to leave first and be identified as less devout than anyone else. They left as a group to keep anyone from being singled out as lazy.

Except Bieberstein. He seemed to be able to come and to go as he pleased, working for different departments on whatever projects they needed him on.

And he wasn't the one. It was clear from Gerry's notes that Bieberstein had been at the office from the time that Lauren had left. It had been an all-nighter for him, even though everyone else had gone home.

"If one of these people went home with Lauren, which one was it?" he asked Gerry.

Gerry looked baffled. "What?"

"If you had to guess which one was going home with her, which one would it be?"

"None of them left with her, exactly."

"It might have been covert. They might have been trying to keep it from the others."

"Hmm." Gerry looked over the list and the notes he had made. "Gordon Drake, Daniel Service... the interns all left around the same time, but they looked pretty wiped out. Honestly, I can't see any of them having the energy to pursue any hanky-panky."

Zachary laughed.

Gerry shrugged, his face turning a little pink. "Really," he insisted.

"I believe you. What were Gordon and Daniel doing there that late?"

Of course, the senior staff could be there whenever they wanted to, but Zachary had gotten the feeling that they didn't stay late like the peons.

"They were together, meeting in Gordon's office."

"I'm surprised they were there so late. And either of them could have joined Lauren after they left?"

"Yeah, they left a few minutes after she did."

Zachary sighed, rubbing the center of his forehead. One name kept coming up over and over again. The one name that he didn't want to associate with Lauren's death.

"Okay. Thanks. If they've blocked you from accessing anything else, then I guess we're done."

"I could try again. I might be able to break in again. They might have changed the password, but won't have had time to put any new security measures in place. They'll be watching, though, waiting for me to show up again."

"It isn't like we're going to get video that proves conclusively which one of them killed her. We can't absolutely eliminate any of them."

Gerry eyed Zachary, brows down.

"What?"

"Before you left, you were saying it was an accident. Now you're saying one of them killed her."

Zachary brought up the text messages on his phone and tapped the threatening one. He turned it face out so that Gerry could read it. His mouth pressed into a straight line.

"And why would they threaten to kill you if it was just an accident?" he summarized.

"Exactly. And some other things came up while I was gone."

"You be careful, man. I wouldn't want to lose a paying customer."

"I will. Send me your invoice. I guess that's all I'm going to need today."

"Well, you know who to call if you need anything else."

———

Zachary paced after Gerry left. He didn't have anything to take to the police. No proof of any foul play. No evidence that it was anything other than an accident, like Kenzie had said. Lauren could have just slipped, hit her head, and drowned, just as the medical examiner had determined.

But Zachary must have been getting close, or he wouldn't have upset someone enough to be getting death threats.

He could show the threat to the police, and they could track down the phone that had sent it, but that still wasn't proof that Lauren was intentionally killed or even that the threats were serious. Zachary got threats from cheating spouses and insurance scammers all the time.

There was a knock on the door. Zachary glanced over at the computer desk to see whether Gerry had left something behind by accident. He didn't see anything, but went to the door and opened it to let Gerry in.

But it wasn't Gerry.

CHAPTER THIRTY-TWO

Gordon smiled pleasantly at Zachary.

Zachary stood frozen, not sure what to do. He knew better than to open the door without checking to see who it was first. But what would he have done if he had looked? Would he still have opened the door for Gordon, or would he have hidden and pretended that he wasn't at home? What good would that do? Sooner or later, he would have to face Gordon.

"You've been trying to reach me?" Gordon suggested. He put his foot into the doorway, preventing the door from being closed again. "Can I come in?"

Zachary allowed him in. Gordon walked through the kitchen into the living room and looked around. He saw the computers on Zachary's desk.

"Is this one of ours?" He pointed at Lauren's laptop. "If you're done with it, I really should take it back. We don't like to have them floating around when they might have confidential information on them."

"Yes. You can take it. And the phone was Lauren's too. It's company issue."

"Ah, very good." Gordon pocketed the phone. He folded down the lid of the laptop, moved it over to deal with the electrical cord, and picked it up. He took it with him as he sat down on Zachary's couch, putting it down at his feet. "How else can I help you, Zachary?"

Zachary looked around. He could run. There was nothing between him and the door, and it wasn't like Gordon was holding a gun on him. He wasn't making any threat at all.

"I was worried about Bieberstein," he ventured. "Especially since he wasn't at work this morning… those interns never miss a day."

"Bieberstein is fine." Gordon's voice was perfectly calm, with no hint of stress. There was nothing in his face that hinted at a lie. His eyes were steady, looking at Zachary but without too much aggression or intensity. He didn't look anything like the egomaniac that Deidre made him out to be. He didn't look like a crazy cult leader who thought he was the Messiah. Zachary saw just what he had always seen. A wealthy businessman, pleasant and cultured, easy to talk to. All of the things that Zachary wasn't. But not a maniac who was going around trying to get rid of any employees who disagreed with him or didn't fit into his corporate culture.

"He's fine? You know where he is?"

Gordon nodded. "You were right to call me last night. It wasn't easy to get him settled down and in a reasonable state of mind. He's going to take a few days off to get the sleep he needs. Paid, of course, and with no impact on his chances at the permanent positions."

"Do you think…" Zachary hesitated.

Gordon raised his eyebrows and waited. His state of calm was almost hypnotic. Zachary could feel his heart slowing and had an intense desire to tell Gordon all of his concerns and theories.

But he still had to consider Gordon a suspect. He'd been around when Lauren had left work that final day. He was on the same floor as the interns, walking by the bullpen half a dozen times a day. He was the owner of the company and could get around and do whatever he desired without anybody questioning it. The company was his baby and, while Zachary couldn't envision him doing anything violent, people often did terrible things to get what they wanted.

Had Gordon risen to where he was without stepping on anyone else?

"Do you think that Bieberstein was right, that he was in danger?" Zachary asked finally, pushing the words out all at once so that he wouldn't get stuck.

Gordon scratched his jaw, thinking about it. "I don't like there being two accidents so close together. I know that Bieberstein only fell on the treadmill at a walking pace, but it could conceivably have been much worse.

Whether it was because someone wanted to hurt him or because he's been working too hard or he picked up a bug... I felt like he needed a rest. Somewhere safe."

"Where?"

Gordon just raised his brows and didn't answer. Zachary got it. If no one knew where Bieberstein was, no one could hurt him. And even if Zachary had been the one to ring the alarm bells, *no one* meant *no one*.

"So was there anything else?" Gordon asked. "Anything at all?"

Zachary wanted to ask him about the health and welfare program, the fraudulent computer records, employee monitoring, information control, and everything else. How much of it did Gordon know and how much of it had been implemented by someone else, right under his nose? Did he really think that he had a company full of happy, dedicated employees, or did he know that they were being manipulated?

Zachary just swallowed and shook his head.

Gordon's phone rang. He looked at the face and tapped to answer it. "Hello, my dear."

Bridget, of course. Zachary couldn't help taking a quick look around his apartment to assess it, as if she might show up at any minute and would be making a list of deficiencies. Everything was reasonably tidy. There were papers out on his desk, his coffee mug that he hadn't washed after his morning cup. It could probably use a good dusting and vacuuming, something Zachary didn't get around to very often. And by the smell of the kitchen, it was time to take the garbage out.

"Yes, I'm there now," Gordon said. He gave Zachary a conspiratorial wink. "I'm sorry I was off the grid for a few hours. Phones had to be turned off."

He listened some more. Zachary imagined Bridget had a long list of grievances to air if he had turned his phone off when she wanted to reach him. Especially since Zachary had called looking for Gordon.

"Yes. Of course, dear. Alright."

After a few more comforting noises, he said his goodbyes and hung up. He slid his phone into his pocket.

"There is a woman who does not like to be ignored."

"No," Zachary agreed with a laugh. "She gets kind of testy if she thinks she's not getting the attention she deserves."

"Well, I do have work to get back to. They'll be calling me too. Actually, they already have, but things will keep until I get back. You're sure that's everything you need?" He smiled once more, and Zachary was again struck by how friendly and trustworthy he made himself appear. He made Zachary feel as if he could trust him absolutely.

And yet, he didn't.

CHAPTER THIRTY-THREE

After Gordon left, Zachary locked the door and reminded himself sternly that he needed to check who was there before he answered it. He had to pay attention and not just open it the moment someone knocked.

He went back to his desk and leafed through his handwritten notes, puzzling through the more cryptic or unreadable ones, trying to remind himself of every step along the way. He should know what had happened. He had all of the details. He'd seen where it happened. He knew the medical examiner's results. He'd talked to all of the players.

He was sure that it hadn't just been an accident. Lauren wouldn't have gone to the bathroom to have a bath without her shower caddy full of toiletries. That meant that someone else had been there and had tried to cover it up. And since there was water in her lungs, it wasn't just a case of her accidentally hitting her head and dying. She had still been alive when he had put her into the water.

It wasn't Mandy. She was too small. Bieberstein was also too small and he had an alibi. He'd been at work that whole night. It could have been one of the other interns. Or Gordon. Or Daniel.

If it were one of the other interns, then it was someone who wanted the position that she apparently had locked up. They were all pretty desperate to sign on permanently. No one wanted to be left out in the cold, the guy who had interned at Chase Gold but didn't make the cut. As the time was getting closer, they were getting more desperate.

Or it was someone in higher authority than the interns, who had reason to stop her. Had her comments about being prepared to have her tubes tied to lock in her position with the company been true? Or had she been bluffing? Or had that just been a story that Aaron had made up to distract Zachary from the truth?

Her family said she wanted children. Had she finally reached the breaking point and decided that was where she drew the line? She wouldn't give up all of her other dreams to get a permanent position with Drake, Chase, Gould?

The firm had had to deal with too many defectors in the previous few months. Too many employees or ex-employees who made the company look bad. If Drake, Chase, Gould were going to be properly positioned to spread internationally and gain a position in the world economy, they had to be clean. They couldn't abide a situation where potential investors looked at the company and saw a problem.

Zachary busied himself with cleaning up while he thought. If he had all of that restless energy, he might as well do something with it. His phone started to vibrate, so he put his coffee mug in the sink and put down his dust rag and answer it. It was Daniel.

"Just wondering if I could come by there to get Lauren's computer, Zachary," he said. "Bev said that she asked you for it but hasn't gotten it back yet. I know you don't want her on your back, so I figured since I was in the area…"

"Gordon Drake was by just a little while ago. He picked it up. And her phone."

"Gordon was by?" Daniel repeated, his tone something of a cross between curious and irritated.

"Yeah. So you can ask him about it, if Bev says she hasn't got it back yet. He could have just put it in his briefcase and forgotten about it. But that's where it is, if you want it."

"Great. That's all I need, then."

After Zachary hung up, he walked back into his living room and looked at his computer. A slide show played as his screen saver, waiting for him to come and wake it up again. The connection came to him suddenly. It had started to form when he'd been at Dr. Boyle's office, and then his attention had been scattered by talking to everyone who had been trying to reach him.

He sat down at his desk, touching the mouse to wake the computer up, picking up his phone to make a call.

"Hey, man, I thought we were done," Gerry complained, as soon as he answered his phone. "If you changed your mind, you're going to have to wait until tomorrow. I have other jobs I need to get finished today."

"I had to give back Lauren's computer, but I cloned Lauren's hard drive, so I can still use that to see everything on her computer, right?"

"You don't touch the cloned drive. That's your failsafe. I created a VM of the cloned drive on your computer, and you need to boot off of that to be mostly safe."

"Mostly?"

"There are still some risks, but it's the safest way we've got for you to access Lauren's data."

"And what's a... VM?"

"Virtual machine. It's like having a second computer system running in a separate window."

"Okay. That sounds like it is going to be complicated... what do I do?"

"It's not that bad, Zachary," Gerry promised. "I'll walk you through it."

He didn't sound angry and impatient with Zachary for taking more of his time. Whatever else he had to finish, he didn't seem to need to get to it immediately.

Zachary put his phone in speaker mode and set it down on the desk so that he could use both hands. Gerry walked him through starting the VM. It wasn't as bad as Zachary had anticipated.

"Now what are you looking for?" Gerry asked. "Do you know how to find it?"

"You said that there was a spyware program accessing her camera."

"Yeah. So you might want to cover yours up now, if you don't want them snooping on you through your own computer this time."

Goosebumps rose on Zachary's arms. He did as Gerry had done and covered the camera lens with a sticky note.

"Okay. Yeah. So what did the program do? Was it on all the time?"

"It was on when the computer was in use. So theoretically, it would stop recording while the computer was idle, and no one had to worry about having their picture taken while walking around the house naked, or steamy bedroom scenes ending up on the company's server. And they weren't videos, but stills taken every twenty seconds. Takes up a lot less space, but still gives them the information they need on what the employee was up to. If they weren't connected to the internet, it would just keep taking pictures and would upload them the next time they connected. Then the company knows what they are doing whether they are online or off. Combine that with keystroke loggers and records of any internet address they visit, and you've got a pretty complete picture of everything your employee is doing while on the company computer."

"So if Lauren had the computer on when she went home that night, it might have recorded something important, without her even knowing it."

Gerry whistled. "Pretty smart, Zachary, pretty smart."

"So how do I access the pictures that it took? I assume it doesn't just put them into the 'pictures' folder."

"No. Do you want me to come tomorrow and take a look? It could be kind of tricky to give you instructions over the phone."

Thinking about Gordon picking up Lauren's laptop and about Daniel's call, Zachary was too uneasy to wait another day. One of them might have figured out there was something incriminating on Lauren's computer, and if they thought he had found it… they might not be willing to wait until he made a move to reveal it.

"I know it's a pain," he told Gerry apologetically, "but if you could just tell me where to look, I'll do the heavy lifting. If there was a picture of Lauren's killer on her drive, I want to find it and get it to the police tonight."

Gerry sighed, but didn't protest. "Okay, you're going to have to tell me what you see as we go through these different folders, because I don't remember exactly where they were stored and it might not be simple to open them to view them. They're only meant to be temporarily stored on the laptop, and are probably compressed and encrypted for transfer."

"I'll do my best."

Zachary reported on each screen Gerry led him through and, although it took longer than he had hoped, he did manage to find the folder of pictures and get them into a viewer where he could page through them as he looked for the ones that were taken on Lauren's last night on earth.

"It looks like these must be the ones that were taken after she got

P.D. WORKMAN

home," Zachary said. "She must have gone online even though she was tired."

"People like to check their social networks," Gerry said. "Touch base with what their family and friends are doing, maybe watch some videos to unwind before bed. Play a game of Solitaire or Sudoku."

Zachary paged through the photos quickly. One person's last hours, divided into twenty-second segments. She was tired. Her eyes were red and she had rubbed off the make-up around them. It made her look strangely childlike. A couple of times, the camera caught her looking over her shoulder, back behind her. But he couldn't see anything going on in the background that should have caught her attention.

He was going through the photos too fast to stop himself when he saw something he wanted to take a closer look at. He backed up through the last couple of photos of an empty room, back to the last pictures of Lauren before her death.

Zachary swore.

"What is it?" Gerry asked.

Zachary swore again.

"Thank you. This is it, Gerry. This is what we needed."

Gerry's answer was drowned out by a knock on the door. Zachary looked toward the door warily.

No one should be coming to his door. Gerry was gone, and Zachary was on the phone with him. Kenzie wasn't coming by anymore. Bridget knew that Gordon had been there, but she wouldn't have come looking for him. If she came to yell at Zachary to back off, he'd have the proof to show her. He could prove that it wasn't just his client's imagination and his own paranoia. He had the proof now.

No one else was likely to come by his apartment without calling first. Not when he could have been off doing surveillance or some other job and the chances of finding him at home were too remote. Not Tyrrell. Heather and Mr. Peterson were too far away. Mario would call first and Detective Robinson was too busy to talk to him and would be closing his file now that they had the medical examiner's ruling.

Zachary stood up halfway, clumsily banging into his desk and making everything on it jump and rattle. Way to be covert and make his visitor think that no one was at home.

He reached out to stop his pen jar from rattling. He steadied the computer, the most valuable thing on the desk, even though its wide base kept it from moving. His sleeve caught on the sticky note he'd used to cover the camera lens. Papers avalanched over his phone. Zachary moved more carefully, quiet as a mouse, tiptoeing over to the door to look into the hallway at the caller.

He never got that far.

He was considering whether he dared go right up to the peephole, or whether looking out the peephole would block the light from inside the room and the visitor would instantly know that he was home. He needed to get a video cam in the hallway, so he could see a clear picture of who was out there without giving his presence away.

Hovering there, just inside the kitchen, considering his next move, he was distracted by the smell of the kitchen garbage. But he'd taken the garbage out, so what was the smell? He frowned at the sink and the microwave, trying to remember what he'd been working on when Daniel had called and interrupted his housekeeping duties.

There was the sound of a key in his door. The building manager coming to check on something? Maybe there was a sewer problem, and that was what he was smelling. He let out his breath, relieved.

There was another sound from the doorknob, like a light hammer tap, and then the handle turned and the door swung open to reveal the building manager.

Only it wasn't.

CHAPTER THIRTY-FOUR

He had on a baseball cap to obscure his face and a loose black hoodie disguised his build, but Zachary knew instantly it was Daniel, even before he closed the door, tilted his hat back, and grinned a self-satisfied smile at Zachary.

"No," Zachary said, backing up a few steps. "Get out of here. You can't break into my apartment. Get out!"

His words might not make much sense, but that was what fell out of his mouth. On TV, the PIs were always great at thinking on their feet, working out what to say to the bad guys to convince them to do something that would let the PI escape and get away scot-free, to return on the next week's episode well and safe.

Zachary's brain was running in overdrive, trying to work out his next move, but his mouth was miles behind.

He backed up a couple more steps and looked over to the desk for his phone. Daniel followed Zachary's eyes and saw the computer.

He looked at the picture on the screen: Lauren looking back over her shoulder, her mouth opening in a scream as Daniel walked into the bedroom behind her. She had clearly not been expecting him, and the next picture in the series was even more wrenching, his hand over her mouth while she struggled to escape his grasp.

"I knew it," Daniel said, his mouth tight and his words clipped and precise. "You little weasel. I knew that you wouldn't give back her computer without finding something first."

"That's you, Daniel," Zachary said, his voice sounding too loud in his own ears. "That's a picture of you breaking into Lauren's apartment and attacking her the night of her 'accident.' Caught right on the company's own spyware. Or was it your spyware? Did you install the spyware to keep an eye on her, just like you broke into her apartment, and broke into mine?"

Daniel chuckled. It was a sound that made Zachary's skin crawl. All of the hairs on his neck stood up as if electrified.

"She thought she had everyone fooled. She thought she had said and done all of the right things and that everyone believed that she would do whatever it took to get that job and hold on to it. She had them thinking that she would give up her family and her future to give herself to that job. But I knew better. I knew she was a liar. I knew they were just words."

Zachary took another step away from Daniel. He couldn't see any weapons on Daniel. Nothing other than the small mallet he had used on the bump key to get in through Zachary's locked door. That mallet wasn't enough to kill him. He must have used something else on Lauren. The skull-crushing blow that she'd received had been from something larger, like the edge of the tub, not from a little hammer. If he got hit with the mallet, it would hurt, but Zachary didn't think it would be enough to disable him.

"How did you know what she was really thinking?" he prompted, side-stepping to prevent Daniel from getting closer to him. "Did she tell you? Or someone else?"

"One thing about being a good liar is you get really good at spotting the signs in someone else. Someone like me or Gordon, we can say anything we want and never give ourselves away. But people like Lauren have tells."

"You and Gordon?"

"Psychopaths. People who don't feel guilt or other inconvenient emotions like the rest of you. You go through your whole lives a slave to your emotions instead of just going all out and getting what you want. You're so worried about everyone's feelings and how your actions affect them, that you don't put yourself first. In this world, if you want to get ahead, you have to put yourself first."

"Gordon? Were the two of you working together?"

"Gordon is a visionary. He knew what he wanted and he was building it. Since I'm not at his level yet, all I could do was help and admire him from afar. I knew that the more I was able to accomplish, the closer I would get to him and the more he would notice me. Until the two of us are equals and can talk openly about our goals and plans for the company, and how we can use it to accomplish our desires."

"The night you killed Lauren, you had a late-night meeting with Gordon."

"You *have* been busy, haven't you?"

Daniel advanced. Zachary again retreated. His escape was cut off. He didn't want to have to fight Daniel hand-to-hand. He'd had enough fights as a teenager to know that he wasn't that skilled. He'd learned a few dirty tricks, but he was no martial arts expert. He was too light to be a wrestler. Too small to be much danger to anyone. But he'd fight if he had to. If he was lucky, he might manage to hold Daniel off or get past him and out the door. He was under no illusions about being able to school Daniel. His best hope was escape.

"Yes, Gordon and I had a wonderful meeting. I told him how much I admired the company he had set up and how I believed we could accomplish great things together. He told me how pleased he was with how I was managing the interns, and that he trusted me to make the decisions that were best for the company, even though they were often difficult." He smiled proudly. "He trusted and admired me."

"He recognized how much you have contributed to the company," Zachary said, hoping that Daniel would hold off on any violence as long as he was being praised. Zachary's stomach turned at the thought of Gordon telling Daniel he trusted him to make the hard decisions. Had he intentionally aimed Daniel at Lauren, or was he unaware of how Daniel would take his words?

"That's right," Daniel agreed. He took a deliberate step toward Zachary. He had told Zachary he could tell when people were lying. Since Zachary was not a psychopath, he assumed Daniel could see that Zachary didn't really admire him.

Zachary swallowed and tried to inch toward the door, but Daniel watched him like a cat watching a mouse, keeping his body in position so that Zachary wouldn't be able to slip past him.

"When did you decide you needed to get rid of Lauren?" Zachary asked.

"I could see she'd made a decision. She wasn't going to stay on and take the job. She was going to make trouble for the company. I knew the instant she decided, and I knew I would have to take action. Drastic action." He took a deep breath and let it out. "Something that I had never done before."

Still, Zachary doubted him. He hadn't been involved in any of the other violence toward the other ex-employees? It might have been the first time he had killed, but Zachary didn't think it was the first time he had ventured into those waters.

"And it was so easy," Daniel said, shaking his head and blinking at Zachary to express his surprise. "I had her address. It was easy to get into her apartment. There was no one else there. So I could just take care of business and get back out again, with no one the wiser."

"No one suspected you," Zachary agreed. He strained his ears for the sound of anyone nearby that he could call out to for help. But it was a quiet evening, he couldn't hear anyone in the hall or the hum of the elevator as it made its way to the floor.

"No one even thought it was murder. Except you. Why?"

"It wasn't me, it was her roommate. She just didn't think it felt right, but she didn't know why."

Daniel shrugged broadly. "That's it? Just instinct? It was easy enough to do, I don't know why anyone wouldn't believe it."

"You did make one mistake, but she didn't catch it. Not consciously."

"What?"

"Lauren had a shower caddy with all of her soap and shampoo and accessories in her bedroom. She wouldn't have left it there, gotten undressed, and gotten into the tub without them."

Daniel made a noise of disgust and shook his head. "How could I have known that?"

"You would have had to have looked around her room and seen it. But you were running on adrenaline. You couldn't be expected to notice."

"That still doesn't prove anything. Even if you took that to the police, that wouldn't convince them it was murder and it wouldn't lead them to me."

"No." Zachary agreed.

Not like the webcam picture.

He could hear the elevator. It was more of a feeling that came up through his feet that an actual sound. He'd noticed it before, standing in the kitchen near his door. He was farther away now, but his body was sensitized by the danger, alert to every change in his environment. He sensed booted feet too. Not in the elevator, but maybe in the hallway. Someone going out to the bar or to visit a friend? Was it someone who could help him if he called out? He didn't want to put anyone else in danger.

He opened his mouth to speak to Daniel, hesitating for a fraction of a second while his brain processed the noises and unusual movement outside his apartment.

CHAPTER THIRTY-FIVE

There was a crash and, unlike with Daniel's quiet breach of Zachary's apartment, the door slammed open and uniformed officers ran into the apartment, their booted feet pounding. They shouted, guns raised to point at both Zachary and Daniel. Zachary held his hands up high, wide-open palms facing them so that they could see he was unarmed. A couple of them threw him to the floor, shouting instructions that he couldn't make out in the cacophony of sound. He put his hands on the back of his head and interlaced his fingers, hoping that would be close enough to their instructions for them to see that he was being compliant and not hurt him.

Daniel, on the other hand, was shouting and struggling and trying to convince them to let him alone.

Good luck with that.

Hands frisked Zachary, and he endured the violation, letting them feel for any hidden weapons. In a few minutes, they had Daniel subdued and the chaos quieted.

One of the cops helped Zachary to his feet and made a show of dusting him off. "Sorry about that, sir. It's not possible for us to tell in a split-second who might be dangerous and who is not. Are you alright?"

"Yeah, I'm fine. Thank you. Can I..." He motioned toward his desk, asking permission to move across the room and to touch things.

"Go ahead."

Zachary went back to his desk, shuffled the papers to find his buried phone, and looked at the name still displayed on the screen in bright letters. The call was still active. He raised it to his ear.

"Gerry."

Gerry swore. "Man, Zachary. I was scared as hell. I thought he was going to kill you before the police could get there."

"They arrived pretty quickly. It just *felt* like an eternity."

Gerry's chuckle was warm and comforting to Zachary. "Did it ever." He swore again and let his breath out in a whistle. "Good to hear your voice, man."

"So when we booted off this hard drive, it was like we were on Lauren's computer, right?"

"Uh… yeah. Exactly like it."

"And when I was looking at the surveillance pictures that the spyware took, did it stop taking more pictures until I shut down that viewer?"

"I'm not there, so I can't tell you for sure, but I doubt it. It would have kept taking pictures and trying to send them back to the server."

"So it was taking pictures of Daniel here, in my apartment?"

"And still taking pictures of you and the cops now. Yeah."

"Good. And could you hear him? Everything he was saying?" Zachary had been worried that Gerry would hang up in order to call the police. But he had apparently stayed on the line.

"Yeah. I tried out 'text to 9-1-1.' Didn't know if they even had text service here, but I guess they do!"

That had been pretty smart. "So you heard him say that he killed Lauren."

"I heard everything."

Zachary exhaled, relieved. It was one thing for him to tell the police that Daniel had confessed. They didn't have his voice recorded—unless the spyware did that too—and they didn't have any physical evidence. Not yet. Maybe there were some of Daniel's hair or skin cells at the scene. The picture of him grabbing Lauren from in front of her computer was convincing, but it didn't actually show the murder. He could say that he was an invited guest and they were just role playing. That she had been alive when he left.

But Gerry had heard the confession too. He could testify as to what had happened at Zachary's apartment. It would all wrap up nicely into a neat package that would ensure Daniel was put away for a long time.

One of the policemen was looking at the picture on Zachary's laptop.

"Is that the woman who was in the papers? The one they said slipped and fell?"

"Yes."

He swore, eyes open wide in disbelief. He looked in the direction of Zachary's door, where they had just escorted Daniel out. "Holy crap! I guess he's going away for a long time."

"Yeah. I hope so," Zachary agreed.

He looked at the door swinging on its hinges. They had broken it through the frame, which meant he wasn't going to be able to sleep there until it was fixed. He pondered who he should call.

———

It was a while before Detective Robinson made it to the scene. Maybe he was out to supper with his wife or was at a kid's school play. Something big and important. Things were quiet when he got to Zachary's apartment. There wasn't much for the police to take pictures of, no evidence to gather other than the burglary tools Daniel had on him. What had Daniel been planning to do to him? Choke him? Slam his head on the bathtub? Use some tool or poison that he found on hand?

They wanted Zachary's computer, but he pointed out that everything was on the hard drive, not his computer, so they could take that for evidence. He emailed himself the pictures first, both the pictures of Daniel with Lauren and of Daniel in Zachary's apartment. He wanted to make sure they were preserved, no matter what happened to the hard drive.

Detective Robinson walked into Zachary's apartment through the open door and looked around. His wrinkled dress shirt clung to his thin body and he gazed over the contents of Zachary's front room through his thick eyeglasses, looking a little like a baffled owl.

"Somebody want to explain to me what happened here?" he asked of the air.

Zachary waited to see if anyone else was going to answer him, but the police who were left were just low-level officers there to make sure everything was cleaned up and taken care of. They looked at him, looked at each other, and shrugged.

"Didn't anyone brief you?" Zachary asked.

Detective Robinson looked at him, giving him a look that Zachary was sure was meant to intimidate him. But Zachary had already been intimidated; a grumpy detective didn't frighten him.

Zachary looked at his watch. "I'm going to have to clear out of here if I'm going to find someone to stay with tonight. I can't exactly stay here, when the door won't shut and lock properly."

"Didn't I tell you to just stay away from this case?"

"Didn't you tell me it was an accidental slip-and-fall?" Zachary countered glibly, irritated by Detective Robinson acting like Daniel being a murderer was somehow Zachary's fault, rather than apologizing for being wrong.

"It would appear... that we were mistaken."

"Yeah, it would appear."

"That doesn't change the fact that you put yourself in danger."

"I didn't provoke him. I was just investigating the case. Looking a little deeper than the police department did."

He didn't make any accusations, but figured his point was obvious. If they had looked at it harder, Zachary would not have been in any danger. They would have figured out that it was Daniel, and no one else would have been put in danger. Not Zachary. Not Bieberstein. Not anybody.

Where was Bieberstein? Could he really believe Gordon's story that he was somewhere safe? Zachary still couldn't decide whether Gordon and Daniel had been in on it together, or whether it was just Daniel, and Gordon was clueless that he had been praising and encouraging a dangerous man.

"How did Daniel Service know where to find you?"

"I imagine he asked around. I've tried not to list it publicly anywhere, I've been using a post office box since... well, since somebody else found me. But Daniel works with... my ex-wife's current partner. So..."

"Bridget's?"

He should have known that Detective Robinson would know Bridget. Everybody in the police department knew Bridget.

"Yeah. Bridget's partner. Gordon Drake."

"The investment banker. Where Lauren worked."

Zachary nodded. It all went in a full circle.

"Was it Gordon Drake who hired you to investigate Lauren's death, then?"

"No. I told you, it was her roommate. I didn't know at the time that I accepted it that she had worked for Gordon's company. I never really clued into... *Drake*... you know."

Detective Robinson looked at him through the thick lenses, his eyes looking slightly warped. Zachary wondered if he were legally blind.

"I would expect a smart private investigator to figure that out."

His expression was so blank, Zachary thought fleetingly of Daniel's brag that he was a psychopath. That he felt nothing toward his victims.

"You would, wouldn't you?" he agreed.

Detective Robinson cracked a smile. "It is the nature of man to make mistakes."

Zachary figured that was as close as he was going to get to an apology.

"So what did you discover in the course of your investigation?" Robinson asked. "I assume there was more, or Service wouldn't have been worried about you discovering him."

Zachary considered this. He motioned to the couch. Detective Robinson followed the motion, then looked back at Zachary.

"Let's sit down," Zachary suggested. "I'll go though the other stuff."

Robinson considered for a moment, then sat down. Zachary picked up his notebook and started filling him in on the details.

CHAPTER THIRTY-SIX

Zachary decided to try Kenzie. He knew he could use Mario Bowman as a fallback if she refused, but it was worth his while to try Kenzie. If she said yes, it might be the beginning of a path back into her life.

He ran several scripts through his head before dialing her number. He knew the conversation would come out nothing like he planned, but he tried anyway to anticipate what she might say and to come up with counterarguments to her objections. In the end, if she really didn't want him there, he wouldn't impose on her.

He tapped her number and waited for it to ring through.

"Zachary?" Kenzie answered it almost immediately. "What took you so long?"

Zachary pulled the phone away from his ear to look at the screen to see if he had any missed calls or messages from her. Nothing. He put it back to his ear as she called to him.

"Zachary? Are you there? Is everything okay?"

"I'm here. What do you mean what took me so long? You didn't call, did you?"

"No. But I thought I'd hear back from you a lot earlier."

"Oh. I told you I'd get you the names of the suspects to check against the forensics."

"Well, yeah, and I kind of heard that you didn't need to guess who the perp was anymore, since he showed up at your door."

Even though she wasn't there, Zachary felt the warmth of the blush that traveled over his face. She had already heard the details from someone in the police department. Maybe Robinson himself.

"Oh, that. Yeah. He did."

"So does that mean you don't need the forensics now?"

"You'll still need to test it to see if he did leave behind any physical evidence. Even though we have his picture and his confession, we need to tie it up as tightly as we can, with every detail we can get."

"I'm teasing you."

Zachary cleared his throat. "Okay. Yeah, you already know what I need."

"Mmm-hm. Started on it today, but I'll have more time for it tomorrow. Detective Robinson wants to push it through as fast as he can. As you say, tie it up as tightly as we can."

"Thanks. I'm sure Lauren's family and friends will appreciate it."

"Have you talked to them yet?"

"No... just sent Barbara a message. I'll have to follow up with her on the details."

"Face-to-face is always better for that kind of thing."

"Exactly," Zachary agreed.

Kenzie was quiet. Zachary decided it was his opening and he'd better take it while he had the chance.

"Did Detective Robinson tell you that they broke down my door?"

"Seems to me he might have mentioned something about that."

"So... I can't stay in my apartment until the building guy gets it fixed for me. It wouldn't be safe."

"So you'll be at a hotel?"

Zachary supposed that the hotel was an option. He was surprised that it was one he hadn't seriously considered. He had immediately thought of staying with a friend. Especially Kenzie. When his apartment had burned down, he hadn't even had a wallet or credit card to book a room at the hotel. He'd been forced to rely on the kindness of his friends. Mario had stepped up then, agreeing to have Zachary stay with him for a few days, which had ended up being a few months before he told Zachary that it was time for him to be getting out on his own again.

"Are you still there?" Kenzie asked.

"Yeah. I was just wondering… I mean, I *could* get a hotel room…"

"Or…?"

"I wondered if you had a spare room where I could crash for a day or two."

"No. No spare room."

"Ah. I guess I'd probably be in your way on the couch."

"Yes. I don't like people sleeping in my living room."

"Okay. I might call Mario. Or maybe I'll just book a hotel room."

"Why don't you come over? I might not have a spare room or a couch you can use, but I might be able to find *somewhere else.*"

A warm, tingly feeling washed from Zachary's head to his toes. He was glad she couldn't see him. She always laughed when he got red. Such a tough guy, turning to mush whenever a girl teased him.

"Yeah…?"

"Sure. You've never seen my house. After all of the times you've entertained me, I should probably return the favor."

Zachary smiled. He'd never asked her why she didn't invite him to her place. He figured that a woman just needed a safe, secure place to go. If she didn't feel comfortable with him being there, then he could respect that. Maybe Kenzie had realized that he hadn't been the only one holding something back in the relationship.

"Do you want the address?" Kenzie asked.

"I've got it."

"Private detective. I should have known. How long will it take you to get here? You need to pack a bag?"

Zachary cleared his throat, giving a little laugh. "I'm already here."

He waited, holding himself tense. Stalker behavior. Looking up her address and sitting in his car outside her house when he called her. He hadn't meant it to be creepy, but sitting there waiting for her response, he knew it could be interpreted that way.

"Well then, come on in."

CHAPTER THIRTY-SEVEN

Zachary had set up a meeting with Barbara before breakfast the next morning. Or maybe it was breakfast. They had coffee, and he never really had much else for breakfast, but he didn't know if it was breakfast for her.

"So does this mean... you have something to tell me, or that you've gone as far as you can and you're telling me that you're done?"

"It means I have something to tell you. Are you ready for that?"

She looked at him, head cocked slightly. "I guess it depends what you have to tell me. You mean that you have a suspect? Is it like Deidre said? Is it Gordon Drake?"

Zachary hesitated and shook his head. "No. And it's more than a suspect. I got a confession."

She blinked. "A confession?"

"Her supervisor, Daniel Service. He followed her home. Broke into her apartment."

"Why? Was it some sex thing? She rejected him?"

"No. He was afraid she was going to do or say something that was damaging to the company. He felt like it was his job to make sure that she didn't."

Barbara stared at Zachary for a disconcertingly long time. She shook her head. "This was… to protect the company from slander? From a bad reputation? I don't get that."

"You know how devoted she was to them… but I guess she had made the decision to make a break with them. It was affecting her health, so maybe she decided that she'd had enough and she'd better stop before it did any long-term damage. Maybe she knew that it would kill her if she kept going like she was without taking care of her body. But once Daniel thought that she was going to betray the company… I'm sorry."

"So it really wasn't an accident. He hurt her on purpose? It wasn't… in the middle of an argument?"

"No. It looks like it was planned and premeditated."

"Because… she had decided not to stay with the company?"

Zachary shrugged. "It's hard to understand why other people do the things they do. Other people's motives don't always make sense to us. But yes… he felt very protective of Drake, Chase, Gould, and he wanted to make sure that she couldn't do anything to harm it. He was set on it becoming a world leader. He wanted to rise to the top of the industry and to be a part of its success."

"Unbelievable. And for that, he would kill someone like Lauren. Just for a job."

"For him, it wasn't just a job."

"It never was for her, either. It was so important to her. It was everything."

"Until she decided that it couldn't be. For what it's worth, I think she made the right choice."

"Even though it got her killed?"

"That wasn't her fault. She couldn't have foreseen the consequences. Her decision was to have a life that wasn't just focused on money and success."

"And that was right."

Zachary nodded. "Exactly."

———

He wasn't sure what to do about Blair Bieberstein and Gordon. He had fudged his answers as much as he dared with Detective Robinson, explaining that he didn't know where Gordon was or if he had been involved. Leave that to Daniel to explain, because Zachary didn't have the answers. He just didn't know what Gordon had known or understood about Daniel. If Daniel could read other people as well as he claimed, did that mean that Gordon could too?

Could he tell when he looked at Zachary or Daniel or Detective Robinson what they were thinking? Or maybe not Daniel, since Daniel claimed not to have any tells.

The case was finished, his invoice to Barbara submitted and collected on, but Zachary decided to keep an eye on Drake, Chase, Gould, just to ensure that everything had settled down and that no one else had been in on the coverup. Had Gordon known? Had Bev? Was there someone who was supposed to review the security pictures? Did he know what had happened and just didn't tell? Or had he been asleep on the job and not noticed those last few pictures?

Or had he told Gordon or whoever his boss was, and Gordon had told them to keep it quiet?

Zachary just wanted to watch the employees as they came and went and to be sure that they were alright. And hopefully to catch a glimpse of Blair Bieberstein returning to work. And Gordon? Did he want to see Gordon?

He didn't want to see Daniel. If they released him on bail and he returned to Drake, Chase, Gould, Zachary didn't want to know about it.

He sat in his car, watching people coming and going. There was one security checkpoint on the way into the building, which made it easy for Zachary, since everyone had to arrive through that one set of doors.

On his second day of surveillance, Zachary saw a familiar little man, not quite as squirrely looking, walking up to the entrance. Zachary jumped out of his car and jogged over to see him. Bieberstein drew back, startled, then took in who it was.

"Oh. Zachary Goldman. I'm glad to see you."

"I just wanted to make sure that you were okay."

Bieberstein's head bobbed up and down. He glanced around to make sure no one was listening to them. "Sure. I'm fine. Just… had to take a couple of days to rest after the accident." He indicated his cast and the bandage on his head. "You know."

"Sure. You just disappeared so suddenly… I was worried about you. I wasn't sure if something had happened."

"Whether they got me?" Bieberstein gave a nervous laugh. "I guess I was talking a little crazy. Just lack of sleep or the side effects of the painkillers."

"I don't think it was crazy. Did you hear about Daniel?"

Bieberstein shrugged uncomfortably. "I don't know what happened with Daniel... I don't get it."

"I don't know if any of us do. He thought he was doing something to protect the company. But..."

Bieberstein looked around, his eyes fastening on something behind Zachary. Zachary turned, but he had a pretty good idea who he was going to see before he did.

Gordon.

"Zachary," Gordon greeted with his trademark friendly smile, and a hand reached out to shake Zachary's. "You came through for us again. You certainly have a knack for digging down and finding out the truth. This company owes you a debt of gratitude."

Zachary hoped that was what Gordon really felt, and not what a disappointment it was to lose his avenging angel. He shook hands with Gordon as expected, pulling back when he felt like Gordon had held on for long enough.

"I just wanted to make sure that Bieberstein was okay," he explained, motioning to the other man.

"I told you he was. I told you I just hid him away somewhere he could get a little sleep, and be away from any other threats. Since you unveiled the threat... he should be safe now. Shouldn't he?"

"As long as you get control of these overtime hours."

Gordon raised his brows. "I beg your pardon?"

"You need to get rid of all of these overtime hours and make sure that employees are getting the medical care that they need. Days off when they are sick. Not working so many hours that they are going to work themselves to death. Lauren's death could just as easily have been karoshi. Her heart showed signs of stress. It was being damaged."

Gordon took this in, frowning. He nodded slowly and patted Zachary on the arm as if comforting him. "You're right. I'll look into it. That shouldn't be happening."

Zachary breathed out. "Good. These people are very devoted to your company. You need to take care of them."

"So many people to take care of," Gordon said ruefully. "Bridget and the babies, and now... several hundred people who work for me. I thought that the structure we had set up would reduce my need to be quite so hands-on with everyone. But it would appear that I need to rethink that decision. I'll consider what I need to do."

He put his arm around Bieberstein and pulled him close, like a father with a teenage son, and talked to him in a paternal tone. "We need to take care of our families, don't we, Mr. Bieberstein?"

Zachary watched them walk into the building, Gordon's words echoing in his head.

Did you enjoy this book? Reviews and recommendations are vital to making a book successful.

Please leave a review at your favorite book store or review site and share it with your friends.

Don't miss the following bonus material:
Sign up for mailing list to get a free ebook
Read a sneak preview chapter
Other books by P.D. Workman
Learn more about the author

PREVIEW OF SHE TOLD A LIE

CHAPTER 1

Zachary tried to stay in the zone he was in, just on the border between sleeping and waking, for as long as he could. He felt warm and safe and at peace, and it was such a good feeling he wanted to remain there as long as he could before the anxieties of consciousness started pouring in.

The warm body alongside his shifted and Zachary snuggled in, trying not to leave the cozy pocket of blankets he was in.

Kenzie murmured something that ended in 'some space' and wriggled away from him again. Zachary let her go. She needed her sleep, and if he smothered her, she wouldn't be quick to invite him back.

Kenzie. He was back together with Kenzie and he had stayed the night at her house. It was the first time he'd gone there instead of her joining him in his apartment, which was currently not safe for them to sleep at because the police had busted the door in. It would have to be fixed before he could sleep there.

Kenzie lived in a little house that was a hundred times better than Zachary's apartment, which wasn't difficult since he had started from scratch after the fire that burned down his last apartment. While he was earning more as a private investigator than he ever had before, thanks to a few high profile murder cases, he wasn't going to sink a lot of money into the apartment until he had built up a strong enough reserve to get him through several months of low income.

Zachary had been surprised by some of the high-priced items he had seen around Kenzie's home the night before. He supposed he shouldn't have been surprised, given the cherry-red convertible she drove, but he'd always assumed she was saddled with significant debts from medical school and that she would not be able to afford luxuries.

Maybe that was the reason that she had never invited him into her territory before. She didn't want him to see the huge gap in their financial statuses.

Once Zachary's brain started working, reviewing the night before and considering Kenzie's circumstances as compared to his, he couldn't shut it back off and return to that comfortable, happy place he had been just before waking. His brain was grinding away, assessing how worried he should be. Did any of it change their relationship? Did it mean that Kenzie looked down on him? Considered him inferior? She had never treated him that way, but did she think it, deep down inside?

Once he left her house, would he ever be invited back? He had only been there under exceptional circumstances, and while he hoped that it was a sign that Kenzie was willing to reconcile and work on their relationship again—as long as he was—he was afraid that it might just have been one moment of weakness. One that she would regret when she woke up and had a chance to reconsider.

With his brain cranking away at the problem and finding new things to worry about, Zachary couldn't stay in bed. He shifted around a few times, trying to find a position that was comfortable enough that he would just drift back to sleep, he knew that it was impossible. His body was restless and would not return to sleep again so easily.

He slid out of the bed and squinted, trying to remember the layout of the room and any obstacles. The sky was just starting to lighten, forcing a little gray light around the edges of Kenzie's blinds and curtains. Enough to see dark shapes around him, but not enough to be confident he wouldn't trip over something. Zachary felt for the remainder of his clothes and clutched them to him as he cautiously made his way to the bedroom door and out into the hallway.

He shut the door silently behind him so that he wouldn't wake Kenzie up. There was an orange glow emanating from the bathroom, so he found his way there without knocking over any priceless decor. He shut the door and turned on the main light. It was blinding after the night-light. Zachary squeezed his eyes shut and waited for them to adjust to the light that penetrated his eyelids, and then gradually opened them to look around.

Everything was clean and tidy and smelled fresh. Definitely a woman's domain rather than a bachelor pad like Zachary's. He needed to upgrade if he expected her to spend any time at his apartment. He'd used her ensuite the night before rather than the main bath, and even though it was more cluttered with her makeup and hair and bath products, it was also cleaner and brighter than Zachary's apartment bathroom.

He spent a couple of minutes with his morning routine, splashing water on his face and running a comb over his dark buzz-cut before making his way to the living room, where he'd left his overnight bag when he and Kenzie had adjourned for the night. He pulled out his laptop and set it on the couch while it booted up, wandering into the kitchen and sorting out her single-cup coffee dispenser to make himself breakfast.

CHAPTER 2

It was a few hours before he heard Kenzie stirring in the bedroom, and eventually, she made her way out to the living room. She had an oriental-style dressing gown wrapped around her. She rubbed her eyes, hair mussed from sleep.

Kenzie yawned. "Good morning."

"Hi." Zachary gave her a smile that he hoped expressed the warmth and gratitude he felt toward her for letting him back into her life, even if it was only for one night. "How was your sleep?"

"Good." Kenzie covered another yawn. "How about you? Did you actually get any sleep?"

"I slept great." Zachary wasn't lying. He didn't usually sleep well away from home. For that matter, he didn't sleep that well at home either. But after facing off with Lauren's killer and dealing with the police, he had been exhausted, and the comfort he had found in Kenzie's arms and the luxurious sheets in her bed had quickly lulled him to sleep. There was a slight dip in her mattress, testifying to the fact that she normally slept alone, and that had made it natural for him to gravitate toward her during the night. It had been reassuring to have someone else in bed with him after what seemed like an eon of lonely nights.

It was the best night's sleep he'd had in a long time.

"You couldn't have slept for more than three or four hours," Kenzie countered.

"Yes… but it was still a really good sleep."

"Well, good." She bent down to kiss him on the forehead.

Zachary felt a rush of warmth and goosebumps at the same time. She didn't seem to regret having allowed him to stay over. "Do you want coffee? I figured out the machine."

"Turn it on when you hear me get out of the shower. That should be about right."

"Do you want anything else? Bread in the toaster?"

"The full breakfast treatment? I could get used to this. Yes, a couple of slices of toast would be nice."

Zachary nodded. "Coffee and toast it is," he agreed.

He saw her speculative look, wondering whether he would actually remember or whether he would be distracted by something else.

"I'll do my best," Zachary promised. "But it better be a short shower, because if it's one of those two-hour-long ones, I might forget."

"I have to get to work today, so it had better be a quick one."

———

He did manage to remember to start both the coffee and the toast when she got out of the shower, and even heard the toast pop and remembered to butter it while it was hot. He had it on the table for Kenzie when she walked in, buttoning up her blouse.

"Nice!" Kenzie approved.

"Do you want jam?"

"There's some marmalade in the fridge."

Zachary retrieved the jar and made a mental note that he should get marmalade the next time he was shopping for groceries. If that was her preferred condiment, then he should make an effort to have it for her when she came to his apartment. He tried to always get things for her when he was shopping, because as Bridget put it, he ate like a Neanderthal. Not one of those fad caveman diets, but like someone who had never learned how to cook even the simplest foods. Most of his food was either ready to eat or just needed to be microwaved for a couple of minutes.

Or he could order in. He could use a phone even if he couldn't use a stove.

"So, your big case is solved," Kenzie said, "what are your plans for the day?"

"I still need to report to the client and issue my bill. Then I've got a bunch of smaller projects I should catch up on, now that I'll have some more time. And I need to get my door fixed. I wouldn't want to impose on you for too long."

Kenzie spread her marmalade carefully to the edge of the toast. "It was nice last night. I'm glad you called."

Zachary's face got warm. All they had done was to talk and cuddle, but he had needed that so badly. He had been concerned that she would be disappointed things had gone no further, so he was reassured that she had enjoyed the quiet time together too. Their relationship had been badly derailed by the abuse Zachary had suffered at Teddy Archuro's hands, which had also brought up a lot of buried memories of his time in foster care. However much he wanted to be with Kenzie, he couldn't help his own visceral reaction when things got too intimate.

"Hey," Kenzie said softly, breaking into his thoughts. "Don't do that. Come back."

Zachary tried to refocus his attention on her, to keep himself anchored to the present and not the attack.

"Five things?" Kenzie suggested, prompting Zachary to use one of the exercises his therapist had given him to help him with dissociation.

Zachary took a slow breath. "I smell... the coffee. The toast." He breathed. "Your shampoo. The marmalade. I... don't know what else."

His own sweat. He should have showered and dressed before Kenzie got up. Greeted her smelling freshly-scrubbed instead of assaulting her with the rank odor of a homeless person.

Kenzie smiled. "Better?" She studied his face.

Zachary nodded. "Yeah. Sorry."

"It's okay. It's not your fault."

He still felt inadequate. He should be able to have a pleasant morning conversation with his girlfriend without dissociating or getting mired in flashbacks. It shouldn't be that hard.

"Are you going to have something to eat? There's enough bread for you to have toast too," Kenzie teased.

"No, not ready yet."

"Well, don't forget. You still need to get your weight back up."

Zachary nodded. "I'll have something in a while."

————

He still hadn't eaten when he left Kenzie's. She was on her way into work, and he didn't want her to feel like she had to let him stay there in her domain while she was gone, so by the time she was ready for work, he had repacked his overnight bag and was ready to leave as well. She didn't make any comment or offer him the house while she was gone.

"Well, good luck with your report to Lauren's sister today. I know that part of the job is never fun."

Zachary nodded. "Yeah. And then collecting on the bill. Sorry your sister was murdered, but could you please pay me now?" He rolled his eyes.

Kenzie shook her head. "At least I don't have to ask for payment when I give people autopsy results."

They paused outside the door. Zachary didn't know what to say to Kenzie or how to tell her goodbye.

"Call me later," Kenzie advised. "Let me know whether you got your door fixed or not."

Zachary exhaled, relieved. She wasn't regretting having invited him in. She would put up with him for another night if he needed her.

"Thanks, I will."

Kenzie armed the burglar alarm on the keypad next to the door and shut it. Zachary heard the bolt automatically slide into place.

"See you," Kenzie said breezily. She pulled him closer by his coat lapel and gave him a brief peck on the lips. "Have a good day."

Zachary nodded, his face flushing and a lump in his throat preventing him from saying anything. Kenzie opened the garage door. Zachary turned and walked down the sidewalk to his car. He tried hard not to be needy, not to turn around and watch as she backed the car out onto the street, checking to see whether she was still watching him and would give him one more wave before she left. But he couldn't help himself.

She waved in his direction and pulled onto the street.

————

Late in the afternoon, Zachary headed back to his apartment, hoping to find when he got there that the door had been repaired and he could feel safe there once more. Of course, if the door had been fixed, he would need another reason to go back to Kenzie's. Or he could invite her to join him and they could go back to their usual routines. Just because she had allowed him over to her house once, that didn't mean she would be comfortable with him being there all the time.

But he could see the splintered doorframe as he walked down the hall approaching his apartment. The building manager had promised to make it a priority, but it looked like whatever subcontractor he had called hadn't yet made it there. Zachary pushed the door open and looked around.

Nothing appeared to have been rifled or taken in his absence. Of course, he didn't have much of value. He'd taken all of his electronics with him and didn't exactly have jewelry or wads of cash lying around. Anyone desperate enough to rifle his drawers and steal his shirts probably needed them worse than he did.

Though he hadn't thought about the meds in the cabinet. There were a few things in there that might have some street value.

Zachary started to walk toward the bedroom, but stopped when he heard a noise. He froze and listened, trying to zero in on it. It was probably just a neighbor moving around. Or a pigeon landing on the ledge outside his window. They spooked him sometimes with the loud flapping of their wings when they took off.

He waited, ears pricked, for the sound to be repeated.

Could it have been a person? There in his apartment?

The last time he'd thought that someone was rifling his apartment and had called the police, it had been Bridget. She'd still had a key to the old apartment. She'd checked in on him at Christmas, knowing that it was a bad time for him, and had cleaned out his medicine cabinet to ensure that he didn't overdose.

It wouldn't be Bridget this time.

She didn't have a key to the new apartment, though he would have been happy to give her one if she had wanted it. Bridget was no longer part of his life and he needed to keep his distance from her, both to avoid getting slapped with a restraining order and because he was with Kenzie, and he needed to be fair to her. There was no going back to his ex-wife. She had a new partner and was pregnant. She didn't want anything to do with him.

There was another rustle. He was pretty sure it was someone in his bedroom. But it didn't sound like they were doing anything. Just moving quietly around.

Waiting for him?

He hated to call the police and have it be a false alarm. But he also didn't want to end up with a bullet in his chest because he walked in on a burglary in progress.

Unlike private investigators on TV, Zachary didn't carry a gun. He didn't even own one. With his history of depression and self-harm, it had always been too big a risk.

Zachary eased his phone out of his pocket, moving very slowly, trying to be completely silent. He wasn't sure what he was going to do when he got it out. If he called emergency, he would have to talk to them to let them know what was going on. They wouldn't be able to triangulate his signal to a single apartment.

Just as he looked down at the screen and moved his thumb over the unlock button, it gave a loud squeal and an alert popped up on the screen. Zachary jumped so badly that it flew out of his hand, and he scrambled to catch it before it hit the floor. He wasn't well-coordinated, and he just ended up hitting it in the air and shooting it farther away from him, to smack into the wall and then land on the floor.

———

She Told a Lie, Book #8 of the Zachary Goldman Mysteries , is coming soon!

ABOUT THE AUTHOR

Award-winning and USA Today bestselling author P.D. (Pamela) Workman writes riveting mystery/suspense and young adult books dealing with mental illness, addiction, abuse, and other real-life issues. For as long as she can remember, the blank page has held an incredible allure and from a very young age she was trying to write her own books.

Workman wrote her first complete novel at the age of twelve and continued to write as a hobby for many years. She started publishing in 2013. She has won several literary awards from Library Services for Youth in Custody for her young adult fiction. She currently has over 50 published titles and can be found at pdworkman.com.

Born and raised in Alberta, Workman has been married for over 25 years and has one son.

———

Please visit P.D. Workman at pdworkman.com to see what else she is working on, to join her mailing list, and to link to her social networks.

———

If you enjoyed this book, please take the time to recommend it to other purchasers with a review or star rating and share it with your friends!

facebook.com/pdworkmanauthor

twitter.com/pdworkmanauthor

instagram.com/pdworkmanauthor

amazon.com/author/pdworkman

bookbub.com/authors/p-d-workman

goodreads.com/pdworkman

linkedin.com/in/pdworkman

pinterest.com/pdworkmanauthor

youtube.com/pdworkman

Lightning Source UK Ltd.
Milton Keynes UK
UKHW020259230721
387625UK00002B/227